meg (handwritten)

KT-403-342

The Adultery Club
and
The Infidelity Chain

TESS STIMSON is the author of three other novels and a biography. She writes regularly for the *Daily Mail* as well as for several women's magazines. Born and brought up in Sussex, she graduated from Oxford before spending a number of years as a news producer with ITN. She now lives in Florida with her American husband, their daughter and her two sons.

www.tessstimson.com

ALSO BY TESS STIMSON

Fiction

Hard News

Soft Focus

Pole Position

Non-Fiction

Yours Till the End:
The Biography of a Beirut Hostage

The Adultery Club
and
The Infidelity Chain

Tess Stimson

PAN BOOKS

The Adultery Club first published 2007 by Pan Books
The Infidelity Chain first published 2008 by Pan Books

This omnibus first published 2008 by Pan Books
an imprint of Pan Macmillan Ltd
Pan Macmillan, 20 New Wharf Road, London N1 9RR
Basingstoke and Oxford
Associated companies throughout the world
www.panmacmillan.com

ISBN 978-0-330-50804-9

1 3 5 7 9 8 6 4 2

A CIP catalogue record for this book is available from
the British Library.

Typeset by SetSystems Ltd, Saffron Walden, Essex
Printed in the UK by CPI Mackays, Chatham ME5 8TD

The Adultery Club

In memory of my mother

Jane Theresa Stimson

3 February 1942 to 3 December 2001

'In my Father's house
There are many mansions.
If not, I would have told you;
Because I go to prepare a place for you.'

Acknowledgements

So many people help with stories and advice when one writes a book, but some have to be singled out for their special contribution.

Without Carole Blake, my agent, I would never have found the self-belief to write this book. Her encouragement, knowledge, meticulous editorial advice, support and – above all – her friendship have been invaluable. I would fly (indeed, have flown!) across the world to have lunch with her.

Imogen Taylor is the editor of whom every writer dreams. Her enthusiasm and vision have been stimulating and infectious, her advice pithy, constructive and perceptive. And she giggles at all the right places. It is a joy to work with her.

Efficient, reliable and always fun to talk to, Oli Munson has also achieved the impossible: rendered conversation about international tax forms entertaining. For him and the rest of the brilliant team at Blake Friedmann, I give thanks.

I am deeply grateful to Trisha Jackson, and to the amazing Pan Macmillan team, including Fiona Carpenter, Emma Grey, Anne Newman, Caitriona Row, Marie Slocombe, Anna Stockbridge, Michelle Taylor and Ellen Wood, all of whose verve and enthusiasm have been inspiring. Thank you!

Every girl should feel like a million dollars at least once.

That most tempting man, Hugo Burnand, gave me *my* moment, when he took my author photographs. *Bliss.*

For anyone enduring the horrors of divorce, let me recommend two people. Firstly, Simon Pigott, of Levison Meltzer Pigott, the most charming, decent and tenacious lawyer in the business. He made my divorce bearable, and I will be eternally grateful that his honourable style allowed my ex-husband and I finally to make peace. And Danusia Brzezina, a loyal and compassionate lawyer and friend. Her legal advice regarding this book was invaluable; her company, as always, is a pleasure.

Eileen Gaulter, of Gaulter Technologies, Inc., interpreted my vague and unhelpfully abstract ideas for a website with creativity, practicality and skill, and I *love* the result. Please check it out: *www.TessStimson.com.*

To Georgie and Charlie Stewart, for their endless generous hospitality every time I fly to London, I cannot say thank you enough. You provide the fluffiest towels and the best company. Your friendship means the world to me.

Thanks, too, to my father Michael and stepmother Barbi, for the dawn airport pick-ups and for allowing my family to wreak havoc in their beautiful home; to my out-laws, Harry and Sharon Oliver, for kidnapping their grandchildren so that I can work, and for providing raspberry martinis as and when required; and to Henry, Matthew and Lily, for tiptoeing away quietly when Mummy has a writing crisis, and for not crashing my computer *too* often.

Above all, to my husband, Erik, for his thousand little kindnesses – and the one very big one: marrying me. Here's to Melville and Milton, and the lifetime in between.

TESS STIMSON
Florida, 2006

1

Nicholas

Divorce is a difficult business. Never more so, may I suggest, than when your client authoritatively declares all men are bastards, and you're left shifting uncomfortably in your seat whilst your penis tries to make itself scarce.

'Not *all* men, Mrs Stephenson,' I venture.

My client ignores my genial smile, grey eyes flicking dismissively around my oak-panelled office. Her gaze briefly snags on the silver-framed photograph of my wife propped beside the leather blotter on my desk; her expression of pity for my spouse places me foursquare with those unfortunates whose parents neglected the legal niceties before bedding down together. Since I have just secured her an extremely generous seven-figure settlement from her ex-husband, I find her disdain for my sex in its entirety a little unfair.

She stands and I rise with her, straightening my silk tie. She extends a scrawny pink tweed arm; her hand sits like a wet fish in mine.

'You may be right, Mr Lyon,' she says drily. 'Maybe it's just the men I marry.'

Her scent is pungent and overpowering: synthetic cat's piss. Far too much make-up; I can't imagine kissing the jammy red lips. She's the kind of woman one would find smeared all over the sheets in the morning, the pillowcase imprinted with her face like the Turin Shroud.

Good legs, though. Slender, neat calves, with nicely turned ankles. But no meat on her bones, and breasts like a boy.

My professional smile does not slip as I escort her to the door. I endeavour not to morally judge my clients: it's distracting and unproductive. There's no place in the context of divorce law for emotion or sentimentality; one has quite enough of that kind of thing from one's clients. My wife, of course – being a woman – begs to differ. I consider myself merely objective. Malinche, however, asserts that my 'brutal kind of truth', as she emotively puts it, is akin to judging a woman's skin only in the harsh glare of daylight, rather than by the softening glow of the fire. I can't quite see her point.

My client stops suddenly in the doorway; I almost run into the back of her. Her head dips as if in prayer, exposing pale, downy vertebrae beneath the stiff blonde bob.

The nape of a woman's neck – so vulnerable, so quixotically erotic.

'I always thought – *hoped*—' she chokes back a sob, 'he'd change his mind.'

I'm at a loss. I certainly did not have this woman pegged as a clinger. Still the right side of forty, she has already acquired a remunerative trio of wealthy ex-husbands, which – despite every effort at objectivity – leads one to make certain assumptions. Put simply: the last thing I expected was for *love* to come into it.

The woman's skinny shoulders start to shake. *Oh, Christ.* I'm so hopeless at this kind of thing. My arms twitch uselessly. Inappropriate in the extreme to hug, but what to do if – God forbid – she starts grizzling all over the place?

Suddenly her head comes up and she squares her shoulders, reminding me of my eldest daughter Sophie on her first day at school. Without another word, she marches through the open-plan secretarial pool and into the hallway beyond. I breathe a hefty sigh of relief. Thank God. What on earth was *that* all about?

As I move to close my door, my secretary, Emma, waves.

'Mr Lyon, it's your wife on line two. She says she's sorry to bother you, but can she just have a quick word?'

'Of course—'

I hesitate in the doorway. There's something I can't quite . . .

'It's my hair, Mr Lyon,' Emma says patiently. 'I had it cut this lunchtime.'

A pity. I rather liked it long.

I return to my desk, glancing at the photograph of Malinche that so aroused my client's compassion as I pick up the phone. It was taken a couple of Christmases ago – by Kit, irritatingly, rather than by me – at the moment she glanced, smiling, over her shoulder, half-bending to pull the turkey from the Aga. I feel a thud of gratitude every time I look at it. It's foolish, I know, but even after ten years I still thrill to the words 'your wife'. Quite how I won the heart of this extraordinary and beautiful woman is utterly beyond my comprehension. I am merely eternally thankful that I did.

'Chocolate–orange sponge cake flavoured with vanilla, orange and lemon zest, or apricot chequerboard cake with chocolate ganache?' Mal demands without waiting for me to speak.

I can tell from my wife's strangled tone that she has the handset wedged between her chin and chest and is no doubt stirring something mouth-watering even as we speak. 'May one inquire—'

'Heavens, Nicholas, don't be so pompous,' Mal says briskly. 'You're not in Court now. Your surprise birthday cake, of course. Metheny insists we finish it this afternoon before you get home.'

I smile at the mention of my youngest daughter, with whom I share a birthday, preternaturally long toes and a wicked fondness for pistachio ice-cream. I had hoped to share a great deal more, but the ultrasound proved itself less than infallible and my much-longed-for boy and potential fishing and cricket companion turned out to be a surprise third petticoat. As a consolation prize I was allowed to name her for my lifelong hero, jazz guitarist Pat Metheny.

'Let me talk to her and ask her which she suggests,' I posit.

'Don't be silly, Nicholas.'

'You were the one who said she was insisting—'

'There's more than one way to insist on something, as you should know.'

Her mellifluous voice takes on an unmistakable bedroom timbre, and there's a sudden rallying cry in my trousers as images of well-toned caramel thighs, silk stockings and coffee-coloured lace flash unbidden across my mind's eye. My witch of a wife is well aware of the effect she's having on me, to judge by the laughter that now replaces the come-hither tone in her voice.

'Anyway,' she lilts, 'you can't talk to her or it won't be a surprise.'

'I'll give you a surprise—'

'Now, it wouldn't really be a surprise, would it?'

'Someone's feeling cocky,' I say. 'What makes you think I'm not talking about the latest council tax bill?'

'What makes you think *I'm* not?'

'Are you?'

'I'm talking cakes, Nicholas. Come on, make up your mind before I have to put two candles on Metheny's instead of one.'

'Will I get candles too?'

'Yes, but not forty-three or the cake will melt.'

'Cruel woman. You too will be forty-three one day, you know.'

'Not for another six years. Now, Nicholas.'

'The chocolate–orange sponge cake, of course. Would it be possible to request bitter chocolate shavings with that?'

'It would. Metheny, please take your foot out of Daddy's bowl. Thank you. How did the lovely Mrs Stephenson's case go?'

'Seven figures,' I report.

'Almost double her last divorce. How wonderful. I could almost consider a divorce myself.'

I hear my wife lick her fingers and my erection nearly heaves into view above the desk. 'If I thought you could procure seven figures from it, darling, I'd draw up the papers for you,' I offer, groaning inwardly as I rearrange my balls. 'Can't get blood out of a stone, unfortunately.'

'Oh, that reminds me: Ginger rang from the garage this morning about the Volvo. He said he's fixed the whatever-it-was this time, but it's on its last legs. Or should that be wheels?' Her voice ebbs and flows in my ear as she moves about the kitchen. 'Anyway, he doesn't think he'll be able to nurse it through its dratted MOT in January. So there's no help for it, I've just *got* to gird my loins and finish the new book, get the rest of my advance—'

'Darling, I think I can afford to buy my wife a new car if she needs one,' I interrupt, nettled. 'Sometimes you seem to forget I'm a full equity partner now, there's absolutely no need for you to knock yourself out writing cookery books these days.'

'I *like* writing cookery books,' Mal says equably. 'Oh, God, Metheny, don't do that. *Poor* rabbit. Sorry, Nicholas, I have to go. I'll see you at the station. Usual time?'

I suppress a sigh of exasperation.

'For God's sake, Malinche, it's William's retirement party this evening! Don't tell me you've forgotten! You're supposed to be on the five twenty-eight from Salisbury to Waterloo, remember?'

'So I am,' Mal agrees, unperturbed. 'I hadn't really forgotten, it just slipped my mind for a moment. Hold on a second—'

In the background I hear a series of strange muffled thumps, and then Metheny's contagious, irrepressible giggles.

Life can be full of surprises. When we learned that Mal was unexpectedly pregnant for the third time I was absolutely horrified. Sophie and Evie were then eight and five; we'd just got them to the stage where they were recognizably human and could do civilized things like skiing or coming out to dinner with us without spending most of the meal crawling around under the table. Now we were to be plunged back into the grim abyss of sleepless nights and shitty nappies. It was only the thought of a son and heir at last that consoled me, and when even that silver lining turned out to be a mirage, I despaired. And yet this last tilt at parenthood has been the sweetest of all. Metheny holds my hardened lawyer's heart in her chubby starfish hands.

An echo of small feet on worn kitchen flagstones; and then a squeal as Mal scoops her up and retrieves the telephone receiver. 'I really *must* go, Nicholas,' she says, slightly out of breath.

'You did remember to arrange a babysitter?'

'Mmm. Yes, Kit very sweetly said he'd do it.'

I have absolutely nothing against those who choose alternative lifestyles. There is, of course, more to a person than their sexuality. I just don't quite see why it must be forced down one's throat, that's all. I do not parade my red-blooded heterosexuality to all and sundry, although it's self-evident. I simply cannot understand why certain sections of the so-called 'gay community' – so sad, the way that decent word has been hijacked – feel the need to rub one's nose in *their* choice of bedmate. However.

I accepted long ago that when I asked Malinche to be my wife, Kit Westbrook was a minor but salient part of the package. *Praemonitus praemunitus*, after all: forewarned, forearmed. And I am not the sort of man to start objecting to his wife's friendships, however unsavoury;

and in any event, Kit is certainly not, and never has been, a threat.

We met, the three of us, twelve years ago in Covent Garden. I had taken my parents to the opera – *La Bohème*, if memory serves – to mark my father's seventieth birthday. Having hailed them a taxi, I was strolling alone through the pedestrian piazza en route to the tube station and thence to my rooms in Earls Court; I remember rather wishing that for once there was someone waiting at home for me. Despite the lateness of the hour, the square still boasted its usual collection of street performers, and I was just fending off a rather menacing young man mocked up in heavy black-and-white face-paint and thrusting a collection hat under my nose, when I noticed a unicyclist start to lose control of his cycle. It swiftly became clear that this wasn't part of his act, and for a moment I watched with morbid fascination as he swung back and forth like a human metronome before waking up and pulling myself together. I barely had time to pull a young woman out of the path of his trajectory before he toppled into the small crowd.

At the last moment, he managed to throw himself clear of the spectators, executing a neat forward roll on the cobbles and leaping up to bow somewhat shakily to his audience.

I realized I was clasping the young lady rather inappropriately around the chest, and released her with some embarrassment. 'I do apologize, I didn't mean—'

'Oh, please don't! If it weren't for you, I'd be squished

all over the cobblestones. You must have quick reflexes or something, I didn't even see him coming.'

She was startlingly pretty. Unruly dark hair the colour of molasses, sparkling cinnamon eyes, clear, luminous skin; and the most engaging and infectious smile I had ever seen. In her early twenties, at a guess; fine-boned and petite, perhaps a full foot shy of my six feet two. I could span her waist with my hands. I find small, delicate women incredibly attractive: they bring out the masculine hunter-gatherer in me.

I noticed that the top two buttons of her peasant-style blouse had come undone in the mêlée, revealing a modest swell of lightly tanned bosom cradled in a froth of white broderie anglaise. My cock throbbed into life. Quickly, I averted my eyes.

She stood on tiptoe and gripped my shoulder. At her touch, a tumult of images – that glorious hair tangled in my hands, those slender thighs straddling my waist, my lips on her golden breasts – roared through my brain.

'Oh, Lord, you've ripped your coat,' she exclaimed, examining my shoulder seam. 'It's all my fault, wandering around in a *complete* daze, I was thinking about the walnuts, you have to be so careful, of course, don't you, not everyone likes them, and *now* look at you—'

I have no idea what nonsense I gabbled in return.

'Malinche Sandal,' she said, thrusting her small hand at me.

I returned her firm, cool grip. 'Ah. Yes. Nicholas Lyon.' I coughed, trying not to picture her hands wrapped around my— 'What a very unusual name,' I managed.

'I know.' She grimaced. 'My mother is this total hippy,

she's convinced our names determine our characters and the *entire* course of our lives – too much acid in the Sixties if you ask me, though perhaps she's right, you can't imagine a romantic hero called Cuthbert, can you, or King Wayne, it just doesn't work – but anyway, she decided better safe than sorry, just to be *quite* sure. My older sister got stuck with Cleopatra, so I suppose I should be grateful I ended up with Malinche, it could have been Boadicea!'

She glanced down, and I realized I was still holding her hand.

With a flush of embarrassment, I released it, praying she hadn't noticed the tent-pole erection in my trousers.

'Of course! I knew it rang a bell. Malinche was the Indian girl who learned Spanish so that she could help Cortes conquer Mexico in the sixteenth century; without her spying for him he might never have succeeded—' I gave a sheepish smile. 'Sorry. Don't mean to go on. Oxford history degree, can't help it.'

Malinche laughed delightedly. 'No, it's wonderful! You're the first person I've ever met who's actually *heard* of her. This is amazing, it must be Fate.' She slipped her arm through mine and grinned up at me with childlike trust. I stiffened, my loins on fire. 'Now, how about you let me cook you dinner to say thank you?'

'Oh, but—'

'Please do. You'd be quite safe, I'm a trained chef.'

'But how do you know *you* would be? You don't even know me.'

'I can always tell,' she said seriously. 'You look like the kind of man who would be honest, fair, and most importantly, optimistic.'

'Well, that is most kind, but—'

'Do you like walnuts?'

'Yes, except in salads, though I don't quite—'

'We were *meant* to meet this evening, don't you see, you knew all about my name and that has to be a sign. And you like walnuts – well, except in salads, which don't count, no one sensible likes walnuts in salads. It's serendipity. You can't turn your back on that, can you?'

'It's not a question of—'

'The thing is,' she added earnestly, tilting her head to one side and looking up at me with those glorious toffee-coloured eyes, 'I'm trying to write a cookery book and my entire family is just fed up with being *fed*, if you see what I mean. Even my friends say they'd give anything just to have pizza and I'm simply *desperate* for a new guinea pig. You seem a very kind, decent man, I'm sure you're not an axe-murderer or anything—'

'Ted Bundy was handsome and charming and murdered at least thirty-six women,' a laconic voice drawled behind us.

Malinche swung round, spinning me with her. I was beginning to feel a little bemused by the unexpected direction my evening was taking.

'Kit, at last! Where have you been?'

A saturnine young man in his twenties thrust a paper bag at her. 'Getting the bloody blue mood crystals you wanted,' he responded tartly. 'Who's the new arm candy?'

'Nicholas Lyon,' I said, overlooking his rudeness and extending my hand.

The young man ignored it, taking possession of Malinche's free arm and glaring at me as he linked us together in an ungainly *ménage à trois* which – though I didn't know it then – was a precursory metaphor for our relationship down the years.

'Oh, Kit, don't be difficult,' Malinche sighed. 'Mr Lyon, this is Kit Westbrook, my oldest and apparently crossest friend, and one of those very weary guinea pigs I was telling you about. Kit, Mr Lyon just saved me from being squashed by a runaway unicyclist, and tore his very smart coat in the process. So stop being so dog-in-the-manger and help me persuade him to come back with us for dinner, he's being *far* too polite about it all.'

'Nicholas, please.'

'I don't mean to be rude,' Kit said, clearly meaning it very much, 'but Mal, you don't know this man from Adam. You *can't* just go round inviting strange men home for dinner, even if they do rescue you from certain death by circus performer.'

'Your friend is right,' I concurred regretfully. 'You really shouldn't take such risks, although I'm not actually a psychopathic serial killer; which suddenly makes me feel rather dull—'

Malinche pealed with laughter. 'See?' she said, as if that settled everything. As, in the end of course, it did.

I realized right from the start that Kit wasn't a rival for Malinche in the usual sense of the word. There was too much of the Sebastian Flyte about him, and he was always too flamboyantly dressed to be anything other than homosexual – in the midst of the dress-down, austere nineties, he sported velvet frock coats and waterfall lace cravats and knew the names for a dozen different shades of beige. But as far as Kit was concerned, Malinche was *his* best friend, and even now, after a decade of marriage and three children, he still hasn't quite accepted that she has a husband who has first call upon her. And then there was the matter of Trace Pitt, of course.

Nothing is ever quite as it seems with Kit. He is, after all, an actor. In fairness though, I must admit he's been a conscientious godfather, always remembering birthdays and the like. And the girls adore him. Not necessarily my first choice; but there we are.

My secretary ushers my four o'clock appointment into my office. I wish I'd thought to remind Mal to bring William's retirement gift with her. In her current mood, she'd be quite likely to bake it in the Aga and wrap the birthday cake instead. For the life of me, I can't recall what she said she'd bought, but I'm quite certain it will be eminently appropriate. Mal's gifts always are, she just has that feminine knack. I always leave Christmas and birthdays entirely to her, even for my side of the family. She's just so much better at it.

Firmly putting personal matters out of my mind, I pull a pad of foolscap towards me and unscrew the lid of my fountain pen. It's not as if Kit could ever do anything to undermine my marriage. We're far too strong for that.

Mr Colman is a new client, so I take detailed longhand notes as he describes the unhappy route that has led him here, to the grim finality of a divorce lawyer's office. He's aptly named, with hair the colour of mustard and a sallow cast to his skin. Once we have established the basics, I explain the bureaucratic procedure of divorce, the forms that must be filed, the documents supplied, the time and the cost – financial only; the emotional price he will soon discern himself – involved.

'We want it all to be amicable,' he interrupts brightly. 'There's no need to run up huge bills arguing over the plasma TV, we've both said that. We just want to get on with it, make a clean break of things. For the children's sakes.'

I refrain from telling him that it's not about the plasma television, it's never about the *television*; at least to begin with. It's about a husband dumping his wife of twenty years for a younger, bustier model. It's about a wife jettisoning her balding husband for a Shirley Valentine affair with the Italian ski instructor. It's about disappointment, hurt, banality and betrayal. But because you cannot quantify any of these things, in the end it *does* come down to the television, and the spoons, and that hideous purple vase Great-aunt Bertha gave you as a wedding present that you've both always hated, and which you will now spend thousands of pounds fighting to own.

All but a handful of my clients – the hardened marital veterans, repeat customers who've been divorced before – sit before me and tell me they want their divorce to be amicable. But if they were capable of resolving their differences amicably, they wouldn't be in my office in the first place.

'And the grounds for the petition?' I ask briskly.

Always a revealing moment, this. For the first time, Mr Colman looks uncomfortable. I know instantly there is another woman in the wings. I gently explain to my client that if his wife has not deserted him or committed adultery – he responds with almost comic indignation that she has not – and will not agree to a divorce, as the law stands he will either have to wait five years to obtain his freedom without her consent, or else cobble together a charge of unreasonable behaviour.

'I can't wait five years!' he exclaims. 'I've only been married to the bitch for four! I call *that* un-fucking-reasonable.'

The path from amicable to Anglo-Saxon has been even shorter than usual.

'Mr Colman, please. Let us be calm. It is my experience that the wife can usually be persuaded to divorce her husband if there are sufficient grounds rather than face a charge of unreasonable behaviour. *Are* there such grounds?' He nods curtly. 'Then I feel sure we can persuade *her* to divorce *you*.'

'Going to cost me, though, isn't it?' he says bitterly. 'She'll take me to the fucking cleaners.'

'It's more a question of weighing up what is most important to you, and focusing on that,' I say neutrally.

It is with relief that I finally bid the intemperate Mr Colman farewell some fifty minutes later. Working at the grimy coalface of marital breakdown is never pleasant, but usually I draw comfort from the thought that my interposition makes palatable what is unavoidably a very bitter pill for most of my clients. At five o'clock on a bleak November Friday, however, after a very long week dealing with the Mrs Stephensons and Mr Colmans of this world, it's hard to feel anything other than despair at the intractable nature of human relationships.

The better part of two decades as a divorce lawyer has brought me no closer to fathoming how people find themselves in these painful imbroglios. I know that old-fashioned morality is very *passé* these days, but having witnessed the destruction and misery that infidelity wreaks – and adultery is invariably the rock upon which the marital ship founders – I can say with some authority that a quick how's-your-father in the broom cupboard is *never* worth it.

My view is skewed, of course, by the scars of my own childhood. But an inbuilt bias towards fidelity is, I think, a *good* thing.

I realize, of course, how lucky I am to have a happy marriage. Mal firmly believes that Fate meant us to be together – her *bashert*, she calls me. Yiddish for 'destined other', apparently (she spent a summer on a kibbutz with a Jewish boyfriend when she was seventeen). I'm afraid I don't believe in that kind of superstitious Destiny nonsense, any more than I do horoscopes or tarot cards; but I'm only too aware how rare it is these days to attain your fifth wedding anniversary, never mind your tenth.

Reminds me. Ours is sometime around Christmas – the eighteenth or nineteenth, I think. I must remember to find her something particularly special this year. She'll kill me if I forget again.

I spend the next couple of hours or so absorbed in paperwork. When Emma knocks on my door, it is with some surprise that I note that it is almost seven.

'Mr Lyon, everyone's going over to Milagro's now for Mr Fisher's party,' she says. 'Are you coming with us, or did you want to wait for Mrs Lyon?'

'I believe she said she'd get a taxi straight to the restaurant from the station. But I need to finish this Consent Order tonight. You go on ahead. I'll be with you as soon as I'm done.'

Emma nods and withdraws.

Quietly I work on the draft Order, enjoying the rare peace that has descended on the empty office. Without the distraction of the telephone or interruptions from my colleagues, it takes me a fraction of the time it would do normally, and I finish in less than forty minutes. Perfect timing; Mal should be arriving at the restaurant at any moment.

I loosen my braces a little as I push back from my desk, reflecting wryly as I put on my jacket and raincoat that being married to a celebrity cook is not entirely good news. I rather fear my venerable dinner jacket, which has seen me through a dozen annual Law Society dinners, will not accommodate my burgeoning waistline for much longer.

Bidding the cleaner good evening as I pass through reception, in a moment of good resolution I opt to take the stairs rather than the lift down the four floors to street level.

As I come into the hallway, I find a young woman of perhaps thirty in a pale green suit hovering uncertainly by the lifts, clearly lost. She jumps when she sees me and I pause, switching my briefcase to the other hand as I push the chrome bar on the fire door to the stairwell.

'Can I help you?'

'I'm looking for Fisher Raymond Lyon. Am I on the right floor?'

'Yes, but I'm afraid the office is closed for the night. Did you want to make an appointment?'

'Oh, I'm not a client,' she says quickly. 'I'm a solicitor. My name's Sara Kaplan – I'm starting work here next Monday.'

'Ah, yes, of course.' I let the fire door swing shut and extend my hand. 'Nicholas Lyon, one of the partners. I'm afraid I was detained on a difficult case in Leeds when my colleagues interviewed you, I do apologize. I understand you come very highly recommended from your previous firm.'

'Thank you. I'm very much looking forward to working here.'

'Good, good. Well, welcome to the firm. I'll look forward to seeing you on Monday.'

I hesitate as she makes no move to leave.

'Miss Kaplan, did you just want to drop off some paperwork, or was there something else?'

She fiddles nervously with her earring. The uncertain gesture suggests she's rather younger than I had at first thought, perhaps twenty-five, twenty-six. 'Um. Well, it's just that Mr Fisher invited me to his leaving party, and I thought it might be nice to meet everyone before Monday—'

'Oh, I see. Yes, of course. It's not here, though, it's at the Italian restaurant across the road. I'm just going over there myself.'

Eschewing the stairs for the sake of courtesy, I summon the lift and we stand awkwardly next to each other, studiously avoiding eye contact, as it grinds its way up four floors. She's tall for a woman, probably five ten or so. Short strawberry blonde hair, wide swimmer's shoulders, skin honeyed by the sun and generous curves that will run to fat after she's had children if she's not careful. Her nose is a little large, but surprisingly it doesn't ruin her appearance – quite the contrary. Its quirky route down her face leavens otherwise predictable, glossy good looks.

I suspect a fearsome intellect and formidable will lurk behind those clear mushroom-grey eyes. Attractive, in a magnificent, statuesque way, but absolutely not my type at all.

Although she does have a certain earthiness. A just-fallen-out-of-bed air.

Christ, *I want her*.

2

Sara

Amazing, isn't it, how an intelligent, streetsmart woman who has the rest of her shit together can be reduced to a gibbering splat of emotional jelly by a man? And not even a lush hottie like Orlando Bloom – as long as he keeps his mouth shut – or Matthew McConaughey. No, *our* Casanova is fifty-one, short, bald – and married.

So, he's a bastard. This is *news*?

'He promised he'd leave her,' Amy says again. 'As soon as they'd sold their house, he said he was going to tell her about us. He *promised*.'

Clearly no point reminding her he also promised he'd be faithful to his wife, keeping only unto her in sickness and in health twenty-four/seven and all the rest of that crap. If promises have a hierarchy, I'm guessing the sacred vows you make to your wife before God and congregation come a little higher in the pecking order than drunken pillow-talk to a bit on the side young enough to be your daughter.

'How long have you been shagging him?' I ask.

'Four years,' she says defiantly.

'And how long has he been promising to leave his wife?'

'Four years,' she says, slightly less so.

In fact, her boss Terry Greenslade has so far sworn to leave his wife just as soon as – and this is in no particular order – (a) he gets his promotion (b) his wife gets *her* promotion (c) his eldest child starts college (d) his youngest child leaves school (e) his dying Catholic mother finally wafts off to limbo or purgatory or wherever it is these incense-freaks go; and (f) the dog (FYI a golden Labrador; how smug-married is that?) recovers from, wait for it, a hysterectomy. I suppose his latest selling-the-house excuse is an improvement on canine wimmins' trouble, but it's all still Grade A bullshit. Every milestone has come and gone and surprise, surprise, *he's still with his wife*. Like, *hello*?

It's not that I have a particular moral thing about affairs with married men, though it's not something I'd shout about from the rooftops either. But at the end of the day, *they're* the ones cheating, not you. A brief, passionate dalliance with someone else's husband is almost a feminine rite of passage; no girl should leave her twenties without one. And married men are usually great in bed – it's the gratitude.

But it's one thing to have a quick fling and send him back home to his wife, self-esteem restored, wardrobe re-invigorated, renewed for another ten years of married bliss with a couple of new bedroom tricks up his sleeve (really, the wives should be thankful). It's quite another to take an unbroken marriage and deliberately turn it into eggs Benedict.

Sorry, but husband-stealing is a bullet-proof no-no in my book. It just wrecks things for everyone. Aside from the poor kids who'll only get to see their dads alternate Saturdays in McDonald's, in the long run it's you who gets shafted. Leopards don't change their two-timing spots: a man who cheats *with* you will cheat *on* you, so how are you ever going to trust him even if you do manage to prise him away from his sad-sack spouse? And let's get real, the odds on that happening are microscopic, despite the friend-of-a-friend everyone knows who finally got to walk down the aisle with one husband, slightly used, previous careless lady owner, after years of patient waiting. It's an urban myth. If they don't leave their wives in the first three months, they'll never leave.

I slug some more white wine into my glass. Bang goes all that hard work in pump class this morning. Screw it, I deserve it.

I scope the wine bar for talent over the rim of my drink, tuning Amy out as she witters on about Terry. I love this girl to death, but I have *so* had it with this conversation. For a tough, ball-breaking corporate tax lawyer, she doesn't half have her head up her arse when it comes to men.

It's raining outside and, depressingly, already dark, though it's still not yet five; the bar smells of wet wool and dirty city streets and damp leather and money. It's one of the reasons I became a lawyer, if I'm brutally honest, to make money; though as it turns out I don't quite have the temperament to go all the way like Amy, and make some kind of Faustian pact to sell my soul to corporate law for sackfuls of filthy lucre. I'm ashamed to admit it, this isn't a desirable trait in a lawyer: but I've discovered I won't actually do *anything* for money. Hence the switch to family law. Less cash perhaps – though still enough to keep me in L. K. Bennetts when I make partner, which I fully intend to do before I'm thirty – but at least I won't die from boredom before I get the chance to spend it.

The windows steam up as the bar fills with randy, rich lawyers kicking back for the weekend and predatory secretaries undoing an extra button as bait. Fortunately Amy and I snagged a table early; though since this is one of those retro eighties places with tall spindly chrome tables and those uncomfortable lemon-wedge stools that'd make a size eight arse look huge (and, let's face it, mine was bigger than that the day I was born) this isn't the advantage it could have been.

Each time the door opens, there's another blast of cold air and wet whoosh of traffic noise as black cabs and red buses – even lawyers can't afford to drive their own cars into London these days – swish through the puddles. Everyone's body temperature goes up ten degrees when they come into the warmth; lots of red cheeks and moist noses.

Hello-o-o. Talking of moist. *Look* who's just walked in. Dark blond hair, tall – by which I mean taller than my five foot eleven or I'm not interested – and very broad shoulders. Ripped jeans, but designer trashed not poor white. Ripped pecs and abs, too. Not a lawyer, obviously. Advertising or journalism, I'd put money on it.

I cross my legs so that my short mint-green silk skirt rides slightly up my thighs, revealing a sliver of cream lace hold-up, and let one killer heel dangle from my toe. Gently I roll my shoulders back, as if to relieve tired muscles, so that my tits perk up – there's plenty of nipple action thanks to the frigging draught from the door – and casually slide one hand up my neck to play seductively with my long hair. At which point I grope fresh air and the silky prickle of my new urchin crop and remember I had the whole lot lopped off for the first time in living memory for my new job. Quickly I turn the gesture into a fiddle with my earring.

I count to ten, then sneak a quick peek at the target. *Shit.* Some skeletal blonde has skewered herself to his hip, and is death-raying the circling secretaries with a diamond solitaire the size of a Cadbury's mini-egg on her left hand. *My fucking luck.*

It's not that I'm especially keen to acquire a husband, particularly when it's so easy to recycle other people's. But perhaps it might be nice to be asked. I haven't even been introduced to a boyfriend's parents yet (though I've hidden from a few under the duvet). Right now, such is my dire on-the-shelfdom, I'd settle for having a boyfriend long enough for the cat not to hiss when he walks in. Amy says – without any discernible trace of irony – that my chronically single state is my own fault for not Taking Things Seriously, Focusing and Setting Goals. Personally, I blame my mother for allowing me to be a bridesmaid three times.

'—sometimes I think he's never going to leave his wife.'

Amy, doll, he is never going to leave his wife.

'Honestly, Sara, sometimes I wonder. Do you think he's ever going to leave his wife?'

There was a time I used to lie and tell her yes, love conquers all, it's a big step, you have to give him time, you wouldn't want a man who could just walk out on his children without a second thought anyway, would you?

'No,' I say.

'Yes, but Sara—'

'No.'

'Sometimes I think you don't want me to be happy,' she says sulkily.

'Oh, yes, that'll be it,' I say tartly. 'I just listen to you go on about this total arsehole ad bloody infinitum for my health. I mean, why chillax at a club when I can spend my Friday nights sitting in a wine bar – and for the record, that's whine spelt *with* the aitch – listening to my best friend make excuses for some pathetic creep who can't just make one woman miserable like most married men, oh, no, he has to ruin two women's lives to feel good about himself.'

'You don't have to be such a bitch about it.' Amy sniffs, getting a face on. 'You're always so cynical—'

'I am not cynical.'

'You are. People can't help falling in love, Sara. You know,' she says, adopting the familiar pitying tone that Couples (however fucked up) use towards Singles the world over, 'when it finally happens to you you'll understand. You can't always choose where you love.'

She pushes the boundaries of friendship, she really does.

'I need to go to the loo,' I say crossly, sliding off my lemon wedge. 'Keep an eye on my bag, would you?'

I smooth down my skirt – two inches above the knee; sexy, but not obvious – and make sure I give it plenty of va-va-voom as I sashay to the toilet. You never know who's watching. The trick, I've found, is to think about the last time you had really hot sex – though, sadly, in my case this is a more distant memory than it has any right to be for a single, solvent twenty-five-year-old female with no immediately apparent drawbacks like hairy armpits, suppurating buboes or Juicy Couture tracksuit bottoms. Not that I'm really in the mood now, to be honest. Amy and her married shit-for-brains have put paid to that. Why do some women insist on believing that any man, even a swamp donkey who doesn't belong to you, is better than no man at all?

But I walk toe-heel, toe-heel to get that hot-model lilt into my walk anyway.

Since I don't actually need to pee, I was just trying to avoid twenty-five to life for strangling my best friend, I loll idly against the freestanding green glass sink – this place takes itself *way* too seriously – and gurn at the mirror. Frankly, this grim fluorescent light doesn't do a girl any favours. Every spot I've ever had since the age of twelve is suddenly ghosting through my make-up, and you could fit Roseanne Barr into the bags under my eyes.

I run my fingers through my new short hair, wondering where the fuck the sassy, sharp, sexy-career-girl crop I had when I left the salon this morning has gone. Thanks to the rain and wet Laundromat warmth of first the tube and now the bar, I'm starting to look disconcertingly like Lady Di *circa* 1982, which is hardly the effect I was looking for. Oh shit. I should never have let Amy talk me into cutting it. I must have been bloody mad. Let's face it: her judgement is hardly without peer.

Despairingly I tug the shingle at the bare nape of my

neck. How long does it take for hair to grow? Five millimetres a month? I'll be an old maid before I look presentable again. No man is going to go near me, I'll turn into a dyke divorce lawyer, I'll never have sex again except with hairy women wearing Birkenstocks. Maybe I'll join the Taliban. At least if you're stuck under one of those black sheets no one's going to know if you have spots or a bad-hair day.

The moment I rejoin Amy, she starts on again about Terry, and I wonder if she even noticed I was gone. *Dear God, if I ever get a boyfriend again, which appears to be increasingly unlikely, please strike me down and cover me with unsavoury rashes if I ever end up like this.*

I glance at my watch. I should be heading over to Fisher Lyon Raymond for the old sod's retirement party now, anyway. Hardly the most exciting Friday night option – although sadly the best offer I have on the table right now – but I couldn't exactly turn him down when he invited me at my bloody job interview. And it probably *is* a good idea to 'meet everyone in an informal setting' before I start there next week. See them all with their hair down – or even their pants, if what I've heard about family lawyers is true.

Astonishingly, given my current run of luck, it's actually stopped raining by the time we finish our drinks and leave. I walk with Amy to the tube station – resisting the uncharitable but reasonable urge to throw her under a train – and then carry on alone down Holborn towards Fisher's, my breath frosting in the icy night air.

It's a five-minute walk that in these heels takes me twenty, so it's gone seven by the time I get to the office block that houses the law firm. To my surprise, the entire building is in near-total darkness. I press my nose to the opaque glass front door: even the security guard has buggered off for the night. I'm puzzled: Fisher told me the party was here at seven, I'm sure of it.

As I straighten up to leave, someone shoves the door open from the inside, almost knocking me out. The suit doesn't even glance at me as I mutter something about an appointment and slip into the warm foyer before the door slams shut. I rub my bruised temples. Lucky I'm not a frigging terrorist, you supercilious git.

I take the lift up to the fourth floor and squint – a little more cautiously this time – through the glass porthole in the door to the Fisher offices. Just the cleaner, moochily waving a duster over the receptionist's desk. *Shit. Now what?*

I wait a few moments, then irritably thump the lift button to go back down. Looks like it's just me, my remote and a Lean Cuisine tonight, then. Marvellous. I'm having the most misspent misspent youth since Mother Teresa.

I hit the button again. Someone must be loading the lift on the second floor; it's been stuck there since forever. The back of my neck prickles, and I shiver. Offices at night creep me out. Too many thrillers where the girl gets it behind the filing cabinets. All those shadows—

The door suddenly opens behind me and I jump about fifteen feet.

A lawyer strides out of Fisher's and is almost through the stairwell door before he even notices I'm there. He pauses, outstretched hand on the chrome push bar.

'Can I help you?' he asks curtly: very Surrey public schoolboy.

'I'm looking for Fisher Raymond Lyon. Am I on the right floor?'

'Yes, but I'm afraid the office is closed for the night. Did you want to make an appointment?'

'Oh, I'm not a client,' I say indignantly. Shit, do I look like a sad divorcée? 'I'm a solicitor. My name's Sara Kaplan – I'm starting work here next Monday.'

'Ah, yes, of course.' He switches his briefcase to his left hand and sticks out his right, practically breaking my fingers with his grip. Right back at you, I think, squeezing his hand as hard as I can. 'Nicholas Lyon, one of the partners. I'm afraid I was detained on a difficult case in Leeds when my colleagues interviewed you, I do apologize. I understand you come very highly recommended from your previous firm.'

News to me. I didn't realize they were so keen to get rid of me. 'Thank you. I'm very much looking forward to working here.'

'Good, good. Well, welcome to the firm. I'll look forward to seeing you on Monday.'

God, he's anal, he couldn't be more restrained if he was strapped to a gurney – but bizarrely, he's kind of sexy too. Can't quite put my finger on it. Maybe it's the mouth: very full lips, and a kind of Douglas dent in the chin. Good-looking, too, though he's quite old: forty at least. And clothes that went out with the ark. Braces, for Christ's sake! But at least he's tall. And that mouth. I bet he'd give great head if someone taught him right—

'Miss Kaplan, did you just want to drop off some paperwork, or was there something else?'

My cheeks burn as if he can read my mind. I realize

my hand is floating aimlessly near my shorn neck again, and quickly turn the gesture into an earring fiddle. My lobes are going to fall off if I don't get used to this haircut soon. 'Um. Well, it's just that Mr Fisher invited me to his leaving party, and I thought it might be nice to meet everyone before Monday—'

'Oh, I see. Yes, of course. It's not here, though, it's at the Italian restaurant across the road. I'm just going over there myself.'

He presses the button and we stand staring in mutual fascination at the steel door whilst the lift takes its own sweet time to come up. Well, this is fun. I've felt less awkward playing Twister. He's kind of gawking at me out of the corner of his eye, probably wondering why the fuck his colleagues hired me and vowing never to go away and leave them to their own devices again. I can tell I am *so* not his kind of woman. Bet he likes them small and dainty, with long girly hair and little nubbin breasts. He's just got that old-fashioned air about him. Poker-straight back like he's ex-military, and that nondescript short-but-not-too-short haircut my father's had since before I was born. At least he's still got hair, I suppose; actually it's thick and dark, it'd probably be curly too if he'd just let it grow a bit. And his eyes are amazing; they're a rather boring, wishy-washy grey–blue colour but they scream 'bedroom'! Mind you, the rest of him is so buttoned-up I bet he'd have a heart attack if he knew.

Surreptitiously I clock his left hand. *Naturellement.* I guarantee the wife's never worked. I can see it all now: she probably started out a size eight but is more like a sixteen now, irons and starches his shirts by hand, cooks him homemade steak-and-kidney pie and has sex by numbers every Saturday night whilst she plans the menu for their next dinner party. Two pre-teen kids, boy and girl, of course, unremarkable private schools, tennis and violin lessons, newish Volvo on the drive, one modest skiing holiday a year – upmarket but not *too* smart – and two weeks every summer somewhere sunny but not package: northern Cyprus, maybe Malta. God, save me from death by domesticity.

The lift finally arrives and naturally he waits for me to go first, shooting me this freaky look as if I'm an alien who's just pitched up on his front lawn after a short sojourn at Roswell. I'd love to get in his trousers just to shake him up a bit. I bet once you got him going he could be a dirty bastard in bed; the funniest part would be watching him find out.

Clearly I am never going to get the chance to put my theory to the test. Lyon edges to the far side of the lift, puts a London bus width between us as we cross the road, and shoots off like an Exocet to the far side of the room the moment we reach the restaurant. Either he's terrified of women or the radioactive waste I ate for breakfast is repeating on me.

I grab a glass of tepid house white from a passing waiter. From the look of it, the law firm has taken over the restaurant for the night. Most of the tables have been pushed back out of the way, which means everyone's standing around in self-conscious knots not knowing quite how to juggle drink, canapés and handshakes. The knack, I've discovered, is not to bother with the canapés.

I'm just reaching for my second glass when the old guy, Fisher, pounces from behind a pillar covered with plastic grapes. Bloody lucky he's leaving, I think, as the dirty git kisses me on the cheek and grabs the opportunity to cop a quick feel of my bum at the same time. Hasn't he heard of sexual harassment suits? Mind you, I suppose you take it where you can get it when you hit sixty and bugger the risk.

I network for a bit, letting Fisher's paw roost between my shoulder blades as he introduces me first to a fiftyish battleaxe called Joan Bryant, their scary-looking 'sleeping' partner – she should be so lucky, she's got a face like a slapped arse – and then to David Raymond, a rather skittish lawyer who looks younger than me but is probably early thirties. You can tell just by looking at him that never in a month of Sundays would he ever be called Dave. I'm guessing his father was the original Raymond on the firm's letterhead.

The conversation turns to the pig's ear the Government has made of its latest legislative proposals for no-fault divorce. Joan immediately – and predictably – says the whole premise is a logical impossibility, since divorce is always the man's fault, and then glares at David as if she's going to eat him and spit out the bones, like Gollum. David gives a sickly grin and feebly starts to point out that there are always two sides to every story – oh dear, not in *divorce*, David, what are you, a frigging Relate counsellor? There's only ever one side: the side paying us – but he subsides into pale sweaty silence when Gollum licks her lips.

Fisher slides his meaty palm down my spine and rests it comfortably on my arse. 'C'mon, c'mon, let the new boy speak. What do you think, Sara?'

'I guess quickie no-faulters could be a good idea,' I muse, resisting the urge to grab his wrinkly dick to even things up a bit. 'You're more likely to get repeat customers if you can recycle the exes quickly.'

'Contested, drawn-out divorces bring in more fees,' Gollum snaps.

Fisher laughs uproariously. 'You girls are two of a kidney,' he splutters. 'Fees first, everything else later.'

I barely have time to register this monumental insult when a rosy-cheeked dumpling in creased Laura Ashley – Fisher's long-suffering wife, I presume – sidles over and gently extracts him from temptation and my waistband. I like her instantly. Mrs Fisher looks like every little kid's ideal mother, all pillowy soft bosom and warm forgiving hugs. Couldn't be further from mine, then, if she tried.

My parents married tragically young – seventeen, the pair of them – and had me six months later. Hmm, you do the maths. My mother likes to relate the 'nightmare' of giving birth to me to anyone who'll sit still long enough: the agonizing three-and-a-half-day labour, the emergency Caesarean, the haemorrhaging, the next-of-kin consent forms, the hysterectomy, the works. Makes you feel kind of guilty from the word go just for existing, really. So anyway: I'm *it*, their one shot at immortality. At least Dad has his job to distract him – he's a financial adviser – but my mother's never worked; I'm her entire focus, and to be honest, it can get a bit wearing. She's always buying me things: a Louis Vuitton handbag for my birthday, Gucci loafers for Christmas; I still get a stocking filled with goodies collectively worth more than I earn in a year. I'm not really complaining; but you get nothing for nothing, not even from your parents. Every time I find myself in a financial scrape – which is pretty much when-ever I walk past Jigsaw – my mother bails me out, then beats me with it for months afterwards. She doesn't do it to be nice, but to control me. Dad doesn't approve but he never interferes; there's no question who wears the trousers in our house.

I toss back the house vinegar and glance round idly for Nick. He's standing in the furthest corner of the room – and staring intently, almost fixedly, at me. I feel a jolt of recognition at the hunger in his eyes. As soon as he catches my gaze he blanches and looks away, but it's too late. You *know* when a man wants you.

I'm shocked. I would never have thought – he doesn't seem the type. Not your usual kind of player. In a previous age I'd have cast him as one of those medieval monks who wore a hair shirt to mortify the flesh and got out a cat-o'-nine-tails whenever he had carnal thoughts. Actually, for all I know he's a paid-up member of Opus Dei. I've read *The Da Vinci Code* too, you know.

He looks so appalled you'd think he'd fallen headfirst into a pit of decomposing plague victims. I almost want to go over and tell him not to worry. He *is* hot, especially with that suppressed slow-burn thing he's got going on. But off limits. I might borrow the odd unattended husband from time to time, but I never do office romances – it's always the woman who gets screwed. No way do I intend to end up like Amy in four years time.

But I can't deny it's going to make encounters by the coffee-machine at playtime more interesting. And if he's got the hots for me, it's not going to do my career any harm either, as long as I tread carefully.

God, that makes me sound like a calculating witch, and I'm really not. It's just that in this business men get to play the Old School Tie card all the time, whereas women have got nothing but the wits – and body – God gave them. You don't often see women reaching down to give their younger sisters a hand up the career ladder the way men do. I'd never sleep my way to the top, but a little flirtation – that's all, I swear – to oil the wheels of fellowship never did any harm. Hey. You play the cards you're dealt.

A middle-aged woman suddenly flusters into the restaurant, her head bobbing frantically as she tries to find a face she recognizes. Probably a clerk's wife. She's missed brushing a bit of her rather wild, dark hair, and it's all bed-heady at the back. No coat, safe, dependable little black dress to the knee, discreet early-marriage jewellery – big on sentimentality, small on diamonds – and a battered bucket handbag the size of the Chunnel. Lovely dark eyes, though, and she's reed-thin, lucky cow. But – oh, God! – she's forgotten to change her shoes. Oh, poor bitch. She's standing in the middle of this snotty Italian London restaurant in a pair of pink towelling slippers.

No one else seems to have even noticed her arrival. I grab another glass of house white from a nearby tray and shoot over.

'Here,' I say kindly, shoving it towards her, 'it tastes like lukewarm battery acid, but it's better than nothing. By the way,' I murmur discreetly, 'you might want to change your shoes in the ladies before you join everyone.'

She takes the wine and shifts her huge bag from one shoulder to the other, shedding a cascade of tissues, broken pens and what looks like a half-eaten gingerbread man onto the floor as it flaps open. I wonder if she's in the right place; surely even a clerk's wife couldn't be this dippy. 'Sweet of you,' she says absently, spilling half the wine on herself as she bends to pick up the shit she's just chucked on the ground. Still glancing distractedly around the restaurant, she mops ineffectually at her dress with one of the tissues, rubbing what looks like flour into the worn fabric.

'Your shoes,' I hiss again.

She looks curiously at her slippers as if seeing them for the first time. 'Oh, yes,' she says equably. 'Well, at least the rain hasn't ruined them.'

I watch disbelievingly as she calmly kicks the slippers off and shoves them into the bulging tardis on her shoulder, seemingly untroubled by the fact that she's now wandering London in her stockinged feet. Is this woman for real? God, I hope I don't get that frigging mental when I'm old.

Abruptly Nick materializes beside us, looking strained. He ignores me completely.

'Malinche, where in heaven's name have you *been*? It's eight-thirty, Will's been asking for you for the last hour! What kept you?'

Fuck, this is Nick's wife?

'Traffic,' she says, waving a hand vaguely in the direction of the street.

'I told you to allow – oh, never mind. Now that you're here, you'd better come and be sociable.'

'I *was*, darling, I was talking to this gorgeous girl here – such a lovely suit, I hate chartreuse itself, of course, the drink I mean, but that's simply a *delicious* colour, especially with that corn-gold hair, how clever of you – what did you say your name was?'

'Sara Kaplan,' I supply faintly.

'Of course, Sara, well, Nicholas, I *was* being sociable as

you can see, I was talking to Sara, she very kindly got me a drink, I was just about to come and find you and Will, and then here you were—'

Does the woman never draw breath? I can't believe the stuffy-but-cute Nick is with this hippy, style-free Alzheimer dingbat. He doesn't look very comfortable either as she latches onto him and grabs his arm, and suddenly I can see it all: the childhood sweetheart he married when he was too young to know any better, the kids that followed before he knew it, the albatross of a mortgage, the arid sex life, the whole nightmare. Poor sod. He looks like he needs some R & R big time.

Hmmm. Now there's an interesting thought.

All of a sudden, Monday can't come quickly enough.

3

Malinche

Kit can be such a total wretch sometimes, *really* he can. I flick the end of a tea-towel at him, but he ducks and instead I catch the saucepan chandelier hanging over the island in the centre of the kitchen, setting pans and ladles clattering against each other. I cover the telephone mouthpiece so that Nicholas won't hear the din, and stick out my tongue at Kit as he sits there shaking with laughter and doing absolutely nothing to stop my wilful baby daughter from putting the rabbit down the waste disposal.

'Oh, God, Metheny, don't do that,' I gasp, quickly rescuing the trembling creature and steadying the saucepans. '*Poor* rabbit. Sorry, Nicholas, I have to go. I'll see you at the station. Usual time?'

Nicholas yelps in my ear. 'For God's sake, Malinche, it's William's retirement party this evening! Don't tell me you've forgotten! You're supposed to be on the five twenty-eight from Salisbury to Waterloo, remember?'

Oh, Lord. I had completely forgotten. It's three forty already, Liz will be dropping the girls off from school at any moment, I haven't made their tea yet – I thought *ravioli di magro* would be nice, I haven't done that for a while; a little fresh ricotta seasoned with nutmeg, sea salt and black pepper and blended with Swiss chard and *pancetta stesa*, and of course freshly grated Parmesan over the top. I haven't sorted out a babysitter, I need to wash my hair, what to wear, how on earth am I going to get to the station in time for the five twenty-eight?

'So I am. I hadn't really forgotten,' I fib, crossing my fingers behind my back, 'it just slipped my mind for a moment. Hold on a second—'

I put the receiver down and thrust Don Juan de Marco back in his cage in the scullery with a couple of wilted leaves of pak choi as consolation, firmly securing the latch with a piece of twine so the baby can't let him out again. Metheny instantly stops what she is doing – picking up spilt Cheerios from beneath her high-chair and putting them one by one into Kit's outstretched hand – to crouch plumply by the rabbit cage, nappy in the air, fat gold curls clinging to the nape of her neck as her chubby little fingers poke and pull at the string. I cross my fingers that the twine holds for at least the next five minutes and throw myself theatrically onto my knees on the kitchen flag-stones in front of Kit, hands clasped in supplication as I try my best to look pathetic.

He ignores my amateur dramatics, fastidiously heaping the Cheerios into a small pyramid on the counter before dipping an elegant pale finger into my cake mix to taste it. I've flavoured it with vanilla and orange and lemon zest, darkened it with cocoa and spiced it up with candied orange peel. The meld of tangy rich scents drifts around the warm kitchen like fog on the moors.

'What?' he says sternly.

I flap my hands at him to be quiet. Nicholas knows Kit is my best friend and comes over to visit, of course he does, but he doesn't have to know quite how often.

'What?' Kit mouths.

I intensify my importunate expression, although I suspect, from the twitch at the corner of Kit's mouth, that the net effect is one of constipation rather than entreaty. He rolls his eyes but nods, as I knew he would. I struggle up from the floor. Dramatic gestures are all very well, but then of course you have to live with the consequences; it's rather like having sex on the beach, not nearly as romantic as you imagine, and of course the sand gets *everywhere*. I scoop up Metheny in the nick of time – my delicious yummy baby, she smells like warm fresh-baked bread – and retrieve the phone. 'I really *must* go, Nicholas—'

'You did remember to arrange a babysitter?'

'Mmm. Yes, Kit very sweetly said he'd do it.'

Quickly I ring off so I don't have to listen to the pained silence that invariably follows any mention of Kit. I've spent the past twelve years variously cajoling, begging and banging heads together, but it's no good, the current wary stand-off between my husband and my dearest friend is clearly as good as it's ever going to get. I have the deepest sympathy for everybody at the UN if the Palestinians and the Israelis are anywhere near this bad, though of course neither Nicholas nor Kit are anything at all like that difficult man Arafat – no, he's dead now, there's a new one, what's his name, I really *must* read the paper a bit more often. It's all a question of finding the time, of course: I get to Saturday evening and I still haven't worked my way through *last* Sunday's papers, though I must say things aren't made any easier by the number of supplements they have these days. Those poor paperboys, I don't know how they carry them up the path: we're creating a generation of twisted spines. I used to think Nicholas didn't like Kit because he was gay, and perhaps in the beginning – though Nicholas isn't like that, he's not racist or sexist or homophobic or anything, well, except in a background wallpaper sort of way, you can't help the way you're raised. But of course it wasn't about that, really, not at all—

'Mal, what an absolutely delicious smell,' Liz says, pushing open the top half of the kitchen stable door. A cold blast of November air carries the scent of bonfires and rotting leaves into the fuggy kitchen warmth. She reaches in to unbolt the bottom half and steps smartly out of the way as Sophie and Evie race past her into the kitchen, throwing coats, lobbing satchels and dropping lunchboxes. 'Hi, Kit. Ooooh, yummy, chocolate and orange, are you doing something Christmassy?'

I retrieve the mixing bowl from Kit's elegant grasp and scrape the lovely gooey chocolaty mixture into a greased baking tin. 'It's supposed to be a birthday cake for Nicholas and Metheny tomorrow, although at the current rate of progress it's going to end up something Christmassy.'

'Oooh, save me a slice. No, no, on second thoughts, don't, I'm supposed to be on another bloody diet for Christmas.' She drools over the photograph on the open page of my recipe book, looking for all the world like a starving Victorian orphan with her nose pressed to a pie-shop window. 'Does look *scrummy*, though. It *is* nearly

Christmas now, and I'm going to do South Beach in January, it's my New Year's resolution. So perhaps one slice.'

'One slice for Nicholas, and one for Metheny,' Kit purrs.

Liz looks flustered. Kit seems to have this effect on women even when they know which way the wind blows for him, bedroom-wise. I haven't yet worked out if it's because they find him so hopelessly attractive – hard not to, with those knife-edge cheekbones and Restoration curls – or because he's just so wickedly louche you can't help but think of s-e-x whenever he's around.

'I don't know how you stay so slim, Mal,' Liz complains. 'It's not fair, you cook such jolly wonderful food and you're as thin as a rake.'

'Family life,' I say, not entirely joking.

'Never works that way for me,' Liz sighs.

Covetously she eyes a platoon of gingerbread men, still warm, that I baked earlier for the school's Christmas Fayre and left out on racks to cool. Dearest Liz. She spends her life locked in an epic battle with temptation, for she adores food, all food, with unbridled passion, but is cruelly fated to wear every bite she eats. I love her dearly, but she's built to last, as Kit mischievously puts it, with childbearing hips squeezed, come rain or shine, into the same pair of worn jodhpurs, a wide, open face with rosy cheeks like two scrubbed apples, and the warmest heart of anyone in the village. She and I share the school run, with me dropping the children off – my older two, her lone poppy – in the morning, after I've taken Nicholas to the station, and Liz doing the afternoon shift so that I can get on with scribbling down a few of my recipes for the new book while Metheny has her nap. At least: that's the theory.

'Gosh, must dash,' Liz exclaims, glancing at her hefty leather-strapped wristwatch. 'Chloe's got a riding lesson at four, it's the gymkhana in a couple of weeks. Cheerio, Kit. See you tomorrow, girls.'

Sophie and Evie jump guiltily, their mouths full of gingerbread men whom they seem to have eaten bodily in one go, like little human boa constrictors. I whip the rest out of their reach as, unabashed, they yell an enthusiastic farewell to Liz, scattering a fine mist of crumbs and saliva across Kit's burnt umber suede jacket and *very* close-fitting brown jeans. No wonder poor Liz doesn't know where to look. You could divine his religion from the tightness of those trousers.

'Oh, God. You two infants are utterly vile.' Kit grimaces, brushing himself down.

'Serves you right for being such a peacock,' I retort.

The girls giggle. They adore Kit, who, for all his posturing, has been an extremely good godfather and will, I'm quite sure, introduce them to all sorts of delightful vices like smoking and baccarat as soon as they are old enough for him to take up to London without me.

'I found a cat today, but it was dead,' six-year-old Evie announces.

I suppress a shudder. 'How do you know it was dead?'

'Because I pissed in its ear and it didn't move,' Evie says.

'You did what?'

'You know,' she explains impatiently. 'I leaned over and went "Pssst!" and it didn't move.'

Kit and I shriek with laughter. Evie looks crossly from one of us to the other, then stomps from the room in a fit of high dudgeon. At nine, Sophie may be the one with the knockout looks – thick chestnut hair, huge black sloe eyes, and tawny skin the colour of caramel, a throwback to my Italian father's roots – but I have the feeling it's Evie's zany interpretation of life that's going to leave a trail of broken hearts when she's older.

Last month, I overheard her doing her maths homework at the kitchen table, muttering to herself, 'Two plus five, that son of a bitch is seven. Four plus one, that son of a bitch is five . . .'

Aghast, I asked her what on earth she was doing.

'My maths,' Evie said calmly.

'Is that how your teacher taught you to do it?' I gasped.

'Course. Three plus three . . .'

The next day I marched into the classroom and demanded to know what Mrs Koehler thought she was teaching my child. When I explained what Evie had been saying, she laughed so much she had to sit down.

'What I taught them,' Mrs Koehler explained, 'was two plus two, *the sum of which* is four.'

Kit now unfolds his long, lean body from the kitchen counter as I pull an onion from the rope overhead to chop for the girls' ravioli. 'What is it exactly that I've agreed to *ce soir*?' he asks languidly.

'Only babysitting. Darling, you don't mind, do you? Only it's Will Fisher's leaving do and I promised Nicholas I'd be there and then of course I forgot all about it – Metheny, no, take Uncle Kit's lovely hat out of the rubbish – and now I have about an hour to get ready and find something to wear and catch the train—'

'Forget the crocheted pasta pillows or whatever it is you were planning,' Kit says firmly, taking the onion out of my hands, 'and get your pert little derriere up the stairs and into the bathtub PDQ. I'll sort out the girls' tea. Sophie, Evie—' this as my middle daughter wanders back to the kitchen with Halibut the cat in her arms, tantrum forgotten already, 'what would you like Uncle Kit to cook you for tea?'

'Pizza!' Sophie cries.

'Frozen! From a box!' Evie adds for good measure.

'Charming,' Kit huffs.

I have walked many a mile in these particular shoes. It's one of those immutable facts of motherhood: the length of time taken and trouble spent preparing a meal is inversely proportional to the enthusiasm with which your children will greet it. Toil for hours in the kitchen producing something nourishing and delicious that hits all the primary food groups and they'll push it around their plates until it gets cold and congeals and even the dog wouldn't want it. Guiltily throw frozen chicken fingers and crinkle chips in the oven and they'll rave about it for weeks.

I shoot upstairs to get ready. I haven't time for the long relaxing bubble-bath I crave – I haven't had that kind of time since I fell for Sophie – or indeed even to wait for the hot water to make its leisurely way through the ramble of furred pipes from the tank in the outhouse to the calcified shower head in the upstairs bathroom, a journey roughly comparable in terms of time and complexity to the Paris– Dakar rally. Instead, I whip off my clothes and brace myself for the ice-cold scourge that passes for a shower in this house. A six-hundred-year-old thatched farmhouse in two acres of breath-snatchingly beautiful Wiltshire countryside is romantic and gorgeous and just oozing with history and charm, and of course as soon as Nicholas and I saw it – house-hunting when I was newly pregnant with Evie – we just had to buy it, there was never any question about that. But it is *not* practical. Overflowing cesspits and lethally exposed live wires are neither romantic nor charming, and there have been times – never publicly admitted to, Nicholas would be mortified – when I have longed for something brand spanking new in vulgar red brick and equipped with the latest in efficient brushed-steel German appliances.

Gasping at the freezing water, I scrape a sliver of hard soap over my chicken skin, able to differentiate between my breasts and goosebumps only by the fact that two of them sport shrivelled brown nipples. I try in vain to work up a decent lather until I realize that it is not in fact soap I am scrubbing over my scrawny pudenda but a piece of the ceiling plaster which has come down *again*.

By the time I finish washing my hair – with supermarket bubble-bath, yuk and bugger, since wretched Sophie has once more pinched the wildly expensive shampoo that Kit gave me last birthday – my lips are blue, my fingers have frostbite, and I feel like one of Shackleton's Antarctic expeditionaries. My dratted hair will frizz into a hideous Afro if I use the hairdryer, and since it's already after five I don't even have time to let it dry naturally by the Aga in the kitchen – the only warm room in the house – as I usually do. I'm going to have to venture out into the bitter November night with my head dripping wet; I will no doubt catch my death of cold, double pneumonia, pleurisy and tuberculosis, but obviously this is entirely my own fault for forgetting about the party in the first place.

'Don't say it,' I warn Kit, as I race downstairs in the safe but dull little black dress I've had since I was about fourteen, 'no time to dither, it had to be this.'

'Quite sure?'

'Not a word, thank you.'

I dispense kisses liberally amongst the girls, fling keys and cash and lipstick into my bag and scramble into Nicholas's Mercedes, then scramble back out and go back for the monogrammed humidor I bought for him to give Will Fisher. I hate driving Nicholas's car, I'm always so scared I'll prang it or something, and although it's so wonderful and safe and huge – I feel like I'm driving a luxury tank – I'm also very aware that even a *tiny* scrape on the bumper will set us back hundreds of pounds. I am really much happier in my old Volvo, so much more forgiving; and every little dent along its sides tells a story, it's like a metal photograph album really, I know I'm going to hate it when I finally say goodbye. But the Volvo's still with Ginger, so it's got to be the Mercedes, and actually – I'd forgotten – it has heated seats, oh what bliss, at least now I'll have a warm bottom when I get on the train.

When Nicholas and I first met, I didn't even know how to drive. At twenty-four I was still gadding about London on the ancient sit-up-and-beg bicycle my mother Louise passed on to me when I followed in her shoes to Edinburgh; although Louise didn't actually graduate, of course, she dropped out in her second year to go to California and 'find herself' with her boyfriend (who naturally made sure he got *his* degree before decamping to join the flower children). The swine stayed around just long enough to get her pregnant with my sister before scuttling home to a lifetime of accountancy in Esher, his brief flirtation with the unconventional firmly over. Louise, not in the least put out by his desertion, joined a Californian lesbian commune and gave birth to Cleo in a pool as the sisters sang 'Kumbaya' in a circle around her. She then promptly fell pregnant again a few months later – 'the lesbian thing never really *took*, you see; when we started having our periods together the amount of hormones swilling around was positively *lethal'* – by a newly arrived waiter from Florence, who this time did at least offer, in very broken English, to marry her. Louise thanked him very gently for being so kind, declined politely but firmly, and came back home to Salisbury so that she could have me at Stonehenge; not quite literally – much to her chagrin, even in hippy 1970 they wouldn't let her do *that* – but in a little country hospital near by.

Once, not long after I met Nicholas, I asked my mother why she had never married after she came back home, fully expecting some sort of Germaine Greer rant about marriage-as-patriarchal-ownership (before she recanted, of course, my mother has never quite forgiven her for that) but instead, 'You think marriage is just about you and him,' Louise said, regarding me steadily, 'but it's *not*, it's not a private romantic thing at all. You take on so many other people, too, a whole network of them, all their problems and fears and difficulties. I never wanted any of that. I knew I didn't have the patience to deal with it. I just wanted it to be *us*.'

I realized then that I didn't actually know my mother at all.

Nor, in a very literal sense, did I ever know my father. But it's from Roberto – Louise never did catch his last name – that I got the impossible hair and an overwhelming desire to cook almost from the moment I could pick up a spoon; it's certainly not from my mother – Louise feels overwhelmed if I ask her to open a can of beans. It's no wonder I'm so skinny, I was practically malnourished as a child; learning to throw a meal together was probably as much my survival instinct kicking in as my genetic heritage. If I'd had my way I'd have run off at the age of seven to become the culinary equivalent of the little drummer boy, working my way up through the kitchen ranks from pot-scrubber to *saucier* to, if I was *very* lucky and worked longer hours than a junior doctor, executive chef. And at least I'd have had enough to eat. But with typical parental hypocrisy – don't do as I do, do as I tell you – Louise refused to hear of me leaving school early; she filled in the application to Edinburgh herself. Feeling it would be deeply churlish if a second generation of Sandal women turned down the chance of a university education, I did actually complete my degree; though even as my pen dutifully churned out analyses of Chaucer and Byron and Nathaniel Hawthorne, my mind dreamed of the perfect soufflé and a hollandaise that, even in the steamiest kitchen, never broke.

After three very dull years I finally marched into my mother's womb-red healing room at the top of our house in Islington, brandishing my examination results, and crying, 'I've done it, I've got my First, now can I go to culinary school?'

Louise lowered herself gracefully from full plank into cobra, assumed the child's pose and said, her face pressed into her yoga mat, 'I've been wondering how long it would take you to find the courage to ask.'

However, I discovered at culinary school that I was more my mother's daughter than I had thought; thankfully not in the actual cooking, *that* came easily – perhaps I was a chef in a former life: Napoleon's, maybe, or some Eastern potentate's, I've often wondered – but in my response to the wretched rules and regulations that hemmed you in and pushed you down and, it seemed to me, got in the way of doing anything novel or creative. I chafed unbearably against the restrictive syllabus whose principal purpose seemed to be to show plump, unimaginative young women in Alice bands and pearls how to find their way to a suitable young man's heart through his stomach. After two terms I quit and moved in with Kit and his latest boyfriend, a shark-like bond trader with dead eyes.

'For pity's sake, what do you really want to do?' Kit demanded one night when the shark was working late and I was driving him potty whining – yet again – about the curdled mess I seemed to be making of my life.

'You *know* what I want to do,' I said tetchily. 'I've been telling you since nursery school. Open my own restaurant, of course.'

'You were three. I thought you'd grow up and put away childish things.'

'So were you. *You* didn't.'

'Acting is different—'

'I don't see why.'

'Put that bottom lip away and stop being such a spoilt brat. Acting is different, as you well know, because you can still have a life whilst you do it. Have you any idea what opening your own restaurant would really be like?' Kit demanded. 'Three-quarters of new restaurants fail within the first year. You'd be working at least eighty hours a week with no evenings off, no holidays, not a minute to call your own, in an industry which has the highest percentage of drug addicts next to dentists—'

'Dentists?'

He waved his hand. 'Never mind that now. The other kitchen staff would hate you just for being there. Half the men in the restaurant business still think a woman's presence in the kitchen curdles the sauce. You'd be eating sexual harassment for breakfast, lunch and tea.'

'All right, all right,' I interrupted. 'I do *know*, Kit. But you did ask—'

'You have a First in English and you cook like an angel. What you should be doing, my love – ' Kit said, his eyes alight with an evangelical zeal I knew well enough to fear, 'I can't imagine how we haven't thought of it before – what you should be doing, Mal darling, is writing cookery books, of course.'

When Kit gets hold of an idea, he's like a dog with a particularly juicy marrowbone. At his insistence, and more to get him to leave me alone than anything else, I put together a slim folder of my best recipes, illustrated with glossy photographs – shot by the freelance who succeeded the bond shark in Kit's revolving-door bedroom – and submitted them to an agent plucked at random from the *Writer's Handbook* by Kit, fully expecting rejection with a generous side-helping of derision by return of post. But, unbeknown to either of us, the agent Kit selected just happened to open my submission ten minutes after returning from lunch with a panicked publisher who had been bending her ear for two hours on the subject of the gaping hole in her upcoming list, thanks to their star cookery writer – a household name with his own TV show and flatware range – eloping to Guatemala with his sous-chef and huge advance; and without delivering his much-delayed, and increasingly urgently needed, manuscript.

Serendipity really is very much underrated. My mother always said it was better to be born lucky than clever, 'although,' she'd add serenely, 'it does help to be both.'

At twenty-two, I had a three-book contract, and then a small guest spot on a brand new satellite channel followed, and when my first book reached number one in *The Times* bestseller list there was even talk of my own TV show in a year or two. I was the Hot New Thing and everything was going absolutely swimmingly and then I met Trace and for a while nothing else mattered. It was wonderful, it was beyond imagining; and then of course it all collapsed into the darkest, most dreadful mess. It was Kit who pulled me out and told me I would get over it and forced me to get back to work when I just wanted to crawl into bed and never come out again, my heart shrivelling with misery against my ribs.

And then, of course, I found Nicholas.

I hover on the restaurant threshold, shifting my bag to the other shoulder as I look for him, anticipating that familiar lurch when I spot his clean, chiselled features – even now, after twelve years – that same strange jolt of knowing I experienced the first moment I saw him, in Covent Garden: that absolutely electric certainty, beyond any shadow of a doubt, that he was The One.

Dear Nicholas, so tall and fine and honourable; so sexy and carnal and unaware.

It's such a relief to be inside, out of the cold. Where *is* Nicholas? The train from Salisbury was freezing, and the cab from Paddington Station wasn't much better. I can't imagine why Louise ever left California.

A waitress thrusts a glass of white wine at me, mumbling something about my shoes. Where *can* Nicholas have got to? The train was a bit delayed, thankfully, or I'd never have caught it; but it wasn't *that* late, he can't have left yet. He must be here somewhere. Unless I've got the name of the restaurant wrong, of course. It wouldn't be the first time.

I scrabble in my bag for the envelope I wrote the restaurant down on, scattering half the contents across the floor. The waitress is still pressing her glass of wine at me so I have no choice but to take it; still fumbling through my bag, I end up spilling most of the wine down myself. Thank God nothing shows on this dress and after three babies it's seen far worse. For heaven's sake, where is Nicholas? Oh, Lord, that wasn't a clean tissue—

'Your *shoes*,' the girl hisses again.

I finally look down and discover that Kit has, quite deliberately, let me walk out of the house in my pink towelling slippers. He is an absolute swine. I will hang him by the neck until he is near death and then cut him down and eviscerate him whilst he is still conscious before burning his intestines in front of him ... or no, I will allow him to babysit Metheny *at his house*.

I can't *bear* to let this stunning girl – clearly *not* a waitress after all; her shoes are far too expensive and far too high – see how mortified I am. She is so pretty and smart and *clean*, and I'm already well aware that she's written me off as barely a fingertip away from senile dementia.

I summon an insouciant smile. 'Oh, yes. Well, at least the rain hasn't ruined them.'

I shove the slippers nonchalantly into my bag as if I do this all the time. Which, of course, I do. Not wear pink towelling slippers to retirement parties in London, this is a landmark snafu even for me; but get caught in the crush as my two worlds – nurturing earth mother and career wife – collide.

Although there is less of the career thing now, of course, which is absolutely natural when you have three children, absolutely to be expected; somehow the book deadlines seem to slither through my fingers like egg yolks. I didn't realize how hard it was going to be just to keep up.

Nicholas abruptly materializes, white-faced and agitated. 'Malinche, where in heaven's name have you *been*? It's eight-thirty, Will's been asking for you for the last hour! What kept you?'

'Traffic,' I say, surprised by his twitchiness. I'm not *that* late.

'I told you to allow – oh, never mind. Now that you're here, you'd better come and be sociable.'

'I *was*, darling, I was talking to this gorgeous girl here – such a lovely suit, I hate chartreuse itself, of course, the drink I mean, but that's simply a *delicious* colour, especially with that corn-gold hair, how clever of you – what did you say your name was?'

'Sara Kaplan,' she supplies.

She really *is* a very striking girl: not conventionally pretty, the nose sees to that, but she has something about her, a sensuality, an earthiness. She must be absolutely freezing in that flimsy outfit, the silly girl: but then she's still too young, of course, to realize that when someone is as lovely and vital as she is, she really doesn't need to wear tons of make-up and short skirts to get attention, she could turn heads if she walked in wearing a dustbin liner and a porkpie hat.

I smile. 'Of course, Sara, well, Nicholas, I *was* being sociable as you can see, I was talking to Sara, she very kindly got me a drink, I was just about to come and find you and Will, and then here you were—'

I can feel the tension coming off Nicholas in waves. I can't imagine what has got him so distraught, it can't just be me, it must be something to do with work; but it's not like him, he's usually so self-contained. It's one of the things that drew me to him in the first place, his assurance, his total certainty of who and what he is – not always *right*, of course, but certain none the less. There are more layers to Nicholas than even he knows, aspects of him I had rather hoped would come to the surface as our marriage went on; but never mind that now, we are still the best of friends, of lovers, so much luckier than most couples these days.

I take his arm and guide him towards his colleagues, chatter soothingly about absolutely nothing in his ear, stroke him emotionally and mentally and even physically as we stand talking and laughing with Will, and finally he pulls me against him and I feel him relax beside me;

though not *quite* enough to totally erase that distant stirring of alarm.

I realize that now isn't the time to mention that Trace is moving back to Salisbury.

4

Nicholas

I awaken from dreams of pale, long limbs and strawberry gold hair with a tumescent erection that makes my balls ache. It's still dark outside, apart from the garish glare of multi-coloured Christmas lights that Evie insisted we hang along the eaves, and for which vulgar display of infectious Americana I risked life and limb atop the window-cleaner's borrowed ladder.

I brush my palm across the warm vale that dips between Mal's shoulder and hips, cupping her buttocks lightly with my hand. My middle finger curls between her legs and strokes the soft fur around her pussy, sliding into the welcoming wetness. Mal doesn't respond, but the change in her regular breathing tells me she's awake.

I slide closer, penis nudging the small of her back. Gently I find her clitoris and increase the pace and pressure of my finger, reaching my other hand over her shoulder towards her breasts. Mal mumbles something indistinct and rolls onto her stomach, taking both breasts and pussy out of my reach.

'Nicholas—'

'It's OK, don't worry, we have time. It's not six yet.'

Easing my way down the bed, I bury my head between her flanks and describe small circles from her coccyx down to her pussy with my tongue. Sweet, like the lavender honey she harvests from our hives in the orchard every June.

Rising up on my haunches, I replace my tongue with my rigid cock at the entrance to her behind. Mal wriggles and squirms in the bed beneath me and flips onto her back, slender legs opening in welcome as she smiles sleepily up at me. She's always loved early-morning sex; we both have. To wake warm and aroused and melt into each other – there's no better way to start the day. She starts to draw me in to her, but I pull back and go down on her again, opening her like a ripe fig. I can feel her impatience as she tightens her thighs. Her juices dribble down my chin as if I've bitten into a rich peach.

My cock throbs as I move my body over hers. It nudges at her pussy and I slide in, savouring her tight, wet grip. Her small breasts crush against my chest. I rock my hips and thrust into her, feeling the familiar heat course through my body, down my cock, sweat slicking our skin together. My feet overlap the foot of the bed and the headboard crashes timpani against the wall. Hot – want – need – want—

Sara.

Christ, I didn't say her name aloud, did I? I glance fearfully up at my wife. Her expression is as serene and untroubled as ever. Thank God. But still.

I sag against Mal as release and shame wash over me. It wasn't my wife's long, dark corkscrew curls I saw spread out on the pillow just now, but Sara's cropped strawberry-blonde head. Even as I kiss Mal's high, little brown breasts, in my mind I am burying my head in Sara's pink, pillowy cleavage.

I haven't been able to get the damned woman out of my mind since she walked into my office. This has gone beyond the reflexive, cursory sexual interest of a breathing male for any attractive female who crosses his path. It's all-consuming. Everywhere I look, I see Sara. I feel as if I'm going insane. It's not as if I'm stuck in an unhappy marriage, looking for an affair; that's the *last* thing I'd ever do, dear God, if anyone should know the damage infidelity can cause, it's me. Christ, I *love* Mal. Unreservedly. No question. I don't even know Sara.

'That was nice,' Mal says, stroking my hair. 'Again.'

'Did you—'

'No. But that doesn't matter.'

'It does, of course it does. Let me—'

She bats my hand away. 'Lovely, but let's wait till tonight, Nicholas. The children will be up soon, we have to get going. It's the girls' nativity play tonight, and I've still got sequins to sew on the Button Dragon and a pterodactyl's wings to superglue.'

I take eager refuge in domesticity, hiding in its comfortable, familiar folds from other, disturbing, thoughts. 'Admittedly it's been a long time since I played Balthasar on the school stage,' I say, climbing out of bed, 'but I'm fairly certain the shepherds didn't watch their flocks all seated on the ground whilst a pterodactyl hovered overhead. It would have eaten the sheep for a start.' I knot the cord of my navy dressing gown at my waist in preparation for the dash down the polar corridor to the bathroom. 'I'm not convinced about the Button Dragon, either.'

'Just be grateful Baby Jesus still gets a part,' Mal says, 'though after the disaster last year with Chloe Washington and the three baby ferrets, I think they're using a plastic doll in the manger.'

I muffle an expletive as I step on a piece of Lego. 'I'm just grateful when we turn up at church for Harvest Festival and it hasn't been replaced by a mosque.'

'You old fraud, you haven't been to church for Harvest Festival since they were using ploughshares instead of tractors,' Mal calls after me as I hop down the hall. 'Don't forget, the service starts at six; you promised you'd catch the early train so you could get there on time.'

I sigh as I fill the sink with icy water and dip my razor into it. I have a pile of work on my desk so high I'm surprised it doesn't have snow on the upper levels. Ten days before Christmas, everyone wants their divorce resolved before the country shuts down for its habitual two-week holiday, and half the clerks and barristers have gone shopping. I wish Mal realized that I want to witness my progeny tread the boards as much as she does, but someone has to keep the family in buttons and pterodactyl wings.

It's still dark and bitterly cold when Mal drops me at the station just before seven. A biting wind skitters litter on the platform and knifes straight through my clothes. I bury my hands deeper in my overcoat pockets and stamp my feet, exhaling plumes of smoke as I wait for my train. On the opposite platform, a young woman shivers in a short denim skirt and lightweight summer jacket, her bare legs almost blue with cold. It never fails to amaze me, the level of discomfort women will endure in the name of fashion. I'm astonished Sara hasn't caught her death, given some of the flimsy outfits in which she turns up to work; though she does always look very attractive. Very. But of course Mal has some lovely warm jumpers, extremely pretty, in fact. And jeans are so much more practical.

The seven-eight to Waterloo pulls in ten minutes late; despite the early hour, the train is dense with Christmas shoppers heading for the bright lights of Oxford Street. The railways appear to farm their customers like foie gras geese: the more they stuff the grubby, stale carriages, the richer they become. By the time we reach Basingstoke, daytrippers are overflowing into First Class, clutching cardboard Starbucks beakers and perspiring in their Puffa jackets. One or two have the grace to look guilty, but most meet our eyes defiantly, grumbling loudly to one another that they've paid for their tickets and there isn't even standing room in the coach. What does British Rail expect them to do: climb on the roof like they do in India?

I have some sympathy with their position – battery hens are more generously billeted – but the disruptive invasion of crisp packets and chattering mobiles makes it impossible for me to concentrate on my case notes. I work instead on my crossword until we get to Woking, at which point a handsome, well-upholstered woman in her mid-fifties – a fellow fixture of the seven-eight train – enters the carriage. She is, like me, an avid enthusiast of *The Times*'s acrostic; over the years we've grown quietly accustomed to exchanging newspapers shortly after she boards the train so that we may compare notes, returning them to one another five minutes before arriving at Waterloo. I assume she is also a lawyer or barrister, since I have occasionally observed her working on ribboned briefs herself; but since we have never actually spoken, I can't be sure.

Since all the seats are taken, I yield mine; she nods her thanks and takes it without fuss. How much simpler is life when there are certain rules and all know and adhere to them.

Two teenage girls in sleeveless padded jackets and combat trousers – I've never warmed to this fashion for down-and-out androgyny – exchange smirks as I take my place in the aisle. I catch a glimpse of my reflection in the train window and suddenly see myself as they must do: a dull, old-fashioned, middle-aged businessman in a buttoned-up overcoat whose idea of rebelliousness is putting foreign coins in a parking meter. I wonder bleakly if this is how I appear to Sara. She can't be more than a few years older than these two.

As every morning for the last month, I feel a guilty, appalled thrill of anticipation as I walk into the office. I refuse to look at the coat rack to see if her cinnamon wool coat is already there.

A loop of wilting silver tinsel is suspended like a hangman's noose above Emma's empty desk. I secure the limp tinsel to the ceiling as I pass – I daren't leave such a potent symbol in plain view of my less stable clients – and take sanctuary in my resolutely unadorned, unfestive office.

'Scrooge,' Mal declared last weekend, when I refused to climb fifty feet up the decaying oak tree at the bottom of the garden to cut some sprigs of mistletoe growing on its upper boughs.

I refrained from commenting on the pagan nature of this particular Christmas tradition, or the stickiness of the bloody berries when trodden by three small children throughout the house. Instead, I drew my wife's attention to the twin facts of our monolithic mortgage, in which we have yet to make a significant dent, and my less-than-monolithic life insurance.

'All right, you can buy a bunch at the garage down the road,' she conceded, after a considered moment, 'now that's not going to threaten our financial security, is it?'

'You haven't see the prices they're asking,' I said darkly.

At home, where I cannot hope to prevail against four women, I have surrendered on the mistletoe – and the rooftop fairy-lights, holly on the picture rails (and, shortly thereafter, embedded in the bare foot), paper chains, strings of gruesome Christmas cards, and the loathsome red poinsettias which Kit insists on giving us every year, just to annoy me; but my office is my own. I will have neither tinsel nor cards depicting drunken elves being pulled over on the hard shoulder of the M25. It's not that I'm a killjoy; actually, I love Christmas – the *real* Christmas, hard to find these days: home-made mince pies and mulled wine, satsumas in stockings and bowls of Brazil nuts, carol singers who know more than the first two lines of 'Good King Wenceslas', midnight Mass; and most wonderful of all, the expression on my daughters' faces when they race downstairs in the morning and discover that Father Christmas ('Santa Claus', like trick-or-treating and iced tea, firmly belongs four thousand miles away across the Atlantic) has filled to overflowing the pillowcases they left in the fireplace along with a raw carrot and warming glass of Harvey's Bristol Cream.

What I *cannot* abide is being wished a 'Merry Xmas' – or, worse, Happy Holidays – by a lip-serving atheist who thinks it perfectly reasonable to put a plastic whistle into a toilet-roll tube with a left-over fortune-cookie slip and malfunctioning banger, and then charge me fifty pounds for a dozen crackers without which my children will consider their mother's sublime Christmas dinner a bitter disappointment. If that makes me Scrooge, very well – it's an epithet I can live with.

I sit down at my desk and slit open my post. For a short while I deal with one or two urgent letters, dictating responses for Emma to type up later, and return a couple of telephone calls; but I cannot wall myself in my office forever. Somehow, I have to learn to temper my atavistic response to Sara. This situation cannot continue.

At two minutes to ten o'clock I gird my loins – rather literally, given the permanent semi-erection I seem to be sporting these days – and join the other partners in the conference room for our weekly case review, suppressing a flicker of irritation when I see that Joan and David are not alone. Will Fisher may have technically retired, but that hasn't stopped him turning up every Friday for the past four weeks; and since we are still in the process of putting the finance in place to buy out his partnership, we must perforce indulge his dead man's hand on the tiller.

'Nicholas, good to see you!' Fisher exclaims as I set down my files.

'Good morning, Will. What a pleasant surprise.'

'Just thought I'd pop in and see how you're all getting

along without me,' Fisher says jovially, as he has done every week. 'Probably all wishing I'd just bugger off and play golf and leave you to get on with it, hmm?'

There's a brief moment of silence before it becomes apparent that denials are required. Naturally young David is the first to slither up to the plate. He could save Fisher a fortune in proctology examinations were he medically qualified. It's hard to believe he's the son of one of the most gifted and charismatic divorce lawyers I have ever met. Losing Andrew Raymond to leukaemia at the age of just fifty-four was a tragedy on both a personal and professional level; that this oleaginous, talentless squirt should be his genetic legacy verges on the criminal.

The door opens behind me, and I tense at the faint scent of 'Allure'. I was at the Chanel counter in Harrods buying Mal's favourite – 'No 5' – for our wedding anniversary last week, when a salesgirl near me sprayed another fragrance onto a nearby customer's wrist. I recognized it instantly as Sara's scent. On some insane impulse I added a large bottle to my other purchases; even now it is delighting the ladies of Oxfam, to whom I donated it in panic on my way home.

'Ah, the lovely lady herself!' Fisher cries, leaping up to usher Sara to the table. 'Have a seat, my dear, have a seat. Joan, if you wouldn't mind moving along – there we are, young lady, that's right, next to me.'

Joan glares, but shifts to the next chair. As Sara takes her seat, her skirt rides a couple of inches up her thighs, revealing a tantalizing glimpse of lace stocking top.

I don't return her pleasant smile, busying myself with my case notes.

Joan launches into her usual polemic on the subject of

client credit; more precisely, our over-extension thereof. A mediocre lawyer but stridently efficient manager, she recognized early in her legal career where her true talents lay and planned accordingly. A hefty legacy from her father enabled her to harness herself to two able, but impoverished, young lawyers, Will Fisher and Andrew Raymond, who founded the firm with the happy combination of her money and their talent; I came on board a decade later. Effectively a sleeping partner, Joan rarely interferes in client matters, but she is as abrasive in manner as Fisher is genial. None the less, under her watchful stewardship, Fisher Raymond Lyon has become one of the most profitable small niche firms in the country.

Joan voted, unsurprisingly, against employing Sara. However, with David so far up Fisher's arse that he could kiss his tonsils, and the old man chronically smitten by Sara's charms, it was evidently a case of two votes to one.

I don't care to ask myself how I might have voted had I not been detained by that case in Leeds. Such a dangerous absence that is turning out to have been.

'—no choice but to go to Court, then, Nicholas?'

I jump. 'Sorry, Will. Miles away. You were saying?'

'Will was talking about the Wainwright case in Manchester, Nicholas,' David says helpfully. 'I believe he's correct in saying there's been no response from the other side to your last offer?'

'None, unless we had something in this morning that I haven't seen yet—'

Sara shakes her head. 'I called them first thing. Claire Newbold's out of the office, but when I spoke to her secretary, she said off the record that Claire thinks our offer's more than generous, but the wife simply won't budge.'

'Damn.' I frown. 'I was hoping this wouldn't have to go to Court. The assets just aren't there to justify it. Two or three days of wrangling in front of a judge and they'll both be lucky to end up with the cab fare home.'

'As long as there's enough to pay *us*,' Joan interjects sharply.

The thin toffee silk of Sara's blouse tautens across her breasts as she leans forward to reach for the file, grey eyes intent. Her nipples jut against the fabric. *Good God, is she even wearing a bra?*

'The husband's not going to get much change out of thirty thousand if it ends up in Court,' she says, scanning her notes, 'and that's on top of the forty he already owes us. It probably makes economic sense for him to give the wife what she wants and walk away with whatever's left—'

I shift uncomfortably in my chair. Christ, my balls ache. 'Hasn't got it. He made his money years ago from a print shop franchise, but lost a lot of it when the stock market plunged, and his business folded about the same time. Apart from the house, his only other serious asset is his pension. He's fifty-six, what else is he going to do?'

'What's the wife asking for?'

'She wants the house, which has no mortgage and is worth about half a million, give or take, and sixty thousand a year for her and the two youngest kids. He's earning thirty-three as a tree surgeon and living in a rented bedsit over a chippie. She's dreaming, but it's going to bankrupt him to prove it.'

'Looks like you're going to Manchester on Monday,' Will says brightly to me.

'Jesus. That's all I need the week before Christmas.'

'Why don't you take Sara?'

I start. 'What?'

'Yes, it's just what she needs, a meaty case to get her pretty little teeth into,' Fisher enthuses. 'It'll be a great learning experience for her, and it already sounds like she's got an in with the secretary which could be very useful. You never know,' he says, leaning over towards me with a wink, 'you might even learn something, Nicholas.'

'But our client can't afford one lawyer, never mind two—'

'This'll be on us. No, Joan,' he says firmly as she opens her mouth to protest, 'think of it as an investment in the firm's future.'

I pinch the bridge of my nose. Two nights in a hotel a long way from home with a woman I haven't been able to get out of my mind for four weeks.

My balls are going to be black by the time I get back.

My mood is not improved when, having raced to Waterloo to catch the early train home, I discover that the station has been temporarily closed because of flooding. The wrong sort of rain, no doubt. By the time it opens an hour later, I have no hope of making my daughters' nativity play on time.

Tired and frustrated, I slink into the darkened school auditorium at ten to seven, just as the Button Dragon and all the little pterodactyls come on stage for their final bow with the Eight Wise Men and the Cookie Monster. Treading on toes and blocking video recorders, I manage to take my seat next to Mal just moments before the lights come up, and am clapping vigorously when our offspring bound from the school stage into the audience with the rest of the eclectic cast.

'Did you see me?' Evie demands.

'I did. You were wonderful—'

'Her tail fell off,' Sophie says scornfully. 'Right in the middle of the Birdie Dance.'

'You mean that wasn't supposed to happen? I never would have known.'

'It didn't *fall* off. Susan Pelt trod on it.' Evie scowls. 'On purpose.'

Sophie looks superior. 'You were in the wrong place and going in the wrong direction, that's why.'

'Was not!'

'Were too!'

'Girls,' I say firmly, confiscating the pterodactyl's wings before somebody gets hurt.

Mal gathers our brood and shoos them gently towards the exit. She smiles wearily at me over their heads, but I can tell from the set of her shoulders that she is annoyed with me, and feel a rare flash of irritation. It was hardly my fault I was late.

On the way home, I explain about the waterlogged station, and later, in bed, she signals her forgiveness by pulling me towards her; but I'm too jittery to do more than kiss the top of her head and hold her close as I stare into the darkness. It's ridiculous to be so nervous about next week; whatever emotional silt Sara is kicking up will soon settle down if I leave well alone. It's just a question of self-control.

My life is perfectly harmonious. I have a wife I love and desire, three beautiful, healthy girls, a job I find fulfilling, satisfying and profitable, a substantial home in an exquisite part of the English countryside – I am truly satisfied with my lot.

And yet, from nowhere, this young woman has suddenly been lobbed into my life like a sexual hand-grenade.

I don't sleep well, and the next morning I'm a bear with the children and distant and uncommunicative with Mal. When she sends me into Salisbury on a fool's errand for red crêpe paper to get me out of the house, I detour into one of those upmarket shops that handcuff their clothing to the rails in the midst of a sea of ash flooring, and purchase an expensive coffee-coloured sheepskin coat that Mal would never consider buying for herself. Only when I have expiated my guilt in an orgy of Christmas shopping do I dare to return home.

On Monday morning, I awaken in more optimistic mood. There's no doubt that Sara is a temptation – or would be, were there the slightest danger of her reciprocating, which obviously there is not; but even if she did, I'm not going to give in to this. I made promises to my wife before God, and I have no intention of breaking them, now or ever.

I do so loathe that modern euphemism, 'the inevitable happened'. To borrow from Benjamin Franklin: nothing is inevitable but death and taxes. Certainly not infidelity.

For the past four weeks, I've run away from Sara, ensuring I have minimal contact with her at work, and that we are never for a moment alone. Whilst technically successful – there has been no opportunity for Fisheresque furtive glances or 'accidental' physical contact on the stairs – this policy of avoidance has merely reduced me to a seething mass of teenage angst and hormones.

Since denial has simply stoked the fires, clearly a change of tack is required. I can't possibly avoid Sara now, so I'm going to have to confront the issue head on and deal with it, once and for all. What am I so afraid of, anyway? Nothing's going to happen. No doubt being thrown together at such close quarters will break the fever, and I will be able to return to my untroubled, comfortable domestic life with no harm done.

I sincerely hope so; my constant hard-on is making it extremely difficult to concentrate on anything other than the chronic ache in my balls.

Sara and I are travelling to Manchester from different parts of the country, so I spend a surprisingly pleasant train journey alone reviewing my case notes and reinforcing my resolve. By the time I arrive at the Piccadilly Hotel in the centre of the city, I realize I have allowed myself to blow this entire matter out of all proportion. What man approaching his mid-forties, married or otherwise, would *not* be visited by erotic thoughts when such a voluptuous, youthful siren appears in his office? The appropriate response is not to panic that moral degeneracy is imminent, but to daydream for a wistful moment of one's youth, heave a regretful inward sigh, and wish the hopeful young pups snapping at her heels the best of luck. Surely the sin is not in being tempted, but in yielding. And I am more fortunate than most; I have a beautiful and sexy wife waiting for me at home.

I can't deny that Sara has awakened disturbingly erotic feelings, yes; but this doesn't necessarily have to be a bad thing. It's just a question of redirection.

Over the years, I've learned from my clients that boredom is a far greater threat to most marriages than the turn of a pretty ankle or a washboard stomach. It's all too easy to slump indifferently into impending middle-age, quarantining sex to weekends and opting for a quick bite at the local Italian on your anniversary so that you can get home in time for *Midsomer Murders* and an early night. Perhaps I *needed* a jolt like this to remind me that I'm only forty-three; it's not quite time for tartan slippers and a mug of cocoa at bedtime yet. Christ, I do still have my own bloody hair and teeth! Even a pair of jeans, somewhere. Maybe Mal and I should try to get away for a weekend soon, leave the children with her mother for a night or two. Might even splash out on some silk French knickers and whatnot.

This whole Sara thing will die down as quickly as it blew up once I deal with these risible feelings of mine head-on. In fact, I'm almost looking forward to the next couple of days. It'll be a relief to meet the challenge and get things back into perspective, back under control.

I check in and leave a message with the hotel receptionist for Sara to call me when she arrives later this evening, then go up to my room to shower and freshen up. Once I've conferred with the office in London and the local barrister handling our case here tomorrow, I telephone Mal to wish the girls goodnight.

'You missed Evie's Bible class recital,' my wife tells me.

'Christ, I'm sorry, I'd completely forgotten—'

'No, I mean you *missed* it,' Mal lilts. 'I haven't had so much fun in years.'

I tuck the handset under my chin and start to lace my shoes. 'Come on, then.'

'Moses – and I quote – "led the Hebrew slaves to the Red Sea where they made unleavened bread, which is bread made without any ingredients. Then he went up Mount Cyanide to get the ten commandos. He died before he ever reached Canada but the commandos made it."'

I snort with laughter.

'No, no, wait, it gets better.' Mal giggles. '"Ancient Egypt was old. It was inhabited by gypsies and mummies who all wrote in hydraulics. They lived in the Sara Dessert. The climate of the Sara is such that all the inhabitants have to live elsewhere."'

Out of the mouths of babes—

'She didn't actually *write* that,' I exclaim.

'She did, I have it here. I can't wait until half-term, they're tackling medieval history then.'

When I ring off later, I discover that Sara has left a message on my voicemail whilst I've been discussing the finer points of Egyptology with my middle child. Since it is below freezing outside and I have no desire to compete with office revellers for a taxi the week before Christmas, I am happy to accede to her suggestion that we meet in the hotel restaurant downstairs at eight to discuss tomorrow's case over dinner. We do have to eat, after all.

Fifteen minutes later, at precisely two minutes to eight, and armed with a stack of legal files, I stand in the hotel lobby and glance around for my colleague.

Oh Christ. Oh bloody Christ. I am in deep, deep trouble.

She's waiting at the entrance to the restaurant, her back towards me as she talks to the maître d'. Her statuesque frame is sheathed in a soft, black wool dress that manages simultaneously to skim and to cling to every voluptuous contour. It ends demurely enough at the knee; but she is wearing black seamed stockings and a pair of scarlet high heels that either ruin the outfit or set it off beautifully. I suspect you need to be a woman to tell.

I realize I am gaping, and close my mouth. Jamming my files across my poker-hard erection, I take a deep breath and go over to her. *This is business. Just business.*

Oh, Jesus.

She turns at my approach and smiles. 'Great. You got my message.'

A deep V of honeyed skin plunges to a generously displayed cleavage. Between her breasts, a silver heart-shaped pendant nestles. I wonder if it is warm from her skin; or perhaps she has only just put it on, it's still cool to the touch.

My cock bucks and for the first time since I was fifteen I wonder if I'm actually going to come in my pants.

'—I said, is a booth all right with you, Nick?'

I nod dumbly. The waiter escorts us to our table, and for a few moments we fuss with napkins and menus and breadsticks. I clear a space on the tablecloth for my files, building a manila rampart between us. It's the only way I can tear my eyes from her breasts.

A silence descends. Awkwardly I clear my throat, squaring the heap of the files in front of me with military precision. 'So – ah – are you going out somewhere later?'

She gives me an odd look. 'No, why?'

Girls are different these days, of course: they dress for themselves. The appreciative physical response they elicit from hapless males is just so much collateral damage.

She snaps a breadstick in two, and puts it to her mouth. Instantly I picture those full pink lips wrapped around my throbbing cock. Grimly I cross my legs and recite my eight times tables.

A tiny crumb falls into her cleavage, and negligently she licks her forefinger and dusts between her breasts to retrieve it. *Six eights are forty-eight—*

'So, have we heard anything back from the other side?' she asks, glancing up.

'Nothing official,' I say, gratefully seizing the conversational lifeline. 'But our barrister, Roger, happened to be in Court on Friday on another case opposite Sandra Reizen, who's representing the wife in our case tomorrow. Sandra couldn't comment directly, of course, but she gave Roger the distinct impression she's going to push the wife to settle out of Court.'

'Interesting. You think the wife will agree?'

'It's certainly possible—'

We spend the next thirty minutes discussing the case; safe on neutral legal territory and with a swift couple of Scotches soon under my belt, I finally allow myself to relax a notch or two. There's no doubting the alarming physical effect this woman has on me, but she's all business, brisk and efficient, and I realize with relief that however lurid my fantasies may be, they are just that: *fantasies*. Unreciprocated schoolboy crushes are hardly a threat to anyone's marriage.

She scans the wine list and orders a decent but inexpensive bottle with dinner; I am impressed by both her *savoir-faire* and her taste. Mal always defers to me over wine. I'm not entirely sure I'd appreciate a woman taking control like this on a permanent basis, but it is certainly an interesting novelty.

During the meal – lamb cutlets for me, fillet of sea bass for her – our conversation broadens to encompass the legal profession in general, and our firm in particular; she permits herself an expression of amused tolerance when Fisher and David are mentioned, but is otherwise commendably discreet.

In fact, *I* appear to be the one doing all the talking; but it's a pleasant change to have such an appreciative audience. Almost hanging on my every word. Especially when the audience in question is so very young. And attractive.

Sara barely touches her meal, which surprises me; she doesn't look like a picky eater. I prefer a woman who tucks into her food; it shows enthusiasm for life.

'Is everything all right?' I ask. 'We can order something else if it doesn't pass muster—'

'No, no, it's fine. I'm just not that hungry. Too many breadsticks, probably.' She leans back and smiles – to dazzling effect – as a waiter tops up our glasses. 'Tell me, Nick, how long have you been with Fisher's?'

'Good God. Let me see. I joined just before my thirtieth birthday, so that's thirteen – no, it'll be fourteen years this winter.'

She regards me for a moment, her clear grey eyes considering. 'I'd only have put you in your mid-thirties now, tops. Although I suppose if I sat and worked it out, you'd have to be older to have gained such a reputation.'

'Reputation?'

'Look, you were the main reason I applied to the firm,'

she says frankly. 'I kept hearing your name mentioned around, and of course you have acted in some landmark cases. I know it's probably not the thing to say, but I couldn't think of a better training than working with you.'

I feel ridiculously flattered. 'That's terribly sweet of you, but—'

'Sweet has nothing to do with it, Nick. It's the truth.'

No one has ever called me Nick before. Even at school, I was always Nicholas. I think I rather like the diminutive; it sounds younger, a little less dull and middle-aged.

She pushes her untouched plate away and leans earnestly towards me. Thank God for the files between us, or I'd have a view straight down her cleavage to her navel.

'The Hopewell case changed divorce law in this country forever,' she says. 'No wife had ever been awarded a third of her husband's future earnings until that ruling. Did you have any idea going into it that you were about to set such a significant precedent?'

'Actually, that was a very interesting case for several reasons, very shrewd of you to bring it up—'

A waiter interrupts to ask if we want coffee.

'I'd love some,' Sara says. 'Let's have it in the bar, Nick, chillax a bit. And maybe a cognac?'

Chillax? Of course: *chill out and relax.* Christ, she speaks a different language.

'Nick?'

I've had more than enough to drink already, and I should go back to my room to reread my case notes and get some sleep.

But I find myself following Sara's swaying hips – *five eights are forty* – to a couple of pseudo-distressed leather sofas at right angles to one another in a corner of the dim bar next door. I dump the legal files on a side-table as Sara kicks off her fuck-me red heels and curls her feet beneath her. She props her chin on her hand and leans on the arm of her sofa, accidentally presenting me with an eye-popping view of her breasts in their lacy black bra. I swear I can actually *see* the dark pink tint of her nipples—

'The Hopewell case,' she prompts.

Once again, her professionalism saves me. I shift in my chair and mentally conjugate Latin verbs, multiplication having worn out its welcome.

Her silver gaze is interested as I delineate the details of the complex case; it really is a pleasure to have such an in-depth discussion about work with someone who really understands and is interested in, rather than bored, by the minutiae. I can't blame Mal for losing interest beyond the headline facts of my cases; she's always happy to listen when I talk shop, but clearly only a fellow lawyer can truly appreciate the technical detail. In parallel, I adore Mal's spring pea soup, of course, happy to lap it up; but the genesis of the home-made chicken stock that constitutes its culinary base isn't necessarily the most fascinating of conversations.

'Did you always want to work in divorce law?' Sara asks as a companionable silence finally falls between us.

I watch her roll the cognac glass between her palms, mesmerized by the sensuous movement of her long hands. The amber liquid, refracted through the crystal, casts gold darts across her face that bring out the tawny glints in her cropped blonde hair.

'Pretty much. I toyed with corporate and tax law for a brief moment—'

'I know.' She laughs a laugh I can feel in my trouser pockets. 'Don't we all?'

I smile with her. Despite the excruciating sexual tension – I have the worst case of blue balls – I feel surprisingly warm and mellow: due in no small part, I realize, to the alcohol I've consumed; but due, also, to her relaxing and attentive company. She has cleverly deferred to me and allowed me to ramble on at length all evening – I'm not a total innocent – but that deference itself is rather flattering. And she really *is* extremely easy to talk to. As well as being exceptionally easy on the eye.

I loosen my tie and braces, sinking back into the comfortable sofa with a contented sigh.

'There have been times I've wished I'd sold out and taken the Corporate shilling,' I admit, 'usually around the same time the next set of school fees fall due.'

'It's cool you didn't, or I'd never have got to work with you.'

'Well, that's very kind, but—'

'I told you, Nick,' she says, lightly brushing my forearm, '*you* were the reason I joined the firm.'

Somehow, her hand lingers. I should pull gently away. I should thank her now for a pleasant evening, pick up my files, and go upstairs. Alone.

I don't move.

Seconds pass. I'm acutely aware of her touch on my arm, of the fact that only a few millimetres of cotton separate my skin from hers. The mellow feeling of just a few moments ago is a distant memory. My cock is as hard as rock.

I'm overwhelmed by the urge to pull this woman – so very different from my wife – into my arms, crush those shiny, pliable pink lips beneath mine, to bury my face in those full breasts and plunge myself into the warm wet core of her. I want to lose myself in her, to get hot and dirty with her; I want to do things to her I'm too ashamed even to put into words.

Her grey eyes meet mine, and I see permission in them.

'So, Nick,' she says, very softly, and her voice is as intimate as the rustle of sheets, 'would you like to come upstairs for a nightcap?'

5

Sara

The words throb in the air between us. *Come on, Nick,*
I will him silently. *Come on, say yes, say yes, you know
you want to.*

Those ditchwater bedroom eyes of his are clearly picturing me spread-eagled naked on a four-poster bed and
covered with blood-red rose petals à la Mena Suvari, but
there seem to be roadworks on the information super-
highway between his brain and vocal cords. God, Nick,
how difficult *is* it? Short of lying down on some Royal
Doulton flatware and sprinkling myself with parsley garn-
ish, could I be offering sex on a plate any more obviously?

If I have to hold this relaxed, inviting smile much
longer I'm going to get lockjaw. Shit, I can't believe how
much I want him to say yes.

I touch my tongue lightly to dry lips and don't miss
the responsive judder in his pinstriped trousers. I don't
know if the public-school poker up his arse is doing
something to his prostate, but this uptight, repressed,

missionary-position Englishman also happens to be the most sexual man I've ever met. He just doesn't realize it yet.

And fuck, do I want to be the one to show him.

Naturally Amy thinks it's hysterical that I've got the hots for my married boss. After all the grief I've given her over her affair with Terry, I suppose I can't blame her. The difference is, *I* know what I'm doing, and more importantly, how this will end, even now, before it's begun. *Especially* before it's begun. You borrow the other little girl's toy for a while until you get bored playing with it and then you give it back. No keepsies in this game.

I'm only going to borrow him, I tell the tiny voice needling my conscience. No one's going to get hurt. No one's even going to *know*.

I lean forward to pick up my bag, treating Nick to another tempting glimpse of my tits, and throw him an amused, cool look: *Coming?* I daren't touch him again, much as I'm longing to. One crass move and he'll run for the hills.

My stomach is fizzing with nerves and excitement. The twanging in my damp knickers is vibrating all the way to my toes. *Say yes say yes say yes.*

Let me tell you, if I didn't fancy the pants off this man, I'd never be going to this much trouble. It was funny at first, the way he kept shooting out of a room every time I entered it, or walking up four flights of stairs if I got into the lift – no wonder he's lost weight. But in the last couple of weeks, it's stopped being so amusing. I really like Nick. I want him to like me. How is he ever going to do that if he never sticks around long enough to hear the second syllable of my 'Hello'?

I've got to say, this is all messing with my head a bit. I've never had a man get under my skin like this; I'm not sure I like it. I just wish to God I knew what it is about Nick that's clicking my mouse.

Professionally, he's confident, surefooted; arrogant, even. I've seen him wring concessions from other lawyers that make our clients want to cast his image in gold – and after Nick's finished with their exes, they can afford to. What's more, he knows how good he is: which is *so* erotic. When he's in full flow, tearing the opposition a new arsehole, I almost feel scared of him myself. Certainly in awe. A brilliant older man at the height of his power, secure and certain of himself – yep, knicker-wetting, no doubt about it.

Then there's the other Nick, so frigging hopeless with women, acting as if he wouldn't begin to know his way around a bedroom; *blushing*, even.

And of course he's totally, but *totally*, off limits. Married, kids, way older than me, and my boss to boot.

Oh, this is *so* not a good combination. And it so *is*.

I could've kissed that lech Fisher when he gave me this Manchester gig, except I'd never prise him off me again. Finally, the chance to scratch the itch that is Nick. So I pulled out all the stops for this evening. The Donna Karan dress set me back a month's salary – shit, sweet Nick, *no*, I'm not 'going out' anywhere afterwards – but way worth it. I borrowed the scarlet Jimmy Choos from Amy – two sizes too small, but this is the twenty-first century: ugly sisters with big feet get to go to the ball too, or we'll sue.

Between them, the dress and shoes did most of the work – with a little help from my Wonderbra – but Nick's so bloody clueless, he couldn't flirt to save his tightly clenched arse. Which means I've had to do it all this evening: draw him out, get him to talk about himself, guide us back onto safe conversational territory whenever he got nervous – and then cut the ground out from under him with the tried-but-true crumbs-down-the-cleavage trick. (About the only food I actually ate tonight. I'm bloody starving: I didn't want to eat too much and put him off. Men hate women with an appetite.)

OK, it's all anti-feminist crap straight from *The Rules*; but then let's face it, so are men. I can impress him later with my sparkling intellect and flair for case law. The way to a man's heart is straight through his ego via his dick: which is what this evening has been all about.

The question is: have I pulled it off?

Only one way to find out. Since he now seems to have lost the power of speech altogether, I stand up, throwing down the bedroom gauntlet with a final flourish.

Do something, Nick. I'm out on a limb here, and it's bloody windy—

Alleluia, he stands up with me. 'I think,' he says hesitantly, 'I think—'

The phone in his pocket rings.

Oh, shit. Not his wife, please, not now. Not when I'm *this* close.

'Good evening, George – no, absolutely not, not too late at all.' Nick mouths *Wainwright* at me, and I breathe again. Our client. It's nearly midnight, but you can't blame the man for being nervous; his whole future is on the line tomorrow. 'How can I help? Of course, fire away—'

It's only the usual last-minute panic-and-reassurance Q & A; but ten minutes later, as Nick snaps shut his phone, I suddenly realize from the rigid set of his shoulders and the shutters screening those muddy eyes that I've lost him. It's more than the moment having passed. He's just had a brief encounter with the Ghost of Divorce Future – all custody battles, maintenance cheques, bedsits and Pot Noodles – and it's terrified him shitless. No doubt he sees that phone call as a Nick-of-time reminder of all he has to lose. *Fuck, fuck and double fuck.*

Or rather, not.

So, isn't this lovely. A happy family Christmas with Ma and Pa, a mixed nuts selection of uncles, aunts and cousins, various freeloading friends and neighbours and – I've stepped into Bridget Jones hell – their 'eligible' collective offspring; not forgetting, of course, the vicar. Who is wearing a paisley Laura Ashley smock, a fashion crime rendered only slightly less shocking by the fact that she is at least a woman. Or so we are given to understand. It's a little hard to tell.

All I need now is for Colin Firth to turn up wearing a hand-knitted jumper featuring Christmas trees and robins. Actually, that *is* all I need. That, and a right good—

'Sara, love, there you are! It's all right, Muriel, I've found her, she's by the sausage rolls. Did you drop something, dear? Almost didn't see you there behind the sofa. No? Well, out you come then.'

'Pearl, sorry, no, actually I was just on my way to the—'

'That's *Auntie* Pearl to you, Little Miss-All-Grown-Up!'

Great-Auntie, if we're going to be picky.

I smile weakly. 'Sorry, I—'

I'm enveloped in a hug reeking of eau-de-mothball and menopause. 'Not too old to give your Auntie a kiss at least, I hope? That's a good girl. Oh, dear, your hair really *is* very short, isn't it, lovey? You look like a boy. Your mum did warn me. Never mind, it'll grow back. Now, then, stop skulking in a corner and come and say hello to everyone. No need to be shy.'

Actually, having to say hello to everyone is precisely *why* I'm skulking in a corner, and trust me, shyness has never been the problem. I cut my teeth on the boys in this room, and from the way most of them are either (a) glaring at or (b) studiously avoiding me, I'd guess they're still nursing the bite marks.

My mother has been throwing her Christmas Day soirées since the days when I still believed that having an old man in red pyjamas sneaking into your bedroom at night with presents was a good thing. It combines her two favourite occupations: showing off (to the downmarket relatives) and social climbing (with the upmarket neighbours). It also gives her a very good excuse to replace the carpet every January because of wine stains.

God knows why my father goes along with it. Poor Dad. He hates parties. He usually slopes off to the greenhouse with Uncle Denny once HRH has addressed the nation, where they while away the afternoon leering over the collection of soft porn Dad thinks no one knows he keeps in a plastic bag under the cucumber cloches. Way to go, Dad; though I'm not sure about the *Busty Beauties* mags. Some of those girls look positively deformed.

Every Christmas the usual suspects pitch up clutching

their home made trifles and hideous poinsettias (what *is* it with these loathsome mini-triffids?) plus or minus the odd newborn/granny at either end of the mortal coil. Which means that over the years, I've played snakes and ladders, doctors and nurses, Monopoly, PlayStation, blackjack, and doctors and nurses again, with the same assortment of cousins and neighbours' sons. In fact, due to extreme amorous laziness on my part, at one point or another I've dated most of them, for periods ranging from an hour to a year. These annual festive get-togethers are an excruciating exhumation of my romantic roadkill.

First was Gareth, who, every time he met my parents, hugged my dad and shook hands with my mother. He was a bit odd, to be honest. I told him I loved kittens and he took me to see a lion cub at the zoo. And he zigzagged when he mowed the lawn.

Mark had even smaller nostrils than me. Our children would have had gills. I dumped him forty minutes after our first snog before one of us suffocated.

Cousin Jonathan was – and still is – the most gorgeous man I've ever dated; a less stroppy Jude Law. He came out three weeks after we started seeing each other – Jonathan, that is. I suppose I should have guessed when I signed us up for a dirty dancing course at the Y, and he asked if they offered ballet.

Daryl was sweet. But dim. I told him I needed space and he spring-cleaned my wardrobe.

And then there was Andrew. Women have a dozen mental channels, and manage to keep all their thoughts separate in their heads. Andrew had only two. The first: 'Can I get sex out of this?' And the second: 'I'm hungry.' Quite often, the two coincided rather nicely.

Andrew and I lasted almost a year purely because of the sex. It was sensational. No problems with that side of our relationship at all. Unfortunately, there weren't any other sides. Things were very simple with Andrew. When he said: 'You have beautiful eyes,' he meant *I want sex*. When he told me I had a pretty smile, he meant *I want sex*. It didn't take a PhD to master the lingo.

Trouble was, he didn't believe in limiting classroom size. I wanted one man to fulfil my every need. Andrew wanted every woman to fulfil his one.

I'm guessing – from Auntie Pearl's *sotto voce* infomercial that having just obtained his second divorce at the age of thirty-one, Andrew is newly eligible, 'so it's not too late, love' – that he hasn't changed in the six years since I caught him teaching linguistics to Mrs-Newcombe-from - two - doors - down's seventeen - year - old daughter, Libby, in my parents' bed.

Looking around, it's clear I'm the tribal bike. But frankly, I think the number of notches on my bedpost is fairly modest, all things considered. It's not my fault that three-quarters of them are currently in the same room.

Oh, God. And Martin. I'd forgotten about Martin. And let me tell you, that hasn't been easy.

If English schools did those American yearbook things, Martin would be voted Most Likely to Die Alone. Put it this way: if he were on fire, I'd toast marshmallows.

'Well, hell-ooo,' Martin says to my breasts.

Nice glasses, Martin. I particularly like the *Star Wars* band-aid holding them together. Neat touch.

'Sorry, just leaving—'

'Leaving? I thought you were staying the night?'

I pull the half-chewed piece of coronation chicken that has just fallen out of his wet mouth from my cleavage. Trust me, this time I'm not doing it for erotic effect. 'I am, but I – er – just have to check in with the office; no reception on my mobile – have to go outside—'

'It's Christmas Day. Isn't the office shut?'

'Yes, it is, but I'm the – ah – duty solicitor. Lot of divorces at Christmas. All that family time. And indigestion, often a trigger.'

'Really? I never realized. Well, we must catch up some time,' he calls after me as I leg it towards the back door. 'Pick up where we left off, hmm, hmm?'

Where exactly *did* we leave off? For the life of me, I can't remember. Little shit probably used a roofie.

I'm halfway up the back garden before it clicks that it's four o'clock on a December afternoon and I'm wearing thin silk jersey and a fixed smile.

Shivering, I plonk myself down on the stone bench beside my mother's new 'water feature', a hideous stone abortion that would be spouting fluid from every orifice if it wasn't frozen solid. Bloody *Ground Force*, they have a lot to answer for. My mother doesn't need any encouragement. I'm really not sure the seven-foot nude bronzes are very Reading, to be honest. We should never have let her go to the Chelsea Flower Show. Talk about putting the chateau into shantytown.

I stamp my feet to get the blood flowing and blow on my hands. Oh, God, what am I *doing* here? My life sucks. I'm twenty-six years old, with my own job, flat, friends and glow-in-the-dark vibrator, and here I am spending Christmas Day shivering in my parents' back garden with assorted pieces of faux classic statuary.

At least when I was a kid there was still the hope of escape. I'd pass round plates of turkey vol-au-vents and dream of one day spending Christmas with a bronzed Adonis on a sun-drenched, white-sugar beach somewhere. I'd watch the twenty-something losers slinking into our sitting room with their parents and sneer at their total *sadness* with all the worldly superiority of my fourteen years. Like, *get a life*. I couldn't ever imagine choosing to come back once parole was granted. I'd certainly never have mashed lips with Gareth/Mark/Jonathan/Daryl/Andrew/Martin if I'd thought there was the remotest danger that ten years later, I'd still be pulling crackers with them.

There was a glorious window, somewhere between sweet sixteen and a year or two ago, when all my friends were single too and we'd spend Christmas skiing in France, surfing in Oz, getting fucked in Phuket. It never occurred to me that it'd ever end. Suddenly they've all paired off, some of them even have kids, and most of the time I *so* couldn't care less; but at Christmas, how can you help but notice you're *still* on your own? So it's either a turkey Ready Meal for one in front of the *Only Fools and Horses Christmas Special* or a trip back to the suburban shagpile-and-pelmeted mock-Tudor nest, where I fit as seamlessly back into my childhood landscape as a Shiite in a synagogue.

I glare up at the nearest Greek statue as it starts to drizzle. God, you really do have a divine sense of humour. You *know* this is not what I meant by a bronzed Adonis. And it was *sun*-drenched.

Oh, why the fuck does Nick have to be married? And

why did I have to let him get to me like this? And why, in the name of Manolo, does he have to be the one married man on the planet apart from my dad who's faithful to his wife?

I don't even try to kid myself we can pick up where we (almost) left off once UK plc re-opens for business after Christmas. You can't reheat a soufflé.

Nick called my room the next morning to say that the other side had abruptly caved – 'Never mind, Sara, the work wasn't wasted. *Si vis pacem, para bellum*: if you seek peace, prepare for war' – and he'd be on the next train home as soon as he'd completed the relevant paperwork. Back to his dippy wife with a heartfelt sigh of relief at his lucky escape from the office Jezebel, no doubt. I didn't even see him check out.

Even now he's probably carving a perfectly cooked, moist turkey at the head of a groaning table as his three pretty little girls excitedly pull crackers in their clean, new party dresses. Beneath the exquisitely decorated tree (real, natch) in the corner is a heap of still-unopened presents, carefully rationed to prevent over-excitement. 'Hark the Herald Angels' is playing quietly on the sound system. On the sideboard, a bottle of Chateau Latour '85 is breathing. And upstairs, on *her* pillow, ready for when the children have gone to bed, is the tiny velvet box containing – oh, God. *Enough already.*

The drizzle suddenly turns into a downpour. Martin is still lurking in the rockery near the kitchen waiting for me, so I make a run for the greenhouse. It's in total darkness as I burst in; it takes a moment for my eyes to adjust to the gloom. It smells of damp earth and compost and dead spiders. Dad is at the far end near the potting shelves, and with an inward smile I make a big show of flapping out my rain-soaked skirt to give him and Uncle Denny time to hide the porn magazines.

But it isn't Uncle Denny who shuffles past me with an embarrassed murmur a few moments later.

It's Libby, Mrs-Newcombe-from-two-doors-down's daughter.

'She sneaked me out a piece of chocolate cake,' Dad says, handing me the crumb-strewn plate. 'You know your mother's got me on another of her bloody diets—' he breaks off as he catches sight of my expression. 'Why, what did you think she was doing in here? Slipping out for a quick bit of nookie with your old man?'

Of course I bloody did, she's got form.

'Of course not,' I snap.

Dad snorts with laughter. 'You *did*, didn't you? You bloody did! I can't wait to tell the lads down the King's Arms. Good Lord, I should be so lucky! The girl's young enough to be my daughter!'

'Younger,' I mutter crossly.

I'm obviously losing it, of course. It's this thing with Nick that's done it: I've got affairs on the brain. As if *my Dad* would ever mess about. He and Mum have been together so long they're starting to look like each other. She *so* drives me up the wall, but she obviously floats his boat. So, whatever.

He gives my shoulders a warm squeeze. 'There you are, then, love. A girl like that wouldn't look twice at an old man like me.'

Wouldn't she? I look at my dad, look at him *properly*, in his creaseless khakis and the light blue jumper Mum gave him this morning 'because it matches your eyes' – as if – and try hard to be objective. He's not as slim as he was in their wedding photos; but, on the plus side, not as spotty either. All right to look at, I suppose; quite nice, actually, if he wasn't my dad, despite that crappy geek haircut, that's one thing that hasn't changed since he was seventeen. At least he hasn't got Uncle Denny's beer gut like the rest of his brothers-in-King's Arms. But he's past *it*, surely? I know he and Mum must occasionally – well, let's not go there. Not a pretty thought. But otherwise. Twenty-six years in, settled, sorted, well-and-truly *married*; past all the flirting and butterflies and assignations in potting sheds.

And then I realize with a shock that he's only forty-three years old: exactly the same age as Nick. Who is most definitely not past *it* at all.

New Year's Eve is worse.

I *had* planned to escape to London and shake down some of my friends to find a cool party to go to. Failing that, I was even considering throwing one (inevitably somewhat *less* cool) if I could round up enough takers; or, as a last resort, staying up till five a.m. with Amy – like all mistresses, forced to fly solo at holidays and weekends – to watch the ball drop in Times Square on CNN, since Improved New Labour has successfully fucked up the fun in Trafalgar. One thing I was most definitely *not* doing: attending the St Edward's cheese-and-wine New Year's Eve parish supper with my parents.

I've got to hand it to my mother. She'd have Machiavelli canvassing for proportional representation if she put her mind to it.

First came the Christmas presents: the latest Black-Berry, a Bose docking system for my iPod, half the Chanel make-up counter (actually, I prefer MAC, the colours are funkier, but my mother insists Chanel is more classy), and a gorgeous Hermès scarf (though I can't imagine what I'll wear it with; I'm not really a scarf sort of person, they make me look like a landgirl). And then, the coup de grâce: a Christmas card containing my latest statements from Visa, Amex, River Island, Gap – all of them paid off. *Fuck*, that must be several thousand pounds right there. More, probably. Agnès B was having a sale last month. Mum must have gone through my in tray – aka my knicker drawer – to find them last time she came to my flat; but I am too busy revelling in the novel sensation of being solvent to object to the invasion. Too much.

Gratitude secure, she moves on to Guilt.

A whispered conversation about Dad in the kitchen: 'Do you think he's lost weight, darling? It's all the stress at work. Hot water first, dear. Warms the pot. Of course he misses you *dread*fully, it's always lovely for him when you come home to visit. He really perks up. I know you're terribly busy with your "career"—' damn her, I can *hear* the quotation marks. 'I don't blame you for not coming back home very often. No, skimmed milk, darling. *Such* a pity you can't stay longer.'

And, 'Mrs Newcombe's daughter won first prize for her sponge last month at the WI Harvest Festival Fayre, did I tell you? Joan was *so* proud. Libby makes the *most* delicious chocolate cake, simply melts in your mouth—

'Would you mind just getting the tea-cosy down from that shelf for me, dear? My sciatica has been playing me up dreadfully, I've never been right since I had you, of course. What a nightmare that was. Did I mention, Muriel's daughter had twins? That's four grandchildren she's got now—'

So when she asked me if I'd like to come to the bloody cheese-and-wine supper with them – it would be such a treat for Dad, we'd love to show our clever girl off, we hardly get to see you these days, darling! – I knew I was screwed.

Now I get it. I am *so* never going to live this down.

'I don't need you fixing me up with anyone, Mum!' I hiss furiously as Martin pumps my father's hand enthusiastically and shoots me a triumphant leer. 'And for God's sake, why him?'

'Don't blaspheme, dear, there's a church on the other side of that wall,' my mother says calmly. 'And I always thought you rather liked Martin.'

'What on *earth* gave you that impression?'

'*You* did, dear. The night your father caught the two of you in the greenhouse and had to have words with young Martin.'

I swear, I don't remember any of this. It's either early-onset Alzheimer's or the little twat *did* slip me a roofie. Although – now I think about it – there was the night I experimented with those little blotting paper tablets; he *might* have been there.

'Be nice to him,' my mother says firmly. 'He only agreed to come at the last minute as a favour.'

This is such a gross misrepresentation of the facts that for a moment I am rendered speechless. And a moment is all it takes for Martin to slide his skanky ass into the plastic chair next to me, trapping me between the wall and a hard place. *His* hard place, to be precise.

'Well, I'll leave you two to it,' my mother says brightly, getting up from the table.

'Mum—'

'Come along, Vincent,' she says to my father. 'I want to get to the cheese before they run out of all the nice ones. Muriel said there's a lovely Crottin de Chavignol, very earthy and flinty, our cheese coach says, and there's the Tomme de Savoie I want to try—'

A cheese coach? Did my mother really just say that, or have I actually fallen down a rabbit hole?

My father throws me an apologetic glance as she drags him away. I want to throttle him. For God's sake, Dad, could you just stand up to the Gorgon for once?

'Well, isn't this nice?' Martin says, oozing closer. 'All on our own at last.'

'With a roomful of people,' I point out. *Witnesses*, Martin.

He pushes his glasses back up his nose with his thumb. 'You were a bit of a tease the other day. Running off like that. You gave me a chest cold, keeping me out in the rain, you know. Mum was quite cross about it. But I know you girls like to treat a man mean, keep him keen, hmm, hmm?'

Oh, God. He's Fisher's secret love child. I grab the bottle of cheap red on the table and fill my water glass with it, then drain it in a single gulp. This could be a very, *very* long night.

Libby Newcombe sniggers as she dumps a book from the pile in her arms onto the holly-sprigged paper tablecloth. Briefly I lift my head from the table to glower at her retreating back. *If you're so fucking cool, you cow, how come you're here on New Year's Eve too?*

'Fancy a quick spin on the floor?' Martin asks hopefully.

'Can't. Got to read this very interesting book about – er – cheese.'

'I didn't know you were interested in cheese.'

'Oh, yes, very. My cheese coach is terribly strict, though, won't let us just dive in half-cocked. Have to read all about, um—' I flick it open, 'the blue-veined cheeses first.'

'Wouldn't mind being a little half-cocked myself,' Martin leers, 'if you get my drift.'

'Sorry. Got to concentrate. Test on Tuesday.'

I suddenly catch sight of the author photograph on the inside jacket flap, and my knickers skip a beat. Shit, but he is *hot*. Talk about fallen angel. Square-jawed, hot-eyed, just-tumbling-into-bed-with-you-if-you'll-let-me expression. Who the hell *is* he?

I flip the book over again. Trace Pitt – oh, of course, I've heard of him. Pitt's Cheese Factory, it's that famous de luxe cheese shop in – God, where is it? Covent Garden somewhere, I think. It's the Harvey Nicks of cheese shops. There's only one other, in New York. Actually, I vaguely remember Mum saying something about the committee getting their cheese from Pitt's this year after the fiasco with the mouse last Christmas.

That is one hot man. Dumb name, sounds like some comic book private eye – Trace Pitt, Ace Detective, what were his parents thinking? – but with a face like that he could call himself Mother Teresa for all I care—

I yelp in shock as Martin sticks his tongue in my ear.

Right, that's it. I whack him with *The Cheese Lover's Guide*, drop to the floor, slither under the table, and flee to the other side of the room. I am not, repeat *not*, staying here a moment longer. Even if I have to walk all the way home to London.

Well, maybe not in these stilettos. OK, where are my fucking parents?

Of my mother there is no sign – probably next door reading from the Sacred Cheese Text with Muriel – but I spot my father straight away.

He's sitting at the bar, and he's not alone. I watch Libby Newcombe cross her legs so that her ridiculously short skirt rides up her thighs, giving Dad a bird's eye view. Her lips are parted as she hangs on his every word with rapt attention – yeah, right, my dad: specialist subject, Motorway Cones on the M25 – flicking her long blonde hair all over the place like she's in a damn shampoo ad. Little tart. Don't you lick your lips and flaunt your cleavage at *my dad*. He's a happily married man. Against all reasonable expectations, admittedly. But still.

I'd like to know what the little ho thinks she's playing at. Blonde hair, legs up to here, no bra: it's like shooting fish in a barrel. He hasn't got a chance. Look, you homewrecker, *he's taken*. It's hard enough holding a marriage together without some twenty-something totty putting pressure on its weakest link. Which, let's face it, we all know men are.

I march over and slide my arm possessively through my dad's.

'Oh, hello, love,' Dad says, clearly surprised by this sudden display of filial affection. 'What happened to young Martin?'

'Nothing fatal,' I say regretfully. 'Look, Dad, can we go now? I'm really tired and I've got to drive back to London tomorrow.'

'What, leave before midnight? What happened to my party girl?' He ruffles my hair. 'Used to be a time we couldn't get you into bed before dawn.'

'Well, she's not twenty-one any more,' Libby says sweetly. 'You know, I can't believe you've got a grown-up daughter, Vinny. You look much too young.'

Vinny? *Vinny?* Since when has my dad been called anything other than Vincent? (Or Dad, obviously.)

'You flatterer,' Dad scolds, the tips of his ears turning pink.

'Dad, *please*, I'm really tired—'

Libby knows when to beat a retreat. I scowl as she kisses Dad's cheek and wishes him a happy new year. *Vinny.* God, men are just so *oblivious.*

'You didn't need to do that, love,' Dad says quietly. 'She's got a bit of a thing for me, I know, but it's harmless. Just a silly crush. She'll grow out of it.'

'Dad, she's not thirteen. And it's not bloody harmless, she was all *over* you—'

'Your mother's enough for me,' Dad interrupts, eyes softening as they rest on Mum, holding court by the cheese table. 'Always will be.'

'I don't know how you put up with her,' I mutter.

My father looks at me with an expression akin to disappointment, and I suddenly feel about twelve years old again.

'You kids are obsessed with being in love these days,' Dad says coolly. 'You think it's all butterflies in the tummy and romantic walks along the beach.'

'I'm not quite that naive, Dad. I know it's got to get a bit boring, after a while. But as long as you love each other—'

'You think that's enough? *Love?*'

I shrug crossly.

'There have been days when I've woken up and your mother has irritated me just by still *breathing*. No doubt she's felt the same about me. There have been weeks – months, even – when we could scarcely stand to be in the same room as each other. But you work through it. You build a life together and you stick with it, no matter how hard it gets at times. You don't dig up a garden every five minutes and replant with something else if the flower you picked out hasn't bloomed, do you? You make your choice, you water and feed it, and then you *wait*. The point I'm trying to make, love, and I'm making a right hash of it, I know, is that marriage is about commitment. And compromise. A compromise with each other; and – ' he sighs – 'a compromise with what you thought it was going to be.'

Not me, I think firmly. I'm not going to settle for second best. I'm not going to end up like Mum and Dad, staying together out of habit and fear.

I want passion! And fire! And romance! The kind of legendary love you read about. Bogart and Bacall. Hepburn and Tracey. Christopher Reeve and – well, Mrs Reeve. Dad's wrong: it *doesn't* have to be a compromise. If you really love each other, you *can* keep the butterflies.

You just have to find your soul mate, and when you do, hang onto them with everything you've got.

The question is: what do you do if someone finds *your* soul mate first?

Life isn't all neat and tidy. Sometimes people make a mistake and end up with the wrong person. Does that mean they have to stay with them forever? Surely it's better to take their chance at true love, wherever they find it? Even if – even if people get hurt.

Dad gives me a quick hug. 'I'm just going to have a dance with your mother before we go. She loves Sinatra. You be all right for a minute on your own?'

I watch my parents take to the floor. They're young enough to be fairly hopeless, shuffling in the same spot whilst toothless pensioners twice their age spin gracefully past like they're on wheels. My parents fit together nicely, covering each other's mistakes and doing the odd safe twirl with the ease of long practice. But they're waving hello at friends as they pass and chatting about the weather, not gazing lustfully into each other's eyes. *And I want more.*

Suddenly everybody starts moving, laughing and jostling, and I realize it's just a couple of minutes to midnight.

Everyone's in couples – even Martin has managed to trap Libby Newcombe in a dark corner. As midnight strikes, I know Dad will give Mum her special Christmas present, the one he saves for the first minute of the New Year – always a beautiful piece of jewellery, some years more expensive than others, but always a one-off, commissioned especially for her: to thank her in advance, he says, for spending the next three hundred and sixty-five (or sixty-six, if it's a leap year, he's nothing if not precise) days with him.

I'm fed up with being single. I want someone to save me from the aunts and dance with me on New Year's Eve. *I'd* like a special present and a first kiss and a man to drive me home when I've drunk too much to walk. I'm so tired of having to put a brave face on being lonely. Dammit, it must be *so nice* to be married this time of year.

As the sound of Big Ben blares from the speaker system, I dig my new BlackBerry out of my bag and pull up Nick's details. Without giving myself time to think too long, I download the song I want, attach it to an email, and hit 'Send'.

6

Malinche

Oh, heavens, it's not often I wish this – Lord knows I'd hate to tempt Fate, she has a nasty habit of taking you a little too literally; I'm always afraid to wish I could lose weight in case I end up having my leg sliced off in a car crash: there, *now* you weigh less – but there are times I can't help thinking how wonderful it would be to be single and child-free at this time of year.

No hot, desperate searches for must-have toys that sold out last October. No three-trolley trips to Sainsbury's for, amongst other things, nine pounds of spuds (which you don't have time to peel until three a.m. on Christmas morning). No excruciating multi-faith carol concerts in which you cannot even see your offspring because of the shadow cast by the tallest child in the school who is always placed right in the centre of the front row.

And, oh dear, no irate publishers left sitting alone in expensive London restaurants because lunch clashed with a carol concert and you forgot to let them know.

That lovely young girl in the low-cut jeans and biscuit suede jacket by the luggage rack, for example. She can't *possibly* be Christmas shopping for three under-tens; not in sexy boots four inches high. She's probably going to be whisked away for Christmas to some glorious white-sugar beach in the Caribbean by a bedroom-eyed Adonis, far from sticky-fingered children high on E numbers and know-better husbands who throw out instructions and then can't put Barbie's Own Recording Studio together.

I cling on to the spring ceiling thingy for grim death as the train barrels round a tight corner. I must be mad. Heading into London to go shopping four days before Christmas is like rowing back to board the *Titanic* for an ice cube. My feet hurt already despite my sensible pumps, and we're only five minutes out of Salisbury station. The train is packed – not a hope of a seat. As it is, I'm nose to gabardine overcoat with the rather large businessman squashed next to me.

And my knickers itch. Well, *scratch*, really. Can't be the label, I cut that out (it's a bit embarrassing when your pants say 'Age 8–10' and you're more 36–38, but Sophie's undies are *so* much more comfortable than mine) so – I *knew* it. Real Christmas trees *are* much nicer, Nicholas is absolutely right; but—

I don't know why Gabardine Overcoat is looking at me so strangely. They're only pine needles.

Christmas is *about* children, of course it is. But three of them does mean rather a lot of presents to buy, what with FC (mustn't call him Santa, Nicholas gets so terribly cross) and then the aunts and grandparents and godmothers who ring up and say, 'Oh, darling, you don't mind getting them something from me, do you, *you'll* know what they want.' And even though it's very kind of them and you know they'll pay you back, eventually, still now that's something else you have to think of and find and buy and wrap. Though after last year – just *what* my mother thought three small children would do with a full-size potter's kiln except try to bake the poor rabbit is beyond me.

I should have started shopping earlier, of course. I meant to; but then I got distracted with planning all sorts of yummy Christmas eats – I thought this year I'd try goose stuffed with persimmon foie gras and a 1985 Chateau d'Yquem sauternes reduction, though I'm rather dreading what Nicholas, such a champion of tradition, will say at the turkey's non-appearance – and so now I'm rather desperately behind. About two months, to be precise. Very sweet of Liz to mind the girls for me, but heaven knows where I'll find a Barbie ski-suit for Chloe. Poor duck, she does rather take after Liz in the hips department, a size 16 at nine years old *is* a bit tricky. Luckily she's stunningly lovely to look at – that delicious pre-Raphaelite hair – but born in totally the wrong century, of course. Seventeenth would have been perfect: Rubens would have loved her. Now if only Nicholas could have nipped into *Snow+Rock* for me, there's one two minutes from him in Holborn, bound to have something; but of course he's away in Manchester. And even if he weren't, presents aren't exactly his thing. Although why possession of two X chromosomes automatically makes them mine, as Nicholas seems to think, he doesn't even—

The Christmas cards. I *did* put them in the post box, didn't I? Or – oh, Lord, I didn't leave them on the front seat of the Volvo? Heavens, I'm not normally *this* scatty.

It's Christmas, it does this to me every year. It's like my brain's on fast forward, scrolling through everything I've still got to do—

I sent them. I'm sure I did.

I wish I was brave enough to copy Louise. She has a three-year Christmas card cycle: she does A to H one year, then I to P the next, and Q to Z the third, so that everyone gets a card every three years. Just often enough that people don't sulk and strike her off their lists.

I stare out of the train window at the pelting rain as we stop for another set of engineering works. It's ten already; I have to be back by four-thirty for Evie's Bible class recital. And as well as scouring London for inspirational stocking fillers I must make time to go to Harrods Food Hall for some Spanish Roncal cheese (so tricky to find, that creamy, buttery Navarre) for the potato gratin. Pitt's would have it, of course, quite certain to have it, but obviously that's not possible, Trace might be there, and it's bad enough that he's moving back to Salisbury; even after all these years—

No, don't think about *that*. Regrets are for cissies, as Kit loves to say.

Another surge of passengers piles onto the train at Woking, and suddenly it really *is* too crammed to breathe. I feel like I'm on one of those cattle trucks to Auschwitz – oh, Lord, I didn't mean it, that's a terrible thing to say, you can't possibly compare—

'I'm not standing for this,' Gabardine Overcoat suddenly announces, levering himself out of the luggage rack whence the latest influx has pushed him. 'The amount they ask for a ticket these days the least I expect is a seat. If they don't provide enough second-class carriages, I think we're perfectly entitled to find seats elsewhere.'

His accent and pale gold silk cravat are true-blue Home Counties. When the much-put-upon silent majority finally finds its voice, you know there's trouble ahead.

Murmured assent runs around the carriage. It really *is* stifling in here; we are all of us kitted out in our warmest winter coats, mittened and buttoned and scarfed and hatted, and the carriage is starting to smell somewhat unwashed. A conspiratorial I-will-if-you-will camaraderie seizes us; it reminds me of playing Knock Down Ginger as a child. (My sister Cleo was always much braver than me, she'd even dare to ring the doorbell of The Perv – I'm sure he wasn't a pervert really, just a lonely old widower whose children lived too far away to visit much – and count to three before running away.)

Two puddingy girls in sleeveless Puffa jackets – I can only imagine what Nicholas would think of their silver nose piercings – push open the connecting door to the First Class corridor. Gabardine Overcoat helps a frighteningly young mother manoeuvre her double pushchair across the swaying threshold. Within minutes, we're all sinking into the posh seats with a delicious feeling of naughtiness.

A pinstriped businessman opposite me snaps his clever pink newspaper in front of his face with a disapproving tut. I giggle and think: I do *miss* Nicholas.

There are many things I have learned from my daughters over the years. For example, a king-sized waterbed holds enough water to fill a three-bedroom Florida condo four inches deep. (Evie, last summer.)

A seven-year-old girl can start a fire with a flint rock, even though a forty-three-year-old lawyer insists it can only be done in the movies. (Evie again.)

Brake fluid from the garage mixed with bleach from the laundry room makes smoke; and lots of it. (Evie. Followed by Kit, and then Nicholas, when they heard about it.)

Always look in the oven before you turn it on – plastic Fisher Price toys do *not* like ovens. (Incidentally, the Salisbury Fire Department has a response time of a little under four minutes.)

And this morning, we all discovered that the spin cycle on the washing machine does not make earthworms dizzy. It will, however, make pet rabbits dizzy.

Pet rabbits throw up twice their body weight when dizzy.

Cleaning up animal sick on your hands and knees before breakfast is not necessarily the most festive way to start Christmas Day, I think, scouring the flagstones with unnecessary vigour. So when Nicholas sneaks up behind me and slides his hands under my dressing-gown to fondle my naked buttocks, I think I can be forgiven for not responding with quite his level of *amour*.

It's not that I don't enjoy sex with my husband. *Per se.* Whisked away to a water villa in the Maldives for two weeks whilst someone else minds the children, with no phones or cross publishers or school runs or laundry, I would like nothing better – well, perhaps not *nothing* better; I must admit to a terrible weakness for home-made bread-and-butter pudding and a fat Jilly Cooper – but anyway, the idea of sex as recreation rather than chore certainly appeals. Whereas these days I seem to find myself thinking, as Nicholas rolls contentedly to his un-damp side of the bed: well, it's Thursday today, so that gives me until at least – oh, the weekend after next before we have to do it again. Which is possibly *not* the most romantic way to approach lovemaking with your soul mate. But a hundred and fifty-two Christmas cards don't write themselves.

I remember, with unexpected nostalgia, surprising Nicholas in his office one evening, not long after we'd met, wearing nothing but a suspender belt and seamed stockings under my raincoat. I'd persuaded the cleaning lady to let me in (it turned out she was a *huge* fan and had bought all my cookery books) and sat there in the darkness for two hours, waiting for Nicholas to come back from Court. He was terribly late; I nearly lost my nerve and went home, but I'd gone to so much trouble, I couldn't bear to just leave. I'd painted my nipples with special edible chocolate paint – I'd trekked all the way out to a ladies-only erotic emporium called 'Sh!' in north London to find it, it was the most embarrassing and exciting tube journey of my life – and even dusted my pubic hair with cocoa powder; I was terrified it'd some-how melt or something before Nicholas got that far, but it didn't, it was *perfect*, it all went off exactly as I'd imagined, just like a late-night movie.

'Don't put on the light,' I said in my most sultry voice, as he walked into his office and reached for the switch.

He jumped about six feet as I moved forward into the

amber puddle of a streetlight and unbuttoned my coat. His mouth simply dropped open; I nearly ruined everything by laughing at the astonished look on his face.

'Close your eyes,' I said, trying not to giggle. 'Now: open your mouth.'

I fed him expensive Belgian chocolates I'd bought in Harrods as I unbuttoned his trousers; one bitter-orange truffle and a cognac-centre later, he laid me across his desk and disappeared between my legs with the rapt expression of a cat that had just got the (chocolate) cream.

I sigh now and reach for the persimmon foie gras. It's been a *very* long time since we made love anywhere but between John Lewis's finest Egyptian cotton (two-hundred threads per square inch). I just don't have the energy.

The rabbit incident aside, Christmas morning passes off relatively well. There's a *slightly* hairy moment after Church when Louise presents Nicholas's parents with a spiky-leafed cannabis seedling; but fortunately to the pure all things are pure, and Kit discreetly (if a little keenly) appropriates it before it can be put in the back of my in-laws' Hillman Imp and innocently repotted in Esher.

'But Daisy says she's in such pain from her arthritis,' Louise protests ingenuously, when Cleo and I corner her in the kitchen, 'and Mary-Jane is the best painkiller there is—'

'Mother, please,' Cleo hisses. 'If you must dabble in drugs, at least refrain from this ridiculous hippy patois and call them by their proper names.'

Cleo professes not to remember playing Knock Down Ginger, or scrumping apples, or pinching lipstick from Woolies for a dare. She claims her crush on Donny Osmond is a figment of my imagination, and that she always thought *Fame* was rubbish. Cleo is now a very respectable chartered accountant ('Blood will out,' Louise sighed when she heard Cleo's decision, 'so much for rebirthing ceremonies') and would probably have made the poor sweet Lyons a much more suitable daughter-in-law than the flaky sometime-chef they're stuck with; but there it is.

At thirty-nine, Cleo is still defiantly single. 'My choice,' she says tersely, when Daisy Lyon tentatively asks her over the sherry if she is *stepping out* with anyone. 'If I wanted, I could have any man I pleased.'

'Yes,' Kit mutters, 'but you never *have* pleased any man, have you?'

I *adore* Edward and Daisy Lyon, of course, impossible not to – she's an absolute lamb, and he's *such* a gentleman, so courtly and correct, with that wonderful ramrod military bearing even at eighty-two; but you can tell they're a bit bewildered by the speed of the world these days, feel somewhat adrift, desperately clinging to the old and the familiar for support. And Nicholas – well, Nicholas *can* sometimes be very much his parents' son. Which just goes to show: it's nurture, not just nature, that will out.

I drag Kit out of the sitting room just before the Queen's speech; if he sees Nicholas and Edward stand to listen to Her Majesty – as they always do – restraining him will be beyond my capabilities.

Christmas dinner for ten is always a little testing, especially when one of the guests decides on the spur of the moment to become a vegan – 'Marvellous idea, Sophs,' Kit enthuses, 'let's start tomorrow, I hate Boxing Day leftovers' – but the goose is thankfully well received and, miraculously, not in the least bit spoiled by the panicked

forty-minute search for Metheny (finally discovered fast
asleep under the potting bench in the boiler room in her
new Pooh slippers) or Evie's disturbingly skilled attempts
at alchemy. Really, Kit is an ass. As if the baking soda
and vinegar incident last month wasn't bad enough, he
has to provide her with the means to cook up H_2SO_4 in
her bedroom.

I feel dreadfully mean about my earlier dressing-gown
briskness when I open Nicholas's present after lunch – not
that sexual favours should be in any way linked to sump-
tuous, nutmeg suede coats from Joseph (though there's no
denying that if they *were*, I've more than earned it this last
month or so. I don't know what's got into my husband,
I might have to borrow Evie's chemistry set to cook up
some bromide for his tea) – but he's obviously spent a lot
of money, an appallingly large sum of money. I mean,
Joseph – whereas I—

'Perfect, darling, thank you,' Nicholas says as he opens
my suddenly-meagre gift – a cashmere sweater the same
moss-grey as his eyes, 'absolutely the right thing.'

'I know it's not terribly exciting, but you did ask for—'

'It's exciting to me,' he says quietly, 'and it will be
wonderfully warm for skiing next week. You are a very
good wife to me, Malinche, a man simply couldn't ask for
better. And I wouldn't ask, obviously. Obviously.'

'Such a very *odd* thing to say,' I muse to Kit later. 'In fact,
he's been behaving rather oddly altogether these past few
weeks. I know it's driving him potty having Fisher looking over his shoulder all the time when he's supposed to
have retired—'

'Oddly?'

'Well, yes. Budge up, Kit, I can hardly move my elbows.'

'I don't know why you don't just *tell* him you smoke,' Kit sighs, gracefully exhaling a smoke ring. 'He's hardly going to divorce you and cite Marlboro Lights as co-respondent. You're as bad as Metheny, hiding out in the boiler room for a quick fag like this.'

'Don't you mean *with* a quick fag?'

'Nothing quick about me, darling. Ask Paul. Or James. Or—'

I cut him off quickly before he recites his entire sexual history (which could take us to Easter.) 'I *don't* smoke, Kit. Christmas Day and birthdays don't count.'

'It wouldn't if you just stuck to *your* birthday, poppet. Now, tell me about sweet Nick. In what way *oddly*?'

I inhale deeply, and spend the next five minutes coughing like a romantic heroine with advanced consumption. Lack of practice; entirely my own fault for not telling Nicholas I smoked when we first met. 'Don't call him Nick, Kit, he hates it. I don't know quite how to put it – he just seems – well, odd.'

'So you keep saying,' Kit observes.

'He's absolutely rampant, for one thing. I mean, he's always been surprisingly keen in the bedroom, though perhaps not *terribly* imaginative – mind you, there was the time with the maple syrup. And of course the nurse's outfit, very boarding school, that, some sort of Matron thing—'

'Malinche,' Kit says, 'sweet of you to share, but not entirely necessary.'

Sometimes I forget Kit isn't actually a girl.

'Sorry. And then he's been terribly grumpy, says it's work, of course, but—'

'He's always grumpy to me,' Kit sulks.

'Yes, well, you don't exactly go out of your way to play nicely with him, Kit.'

'I make *every* effort—'

'Kit, you gave him *purple anal beads* for Christmas.'

'Just trying to share the fun, darling.'

'It's lucky for you he assumed they were part of Sophie's jewellery kit; you must get them back before she turns them into a necklace for her teacher or something.' I stub out my cigarette. 'I don't mean Nicholas has been grumpy, exactly; more *moody*, I suppose. A bit bearish, at times. And then suddenly terribly, *terribly* nice and attentive—'

Kit pointedly says nothing.

'Don't even *think* it,' I warn. 'Not after—'

'Yes,' says Kit, 'point taken.'

'Although,' I muse, 'he did say this girl's name the other morning in bed, it was actually rather funny—'

'*Funny?* Are you quite mad, Malinche?'

'Don't look at me like that, Kit. He's just having a naughty little fantasy about this girl at his office – Sara. I met her once, rather shy as I recall – but you know as well as I do he'd never *do* anything. He's positively phobic about adultery, hardly surprising, given what happened to his parents. It was quite unconscious. I'm sure he had no idea what he'd said; he'd probably die of embarrassment if I ever told him.'

'Sadly, Pollyanna, I fear for once your optimism is well placed,' Kit says regretfully. 'I can't quite see Nicholas doing the old inny-outy on his desk with the office floozie, much as the image delightfully boggles the mind. No, I think it probably *is* just work, sweets, or quite possibly a brain tumour—'

'*Not* funny, Kit.'

'Now, *you*, on the other hand, I can quite see getting up to all sorts of mischief.'

He's lost me. 'Mischief? Me? What sort of mischief?'

Kit unfurls his elegant frame from the potting bench and saunters towards the door. 'I meant to tell you,' he says negligently. 'Trace Pitt is opening his own restaurant in Salisbury, that's why he's back. And I hear—' He turns to me with a dark, amused smile, 'I hear he's hoping *you* will be his new head chef.'

'Oh, Nicholas, isn't it breathtaking?'

I jam my ski poles into the snow, biting off my gloves finger by finger and unwinding my scarf as I drink in the spectacular view. Below us, the Briançon valley looks absurdly like a Christmas cake dotted with little green plastic pine trees. The vicious snowstorm of yesterday has cleared, leaving behind a foot of glorious fresh powder and acid blue skies.

'Fine,' Nicholas says shortly.

Oh dear. I thought the hard skiing this morning might have cheered him up a bit. Taken his mind off it, so to speak.

I do love him, and I *do* still fancy him – 'Is it something I'm doing? or not doing? Please, *tell* me,' he said this morning, desperately earnest – but I just don't want sex as much as he does. Not these days. Not with three children, for heaven's sake. And I'm sorry, but I've always *hated* it in the morning. I don't feel quite fresh. There's too much raw life going on, too much spinning in my head – PE kits and lunchboxes and feed the rabbit and fix stuck window – and not enough sleep. *Never* enough sleep. It's hard enough to get in the mood at night, when you can't help but keep an eye on the clock: it's midnight, six hours till I have to be up, if this takes another twenty minutes, then—

But in the morning, when you'd *kill* for just another five minutes' sleep. And knowing the girls could come in at any minute. You would have thought, after ten years of marriage, you would have thought he'd *know* when I'm in the mood—

'Better get going,' Nicholas says now, 'the others will be waiting.'

He shoots off down the piste before I even have my gloves back on. I'm still trying to tuck my scarf back into my ski jacket and do up the zip with clumsy fingers as he reaches a sharp left bend. I glance up, squinting slightly at the brightness of sun on snow, to see where he is, and watch it all unfold before me: the pack of snowboarders appearing over the crest of an adjoining run as if from nowhere, Nicholas stationary on the bend, adjusting his boot, waiting for me to catch up, the snowboarders suddenly bearing down on him, the edges of their boards glinting like knife blades in the sunlight. And then Nicholas glancing up, astonished, as two of the snowboarders cut in front of him, giving him nowhere to go, and four more head straight towards him, so that he has no option but to throw himself bodily into the snowdrift at the side of the run if he wants to avoid being mown down.

And just as suddenly, it's all over, and Nicholas is

picking himself out of the snow, the boarders' mocking jeers – 'Get out the way, Grandad!' – echoing down the mountain.

To my surprise, Nicholas tells the story against himself when we join Liz and her husband, Giles, at the piste-side mountain café twenty minutes later, his moodiness melting with the snow on his jacket.

'My own bloody fault,' he observes, 'standing in the middle of the piste like that. Should've known better. Right on a bend, too. Bloody idiot.'

'They should have jolly well watched where they were going,' Liz protests.

'Ah. Not as easy to manoeuvre as skis, snowboards,' Giles says.

Giles is the kind of man who sees the good in everyone, even homicidal Antipodean snowboarders. He has been heard to remark that Osama bin Laden, being one of approximately ninety-five brothers, is clearly very much a family man.

'But are you all right?' Liz presses anxiously. 'I've ordered you an extra plate of *frites*, for the shock.'

Nicholas laughs ruefully.

'I'm going to have the devil of a bruise on my backside in the morning, and my sunglasses are wrapped around a pine tree, but apart from that, the only casualty is my pride. You ever tried snowboarding, Giles?'

'Young man's game,' Giles harrumphs.

'Giles! You're only thirty-five,' I say, laughing.

'Not wearing the years as well as you, Malinche,' he says gallantly. 'And I'm certainly an old enough dog to know when new tricks are beyond me.'

'I rather think it's trying new tricks that keeps you

young,' Nicholas says thoughtfully, blowing on his *vin chaud*, and surprising me for the second time this morning.

In fact, Nicholas surprises me rather a lot during the second half of our holiday; and *I* surprise both of us by finding this unfamiliar Nicholas rather erotic. So erotic, in fact, that Nicholas has to brave the ordeal of purchasing condoms in French from the local pharmacy at ten past eleven one night; it (shamefully) never having occurred to me to pack any.

'*Edepol nunc nos tempus et malas peioris fieri*,' Nicholas says triumphantly as he throws the packet on the bedspread and his clothes on the floor. 'Now's the time for bad girls to become worse still.'

'Who said that?' I ask, pulling his beautiful naked body onto mine.

'Plautus.'

'I *like* Plautus,' I say firmly.

It all starts the morning after his near-miss with the snowboarders. I come down to breakfast late after struggling for twenty minutes to get a demonic Metheny into her snowsuit for the village crèche, only to find Nicholas has disappeared.

Evie lifts her face out of her breakfast bowl and displays a Cheshire Cat hot-chocolate grin that reaches to her ears. 'Daddy said he'd see your pussy in the van show at lunchtime,' she announces.

I look to Sophie for translation.

'He'll see you at Le Poussin for a *vin chaud* at lunch,' Sophie sighs. 'Evie, you're useless. As if Daddy would ever drive a van.'

In the event, had Nicholas arrived at the piste café at the wheel of a white Ford transit demanding sexual satisfaction, I would have been less surprised.

'Snowboarding?' Kit exclaims, when I called on my mobile from the café lavatory to share the apocalyptic news. 'Nicholas?'

'Snowboarding, Nicholas,' I confirm. '*Not* two words I ever expected to use in the same sentence.'

'Suddenly abduction by aliens is sounding perfectly reasonable,' Kit observes, 'I'm looking at the whole business of Roswell and Area 51 in a whole new light. By the way,' he adds meaningfully, 'I noticed, when I was feeding your rabbit, that you have rather a lot of messages on your answer machine.'

'Don't, Kit.'

'I don't understand you,' he says crossly. 'How can you not be curious, after all these years?'

Trace always did have the power to tempt, I think, as his satanic smile fills my mind. But of course it's out of the question. I mean, the hours, for a start. The girls would need to keep photos of me by their beds so they didn't think we were being burgled if they ran into me in the hallway in the middle of the night.

But my own restaurant—

Impossible. No point even thinking about it: so I very carefully don't.

No matter what hours Trace offered me, accepting would be unthinkable; far, far too dangerous on every level. I love Nicholas more than I thought possible; but I'm not going to risk it all by putting myself in the line of fire again.

It turns out he has rather a knack for snowboarding.

After two days in which he acquires a collection of bruises that has Evie emerald with envy, it suddenly all comes together for him, and on the third morning, he and his snowboard join the rest of us ski-bound mortals on the piste.

He's even found time to buy a new khaki jacket and grey cargo pants, I notice in astonishment. Thankful though I am to see the back of the vile navy all-in-one he's had since we first met, this is all taking a bit of getting used to.

I'm also taken aback to see him sporting white earphones – *earphones*! And this a man who resolutely refused to switch from vinyl until 1994 – and listening to a song by some girl I've never even heard of.

'I wouldn't complain,' Liz mumbles through her pain au chocolat elevenses. 'As mid-life crises go, buying an iPod and taking up snowboarding is fairly harmless. And you have to admit it suits him.'

Liz is right: the changes in Nicholas *do* suit him. Watching my husband shooting past on his board, arms outstretched for balance, knees bent, the wind whipping back his hair – goodness, it needs cutting – I'm suddenly punched by the thought: *this is the real Nicholas*. There have been glimpses in the past – usually in bed – but in a dozen years together I have never seen him as clearly as I do now.

It's always been the one sly disappointment of my marriage, that I've never managed to breach Nicholas's fettered self-control. Edward and Daisy Lyon's meticulous British upbringing, it turns out, was more thorough than I'd realized.

And yet – perhaps not thorough enough.

No. Trace Pitt can build the Taj Mahal in Salisbury town centre and I'm still not going to return his calls.

'Sophie, will you hurry up!' I yell up the stairs, shifting Metheny to the other hip. 'I told you, I've got things to do this morning, we're going to be late!'

Sophie appears on the landing. 'But Mummy, I can't find any clean knickers! They've all just vanished! I can't go to school without any knickers!'

Oops. 'Darling, just grab any old pair from the clean laundry basket. We can sort it all out tomorrow. The first day back at school is always a bit of a rush, you know that.'

Minutes later, Sophie thunders down the stairs past me and piles into the back seat of the Volvo next to Evie. I move round to the other side to strap Metheny into her car seat. Scarcely have I secured the hold-all-five-points-and-click-together-whilst-your-baby-squirms-resentfully harness (I swear, it would defeat navy SEALS) than she sicks up porridge all over herself, the car seat, me and – I don't *believe* it—

'Evie! What on *earth* is Don Juan doing in the car?'

'But Mummy! It's show and tell this morning—'

'Take him back to his cage in the scullery. *Now!* Sophie, help me get Metheny back inside so I can change her. Oh, Lord, the phone—'

It's my gynaecologist's secretary, calling to reschedule because an elective Caesarean has suddenly 'come up' – for which read an invitation to golf and a long lunch at the nineteenth hole. Can I please come in an hour earlier – *earlier*? oh, have pity – this morning for my well-woman check. The secretary sounds deeply apologetic, but we both know there is nothing to be done. The gynaecologist is, after all, a man.

I could cancel my appointment altogether, but then the gynaecologist will sulk, and make me wait three days to see him next time I have an excruciating bout of cystitis (which, if Nicholas stays on present bedroom form, may not be too far away).

So instead I race to the girls' school at breakneck speed – 'Mummy, did you see that lady's face at the traffic lights? She looked really funny, can we nearly hit someone again?' – deposit Metheny at Liz's, and arrive back home with two minutes to spare before I have to leave again.

I usually like to make a little extra effort on the hygiene front when I'm going to the gynaecologist (it's like brushing your teeth before having them cleaned, or Hoovering under the bed before the cleaner comes) but clearly this time I'm not going to have time for more than a lick and a promise. I rush upstairs, throw off my kaftan – *such* a sartorial lifesaver, I can't imagine why these ever went out of fashion – wet the flannel sitting next to the sink, and give myself a quick wash down below to make sure all is at least *presentable*. Flinging the flannel into the laundry basket, I throw the kaftan back on, hop back into the car, and race to my appointment.

And this headless-chicken chaos is just an ordinary morning, I reflect as I spend the next twenty minutes sitting behind a horsebox and grinding my teeth in frustration.

I realize that Nicholas, like most husbands whose

wives don't actually go *out* to work, secretly believes that I lie around all day eating chocolate digestives and trying on shoes. And he is right, to a certain extent, since this is exactly what I *would* do – once I have taken the girls to school, swept the kitchen floor, stacked the dishwasher, hunted down dirty socks (my last sweep behind the Aga, under Don Juan's cage and, revoltingly, in the biscuit tin, yielded four), put the washing machine on, dropped off Nicholas's dry-cleaning, played with Metheny on the swings at the village green, put a casserole in the Aga, mopped up the mess from the leaky dishwasher, called a plumber, done all the washing-up by hand, pegged out the laundry, put Metheny to bed for her nap, brought in the laundry when it starts to rain, arranged a service for the Mercedes, scribbled down a sudden idea for a new sort of soufflé, pegged the laundry back out again when it stops raining, answered the phone four times to salesmen trying to sell me double glazing, collected the girls from school, glued cotton wool on a cardboard snowman, written five sentences using adverbs ending in –ly, fed the girls, bathed them, dressed them, read them a story, put them to bed, discussed arrangements for his parents' golden wedding anniversary party for forty minutes with his mother on the phone, checked under Evie's bed for monsters with a torch, read them a story *again*, ironed Nicholas a shirt for the morning, cooked our dinner, washed up, tidied up, bathed myself and gone to bed. Just line those shoes up for me to try on, I'm sure there'll be time tomorrow.

Kit says I should stop trying so hard, let Nicholas see some of the frantic paddling below the surface instead of just the cool, calm swan above; but I can't, he thinks I'm so capable, so organized, so unflappable. I couldn't bear his disappointment.

Thanks to the snail's-pace horsebox, I'm ten minutes late for the gynaecologist. The secretary whisks me through to an empty examination room with a rather-you-than-me smile, and I whip off my clothes and pop up onto the table, sliding my ankles into the stirrups and trying to look suitably contrite. It doesn't do to antagonize megalomaniacs armed with cold specula.

I stare up at the ceiling, letting my mind drift. If I were going to be Trace's head chef – obviously I'm *not*, but if I *were*, there are some fascinating things happening in micro-gastronomy at the moment – oh, that sounds dreadfully dull and scientific, not at all to do with making strawberries taste of chocolate and potatoes taste like peas, which is what it *really* is—

(Relax, *relax*, he's seen it all a thousand times.)

—and if anyone was going to take that sort of gastronomic plunge, it would be Trace, I'm amazed it's taken him this long to open his own restaurant—

(Oh, *cold* hands.)

—though obviously I can quite see how sardine ice-cream in Salisbury might not—

The gynaecologist chuckles between my thighs. 'My, my, Mrs Lyon, we have made an extra effort this morning, haven't we?'

I peer through my splayed legs at the top of his head. 'I'm sorry?'

'Always a pleasure when someone goes the extra mile. All right now, try to relax, this'll just take a jiffy—'

I puzzle briefly over his remark on the drive home,

squirming damply in my seat – so much lubricant, necessary of course, unless one is turned on by the cold metal probing of strangers; not that there's anything *wrong* with that, though it's all a little Black Lace for me – but then as I walk in the back door, the phone is ringing, and by the time I've placated Ali, my increasingly tetchy agent, with reckless promises of a dozen new recipes and a complete synopsis (a dozen! By mid-February!) the entire incident has completely slipped my mind.

The penny, however, drops with a resounding echo when the girls get home.

'Mummy,' Sophie calls from the bathroom, 'where's my flannel?'

'What flannel?' I yell back, my head still in the Aga (from which I am extracting a slightly burned casserole, not contemplating anything Sylvia Plathish).

'The one that was here by the basin,' Sophie says with exaggerated patience. 'It had all my glitter and sparkles in it.'

I'm naked and about to step in the shower – oh, the shame! – when Evie runs into the bathroom, her eyes wide in her bleached, shocked face. 'Liz is here and she didn't even see the shortbread you left out to cool she just came running through the kitchen she's still got her slippers on and she says you have to come downstairs and watch the TV *now*.'

A cold drool of fear slides down my spine as I grab a towel. Instinctively, I know that something terrible has brushed my family.

Liz is hunched forward on the sofa in front of the

television, her elbows on her knees. She leaps up and rushes over as if to throw her arms around me – then, at the last moment, seems to realize that this is inappropriate: *for now*, I think in terror, and stands there awkwardly fiddling with the hem of her bobbly old cardigan instead.

'What, Liz? What is it?'

'A bomb,' Liz says helplessly. 'Actually, five of them. In London again, it seems they were timed to go off together in the middle of the rush hour—'

'Where?' I say thickly, as if talking through a mouthful of peanut butter.

'Trafalgar Square, Marble Arch – it's terrible there, oh, God, Mal, the pictures – Victoria Station, Knightsbridge and—'

She pauses. I can't bear the pity in her eyes.

'Holborn – oh, my God, Nicholas.'

How unoriginal, how desperate, the bargains we make with God. Please keep him safe and I'll go to church every Sunday. Please keep him safe and I'll give a hundred pounds to charity. Please keep him safe and I'll never get cross when he leaves his clothes on the floor, I won't mind that he never makes the bed, I'll devote myself to being a perfect wife, a perfect mother, I'll do anything, only please, please keep him safe.

Kit arrives ten minutes after Liz. He scoops up the children and whisks them home with him – 'Who's for a sleepover at Uncle Kit's? No, Evie, you appalling child, you may *not* bring that revolting rabbit, not unless you bring carrots and onions to have with him' – and I sit riveted in front of the television, gripping my towel to my chest with white-knuckled fingers, unable to tear myself away from the horrific news footage, my mind blank with fear.

The terrorists have outdone themselves this time and blown up a power station too, it seems. So much of London is blacked out and of course the telephones are down, landlines *and* cell networks. There's no way of communicating, of finding out, and all I want to do is leap in the car and drive up there and *see*; but of course I can't, the roads into central London are closed, half the city is cordoned off, so I sit here, taut as a bow, not daring for one second to stop the silent mantra in my head – *keep him safe keep him safe keep him safe* – in case I snap the thin thin thread connecting my husband to life.

I watch the live images with an eerie detachment. The smoking ruins, the carnage – this is Tel Aviv, surely? Baghdad, or Kabul; not London. Not *again*.

None of it seems real. In a moment that old woman, covered in a blanket of grey dust, will open her eyes again, they'll wipe all the tomato ketchup off that dead-eyed teenage boy, those people will stop shivering under the foil emergency blankets and get up for a cup of coffee, laughing and complaining about the canteen sandwiches as they stretch their legs and wait for the next take. Except, of course, that those crumpled mounds beneath blue sheets aren't carefully arranged props, that isn't red paint on the pavement there, that lost teddy bear – somehow there's always a teddy bear, isn't there? – belongs to a real child.

Even though I know the lines aren't working, I press redial again and again until Liz finally takes the phone away from me. 'He'll call you,' she says brightly, 'as soon as the networks are back up. He'll be fine. You know Nicholas, fit as a fiddle. Look at him snowboarding.'

So what! I want to scream. A whole orchestra of fitness can't protect you against nails and glass and bricks and concrete!

By midnight, the news networks have shifted into aftermath mode; their reporters, more composed now that the initial adrenaline rush of 'Breaking News!' has eased, tell us little new information as they stand in front of arc-lit heaps of smoking, blackened rubble, grim-faced rescue workers slowly toiling in the background. In the studios, terrorism 'experts' and politicians bicker. And still I have no idea if my husband is alive or dead, if he is already one of the two hundred people – dear God! *Two hundred* – blown into flesh-and-bone smithereens by the blasts; or if he will be a statistic added in later.

Eventually, I send Liz home, to cherish her own husband. I call Nicholas's parents again and promise to let them know the minute I hear anything at all. 'No news is good news,' Edward says bravely, but I can hear Daisy sobbing quietly in the background. And then I curl up on the sofa, still in my bath towel, dry-eyed, wide awake, waiting. Waiting.

Because we've all had to learn, haven't we, that this is how you find out that your husband, your child, has been killed by a terrorist bomb on the way home from work; there's no flight manifest, nothing to say clearly, in black and white, one way or another. You tell yourself there's more chance of someone you love being hit by a bus than blown up on one, but fear washes through you as you wait anxiously for the phone to ring, and an hour later you're still waiting, and the dread coagulates in your stomach; and *yes*, the lines are down, and *yes*, he's prob ably stuck in gridlocked traffic somewhere, but the hours pass, and the next day breaks and *he* still hasn't phoned, and somewhere out there, for two hundred families the worst *has* happened, even if they don't yet know it. The fear blossoms like a mushroom cloud in your soul and you're left clinging to a tiny shred of hope as if your sanity depended on it: which of course it does.

And at quarter to seven the next morning, my phone finally rings.

'Mal? It's me,' Nicholas says.

Thank you thank you thank you thank you thank you thank—

'Mal, are you there? Dammit, these lines—'

'I'm here,' I whisper dizzily.

'You saw the news, obviously. I'm fine, bit shaken up, as you'd expect, but we were lucky, office lost a few windows but the main damage was the other end of Holborn.' His tone is flat, leached of emotion. *Shock, obviously.* 'It's not as bad as it looks on television, but Christ, it's bad enough.'

The words spill out of me with all the pent-up force of twelve nightmarish hours. 'But are you *sure* you're all right? Where were you when it happened? What did you do? Where have you been, I tried to call you but—'

'I'm fine,' he says again. 'Look, I'm sorry you were worried but – hang on.'

There is a strange noise, like rushing water, and then a clatter as Nicholas picks up the phone again. His voice sounds muffled, as if he's climbed into a wardrobe. 'Mal, it's been a hell of a night,' he says wearily. 'I know you must have been going frantic, but it was out of my hands.

I'll do my best to get home as soon as I can, but you can imagine what it's like trying to move anywhere at the moment. I don't even know if the trains are running yet.'

'Waterloo's open again, I heard on the news. Where are you now?'

'Oh. Yes. At the office, obviously. Spent the night here. Look, Mal, let me go now, OK? I'll be home when I can. How are the girls?'

He sounds more shaken than I've ever heard him. He clearly isn't telling me the half of it, and a fist twists my insides. Lord knows what he's been through, what horrors he's seen. *How close I came to losing him.*

'The girls are fine,' I say, 'they're with Kit—'

'Of course.'

'Nicholas, please. He was worried sick about you – we all were.'

'Sorry. Yes.'

'I love you,' I say, suddenly overwhelmed. 'I do *love* you, Nicholas.'

He hesitates, and I smile through my tears. Embarrassed to say it in front of everyone at the office, even now. How very Nicholas. 'You too,' he mumbles finally.

It's only after he's rung off that I realize I haven't asked if he's spoken to his parents. I try to ring him back at the office, but get a disconnected tone – clearly the phone network is still very patchy, Nicholas must have been lucky. I telephone the Lyons myself with the news, and then drift slowly into the kitchen, suddenly rather light-headed.

It's like I've been holding my breath for the past twelve hours. I feel sick, elated, tired, anti-climactic, angry, foolish, all at once. I never want to have to go through a night like that again. How dreadful that it takes something this appalling to remind you how very much you have to lose.

I suddenly feel very small and ashamed of myself. I spent most of yesterday mentally raging against Nicholas simply because he was out working whilst I was stuck slaving over a hot ironing board and picking up raisins of rabbit poo from the fruit bowl. But his job nearly cost him his life. What is a little boredom or the odd steam burn on your wrist compared to that?

A thrill of pure happiness sweeps over me. He's safe, he's alive. I do a little jig of relief and delight and pleasure by the Aga, I just can't help it.

Which is why, when Trace Pitt pushes open the top half of the kitchen stable door and sees me for the first time since the day I lost our baby, I am standing there stark naked with sparkles and glitter in my pubic hair.

7

Nicholas

Standing up was an egregious error. Not only is my tent-pole erection now clearly visible should anyone care to cast their gaze thither, but I am perfectly positioned to see straight down Sara's raspberry silk blouse – Christ Almighty, *no bra* – thus profoundly exacerbating the problem which I originally rose to alleviate.

I pick up the manila case folder on the conference table and hide behind it: literally and metaphorically.

'So. Ah. Mrs Stockbridge. We've heard from your husband,' I say briskly to my client, 'and it seems that he has now made a sensible proposal to resolve our concerns regarding your being divorced whilst your financial claims remain to be determined. He has renewed his commitment to nominate your son to receive his death-in-service benefit and, moreover, he has nominated you—'

Sara's eyebrow quirks. I have noticed that her eyebrows attain particular mobility in response to my use of

such words as *heretofore* and *whence*. She really is the most
unlikely lawyer.

'—he has nominated you,' I continue hastily, 'to receive
all funds payable under his Life Insurance policy. We are
told by his Counsel that this will produce two hundred
thousand pounds upon his death. This will remain the
status quo pending the resolution or determination of
your wider application—'

'So he can go ahead and marry his floozie anyway?'
Mrs Stockbridge interrupts.

I regard my client in confusion, disconcerted by this
abrupt departure from the legal niceties. Stolid, pow-
dered and neatly dressed, she has that rather musty, fishy
smell of a woman on the Change. Mrs Stockbridge is *not*
a woman I wonder about kissing. I do not imagine her
slipping her tongue between my lips, if she'd run away, if
she'd stay, or if she'd melt into me, mouth to mouth, lust
to lust—

Christ. That damn song Sara sent me. I can't get it out
of my head.

Across the table, Sara shifts in her chair, her untrammelled pink nipples jutting tightly against the silk.
I defy any man to remain unaffected.

'Mrs Stockbridge, I realize this situation is distasteful
to you—'

'*Distasteful!*'

Tears and raised voices: to my mind, Dante's tenth
circle. When someone cries in front of you, *anything* could
happen. My discomfort is perfectly natural. I cannot
remember my parents' fiery battles, as Malinche alleges, I
was only six months old; it is just normal, natural British
rectitude. Obviously.

I edge around the table, wondering how best to handle my emotionally imploding client. Perhaps some tea—

With a slight shake of the head, Sara quells my ministrations at the tea tray. 'Mrs Stockbridge, I know it doesn't seem fair,' she says quietly, 'after thirty-four years of marriage, for him to leave you for a girl who wasn't even born when you started your business together. And now you have to sell it, and your lovely home, and move to a little flat on your own, whilst he gets to walk away and start a new life without looking back. I can quite see it doesn't seem right.'

Thank heavens. Sometimes a woman's touch is essential. A man can't be expected to deal with waterworks and precipitate emotional outbursts. It's not in his nature.

'She was our granddaughter's babysitter,' Mrs Stockbridge says thickly. 'I thought he was going to our Sandra's house every night to see the new baby.'

'We can't make it right,' Sara sympathizes. 'But we *can* try to help you make the best of it. He'll get his divorce, that can't be helped, but we'll make him pay dearly for it. And sometimes,' she adds shrewdly, 'when you tell people they *can't* have something – or some*one* – they just want it all the more.'

Mrs Stockbridge and I reflect on this for a moment. Our client is no doubt thinking, perhaps with a modicum of surprise, that her attractive blonde lawyer has a rather sensible head on her strong young shoulders. Indeed, Sara is quite correct in her supposition: I have helped sunder many second marriages precipitated in no small measure by contested, drawn-out first divorces. What may have started off as a brief fling is often forced to become something far more serious than it warrants by the sheer weight of chaos it has caused.

I, on the other hand, am wearily thinking, with a great deal less surprise, how much I should like to take Mrs Stockbridge's attractive blonde lawyer to bed. And how *very* fortunate it is that the firm has no cases that are likely to be heard outside London in the foreseeable future.

'Mrs Stockbridge,' I say, returning to the matter in hand, 'the offer is fair – certainly in financial terms – and my advice would be that you accept it, albeit with reluctance. It was only because there was no financial security in place for you that we had any chance of resisting his application for the Decree to be made Absolute.'

'Don't let him see how much it hurts, Joan,' Sara urges. 'Walk away with your head held high. And don't forget, this isn't over yet. By the time we've finished, he'll have to send his new wife out to work just to pay his maintenance to *you*.'

I am not entirely comfortable with Sara's fiercely adversarial attitude, but it appears women know each other better: Mrs Stockbridge certainly seems to respond to it. Betwixt us, we prevail upon our client to accept the advice for which she is paying us handsomely, and having signed a brace of documents, the lady finally takes her leave. I feel deeply sorry for her. It is most unfortunate that she caught her husband and the babysitter *in flagrante* on her daughter's sofa; had she not done so, I am quite sure the young woman would never have induced her foolish middle-aged lover to quit his three square meals a day and neatly ironed shirts for her own undeniable, but fleeting, bedroom charms. No doubt the entire affair would have petered out within a very short while of its own accord. Now, however, the damage is done. Instead of the comfortable retirement which should have been his in less than three years, he will no doubt soon find himself treading upon Lego in the middle of the night once more.

Emma, my secretary, knocks and puts her head around the door. 'Mr Lyon, I have the Wilson Form E, it's been notarized. Did you want me to send it out to Cowan Finch in the morning?'

'We're getting a little tight for time on the Wilson hearing.' I glance at my watch. 'It's nearly six now; I'll drop it off at Cowan's on my way to the station, earn us a couple of days' grace. Could you give them a call and let them know to expect it before you leave for the day?'

Emma nods and withdraws. As I gather the Stockbridge files and follow her out of the conference room, Sara falls into step beside me. I don't say anything: because I cannot think of anything safe to say.

The song she sent me at New Year changed everything. It said that Manchester was not an aberration, the result of too much alcohol or the temptation of proximity. It said that I wasn't imagining the subtext of her invitation to *come up for a nightcap*. Sara knew precisely what she was doing when she used a song to ask a married man to imagine what would happen if we kissed.

I don't want this. I love my wife. *I love my wife.*

I want this. I want to sleep with this woman more than I want to breathe. But I am still not going to do it. I am Renaissance man, not a brute animal.

I exchange the Stockbridge files for the substantial stack of documents destined for Cowan Finch, shrug on my overcoat, and reach for my briefcase.

'Here, let me take some of those,' Sara says, forming a tray with her forearms.

I hesitate, but I am indeed heavily laden. To refuse would be ostentatiously churlish. With a curt nod, I heft the Wilson deposition into her arms. A breath of Allure washes over me, and something else I cannot readily identify – a sweetness that is Sara's alone.

We exit the office and walk towards Holborn in tandem. As we cross a narrow side street a short distance from the underground station, Sara's heel sticks in the gutter. She stops to free it, slipping her foot from the shoe and laughing as she tries to balance without touching her stockinged toes to the wet pavement or dropping the documents. Naturally, I pause beside her. And so we are protected by the two solid office buildings on either side of the street from the full force of the blast that tears through High Holborn a split second later.

Had it not been for Sara's shoe, we would have been ten feet further down the main road. Precisely where a thousand lethal shards of plate glass skewer down, any one of which would have been enough to kill us.

It's quite extraordinary, how your instinct for survival takes over. I throw myself across Sara and propel the two of us into a shop doorway, our ears ringing from the explosion. The blast has sucked up all the air and ripped the oxygen from our lungs. We crouch against the wall, tenting our overcoats above our heads to block out the choking brick dust billowing around us, gasping great gulps of dry air as our eyes stream.

And then our ears pop and we flinch at the abrupt wail of a thousand car and burglar alarms. Within minutes, fire engine and ambulance sirens fill the air. The injured city itself seems to be groaning. It takes me a moment to realize the muffled sound is the collective moans of the trapped and dying.

Sara and I look at each other. Our faces, hair and clothes are thick with grey dust. I see no fear in her silvery eyes: just curiosity, relief – and a spark of adrenalin-fuelled excitement.

'D'you think it's over?' she asks calmly.

Her *savoir faire* in the face of such crisis is startling. I can only imagine Mal's panic in a similar position; although, of course, it would be for the children rather than herself. But Sara has the emotional self-control of a man; I find it both refreshing and dangerously attractive.

We both jump as more glass and debris crash to the ground.

'I think it probably is, unless they've booby-trapped it so another one goes off once the rescue services are here,' I say, wondering when we all became so terrorist-aware. 'This may just be one of several in the city, like last time—'

Another crescendo of shattered glass, this time just feet away.

'We shouldn't stay here,' I urge. 'Christ knows how unstable the blast has left the buildings.'

Sara stands up, brushing brick dust from her clothes. 'My flat's in Theobald's Road,' she says, 'ten minutes away.'

A close brush with death has a salutary effect. One is forcefully reminded of one's mortality; the brevity – and fragility – of life.

Carpe diem. Seize the day.

A brief glance down the road confirms that our office building has survived relatively unscathed, apart from a few shattered windows. My first instinct is to run to the scene of the blast, where I will no doubt prove a hindrance rather than a help; but a lone police car is already barricading the through road. And so there is nothing to save me from myself.

My mobile phone has no signal – standard procedure, these days, to shut down the networks during terrorist attacks to prevent further remote-controlled blasts – but I turn it off anyway.

Holding hands, Sara and I run towards High Holborn in an instinctive – if absurd – half-crouch against further onslaught. We jolt to an appalled halt as we reach the main thoroughfare, stunned by the sheer level of destruction. It is as if our capital has metamorphosed into the stricken streets of Baghdad. Upended cars, pulverized buildings, toppled street lamps; and over it all, a pall of thick, heavy dust and smoke. I'm astonished by the speed of the rescue services, who have cordoned off the entire site; but then they have had a grimly thorough apprenticeship.

We cross Holborn, broken glass crunching beneath our feet, and up Hatton Garden, paying little heed to the eviscerated shop fronts of the diamond district. We barely register the eerie silence in the undamaged backstreets, the dearth of traffic and pedestrians. I am too busy unbuttoning her blouse even as we run, her hands are too frantic against my belt buckle as we skirt cars abandoned in panic in the middle of the road.

We burst through the front door of her apartment building, and I push her down on the grubby communal stairs. Shoving her skirt up to her waist and peeling off her knickers, I thrust my knee between hers and spread her thighs as I yank down my trousers. And then I'm inside her, and my blood is pounding, roaring, *thundering* as I come.

After a moment, I pull out of her and grip the newel post to haul myself upright, panting as I shove my wilting cock back into my pants.

'Well, that may have been good for *you*,' Sara says drily, 'but it didn't do a thing for me.'

She wriggles upright, pulling her skirt down smartly and picking up her knickers. I rub my chin ruefully, a little appalled – and thrilled – by the brutishness of my behaviour.

'Sorry. Couldn't help it.'

'Fuck you couldn't.'

'Fuck I couldn't,' I acknowledge. 'But don't worry. I'll make it up to you.'

'You bet your sweet arse you will,' she says cheerfully.

'Here?'

'Yes—'

'Here?'

'Christ, *yes*—'

'Like this?' She kneels up between my thighs, strawberry-tipped breasts glistening with sweat. 'Nick. You have to tell me what you want. How else am I going to know?'

No woman has ever asked me that before.

'I love that thing you did – on my – with your nails,' I mumble finally.

'This?' she purrs.

'*That,*' I gasp.

Sara talks during sex. Not mindless chatter or Nazi instructions or porn-movie dirty; she *talks* to me.

Do you like this? What about this? Faster? Slower? Is this better? Does this turn you on? I love it when you do that. Can you put your mouth where your fingers just were? Amazing, that's *amazing*. Would you like to try this? Or that? Let's see if we can. I think we. God, that's making me wet. If you could just. Maybe we should try. Oh, perfect, *perfect*.

Nothing bothers her. She giggles when our sweat-slickened bodies fart against each other. She laughs when we get stuck in a particularly gymnastic position and have slowly to unwind from one another limb by limb as if from a game of Twister. A condom is produced from her bedside drawer – 'Lucky my period is due in two days, or that fuck on the stairs could have been a frigging *disaster'* – with insouciant efficiency: 'Lemon-and-lime or plain?'

Afterwards, she rolls onto her side and lights a cigarette. I stare at her, more shocked by this than by the huge (black) dildo I found whilst groping for a box of tissues under the bed.

'I didn't know you smoked!'

'I don't. Only after sex.' She flips the box open. 'Ah. Just one left. Seems a shame to keep a whole packet for just one cigarette.'

'It does?'

She reaches for my cock again. 'Yes, Nick. It does.'

*

It is only as daylight streams through Sara's begrimed bedroom window that I allow myself to think of Mal. My wife. The woman I have just betrayed in the most unforgivable of ways; *four* times, to be precise. Though obviously this is nothing to be proud of.

An excoriating wave of shame swamps me. Christ Almighty, *what have I done*?

I get out of bed, careful not to disturb Sara, grope in my jacket pocket and switch on my mobile phone. I listen to the fourteen messages on my voicemail – all but one of them from my wife – feeling increasingly sickened as I register Mal's mounting panic. Jesus, I shouldn't have turned off my phone. What must she have gone through last night?

Glancing once more at the bed, I move quietly into the sitting room – extraordinary how the girl manages to be simultaneously minimalist and messy – and call home.

She picks up on the first ring.

'Mal? It's me.'

Silence. I wonder if my phone battery has just died and check the display. 'Mal, are you there? Dammit, these lines—'

'I'm here,' she whispers, sounding half-asleep.

'You saw the news, obviously,' I say, trying to sound normal. *What is normal, when you've just broken every promise you ever made?* 'I'm fine, bit shaken up, as you'd expect, but we were lucky, office lost a few windows but the main damage was the other end of Holborn. It's not as bad as it looks on television, but Christ, it's bad enough.'

'But are you *sure* you're all right? Where were you when it happened? What did you do? Where have you been, I tried to call you but—'

I feel a surge of guilt-stewed impatience. Does she have to make such a *drama* out of it?

And then appalled remorse: she's been up all night sick with worry. *Whereas I—*

'I'm fine. Look, I'm sorry you were worried but – hang on.'

Sara has stumbled out of bed and into the bathroom, leaving the door ajar. I don't particularly want her to know I'm phoning my wife – no need to rub salt into the wound – but more importantly, I don't want Mal to hear another woman's ablutions. I move into the tiny hallway and shut the door. 'Mal, it's been a hell of a night,' I mutter, cupping the phone. 'I know you must have been going frantic, but it was out of my hands. I'll do my best to get home as soon as I can, but you can imagine what it's like trying to move anywhere at the moment. I don't even know if the trains are running yet.'

'Waterloo's open again, I heard on the news. Where are you now?'

Panic flares, and I force myself to damp it down. *She doesn't mean anything by it. It's a perfectly normal question.* 'Oh. Yes. At the office, obviously. Spent the night here.' I'm aghast at how swiftly, how easily, the lie comes. 'Look, Mal, let me go now, OK? I'll be home when I can. How are the girls?'

'The girls are fine, they're with Kit—'

Bloody would be. 'Of course.'

'Nicholas, please. He was worried sick about you – we all were.'

'Sorry. Yes.'

'I love you,' she says, and I can tell she's crying. 'I do *love* you, Nicholas.'

I have never felt such a contemptible heel in my life. How can I sleep with another woman and still love my wife? How can I tell my wife I love her with another woman's juices still sticky on my skin?

I spin as Sara opens the hall door: gloriously, magnificently naked.

'You too,' I say quickly into the phone, and click it shut.

Sara doesn't ask to whom I was speaking, and I don't proffer an explanation. I feel my cock stir yet again as I follow her back into the bedroom, searching for the words to tell her I'm about to leave her high and dry. It was undeniably the most physically satisfying night of my life; but it was also, without doubt, unrepeatable. I know better than most where this road will lead if we pursue it further. The pain, the grief, to all involved. Better to end it now. She's a woman; she's bound to have started to read things into this. Get feelings for me. I need to let her down gently, before she gets hurt.

I pick up my trousers from the sitting room floor and am clumsily struggling into them when Sara comes back out of the bedroom, knotting the belt of a scarlet coffee-stained kimono.

'Look, Nick,' she says, pulling at her earlobe, 'last night was great – wonderful – but it was just a one-off, right? I mean, I think you're cool, but to be honest, I'm just not that into the whole office romance thing.'

I stand there, one leg in my trousers. What was wrong with last night? Wasn't the sex good? *I* thought the sex was good. Unbelievable, in fact. So why—

'It's not you,' she says, perching on the arm of the

white sofa. 'I had a great time, really. But you've got to admit, the whole bomb thing – well, it kind of suspended the normal rules for a bit, didn't it? We made the most of it, and I'm cool with that. But we have to work together and I don't want last night to get in the way, so I thought I should just be, you know: upfront about it now.'

I should feel relieved. She's let me off the hook.

'You're OK with that?' I ask.

'Oh, fine. Really. Don't worry about me.'

She doesn't sound at all regretful. 'Good. Good. That's – good.'

'Our little secret,' she says.

'Absolutely.'

'So.' She stands up. 'I'm going to make myself some coffee, and then go back to bed, I think. No work today, obviously. Want a cup?'

'No, I'll – uh, I'd better get back to – I've got to – the train. But thank you.'

'OK. Make sure you really slam the front door downstairs when you leave, it tends to stick and you think you've shut it but you haven't. We've already had to get police to evict bums twice this year.'

'Will do. Right.' I match her businesslike tone. 'I'll get Emma to email everyone to let them know when the office is up and running again. The sooner the better, really. Tomorrow if possible, even if we can't get the windows fixed for a day or two.'

She reaches for the remote control. 'Thanks, Nick. I can work on the Yeates file from home in the meantime, I've got all the paperwork here from last weekend. By the way,' she adds, eyes on the screen as a correspondent reports live from the clean-up operation in Trafalgar Square, 'love the hair. Knocks ten years off you. I told you it'd look better long.'

'Oh, Nicholas! You look *dreadful*!'

'Thank you,' I say tightly. 'I feel so much better now.'

Mal throws her arms around me, burying her face in my shoulder, and I stiffen in horror. *I should have showered at Sara's.* Washed away the warm, honeyed scent of her skin, toffee in the sun; I can still feel the dry stickiness of her cum on me – I have never slept with a woman who ejaculated before, it was the most erotic sensation I've ever experienced. Surely Mal can tell, *surely—*

With a sob of relief, my wife releases me and I follow her into the warm fug of the kitchen. Every available surface is covered with pans and crocks of freshly cooked food, still warm from the Aga: gingerbread loaf, blue cheese polenta, chèvre and garlic timbales, apricot-glazed foie gras, peach and champagne cobbler, olive bread, grilled quail. Enough to feed an epicurean army. Mal's usual answer to emotional crisis. I just hope it freezes.

She whips a milk pan of crème en glace from the heat. 'Darling, I'm sorry, I didn't mean you look dreadful, it's just you're so crumpled and dishevelled – I can *smell* the bomb on you, so terrible, it's like Guy Fawkes night only of course much, *much* worse. All this dust in your hair – goodness, it's getting long, isn't it, your hair, I must make you another appointment at—'

'Malinche,' I interrupt. 'I've just survived a terrorist explosion, I've barely slept in forty-eight hours' – this much is true – 'it's taken me the entire day to get back home and you're worried about grime on my jacket and the length of my hair?'

She looks stricken.

'Nicholas, I've just been so terribly worried about you, you can't imagine – and I know you've had such an *awful* time—'

'Better than many,' I say soberly.

'Yes. Of course. Oh, *Nicholas*.'

'Anyway,' I say quickly, before she goes off again, 'I *like* my hair like this. Knocks ten years off me. Where are the girls?'

'Metheny's in bed, she couldn't wait up any longer, but Sophie and Evie are in the dining room, doing their homework. Can I get you a cup of—'

'I could do with a Scotch. Don't worry, I'll get it.'

I am aware of Mal's hurt and bewildered expression, but deliberately fail to catch her eye as I leave the kitchen. I didn't think it would be this difficult.

Sophie flings herself on me the moment she sees me with melodramatic gusto; her godfather would be proud. Evie, however, doesn't look up from what she's doing, the tip of her tongue protruding with concentration as she pores over her work. Mal does exactly the same thing when she's working on one of her cookery books.

'Hey, Sophs,' I say, ruffling my eldest daughter's hair. I peer over Evie's shoulder. 'What are you doing, sweetheart?'

'Stuff,' Evie says succinctly.

'What sort of stuff?'

'About God and mothers,' Sophie scorns. 'We did that *years* ago.'

'Well, you were Evie's age *years* ago,' I say reasonably.

'Who's the boss at our house?' Evie demands, looking up.

'Your mother allows me the honour,' I say drily.

'Mummy is, of course,' Sophie says. 'You can tell by room inspection. *She* sees the stuff under the bed.'

I don't need reminding of Mal's all-seeing eye. I reach for Evie's homework handout, scanning her startling answers, which are written in vivid purple pen: Evie naturally assumes the school's edict that all homework be completed in boring HB pencil does not apply to her.

It appears that Charles Darwin was a naturist (not a pretty thought) who wrote the Organ of the Species in which, apparently, he said God's days were not just twenty-four hours but without watches who knew?

Evie's eyes narrow, daring me to laugh. It is a struggle. I cannot imagine what trendy modern teaching methods lead primary school teachers to think it a good idea to ask a classroom of precocious six-year-olds what God made mothers from, but Evie's answer – 'He got his start from men's bones, then he mostly used string' – suggests my middle daughter has significantly more imagination than do they.

I'm muffling a howl at Evie's answer to the disingenuous query, 'What would make your Mummy perfect?' 'Diet. You know, her hair. I'd diet, maybe blue.' And then a sudden cold thought slices across my laughter, silencing me so sharply that Evie stops scowling and looks at me in surprise. *These are the moments you'd miss if you lost Mal.*

Divorce turns children into flesh-and-blood timeshares. Residence with one parent, alternate weekends and Wednesday evenings with the other. Christmas Eve with Daddy this year, Christmas Day next. We may dress up the inequity and call it joint custody, but the hard truth is that a child only has one home; anywhere else and it's just visiting.

I can't believe I've been so damned stupid. Dear God, if Mal *ever* finds out—

I put Evie to bed, and circumvent the usual four rounds of SpongeBob Squarepants – a perverse concept, particularly the aquatic Texan squirrel; whatever happened to Pooh? – with a contraband tube of Smarties; Mal would have a fit if she knew, but tonight I lack the emotional and vocal reserves to essay the demanding roles of Mr Krabs, Squidward and the rest.

Sophie settles herself happily in the saggy kitchen sofa with *The Lion, the Witch and the Wardrobe*. Pretending I haven't heard Mal's request to stay and chat whilst she finishes up dinner, I slope off to my study.

Slumped in my leather armchair, I stare moodily into my glass of Scotch. Everything seems so normal. Except that for the first time since we met, I can't tell Mal what's weighing so heavily on my mind. We've always had such an honest relationship; we know each other so well. How *could* I have jeopardized that?

It was a one-off. The bombs and – *force majeure*, the insurance people call it. Clearly I *could* help it, but – events, dear boy. Events. As Macmillan observed.

What's absolutely certain, perfectly apodictic, is that it won't happen again. I *cannot*—

'Da-aa-addy!'

'Mal!' I call through the open study door.

I hear the clatter of pans, but Mal doesn't respond.

'Da-aa-addy!'

'Mal! Evie wants something!' A cold draught whisking

up the kitchen passageway suggests Mal is outside in the scullery. Suppressing my annoyance, I put down my drink and go to the bottom of the stairs. 'Yes, Evie?'

'I'm thirsty. Can I have a drink of water?'

'No, you had your chance. No more messing about, it's lights out.'

I've just picked up my glass of Scotch when her voice rings out again. 'Da-aaa-ddy!'

'What now?'

'I'm really, *really* thirsty. *Please* can I have a drink of water?'

Where the hell is Mal? 'I told you, no! Now settle down, Evie, you have school in the morning. If you ask me again, you'll get a smacked bottom.'

This time the glass gets as far as my lips. 'Daa-aaa-aaa-ddy!'

'What?'

'When you come in to give me my smacked bottom, can you bring me a glass of water?'

I relate this exchange to Mal later as we brush our teeth companionably in the bathroom together. We exchange complicit parental smiles – 'She got the water, didn't she?' 'Yes, what I didn't spill from laughing on the way upstairs' – and I tell myself, *See, it's going to be OK, you can get past this.* Last night was a mistake, an unconscionable mistake, but what's done is done. You just have to put it behind you. Forget about it. It never happened.

But when we go to bed and Mal's hand drifts gently across my chest and then lower, questioning, I pull the bedclothes up to my shoulders and roll away from her.

*

The next morning I leap out of bed, shushing Mal back under the covers. I organize the girls in a trice – I really can't see why Mal finds mornings so taxing, especially since Evie lets the cat out of the bag and admits her mother gives them fondant fancies every day for breakfast – and whisk them off to school. The Daddy-you-forgot-to-do-packed-lunches crisis (I could have sworn I paid for school dinners) is averted with a ten-pound note which will no doubt be spent solely on slimy canteen chips. I am beginning to see that the principal consequence of my indiscretion will be rotten teeth and childhood obesity.

Buoyed by an energy and optimism attributable to my new-leaf frame of mind, I stop at Margot's Flowers on my way back home and demand the most extravagant arrangement the shop purveys. 'For my wife,' I add needlessly.

The girl messes with secateurs and raffia and I resist the urge to tell her to hurry up.

'Anniversary or birthday?'

'Neither.'

She grins pertly. 'Oh, dear. In the doghouse, are we? What did you do?'

'I didn't *do* anything,' I say stiffly.

'Never mind.' She winks. 'This should earn you a few brownie points.'

Mal looks astonished when I walk into the kitchen with the flowers, which are roughly the size and weight of a small child. She tightens the belt of her ratty candlewick dressing-gown before opening her arms to receive them. 'What have I done to deserve this?'

'Do I need a reason to give my wife flowers?' I say, stung.

She hesitates. 'It's because of what happened in London, isn't it?'

I thank God that her back is turned to me as she reaches for a vase. The shock must surely register on my face. *She knows. How can she know?*

'Ah – London?'

She cuts open the cellophane and buries her face in the blooms. 'Oh, gorgeous! The bombs, Nicholas. Post-dramatic stress or whatever it is. You come close to death and suddenly you start to value what you could have lost, it's like you're born again or something, there was an article in the *Daily Mail*.'

My relief is such that for a moment I cannot speak. 'Yes,' I stumble. 'Yes. In a way.'

'It's dreadful about those poor people – they've identified a hundred and seventy-nine, so far, and you know there'll be more, it doesn't bear thinking about – but we were lucky, darling, nothing terrible happened to our family yesterday. We can't let these people win, we can't give in to them.'

I smile awkwardly and reach past her for the pile of post on the kitchen table. Mal turns back to the flowers, giving a satisfied murmur as she tweaks the final bloom into place.

'I can drop you at the station on my way into Salisbury,' she says, hefting the vase towards the sitting room. 'I guess you'll be needed at the office to get things back up and running again.' She hesitates on the kitchen threshold. 'Nicholas. I've been meaning to tell you, I saw Trace Pitt yesterday, he stopped by to – actually, to offer me a job.'

I sift through the brown envelopes, pulling out the renewal notice for my subscription to the *Lawyer*. I must make sure Emma doesn't forget to deal with it. 'Mmm?'

'Working at – well, managing, really – his new restaurant.'

Emma has sent out emails asking the staff to return to work today; apart from the broken windows, which she has already had replaced – 'I know a charming man in Epping, Mr Lyon, cash in hand, but he'll get us sorted in a jiffy' – our office suffered little damage. I feel mingled terror and reluctant excitement at the thought of seeing Sara again.

'He's very keen – silly amounts of money really – and he promised no late nights, plenty of staff to cover for me, but of course I wanted to ask you first—'

'Ask me what?'

'If I should do it.'

'Oh. Yes. Of course you should.'

'I should?' She sounds surprised. 'Really?'

'Absolutely,' I say absently. 'I really do need to get going, Mal.'

'Sorry, sorry, yes, let me just go and get dressed.' She brushes by the cork noticeboard next to the Aga; a sheaf of yellowing papers flutters to the ground and Mal picks them up and re-pins them with infuriating slowness. 'Oh, yes, that reminds me. It's the girls' Open House next week, Nicholas, you need to be home early that day, we absolutely *can't* be late. Not after the school play.'

I don't need reminding of that little fiasco. 'Fine. I'll make sure I'm there. When?'

'Friday the nineteenth. It starts at seven. And *please*

don't be late, Nicholas. I'm not sure I can stand Evie wearing her wellingtons to bed for a month again in protest.'

'Friday the nineteenth?'

Sara grimaces. 'I know it's short notice, but press tickets are always like that. Michèle can't go, she's working in Paris that weekend, but she knows how much I love opera and wondered if I'd like them. I know it doesn't float everyone's boat – *Tristan und Isolde* can be a bit heavy—'

'Good Lord, no, I love Wagner! My favourite composer, in fact. And I haven't seen *Tristan* for years.'

'Really? How funny, he's my favourite composer too.'

Christ, she looks amazing in that plum shirt. So decadent; so *bedroom*. Tiny beads of sweat glisten in the shadowy vale between her breasts.

I sigh. 'It's just—'

'I'm sorry, Nick, you're probably busy. I shouldn't have asked.'

'Any other night and I might have been tempted,' I say truthfully. 'But the nineteenth is out, one of my daughters has a thing at school, I *have* to be there—'

She shrugs. 'Another time. Probably just as well,' she adds, her grey gaze direct, 'since I can't guarantee you'd have made the last train home.'

It sounds like a statement.

We both know it's a question.

8

Sara

Fuck, I hate opera. I don't know what possessed me to suggest this; I must be off my head. And Wagner, for Christ's sake. So bloody dark and depressing. I'm not exactly into the fat-lady *oeuvre* at the best of times, but at least a cheery bit of Mozart would have been bearable. *Figaro*, maybe; I almost like that. Wagner was great mates with Nietzsche, according to my programme blurb; which explains a good deal about the pair of them. No wonder poor Nietzsche came all over nihilistic if he had to listen to this misery all the time.

I pinch a sideways glance. Nick's tipped forwards in his plush velvet seat, long fingers steepled, absolutely still as he gazes up in rapture at the stage. Bless.

I stifle a yawn behind my programme. The things we do for love. Look at *über*-citygirl Princess Diana schlepping off to Balmoral in her green wellies to convince Prince Charles there was nothing she liked better than standing around in the pissing rain all day, whilst men who smelled of horses and women who looked like them took pot shots at innocent pheasants.

And OK, there's no denying I have a developed a certain *fondness* for Nick. A penchant, as it were. Or I wouldn't be here. Mind you, the grief he gave me over the tickets! Jesus. He had a *total* shit fit when we were shown to the best seats in the house, ranting that no wonder the BBC was in trouble, we all end up paying for these press junkets, it's taxpayers' money after all, do I have any idea how much front row orchestra seats cost?

Er, yes, actually, Nick. Nearly four hundred quid. I could have bought that gorgeous russet chiffon corset from La Petite Salope; they had it in my size.

(Note to self: next time am inventing freebies from imaginary journo friend to facilitate shameless seduction of boss – again – make sure they v. cheap freebies.)

I swear I've aged ten years by the time the lights come back up and the audience – average age: ninety-five and three-quarters – creaks to its bunioned feet to applaud. The fat woman next to me almost knocks me out as her pink taffeta arms pump like fleshy pistons. Somebody shoot me if I ever end up with bingo wings like that. Another encore and she'll take off.

Thank God I'm not married to Nick. Imagine having to sit through this on a regular basis—

And then he turns and smiles at me with such boyish pleasure that my heart flips and trades places with my stomach.

'You really enjoyed that, didn't you?' Nick says fondly as we thread our way along the crowded aisle. 'You looked as if you were absolutely lost in the music.'

I'd sit through anything for you, lover. 'Mmm.'

'It's unusual to find a woman who really appreciates Wagner. He appeals to a more sophisticated musical palate. Very much your red Zinfandel, as it were. Mal – uh – many women prefer something a little more frivolous. Mozart is very popular. That's if they like opera at all.' His hand on the small of my back guides me through the crowded foyer. 'Not that one can dismiss Mozart out of hand, of course, but to my mind one cannot compare *The Magic Flute* with the solid genius of *Der Ring*.'

I turn another yawn into a cough. Killing the sex buzz here, Nick, with all the opera chit-chat: sweet-talk it is *not*. And don't think I missed that little Freudian slip, either. Ouch.

Not that hearing her name makes me feel guilty, or anything. I mean, what goes on between Nick and his wife isn't any of my business. Is it? To be honest, I feel sorry for both of them. She obviously can't keep up with him, poor thing. She must feel totally out of her depth when she ventures into his world. And how frustrating for a man as bright and sophisticated as he is to be stuck with such a dull, suburban sort of woman. I mean, what do they find to *say* to each other? Conversation in their house probably revolves around the children and what joint to have for Sunday lunch. He must be so *bored*: in and out of the bedroom. No wonder he has to look elsewhere.

When you think about it, I'm probably lightening the load for her too. Having me to talk to must take the pressure off, even if she doesn't realize it. I bet he goes home in a much better mood when he's had a chance to offload some of his stress with a woman who really understands him. And it's not like I'm ever going to break them up, or anything. I'd *never* do that.

I thank God I boned up on the bloody opera at the weekend. Got to stay one step ahead if I want to be Ms *Simpatico*.

'Of course, you can't ignore the fact that *Tristan und Isolde* changed the course of musical history,' I offer. 'Driven by his unconsummated passion for Mathilde, the wife of one of his patrons, Wagner took the iconographic adulterers of medieval literature, and underpinned their tragedy with Schopenhauer's quasi-oriental philosophy—'

'—and as the end result rewrote the entire harmonic rulebook! Absolutely! A woman who's beautiful *and* bright. Now, tell me, do you think—'

Shit, don't ask me any questions, I only memorized the one paragraph from *Opera for Morons*.

But beautiful and bright: I *like* that. And I especially like that *he* likes it, too.

Why is it savvy women usually want men with smarts, but most intelligent men are happy with the dumbest of fuck puppets on their arms? Is our biological imperative for a protective hunter-gatherer/pneumatic walking womb (delete as appropriate) really that strong?

Nick Lyon is a very unusual man. I just hope his dippy wife appreciates him.

I spin on my four-inch heels – I am *so* going to pay for these tomorrow: I have blisters you could trampoline on – and allow the jostling crowd to crush me right up against Nick's chest as we spill into the Covent Garden piazza. 'You know, Nick, all that passion has left me *beyond* starved,' I say. 'I know this cool little sushi bar round the corner, Yuzo's, it's always open late. Their sashimi is out of this world, though of course if you don't like sushi—'

A pinstriped-wool rod of iron presses against my thigh. 'Not at all,' Nick chokes out, turning puce. 'Perfect choice, actually: my favourite restaurant, in fact. Extraordinary coincidence—'

Not *that* extraordinary, to be honest. Marvellous search engine, Google. Can find all sorts of useful little nuggets when you type someone's name into it. Like interviews they gave to law magazines a couple of years ago in which they listed all their favourite things for some boring *Desert Island Discs* thing. What, you think I plucked the wretched German miseryguts out of thin air?

Sushi *was* a bit of a surprise, I must admit. I had Nick down as a steak-and-kidney pie, spotted-dick-and-custard school dinners kind of man. Still waters do indeed run deep.

My stomach rumbles as if I haven't eaten for a day (which I haven't: it's the only way to get the zip on this satin cocktail dress of Amy's to close) and now it's my turn to sizzle with mortification. Well, shit, a vociferous digestive tract, *that's* attractive. Men don't like women who actually *eat* to stay alive. At least raw fish is a minimalist kind of food (as opposed to Italian, which should only ever be eaten in front of people you *never* intend to have sex with). My enthusiasm for opera may be complete bullshit, but fortunately, I *do* really love sushi. I'm not sure even Princess Di could've choked down raw eel for love alone. Mind you, I suppose she could have always thrown it up again.

As we reach the far side of the piazza, the general vague thrum of background chatter suddenly distils into the distinct sound of (female, screechy) yelling, and the next moment I'm nearly knocked off my feet as a skinny blonde girl in chocolate suede hotpants and bronze kinky boots barrels out of a nearby shop and straight into me.

Without even bothering to apologize, she ricochets off my admittedly pneumatic chest and springs towards the (*very* cute) guy who's followed her out, a tiny cell phone still clamped to his ear.

'You fucking *bastard*!' the girl yells at the cute guy. 'You're talking to her *now*, aren't you? Nobody dumps *me*, you shit!'

I wince as she slaps his face with a crack that echoes around Covent Garden.

'You're bloody welcome to each other! She'll never leave her husband, you know that, don't you? I hope she makes you fucking miserable!'

It's mesmerizing street theatre. A crowd gathers instantly; one or two actually throw coins, clearly under the impression that this is staged entertainment. For some reason, he looks strangely familiar, though I can't begin to place him. God, she has a *tiny* arse. You wonder how girls like that sit down without perforating their buttocks.

She storms off, the crowd parting swiftly on either side of her. He shrugs ruefully, and disappears back into the cheese shop behind him.

As people start to drift away, I wander over to the shop window. That bloomy-rind cheese in the front looks killer. I press my nose to the glass to read the tiny flag next to it. Brie de Meaux; God, I *love* that. *And* some Brillat-Savarin, and another delicious-looking Fourme d'Ambert. I'd know fuck all about cheese normally, but they had pictures of these in that book I got at New Year's and what with that and Mum's bloody cheese lessons—

'Shit, that was Trace Pitt!' I exclaim. 'I *knew* I'd seen his face before!'

'Hmm?'

'The guy who got slapped. Come on, you must have recognized him—'

'I wasn't really paying attention,' Nick says vaguely, peering over my shoulder at the cheeses. 'Actually, my wife used to be engaged to him. If it's the same man. Years ago. Can't quite remember who broke it off—'

That ditzy woman used to be engaged to *the hottest man on the planet*? 'You're kidding!'

He shrugs. 'It was a long time ago.'.

God. For a moment, I wonder if there's more to Mrs Lyon than meets the eye.

Nick smiles at me and squeezes my shoulders. I risk slipping my hand casually through the crook of his arm as we stroll towards Yuzo's; to my delight, he doesn't flinch from my touch despite the fact that we're out in public and People Might See Us. Then again, maybe he's too busy thinking about what we'll be doing once we're in private to really notice.

Sex with Nick was *über*-hot. I had this hunch it was going to be seriously down-and-dirty with him, he's just got this sexy subliminal *thing* going on; but even I was taken unawares (*oh, be still my beating knickers!*) when he threw me down on the scuzzy communal stair carpet for our inaugural shag. *Mercy, Mr Lyon, you're so strong! What's a poor helpless girl to do but surrender?*

Four times in one night. Gotta say, that's good for any

man, never mind one *his* age. And he was positively bursting with pride; though he'd have cut his own throat rather than say so.

I was shit-scared when the bomb went off. I know Nick thought I was being all calm and cool, but that's just how I get when I'm terrified out of my skull. It's like my brain goes offline until the crisis is over. The shock hits me later: three days after the bombings, I got the shakes bad enough to turn my morning café latte into yoghurt.

The thing is, the *trouble* is, when Nick threw me into that shop doorway and protected me from the blast with his own body, something unexpected clicked inside me. He did it instinctively, without even thinking about it. Much as I'd like to believe it was about me, I think he'd have done it for Osama bin Laden if he'd been strolling by, it's just the kind of man he is. Which makes it even more heroic. He probably has 'Superman' stencilled discreetly on his Fruit of the Loom boxers.

And now I'm in a bit of a fix. Feelings-for-Nick-wise.

Such a pity the role of Lois Lane is already taken. I can't help it, I really *like* him now. And it's not just the smoking sex or the thrill of the chase. (Though I have to admit to being meanly thrilled when he suddenly ducked out of his daughter's school thing to come to the opera with me, even though it meant the only tickets available at the last minute required my entire life savings and a promissory note for my firstborn child. But I'm sure his daughter didn't even notice he wasn't there, anyway. Kids don't, do they?)

He reaches past me to hold open the restaurant door,

sweet old fashioned boy that he is. As I pass him, he drops the lightest, sweetest of Sunday morning kisses on the shingled nape of my neck, and my knees practically buckle with lust and longing.

He has *no* idea how hard it was to play it cool after that first night together, to act like I wasn't interested in anything other than a one-night stand. But it was the only way to keep him hooked. I had to Dear John him before he got the chance to do it to me. He'd have run for the hills otherwise.

I know Nick isn't mine. I know I'm just borrowing him; and I shouldn't even be doing that. I am a very, very bad girl and I will die a lonely spinster's death with my fourteen cats and go to hell.

But knowing it's not allowed under any circumstances somehow just makes it all the more sexy. And OK, call me pathetic, but the fact that he'd risk so much to be with *me* makes me feel like a million dollars. He could lose a wife he presumably cares about, in his own way, and end up stuck in some cruddy bedsit without his kids, whom he clearly adores; all our lives could so easily become a massive screw-up. And yet here he is. With me.

But I'm still going to give him back. I swear.

Nick starts to help me out of my coat; then suddenly petrifies, his hands frozen on my shoulders. I glance back at him. His face is grey, and for a horrified moment I think he's having a heart attack.

Then I follow his appalled gaze. A fat, middle-aged woman in a totally minging flowered smock is steaming towards us, trailed by a man in tweeds and – you have *got* to be kidding me – a spotted red cravat. From the

appalled I've-just-dropped-my-newborn-on-its-head terror
in Nick's eyes, I take it she knows him. Either that, or he
feels the same way as me about the cravat.

His hands fall from my shoulders as if scorched.

'Nicholas! What a lovely surprise! Giles, look who it is!
We didn't expect to see you here!'

No shit. And there was me thinking Nick had arranged
this little rendezvous between his wife's friends and his
mistress on purpose.

'Business meeting,' Nick manages. 'Clients. Ran on a
bit.'

'You poor thing!' she sympathizes. 'And isn't it Evie's
Open House tonight? Chloe's year had theirs last week –
such a shame, little Evie must be *so* disappointed you
couldn't go—'

Shit, now I *do* feel guilty.

'These things can't be helped, Liz,' Giles chides gently.

'At least you had some company,' she adds guilelessly.
'Makes all the difference, doesn't it?'

She smiles at me, clearly waiting for an introduction.
Nick appears terminally fascinated with his briefcase handle, so, feeling just a tad sleazy at dragging these people
into our mess, I stick out my hand and pray she's as
clueless as she appears. 'Sara Kaplan. I'm Nick's junior
partner. One of those tedious cases that drag on, you
know how it is.'

'Oh, yes! Well, no, obviously – you glam career girls,
I don't know how you do it. Having it all. I'm just a
housewife. I'm sure that seems jolly dull to you.'

'No, of course not.'

'Oh, Nicholas – sorry, Sara – but look at the time!

You'll miss the last train if you're not careful! Well, don't panic, no need to rush, we don't mind waiting till you've had a bite and giving you a lift back, do we, Giles? As luck would have it, Giles brought the Range Rover up today. We had to pick up his great-aunt's whatnot, Sotheby's simply *couldn't* shift it—'

'No call for these things nowadays,' Giles says sadly.

'We'd never have managed it on the train. Bit of a squeeze in the car, to be honest, but there's still a bit of room in the back, so that's all right,' Liz smiles. 'As long as you don't mind sharing with Chloe's tack. Isn't it lucky we ran into you?'

'Isn't it?' Nick echoes.

'Can we give you a lift anywhere, dear?' she asks me.

'No, I'll be fine. Couple of hops on the tube and I'll be home.'

'At this time of night? Are you sure that's safe? Shouldn't you get a cab?'

'I'll be fine,' I say, suddenly desperate to escape. She seems such a decent woman. 'Do it all the time. Not that hungry anyway, actually. Better go. It was lovely to meet you both. I'll see you on Monday, Nick.'

I skitter down the tube steps in my hussy heels like the hounds of hell are after me. Jesus Christ, that was close. Thank heavens, if we had to run into anyone, it was Pollyanna and Farmer Giles. Fuck, what are the odds? A city of ten million people and of all the sushi bars in all the world, they have to walk into ours—

Nick's never going to come within a ten-mile radius of me after this. And frankly, I'm not sure I blame him. This is suddenly all getting rather too complicated for my liking. I'm beginning to feel a bit crappy, to be honest. Less like the siren temptress I thought I was, and more like a cheap little tart.

Shit shit *shit*.

'La Perla?' Amy whispers reverently.

'La Perla,' I say, trying not to sound smug.

'Terry's never even got me M & S,' she says wistfully, fingering the exquisite wisp of coffee silk and lace poking out of my gym bag. 'How come he's buying you La Perla already? You've only done it once.'

'It's when you've only done it once that they buy you La Perla,' I observe.

'So why on earth do you want to *end* it?'

'What can I tell you?' I sigh, shoving the silk teddy back in my holdall. 'Some of us are born with consciences, some achieve consciences; and some have consciences thrust upon them. Mine was very much of the thrust variety, trust me. You have no idea what I'm turning down.'

'You're mad. It'll be something from Tiffany next, I bet you. See if you can hint about something from their 1837 collection—'

'Good idea, Amy. He could give them, oh, I don't know – his *wedding ring* in part exchange.'

'No need to get all narky. I'm only saying,' Amy sniffs. 'I just don't know why you're being such a martyr, that's all. It's nothing to do with you if he's unfaithful to someone else. Sometimes a marriage just comes to a natural end, and there's nothing anyone can do about it. Look at me and Terry—'

This is *really* not a comparison I'm happy with.

The truth is: I'm not sure why I'm being such a martyr, either. Maybe it's less my guilty conscience than a growing fear that I'm in over my head. I need to get out now, while I still can.

'You two at the back,' a voice snaps. 'Were you planning to join us, or are they selling tickets to watch today?'

We jump guiltily. Roj, our sadistic Pilates instructor, is balanced on his big rubber ball like a performing seal. The rest of the class glare at us reprovingly. Teacher's pets.

Heads down, we scurry to our allotted places: right up at the front, where you can't skive off and keep your arse – sorry, *sits bones* – on the floor when he's not looking.

We all adopt the Half-Dead Cockroach Pose: flat on our backs, feet on the balls, hips raised twenty centimetres above the mat. It's a position I can hold for approximately ten seconds, and only then when a man is making it worth my while somewhere in the vicinity of my (overdue) bikini wax.

I slouch. Roj pounces. 'Ow!' I yelp.

'Hips up! It's for your own good! Two minutes to go, everyone.'

'He hit me!' I hiss to Amy. 'With his pointy stick thing!'

'He does that now,' she whispers back. 'He's allowed, I checked. It's in that thing we signed when we joined his class.'

Oh, good God. What am I doing here? It's not like I'm going to need taut thighs and toned buttocks any time soon. With Nick out of the picture, no doubt I will soon be once more enjoying the Great Sex Drought that preceded him. And finding a frog worth kissing will be doubly hard now that I know what I'm missing. Call me spoilt, but *X-Men: The Director's Cut* and a quick bite at

Pizza Express no longer has quite the same allure as dinner for two at Yuzo's and a night at the opera.

OK. Bad example. But you get the point.

After Friday's sushi bar fiasco, I spent the entire weekend closeted in my apartment, guzzling Ben & Jerry's and watching the complete fifth season of 24 – I have a bit of a thing about Kiefer Sutherland, what can I say? – on DVD in one sitting. I don't know if it was the chronic sleep deprivation or if I've got a fraction more emotionally involved with Nick than I thought I had: but when I found his red braces under my bed I couldn't help thinking about the last use we put them to; which made me remember the easy way our hips slotted together when he pulled me towards him, and how he smiled in his sleep when the sunlight slid through the blinds and striped his face, and before I knew it I was howling for two hours straight.

I lower my bottom back onto the mat. How can I miss him this much when the two of us barely even got off the ground? It's not like I was falling in love with him or anything. I mean, it was just a fling, after all. Just sex. And I was *going* to give him back.

Just not quite yet.

A pair of ridiculously tiny feet stop ominously beside my left ear. (Christ, does he bind them or something?) 'Miss Kaplan. If *you* can't be bothered to squeeze your tush, how can you expect anyone else to want to?'

Oh, please. Give me a break and go back to California.

'Up. *Up!* Better. Everybody, dynamic squeezing. *And hold.*'

I was so convinced Nick was henceforth going to treat

hme like I'd got an advanced case of bird flu, I'd (almost) resigned myself to that night together having been a great one-off.

A really great one-off. But a one-time-offer, no-repeat-special all the same.

So the flowers on Monday threw me a bit. It was a very lovely thing of Nick to do – if a little clichéd – but since he didn't include a note, I had no idea what they bloody meant. Kiss-and-make-up or kiss-off?

The boxed set of Wagner on Tuesday was a very romantic thought (and, fortunately, easily exchanged for the Arctic Monkeys). By Wednesday – a book of First World War poetry: how sweetly resourceful, he must've checked out my book shelves to see what I like – I was getting the picture; and then the La Perla yesterday dotted the i's for me. I'm absolutely *not* going to get drawn back in by his unexpected and rather touching twelve-days-of-Christmas routine, I've made up my mind: it's over, it's too complicated and dangerous and messy, and more importantly my mother would kill me if she ever found out; but all the same, I can't help it, I'm curious as all get-out to know what he's got planned for today—

'It's not how many you do, it's the *quality*,' Roj scolds as I fake quick little crunches.

I hiss at Amy, 'Are we talking men or muscles here?'

Nick slipped a Claridge's keycard in with the silk knickers; very sexy, very discreet, very *not allowed*. I've never stayed at Claridge's. I'd love to try their health and fitness spa: it's supposed to be fabulous. Not that I'm going to change my mind, obviously.

I can't believe this is the same man who practically

hid in the document vault every time I walked into the room just a few weeks ago. Now it's like he's one part Mr Chips to two parts Casanova. It's a bit disconcerting, to be honest. There's hidden depths; and then there's schizophrenic.

Or maybe – and this thought gives me the kind of rosy glow Pilates has never achieved – maybe I just bring out the crazy wild romantic in him.

Amy is *exactly* the kind of friend a girl needs when she's having an inconvenient attack of conscience.

'Passion isn't something you can help,' she says for the ninth time. 'It's not like you wanted any of this to happen.'

Not *entirely* true, as I recall, bringing to mind the lethal little Donna Karan dress I wore in Manchester. But let's not split hairs.

There's a ping from my computer, and I switch the phone to my left ear so that I can access my emails while I talk. 'He's sent me *another* one. I can't believe he's doing this at work. Supposing someone else saw them?'

'What's it say?'

'Hang on, let me open it – God, something in Latin, he's always doing that. It's weird, but kind of cute, really. *Amans, sicut fax, agitando ardescit magis.* Whatever the fuck that means.'

'Say again?'

'*Amans, sicut fax, agitando—*'

'"A lover, like a torch, burns brighter when shaken." Oh, that's clever. After the shock of what happened on Friday at the sushi bar, he—'

'Yes, yes, I get it. How'd you know what it means?'

'Classical education,' says Amy. 'I blame my parents.'

'*You're* the one who should be having the affair with him,' I grumble. 'You've got the temperament, not to mention the languages, for it.'

'But it's *you* he's buying Tiffany bracelets for,' Amy points out crossly.

When I got back from the gym earlier, Friday's present was waiting on my mouse mat in its trademark yummy blue box and white satin ribbon. I wiggle my left wrist back and forth delightedly. I have wanted this silver bangle – from the 1837 collection, natch – for about half my life. It's the one thing my mother's always been annoyingly firm about: no matter how much I pleaded, she insisted a woman should only ever be bought jewellery by a lover. Not that a bangle is going to change my mind about ending it with Nick, clearly.

Amy showed commendable told-you-so restraint when I informed her of my latest love token; though she couldn't resist emailing me the link to Tiffany solitaires.

'But he's married,' I tell her again, without much conviction.

'And you said you're happy for him to stay that way.'

'Ye-e-e-ss,' I say.

'So what harm can seeing him do? Let's face it, if they break up over you, it can't have been much of a marriage, can it? It's not like you're *dragging* him into bed. He's a grown up, he's made his own decision. And if it isn't you, it'll be someone else,' she adds cynically. 'Once they start screwing around, they don't just stop.'

I get the feeling Amy is enjoying my comeuppance a little too much. Frankly, I can't blame her; my hubris regarding affairs with married men has certainly invited it. But it doesn't mean I have to *like* eating humble pie.

And I'm not going to change my mind.

'You think I should see him again, then?'

'Oh, for Christ's sake,' she snaps, sounding uncannily like me in a previous life. 'You're going to do it anyway, and you know it. *End it*, my arse. What are you waiting for, me to talk you into it so you don't feel bad later?'

Yes, actually.

'Fine. I'll write you a note. Look –' she sighs – 'if you really like him and you want this to work, take some advice from someone who's been there, bought the T-shirt and knitted a matching sarong—'

'What? *What?* Don't mention his wife? Never ask him to stay the night?'

'Don't *ever* forget to wax.'

Amy is a professional mistress (I don't mean she's got an S & M dungeon in her basement or anything; just that she's been doing this for four years now, so she presumably knows what she's talking about) and I therefore take her at her word. If she says wax, I'm saying how high.

I glance up at the clock. I'm supposed to be meeting Nick at Claridge's in an hour. Buggery buggery fuck. A little notice for our much-postponed hot second date would've been nice. But I suppose he wasn't to know that his new client would suddenly cancel and create a nice hotel-bedroom-shaped hole in his schedule. The kind a wife doesn't notice.

I open my bathroom cabinet and dig around until I

locate the cold wax kit Amy gave me two Christmases ago. (Now I think about it: an odd choice for a present.) No way am I putting hot wax on my bikini line, thank you very much. With this you just rub the strips together in your hand until they're warm, peel them apart and press them to your inner thigh (or wherever). No muss, no fuss. I've never done this myself before, I usually go to the salon, but how hard can it be?

I nip back into my bedroom and use the hairdryer instead of rubbing the strips together to save time. Would my new fuchsia silk dress be too much? It's a bit tight, but it makes my cleavage look sensational. And I could always tone it down with a pair of kitten heels instead of my usual skyscrapers.

Back in the bathroom, I put my hair straighteners on to heat, get naked and prop one foot on the toilet. I scan the instructions again, then apply the warmed wax strip to the right side of my bikini line, covering the right half of my girly bits down to my thigh. I brace myself for the pain. God, these strips are long—

Jesus H fucking Christ! I'm blind! Blinded by pain!

Slowly the world stops spinning and my vision returns. I glance down, and realize I've only managed to pull half the strip off. Another deep breath, and the bathroom disappears into a renewed swirl of lights and stars.

When consciousness returns, I peer at the wax strip for evidence of my endurance. It's as blank as a newborn's diary.

I look down. The hair – and the wax – is still there. *On me.* The most sensitive part of my body is now covered with congealing wax and matted hair. Oh, for God's sake.

I'm just going to use my razor and have done with it. With any luck, my shaver's rash will blur with stubble rash if I play my cards right tonight.

I take my foot off the toilet, put it down, and instantly realize my mistake.

I am now – not to put too fine a point on it – *sealed shut*.

I penguin-walk around the bathroom trying to figure out what to do. Six-twenty-five. *Oh shit, oh fuck*. Water! Hot water, melt the wax. Then shave, dress, run. I'll get into the hottest water I can stand, the wax will melt, and I'll just wipe it off with a sponge. Simple.

I run a bath hot enough to sterilize needles, and step into it. *Not* the fuchsia dress, I decide, as I start to steam. Nick won't be able to see where it leaves off and I begin.

It's at this point I discover there's one thing worse than having your nether regions glued shut with wax: and that's having your nether regions glued shut and then sealed to the bottom of a cast-iron bath of scalding water – which, by the way, may sear human flesh but does *not* melt cold wax. So I am now stuck to the bottom of the fucking bath.

When I call Amy for help on my mobile – thank God I brought it in here with me in case Nick called – it takes her a full two minutes to stop laughing long enough to take a breath. 'Have you tried calling the customer help number on the side of the box?' she suggests eventually.

'Great idea, Amy,' I say, leaning over the side of the bath and trying not to pass out from the heat. Steam billows around my shoulders and I nearly drop my phone into the water. 'I could be the joke of someone else's night.'

'What about emptying the bathtub and just yanking yourself free?'

Five minutes later, I am still glued to the bottom of an empty and rapidly cooling bath. I start to shiver. This could only happen to me. It makes forgetting to change out of your bedroom slippers look positively chic. 'OK. Next bright idea?'

'Is there a lotion in the box?' Amy queries. 'They usually give you one to get rid of excess wax. You could try rubbing that on—'

It takes a complicated bit of manoeuvring with a loofah, but eventually I knock the bottle of lotion near enough for me to reach it from the bath. I take a sniff as I open the lid: it smells foul. I rub it on my bits doubtfully, hoping I haven't just ruined my chances of multiple orgasms forever.

'It works! *It works!* Oh, thank God, thank God. Amy, you are a star. And if you ever, *ever* tell anyone about this, I will strangle you with your own intestines.'

'How *very* interesting,' Nick says, raising his head from between my thighs an hour later. 'I don't think I've ever – isn't there a name you girls have for this?'

I believe the technical term is Monumental Fuck-up. 'It's called a Brazilian wax.'

'Ah. After the girl from Ipanema and her thong, presumably. Doesn't it hurt?'

'Less than being superglued to an cast-iron bathtub,' I sigh. 'Never mind. It's a long story.'

Nick grins, and dips his head again. 'Well, it looks very

tender to me. Very much in need of some careful attention. Here. And perhaps *here*—'

'I think you missed a bit,' I say, arching my back
against the pillows.

'You can always stay here, if you want,' Nick offers; as
he has done on each of our five previous visits to the
hotel. He towels his hair dry, then drops it carelessly on
the bathroom floor. 'You don't have to leave with me. I've
paid for the night, you might as well enjoy it.'

'I've told you, we could just go to my place, this must
be costing you a fortune.'

'Not your problem.' Naked, he sits on the side of the
bed and picks up my hand, tracing patterns on my palm
with his thumb. He doesn't look up. 'And it's a bit safer
here, Sara. More anonymous. I could be meeting any
number of clients in a hotel restaurant, especially during
the day. If I was spotted coming out of your flat again, it
would be a lot harder to explain.'

We had another near miss a couple of weeks ago, when
Joan, the office battleaxe, walked straight into Nick as he
was leaving my building one evening. He managed to
flam up some excuse about dropping off some paperwork,
but I'm not sure she was convinced. She's been giving
me some very suspicious looks recently, especially when
I'm working on my own with Nick.

I can't believe how complicated having an affair is. I
thought the big adultery dilemma was supposed to be
about morals, not bloody logistics. Christ, his wife doesn't
even live in the same county as me. How on *earth* women
manage to have affairs with their brothers-in-law two

doors down without getting caught is beyond me. Homeland Security or MI5 or whatever they are now could do worse than start looking for double agents in the adulterous 'burbs, if you ask me.

Several times, we've come to Claridge's for wickedly sexy afternoon romps when clients settled out of Court; I almost prefer those quick impromptu trysts to our carefully planned evening rendezvous. I always feel a bit flat when Nick has to leave in time to get the last train home.

He picks up his watch from the bedside table and fastens the leather strap around his wrist. As he gets up from the bed, I suddenly slither forwards on the crumpled, damp sheets and take his semi-hard cock in my mouth, pulling his buttocks towards me. For a moment he resists, and then I feel him yield, his body shuddering against me as he grips my shoulders hard enough to leave handprints.

Just as I taste his salty pre-cum, he pulls himself free, pushing me back down on the bed. For a moment I think he's about to walk away; and then, in a sudden, erotic change of pace, he flings himself down beside me and starts to trail kisses between my breasts, over my stomach, his tongue darting into my belly button – 'Christ, what the *hell* is that?' he said the first time he saw my piercing. 'Doesn't it chafe?' – before snaking wickedly lower; but not yet low enough. He drops kisses on my eyelids, my nose, my cheeks, my lips, my throat, his eyelashes butterflying my skin as he moves. My breasts are squashed hard against his chest. He smells so sweet and warm, like cinnamon in mulled wine, like cloves in oranges, like pine cones on a bonfire.

Treated with such expertise, the whole of my body is

an erogenous zone. The skill with which he's holding back, controlling the pace, not giving in to my craving to go faster, have him now, drives me absolutely *wild*.

Just as I'm about to scream loud enough for the entire hotel to hear, he plunges his head between my legs and I tangle my hands in his hair, my body bucking electrically as he tongues my clitoris. Feverishly I wrap my legs around his shoulders. He thrusts two fingers inside me, moving them like leaping fish against my inner wall, still lapping my clitoris, and it's a sensation like nothing I've ever known, an erotic roller-coaster speeding ever upwards. Stars explode behind my eyes. Lightning rips along my nerve endings. I come faster and harder than I have ever done in my life, my body ricocheting against the bed as the waves break, and keep on breaking, across my body.

Finally, Nick lifts his head and moves a little further up the bed, resting his cheek against my stomach as I quiver with spent passion. 'I love – I love to be here,' he says quietly. 'I feel safe, safer than anywhere else in the world.'

Did he – *did he nearly say the L word just then*?

He rolls onto his back next to me. After a few minutes, I envelop him with my body, and cover his face with kisses, his stubble sandpapering my mouth. Straddling him, I kiss my way down his chest, nibbling little fish kisses, relishing the salt and sweet taste of his skin. I suck his left nipple and he groans his appreciation. An answering beat throbs between my legs as I grasp his cock, steel covered in velvet—

His mobile telephone rings, and I don't have to ask who's calling.

I stretch languorously on the bed, trying to look un-ruffled by the fact that he bothers to answer it. A sexy, cool mistress, not a frustrated and demanding girlfriend.

Nick throws me an embarrassed half-smile as he clum-sily pulls on his clothes, gripping his phone between neck and ear.

'I'm on my way. Just finished now. Yes, I know, and I'm sorry, but—'

I hand him his shoes. He doesn't meet my eye, his expression closed as the phone squawks. She doesn't sound very happy to me. Poor Nick, the last thing he needs is some nag of a wife bitching at him after he's worked his arse off all day keeping her in bloody bon-bons. If I were married to him, I'd never gripe at him like that; after all, I know from the inside what he has to go through, the stress he's under, every day. I'm in the business. She can't *possibly* understand.

'I don't know what time. I might be working, anyway. Yes, I realize that, but it can't be helped. Look – *look*, Malinche. I said I'm sorry, but the Court doesn't see February the fourteenth as anything other than the day that happens to fall between February the thirteenth and February the fifteenth.' Wearily, he rubs his hand over his face. 'I know; I *know* you have, but—'

Another burst of indistinct babble. He stalks over to the mirror, running his fingers through his hair and checking his suit jacket for tell-tale blonde hairs. It's lucky he's cautious. I'm glad he is. I don't mind it in the least.

'Look, we'll talk about it when I get home.'

'Are you sure tomorrow night's going to be OK?' I ask, knotting my bathrobe. 'We can always do it another evening if it's going to cause a problem, I won't mind.'

'Of course you will,' Nick says, with unexpected shrewdness. 'And I wouldn't blame you. I promised I'd take you out for Valentine's Day, and I will. Now,' his voice softens, 'hand me my briefcase and lock yourself in the bathroom, you temptress, or I might just find myself unable to let you go.'

I feel shivery and glittery inside, like this is our first date. In a way, it is; well, our first special event date, anyway. I spent last year's Valentine's Day in Andorra with Amy, the two of us trying to drown our mutual despair over our romantic ineptitude by hiding out somewhere Hallmark-free. We weren't to know an internet dating agency had chosen our hotel for their annual Celebration of Love weekend. Forty-two loved-up couples holding hands and smiling all the time. It gave me a migraine.

I scan the sushi menu again, sipping my mimosa and hoping Nick hurries up and gets here. I've been stuck in bloody Birmingham on a case all day, so I haven't seen him since he left the hotel last night. I can't wait to give him his present. Well, wear it for him, at least.

I tick off my sushi and sashimi choices – I'm glad Nick picked Yuzo's again; let's hope we break the jinx this time – and dither over seaweed or cucumber salad. Maybe I'll wait till Nick gets here and see what he wants. Actually, now I come to think about it, we haven't ever had a proper dinner date at all, unless you count Manchester that time. It'll be quite nice to sit and *talk*, like a normal couple, before jumping into bed.

Quarter past eight. Fifteen minutes late. Oh, come *on*, Nick, I *hate* waiting at a table on my own. There's only so long you can fiddle about with a menu trying not to look sad and stood-up, even one as complicated as Yuzo's.

A waiter hovers discreetly by my elbow. 'Are you ready to order, Miss?'

'No, I'm just waiting for someone. I was a bit early; he should be here soon.' I glance hopefully towards the door as it jangles open. My whole body fizzes with pleasure and relief. 'Oh, look, *there* he is!'

'Whenever you're ready, Miss.'

Thank God. For a moment there I thought—

The welcoming smile on my face dies as Nick walks coolly towards my table, which suddenly seems very prominent and exposed.

Two paces behind him is his wife.

9

Malinche

A woman always *knows*, doesn't she – it's an intuition thing. Nicholas doesn't believe in intuition, he says it's just your unconscious mind picking up subtle signals and body language that your wide-awake self hasn't noticed, putting two and two together and then *ping*! presenting you with four; so then of course you think (when four turns out to be the right answer) oh, four! How amazing, it must be my intuition.

So perhaps it wasn't a psychic sixth sense at all, but my clever old unconscious mind jabbing me in the mental ribs: look, he's wearing jeans, he's always hated jeans; look, he's packing his own suitcase for business trips these days instead of leaving it to you; look, is that a different after-shave, a new shirt, has he always locked that drawer, since when has he been interested in playing squash?

If it had been your best friend sitting at your scrubbed pine kitchen table, a mug of cooling coffee untouched in front of her, fretting aloud over her latest psychic poke, adding it to the catalogue of sharp, pointed little prods and digs and nudges of the last weeks and months – an affair, you'd have said (inside your head, of course, because this isn't something you can say aloud until *she* sees it too), an affair, *he's having an affair*!

Kit being Kit, however—

'He's having an affair, darling,' he'd said baldly, heedless of the social niceties *vis-à-vis* other people's cheating lovers, calmly blowing smoke rings across the table. 'It's as obvious as the *very* pretty freckled nose on your face.'

'Kit!'

He thunked the kitchen chair back onto all four legs. 'Sweetheart. Staying out late: check. New haircut, new clobber – not sure about the black jeans, but however – new and hitherto unprecedented desire to play sweaty macho sports: check. Either he's having an affair or,' he'd smiled evilly, 'he's crossed to my side of the street and can't bear to tell you.'

'For heaven's sake, Kit, Trace isn't *gay*.'

Kit had spread his elegant hands: I rest my case.

'But Kit,' I'd whispered, wrapping my arms about the barely-there bump beneath my shirt, the bump only Kit yet knew about, 'how can he be having an affair, are you sure, are you quite, *quite* sure?'

'It's not that I don't care, darling girl. I love him too, you know. I realize this is absolute hell; but at the end of the day, it is best to know,' he'd sighed, getting up to make some fresh coffee. 'All the signs are there, I'm afraid,' and with those few words my safe, glorious, perfect young life had teetered on the brink for the final time and then crashed irreparably about my shoulders.

I stop now beside a bush of winter sage, drawing in a deep gulp of perishing February air as the thirteen-year-old memory pounces, landing a blow to my solar plexus so powerful that for a moment I can't quite breathe. Kit was absolutely right, of course. All the signs *were* there. And I hadn't even told Kit about the dropped phone calls, the taking up smoking, the new willingness to walk the dog for hours each Sunday afternoon on the common. Classic, textbook signs. Trace was having an affair. It was obvious.

Obvious.

And wrong.

I push open the latch gate – trust Trace to have the most sweetly picturesque cottage in the village, all thatched roof and creeping roses and winding Wizard-of-Oz brick pathway – and do my best to feel like the happily married thirty-something mother-of-three I am, and not the distraught pregnant twenty-two-year-old child I was when last I stood at Trace's front door.

Butterflies whisk around my insides. I take short, choppy steps to avoid slipping on the path, my breath gusting in icy plumes. I should have worn sensible flat boots, of course. Kitten heels sound so chic and girly, don't they, and with their pretty sequins and bows – but so hopelessly lacking in traction, I could break my leg or my neck, or worse.

Kit tried to stop me from going to confront Trace that day, of course, but I wouldn't listen, I locked him out of my car; I can still hear him hammering on the passenger window as I screeched recklessly down the gravel drive, determined, now that the poisonous thought was in my mind, to have it out with Trace immediately. It was a miracle I didn't crash and smush myself into jelly on the way; though of course there were times in the next few appalling, grief-sodden days and weeks I wished I had. Wished I hadn't survived the helter-skelter journey to throw those ugly accusations at Trace as soon as he opened his front door, to spit out the wonderful, amazing, precious news I'd been saving and savouring, and instead fling it at him like a gilded weapon, to wound and hurt.

I hadn't given him a chance to explain or defend himself, because *all the signs were there*; instead, I'd run back to my car, blinded by tears, and of course I hadn't even seen the slick of oil pooled in the driveway, oil from the leak in my car that Kit had been nagging me for weeks to get fixed. How could I ever put that right, how could I tell my poor little nearly-baby: you'd exist if only I hadn't been so angry, if I hadn't listened to my 'intuition', if I'd just remembered to get the wretched car *fixed*—?

The front door opens and I nearly fall into a rose bush.

'I've been watching you dithering for the past five minutes,' Trace says, the corners of his beautiful mouth twitching. 'I actually thought you were going to go back home at one point, I was all set to come out and bodily drag you in.'

'Lord, don't do that,' I say, alarmed, 'you have *no* idea how the neighbours gossip in this village.'

Quickly I step past him, trying not to notice how good he smells, and straight into the sitting room, where Trace has effortlessly managed to combine his passion for angled Swedish minimalism with chintzy English country cottage. Quite how Tudor beams and horse brasses hit it off with a flat-screen television and black leather sofa I'm not sure, but in Trace's sitting room they give the distinct impression of being more than just good friends.

Rather like Trace himself, I think distractedly; all angles, charm and contradictions, yet such a perfect blend of everything you ever thought you wanted—

'May I say, Mrs Lyon, how very lovely you look with your clothes *on*,' Trace drawls, closing the door behind me. I jump at the sound like a rat in a trap. 'Not that I didn't appreciate the effort you went to last time we met; it gave a whole new meaning to the concept of the Naked Chef.'

'You promised,' I wail, my cheeks flaming.

'Relax. My lips are sealed. Though the glitter *was* a nice touch, I have to say.'

'Trace!'

He holds his hands up. 'All right, all right. I'll never mention it again, yes, I promise. Now. Into the kitchen. I've been cooking up a storm, Mrs Lyon, as instructed – it's not been easy, let me tell you, Christ knows what sadistic bastard invented the bloody Aga, it's either on or it's off with nothing in between. I need to know exactly what you think of my white onion risotto with Parmesan air and espresso—'

'You tried it!' I cry delightedly.

'You told me to,' Trace says ruefully.

I follow my nose – such a delicious smell, I hadn't realized until now how hungry I am; but then I couldn't eat at breakfast, or at lunch, far too nervous, which is so silly, really, it's not as if Trace and I— Of course I haven't seen him in *so* long (apart from the humiliating glitter incident, of course), not properly, not since we were lovers, in fact, and somehow I'd forgotten quite how *attractive* he is in the flesh—

I concentrate furiously on the kitchen. Trace's bête noire, a glorious French blue four-oven Aga, takes pride of place, but everything else could have been taken straight from the pages of *Bon Appétit* – all that stainless steel, so wonderfully stylish, of course, though can you *imagine* the jammy handprints? – and I spin from one delight to the next like a child in a sweetshop: all-clad sauciers, a Robocoup, a full set of Global knives (what *is* it about the Japanese and cold steel?), a tilt braiser; and oh, *what bliss*, an antique Griswold cast-iron skillet. He must have stayed up half the night on eBay to get hold of one of those.

Trace lifts the lid of a saucepan simmering on the Aga and dips in a wooden spoon. 'Come on, then. Try it.'

Obediently, I open my mouth. Trace leans in, palm cupped beneath the spoon to prevent drips, and I know it really *is* the most appalling cliché, feeding each other food, so overused in cinema, I always think; but still forbiddenly, stomach-fizzingly erotic.

Hypothetically speaking.

'De-mm-shous,' I mumble through a mouthful of heaven.

'Against all reason,' Trace agrees.

People always forget that cooking is a science as much as it's an art. All you have to do is think about the mystery of mayonnaise: it's the sauce most tightly packed with oil droplets, up to eighty per cent of its volume is oil, in fact;

and you can make them more-stable small droplets by whisking a portion of the oil into just the yolks and salt to start with, so that the salt causes the yolk granules to fall apart into their component particles, and there you are, no curdling. Straightforward science.

How can anyone not find molecular cooking absolutely fascinating? It really is the next great trend in cooking. There hasn't been a culinary revolution like this since – well, since Escoffier, really. As I explained to Trace, and I could kiss him for saying yes to all this, the way it works is that to create unusual and original recipes, you analyse the molecular make-up of the ingredients with an infrared spectrometer nuclear magnetic resonance machine – any synthetic chemist or physicist will have one – and foods with similar composition just pair well together, even when you're sure they really, really shouldn't, sort of like Elizabeth Taylor and Richard Burton, if you see what I mean. Heston Blumenthal is just so brilliant at this; his recipes are nothing short of genius. And so—

'Bacon-and-egg ice-cream?' Trace asks doubtfully the next week, when I present him with a draft menu. 'Sardine-on-toast sorbet and meringue cooked in liquid nitrogen at your table?'

'So much more exciting than crêpes flambées, don't you think?' I enthuse.

He reads down the page. 'Envelopes of squid filled with coconut and ginger butter, monkfish liver with tomato seeds, freeze-dried foie gras shaved over consommé, thermo minted pea soup—'

'That'll be hot at the top and cold at the bottom,' I explain helpfully.

'Of course. Followed by roast breast of duck with olive oil and chocolate bonbons, and a dessert of fig and black olive tatin with brie ice-cream, no doubt.'

'It's all about working with natural flavours rather than adding something chemical to make it whizzy,' I burst out, unable to contain my excitement any longer. 'It's essentially the creation of flavours and textures that will transport your taste buds to a happier world.'

'You dippy hippy, you *are* your mother's daughter,' Trace grins. 'Though I'm not sure what she'd say about the snail porridge. Poor old snails.'

'I need to work on a signature dish,' I muse, twisting up my hair and skewering it with a pencil, so it'll stay out of my way. 'Pino Maffeo is famous for his seared foie gras with a twenty-four-carat golden egg – he takes this small, oblong meringue and dredges it in lightly whipped cream, then dunks it in the liquid nitrogen – nearly two hundred degrees below zero, *imagine!* – which flash-freezes the cream, creating a texture like an eggshell. And then he injects mango sauce into the meringue with a syringe, and wraps the whole thing in twenty-four-carat gold leaf. Once it's cracked, it oozes with the yolk-like mango sauce—'

'*I'm* the one who's cracked,' Trace mutters. 'I must be, to have agreed to this. It looks like Frankenstein's laboratory in here, not a bloody kitchen.'

'Oh, that reminds me,' I add, 'I'll need to move some of this stuff over to my kitchen at home. Nicholas has got so much work on at the moment – ever since Will Fisher retired, really, he seems to *live* at the office these days – he's often back so late I'm not even awake. It would be *so* much easier if I could work on my recipes at home in the evening, after the children are in bed, instead of having to get a babysitter and keep coming over here.'

All absolutely true, of course (poor Nicholas, even at weekends he's taking calls from the office); but perhaps not the *whole* truth.

Which is that Trace is still dangerously and wildly sexy and gorgeous, and I'm really not at all sure that being shut up with him in this cosy little cottage cooking every day – when, as we all know, a kitchen is a more sexually charged environment than the Moulin Rouge – as we have been doing all week is such a frantically good idea. I *adore* Nicholas, of course, absolutely smitten, no question of me ever *doing* anything, that doesn't even come into it; but the thing is, Trace is unfinished business, as it were; and it's all *so* much better if the question of tying up loose ends never arises. For all concerned.

After I lost our baby, Trace never once reproached me; he didn't need to. I could do enough of *that* myself. It all seems so sad and silly and *unnecessary* now. I should have talked to my mother, of course; more importantly, I should have talked to Trace. But I was barely twenty-two years old, inexperienced and desperately naive. I could whip up a feather-light soufflé with my eyes shut, but I knew nothing about love. How strong it could be.

I couldn't stand even to look at my face in the mirror. The thought of seeing in his eyes the loathing and disgust I saw reflected each day in my own was simply more than I could bear.

And so I refused to see Trace at the hospital, refused to take his calls after I returned home, refused to answer the door no matter how much he argued and pleaded and –

finally – yelled at me to come out and face him. Because I couldn't, you see. Couldn't face the man whose child I'd killed through my own stupidity and lack of trust. Trace wasn't having an affair, of *course* he wasn't; it turned out he'd taken a second job (in the midst of the nineties' economic recession, the fledgling cheese shop was floundering), a job he hated and despised, but needed: to pay for an engagement ring. An agent – someone he'd met, with bitter irony, through Kit, in fact – had offered him obscene amounts of money to become the Face (if that's the right word) of a funky new jeans label: hence the new clothes, the sudden need to keep fit, the secretive phone calls. Trace had learned to smoulder from billboards and newspapers and magazines and imbue a rather ordinary pair of jeans with enough sex-by-association to have them flying off the shelves in record numbers.

Such numbers, in fact, that they'd paid not just for one-and-a-half sparkling carats but also for the deposit on a flat off the King's Road, over whose threshold Trace had planned to carry me just as soon as I said 'Yes'.

Which I would have done, of course. Only by the time I knew what Trace was about, it was all *far* too late.

The only person to threaten my monopoly on self-loathing was Kit. He tried to fix things, of course, to persuade me to let Trace back into my life. He didn't understand – neither of them understood – that this wasn't something I was doing out of choice. That I loved Trace more than I ever had, but I knew – or *thought* I knew, child-woman that I was – that our poor little baby would always be there, a shadow between us, its loss darkening and souring every sweet moment, locking us both into a grey spiral of misery and despair until nothing was left in either of us to love. I couldn't do that to Trace. Not after everything else I had already done to him.

Five months later, I met Nicholas.

'It absolutely isn't *on*, Trace. Not at this time of night—'

'You weren't asleep, were you? I can tell.'

'That's not the point.'

His voice is teasing. 'I rather think it *is*, though. Isn't it?'

I put the phone down for a moment, and shut the door to Nicholas's study a little more firmly so as not to wake the girls. 'It's ten-thirty at night, Trace. I have three small children asleep upstairs, not to mention a psychotic rabbit, a cat and of course now four hamsters.'

'Four hamsters?'

'My mother gave the girls four Russian hamsters for the Chinese New Year, one for each of them and one just in case, and so far they all appear to be cohabiting in homosexual bliss.' I sigh. '*Not* one of her easier presents, they shit like, well, like hamsters, I suppose. Though I have to say as presents go it's not *quite* as bad as the bicycle horns in each of their stockings last year – she must have stuffed them in when she was babysitting during Midnight Mass. I wanted to strangle her at five-thirty on Christmas morning – but never mind all that now, you really *can't* call me this late, supposing Nicholas had answered—'

'I was bored,' Trace says carelessly, and I can't help thinking, amused and frustrated in equal measure; no wonder Kit loved him, they're both so much *alike*. 'And you *unbore* me. Besides which, I have to talk to you about sourcing.'

'Can't it wait until the morning?'

'Not if you're coming with me, it can't.'

'Coming where?'

'I've just unearthed this amazing new supplier in Normandy, *fantastic* cheeses, Mal, out of this world, you'll love them. If we get the first Chunnel train after six, we can—'

I laugh. 'Trace, don't be absurd, I can't do that. It's Saturday tomorrow, Sophie has Pony Club, though I must say I rather think she's growing out of this particular phase, thank God, you have no idea how expensive it is; and then Evie's got a birthday party in the afternoon. I'm sure Metheny's getting a cold, too, it's just out of the question, I'm afraid.'

'Bugger. Can't Nicholas look after them for the day?'

Nicholas is a good father, a good husband, but the idea of leaving him to cope with the three girls all day on his own whilst I gallivant off to France in search of cheeses – of course, Trace has never actually *met* Nicholas—

'He isn't even home from work yet, Trace, I can't expect him to mind the children tomorrow. He needs a break, he works incredibly hard.'

'So do you,' Trace says, 'harder, actually, I should imagine.'

For a mildly hysterical moment I think of the laundry room, the dirty clothes hamper filled to the brim, the overflowing ironing basket practically an archaeological dig. Of the dishwasher still full of dirty plates from last night – I just haven't had a spare moment to crawl in it and fish out the soggy spaghetti clogging the filter – and the kitchen bin squished full with so much compacted rubbish I can't actually get the plastic liner out. The empty larder – 'Mummy! These Cheerios aren't Cheerios, they're *dust*, we're going to starve, Evie says she'll call social services' – the overdue car insurance, the forgotten dry-cleaning, the late birthday cards, the unreturned library books. The burnt-out bulb in the fridge that I keep *meaning* to replace, the dirty bed-sheets I simply *must* get round to changing before they climb off the beds themselves. The Christmas thank-you letters I haven't written, the name-tapes I need to sew in, Sophie's science fair project, the manuscript I *still* need to deliver, oh God, oh God—

'Where is your husband at this time of night, anyway?' Trace asks. 'Didn't you say Evie had a school thing on tonight?'

I don't often feel angry – it's so demanding: time, energy, I don't have enough of either to squander on just being *cross* – but I could have cheerfully killed Nicholas this evening. I chose him precisely because he seemed like the kind of man who would never let you down.

'He had to work, some eleventh-hour settlement that needed to be thrashed out,' I say through gritted teeth. 'Poor Evie, she was *so* disappointed. They've been doing a special project on Stonehenge and she spent hours on it. All the girls in her class did presentations and of course she was the only one there without a father watching. It broke my heart.'

'Bring her with you tomorrow,' Trace suggests. 'Go on, why not? Nicholas could cope with the other two, surely, and it'd cheer Evie up, a trip to France.'

When Trace says it like that, it seems so do-able. Everything always seems so simple, so easy, to him. He has such energy, such passion and determination: enough to carry you with him even when you *know*, in your heart of hearts, that it's not that straightforward.

He fills the world with such possibility. Whereas Nicholas—

But I can't start to compare them. Or I really *will* be in trouble.

Kit must think me still twenty-two, foolish and wide-eyed. I do *know* why he exerted himself to persuade me to take the job with Trace; and it has nothing to do with the fantastic career opportunity, the dream come true, that it absolutely is. Kit has never really forgiven Nicholas for coming into my life when he did, closing the door on Trace and thus any chance Kit might have had to redeem himself. When I said I was marrying Nicholas, Kit insisted it was too soon, I hadn't yet worked Trace out of my system, I needed Nicholas for all the wrong reasons. When what he *really* meant was that he didn't want to live with his own guilt.

'Come on, Mal,' Trace wheedles, 'come to Normandy with me.'

'It *would* be nice to just drop everything for once,' I say longingly.

'And it *is* business. We can be there and back in a day. You know it'll be fun, Evie can play chaperone – oh, shit. Look, I have to go—'

Over the distant thrum of street noise, I hear a girl's high-pitched voice; I can't make out the words, but her sentiments are clear. I smile, wondering what hot water Trace has got himself into now. Over the years, I've spotted him popping up now and again in the odd gossip column – one of London's most eligible bachelors, apparently; not that I'm jealous, of course – usually accompanied by one in an interchangeable series of whippet-thin girls with ribs like famished saints. I suppose it was only a matter of time before it all caught up with him.

'See you tomorrow,' Trace says quickly, clicking off the call.

'We'll see,' I reply to dead air; that favourite parental euphemism for *No, but I'm too tired to argue any more*, smiling despite myself as I replace the phone.

He could always do this to me. Make me smile, make me believe that whatever insane idea he'd come up with – write a book, run a restaurant, *marry me* – was the right, the only, thing to do. Which is why I didn't dare see him again for thirteen years, until I was sure I was quite, *quite* safe.

I don't leave Nicholas's office for a long time, staring at the framed picture of the two of us on his desk. Our wedding day, ten years ago; we look so young, so carefree, so certain.

Kit wasn't entirely wrong in his assessment. I *was* a little bit reboundish when I met Nicholas; after what had happened with Trace, who wouldn't be? But I knew without doubt that he was the right man to marry, in a way that Trace never had been. Not quite as dashing, perhaps, not as knicker-wettingly, stomach-churningly disturbing; but you can't live on a perpetual knife edge of excitement all your life, can you? If Trace was the ideal lover, I knew instantly that Nicholas was the ideal husband. Men are like shoes: you can have sexy or comfortable, but not both.

Not that Nicholas wasn't sexy, too. In his own way.

There was a depth to him that was shadowed and dark, a carnal, sensual undercurrent of which he seemed totally unaware. All it needed was the right woman to tap into it. And I was so sure then that that woman was me.

'You didn't tell me Liz gave you a lift back from London last night,' I say, bending to pull off Metheny's muddy wellies as Nicholas comes down the stairs a little after ten the next morning. 'She said it was well past midnight by the time you all got back. I think she could've done without taking Chloe to Pony Club this morning, to be honest, she looked done in when I saw her—'

'How could I have told you? I've only just woken up.'

I look up in surprise. 'No need to bite my head off.'

'Christ. I'm barely downstairs before you're giving me the bloody third degree. Didn't realize this had become a police state. Where are we, Lower Guantanamo?'

'Mummy! That's ow-eee!'

'Sorry, sweetpea. There we are, all done.' I watch Metheny toddle happily towards the sitting room, then follow Nicholas into the kitchen, unwinding my scarf and pulling off my woollen gloves. My nose starts to run in the warmth. 'Nicholas? Is something the matter?'

He ignores me, flinging open cupboard doors at random. 'I don't suppose there's any danger of a decent coffee in this house?'

'There's a jar in the end cupboard, by the cocoa. Nicholas, is everything at work—'

'Not bloody Nescafé! I meant *real* coffee! You would have thought I could get a decent cup of proper coffee in my own bloody house! Is that really too much to ask?'

I stare at him in astonishment as he crashes and slams his way around the kitchen. Nicholas has always been a tea-drinker; rather a fastidious and demanding tea-drinker, actually, a warming-up-the-pot, milk-first, Kashmiri Chai kind of tea-drinker, to whom tea bags are anathema and Tetley's a four-letter word. I cannot recall him ever drinking coffee in his life.

In another life, I might wonder if Nicholas – but no; if nothing else, the disaster with Trace taught me the value of trust.

There's a knock at the kitchen window, and the window-cleaner waves cheerily. I sigh inwardly. I'd forgotten he was coming today; and he only takes cash. Things seem to be a little bit tight this month – we must have spent rather more at Christmas than I'd realized – that wildly extravagant Joseph coat, of course. I can't wait for a chance to wear it. And Nicholas has been taking rather more cash out than usual recently; expenses, I should think – they'll be reimbursed eventually; but in the meantime— And I *had* been hoping to get to the beginning of February without having to dip into the housekeeping money for any extras—

'Nicholas, do you have any cash on you?'

'God, I suppose so. Never bloody ends, does it? In my wallet, should be on my desk. I'm going to have a shower before this place turns into Piccadilly Circus.'

Pausing only to grab his mobile phone charger from the kitchen counter, he stalks up the stairs, his stiff paisley back screaming resentment. I wipe my streaming nose on a wodge of paper towel. Resentment at what I'm not quite sure. *He* wasn't the one up at six with three children.

His battered leather wallet is lying on his desk. I pull

out a couple of twenty-pound notes, dislodging several till receipts and a photograph of the children as I do so. I stop and pick up the snap, my irritation melting. I *love* this picture. It was only taken a couple of months ago; Evie has a large purple bump right in the centre of her forehead, forcing her fringe to split in two around it like a shallow brook around a rock. She did it running down Stokes Hill with Chloe and Sophie; she was so determined to win the race, she couldn't stop and ran full-tilt into the side of a barn at the bottom. Absolutely refused to cry, of course. It took two weeks to go down. And Sophie, just learning to love the camera, her head tilted slightly to one side, looking up from under those dark lashes – oh dear, she's going to be devastating sometime really rather soon. And Metheny, cuddled in the centre. My milk-and-cookies last-chance baby. So plump and sunny, beaming with wide-eyed, damp-lashed brilliance at me. The photograph is a little out of focus and all three of them could have done with a wash-and-brush-up first; but it captures them, the *essence* of them. This is who they are.

Judging from the creases in the picture, Nicholas loves it too. I can see marks in the print where he's traced his thumbnail fondly over their faces, just as I'm doing now.

A childish shriek emanates from the other room, followed by a crash and the sound of running feet. I shove the picture back in the wallet, and pick up the folded till receipts scattered across Nicholas's desk.

A name on one catches my eye. I pause. La Perla? I didn't even know he'd even heard of them. *I* certainly wouldn't have if Kit didn't keep me *courant*. And he spent – I blanch – *how much*?

Good Lord. How very sweet and generous and romantic of him; and how very, very lovely. Things have been rather – well, quiet, in the bedroom recently. After the sexual feast at Christmastime, it has been very much famine this last month or so. This is clearly his way of putting things right.

Smiling inwardly, I fold the receipt carefully and replace it, so that Nicholas won't know I've seen it and spoilt his Valentine's Day surprise.

It takes me ten days to find a dress worthy of bedroom naughtiness from La Perla. I used to *love* shopping, of course, but these days I'm always so conscious of the cost. Sometimes I look at my yummy Gina strappy sandals or the silly pink Chloe bag I just *had* to have the summer I met Nicholas, languishing at the back of my wardrobe now, pockets filled with coins that are probably out of circulation, it's been so long since I used it; and I think, that'd pay for the girls' school uniforms for the entire year. How could I be so wickedly extravagant, what was I thinking?

But Nicholas has obviously gone to such trouble. So I scour Salisbury for something truly special, a miracle of a dress that will successfully hide the fact that whilst I may technically be the same size ten I was before I had three children, there's no denying that everything has shifted a little further – well, south. At what age do you give up on your looks, I wonder. Sixty? Seventy? When do you decide, OK, I'm done, no more mascara, no more highlights, no more diets, I'm just going to get saggy and grey and wrinkled and fat and *happy*?

You know, I can't wait to be old. It's middle age that petrifies the life out of me.

I finally find what I'm looking for in one of those dreadful boutiques where the shop assistants look like Parisian models and you have to ring a doorbell to get in. I would never have even dared to enter if I hadn't been desperate. But it really is a lovely dress, I think, as I stand in the middle of the shop floor and wrestle with my conscience. It fits me perfectly. It might be expensive but it's such good quality, it'll last for ages. *And* it's in the sale; only ten per cent off, but still, ten per cent is ten per cent. I know I wasn't going to buy black again, but this is totally different from my other black dresses. I haven't got one that's above the knee like this, and anyway black is timeless, it'll never go out of style, and so *slimming*. And of course I won't have to buy new shoes, my old black courts will go perfectly, so that'll save money. It'd be a false economy *not* to get it.

And then at the till, as one credit card after another is declined, and I pull out the emergency only-if-the-roof-comes-down plastic, only to find that it too is over the limit – though since I haven't seen a bill for ages, I have no idea by how much – I wonder if I can possibly persuade Nicholas to take back the extravagant La Perla without offending him.

Scarlet with embarrassment, I turn to slink out of the shop, feeling like a criminal. The smart assistant probably thinks I'm a bankrupt, one of those shopaholics you read about, or worse, that I stole the cards –

'I thought it was you,' Trace grins, barring my path.

*

I'm not quite sure why Nicholas is being so *strange*. First yesterday, when I called to ask him what time to get Kit over to babysit for Valentine's Day—

'I don't know what time,' he said tightly, 'I might be working, anyway.'

'But it's all organized! I've booked the Lemon Tree!' I exclaimed.

'Yes, I realize that, but it can't be helped.'

'Nicholas, we're talking about Valentine's Day,' I said, disappointment sharpening my tone. 'I've barely seen you for *weeks*, you're working the most ridiculous hours these days, ever since you made partner – well, ever since Will Fisher retired, really – and I'm sorry to call you on your mobile when you're clearly in the middle of an important meeting, but frankly, what else am I supposed to do? You miss the children's special events, you're shut in your office at weekends, some nights you're barely home before it's time to go back to work again; if I didn't see the sheets crumpled in the spare room I wouldn't even know you'd *been* here. I think the least you can do is spend one day – *Valentine's* Day – with your wife.'

'Look—'

'I really don't think it's too much to ask, do you?'

'*Look*, Malinche. I said I'm sorry, but the Court doesn't see February the fourteenth as anything other than the day that happens to fall between February the thirteenth and February the fifteenth.'

It was his *tone*, really, rather than anything he'd actually said. As if I was a tiresome child, a nagging wife; so unfair, when that isn't me, has *never* been me.

'I've been so looking forward to it,' I said quietly.

'I know; I *know* you have, but—'

'Nicholas. Please don't sigh.' I interrupted, really hurt and angry now. 'If you think your work is more important than—'

'Look, we'll talk about it when I get home.'

'When?' I demand. 'When would that be? Precisely, Nicholas? Because I can't see exactly how you're going to fit us into your very busy schedule. Actually.'

When he hung up on me, I couldn't quite believe it. He's never hung up on me in all the years we've been married. We've always talked things through, however difficult and painful that has been – and we've been married ten years, of *course* it's been difficult and painful at times.

And then after that row, that rather *horrid* row, when I phoned the office this morning, Emma said he *wasn't* working tonight after all, at least there was nothing in his diary – that tricky case must've settled. So I thought I'd surprise him by coming up to London and taking him out to his favourite sushi restaurant in Covent Garden (so funny, that Nicholas loves sushi; to people who don't know him, he always seems more of a school-dinners treacle-pudding kind of man); we haven't been there for *ages*.

I'd meant it as an olive branch, my way of saying sorry that we'd argued. But somehow, it's not going quite as I hoped.

The orange glow from the street lamps casts strange shadows across his face as he leans against the side of the black cab next to me. It makes him look suddenly old; and very tired.

A cold hand twists my stomach. He looked so shocked when I walked into his office half an hour ago, I thought

Banquo's ghost must be behind me. He still seems – oh, Lord, perhaps he's *ill*. What if *that's* it? He's ill and he hasn't told me? Cancer, even.

'Is everything all right?' I ask anxiously as the cab drops us off in Covent Garden. 'Are you *sure* you feel—'

'I'm fine. Please don't keep asking.'

I follow him nervously into Yuzo's, slipping off my coat and wondering if he'll notice my new dress. Heat rises in my cheeks. *So* sweet of Trace – totally unnecessary, I'm sure he wasn't planning to buy all the front-of-house restaurant staff black Max Mara outfits – but after he stepped in and saved the day like that, how could I say no to the sourcing trip in Italy? After turning down France. Especially when he explained that Cora and Ben, his business partners, were coming too; it's not like I'm going to be *alone* with him – it's only five days – I just don't know if Nicholas is going to see it the same way—

'Isn't that Sara!' I exclaim.

'I don't know. Is it?'

'Well, of *course* it is, darling.' I nudge his elbow. 'We can't just ignore her. Come on, say hello to the poor girl. She looks absolutely terrified of you.'

Which is rather strange; because I thought they got on quite well.

'I'm sure she doesn't want us to interrupt—'

Men. Sometimes you *do* wonder.

'How *lovely* to see you!' I say warmly, to make up for Nicholas's scowl. 'What a funny coincidence! Are you meeting someone – but of course you are, it's Valentine's Day, what a silly question. I'm sure you've had dozens of exciting cards too, it's *so* lovely to be young and single.'

She blushes rather sweetly. 'Not really—'

'Malinche, let's go and sit down.'

I remember how horrible it is to be sitting and waiting at a table on your own, feeling as if everyone is looking at you and wondering if you've been stood up. 'What a *lovely* bracelet, Sara. Tiffany, isn't it? Lucky, *lucky* you, I've always wanted one of those.'

'Malinche—'

'Nicholas, do stop. So, is this your first Valentine's together, Sara? Or is it wildly indiscreet of me to ask? It's always so romantic, I think, when—'

Her phone beeps twice; she scans her messages, and then suddenly jumps up and grabs her coat. 'Oh, God, I'm a complete idiot, he's in the sushi bar on the *other* side of the square, I must have got it wrong. So lovely to meet you again, Mrs Lyon, have a lovely evening. See you tomorrow, Nick, bye.'

I can't quite explain the feeling of relief. Sara is a *very* attractive girl – even dear loyal Nicholas couldn't help but notice she exudes a sensuality no red-blooded male could ignore; but she is clearly taken, off the market, as it were, which is so wonderful. For her.

'Well, she seems very keen,' I smile. 'How lovely.'

'Can we order, please, Mal?' Nicholas says tiredly.

I'm sure he's sickening for something. The last time he was like this, he ended up in bed for four days with a temperature of a hundred and two. He's so distracted he can barely hold up his end of the conversation through dinner, and nearly forgets to give me the glossy paper bag he was putting into his briefcase when I walked into his office. Only when I teasingly remind him does he hand it over to me with a faint smile.

'I'm sorry. I – um – I didn't get you a card,' he says, not quite meeting my eye.

'Oh, Nicholas. As if that matters.' I open the bag and unwrap a flimsy parcel of pale pink tissue. A slither of plum silk whistles into my lap. 'Oh, how *beautiful*!' Holding the delicate bra-and-knickers set up against my chest, I take care not to let the fragile lace brush against my dirty plate. 'Do you like them?'

'Of course. I wouldn't have bought them otherwise.'

I glance at the labels and laugh. 'I can tell it's been a while. These are two sizes too big, I'll have to take them back and exchange them. You kept the receipt, didn't you?' I hesitate, suddenly spotting the tiny duck-egg-blue box at the bottom of the bag. 'Oh, Nicholas. You *didn't*—'

I draw a breath when I see the silver hoop earrings. 'Nicholas. They're exquisite. I don't know what to say.'

For a moment, neither of us speaks. I have the strangest sensation, as if I'm standing on the edge of a cliff, my life hanging in the balance.

Then, 'Happy Valentine's Day,' Nicholas says softly.

He smiles at me, a quiet smile that reaches his eyes; and it's as if a warm Caribbean breeze sweeps gently across our table.

I kiss his cheek. 'I don't know why I deserve all this, but thank you. You really are the most romantic man – and I'm sorry I got so upset yesterday, I didn't mean—'

'No, *I'm* sorry,' he says quickly. 'I'm sorry about everything.'

'What do you have to be sorry for?'

'For not appreciating you the way I should. For not being grateful for what I have. For not telling you that I love you often enough. And I *do* love you, Mal.' His expression is suddenly hunted. 'I love you more than I can tell you. I don't ever want to lose you.'

'You're not going to lose me—'

'Don't laugh. I mean it, Mal. Sometimes things happen – people make mistakes – and you don't realize what you have until it's too late.'

The purple silk lies pooled in my lap. 'What are you trying to say, Nicholas?'

'Nothing. I just – you and the girls, you come first, you know that. Don't you?'

'Of course I do,' I say uncertainly.

Suddenly, I'm afraid. A door opens up in my mind, leading somewhere I don't want to go. Firmly, I close it.

'Mal, why don't we go away somewhere, spend some real time together?' Nicholas suggests suddenly. 'Just the two of us, we can leave the girls with my parents or Louise. The Lake District, maybe, or Paris, you've always loved Paris. Or even Cornwall – we could go back to Rock, I know it's changed a bit since our honeymoon days, but we could try to stay at the same cottage we rented then, sit in front of the fire, just *talk*. Get to know each other again. Couldn't we?'

My eyes prickle. Maybe Nicholas isn't ill, but he's certainly strained and tired. How long has he been over-worked like this, and I haven't noticed? Too preoccupied with the girls and recipes and book deadlines – and Trace.

I've barely noticed Nicholas's comings and goings this last month or two, I've been so caught up in the distractions of my own life. Including fretting about a relationship that was over thirteen *years* ago. If there's an unexpected distance between Nicholas and me, isn't it as much my fault as his?

'Let's go home,' I whisper.

That night, after we make love with more tenderness and sweetness than I can remember for a long time, after he's brought me to orgasm three times and fallen asleep in the warm, tanned curve of my arms like a trusting child, I stare up into the darkness and realize how incredibly lucky I am to have this man. Trace may offer exciting possibilities, but Nicholas gives me things that are *real*. The things that matter. Happiness, security, contentment, love.

I smile to myself. Even if he does forget that I don't have pierced ears.

10

Nicholas

There was an Australian girl, when I was barely nineteen. It was Oxford's long vacation; impecunious and newly jilted by a girlfriend whose name I've long since forgotten, I was spending the summer with my parents in the Rhônes-Alpes, in a tiny village called La Palud, half an hour north-east of Grenoble.

I awoke one morning to find my parents had gone hiking, leaving me alone with my law books (whose spines, I regret to say, had yet to be cracked; a state of affairs presumably noted by my all-seeing mother). This being *Jean de Florette* country – a simmering feud between the villagers over the communal well had led to scythes at dawn just a few weeks before our arrival – if you wanted a reviving morning shower before turning to your neglected studies, you had to make the short walk from our remote mountain chalet to an impossibly photogenic lake near by.

And so began the headiest ten days of my life.

The erotic imprint left by Kristene as she rose naked from the lucent water, a modern-day siren, is such that even now, nearly twenty-five years later, I grow hard at the thought. Her skin glistened in the morning sunlight as if she'd been dipped in syrup. I watched as she smoothed back her wet hair from her face with the palms of her hands, her back arched, presenting high, firm, raspberry-nippled breasts to the sky. A burl of chestnut hair wisped between long, endlessly long, brown legs.

When she saw me standing there, open-mouthed and overcome, she simply smiled, winked, and dived grace-fully backwards into the water.

She was twenty-nine, her mood as pliant as her warm and willing body. I'd shed my burdensome virginity at seventeen to a girl my own age scarcely more experienced; two years on I still knew less about the way a woman worked than I did about a jet engine. Kristene rectified my woeful ignorance. She guided my hands, my tongue, my cock, my mind, with wanton, audacious confidence, unashamedly taking as much pleasure as she gave.

It was clear from the beginning that our relationship, which occupied no dimension other than the gloriously physical, had no life outside this particular time and space. I was being admitted to a sensual Eden for reasons I neither knew nor cared to discover; soon, the door would close again. So I greedily slaked my thirst whilst I could. I returned to that lake day after day, gorging myself on her, determined to wring every moment of pleasure from her body in the hope that the memories would be enough to sustain me when she was gone.

They were not. For years afterwards, sex with every

woman I bedded seemed as dry and stale as week-old biscuits when you have tasted nectar.

I'd forgotten how Kristene made my body feel until I met Sara. One remembers the taste of a strawberry: but even the most vivid memory is but a faint, dull facsimile compared to the sybaritic pleasure of biting into the strawberry itself.

That one night with Sara has reawakened senses I've not felt since those halcyon days by the lakeside when I was a priapic nineteen-year-old. How to describe the indescribable? Losing myself in her lush, ripe body, it was as if I was all cock, every muscle and sinew of my body throbbing with the heat of her. I felt her sweet wetness down to the tips of my toes. For the first time in my life, I actually lost my mind when I was inside a woman; even Kristene hadn't come close to *this*. I was conscious of nothing else but the need to possess, and be possessed by, her.

A need utterly at odds with the fact that despite everything I still love my wife.

'Not really *on*, is it, old man?' Giles says. 'With the best will in the world. Not blaming you, of course, old chap, seen the girl myself; hard for a fellow to resist, absolutely. But the thing is, Nicholas, Mal's a lovely woman. Man would be a fool to lose her for a pretty face.'

I stare morosely into my pint. 'She's a wonderful woman. I don't deserve her.'

'So what's this all about then?' Giles says kindly. 'Not like you. Always such a *sensible* chap.'

'Not so sensible now, it would seem.'

He nods at the landlord. 'Same again? Look, Nicholas, we all make mistakes. Fellow's got to be a saint sometimes – the girls these days. Lot more forward than they used to be. Had a bit of a brush myself a few months ago, matter of fact. Girl on the seven-nineteen, always sits in the first carriage behind the engine, same as me. Charming girl. Works in advertising. Got chatting after a while, as you do. Quite brightened up the journey, if I'm honest. Anyway, next thing I know, she's asking me to come with her to a gallery opening.'

'What did you say?' I ask curiously.

'Said no, of course,' Giles says briskly. 'Look, old chap. Don't mean to be a killjoy. But once you open that door – well, who knows where it'll lead? I know I'm not every girl's cup of tea, never been an oil painting, I know that; but Liz is rather *fond*, you know. Break her heart if she found I'd been dipping my wick elsewhere. Thing is, you and Mal have a good thing going. And there are your girls to think of. Why take the risk?'

I've asked myself the same thing a thousand times. Sleeping with her once, after the bombings, I could almost explain away; danger makes us all do things we wouldn't normally. And perhaps that would have been it, if Sara hadn't produced the opera tickets – how magnificent, that she should love Wagner! – and made it clear she *was* interested in a repeat performance, after all. If we hadn't run into Liz and Giles, I *would* have taken her to bed again. And this time, the only danger would have been of my making.

'Liz told Mal about last night, you know, Giles. Said you'd run into me in London and given me a lift back.'

'You were jolly lucky there, Nicholas. *Jolly* lucky. Could've been very different if it'd been anyone else. But Liz is a good woman. She takes things at face value. You'll be all right with her.'

I drain my pint and set it down. Giles is absolutely right. Five minutes earlier, and Mal's best friend would have seen Sara all over me like a cheap suit. I should never have let her touch me in public; it was pure bloody recklessness. I should never have gone out with her again at all.

Amare et sapere vix deo conceditur. The gods never let us love and be wise at the same time.

The thing is, one night with Sara wasn't enough. *Nowhere near enough.*

I know this thing has to end, and soon; the stakes are too high. I could lose everything I care about. Christ Almighty, I deal with marital train wrecks every day of the week. I had a client in my office just last Friday, been married two years and nine months. Wife had a couple of miscarriages, and the bloody fool ended up in bed with his secretary. He's now looking at giving his wife his house and a rather nasty slice of the next few years of his life; and that's a best-case scenario, *if* we pull the right judge. Meanwhile, the secretary has taken one look at the interim maintenance order and made for the hills.

I have to get Sara out of my system, once and for all. But denying myself only seems to feed the fever. Perhaps if she *stops* being forbidden fruit, if I let this thing run its natural course, it'll burn itself out. I'm sure of it.

Valentine's Day. Less than a month away. I'll give

myself till Valentine's Day, the day associated with love and romance the world over; and then I'll put an end to it. We'll have a final passionate liaison, and then bid each other a regretful, but amicable, farewell.

Somehow, putting a time limit on the affair eases my excruciating guilt. I've already broken my vows; the damage is already done. A few weeks longer, that's all I ask.

I'm not leading Sara on under false pretences. She's a young girl with everything going for her. It's not like she's in this for the long haul. She's a smart woman; she knows I'm not a good bet for the future. And at her age, she's probably not even thinking about the future anyway. She's enjoying this for what it is: fun, good conversation, and bloody fantastic sex.

I send her half a florist's stock on Monday by way of an apology for our ruined evening; and then a boxed set of the Wagner she loves so much the next day. I haven't been caught up in such a romantic rush for years; on Wednesday I surprise myself by tracking down a rare out-of-print book of poetry – a revelation, that, to discover a dozen well-thumbed volumes of First World War poets on her book shelves; I had expected airport bricks of the type Mal favours – whilst Thursday's gift is inspired by a comment from one of my female clients.

'La Perla!' the woman says furiously, as she storms towards my office waving what turns out to be an American Express credit card statement. 'I was married to the bastard twenty-seven years, and he never bought *me* bloody La Perla!'

Google divulges the nature of this particular feminine Holy Grail; unfortunately, I'm left to fend for myself when it comes to the delicate matter of making the actual purchase. I have no idea what size to buy Sara; cupping my hands in a broadly indicative mime elicits more hilarity than helpfulness. However, eventually we establish the parameters of my quest by dint of a rather unseemly comparison with several shop assistants' *embonpoint*; soon I am left to choose between a coffee-and-cream all-in-one lace confection, and an enticing plum brassière and panties set so flimsy it looks as if it will barely last the anticipated five-minute interlude between revelation and removal.

I buy both: one for now, and one for Valentine's Day. It will be my farewell gift to her; a memento of one last spectacular night together before we say goodbye.

Into the folds of the coffee-coloured silk, I slip a Claridge's key card. And it is at Claridge's that our affair moves up a gear, the day after I give her my final gift: a silver Tiffany bracelet I know she covets.

Valentine's Day creeps ever closer as, over the course of the next few weeks, we meet up at the hotel again and again. I daren't risk a late night more than once or twice a week, but there is the occasional afternoon tryst, when a client cancels; almost more passionate for its spontaneity. It's costing me a fortune (my credit cards are near their limits; thankfully the firm's profit share at the end of the financial year in April will clear them before Mal notices) but with the recklessness that characterizes this whole liaison, I find I don't care. It'll be over soon. When I run out of credit, I will simply pay cash.

I can't tell Sara that I already plan to end our affair, that would be unkind; but I am careful, very careful, not to offer her more than I can give. Beyond the pleasure our lovemaking affords me, I *like* her; very much. The last thing in the world I want to do is hurt her.

But none the less, there is a moment, the day before Valentine's Day, when I almost slip.

I'm about to leave for the last train home after another wonderful evening with her when Sara takes it upon herself to treat me to one of her mind-blowing blow-jobs. I should leave – I'm late already – but oh, God, it's as if she has a dozen tongues, all conspiring to drive me out of my mind. Train times and anxious wives mean nothing. Promises, lies, love and truth – nothing matters but the woman on her knees in front of me. *Hot, warm, wet* . . . Jesus Christ Almighty.

I let her take me to the brink, then abruptly pull away from her. More than anything, I want to drive her to lose control the way she does me; I want her writhing on the bed frantic for my touch. I taste her hot sweat when I kiss her skin, my mouth moving from breasts to belly-button to her strangely naked mound. It's like the whole of her body is an erogenous zone as she squirms erotically beneath me. I hold back, carefully controlling the pace, deliberately refusing to let her breathy little cries spur me faster.

Finally, when I know I've got her where I want her, I tongue her where she's aching to be touched.

After she comes, I slide up the bed and rest my cheek on her belly, relishing its soft, cushiony feel. A relaxed warmth seeps through me as her heartbeat thuds, slowing now, a little above my ear. Unbidden, words float to the surface. 'I love—'

I want to bite my tongue off. Good God, the blood-rush to my cock must have caused a severe lack of its flow to my brain.

In the *here and now* I love her, certainly. But a woman reads far more into those three overused words than a man often means her to hear.

'I love to be here,' I amend hastily. 'I feel safe, safer than anywhere else in the world.'

She's quick to hide it; but not quick enough. I see hope in her eyes, and roll away from her, onto my back, so that she won't see the answering pity and incipient claustrophobia in mine. *I thought she was smarter than that.*

A beat later, and she's astride me, hands guiding my cock towards her, and I wonder if I imagined it after all. And then, with infuriating inevitability, my mobile telephone rings.

'Emma, would you mind getting Simon Jailer on the phone? I need to clarify a couple of points on the Wasserstein case before Friday, and I know he's tied up in Court all day tomorrow.'

I go back into my office, glancing at my watch as I pick up my briefcase. Nearly seven; I should get going as soon as I've spoken to Counsel. I don't want to leave Sara sitting alone at Yuzo's; tonight of all nights.

This time tomorrow it will all be over. I know this is my choice, it's what I planned all along; but it's going to be harder to say goodbye than I thought.

I take out the glossy bag containing my farewell gifts to Sara from my desk drawer, and flip open my briefcase. As I slip it in between a legal file and my newspaper, unable to suppress a shiver of erotic anticipation, my office door opens and I shut the briefcase quickly, not wanting Emma to see.

But it isn't Emma standing in the doorway.

Saying no to my wife's invitation wasn't an option. Not only was I wrong-footed by her improbable materialization in my office, barely able to summon the wit to utter her name, never mind fabricate a plausible excuse to flee; but the searing guilt which I have successfully banished from my mind these past few weeks is now rising up a thousandfold stronger for its exile.

I have no idea what will happen in the next twenty minutes; nor any control over it. In some ways this enforced abdication of responsibility is almost a relief. Perhaps Sara will betray me: inadvertently or by choice, a woman scorned. Maybe Mal will guess the moment she sees my colleague sitting in my favourite restaurant, which has, of late, acquired some of the less pleasing characteristics of Piccadilly Circus. If I am truly fortunate, this noisome taxi will disappear down an abyss in the road and swallow me whole.

Clammy and sick with fear, I try to imagine a life without my wife and daughters in it, and fail utterly.

I cannot even meet Sara's eyes when my wife rushes over to greet her – dear Christ, did she have to comment on the bloody bracelet? – and grip the back of the nearest chair as Mal chatters relentlessly.

It seems Sara has more presence of mind than I could ever have anticipated. Within moments, she has confected some excuse and vanished.

'Well, she seems very keen,' Mal says brightly, shaking out her napkin. 'How lovely.'

Nausea rises. 'Can we order, please, Mal?' I say desperately.

I can barely concentrate on a word she says as we plough through the meal. *Dear God, how am I going to unravel this unholy mess?* I cannot believe that I, of all people, have managed to get myself into such a fool-hardy, melodramatic position. Dammit, I was going to end it tomorrow! Mal seems blissfully unaware; but the possibility still exists that Sara will be so incensed by what can only seem to her as my betrayal, that she seeks revenge by confronting my wife. The hurt that would inflict on Mal doesn't bear contemplating. And my girls. How can I ever look them in the eye again if they find out what I've done? I have been seven types of idiot, led by my genitals like a schoolboy. Christ Jesus, let me walk away from this unscathed and I swear to God, I will *never*—

'—So go on, don't keep me in suspense.'

I startle. 'Sorry?'

'Oh, Nicholas, don't be mean, you know I saw you put it in your briefcase,' Mal teases, 'and I just can't wait any longer, I'm *dying* for my present, *please* can I have it now?'

This unedifying, shameful farce is clearly destined to play itself out to the bitter end. I reach beneath the table for my briefcase.

'I'm sorry. I – um – I didn't get you a card.'

'Oh, Nicholas. As if that matters.'

She opens the bag and unwraps the underwear I selected for another woman. I feel sick with shame as she innocently holds the wisps of silk and lace up against herself. 'Oh, how *beautiful*! Do you like them?'

'Of course,' I mutter. 'I wouldn't have bought them otherwise.'

'I can tell it's been a while,' she laughs, examining the label. 'These are two sizes too big, I'll have to take them back and exchange them. You kept the receipt, didn't you?' She peers back into the bag and gasps. 'Oh, Nicholas. You *didn't*—'

Please don't notice that these match the bracelet Sara was wearing, please don't put two and two together, please be your usual sweet, trusting, innocent self.

'Nicholas,' she breathes, gazing at the earrings. 'They're exquisite. I don't know what to say.'

And suddenly, in a moment, the fog lifts. *Non pote non sapere qui se stultum intellegit*: a man must have some wit to know he is a fool.

I love Mal; I always have. From the moment I first met her, I've known she's The One. She's my dearest friend, my love, the mother of my children. There is a sweetness to her, a purity of heart and spirit, that I have never known in anyone else. And she loves me; far more than I deserve. I know she would never contemplate betraying me; her loyalty and fidelity are absolute. How can I have risked all of this for what amounts to no more than a glorified roll in the hay?

'Happy Valentine's Day,' I tell my wife; meaning it.

Later that night, after Mal and I have made love for the first time since I slept with Sara – not the roller-coaster of eroticism that it is with Sara, granted, but laced with a love and gentleness I can only ever find with my wife –

we make plans for a romantic break in Cornwall, where we honeymooned; we build castles in the air and articulate our dreams for our children, for ourselves. I fall asleep with my head in the curve of her arm, and promise from the depths of my soul that it will all be different from now on.

For four days, Sara manages to avoid being alone with me for a single moment with the same expertise with which I once evaded her.

She whisks in and out of my office with armfuls of files, careful to make sure that Emma is within earshot before doing so. Christ knows how her bladder is holding up; I've stationed myself outside the women's toilet for hours without glimpsing her. Much as I'd be happy to play ostrich with her, I know we can't bury our heads in the sand forever; I need to end this liaison cleanly, and with as little acrimony as possible. I have to explain, for my own peace of mind; and to somehow find the right moment to discuss a very good job opening at Falkners Penn for a young, ambitious lawyer keen to make partner before she's thirty.

I have to be certain she's not going to betray me.

My chance comes on Friday, when Emma's sister unexpectedly arrives from Worcester, and she begs for an unscheduled afternoon off.

Joan and David are out of the office; a secretarial leaving party has decimated the remainder of the staff. I give the one temp on duty a free pass, and she scuttles off, delighted, to join her colleagues across the road.

Sara looks startled as I walk into the conference room, and instantly leaps up from the table. 'I just have to get this FDR statement to Emma—'

'She's not here. She's taken the afternoon off to go shopping with her sister.'

'Perhaps one of the other girls—'

'They're all at Milagro's for Jenny's leaving party. Sara,' I put out a hand to detain her, 'I need to explain.'

She stiffens.

'I don't think that's necessary.'

'I know this must be hard to believe, but I had no idea she was going to turn up until she appeared in my office. *I swear it.* I wouldn't do that to you; you *must* know that. I didn't have a chance to phone you, she was with me the whole time, and then she insisted on Yuzo's – Christ, what are the odds—'

'Quite high, I should imagine, when you declare your preference to the world in the *Lawyer*,' Sara says acidly.

'But I really had no idea she—'

'Nicholas, please. I think we both know the situation. You're a married man; I knew that from the beginning. There's really no need to rake things over any more. We had a good time, but we knew all along it had to end sooner or later. At least this way no one's got hurt.'

Her eyes are suspiciously bright. I brush my thumbs beneath them. 'Haven't they?'

I sought her out with the most honest of intentions. I truly meant for this to be a tying up of loose ends.

But that touch is all it takes. A fire ignites between us; my cock is rock-hard in an instant, and as Sara's eyelids flutter, I smell her arousal. Gripping her face between my palms, I bruise her lips beneath mine. I taste the metallic tang of blood and don't know which of us is cut.

She yanks my shirt out of my trousers as I propel her backwards towards the glossy mahogany conference table and shove her skirt up over her thighs. She fumbles with my belt buckle. Buttons plink across the table as I rip open her shirt. I push aside her panties with fierce fingers. In a moment I'm inside her, forcing her down onto the surface of the table, frantic and angry and hot with desire. My mouth descends on one cinnamon nipple, biting it roughly through the flimsy fabric of her bra. There's a crash as her heap of files tumbles from the table to the floor.

Her legs curl around my waist, and I drive my cock deeper into her. She pulls my shirt free from my shoulders as I unhook her bra; our skin hisses as it hits. She smells of vanilla and sweat and peppermint and sex. Her ripe breasts splay lushly either side of her breastbone, eddying with every violent thrust. Throwing back her head, a guttural growl vibrates low in her throat, her sharp white teeth biting down on her swollen lower lip. Her nails dig deep into my shoulder blades and I flinch *don't leave marks* and then oh God oh God *oh God*—

She comes a moment later, her body jerking so hard that her spine thumps against the table. I feel her juices flood us both and it's almost enough to get me hard again.

'Oh, Christ, I've peed myself—'

'No. You just came. You know. Ejaculated.'

She laughs disbelievingly. 'Fuck off.'

I pull out of her and yank up my trousers. 'You've done it before. Not many women do it, but those that can – *Jesus*. You have no idea how erotic it is.'

'Are you kidding me?'

'Would I joke about something like that?'

'You tell me.' She sits up on the table and pulls down her skirt. 'Shit, you've ripped half the buttons off my blouse. You couldn't have just waited a moment and undone them, could you?'

'Could you?'

Her expression is dark and hot. 'No.'

'It's not over, is it?' I whisper, cupping her breast in my hand and pulling her buttocks towards me with the other. 'Between us.'

Her nipple stiffens instantly. My cock is already half-way to being ready for her once more. I drop to my knees and spread her legs as she sits on the edge of the table, burying my face in her wet pussy.

'We haven't even started,' she groans.

My mother had a saying: *No one misses a slice of cut cake.* She meant that the first cut is the one you notice. After that, the difference is much harder to see.

The first night I slept with Sara, I was tormented with guilt. Each subsequent liaison has compounded the betrayal; but somehow, where once guilt blistered my skin and rubbed my soul raw, now it merely chafes like an ill-fitting shoe.

If I'm honest: all I care about now is not getting caught.

'You can't mark me again,' I whisper, stroking Sara's bare shoulder as we lie in the darkness of her bedroom, both of us spent. I can't afford Claridge's on a long-term basis; we have no choice now but to use her flat, whatever the risk. 'After the conference room, I had to get up half an hour earlier for a week so that I could finish showering before Mal was awake.'

'I'm sorry. I didn't do it on purpose.'

'I know. But we have to be careful—'

'Enough, already,' Sara says tightly. She leans over me to pick up her cigarettes from the bedside table. 'What do you want me to do, wear surgical gloves?'

'I wish you wouldn't do that. *Smoke.* It's not like you smoke the rest of the time; I hate that you do it in bed.'

'So let's stick to having sex in the great outdoors.'

'Now you sound like a petulant child.'

'So stop talking to me like one!'

She swings her legs out of bed and stalks naked towards the window, parting the blinds with one finger and exhaling moodily. 'I'm fed up with being fitted in between lunch and conference with Counsel. It's like you get here, we have sex, and then you leave. It's not exactly romantic, is it?'

'We have dinner – we went to the opera—'

'Fucking Wagner!'

'I thought you *liked* Wagner. *Tristan und Isolde* was your idea—'

She drops her cigarette into a revolting mug half-full of cold coffee and sits back down on the bed beside me, her expression instantly contrite. 'I *do*, Nick. I'm sorry. I don't mean to be a pain in the arse. I just like being with you, that's all. I hate that it has to be like this—'

'How else do you expect it to be, Sara?'

'I'm not asking for anything,' she answers quickly. 'That's not what I meant.'

'I stay here as late as I can,' I say tiredly. 'I missed the last train from Waterloo last week, I had to get a taxi from

London all the way to bloody Wiltshire; do you have any idea how much that cost? I'm sorry that I can't stay here more often, and I'm sorry that I can't stay all night; but you *knew* it was going to be like this.'

She gives a light half-laugh that doesn't quite come off. 'You *could* call me a bit more often at the weekend.'

'It's not that easy. I can't call you from the home phone; it's too risky. Mal could overhear me, or the children could pick up the extension.' I throw a pillow behind my head. 'And my mobile doesn't pick up any reception at home, we're in a network-dead zone. I have to drive halfway to Salisbury to use it, and there's a limited amount of excuses I can come up with to do that. I'm sorry.'

'Nick, I know the score. I'm not asking for any kind of commitment, you know that.' She averts her gaze. 'I'd just like to wake up with you once in a while, have breakfast, read the newspapers, that kind of thing.'

No, I want to tell her, *those are the kinds of things you do with your wife, and I already have one of those.*

I watch her picking fretfully at a loose thread in the sheet with a mixture of pity and exasperation. She's in too deep. She is starting to have feelings for me, whatever she may say now; and I am going to end up hurting her. I have to end it. *I have to end it.*

But carefully. I can't risk her running to Mal afterwards. Perhaps if I take her away, explain it all, let her down gently.

'Look,' I say, 'Mal mentioned something about a trip to Italy around Easter – some sort of sourcing trip for her new restaurant, I didn't pay much attention. She'll be away for a few days, the girls will be with her mother. I might be able to arrange something then.'

Her naked left breast is an inviting two inches away from my shoulder. Jesus. My cock stirs, and I reach for her; but she pulls away from me, chewing her lip and looking down at her nails. 'Nick?'

Christ, what now?

'Nick, do you and Mal – do you still, you know?'

'Do we still what?'

'God, do I have to spell it out?' She flushes. 'Do you still have *sex*?'

There's no right way to answer this question. *I'm married*, I want to tell her, *of course I still have sex with my wife*; not as often as we did once, our bedroom could not be mistaken for a French brothel, but yes, we have sex, and yes, it's very nice, thank you, sometimes quite a bit *more* than nice. And it's very different from sex with you, which is to nice what interstellar travel is to a trip to Bournemouth; but I'm a man, which means that some-times I'm in the mood for a trip to Bournemouth, and sometimes I want to don a spacesuit.

But this isn't what Sara wants to hear. And I want to keep Sara happy, for her sake, because I truly like and respect her, I don't want to hurt her; and for my own.

'She's not really that interested in sex any more,' I say, flinching inwardly at this new betrayal. 'What with the children and everything, she's never really in the mood. And since I met you,' and this time Sara doesn't move away when I reach for her, '*I* haven't been in the mood either.'

She slides astride me, satisfied now. 'Really?' she says,

easing me inside her. 'I can't say that's a problem *I've* ever noticed.'

Three weeks later, I pad barefoot down the narrow stairs of our rented cottage in Rock and find Mal already busy in the kitchen. Something rather foul-smelling is cooking on the stove. I lean over to peer into the frying pan and do a double-take.

There, being skilfully sautéed to a crisp, is one of my black wool socks.

'Mal, what on *earth* are you doing?'

'What you asked me to do last night,' she says, flipping it expertly with a fish-slice, 'when you came to bed very drunk.'

'I don't remember asking you to cook my sock.'

She grins wickedly at me, her dark eyes dancing, and the penny drops. 'Oh, very funny,' I say, grabbing my burnt sock out of the pan and blowing on my fingers. 'How long have you been waiting to set me up with that witty little play on words?'

'Since about eight this morning,' Mal giggles.

Sometimes my wife seems little older than the children. It's at moments like this I realize from whence Evie has acquired her unorthodox sense of humour and attitude to life.

I arranged this long weekend because I'd promised it to Mal; I packed for it with a heavy heart and deep sense of misgiving. Four days together at close quarters, without the distractions of children and work, lacking even the diversion of household chores or television to dilute our unaccustomed intimacy. A delightful scenario for newlyweds; a testing one for even the most devoted long-standing marriages. How much more so for a husband in the midst of an adulterous affair?

I expected it to be awkward, difficult, even; with long silences and stilted conversation. I thought the distance between us would be painfully obvious to us both.

What I did not expect was to fall back in love with my wife.

I stayed up into the small hours last night, trying to make sense of the chaos in my heart and head. Intoxicated as I am with Sara, I am not such a fool as to mistake my feelings for love; or anywhere close. The nature of my betrayal is entirely sexual; there is no question of any emotional involvement. I'm not sure whether that makes it better or worse.

Sex with Mal is pleasant. Tender, in a way it never is with Sara. But with Sara, it's like nothing I've ever known. I can ask for anything, be anyone, I want. There's no fear of being judged, of being thought dirty, or perverted, or selfish. She won't look at me as I slice the tops off the girls' boiled eggs at breakfast and remember what I did to her the night before. To have to turn my back on that sexual freedom forever, to give her up; it'd be like waking up blind and knowing you'll never see a sunrise again.

When Mal goes away, I remind myself. I have to tell Sara it's over then. If I don't, sooner or later, Mal is going to find out, and I will lose her. And I love Mal: more than I crave Sara. It should be easy.

It won't be, of course.

I wrap my arms around my wife and kiss the top of her head. '*Mea culpa.* I guess I got through rather more of the malt than I'd realized after you went to bed—'

'My own fault for not staying awake and supervising you. But it's not like the ending to *Casablanca* is ever going to change, and I was *so* tired after yesterday—'

She blushes, and I can't help but smile. My wife of ten years, the mother of my three children, reduced to flushing like a teenager when she's reminded of our agreeable afternoon in bed. 'I meant the climb down to the cove, Nicholas.'

'Ah. Fancy doing it all again today?'

'We don't want to keep going down the same old paths, do we, Nicholas, that would get rather dull, wouldn't it?'

'Would it?'

'It would.' She pulls a freshly baked pie out of the oven – even on holiday, my wife the cook – and bats my hand away. 'Wait. A little anticipation will do you the world of good. This is for lunch. I thought an alfresco picnic would be fun, and the weather is supposed to be rather nice, later, for March; we can wrap up warm and sit on the beach.'

'Alfresco works for me.'

She giggles again. '*Nicholas*—'

My mobile telephone shrills. It's on the windowsill beside Mal; she reaches for it, but in a moment that lasts a lifetime I just manage to get there first. 'It might be a client,' I say quickly. 'I had to give Mrs Wasserstein my number; it was the only way to get Friday and Monday off.'

Mal looks surprised. 'Don't do that too often or you'll never get a break.' She covers the pie with a linen tea-towel. 'I need to get my tennis shoes out of the car boot if we're going to go for a walk – have you seen the keys?'

'In my jacket pocket, on the banister.'

I take the phone out into the back garden, shivering in my dressing-gown and bare feet. 'Sara, what the *hell* are you doing calling me at home?'

She sounds stricken. 'Oh, God, Nick, I'm *so* sorry. I didn't mean to call you; I must've hit redial by mistake. Jesus, I hope I didn't cause a problem – I'm *really* sorry.'

I sigh. 'Never mind, I've done that enough times myself.' The incriminating potential of my mobile terrifies me: the text messages, the call records. I've started charging it at the office, just in case Mal should see something on it she shouldn't. 'Is everything OK?'

'I suppose. I'm at my parents. Dullsville, you have no idea. They want me to come down on Easter Sunday for some village egg race or something; as *if*. How's it going in Wiltshire?'

'What? Oh, yes, Wiltshire. Fine, fine. Look, I've got to go. I'll see you on Tuesday—'

'Can you come round after work?'

'Maybe.' I glance up as Mal appears in the back doorway. 'Look, I have to go.'

I click the phone shut. I always knew having an affair involved deception; that I would end up lying to not just one woman, but *two*, I had no idea.

Mal waits until I reach her, and then holds out her hand palm upwards, her eyes never leaving my face.

'Nicholas,' she says evenly, 'whose lipstick is this?'

11

Sara

'Oh, Nick. You fucking bastard,' I breathe.

I tap my finger on the urgent DHL package Emma
has left out on her desk for the courier to take to Nick for
signature. He's *not* at home in Wiltshire with his ditzy
wife and cute photogenic children. The lying shit is in
bloody Cornwall getting his – forgive the pun – rocks off.

Well, aren't you a quick learner, Nick Lyon. Amazing
just how fast you've got the hang of this lying-through-
your-teeth shit. You're right up there with the pros.

I do what I always do when the Big Bad World gets
too much for me: I decamp to my parents' for the weekend.

There's something deeply reassuring about sleeping
in my tiny single bed with its Barbie-printed sheets. My
old, cuddly teddy bear (from Harrods, natch) is waiting
for me on top of my pillow, still wearing the holey jumper
I knitted for him the Christmas I turned ten on my new
automatic knitting machine (Nagged for: 364 days. Used:

forty seven minutes). I wouldn't mind growing up if it was all late nights watching cartoons and chocolate ice-cream for dinner, like you think it's going to be when you're seven. I just don't want to end up like my mother, stuck with a ton of carrots to peel and an ironing basket the size of Everest. Where's the fun in that?

By the time I show my face downstairs on Saturday, it's gone eleven. My mother is at Sainsbury's. (Planning Your Meals: another very good reason not to grow up. I prefer to hit the local 7–11 approximately fifteen minutes prior to dinner. Nick practically had a coronary when he opened my fridge to make a post-shag sandwich and beheld the sum total of my larder: two out-of-date plain live yoghurts left over from my last failed diet, three cans of Red Bull and, in the freezer section, a half-empty bottle of vodka.) My mother actually aspires to be a Waitrose shopper, but she can't bear to pay their prices when Sainsbury's does the same things so much cheaper. She consoles herself with the fact that at least she hasn't sunk as low as Asda.

Dad, however, is very much in evidence: propped up at the breakfast bar with bloody Libby Newcombe.

'Men give love to get sex,' Dad opines as I walk in. 'Women give sex to get love. There's your battle of the sexes in a nutshell.'

'But Vinny, he said I was The One!' Libby wails.

'They all say that Before. Hello, love,' Dad says to me as I slouch towards the kettle. 'Libby and young Martin have just split up, I'm afraid. Made off with the fancy piece from the Duke's Head. She's a bit upset about it, they've been together since New Year's Eve.'

'She should be bloody grateful,' I mutter.

'The thing is, Libby, love, you've got to play a bit hard to get,' Dad says, resuming his role as Dr Phil with disturbing ease. 'Chap's not going to pay for the cow if he's getting the milk for free, is he?'

I'm not sure I can deal with this fresh insight into the dynamic of my parents' marriage this early in the morning. Early for a Saturday, I mean.

I slouch back out of the kitchen with my tea, once Dad remembers his manners and gets up to make it for me.

And thus passes the rest of the weekend. I skulk, mooch and saunter, occasionally interspersing this frenzied activity with a bout of ambling, meandering, roaming or rambling, as the mood takes me. There are even moments of slumping and drooping, just for variety.

I check for text messages so often I'm surprised my phone doesn't howl, 'Gerroff Me!' and leap out of sight behind the sofa when I walk in the room.

On Sunday I call Amy. 'What?' she says sharply.

'Way to go, Ames. I love you too.'

'I'm waiting for a call,' she snaps.

'Who from?'

She hesitates. 'Terry, if you must know.'

'You're at your parents' again, aren't you?' I speculate.

'How did you know?'

I sigh. 'Lucky guess. So, did Terry say he'd ring you?'

'No. But he *might*.'

'Does he usually call you at weekends?'

'Does Nick usually call you?'

There's a silence as we contemplate our respective adulterers. Not for the first time, I am struck by our self-deluding masochism. There are plenty of men out there having affairs with married women, but I bet *they're* not benched at their parents' houses chewing their fingernails back to the elbows waiting for her to ring. I bet they're having a good ole time, hanging with their mates down the pub, sinking a few whilst they wait till it's late enough to go clubbing, where they'll undoubtedly end up pulling a fit teenager and getting laid just to keep their hand in. Sure as shit *they're* not riding the pine in suburbia.

'Are you going to the Law Society dinner next month?' Amy asks suddenly.

'Hadn't thought about it. Probably. Why?'

'Well. It's plus spouses,' she says meaningfully.

So Nick will bring the ditz. 'Maybe we can take turns with him,' I suggest.

'You won't be so flippant after four years,' Amy reproves. 'Look, I have to go. Terry might be trying to get through. I'll talk to you on Monday.'

I wander disconsolately into the kitchen, where my mother is peeling potatoes for Sunday lunch. There's no way *I'll* still be doing this in four years. Jesus, I don't intend to still be doing it in four months. I'm not going to end up like Amy, wasting my life waiting for a man who's never going to make the break. It should never have got this intense in the first place. It was supposed to be a bit of fun, good conversation and some way-fantastic sex. I wasn't supposed to fall in *love* with the bastard.

'Don't hover, Sara, it's distracting,' says my mother.

'Sorry.'

She hands me a knife and points to the vegetable rack. 'Might as well make yourself useful with the sprouts now you're here.'

For ten minutes or so, we peel and chop in silence. I can't say it's companionable; my relationship with my mother is, at best, a wary truce. At worst, it puts the Middle East conflict to shame.

'Man trouble, is it?' my mother sniffs.

'Is what?'

She reaches past me to put another potato in a saucepan of cold water. 'You've been mooching round the house all weekend with a face like a wet Sunday. That phone is practically attached to your hip. You were like this over young Martin, as I recall.'

'I was *not*!'

'Have it your own way.'

I slice sprout stalks with unnecessary vigour.

'Not interested, is he?' my mother says after a moment. *Scrape, peel.*

'Who?'

She plops another spud in the pan. 'The man you're eating your heart out over.'

'Yes, he's interested, thank you,' I say, stung.

'Married, then?'

'Dammit, Mum! Now look what you made me do!'

'Don't bleed on the sprouts, dear.' She hands me a piece of kitchen towel; I ignore it and suck my finger. 'Girls your age don't choose to spend the weekend with their parents unless he's either not interested or married.'

I'm shocked: both by the unexpected perspicacity of what she's said and the fact that she's said it at all. My mother and I don't go for soul-baring and girlie intimacy. She tells me she loves me with Hermès scarves and Prada backpacks. I show her I love her by wearing them.

I've always envied Amy's warm, close relationship with her mother. She told me once that when she goes home at the weekend, her mother sits on the loo seat and chats to her whilst she's in the bath. The image of cosy familiarity it conjured up made me so jealous I couldn't speak to her for a week.

My mother never asks me about my love life; presumably because she has a pretty good idea of its nature. And in fairness, I've always returned the compliment.

'Married men aren't fair game, young lady,' she says sharply.

'Mum, I *know*—'

'Wanting someone is no grounds for trampling all over another woman's marriage. And falling in love is no excuse either. Pass the salt cellar, please.' She grinds with swift, angry movements. 'We all have choices. Men are fools. It doesn't take much to tempt them. It's up to us not to let each other down.'

I don't know why she sounds like she's talking from experience. My dad would never cheat on her. He *said* so.

'And they never leave their wives,' she adds coldly. 'Whatever sweet words they tell you to get you into bed. Remember that.'

'I've no idea what you mean,' I say. 'Is there any wine open?'

She nods, purse-lipped, towards the fridge. I pour myself a heftier glass than I want just to annoy her, and go out into the back garden. It's surprisingly mild for March; I sit on the stone bench near the greenhouse, sipping my wine – passable, given that it came from a box not a bottle – and enjoy the play of watery sunshine across my face. Dad has already turned the earth for his broad beans; the air smells rich and peaty. Maybe I'll offer to help him plant them this year. I haven't done that since I was about twelve. I used to love crouching beside him in my red wellies, pushing the big beans into the freshly tilled soil with my thumb. I remember when I was six, I couldn't wait for them to grow, and snuck out of my room every night with a torch to check on them until I trod on a slug in my bare feet and screamed so loudly I woke the neighbours. My mother hates that Dad grows his own vegetables, of course; she calls it his 'allotment fetish'. She thinks the neighbours will assume we can't afford to buy them shrink-wrapped and genetically modified at the supermarket. Poor old Dad. I don't know how he puts up with her.

I drain the wine glass and set it down on the bench. My mobile is burning a hole in my pocket. The trip to Rock might have been a last-minute thing. Maybe Nick didn't even know about it; maybe it was all *her* idea. Like Valentine's Day. It's not as if he actually *said* he was going to be in Wiltshire as usual this weekend. I just assumed.

In the beginning, I never used to really think about Nick and his wife together. Now I can't stop.

It was seeing them both at Yuzo's. What I should have done after I bugged out of the sushi bar was take a cab home, eat a full tub of Cherry Garcia, and finish the bottle of vodka in front of *The Way We Were*. What I actually *did* was skulk around Yuzo's for two hours in the freezing cold feeling sorry for myself and dreaming up ways to castrate the bastard with piano wire. I saw them come out, his arm wrapped protectively around her teeny-tiny shoulders. They stopped for a moment in the street and kissed. Brief, but affectionate: you could tell. He stroked her cheek afterwards. Not the actions of a man who's sleeping with his junior partner on the side. Not the actions of a man who *isn't* sleeping with his wife.

Watching them, I felt as if I'd been punched in the stomach. My head hurt. How could he lead me on like this; how could he *lie* to me like this? Make me think—

Think what, exactly?

He never said he'd leave his wife. *What did you expect, you love-struck cow? That he was going to fall in love with you too and suddenly it'd all be different?*

I finger my phone through my fleece pocket. He could at least ring. That couldn't be too hard, could it? To make one simple phone call now and again?

I should never have let it all start up again. I'd been doing fine up to that afternoon in the conference room, even if I'd nearly passed out from the pain of not peeing so he couldn't catch me by the toilets. Well, not *fine*; but I'd managed to avoid being alone with him, anyway. I hadn't slit my wrists.

And then he touches me, and every sensible, look-both-ways, self-preserving thought flies out of my head.

Some men never listen to you in bed; in the end you give up asking for what you want. It's like when you mishear someone's name, and you ask them to repeat themselves: do it more than twice and it starts to get embarrassing. Why do some men always think they know what you want better than you do? You can be getting it on, moments away from orgasm, and you moan, 'Right there, don't stop!' and they think, oh, she likes that, then she'll really like *this*; and they stop and do something different. I want to take out a full-page newspaper ad': when I say, 'Right there, don't stop!', I mean, 'RIGHT THERE, DON'T STOP!'

With Nick, sex just gets better every time. I've never felt so connected to another person in my life; it's like he's inside my head. But now scary, grown-up feelings have got all jumbled up with that mind-blowing sex. I don't want to give him back any more. I don't want to share him. Everything's changed. And I don't know what to do about it.

Suddenly I desperately need to hear his voice. I just want to know he's missing me, too. I break my cardinal rule: I drink and dial.

It rings twenty-four times before he answers. And then—

'Sara, what the *hell* are you doing calling me at home?'

Talk about reality check. He sounds really annoyed. Dammit, this was a fucking, *fucking* stupid thing to do. What was I thinking?

'Oh, God, Nick, I'm *so* sorry,' I say quickly. 'I didn't mean to call you; I must've hit redial by mistake. Jesus, I hope I didn't cause a problem – I'm *really* sorry.'

To my intense relief, he actually buys it. 'Never mind, I've done that enough times myself. Is everything OK?'

'I suppose. I'm at my parents. Dullsville, you have no idea. They want me to come down on Easter Sunday for some village egg race or something; as *if*.' I pause, steeling myself to ask the question. *Don't lie to me, please don't lie.* 'How's it going in Wiltshire?'

'What? Oh, yes, Wiltshire. Fine, fine. Look, I've got to go. I'll see you on Tuesday—'

'Can you come round after work?'

I slam my fist against the stone bench. I hate how weak and desperate that sounds. What's happening to me? I should be tearing him a new one right now, not going back and begging for more.

'Maybe. Look, I have to go.'
Bastard. Bastard, bastard, *bastard*.

Staying with a man who lies to someone else is dumb enough. Staying with a man who lies to *you* is just plain retarded.

Maybe he was telling the truth about Valentine's Day; perhaps she *did* just turn up at his office. Which is a little out there in itself. Either she's a suspicious bitch or their relationship isn't quite the Cold War standoff he likes to make out. But he sure as shit lied to me about spending a long weekend alone with her in Cornwall.

And I'm not going to call him on it.

Without even noticing it happen, I've crossed the line. I can't give him up now; it's as simple as that. I want him for myself. I want him to leave his wife, walk out on his kids, move in with me and for us to live happily ever after. I want his ring, his name, the whole shebang. Even though I know it's selfish and wicked and will break the heart of not just his wife, but the three innocent little girls whose picture he touches, like a talisman, every time he opens his wallet.

It's not that I don't care. I used to think I was a decent person; before I met Nick, the worst thing I'd ever done was to back into a white van in the multi-storey car park and not leave a note. (Which, if you think about it, is probably just karmic payoff.)

But you can't help who you fall in love with. I know it's wrong, but I can't help it. It's not as if *I've* wrecked their marriage; it's impossible to break up a good relationship, isn't it? If he was happy with his wife, he wouldn't be with me in the first place. And she can't want him to stay with her out of guilt. No woman would. What kind of second-hand relationship would that be? It's got to be fairer to both of them if he leaves, and gives her a chance to find someone else too. If she really loves him, she'll want him to be happy.

I can make him happy. I *understand* him. I love him; and I know he loves me. He's as good as said so. And you can't have the kind of amazing, soul-baring sex we have if you don't love each other, can you?

The day Nick's due back at work, I put on a vintage black nipped-in Fifties suit I know he likes, and a gorgeous apple-green bra and knickers set, just in case. It's only been four days since I last saw him, but I've got first-date butterflies; I'm so nervy I have to reapply my lip liner twice. I even get to the office half an hour earlier than usual, and sit at my desk pretending to work whilst I wait for him to get in. I've decided I'm not going to tell him I know about Cornwall. I'm not even going to mention—

'What the hell was this all about?'

He storms into my office, slams the door and flings something on my desk; I want to look but I can't take my eyes off his face. I've never even seen him slightly angry, never mind like this. His grey eyes are as cold as granite, his jaw clenched as he fights to keep his fury under control.

I flinch when he puts both palms down on my desk and pushes his face into mine.

'I'm waiting,' he spits furiously.

'Nick – someone might hear.'

'It's a bit late now!'

I drop my eyes. My gold Estée Lauder lipstick rolls gently to a stop against my mouse mat.

When I was nine, I dropped my grandmother's precious Royal Worcester coronation figurine on the floor. I'd taken it off the dining-room mantelpiece, despite express instructions *never* to touch it. I stared at the broken shards on the fireplace tiles in an unthinking, blind terror, as if I could *will* the last few seconds not to have happened. In my mind's eye, I ran a spool of tape backwards and saw the pieces jumping back together again, becoming whole, like a cartoon. My craving was such that I could almost *see* them move.

What possessed me to put my lipstick in his jacket pocket? *What?*

A wave of heat washes through me, instantly followed by a cold sweat that chills to the bone. I concentrate very hard on not licking my dry lips, unable to tear my eyes from that small gold tube.

'I think that's answer enough,' Nick says disgustedly.

He turns on his heel. I watch him walk towards the door, and know that if I let him leave this room now I will never have another chance.

'Where did you find it?' I ask, somehow squeezing surprise into my voice.

He freezes. 'Where did I find it?'

'It's my favourite, I've been looking for it *every*where.' I pick it up; my hand shakes, and I put it down again. 'I thought I must have left it in the hotel the last time we stayed there; I can't remember seeing it since then.'

For a long moment, he doesn't move. I can't breathe. Then he turns round, his eyes dark with suspicion.

'It kept rolling off the marble vanity in the bathroom,' I say, 'so – of course! – I left it in that china tray by the television, where you always put your keys and wallet. You must have picked it up without noticing when you left in such a rush to get the last train.'

'I picked it up?'

I shrug. 'You must have done. So where did you find it?'

'*I* didn't,' Nick says, his eyes fast on mine. 'My wife did. In my jacket pocket, when she went to get my keys.'

I don't have to fake my appalled expression. I just have to think what will happen if he doesn't believe me.

'What did she say?' I whisper.

'She's my wife. She found another woman's lipstick in my jacket pocket. What do you *think* she said?'

'Does she – have you—'

'Told her about us?' he asks curtly. 'No. Fortunately, my wife is a very trusting woman. When I tell her an obscene pack of lies about finding lipsticks in hallways, she tends to believe me.'

I nod. I'm relieved; of course I am. Hot shame washes over me again. I'd never have believed myself capable of being this sly and manipulative. I didn't understand how much I love him until I realized what I'd do – and what I'd put up with – to keep him. But if I naively thought for one moment that planting a lipstick where his wife would find it would push him into choosing me, I'm certainly disabused of the idea now. He's not going to leave his wife for me. *Of course* he's not going to leave his wife. They never do.

'Nick?' I say carefully. 'Are we OK?'

He hesitates. A chink opens; it's all I need. I move out from behind my desk, aware that I look just the right side of slutty in this figure-hugging suit. My top button has come undone; I don't bother to fix it. I let my eyes flicker to his groin just long enough to put the idea into his head. I'm close enough for him to smell my perfume and the warmth of my skin, but I leave him a little ground to cover between us. The last thing I need is for him to feel cornered.

'I'm sorry,' he sighs, wrenching his eyes from my cleavage. 'I thought – I don't know what I thought. It's been a difficult weekend.'

'Will I see you later?'

'Not tonight. It's not that I don't want to – I can't,' he says quickly. 'We're having my parents over for dinner. But tomorrow. I could come over tomorrow. As long as—'

I look away so he won't see the resentment on my face. 'The last train. Yes. I know.'

Is it my imagination, or is Nick – is he cooling on me? I can't put my finger on it, but he just doesn't seem as *hungry* as he was before. It's nothing he's doing – or not doing – in bed. It's more a sense that the closer I move towards him, the further he moves away.

I push myself up on one arm as he rolls out of bed and reaches for his trousers. 'You're leaving already? It's not even eight!'

'I can't keep arriving home at midnight, Sara.'

I watch silently as he buttons his shirt and fastens

his cufflinks. The power has inexplicably but undeniably shifted in our relationship. A couple of months ago, he was the one showering me with presents and besieging me with attention. Now, the sex is as vigorous and satisfying as it ever was, but he's barely whipped off his condom before he's shooting out the door.

He shrugs on his jacket and picks up his briefcase. 'I'll see you at work tomorrow.'

I nod tightly. He sighs, and comes over to sit on the bed. I pull up my knees and rest my chin on them, and he rubs my bare back as if I'm a child. 'Sara, I'm sorry. I'd understand if you wanted to stop this. I wouldn't blame you. I can't offer you a future, or make you any promises. You deserve better than me.'

Ice trickles down my spine. Men always say that when they're too spineless to dump you.

'I'm fine with it,' I manage. 'No strings. It's the way I like it.'

'Look. Mal's going away the week after next, remember, this bloody sourcing trip of hers,' he says gently, turning my face towards him with his finger. 'The girls will be staying with her mother. I've booked us into a country house hotel in Kent. Four-poster bed, hot tub, roaring fires, the works. The office is closed over Easter; we can spend five whole days and nights together. How does that sound?'

'Bliss,' I laugh, folding myself into his arms.

Of course he's not going cold on me. I'm just being paranoid. He'd hardly arrange a romantic break away *à deux* if he wanted to end it.

He kisses the top of my head. 'We'll get a chance to

talk. After that, we'll know where we are.' He hesitates. 'And where we're going.'

'You have *got* to be kidding me!'

'Christ, Sara! What do you want me to do? Say no, sorry, darling, you can't change your mind and come back, I've got a dirty weekend planned with my mistress?'

'Dammit, Nick!' I almost wrench the phone out of its socket as I storm across my bedroom. 'I've just finished packing; the taxi is outside waiting at the kerb for me! What the fuck am I supposed to do with myself for the next five days? You can't just mess people about like this!'

'You're right,' he snaps back. 'I'm clearly making you bloody miserable. Why don't we just call it a day and have done with it?'

'Fine. Why don't we?'

Because we can't.

No one knows how painful it is to be a woman in love with a man who goes home every weekend to his wife and family unless they've been there. It's too easy to judge her, to paint her as a scarlet woman, a home-wrecker, a destroyer of lives. Easy, too, to forget that the life she destroys most is her own.

I think of him day and night. I ride a roller-coaster of emotion: rising to dizzy heights working with him during the day, and in the evenings when I steal him to my flat; through the dreaded anticipation of his going; to bleak pillow-sobbing desolation as the door shuts behind him.

'I can't be in a position where your happiness depends on me,' he sighs one day, when the tears start before he even leaves. 'I don't think I can take the responsibility.'

Despair descends on me like a cloak. Does that mean he doesn't want to be with me after all? Is he working up to telling me it's over?

And then I come downstairs the next morning, to find a huge cardboard box with my name on it just inside the threshold. I open it, and a chocolate-box calico kitten leaps into my lap and kneads it as if she's been there all her life.

Now the responsibility is halved reads the note attached to her collar.

I scoop her up and take her upstairs. I was right: I will die a lonely old spinster with fourteen cats. At least my mother will have the satisfaction of being proved right.

Four months ago I believed mistresses could be divided into two groups: those who, like me, had chosen their role deliberately, and delighted in the intoxication of forbidden sex; and naive victims – like Amy – hanging on in there, hoping for marriage.

It never occurred to me that the line between the two wasn't fixed.

The thrill of sneaking around to meet him has long since gone. *That* vanished one afternoon as we checked out of Claridge's, a giveaway two hours after checking in. As Nick paid the bill, I hung back, pretending to reapply my lipstick, feeling slightly self-conscious in my slinky dress and too-high heels. I waited until Nick had gone outside and hailed a cab, so that no one would see us emerge together. As I was about to leave, the concierge materialized at my elbow.

'Word to the wise: tell your clients not to use their credit cards in future, love,' he murmured. 'Too easy to trace.'

Nick has made a liar and a cheat out of me; he's turned me into a person I don't recognize, someone who can actually be mistaken for a freaking hooker.

And *still* I can't give him up.

'If it wasn't for your wife – if you weren't married – do you think we'd be together?' I ask him casually one day.

He hesitates. 'Yes, of course. But I *do* have a wife. And three children.'

So he *does* want to be with me. He must have considered the idea of leaving, then.

Which is only a small step from actually *doing* it, isn't it?

'I told you not to come,' Nick hisses.

'And I told you I was coming anyway,' I hiss back. 'So nice to meet you again, Mrs Lyon,' I say brightly, as she stops gossiping with Will Fisher's dowdy wife and catches up with us. 'I *love* your dress.'

She glances down doubtfully. 'You don't think it's a little, well, *orange*? I was in Rome a few weeks ago – the Italians wear colour wonderfully, don't you think, but then the light there is so *luminous* – of course I got it home here, not the same light at all. I feel rather like a giant nasturtium.' She smooths her palms nervously on her skirts. 'Rome is such a wonderful city, but don't *ever* go over Easter weekend; just heaving with tourists, I can't imagine what I was *thinking*.'

Ah, yes. My five-day romantic break, over before it began as I was about to jump into a taxi. *Alas, alack, the wife is back.*

'Nicholas gave me the necklace for my birthday last week. Venetian glass,' she adds dreamily, fingering the delicate blown beads at her neck. 'It's antique; very extravagant of him. I don't know what I did to deserve it, but I shall have to keep on doing it, evidently.'

I shoot Nick a vicious glance. He gave me an identical necklace as a kiss-and-make-up present after our last row. What was it, a job lot off the back of a gondola?

'I do *love* the Law Society dinner, every year, don't you?' his wife prattles. 'Such fun catching up with everybody. Oh, look, Nicholas, there's Will Fisher, talking to that pretty little thing in blue; what an amazing dress, positively gravity-defying, one wonders how it stays up. He really is *so* naughty, his poor wife. Come on, darling, we need to go and save him from himself before he actually climbs into the girl's cleavage. He could be lost for *weeks.*'

'If looks could kill,' Amy murmurs behind me as Nick's wife drags him away.

'Give me a break,' I say, reaching for a glass of champagne from a passing waiter.

'I don't know how you had the balls to come tonight,' she says, following suit. 'I've never even seen Terry's wife, never mind chatted to her over the canapés. Don't you feel weird talking to her?'

Weird doesn't begin to cover it. I'm so consumed with jealousy, it's like a vice around my chest. Bile, bitter and choking, rises in my throat, and I knock back my drink to wash it away. I should never have come. I knew it would be like this; and yet I couldn't keep away. Some insane impulse drags me back to this woman, whom I'm beginning to hate, again and again and again. Why? *Why* am I so obsessed with her? What is it that drives me to Google her name and order every one of her freakin' cookbooks? Or steal the picture of her from his wallet so I can brood over it at night, and wonder what the hell he sees in her? She's nothing to me. *Nothing.* A rock in the path between me and Nick.

I narrow my eyes, watching her.

'That dress is minging. *So* not her colour. And it makes her look even scrawnier than usual.'

'I'd kill for her figure, though,' Amy sighs.

'Look at her. Hanging on to Fisher like that, bending his ear, like he even cares what she thinks. It's not like she's one of us, is it? She's just a wife.'

Amy stares at me. 'You're getting very *hard* these days, Sara. You never used to be such a bitch. I know how you feel about Nick – no one knows better than me – but it's not her fault she married him first. Whatever happened to *poor thing, I feel sorry for her, she doesn't understand him*?'

I bite my lip. Amy's words are a little too close to the mark for comfort. She's right: I never used to be this way. I'm turning into a hateful, jealous cow. But this is war. I can't afford to feel sorry for Nick's wife now.

'She should make way for someone who *does* understand him,' I snap. 'Why is she hanging on to him like this, making them both miserable? Why can't she just accept that he's moved on and let him go?'

'Maybe she still loves him.'

'Well, he doesn't love *her*,' I say fiercely.

'Has he told you that?' Amy asks, surprised.

'Not in so many words. But he wouldn't be with me if he loved her, would he?'

'Welcome to the adultery club,' Amy says cynically, clinking my glass. 'To liars, cheats and bastards everywhere. Where would we be without them?'

A man coughs behind us. 'Excuse me? It's Miss Yorke, isn't it?' he asks Amy. 'Tom Stewart. I was opposing Counsel on the Brennan case a month or two ago.'

'Oh, yes,' she says, without much interest.

'I was wondering if I could have a quick word: it's about a feature they're running in the *Lawyer* next month on collaborative law—'

Collaborative law my arse. He fancies the pants off her, it's as clear as day. *And* he's single. I wander off to work the room, giving him a clear field. It's about time Amy had a decent, available man in her life.

'Well?' I demand when we nip to the toilet forty minutes later for a quick debrief before the formal dinner gets under way. 'Did he ask you out?'

'Yes. Invited me to a conference in Paris, actually.'

'Paris? What do you mean, *Paris*?'

'What do you think I mean? Paris, big city on the other side of the Channel, tall tower thing in the middle, men in stripy shirts riding around on bicycles with onions round their necks—'

'Ha bloody ha. What did you say?'

'No, of course.'

'Are you kidding me? What did you do *that* for? He's cute, successful, *single*—'

'I couldn't do that to Terry,' Amy says, shocked.

I want to hang my head against the mirror. 'Amy, you are so sad. *We* are so sad. Wasting our lives on lying, cheating married men, whilst the good, single guys are getting snapped up by girls with sense enough to know a keeper when they find one. What's *wrong* with us?'

'Terry's not like that—'

'Of course he bloody well is. They're *all* like that.' I switch off the hand-drier. 'I just don't understand why Nick doesn't *leave* her. You saw her; she's so *old*. She's got to be nearly forty, at least. What does he see in her, when he could be with me? It must be the children. It's got to be. I'm sure he'd leave her otherwise. He's practically said as much.'

Amy reapplies her lipstick carefully and presses her lips together to blend. 'I really think Terry *will* leave soon. He's promised, by the end of the summer—'

'Maybe I should give Nick an ultimatum,' I muse.

'You can't. Then he'll feel trapped, and he'll choose her because it's safer. You just have to wait until he's ready to make the move.'

'But for how long? We could carry on for *years* like this.' I sigh. 'I left a lipstick in his jacket pocket on purpose once. I thought it might, I don't know, speed things up a bit. She found it, but they're *still* together – he got out of it somehow.'

'She obviously doesn't know about you. Look how *nice* she was to you earlier—'

There's a sound from the disabled cubicle at the end. We both jump; neither of us realized anyone was in here. Shit, I hope whoever it was didn't hear any of that. The last thing I need is for it to get back to his wife, Nick'll go mad.

Then the ladies' door opens, and Emma sticks her head round the jamb. 'You'd better come,' she says, her voice brittle with fear. 'There's been an accident on the stairs. It's Mr Lyon.'

12

Malinche

Trace and I face each other from opposite sides of the ornately carved double bed. I'm not sure if my giddiness is from the delicious wine we consumed at dinner with our *polenta pasticciata con le acciughe* – I do *love* anchovies, though they are of course very much an acquired taste – or from something else entirely.

'Cora and Ben aren't coming, are they?' I say slowly.

He gives me a boyish, embarrassed smile, and shrugs.

'They were *never* coming, were they?'

'Tucked up in bed in Bath without a care in the world,' Trace admits unrepentantly.

I sink onto the damask bedspread. 'Oh, Trace. What were you *thinking*?'

'You know the answer to that,' he says urgently, moving around the bed. 'Come on, Mal. Don't tell me you don't feel it too? Every time I come within five feet of you, I'm twenty-two again. It's like I've got goldfish tap-dancing through my veins. Nothing's changed for me. Can you honestly look me in the eye and tell me you don't feel the same?'

I daren't look at him at all. I'm so afraid of myself right now, I scarcely dare breathe.

I think I knew we'd end up here from the moment Cora and Ben failed to turn up at the airport this morning – 'Crisis at the restaurant,' Trace said carelessly, 'they'll join us tomorrow' – and, recklessly, I decided to come anyway. Perhaps I even knew when he paid for my Max Mara frock; such an *intimate* thing to do, to buy a woman clothing – Robert Redford knew precisely what he was about when his indecent proposal started with the purchase of a cocktail dress. And then again, this afternoon on the Via Condotti, the exquisite burnt umber gown in the window of Armani: I only stopped to *look*, I'm a woman, it was reflexive; I certainly didn't mean for Trace to go in and *buy* it.

Afterwards we sat at a chrome bistro table in Piazza di Spagna, sharing a plate of delicious *antipasti vegetale* between us, the achingly expensive dress in its discreet cream cardboard bag sitting in state on a chair of its own.

'You'll have to take it straight back, of course,' I said, spearing a piece of *carciofi alla provenzale*. 'Oh, have you tried this?'

Trace opened the cardboard bag, took out the receipt for the dress and ripped it in two, and then four, the pieces fluttering onto the cobbles. 'Can't return it now. You'll just have to wear it and look stunning and think of me.'

'That,' I sighed, 'is precisely the problem.'

'I can't see why.'

I teased a sliver of prosciutto from its companions.

'Trace, you are so completely *impossible* sometimes. I'm married, I can't go around wearing clothes another man has bought me all the time. It's – it's—'

'Inappropriate? Unseemly? *Improper*?'

'Well,' I said, half-cross, half-amused, 'yes. Yes it is.'

'Christ,' Trace exclaimed, 'women. Why do you have to make everything so damn complicated? You see a dress you like, you can't afford to buy it – and Jesus, you actually *don't*; does Nicholas know how unique that makes you? – and so I buy it for you, because I want to and I can. Why can't it just be that simple?'

He raked his hand exasperatedly through his thick blue–black hair, his T-shirt rising with the movement of his arm and exposing several inches of firm, tanned stomach above the low-slung waistband of his threadbare jeans. Every female heart in the square simultaneously missed a beat; including mine.

The waiter exchanged our decimated platter of char-grilled aubergines, peppers and asparagus for a bowl of *fagiolini al parmigiano*. I heaped a scoop of the beans into my mouth – heaven! – and waited.

'It's like colours,' Trace said, jabbing at a *crocchette di cavolfiore* with his fork. 'Men only see in sixteen colours, like Windows default settings. Peach, for example, is a *fruit*, not a colour. Pistachio is a nut. Aubergine is a vegetable. We have *no* idea what mauve is.' He crunched a raw cauliflower floret and speared another. 'I swear, you all speak a different language. Never a straight bloody answer to anything. We'll ask you what's wrong, and you'll tell us nothing; so we will – forgive us for the absurdity – assume that nothing is wrong and thus ruin the entire evening for both of us.'

'Have you tried some of the heirloom tomatoes?' I asked mildly.

Trace was not to be deflected.

'Anything we said six months ago should be inadmissible in an argument. In fact, all comments should become null and void after seven days.'

'In that case, I'll wait a week and then return the dress,' I said firmly. 'Now, Trace. If you've finished. About Cora and Ben. What time did you—'

'When someone loves you,' Trace interrupted, dropping his fork abruptly and putting his finger across my lips, 'the way they say your name is different. Did you know that?'

And the careful, casual friendship we've both nurtured these last few months was blown wide open in an instant.

When you've loved each other as much as Trace and I have done, and when those feelings have been cut off in their prime and never given the chance to grow and change into a different sort of love, the softer, less *concentrated* kind of love you find in a marriage, moderated by time and familiarity; never given the chance, perhaps, to fade to white nothingness like a Polaroid photograph and gently disappear – when you have had that kind of love, can you can you ever go back and share something less?

After lunch, we strolled around the Eternal City as if we had nothing on our minds but touristy pleasure. We admired the pavement artists in Piazza Navona, threw coins into the Trevi Fountain, and gazed in awe at the marvels of the Forum. We ate hot chestnuts from a street stall and brought little leather handbags for the girls, we washed down our delicious dinner with cleansing grappa, and we talked about everything but the only thing we each could think about: *what happens next?*

The ornate carved bed creaks as I stand up. Automatically, I turn and smooth the wrinkles in the damask bedspread. Somehow, I have to find a safe path for us through this minefield of nostalgia and unfinished business. I have to keep my head, even though my toes are tingling and my stomach is fizzing with excitement: because of course new love is intoxicating, addictive, in fact; and that is where we are, the stage we're still at, the heat between us preserved all these years like a fly in amber. But it isn't *real*. I have to keep telling myself that. *None* of this is real. However vivid and dizzying it seems.

Trace forgets that we aren't irresponsible teenagers any more. Other people are affected by the decisions we take, and the mistakes we make. And so—

'Get up, you twit,' I scold, deliberately refusing to take him seriously. 'It's a bit late for bended knee.'

His expression darkens. 'Would it have made a difference? If I'd asked you to marry me before you – *before*?'

'No, Trace,' I say softly, 'it was never about that.'

He gets to his feet, and throws wide the doors to the roof garden. I follow him out onto the terrazzo. We stand side by side without touching, gazing over the starlit roofs of Rome, breathing in air that smells so very different from the air back home: city air, yes, but with rich, deep low notes of roast chestnuts and spicy lemon, mimosa, bougainvillea and heady, feminine perfumes. Easy to get intoxicated on a midnight terrace in a foreign country with a man who, still, has the capacity to make your soul sing.

'You've put me in an impossible position, you know,' I say quietly. 'I can't stay here in Rome alone with you. Much less in the same room.'

'You could.'

I sigh deeply. 'Yes. I *could*. But we both know it would be a terrible mistake. What happened thirteen years ago – it's in the past, Trace. We can't go back. Too many people would be hurt; people I care about very much. You can't build happiness on someone else's misery.'

Furiously, he swings round to face me. 'What about me? What about *my* misery?' he says fiercely. 'Tell me you don't still love me, and I'll never mention it again. I'll be the dearest, most respectful friend a very proper married woman could ever have. Just tell me, Malinche, and I swear, I'll never ask you for anything again.'

'I love Nicholas,' I say steadily.

'More than me?'

He really is *so* beautiful. Tall, lean, just the right side of louche with his bare feet and faded jeans and layered T-shirts – really, he should be whizzing down a snowpipe in Colorado – and that black, black hair sweeping back from his forehead in a startling widow's peak; and then of course those extraordinary hazelnut-whirl eyes, fringed with lashes that no man has a right to. It's about symmetry, isn't it, beauty: our unconscious mind busy again, matching, measuring, weighing up, looking for patterns and points of reference. In a chiselled jaw or the curve of a cheekbone; or a relationship between two people who once believed themselves destined for each other.

'I love Nicholas,' I whisper.

He steps closer, so that we are drinking in each other's breath.

'Then why the tears?' he says softly.

Our gaze snags and hangs in the air, a dewdrop on a blade of grass. The smell of him – cedar, spiced rum and clean sheets – drifts over me like woodsmoke from an autumn bonfire.

I shiver, and the next moment Trace has caught my head with both of his hands and bent his lips to mine. His kiss is so familiar, and yet so *other*. He tastes cool and minty and smoky and honey-sweet. His stubble grazes my chin; I feel the rough calluses of his thumbs against my cheeks. My arm snakes around his back and tangles in his hair and as he scoops me up and carries me back into the bedroom without breaking our kiss, a kiss that speaks roughly to every cell in my body, as he lays me gently on that damask bedspread and starts to unbutton my dress, it's as if the long years without him have been the betrayal, and this, *this* is where I'm meant to be.

Of course I can't stay in Rome *now*. I call Nicholas and explain that we have, Trace and I, foolishly failed to take into account the fact that it's Easter, and this very Catholic country has effectively closed down; apart, of course, from those bits of it making huge sums of money fleecing the hordes of devout tourists. I tell him I will be returning home that afternoon; which Nicholas seems to accept without demur, without any real expression of his opinion at all, in fact, something I would find very perplexing were I not so caught up in this hideous, *hideous* guilt.

Which is only exacerbated when Nicholas then organizes, for the first time in our married life, a birthday party for me the following week; and even includes Kit, which must have pained him.

Grown-up birthdays have never been very big in our house; not for want of trying on my part. Nicholas belongs to the half of the population (generally male) who thinks they're a big fuss about nothing. Which is rather a disappointment to the other half (generally female) who thinks fax machines and new vacuum cleaners are *not* the way to celebrate being another step closer to forty.

As we all sit down to dinner, which he has, astonishingly, refused to let me cook, he hands me a long, thin, scuffed cardboard box.

'Oh, Nicholas!' I exclaim, as I draw out the string of exquisite hand-blown Venetian glass beads. 'It's the loveliest thing you've ever given me!'

He fastens them about my neck, dropping a light kiss on my cheek. I certainly can't complain about his attentiveness. I don't think I've felt so cherished since our honeymoon.

Which only makes me feel so much worse.

'Come on, Evie,' I whisper, as Nicholas moves to the sideboard to carve. 'It's your turn to say Grace.'

'I don't know what to say,' Evie hisses back.

'Duh!' Sophie says scornfully. 'It's only the same every Sunday!'

'Just say what I always do, sweetheart,' I encourage.

Evie respectfully bows her head. 'God,' she intones gravely, 'why on earth did I invite all these bloody people to dinner?'

'It wasn't funny,' I say to Kit later as he helps me wash up, whilst Nicholas drives his parents to the station to catch their train back to Esher. 'I know you and Louise think it's hysterical, but Nicholas's parents probably won't accept an invitation here for the next five years.'

'I would imagine—'

'*Sssh!* Little pitchers, Kit.'

Sophie lolls against the kitchen island, ears waggling avidly. Kit is always so wildly indiscreet; I dread to think what outrageous gossip they pick up when he's around.

'Mummy?' she asks. 'When's the right time to get married?'

I'm grateful for the change of subject. I dunk a copper saucier into the sudsy water.

'I don't know, darling. Why?'

'Evie says she's *never* going to get married. She says you have to kiss boys if you get married. Mummy, when is it OK to kiss someone?'

When your husband isn't looking.

'When they're rich and handsome as sin,' Kit quips, watching me carefully.

'Kit! You have to date someone a bit first, Sophie darling,' I explain, elbowing him in the ribs. 'Dates are for having fun, and people use them to get to know each other.'

'On the first date, you tell each other lies, and that usually gets people int'rested enough to come back for a second date,' Evie opines. 'Even boys have something int'restin' to say if you listen long enough.'

I try not to laugh. 'Not *lies*, exactly, Evie—'

'Daddy wishes he wasn't married,' Sophie says casually, running her finger around the birthday-cake plate to scoop up the last of the icing. 'I heard him on the phone yesterday; he said everything would be different if he wasn't already married.'

My chest tightens. Nicholas was no doubt talking to Giles, all boys together, moaning about the wife, that kind of thing. But for no reason that I can think of an image of the gold lipstick I found in Nicholas's pocket a month ago swims into my mind. He found it in the corridor at work, he told me so. And *of course* I believe him. That horrible feeling in the pit of my stomach is *my* guilt, not his.

'I can't see *why* you feel guilty,' Kit complains, after I've shooed the girls upstairs to bed and we stand on the kitchen doorstep enjoying a furtive smoke. 'It's not like you did anything to feel guilty about.'

'Kit! I kissed another man! And what's worse, I enjoyed it – very much, if you want to know the truth.'

'Darling girl, if that was the criterion for adultery, there'd be very few people left married at all. Temptation isn't a crime.' Thoughtfully, he watches me stub out my cigarette and carefully wrap the butt in a piece of kitchen foil. 'You sweet romantic child, did you really think you could sail through to your golden wedding anniversary without the odd little slip now and again?'

'I'm sure Nicholas hasn't slipped,' I say miserably.

'Dear one,' Kit chides, 'you didn't go to bed with the man, you silly girl: which if you ask me is where the real crime lies, but that's a different matter. In the end you Just Said No, like the good little girl you are, and ran back home to mother, no harm done. Although if you're going to cut up this rough about it, you might as well have thrown caution to the winds and bonked him silly.'

'I very nearly did,' I admit. 'Oh, Kit, you can't *imagine* how much I wanted to—'

'You'd be surprised.' Kit sighs.

'We were kissing and kissing and it was *wonderful*, and then at the last minute he stopped and said, "Are you sure?" and of course I wasn't, and he was very sweet about it, said of course he understood, it didn't matter at all, he didn't want to rush me into anything I didn't really truly want—'

Kit exhales. 'Oh, he's good.'

'He *was*,' I say, deliberately misunderstanding. 'He was very good. He slept on the sofa – it was too late to book another room – you should have seen him, his feet hanging off the end. And then he very kindly ran me to the airport in the morning and – and—'

Suddenly it's all too much. I flee inside and crumple on the kitchen sofa, wailing like a child.

Kit sinks down next to me and gently rubs my back. 'Sweet girl, don't cry. Not on your birthday. Nothing happened, it was just a silly little kiss, everything's going to be absolutely fine—'

I raise my head. 'But I *wanted* to sleep with him, Kit, don't you see? It doesn't actually matter if I *did* it or not. I wanted to go to bed with Trace, which is just as bad as if I'd gone ahead and done it. It's *worse* than if we'd had meaningless sex and forgotten about it in the morning. That would've just been physical, but I've betrayed Nicholas emotionally. I've got involved with another man: to all intents and purposes I've committed adultery. Whether we got our kit off doesn't really matter.'

'Bullshit,' Kit says succinctly. 'If you really believe that's true, why *didn't* you sleep with him in Rome?'

I hesitate, sniffing noisily. Kit hands me a tissue.

'You don't jail people because they *think* about robbing a bank. This kind of self-flagellating nonsense is what keeps the bloody Church in business. You *didn't* fuck him. You thought about it, you kissed him, and then you backed off.'

'But—'

'Malinche, get over it already. Worse things happen at sea. Just try not to call your husband Trace in bed; he might not be quite as understanding as you were—'

We both startle as Nicholas lets himself in through the kitchen door.

'Well, I think I got them to see the funny side by the time we reached the railway station,' he says, shrugging off his jacket. 'I'm not sure my mother's entirely forgiven us, but if we promise to—' He stops, one arm still caught in his sleeve, as he sees my reddened, blotchy face. 'Malinche? What's the matter? Has something happened?'

'Bit of a ding-dong with Louise,' Kit says cheerfully. 'I'm sure it'll all blow over by the morning.'

Nicholas frowns. 'Things seemed fine when I left.'

I feel absolutely wretched. *Oh, what a tangled web we weave!* I hate deceiving him; and yet the lies keep growing, spiralling out of control, each one sprouting two more like some mythical Greek monster.

'Mal?'

'It's nothing,' I mumble. 'Like Kit said. It'll all blow over in the morning.'

'I hope so,' Nicholas says, hanging up his coat. 'It's the Law Society dinner next week, and Louise said she'd babysit for us since Kit's in New York. It'd be a nuisance if you couldn't come, Will Fisher asked for you especially.

And with this mess over buying out his partnership, I do really rather need you to be there.'

'You are one of the few women I trust within a ten-foot radius of my husband,' Meg Fisher tells me sadly. 'Look at him. Bee to a blasted honeypot.'

We both watch Will all but disappear into the cleavage of a rather flashy young girl in a plunging blue dress. My heart goes out to Meg. Does Will have no shame, that he treats his loyal wife of twenty-five years like this in front of everyone? And yet, in every other respect, he's a very likeable man.

'He doesn't mean anything by it,' I say kindly.

Meg sighs. 'You're so lucky with Nicholas.'

I glance at my husband, talking shop with Sara. I know Nicholas wants to buttonhole Will this evening, to get to the bottom of this problem over his partnership share; now would be the perfect time to distract the old rogue from his shapely companion.

'*So* nice to meet you again, Mrs Lyon,' Sara says brightly as I join them. 'I *love* your dress.'

Heat rises in my cheeks. Kit said it was silly to refuse to wear the dress just because Trace had bought it when it's so perfect for me; but I feel as if I have a huge red 'A' for Adultery painted on my frock.

'You don't think it's a little, well, *orange*?' I say, flustered. 'I was in Rome a few weeks ago – the Italians wear colour wonderfully, don't you think, but then the light there is so *luminous* – of course I got it home here, not the same light at all.' I tweak my skirts. 'I feel rather like a giant nasturtium. Rome is such a wonderful city, but don't *ever* go over Easter weekend, just heaving with tourists, I can't imagine what I was *thinking*.'

It's quite clear from her bemused expression what *she* is thinking, and I can't blame her. I have verbal diarrhoea. Even Nicholas is looking at me strangely.

'Nicholas gave me the necklace for my birthday last week,' I add, a little desperate to get off the topic of Trace's dress. 'Venetian glass. It's antique; very extravagant of him. I don't know what I did to deserve it, but I shall have to keep on doing it, evidently.'

Oh dear. Too much information. Nicholas hates me to talk about anything personal, and Sara seems equally embarrassed by my domestic prattle.

Suddenly I feel acutely uncomfortable, as if I've walked into the wrong classroom. I've accompanied Nicholas to these dinners for years, I know almost everyone here. And yet unexpectedly I feel like a fish out of water, as if I don't belong any more, and the sensation is unnerving.

I chatter to fill the silence.

'I do *love* the Law Society dinner, every year, don't you? Such fun catching up with everybody. Oh, look, Nicholas, there's Will Fisher, talking to that pretty little thing in blue; what an amazing dress, positively gravity-defying, one wonders how it stays up. He really is *so* naughty, his poor wife.' I slip my arm through his, pretending not to notice him stiffen. 'Come on, darling, we need to go and save him from himself before he actually climbs into the girl's cleavage. He could be lost for *weeks*.'

Will Fisher obligingly desists from pawing the young lady chatting to him, and tries instead to work out if he can actually see a nipple through the flimsy silk of my dress.

His plump hand rests on my bottom as Nicholas talks to him about the partnership, and I resist the urge to tweak his willy to even things up a bit.

I already know from Meg that Will has no plans to come back out of retirement, as Nicholas fears; the only reason he hasn't signed over his share of the firm before now is because he can't quite bear to give up his chance to attend dinners like these. If the partners offer him a sinecure of some sort within the firm that keeps the social door propped open, he'll hand over the shares without a murmur.

'Thank Christ for that,' Nicholas says fervently, when I explain this to him later, 'I thought the old bugger was going to keep a grip on our balls forever.'

'He just doesn't want to be shut out of the sand-pit, darling,' I say. 'If you talk to David and Joan I'm quite sure – oh, blast. I *hate* strapless bras. Nicholas, I'm just nipping to the Ladies to do a quick bit of repair work before my bosoms fall out, or Will Fisher will have a field day.'

'Well, hurry up. They'll be calling us in to dinner in a minute.'

I bolt to the toilets. The ordinary cubicles are too cramped for me to take off my dress and put my bra on properly, so I slip into the disabled cubicle at the end – are we allowed to say disabled these days? Isn't it supposed to be ambulatorily challenged, or something? – and cross my fingers that no one in a wheelchair comes in during the next five minutes.

I'm twisted like a pretzel trying to hook up my bra when two girls enter the toilets, chattering nineteen to the dozen. At first, I can't hear what they're saying through the noise of running water and the whirr of the hand-drier. Then suddenly the drier stops, and I recognize Sara's voice.

And she's talking about my husband.

Nicholas's accident saves our marriage; for the time being. Even as I'm struggling to digest the conversation I have just overheard – *I don't understand why Nick just doesn't leave her* – the news that my husband is hurt instantly overrides everything else.

I scrabble stupidly with the lock on the cubicle door – *What does he see in her, when he could be with me? It must be the children* – and run out of the ladies', moments behind Sara and her friend. A thousand images race through my mind: Nicholas crushed beneath an ornate chandelier; Nicholas crumpled on the floor, clutching his heart; Nicholas choking on a canapé.

Nicholas kissing Sara on her full lips, his long legs entwined with her brown ones, his hand on her breast, his penis buried inside her.

A small crowd has gathered at the head of the marble staircase. Nicholas – *I'm sure he'd leave her otherwise. He's practically said as much* – is being carried up it by two burly rugger-buggers in dinner jackets who have made a seat for him from their mammoth forearms. He looks pale but is already laughing ruefully at his plight.

My heart slows a little. He's all right then. Not dead. Not mortally injured.

'Sprained an ankle, that's all,' one of the men says, as they carefully put Nicholas down on a gilt chair someone has whisked from the dining room. 'Missed his footing on the stairs. Going to hurt like hell in a bit, but it looks worse than it is.'

'Hurting already, if you must know,' Nicholas manages.

'What was it then?' someone asks. 'Banana skin? Cleaner left her mop out?'

A ripple of amused laughter. 'Picked a good night to get themselves sued, didn't they? The bloody Law Society dinner!'

'Need someone to call you a cab, old man?' Will Fisher asks.

'I'm not leaving now,' Nicholas says, uncharacteristically jovial. 'Takes more than a sprained ankle to keep a good lawyer down. Just make sure the port gets passed my way first, that's all I ask!'

The two men pick Nicholas up again, gilt chair and all, and carry him into the main stateroom, and it looks for all the world as if he's being hoisted up on their shoulders, the wounded hero held aloft by his loyal team mates, the man of the hour, as they laugh and josh and banter their way in to dinner.

Kit was right. *Wanting* to go to bed with someone and actually *doing* it are very different things. I see that now.

Somehow I stay serene through dinner. I talk to the man on my left for the first course, the man on my right for the second. I acknowledge compliments passed Nicholas's way through me, and pay a few in return. I join in the laughter and general *bonhomie* as Nicholas is carried back downstairs like a Little Emperor and put carefully into a cab, and even though I have to curl my fingers into my palms until they bleed tiny little half-moons, I don't throw myself at Sara and scratch her silver cat's eyes out as she leans into our taxi and solicitously wishes him well, much as I want to.

The moment for confrontation with Nicholas passed with the words *'There's been an accident,'* and even though his injury turned out to be nothing, far less than he deserved, in fact, it created a diversion, just long enough for my mind to clear. And so I say nothing to my adulterous husband: because I have yet to work out what, if anything, I want to say.

I'm in shock, I know that. I am sure the pain and grief and anger will come flooding soon; but in the meantime I am like a man who has lost a limb, foolishly staring at the bloody stump, unable to feel it even though he knows it must hurt like nothing he has ever known.

Nicholas doesn't notice my quiet mood on the train home. Why would he? His mind is filled with images of his lush young mistress, her gym-honed body unmarred by bearing his children, her strong shoulders unburdened by the responsibilities of wifedom and motherhood.

And I was nice to her, I tried to put her at her ease. How could she look me in the eye and make polite small talk when all the time—

Silently I help Nicholas hobble into the house; though away from his friends and colleagues, it appears he can actually manage rather well without me, limping up the garden path with surprising energy. We don't speak as we undress on opposite sides of our double bed, and I am saved the dilemma of whether to avoid his goodnight kiss by the fact that he doesn't bother to give me one. Now that I think about it, he hasn't kissed me goodnight for quite some time, a habit that *had* carried through a decade of marriage; shame on me, for not noticing before. Was that when the affair started: when those goodnight kisses stopped?

Nicholas rolls onto his side, his back towards me, his bad ankle propped on my spare pillow, and within moments he is asleep. Whilst I lay wide awake, eyes staring into the greyness, spooling back every moment of our ten years together, sifting for signs of his affair. I sort the good memories from the bad, the pros from the cons. The look in his eyes as Sophie was handed into his arms, still slick with vernix and blood. The camping trip in Oxfordshire five years ago, when a swan chased us all, screaming with laughter, into the river. The strength of his grip around my shoulders when we waited for Evie to be tested for meningitis a week before her second birthday. The twenty-five-year-old he has bedded and to whom he has made Lord-knows-what snake-in-the-grass promises, before coming back home to me.

I wish I knew when it started. Which is our last true memory, before the lies began. If there have been other affairs, before her. If he still loves me.

If he is planning to stay.

As dawn steals into our bedroom, I have two unequal heaps of memories before me: reasons to stay with Nicholas and reasons to leave.

And the second pile is dwarfed by the first because it contains the one immutable fact that overshadows and overrides everything else: despite everything, I still love him.

*

The days bleed into each other, long and sluggish. At night I go to bed exhausted, reading for a short while before falling into a heavy slumber or tossing restlessly half the night and waking too early. And still I say nothing.

The blessed numbness doesn't last. When the pain comes, it is so lacerating I want to eat my own soul. I feel hugely, blindingly angry. At both Nicholas, for being so spineless and weak and *just like a man*; and at myself, for having allowed this to happen.

How could I have not seen it coming? Everyone says the wife is always the last to know, but even still. I've been such a fool. The wretched lipstick, for example. If Nicholas had erected a neon billboard in the back garden which proclaimed *I'm Having an Affair*, it couldn't have been more obvious.

And Valentine's Day. How they must have laughed at me in bed together later, the poor silly wife believing their stories of 'coincidences' and 'who would have guessed!' Blind to their lies, because she didn't want to see—

Oh, God. The beautiful sexy underwear from La Perla, and the earrings for pierced ears. They were never for me at all.

I sob as I force them down the waste disposal, first the fragile wisps of lace and silk, then the delicate silver earrings. They rattle like a trapped teaspoon and I cover my ears. Why was I so determined to believe in him? The signs were all there—

But of course I've been here before, haven't I? When the signs have all been there.

I can't cope with seeing Trace when I'm this vulnerable, so I fib that the girls are ill, I tell him that I can't possibly consider working just yet. A part of me yearns to run to him and cry on his shoulder, but I daren't. I only held out against him last time by the skin of my teeth. And two wrongs don't make a right. They don't.

I can't tell Kit what's happened when he gets back from New York either, because he would refuse to sit idly by; and I know that sitting idly by is exactly what I have to do.

Nicholas is the divorce lawyer. He has rinsed a thousand broken marriages off and sifted through the shards, to salvage what's left. If anyone is qualified to talk about the implosion of a family, it is he. And so I take his advice; though surely he never meant it to be applied to *our* marriage.

'The mistake women always make,' he said once, holding court at a smart dinner party, 'is to *over-react*. Most husbands don't dream of leaving their wives until push becomes shove. Half the allure of a mistress is that she's a fantasy. He doesn't want her to become his wife. Confronting him,' he added, examining his port against the light, 'is the worst thing she can do – always assuming she wants to keep him, of course.'

And even though I could cheerfully castrate my husband with a pair of blunt paper scissors – I can scarcely bear to even *look* at him right now – I want to keep him.

I married him and created this family with him. He isn't perfect; he isn't necessarily the man I could have loved most in this world. Not necessarily my soul mate. But he is my husband, and I believe passionately that my children need to grow up with their father. I didn't throw away everything even for Trace; I am certainly not going to now because some silly girl has taken a fancy to Nicholas.

The irony is that to fight for him effectively I must do nothing.

'Not weak at all, actually, Malinche,' Louise says, when she catches me crying over an M & S lasagne one afternoon. ('*Frozen* dinners?' she said as she walked unannounced into the kitchen, 'either the apocalypse is upon us or one of you is having an affair, so which is it?')

'You don't think I should leave him, then?'

'I didn't say that,' Louise says, 'though I've never been of the opinion that an affair has to wreck a marriage. Sex is just *sex*, after all, especially for a man. I simply said it wasn't weak to stay. Sticking it out like this takes a huge amount of strength and courage. Although,' she looks at me closely, 'there's a price to pay. When was the last time you slept through the night? You're looking very pale, Malinche, and I don't mean that as a compliment.'

'To be honest, I can't quite see how I could take it as one.'

'Have you considered talking to the girl?'

I gape.

'I couldn't! What on earth would I *say*?'

'I would have thought that was obvious,' Louise raps back smartly. 'You tell her you haven't quite finished with your husband yet, and if she doesn't mind, you'd like him back.'

'Louise, he's not a ball the children have kicked into next door's garden by mistake! Apart from anything else, if I go and speak to her, she'll tell Nicholas the cat's out of the bag, and then there's no going back. The last thing I want to do is to force his hand.'

'He might choose *you*,' she observes. 'Most men are cowards, when it comes down to it.'

'But what if he doesn't?' I cry out in anguish. 'What if he's fallen in love with her? What if he can't decide what to do? Louise, what if he chooses *her*?'

I know I'm right. I daren't take the risk. I have to wait and hope it burns itself out, no matter how much it hurts. And oh, God, it hurts. It's the hardest thing I've ever done. Every time he works late, I know he's with *her*. Every call he takes in his study, carefully shutting the door behind him, is from *her*.

I spend my days wishing for the nights to come so that I can take off my brave face; and the nights of haunted wakefulness longing for daybreak and the release it will give.

The children are what keep me sane; I do my best to carry on as normal, but it's so difficult. My temper is short, and my patience shorter. Little things that I would ordinarily take in my stride – Evie forgetting to water the herbs on the windowsill, or Sophie taking it upon herself to iron her new school shirt and burning it – floor me completely. I snap at them over nothing, and then I have maternal guilt to add to my many shortcomings.

One afternoon, when we have got home from school, Metheny backs into the Aga door just as I'm taking out a casserole dish, and our dinner ends up all over my feet and the kitchen floor.

I make sure Metheny is unhurt, and then scream at her as I kick off my ruined shoes, reducing her to hiccoughing tears. Evie and Sophie come running into the kitchen, straight into the congealing pool of Lancashire hotpot. When I shriek at them to move, they run back into the sitting room, leaving two pairs of little gravy footprints on the expensive wool carpet behind them.

I collapse onto a chair, and bury my face in my hands, sobbing uncontrollably. Louise was right. I can't keep doing this. It's killing me.

When the phone goes, I ignore it. It rings out a dozen times, stops for thirty seconds, and then rings again.

Wearily – *duty calls* – I finally get up and answer it.

It is the casualty department of a hospital in Esher. Edward Lyon has had a massive stroke, and at eighty-three, the prognosis isn't good. His wife is by his bedside, but of course his son needs to get there as soon as he can. The nurse is too tactful to add, *before it's too late*, but she doesn't need to.

Poor Daisy. Poor, *poor* Daisy. How will she possibly cope without Edward? Forty-seven years together. A lifetime.

I call Nicholas at work, but it's after five on a Friday night and the office answerphone kicks in; everyone must already have left for the night. I try his mobile; it goes straight to voicemail. I wait ten frantic minutes, get his voicemail again, and then call Liz.

As soon as she arrives to collect the children and take them to hers for the night, I grab a pair of shoes from the scullery and drive hell-for-leather to the station. I can't punish Nicholas by letting him miss the chance to say goodbye to his father. No matter how much I'm hurting, he doesn't deserve that.

It's seven-forty by the time my cab pulls up outside

her flat. I hand the driver twenty pounds and ask him to wait.

The door to her building hasn't properly closed; I'm able to go straight up to her flat on the first floor. She answers my knock still knotting the belt of her cheap red kimono, and I take advantage of her absolute shock to walk briskly past her towards my husband, who is sitting, naked from the waist up, on the edge of her large unmade bed. If this weren't all so awfully, horribly serious, the dumbstruck expression on his face would make me laugh. The air smells of sex and smoke, and I realize I have never wanted a cigarette as much in my life as I do now.

'It's your father,' I tell Nicholas clearly, 'he's had a massive stroke. There's a taxi waiting outside to take you straight to the hospital. Please tell Daisy I'll come whenever she needs me. And Nicholas,' the blood is pounding in my ears, but I know exactly what I have to say, 'there's a holdall with your things in it on the back seat. If you need anything else, we can arrange it at the weekend. I don't plan to say anything to the children just yet. One thing at a time.'

I walk unsteadily back into the sitting room. And, when the vomit rises in my throat, I don't seek out the bathroom but, in a small but intensely satisfying act of revenge, allow myself to be violently sick all over his mistress's beautiful, expensive white sofa.

13

Nicholas

I open the fridge door and am confronted by precisely the same rotting fare as when I quit the flat this morning. 'Jesus Christ, Sara! I thought you were going shopping!'

'I was in Court all day, I told you that. When was I supposed to have time?'

I remove two putrescent tomatoes and something that may once have been a block of cheese but which is now a homage to Alexander Fleming, and cast wildly about for the dustbin. Of course this is pointless, since Sara uses supermarket plastic bags hung on the knob of the cupboard nearest the door in lieu of the traditional rubbish receptacle, a dustbin; a practice rendered even more irksome when the bags leak, as they frequently do, all over the floor. Only this morning I found myself standing in a puddle of last night's Chinese takeaway as I spooned fresh coffee into the percolator.

Rotten tomato is oozing through my fingers by the time I locate the bag and dispose of them. I swear under my breath as I rinse my hands in the sink. Dear God, I haven't lived like this since I was an impoverished student at Oxford.

Sara skulks into the galley kitchen. 'You didn't have to throw out the cheese, Nick! I could've scraped the mould off.'

'And poisoned us both.'

'Cheese is milk gone mouldy, everyone knows that. It doesn't go off.'

'Fine.' I fling open cupboard doors. 'I gave you two hundred pounds on Tuesday to go to Waitrose, and the only thing in the damn larder is a bottle of Tabasco and four tins of fucking anchovies. What the hell happened?'

'I spent it,' she mutters.

'On what? Bloody truffles?'

'I left my credit card at home, and I saw these shoes. I was going to pay you back,' she adds defensively as I storm into the sitting room, nearly tripping over the wretched cat. I wish I hadn't bought her the animal, this entire apartment stinks of piss. She picks up the kitten and follows me. 'I just haven't been to the cash-point yet.'

'It's not the damn money, Sara. It just would've been nice to come back and find something to eat—'

'I'm not your freakin' servant,' Sara spits.

'Sara, I've just buried my father!'

Startled, the cat springs out of her arms. Sara deflates like a pricked balloon, and I'm reminded, yet again, how *very* young she is.

Moving in with her was a mistake. I knew it even as I unpacked the holdall of clothes Mal had left in the taxi for me – each of my shirts carefully folded so as not to crease

– and crammed them into Sara's overstuffed wardrobe on cheap wire coat-hangers. I had nowhere else to go, other than a hotel; but in the end, practicalities were the least of it. It was the desperate need to salvage *something* from this whole sorry débâcle that made me agree to Sara's feverish suggestion. For the misery and grief I have caused to have been for a reason.

If we work at it, it's bound to get better. It's just a question of adjusting.

'I thought there'd be something to eat,' she mumbles now, eyes on the ground, 'at the wake. I assumed you'd just come home and we'd – you know.'

'We'd *what*?'

She grinds her toe into the carpet like a small, embarrassed child. 'In the midst of life we are in death, and all that. Amy said when people die, you want to celebrate life. Oh, come on, Nick, do I have to spell it out?'

I suddenly notice that she's wearing a very brief pleated grey skirt and has her hair in short schoolgirl bunches. Even as I sigh inwardly at her naivety, my cock springs to life.

'Man cannot live on sex alone. Although,' I add, 'I appreciate the thought.'

She drops to her knees in front of me, unzips my trousers and releases my semi-erect cock from my boxer shorts. Through the uncurtained window behind her, I can see straight into a block of flats opposite. I watch a fat woman struggle out of a green wool jacket. She glances up as she hangs it on the back of the door, and I realize that if I can see her, the reverse must also hold true. She's too far away for me to see her expression, but the way she snaps her curtains shut speaks volumes.

I'm not really in the mood; but the thought of being watched as Sara kneels and sucks my hardening dick is an unexpected aphrodisiac.

In fact, I realize, I'm about to come: too soon. I grab her shoulders and pull her upright, then shunt her up onto to the breakfast bar. She pulls her white blouse over her head without troubling to undo the buttons, and I scoop her breasts from the lacy bra and clamp my mouth around a cherry-red nipple. She groans and buries her hands beneath my shirt. I bite and nip, not troubling to be careful. Her fingernails scrape and claw at my back. I bunch her skirt up around her waist, pulling off her panties and thrusting my fingers forcefully inside her. She's slick and wet, and I lick my fingertips afterwards. Her eyes half-close as she leans back on her elbows, opening her pussy to me.

I taste her, relishing the musky sweetness. And then I lift her off the counter, push her forwards over the uncomfortable white sofa, and plunge my dick into her backside.

She gasps in shock, but after a moment's hesitation, starts to grind her hips in time with mine. As her movements get more frantic, I thrust faster, reaching around to knead her breasts, trapping her nipples – none too gently – between thumb and forefingers.

I come in an explosion. As I slump over her sweat-slicked back, I glance up through the window again. The fat woman is staring right back at me.

'Fuck,' Sara pants, twisting round. 'Can we finish up in the bedroom? This sofa still *stinks* of puke.'

*

It took my father three weeks to die. He survived the initial massive stroke, only to succumb to an infection originating at the site of his IV line. The cause of death, according to the sombre grey certificate with which I was presented upon registering his passing: septicaemia leading to multiple organ failure.

I don't know if I could be said to have got there *in time*. He was still, technically, alive when I arrived post-haste from London, so consumed with fear that I was able, briefly, to banish the excoriating circumstances of my summons in some uncharted corner of my mind to deal with later. But he was already unconscious by the time I reached his bedside, and so we never had a chance to exchange a last word, a final farewell. I was left to sit helplessly beside the husk of the man who had once been my father, stroking his hand – occasionally his cheek – and trying to talk to him as if I really believed he could still hear me.

Since we are being technical, Edward Lyon wasn't actually my father at all, but my father's elder brother. My biological parents achieved the unusual distinction of being killed in the same car crash in two separate cars.

Andrew Lyon had been having an affair with his dental nurse. My mother, upon discovering this – quite how never became clear – confronted him and a domestic fracas naturally ensued. She fled in her car; he pursued her in his. It was subsequently impossible to establish which of them lost control on a sharp bend first, and which smashed into the other's wreckage. Very little survived the fireball, and of course forensic science in the Sixties was not what it is now.

Edward and his wife Daisy took me in. I was six months old; they have always been my parents in every sense that matters.

I have often wondered what kind of man could embark upon an affair when his wife had just presented him with their first child. Now, perhaps, I know.

Bad blood. Is there a gene for infidelity, I wonder, like those for baldness or big feet? All my life, I have tried to atone for the sins of my biological father. Made a career out of picking up the pieces of adultery, in fact. Hubristically, I believed that of all the men I knew, I was without doubt the least likely to have an affair.

This afternoon I stood at my father's graveside, my arm around my mother, and watched my wife, her face undone by tears. Of course I grieve for my father, his death has left a void in my life that nothing can fill; but there is a point every adult child reaches when they unconsciously begin to prepare for their parents' deaths. You ache for your loss, but it is the natural order of things. Nature renders us heartlessly resilient when necessary.

Losing the woman you love through your own stupidity, weakness and mendacity is another matter. *Stultum est queri de adversis, ubi culpa est tua*: stupid to complain about misfortune that is your own fault. Nature erects no self-protecting carapace for such preventable misery. Nor should she; I deserve the obloquy now being heaped upon me from all quarters.

Except, astonishingly, from Malinche.

'This isn't what I wanted,' she said quietly, stopping beside me as I handed my mother into the waiting funeral car. 'I wanted to wait you out. I did *try*.'

A sea of mourners washed past on either side of the

car, newly turned earth sticking like coffee grounds to their stiff black shoes. Muted snatches of consolation – '*So sorry, Nicholas*' – eddied around us. April seems such an inappropriate month in which to bury someone, with its pledge of life. I wanted bare branches scraping at leaden grey skies, not this green-bladed promise and birdsong.

'How long have you known?'

'Since the Law Society dinner.'

'How did you—'

'Nicholas,' she whispered.

I looked away. On the gravel path behind us, a knot of black-clad mourners stopped to chat; a rising laugh was hastily smothered with a quick, abashed glance in our direction. We can only do grief and pain for so long, before life surges back out of us, bidden or not.

I took a deep breath. 'Malinche, is there any chance I could come—'

'No, Nicholas. I'm sorry.'

Inside the car, my mother glanced fleetingly at us, and then looked away.

'I know how this must sound: but it didn't mean anything. Please—'

'Of course it *meant* something,' she said sharply, 'to me, if not to you! You aren't the only one affected by this. It's not up to you to decide if it meant something or not.'

'I realize you're angry now, but—'

'Angry doesn't begin to cover it.'

'You can't mean to go through with this. Separation. A divorce. Surely?'

She stepped backwards slightly, as if I had just dealt her a physical blow. 'What else did you expect, Nicholas?'

'Can't we at least *talk*?' I said desperately. 'What about the children? Did you think about what this will—'

'Did *you*?'

In the distance, two men in blue overalls walked towards my father's grave, chatting, clods of dry earth falling from the shovels over their shoulders.

Mal watched me watch them and sighed. 'Nicholas, now isn't the time. I've told the children you're looking after Grandma at the moment. When the time is right, we can tell them that you – that we—'

'Can I see them?'

'Of course you can see them!' She touched my arm, briefly. Her face softened. 'I would have brought them to see you before, but you were always either working or at the hospital. It didn't seem right to involve them in all of that.'

I should have established a pattern of access immediately. Set a precedent, worked out ground rules for visitation. How many times have I rebuked a client for failing precisely in this regard, thus enabling the other side to allege non-involvement, disinterest, neglect? Never considering for one moment that they simply couldn't face the children they'd so badly let down.

Mal shifted on her feet, imperceptibly, but enough to tell me that she was finished here. My heart clenched. Suddenly my head was filled with a thousand things I wanted to say to her. I wanted to tell her that I loved her more than I could have thought possible, that I had never stopped loving her, that I had been a complete and utter fool. I would do anything, promise everything, if she'd just give me a second chance. That my life without her was ashes. And yet, like Lear's daughter, *unhappy that I am, I cannot heave my heart into my mouth.*

I pinched the bridge of my nose. 'I'd like to see them this weekend, if that's all right.'

Her expression flickered, as if she'd been expecting me to say something else.

'They'd love to see you, too,' she said, after a moment. 'Where?'

'I couldn't come—'

She half-turned, presenting me with her profile. 'No.'

'Not McDonald's. Or a park. I couldn't face it.'

'And not—'

'I wouldn't dream of it,' I said quickly. 'My parents', then? Or,' I added, 'rather, my *mother's*. I wonder how long that will take to get used to?'

'He was a good man,' she said warmly, 'your father.'

'Thank you for coming.'

'Nicholas. I loved him too.'

Perhaps ten feet away from us, a man hovered. I hadn't noticed him before, but now that he'd caught my attention, I couldn't imagine why not. He was extremely good-looking, with that rumpled Steve McQueen edge women inevitably find attractive. And he was clearly waiting for my wife. She smiled sadly, briefly, at me, and then turned, walking towards him. He didn't touch her, but there was something in the way he bent towards her, like a poplar to a riverbank, that told me there was a history between them of which I was not a part.

And for the first time it hit me that I'd lost her.

*

He's there too when she drops off the girls at my mother's house the following Saturday, sitting in the passenger seat of my wife's car.

I take Metheny from her mother and nod towards the Volvo.

'Who's that?'

Mal unshoulders a cumbersome quilted bag filled with Metheny's detritus: nappies, cream, plastic beaker, Calpol, spare dummy, spare clothes, spare blanket. 'Make sure she sleeps for at least an hour in the afternoon, but don't let her go beyond two, she'll never settle for the night. She's started taking the beaker of apple juice to bed, but don't forget to water it down first. And for heaven's sake, don't lose the *Wiggle-Wiggle* book, she had the house in an uproar last week when we couldn't find it—'

'Malinche, I do *know*.'

She stops rummaging. 'Yes. Of course.'

Sophie and Evie bound up the garden path towards me, hair flying.

'Daddy! Daddy! Mummy said we can stay all night at Grandma's house! I brought my new satin pyjamas, Uncle Kit gave them to me for Easter, he said they were much better than chocolate, I look like Veronica Lake, who's Veronica Lake, Daddy, do I look like her?'

'You don't look like a lake, you look like a big fat puddle,' Evie says crossly, 'you're a big muddy fat puddle.'

Sophie smirks and folds her arms. In an irritating, singsong voice, she chants, 'I know you are, but what am I?'

'Puddle head. Puddle head.'

'I know you are, but what am I?'

'Puddle head—'

'I know you are, but what—'

'I'll see you all tomorrow afternoon, girls,' Mal says blithely, kissing each in turn. 'Be good for Daddy. And give Grandma lots of extra cuddles, she's missing Grandpa and she needs them.'

Metheny's sweet brow furrows as she watches her mother walk down the garden path. For twenty seconds she is silent, and then as Mal gets into the car, she starts to squirm in my arms, plump fists flailing as she realizes her mother isn't coming back. I march firmly into the house and shut the front door as she starts to turn red, then blue, with temper, waiting for the familiar bellow of sound.

'Oh, dear Lord,' my mother says nervously. 'What's wrong with the child?'

'She'll be fine in a minute, Mother. Sophie, leave your sister alone. Evie, stop fiddling with that lamp—'

We all wince as the scream finally reaches us. I'm reminded of counting the seconds between flashes of lightning and the thunderclap to work out how far away the storm is.

I jounce my youngest daughter against my chest. Her screams intensify.

'Metheny, sweetheart, calm down, Daddy's here. Mummy will be back soon. Breathe, darling, please breathe. Sophie, *please*. You're the eldest, you should be setting an example—'

There's a crash. Evie jumps guiltily away from the kitchen windowsill.

'Not the Beatrix Potter!' my mother wails. 'Nicholas, I've had that lamp since you were a baby!'

Metheny, shocked into silence by the sudden noise, buries her wet face in my shoulder. I apologize to my mother and hand the hiccoughing toddler over to Sophie with relief. 'Take her into the back garden for a run around while I clear up this mess. You too, Evie. We'll talk about this later. Oh, and Sophs?'

I have always despised clients who use their children to snoop on their spouses.

'That man who came with you today,' I say, with studied casualness. 'I don't think I recognized him—'

'He's a friend of Mummy's,' she shrugs, banging out into the garden. 'The one she does all the cooking with.'

I digest this news as I sweep up the shards of broken china. So *that* was the famous Trace Pitt, Mal's onetime boyfriend and current boss. I hadn't realized he was quite so young. And attractive. And close to my wife.

I wonder if his sudden ubiquity is the staunch support of an old friend in times of need (in which case: why not Kit?); or altogether something more.

And if the latter, *how long has it been going on*?

I am thoughtfully emptying the dustpan into an old newspaper when Evie runs back in with muddy feet and a bunch of flowers almost as big as herself. 'I got these for Grandma, to say sorry for the old lamp.' She beams from behind the blooms. 'Aren't they pretty?'

My mother moans softly. 'My prize cheiranthus.'

She retreats upstairs for a lie down, whilst I struggle dispiritedly to impose order on the childish chaos Mal normally keeps efficiently in check. I dose Metheny up with a pre-emptive teaspoon of Calpol and finally manage to get her down for her nap, but Sophie and Evie squabble continuously for the rest of the afternoon, refusing to settle to anything approaching sibling harmony even when I break every household rule and permit unrestricted access to the television on a sunny day.

'The stupid TV's too small,' Sophie says sulkily, drumming her heels on the base of the overstuffed sofa. 'And there's no Cartoon Network.'

'Please don't kick the furniture, Sophie. Evie, if you need to wipe your nose, use a handkerchief, not the back of your sleeve.'

Defiantly, Evie scrubs at her face with the starched antimacassar. 'I want to watch *Charlie and the Chocolate Factory*. I brought my new DVD—'

'Duh! Grandma doesn't have a DVD player.'

'We've got one at home,' Evie whines. 'Why can't we go back home and watch it? Why do we have to come here anyway?'

I sigh. 'It's complicated.'

Abruptly, Sophie leaps to her feet. 'Daddy doesn't live with us any more, stupid! He's not coming home! Ever, ever, *ever*! They're getting a divorce, don't you know *anything*?'

'Sophie, nobody said anything about—'

She turns on me, her eyes large and frightened in her angry, pale face. 'You *are*! You're going to get divorced and marry someone else and she'll have babies and you'll love them more than us, you won't want to see us any more, you'll forget all about us and love *them* instead!'

I stare after her as she slams out of the room. Guilt

makes a fist of my intestines. And I know from bitter vicarious experience that this is just the start of it.

When Sara telephones at teatime, and suggests coming down and taking the girls out to Chessington with me on Sunday, I fall upon the idea. My mother is clearly in no fit state to cope with the children at the moment, particularly when they are acting up like this, and I certainly don't have a better idea. I have never had to fill an entire weekend with artificial activity and entertainment for three small children before. I have no idea what to *do* with them. Weekends have always just *happened*. A spot of tidying up while Mal goes to Tesco's, changing lightbulbs and fixing broken toys. Mowing the lawn. A game of rounders now and then; teaching the girls to ride their bikes. Slumping amid a sea of newspapers after Sunday lunch whilst the girls play dressing-up in their rooms.

I love my daughters; of course I do. But conversation with children of eighteen months, six and nearly nine is limited, at best. In the normal course of events, we are either active in each other's company – playing French cricket, for example – or each doing our own thing in separate parts of the house. Available to each other, but not *foisted*. Not trapped in a cluttered house of mourning in Esher without even the rabbit's misdemeanours for petty distraction.

For the first time, I realize that access and family life are not even remotely related.

Clearly Mal isn't scrupling to introduce our daughters to her 'friend'. And they may actually *like* Sara. Relate to her, even. In time, perhaps, she could become more of a big sister than anything else—

'I *hate* her!' Sophie screams the moment she sees Sara getting out of her car the next morning.

'Sophie, you've never even *met* her.'

She throws herself at the lamppost at the end of my parents' drive and sits on the filthy pavement, knotting her arms and legs about it as if anticipating being bodily wrestled into the car. 'No! You can't make me go with her!'

'Sophie, you're being ridiculous! Sara's a very nice—'

'She broke up our family!' Sophie cries. 'She's a *home-wrecker*!'

I stare at her in shock. I can't believe I'm hearing such tabloid verbiage from my eight-year-old daughter. 'Who told you *that*?'

'I heard Mummy talking to Uncle Kit on the phone! She was *crying*! Real, proper tears, like when Grandpa died! Her face was all red like Metheny's and she had stuff coming out of her nose and everything! And she told Uncle Kit – ' she hiccoughs – 'it's all *her* fault!'

Involuntarily, I glance at Sara.

'*Please*, darling. Let go of the lamppost. The entire street is looking at you.'

Sophie pretzels herself even tighter. 'I don't care!'

My arms twitch helplessly.

'Why are you being so difficult? Sara is trying to be *nice* to you. Chessington was *her* idea.'

'So what! It's a stupid idea!'

Evie climbs into the back of our car and sticks her head out of the window. 'We could always push her off the roller-coaster,' she suggests cheerfully. 'She'll splat like strawberry jam on the ground and the ambulance men will have to use spades to scrape her off. We could put the bits in a jar and keep it next to Don Juan's cage—'

'Evie, that's enough!'

'Why don't you sit in the front with Daddy?' Sara says nicely to Sophie. 'I'm just along for the ride, anyway.'

'You'll get carsick,' Evie says, pleased.

'If I was going to cling onto something,' Sara whispers loudly to Evie as she gets in beside her, 'it wouldn't be to a *lamppost*. Dogs love lampposts. Just *think* what you might be sitting on.'

Sophie quickly lets go and stands up. She pulls up her pink Bratz T-shirt and wipes her damp face on the hem. 'I'm not sitting next to *her*, even if we go on a scary ride. I'm not even going to talk to her.'

'Fine. I don't suppose she wants to talk to you much, either, after that little display.'

'She'll get cold,' Sophie warns, ruinously scraping the tops of her shoes on the pavement as she dawdles towards the car, 'in that stupid little top. She'll probably get pneumonia and die.'

'Seatbelt, Sophie.'

She slams home the buckle. '*She* can't tell us what to do. She's not our mother, anyway. She's not anybody's mother.'

'Thank goodness for that,' Sara says briskly, 'I don't like children.'

Evie gasps.

'Not *any* children?' Sophie demands, shocked by this heresy into forgetting her vow of Omerta.

'Nope.'

'Not even babies?'

'Babies most of all.'

'Metheny *can* be a pain,' Evie acknowledges, regarding her sister, who is sleeping peaceably in her car-seat, with a baleful glare. 'Especially when she pukes. She does that a *lot*.'

'Don't you like *us*?' Sophie asks, twisting round.

'I haven't decided yet,' Sara says thoughtfully. 'I like some people, and I don't like others. It doesn't really matter to me how old they are. You wouldn't say you loved everyone who had red hair or brown eyes, would you? So why should you like everyone who just happens to be four?'

'Or six,' says Evie.

'Or six. I just make up my mind as I go along.'

'You're weird,' Sophie sniffs, but her voice has lost its edge.

I glance in the rear-view mirror. Sara smiles, and the tension knotting my shoulders eases just a little. Clearly my intention to present her as a friend was arrantly naive; certainly as far as the precocious Sophie is concerned. I must discuss how much she knows with Mal as soon as possible. But I could not have maintained the subterfuge of remaining at their grandmother's in order to console her for very much longer in any event. Perhaps it's better to have the truth out in the open now. Rip off the sticking plaster in one go, rather than pull it from the wound of our separation inch by painful inch.

Children are remarkably resilient. And forgiving. As Sara and Evie debate the relative merits of contestants on some reality talent show, I even dare to hope that today may turn out to be better than I had expected.

My nascent optimism, however, is swiftly quenched.

Before we have even reached the motorway, Metheny wakes up and starts to scream for her mother, Evie and Sophie descend into another spate of vicious bickering over their comic books, and I am forced to stop the car in a lay-by so that Sara may be, as predicted, carsick.

I turn off the engine. We had a Croatian au pair one summer: sick every time she got in the car. Couldn't even manage the bloody school run. Fine on the back of her damn boyfriend's bike, though.

As Sara returns from the bushes, there comes the unmistakable sound of my baby daughter thoroughly filling her nappy.

Naturally, I have forgotten the changing bag. And naturally again, we are far from any kind of habitation where I might purchase anything with which to rectify the situation.

I unbuckle Metheny and lay her on the back seat with some distaste, wondering what in God's name I do now. Clearly I cannot leave her like this: mustard-coloured shit is oozing through the seams of her all-in-one. I struggle not to retch. We're at least half an hour from anywhere. Jesus Christ. How can a person this small and beautiful produce substances noxious enough to fell an army SWAT team at a thousand paces?

I look around helplessly. The car rocks alarmingly as vehicles shoot past at what seem like incredible speeds from our stationary standpoint. It isn't that I'm not versed in changing foul nappies; I have handled several bastards, in fact, from each of my daughters. But not unequipped. Not without cream and wipes and basins of hot water and changes of fresh clothes.

Metheny's screams redouble. There's no help for it; I

will have to clean her up as best I can and wrap her in my jacket. I offer a silent prayer that we reach civilization before her bowels release a second load into my Savile Row tailoring.

Sophie watches me struggle for ten minutes with a packet of tissues from Sara's handbag and copious quantities of spit, before informing me that her mother always keeps a spare nappy, a packet of wet-wipes and a full change of baby clothes beneath the First Aid kit in the boot.

I grit my teeth, aware that I now smell like a POW latrine. I have liquid shit on my hands, on my trousers and – Christ knows how – in my hair. I tell myself the children are not being much worse than normal. It's just that normal childish awfulness is infinitely worse when endured alone. And despite Sara's physical presence, I realize that without Mal beside me, I am very much on my own.

Each of the next four weekends is successively worse. This for a number of reasons: not least of which is the unexpected, but undeniable, new spring in Mal's step.

'You've cut your hair,' I accuse one Saturday in mid-May.

She blushes. 'Kit persuaded me to go to his stylist in London. Do you like it?'

'I love it,' I say grudgingly. 'It's very short, very gamine, but it really suits you. I don't think I've ever seen you with your hair short like this before.'

'I used to have it this way,' she says, 'before we met. But you never let me cut it. You always insisted I keep it long.'

'Did I?'

'You used to insist on a lot of things, Nicholas.'

She smiles and shrugs. I watch her flit across the pavement to the car, where Trace is once again waiting. I can't fool myself that there is nothing in it any more. It's manifestly evident that the sparkle in her eyes is entirely down to – and for – him.

Jealousy, thick and foul, seeps into my soul.

That Mal would so simply slough off our marriage like an unwanted, outgrown skin, emerge somehow brighter and sharper, an HDTV version of her blurry, married self, was an outcome of our separation that I had, narcissistically, never even considered. But every time she drops off the children, she seems to have grown younger, closer to the free-spirited nymph I rescued in Covent Garden. For the first time in perhaps years, I find myself *noticing* her. The ethereal fragility – so deceptive – the dancing, bottomless eyes. The way she has of drawing you in, making you feel like the king of the world with a look, a quirk of the eyebrows. All this extraordinary beauty and happiness was mine; I held it in the palm of my hands. And now I don't even have the right to know how she will spend her days; or, more pertinently, nights.

Nor have things become any easier between Sara and the children. I had thought – hoped, rather – that their hostility towards her would diminish as they grew used to her. To my perturbation, the reverse appears to be the case. Sophie, in particular, is sullen and uncommunicative. Evie is simply rude. Metheny, who can have little comprehension of the grim changes stirring her life, picks up on the general air of familial misery and responds by being fractious, grizzly and demanding.

Understandably, Sara's initial well-meaning patience soon wears thin.

'I didn't expect rave reviews,' she says one day, after Sophie deliberately leaves a wet umbrella lying on top of her new suede jacket with predictably disastrous results, 'but do they have to make it so freakin' clear how much they *hate* me?'

I put down my newspaper.

'I'm sure it was an accident—'

'Of course it damn well wasn't, Nick, but I'm not just talking about the jacket. It's *everything*. We never have a moment to ourselves any more. We daren't be in the same room together at work in case it looks like favouritism – for God's sake, Emma's quit because of me. Joan practically hisses when I walk past, and Fisher seems to think he's now got carte blanche to grope my arse every time he comes into the office. My fucking reputation is shot to shit—'

'You're not the only one,' I say grimly.

'Yeah, well, you're partner already. No one's going to accuse *you* of sleeping your way to the top. But whenever *I* pull off a coup, everyone will say it's because I'm screwing the great Nick Lyon. And then,' she snaps, returning to the subject in hand, 'then, at weekends, we have the children twenty-four/seven. We saw more of each other when you were still living at home!'

'It's family life,' I say powerlessly. 'It's the way it is.'

'But it's not *my* family, is it? Ruining everything.'

I stare at her. 'They're my children.'

She stalks to the window and peers between the blinds in a gesture of frustration I'm starting to recognize.

'I'm beginning to think your wife has planned it all this way,' she says spitefully. 'Dumping the children on us every weekend whilst she gets it on with her new hottie. She's got it made, hasn't she? Whilst we're crammed in this tiny flat with three out-of-control kids—'

I reel from the sickening punch of jealousy to my stomach at the thought of my wife with another man.

'At least she lets them stay here now,' I manage. 'That can't have been easy for her.'

Sara's mouth twists into an unattractive smile.

'Poor cow. Stuck shagging Mr Sex-on-Legs whilst we get to wipe snotty noses and change fucking nappies all weekend. My heart bleeds.'

'You make it sound,' I say tightly, 'as if you'd rather be her.'

A silence falls. Sara drops her head, abashed.

'I didn't mean that,' she says. 'It's just—'

'I know,' I say.

And I do. Most children are not, if we're honest, lovable, except to their own parents, and then not all the time. Or even much of it. For every heart-warming, couldn't-live-without-them moment, when plump child-ish arms are wreathed about your neck and sunny smiles bottled in some corner of your mind, there are many more bleak, never-admitted, what-was-I-thinking ones. Children demand and insist and control. They force you to be unselfish, and since this is not a natural human state, yielding to their needs breeds resentment and refusing to do so evokes guilt.

I can't blame Sara for not wanting my children around too much. In such intense, concentrated, artificial parcels of time, frankly, neither do I. Until now, I'd thought divorce for a man meant not seeing his children enough. It hadn't occurred to me that *too much* was worse.'

'There's a party next Saturday,' Sara says, lighting a cigarette. The smoking, it seems, is no longer just post-coital. 'A friend of Amy's. I'd really like to go.'

'I don't mind staying here and babysitting the girls—'

'To go,' she says firmly, 'with *you*.'

I wave my hand in front of my face, to make a point.

'Give me a break,' Sara snaps. 'It's *my* flat.'

I don't want to go to a party at Amy's friend's house. I already know what it will be like: dark, noisy, cramped, with appalling music and even worse wine. I will feel like an invigilating parent, and will be regarded as an object of curiosity and derision. Sara will want to let her hair down and smoke drugs on the staircase – yes, I was a student once – and feel she can't because she has to look after me.

But she *needs* this. She needs to float me into her other life for our relationship to be real. And perhaps without the children we can have the wild, untrammelled sex we used to have, instead of the furtive suppose-they-walk-in *married* sex we've been having recently.

I call Mal, and tell her that I can't have the children this weekend. She sounds neither surprised nor put out; in fact, she exclaims cheerfully, that's perfect, they – *she and Trace*, I think sourly – were planning to take the Chunnel to France for the weekend anyway, another sourcing trip; the children can come too, it's not a bother, be lovely to have them for a change, actually: next week, then?

*

I picture my daughters, laughing and bouncing up and down excitedly in the back of his flash car, singing 'Frère Jacques' at the top of their young voices. Thrilled by the thought of a tunnel that goes all the way under the sea, by the adventure of travelling to foreign lands, by sleeping in beds with French bolsters instead of English pillows. I picture Mal leaning across in the front to kiss his square-jawed matinée-idol cheek, smiling contentedly at some erotic memory from last night, 'dormez vous, dormez vous'—

'Nick? Are you OK?'

I jump, spilling my wine – execrable; I'm surprised it doesn't dissolve the carpet – from its plastic cup. 'Sorry. Miles away.'

Sara leans in to be heard over the music. 'How's it going?'

The party is everything I had feared it would be. I am indeed the paterfamilias of this social gathering, doubling the average age of the participants at a stroke (literally, I fear, if the music continues to be played at this bone-jangling level). In the semi-darkness around me, couples who probably don't even know each other's names exchange saliva, if not pleasantries. A number of pairings are not the traditional boy–girl. It is impossible to conduct a conversation anywhere but in the kitchen, whose harsh fluorescent light illuminates the pallid, vacant faces of our legal elite in variously mentally altered states. I was wrong in one particular: the sweet smell of marijuana I remember from the parties of my student days is absent, replaced by a dusting of chic, expensive white powder on the lavatory cistern and arranged in neat Marmite-soldier lines across the surface of a small square hand-mirror, quixotically imprinted with a lithograph of the engage-ment photograph of Prince Charles and Lady Di, complete with hideous pussy-cat bow.

Mal and I found ourselves at a party not dissimilar to this shortly before we got engaged; at Kit's invitation, naturally. He vanished as soon as we arrived to pursue the travel writer to whose column – in every sense of the word – he had taken a fancy. Mal and I clung to each other's fingers like lost children, excusing ourselves in that peculiarly British fashion every two minutes whenever someone trod on our feet or jostled us as they barged past.

'Oh God, I'm too old for this,' she exclaimed suddenly, as a louche youth brushed against her, burning her bare shoulder with his cigarette. 'Please, Nicholas, *please* get me out of here.'

We spent the night in our own safe, dull double bed at my flat, a little ashamed of our prematurely middle-aged flight, but thrilled and relieved to have found *simpatico* company in our retreat, to not have to pretend. And of course, we were still at that stage in a relationship when one does not need the ameliorating presence of others. We were each enough for the other.

I woke up that morning, Mal's tawny limbs tangled in my Egyptian cotton, her dark hair streaming across the cream pillow, small brown nipples proudly erect even in her sleep. She was exquisite; and I knew then, without a doubt, that I wanted to wake up next to this amazing woman every day for the rest of my life. The following weekend, having procured the ring – an opal: its pearl-escent creaminess seemed, to me, to encapsulate the image of Mal that defining morning – I asked her to marry me.

Sara's hand snakes possessively down my wool trousers – 'Are you really wearing a suit?' she said to me as we dressed this evening, 'don't you have any jeans?' – and grasps my erection. 'Looks like the party's happening elsewhere,' she purrs in my ear.

I smile faintly. She wraps her body sinuously around mine, pleased. She isn't to know that my arousal stems not from her young, vibrant presence, but from a ten-year-old memory of another woman in my bed.

'I'm sorry—'

'Forget it. It happens. It's not a big deal.'

We both know she's lying. Sex is not just an important part of our relationship: it defines it. When things have started to go wrong in the bedroom – which has, until now, been the one place they can be guaranteed to go right – for us it is not just a little hiccough, one of those things to be put right with a change of scene or a good night's sleep.

I fold my arm beneath my head and stare up at the ceiling. The bald truth is that the hot, frantic passion I had for her, the desperate *need*, has vanished as quickly and inexplicably as it came. Suddenly, after all these months of lust, I don't want her any more. She hasn't done anything wrong. She is still just as sexy, as attractive, as she was the day I first saw her. Just not to me.

Sara gets out of bed and wraps her red kimono about her voluptuous curves, clutching it to her body as if cold.

'Just getting a drink of water,' she says.

I nod, and she goes out into the kitchen.

It's my fault, of course. I knew this would happen.

Love lasts; passion doesn't. Without warning, there's nothing left. If only it had burned itself out before Mal discovered us. Why *now*? When all this can cause is more pain?

Sara may have been a willing partner: the instigator, even, of our affair. But she's so *young*. So – despite the worldly facade and bedroom skills – very inexperienced when it comes to men. I know her feelings for me are not as transient, or as lightly dismissed, as my more carnal sentiments towards her. I'm very fond of her; I like and respect her; the last thing I want to do is hurt her – but that's it. She fancies herself in love. Calf love, perhaps, but no less powerful for that.

Above all, I should never have agreed to move in with her. Permitted her to entertain fantasies of a happy-ever-after together. It was stupid of me; cruel, actually. When I am still in love with my wife.

I hear the sound of the shower, and slide out of bed. It's three in the morning; Mal will be in France now, cosying down with her lover at her charming Normandy *pension*. But, suddenly, this can't wait.

I stand at the window, looking down into the street, my mobile pressed tightly against my ear. After four rings, the answerphone kicks in. I listen to Mal's voice explaining that *we can't come to the phone right now*, imagining it echoing around the darkened kitchen, startling the poor rabbit in his scullery.

'Mal,' I say desperately. 'I know I've been a bloody fool. What I did was unforgivable. I don't deserve a second chance. But *please*, Mal. Please don't shut me out. I love you so much. I know you've—' I hesitate, 'I know you're not alone. It kills me, but I swear, I don't even care about that. I just want you back. Nothing else matters besides being with you.' My voice cracks. 'Jesus, Mal, I wish more than anything I could turn back the clock. I wish I'd told you before how happy you've made me, how much I love coming home to you every night, waking up next to you every morning. I know what I did was wrong. I have no excuse. But *please*, Mal. Give me a second chance. I swear I won't let you down. *Please*.'

I don't know what else to say. After a long beat of silence I click off my phone. Behind me Sara is silhouetted in the bedroom doorway. I have no idea how long she's been standing there, or what she's heard.

I know, in some deeply instinctual way, what she is going to say, even before she opens her mouth and changes things forever.

'I'm pregnant,' she says.

14

Sara

No,' says my mother.

'But Mum—'

'I said *no*.'

Her voice sounds strangled. I picture her at the kitchen sink, phone crooked between shoulder and chin, peeling Dad's bloody potatoes for dinner tonight.

I attempt a conciliatory tone.

'He's really nice, Mum. You'd like him. If you just met him, you'd—'

'Nice men don't up and leave their wives for the first floozie to lift her skirts,' Mum says sharply. 'And they certainly don't have the brass neck to pitch up at her parents' for tea and sandwiches afterwards. I'll have no truck with it. He's not welcome here, and you can tell him so from me.'

I flush.

'Do you have to make it sound so sordid, Mum?'

Scrape. Scrape.

'Those poor children. Never mind his poor wife. I don't know how you sleep at night.' A soft phlish, as she drops a potato into the pan. 'Imagine how *you'd* have felt, if your father had upped and—'

'If you ask me, it's a bloody miracle he didn't,' I retort, 'I certainly don't know how he's put up with you all these years.'

I fling the phone on the sofa. *Shit*, I shouldn't have said that. Now I'm doubly in the wrong. I'll have to phone her back and apologize for being rude and hanging up on her; and then sit through another of her pocket sermons on Sins of the Flesh and Why Married Men Are Not Fair Game.

I don't know why I feel so bloody guilty about it. After all, I've been praying for months that Nick would leave his wife. OK, the thought of his three little girls sobbing themselves to sleep at night because Daddy's gone didn't exactly make me feel good about myself – I'm not Cruella De Vil – but I never thought it'd bother me *this* much. Some nights, I toss and turn for hours, picturing their pale, tear-stained faces, whilst Nick sleeps like an innocent babe next to me. It seems my mother has managed to hamstring me with a bloody conscience after all.

I kick the damp towel Nick has left in the middle of the sitting room floor out of my way and go into the kitchen. Coffee grounds are scattered all over the counter, and the sink is full of dirty cups and plates from last night. He made enough bloody noise clattering around in here at six this morning when I was *trying* to have my Saturday morning lie-in. You'd have thought he could've managed to load the freakin' dishwasher, for fuck's sake—

I shriek as a cockroach the size of a small cat shoots out from behind the fridge.

It stops in the middle of the floor halfway between me and the door, its disgusting antennae things twitching back and forth. I shudder, acutely conscious of my bare feet. If that thing runs over them I'll have a fucking heart attack, I swear.

Gingerly I reach for something to throw at it. Christ Almighty, where's a man when you need one? Although Nick's more the type to leap up on the kitchen counter at the sight of a mouse. Somehow I can't quite imagine him scooping up cockroaches with his bare hands.

I lob a wet J-cloth. The cockroach skitters beneath the sink. Well, that's washing up out for the rest of the day. I'm not going near the sink till I know that thing's dead.

Keeping a wary eye out for other roaches hot to party, I make myself a mug of tea – 'Good God,' Nick said, 'not tea-bags, don't you have any loose Earl Grey?' – and curl up on the sofa, keeping my feet safely tucked up under my bottom. The cushions still smell of puke. I've bleached the sofa so many times it's started to hang out white flags when I approach, and I still can't get rid of the stink.

It kills me to say so, but I've got to give Nick's wife props. Spewing all over the pristine white *not*-bought-in-the-sale Conran is one helluva way to diss your rival.

Aw, sod it. She can have the sofa. After all, I've got the man.

A swirl of pleasure whisks its way down my body and I grin into my mug. Conscience be damned. *He actually left his wife.* OK, so he was pushed a little bit; but still, I am the stuff of urban legends. The mistress who got to waltz off into the sunset with her man. No wonder Amy's spitting blood.

I couldn't believe it when she crashed my flat and handed him to me on a plate. Just like that. Didn't even put up a fight.

Nick muttered something about finding a hotel, but of course he was just saying that so I didn't feel I *had* to ask him to move in. As if I was going to let an opportunity like *that* slip through my fingers. It's not quite the way I would've liked it to happen – it would've been nice if he'd left his wife by choice and told me he couldn't live without me, begged me to let him stay, rather than ended up here by default; but it comes to the same thing in the end. The important thing is we're *together*.

Every relationship has a few teething troubles at the beginning. It's only to be expected. Things are a bit cramped with two of us in the flat, and Nick isn't exactly house-trained. Too many years having someone run around after him, cooking him hot dinners and ironing his shirts. And it's a bit of a strain having to look sexy and fabulous twenty-four/seven; I keep having to get up early to sneak in the bathroom and shove on some slap before he sees me. He looked a bit shocked when he beat me to it the other morning and caught sight of me *au naturel*. It's his own fault: I was having my own *There's Something About Mary* moment after some rather pervy sex the night before.

But actually, I think he's finding it all rather romantic, really. Bohemian. Sort of like being a student again, young and footloose and carefree. I bet it makes a nice change from all that family responsibility.

I pick up the phone and dial. 'Hey. S'me.'

'If you go all loved-up on me again, I'm hanging up,' Amy says warningly.

'Sorry, doll, the honeymoon's over. Didn't I tell you? He leaves dirty clothes all over the floor and wouldn't know an ironing board from a vibrator.'

She snorts. 'No wonder you need a king-size bed.'

'D'you fancy going to Camden Market this morning?' I ask. 'If we get a wiggle-on we could get there before eleven. I was thinking about trawling round the covered market for some silver earrings, I think I lost one of my Indian ones at the gym.' I giggle. 'Roj probably nicked it for his Prince Albert.'

'Eeuuw. Do you mind? I haven't finished my breakfast.'

'Meet you there?'

'I don't know. I *was* going down to my parents'—'

'Oh, live dangerously, Ames,' I wheedle. 'C'mon, it's a lovely day. And we could do lunch at the Dôme, we haven't been there for ages.'

I feel her weaken at the thought of bouillabaisse.

'Where's lover boy, then?'

'He's seeing his kids. It's the first time since they split up; his wife is dropping them off at his Mum's for the weekend. He won't be back till tomorrow night. Please, pretty please? I'll lend you my new James Blunt—'

'Throw in your Oasis dress for a week and I'll see you in forty minutes.'

She's already waiting for me when I reach the entrance to the covered market. We stroll round the stalls of knick-knacks, bric-a-brac and vintage crap for while, pawing over the junk of yesteryear and muttering ribald remarks to each other. For some reason, a kitsch nest of chamber pots – his 'n' hers – reduces us to tears of mirth. Eventually, I buy a delicate pair of amber and silver earrings – 'God, look at the tiny fly stuck in that one,' Amy marvels, 'can you imagine how old it must be?' – whilst she bargains for an antique game of bagatelle for Terry's next birthday. 'I know it's not very romantic,' Amy admits, 'but at least he can take this home without his wife suspecting it's from another woman.'

'I have to say,' she adds crossly as we sit down to lunch, 'you look positively glowing. Living the happy-ever-after, are you?'

'More or less,' I grin, flipping open my menu.

'Tell me the less,' she sighs, 'I don't think I've the stomach for more right now.'

'Well, his father died last week, so to cheer him up I dressed as a schoolgirl and shagged him over the back of sofa in full view of the neighbours,' I start.

Amy chokes on her sparkling water.

'And,' I whisper, leaning across the table, 'he shoved his – you know – up my bloody arse.'

'You're kidding? What, without even asking?'

'Without any bloody lube, either,' I say feelingly. 'I had to perch on one cheek for three days.'

'Well, he did go to public school. I suppose it's only to be expected.'

We drop the subject of anal sex as the waiter takes our order. I don't really feel like wine, though Amy opts for a glass of Sancerre. I guess I'm not in the mood.

I snap a breadstick between my fingers. 'Joking apart, I do sometimes wonder, Amy. I know Nick and I have always been *about* sex. I mean, obviously: that's the whole point of having an affair. But sometimes, especially lately, it seems so impersonal. We do all this wild stuff in bed – and out of it, come to that – and generally I'm cool with whatever he wants to try as it doesn't involve lit cigarettes or live goldfish up my fanny.' I lick my forefinger and dab restlessly at the crumbs. 'But there's not much tenderness. He hardly ever kisses me. I just – I don't know, Ames.' I surprise myself by suddenly feeling close to tears. 'It's just this feeling I have. It's like he doesn't even *see* me sometimes.'

There's a short silence. Amy looks understandably bewildered at the speed of my transition from smug unmarried to oops-worms-in-Paradise.

I'm a little confused myself. I didn't realize that was there until I opened my mouth and it all spilled out.

'Are you sure it's not just *you*,' she says, 'wanting more from him? Now that you're living together.' She moves the bread basket out of my reach. 'Having an affair is one thing. Now you're in a relationship. Everything's changed all of a sudden. Of *course* you want more than a good seeing to over the back of the furniture. And I'm sure it's going to be fine, but it's just going to take a little time, that's all. It's a big adjustment for both of you.'

I recover quickly. After all, I'm the poster girl for Other Women. The proof it *can* all work out in the end.

'I'm sure you're right,' I say brightly. 'After all, what goes on in the bedroom says a lot about the rest of your relationship, doesn't it? As long as things are good there, everything else will fall into place eventually. It's just a question of us getting used to living with each other.'

'I'm sure everything's going to be fine,' she echoes.

I narrow my eyes. 'What? Spit it out.'

She leans back as the waiter places her soup in front of her, choosing her words.

'It's just – I'm not sure I'd let him spend quality time with his wife and kids yet. No need to remind him what he's missing, if you see what I mean.'

I stare at her, surprised.

'Look,' she says. 'The kids are his one weak point. Come on, Sara, how many times have you had a client change his mind and go back to his wife once it gets down to custody and a week at Christmas and two in the summer?'

I realize Amy has prodded precisely where it hurts.

'I'm not saying for a minute he'd go back to her,' she reassures me. 'But why take the chance? She knows him better than anyone, remember. She'll know which buttons to press. She could be cosying up to him in the kitchen right now, dandling that cute little baby on her lap, getting him all nostalgic for family life.' She stirs her bouillabaisse. 'It's a really delicate time, the first few weeks after they leave. And he's just lost his dad. If I were you, I wouldn't let him out of my sight.'

'I can't stop him seeing his kids – I wouldn't want to—'

'I'm not saying you should. Just make sure you're part of the picture, that's all, rather than her. The battle's not over yet. Don't give her a chance to talk him round. I know kids aren't your scene, but you've got to play it like they are for a bit. Take them out to – I don't know, Chessington or something. You can always ease up later, once things are more settled.'

I look down at my plate of calamari. 'I don't feel all that hungry, Ames. I think it's your fish soup, it's making me feel a bit sick.'

Amy cheerfully digs her fork into a deep-fried baby octopus.

'At least it's not morning sickness,' she grins.

Ten days late. That's not much, surely? I know I haven't missed a pill. I checked. There could be lots of reasons my period's a few days late. That dodgy Chinese, for example, I was as sick as a dog for two days. Lack of exercise: I've barely seen the inside of the gym since Nick moved in. He likes me to be there when he gets home. Not to mention the bloody stress. This flat is a little on the crowded side with two adults sharing; throw in three children every weekend as we've been doing for the past few weeks and it's total fucking chaos.

I part the blinds with my finger and peer down into the street as Kat winds around my ankles. Chessington was a freakin' fiasco, it pissed with rain and the kids hated me, but at least I was there. And I suppose I should be grateful Nick's wife lets the children come and stay here at all. His mother refuses to allow me to darken her doors – she'd get on with mine like a house on fire, I think sourly – so otherwise I'd never see Nick at weekends at all.

I watch his wife lift the baby out of her car-seat and start to unload bags from the boot. I couldn't believe it the first time I saw all the baby shit heaped around my tiny flat. All that paraphernalia for one small child. You can hardly move for tripping over plastic sacks of nappies and bottle warmers and buggy wheels. Not to mention the moth-eaten old toy lamb that invariably gets lost five minutes before bedtime and requires a two-hour search before it's finally located somewhere obvious like the *fucking microwave oven*.

'Look, Kit-Kat,' I say, picking her up, 'the *über*-hot sex-god is here again, too.'

I press my nose to the window as he takes the bags from Nick's wife, laughing at something she says and throwing an arm casually around her shoulder. Jesus, look at his cute butt in those low-slung jeans. I certainly wouldn't kick him out of bed. How the fuck does she manage it? She's only been single for a minute and she's got this shaggable babe warming her sheets. No wonder Nick has steam coming out of his ears.

Happy for her, my arse. He's so jealous, he wants to eat his own elbow. Not that I'm in the least worried: it's just a macho guy thing. Territorial. Nothing to do with how he feels about *her*. And it certainly makes things a bit easier for me; a bit more secure. Even if he wanted to go back to her, which he *doesn't*, the fact that she's playing hide-the-sausage with a hottie like that pretty much closes the door on the whole kiss-and-make-up routine. How very Hollywood of us: a perfect happy ending.

Well; almost.

Sophie looks up from the street and makes a fingers-down-the-throat gesture in my direction that neither of her parents sees. She's a real piece of work, that one. I scowl, resisting the temptation to stick out my tongue at her. Maybe Nick's wife isn't being so altruistic letting them stay here after all.

The baby's OK – well, all she does is shit and cry, but she's quite sweet when she's asleep. Which is fortunately fairly often. And Evie's not too bad either; we got quite a thing going over *The X Factor*, she's as much of an addict as I am. But then Sophie put the frighteners on her – I heard the little witch telling her Daddy would come back home and 'love Mummy again' if they could just make me go away. I'm feeling less guilty about *her* by the minute.

Last weekend, I caught her scrubbing out the loo with my toothbrush. That was after finding glue all over the keys of my very expensive new laptop (Pritt Stick, thank God, not superglue, though it still took hours to get it off); and then there was the full bottle of Chanel's Rouge Noir nail varnish that mysteriously spilt all over my new pale pink L. K. Bennetts.

I could tell Nick, of course, but that's exactly what Sophie wants me to do. I run to Daddy, he bollocks them, and we all sit and glower at each other over Pizza Hut's finest. Eventually Daddy gets tired of all the aggro and decides it'd be better for the children if he saw them when I wasn't around. Before you know it, hey presto, he's going back home to her.

The very thought of it makes me feel ill. I shoot into the bathroom and dry heave over the toilet bowl. Ten days is nothing. Just an iffy chicken sandwich, that's all. Nick told me not to eat it, said it was a week past its sell-by date. Next time I'll listen.

Nick and the children tumble through the front door as I wipe my mouth and go back into the sitting room. The baby's sweet face lights up with recognition. Nick puts her down; holding out her chubby little arms for balance, she toddles towards me, gabbling something that might, or might not, be my name. Despite myself, my heart melts as I scoop her up. Precious. She smells so sweet: for a change.

She snuggles into my neck, and I feel a bit of a lump rise. I catch Nick's eye over the top of her golden head, and he smiles: the first honest, warm smile I've had from him in days. The girls must be finding this whole thing really hard. It's no wonder they're playing up a bit. Their world's been completely turned upside down; it's bound to take a bit of getting used to—

'Ooops,' Sophie says, not troubling to hide her smirk as a big orange felt-tip pen stain spreads outwards next to where she's sitting on my poor beleaguered sofa. 'Sorry, Sara.'

Enough is enough. My sofa is trashed, half my mugs are broken, there's crayon scribble all over my walls, a dozen earrings – one from each pair – have gone missing, the last ten pages of my new Grisham thriller have been ripped out before I've had a chance to read them, an entire pot of my £100-a-throw La Prairie face cream has been wasted on nappy rash because *somebody* lost the Sudocrem, my suede Joseph jacket is fit only for lining the cat's litter tray, there are sleeping bags and pillows and inside-out pyjama bottoms all over the floor, dirty nappies are stinking out the bathroom, and I haven't had a decent lie-in for weeks; never mind a fucking orgasm. I defy any girl to come when three small children with a propensity to barge in without knocking are supposedly asleep on sofa cushions next door.

I tell Nick in no uncertain terms that I need a weekend off. A barrister friend of Amy's is having a party over in

Swiss Cottage and, for once, I want to forget about children and responsibility and just go. I'm so tired of the chaos and bullshit from the damn kids. We sound like an old married couple arguing over the children. We need a break; to have some fun.

To my surprise, Nick agrees. Maybe he'd like to get hot and heavy again between the sheets, too. A good shag is probably what we both need. Get things back on track again.

I blow a fortnight's salary on an amazing Matthew Williamson dress, and borrow Amy's GHD straighteners to get my hair (finally out of its Pantomime Boy/scary dyke phase, thank God) to behave. Actually, the crop's done it some good, I've got all these cute little strawberry-gold kiss curls tumbling sexily onto my bare shoulders, and my hair seems much thicker than usual. I blow myself a kiss as I finish my make-up in the bathroom. Not even the usual pre-party break-out of zits to ruin my day. I look pretty damn good, if I say so myself.

Nick doesn't even notice.

He's unusually quiet (even for him) in the cab on the way to the party. I begin to wonder if this was a good idea after all. He hasn't even changed out of his bloody suit, for God's sake. He looks like my *father*.

But we've been living together for nearly two months now. Sooner or later, he has to meet my friends, mix in my world; particularly as nearly everyone in *his* world isn't talking to him any more. Even Giles blew him off when he called. No doubt Liz has threatened to withdraw bedroom privileges if Giles dares to socialize with The Slapper (i.e. yours truly); but Nick still took it hard.

Apart from one or two rather unsuccessful trips to the movies (he loathed the Matthew McConaughey rom-com I picked, and I fell asleep during his choice, some subtitled Vietnamese crap) we haven't been out at all since his father died. Our social life isn't helped by the fact that Nick's giving most of his salary to his wife out of guilt. Which means I'm the one keeping us both. Much more of this and I'll be pawning the Tiffany bracelet to pay the phone bill. So much for dirty weekends away at Michelin-starred country houses. Romantic it's not.

The moment we arrive at the party, Amy drags me away to meet this new guy who's started working at her office. Since it's been five years since she dragged me away to meet anyone other than Terry the Lying Slimeball, I'm duty-bound to fan the flames of romance, however feebly. Nick's old enough (hah!) and ugly enough to look after himself for five minutes. There are plenty of lawyers around for him to talk to if he gets desperate.

But then I run into this girl from law school I haven't seen in years, it turns out she's now engaged to a man I used to date, how weird is that? And then on my way back from the loo I get chatting to my opposite number on a new case I've just picked up, and we get stuck into one of those long, involved conversations on the stairs, ducking and diving around people as they push between us every two minutes. Then I need to top up my drink again, and I'm laughing with my friends, with my young, irresponsible, child-free friends, and I can't help it, right now I just don't want to go back to Nick and his here-on-sufferance, well-if-it-makes-you-happy, miserable bloody attitude. No doubt he hates the music, and the cheap plonk, and the plastic cups, and the couples snogging all over the room. Heaven help us if he finds out the bodies writhing on the crappy velour sofa are both *men*.

Someone offers me a line of coke, throwing Nick a wary look. Even though I decline, because I've never done hard drugs, something about the awkward, pompous way Nick is standing on his own, aloof from the rest of the party, annoys the fuck out of me.

A small worm squirms somewhere deep inside my brain: *this isn't working*.

I shock myself. After all the pain and misery we've caused, after everything we've risked to be together, of course it's going to work. I'm getting all het up over nothing. It's just one stupid party! This just isn't Nick's scene, that's all. Let's face it, this is barely one step up from a student bash, and with the best will in the world, it's a long time since Nick was a student.

It's nothing to do with *us*. We love each other. We're going to be fine. Absolutely fine.

I shake my head as someone else offers me a reefer and thread my way through the crowd towards Nick.

'Nick? Are you OK?'

He jumps, spilling his wine on the floor. 'Sorry. Miles away.'

I bend over to make sure he gets a good eyeful. 'How's it going?'

He smiles absently. *Come on, Nick, meet me halfway here.*

My hand drifts lightly down his trousers, and I'm gratified to discover that he's rock hard already. *That was quick work.* I must remember to wear this dress again. 'Looks like the party's happening elsewhere,' I tease.

Nick's all over me in the back of the cab home, pawing

at my skimpy dress with an urgency that seems almost frantic. We fall through the front door of my apartment ripping at each other's clothes. Naked but for my high heels, I back towards the bedroom, pulling him with me. He shucks off his shirt and kicks away his shoes. I lay back on the bed as he steps out of his trousers, and moisture floods me at the sight of his beautiful, big cock. My body flames. I've never felt hungrier to have him inside me. *It's all going to be fine.*

He falls on the bed beside me. Hunger zings up and down my skin. He shoves my thighs apart with his knee, cupping his hand over my pussy and bending his middle finger to caress me as he slides his body over mine. Gently he eases his cock between my thighs. Without entering me, he lets the head of his dick rub my clit. My whole being is now centred on the few inches of nerves and sensation between my legs. Lust races through my body, making my toes tingle, my whole body jerk.

Nick abruptly pulls away from me. Even as I grab for him in frustration, he's sliding a pillow beneath my hips and slithering down the bed between my legs. He dips his head and starts to kiss me softly, using only his lips as though he's kissing someone hello at a party. My fingers twine through his hair, pushing him into me, but Nick resists my pressure and holds back, teasing my clit with his lips, lightly nibbling me with his teeth, swirling his tongue around the very edge of my pussy.

My body burns with need. I feel as if I've been awakened from a very long, deep sleep by a pornographic Prince Charming. I'd almost forgotten it could be this good.

He moves up my body, kissing my tummy, my belly-button, my breasts. I taste myself on his lips as he reaches my mouth.

'I want you inside me,' I moan.

I reach for him, and he's firm, but no longer hard; I've kept him waiting too long. I push him back on the pillows and slide down his body to take him in my mouth. I suck and tease and stroke, my fingers feathering across his thighs and balls, and after a few minutes I feel his cock spring to life.

I disengage myself and ease astride him, welcoming him home, drawing him deeper inside me. His thrusts grow harder and faster, and I feel my orgasm start to rise, the heat building between my legs. Before I can come, Nick spins me round and moves on top of me. I don't mind the change in position – but all of a sudden he isn't thrusting deep inside me any more. He loses his rhythm and slips out of me. I put my hand between our legs to help him back.

'Oh,' I say.

'I'm sorry,' Nick mumbles.

'Forget it. It happens. It's not a big deal.'

He rolls away from me and stares up at the ceiling, head resting on the crook of his arm. We both know I'm lying. Whether I like it or not, sex is not just an important part of our relationship: it defines it. If it goes wrong in the bedroom then we are, forgive the pun, screwed.

Or rather: *not.*

I get out of bed and grab my red kimono. I suddenly feel very very sick and very, very scared. 'Just getting a drink of water.'

In the bathroom, I switch on the shower and stand

beneath it, closing my eyes and leaning my head against the cool tiles. How has it all gone wrong so fast? Or – or was it always wrong, and I just refused to see it? Too busy enjoying the thrill and the secrecy and the danger and the unattainability to acknowledge the truth. Which is that much as I love him – and I do, oh, God, *I do* – Nick and I have nothing in common except the pleasure we share in bed, and without that, there is absolutely nothing holding us together.

Except that's not quite true.

Instinctively, my hands curve protectively around my belly. Soft, squishy, still looking exactly the same as it always has.

But three-and-a-half weeks late isn't nothing, much as I've tried to tell myself it is. Three-and-a-half weeks late is *something*. Morning sickness, glowing skin, lustrous hair, and heavy, tender breasts are all *something*. And it has nothing to do with questionable takeaways or insufficient sit-ups or stress.

I can't do this on my own. Alarm bells about Nick are going off in all directions, but *I can't do this on my own*.

The hot water starts to run cold. I step out of the shower, and dry off. Knotting the belt of my robe, I pad back towards the bedroom.

He's whispering, but the flat is very small, and very quiet. My footsteps don't make a sound on the pale ash floor. And so I overhear my lover tell another woman – his wife – how much he loves her, as he begs her to take him back.

When he finally ends the call and looks up, I tell him.

*

I find Dad in the greenhouse at the end of the garden, tenderly separating a tray of tiny seedlings into individual pots. Slumping onto a wooden bench out of his way, I watch him press each small plant in gently with his thumbs. He nods at me to show he's noticed I'm there, but quietly goes on with his work for ten minutes or so, until the tray is empty.

Finally he straightens up, brushing his hands together to get rid of the loose soil. He surveys the neat row of pots with satisfaction. 'Should do nicely this year,' he says. 'Good and strong, this batch are. And the beds should be fertile, thanks to your mother's compost. All those potato peelings and such.'

'Don't let her hear you say that, Dad. She'll have a fit if she thinks she's helping.'

He starts to tidy his tools away. 'Well, that's your mother for you. Not likely to change now.'

I pick up a cloth rag and start to clean earth from a small trowel. Beside me, Dad rolls a length of green gardening twine into a ball. It's hot and humid in here; sweat collects beneath my breasts, and trickles between my shoulder blades. The air is close and has the sickly-sweet smell of rotting fruit. A fly buzzes against a window-pane, and Dad leans over me to open the window and let it out. The cooler outside air brings with it the familiar scent of freshly mown grass and blossom from the may tree at the end of the garden. I'm reminded of all those summer days I spent cooped up indoors, frantically cramming for exams, whilst outside the rest of the world turned, carefree.

'If you could just talk to her, Dad,' I start.

He grunts. 'Won't make any difference.'

'I know it's not what she would've chosen for me, Dad, but it's my life. I love Nick, and he loves me. Can't she just accept that and be happy for me?'

'She just worries about you, love. We both do.' He reaches up to hook the ball of a twine on a nail in the wall. 'When you have children, you'll understand. It's not a question of whether we approve or not. We just don't want you to get hurt.'

I swallow a great big ball of guilt. I can't tell them about the baby, not yet. Christ, they haven't even *met* Nick; the last thing they need to know is that he's already knocked up their precious little girl.

I fold the cloth rag neatly into squares.

'The only person who's going to hurt me is Mum, if she keeps this up,' I mutter.

Dad looks at me for a long moment, then sits down heavily on the bench. He leans his hands on his knees, rubbing his palms gently up and down the worn corduroy. 'Love, are you *sure* you've really thought all this through? I know you think you have, but it's never that straightforward. This man, this Nick, he's not just older than you. He's done so much more. A wife, a family – love, you've got your whole life ahead of you. You're only twenty-six. The world's your oyster. I hate to see your wings clipped before you've even had a chance to spread them.'

'He's asked me to marry him,' I say defiantly. 'As soon as his divorce comes through. And I've said yes.'

My father nods slowly several times.

'I do love him, Dad,' I say, crouching in front of him. 'Please be happy for me.'

'He's a married man, love,' my father says softly.

'There's no getting away from it. You'll be taking on a man who's already walked away from one family. What's to stop him from doing it to you?'

After Emma quit as Nick's secretary, handing in her resignation the morning our affair became public knowledge, he hired a new girl. Twenty-two years old, legs up to here, the spitting image of Scarlett Johansson. Nowhere near as efficient as Emma; she seems to require a lot of direction from Nick. A lot of hands-on, one-on-one attention.

'He wouldn't do that to me, Dad. He *loves* me.'

Dad sighs, and pats the bench beside him. 'Sit down, Sara.'

I do as he says. For a long moment, neither of us says anything.

Then, 'When you were about three or four,' Dad says, 'your mother and I went though a bit of a rough patch. Things were rather strained at home. She'd just started a new job, and I didn't much like coming home to fix my own dinner. Caused a few rows, I don't mind telling you.' He smiles wryly. 'Don't forget, it was different then. A man had certain *expectations*. It was my job to put bread on the table, and hers to make something out of it. I didn't hold with her going out to work, and I told her so. But you know your mother. She went out and got herself a job anyway. Receptionist at some posh law firm in town.'

I stare at him in surprise.

'I didn't know Mum had ever worked.'

'Yes, well, there's a lot you don't know about your mum and me.' He rubs his hand over his jaw. 'I know the two of you don't get on, and you lay the blame for everything that goes wrong between you at her door. She can be difficult to live with, I grant you that. But it's not always been easy for her, either.'

A field mouse darts between the potting benches. We both watch it skitter down the centre of the greenhouse and disappear beneath an upturned terracotta pot.

'Anyway. I used to get home earlier than your mother did, and I took to stopping by a neighbour of an evening. For a chat, sometimes a drink or two. She was married, too, but her man was out late most nights. After a while, we got to be friends. *Good* friends.'

The words hang in the air.

'You had an affair!' I gasp.

'I suppose you'd call it that. Turned both our heads, for a while, I'll admit. I was all for upping and leaving your mother, but she wouldn't hear of it. Said she couldn't do that to a little 'un like you. She was the better woman, I'll say that. I was so head-over-heels, I couldn't see straight.' He swallows noisily. 'Went on for the best part of six months. I kept meaning to put an end to it, but I could never seem to find the right moment. And I was so angry at your mother. I never stopped to think of the damage I was causing.' He closes his eyes briefly. 'And then, of course, she found out. Caught us bang to rights – here, as a matter of fact, right in the middle of this greenhouse. Jan had come over—'

'Jan?' I exclaim. '*Mrs Newcombe?*'

He nods.

'Oh, Christ,' I say, covering my face with my hands. 'Libby's about four years younger than me. Please don't tell me—'

'Of course she's not mine! What do you take me for?'

'Well, I'm beginning to wonder,' I say bitterly. 'I can't

believe all this, Dad. It's too much to take in. What did Mum say?'

'She gave me a second chance,' Dad says simply. 'And I took it. I've never regretted it for a moment. Yes, she gave me a dog's life for a year or two, and she still has her moments, but we got past it in the end. And we've been stronger because of it. It taught us to value what we have, and look after it. She gave up the job, not because I asked her to, but because she wanted to show that she was willing to meet me halfway.' He takes my hands in his. 'Sometimes a man makes a mistake, Sara. Gets carried away. And when there are children involved, you owe it them to think twice before you tear their lives apart. I know you love this man, and you believe he loves you.' He shrugs. 'Maybe he does, I don't know. But are you sure, are you really *sure*, that their marriage is over? Because if you're not, Sara, you're ruining an awful lot of lives for nothing; including your own.'

I pull the car over and peer at my *A–Z*. Stapleford has to be around here somewhere, surely to God. I've gone up and down this section of the A36 for forty-five minutes. I must be missing the bloody turn-off.

Slamming the wheel with frustration, I move back into the flow of traffic. This is terrifying enough to do as it is, without getting fucking lost.

Nick asked me to marry him as soon as I told him I was pregnant. And despite the conversation I had just overheard, despite hearing him tell his wife he still loved her and wanted to come back, despite all my doubts and misgivings, I said yes.

I want this baby. I want his child too. Maybe this one will be a boy. A son, someone he can take fishing and teach to play cricket or whatever it is men do with their sons these days. Giving him a child will make *me* just as important to him as *she* is. I won't just be his mistress, I'll be the mother of his baby. We can build on that, work at it, fashion a real relationship out of the bits and pieces we've got now. A child will make all the difference. He loves me, in his own way, I'm sure of it. With a little time and attention, that will grow.

But not if she crooks her finger and he goes running back. I can't live like that. Can't bring a child into that.

I have to know that the door's closed for good.

Finally. I take the turning to Stapleford and sit behind a horse-van, drumming my fingers impatiently on the wheel as we crawl along at fifteen miles an hour. As we stop altogether to let a herd of cows cross the road, I flip down the sun visor and study myself in the mirror. Great. A huge fucking zit, right in the middle of my chin. Just what I need.

I flip the visor back up. It's not only a question of wanting to be sure of Nick. I never thought I'd say it, but – I need absolution. I can't go forward otherwise. It may be impossible to turn the clock back and undo the damage Nick and I have caused, but if I know his wife is at least happy now, perhaps I'll sleep better. Something my mother once said sticks in my head: *you can't build happiness on someone else's misery*. I guess it's a karma thing.

What am I talking about? Of course his wife is happy now. She's got the thinking woman's tottie to warm her bed. I just want her to promise she'll steer clear of my man.

Yes. The irony is *not* lost on me.

We reach a T-junction, and I turn into a narrow track leading up a steep hill. Twice I have to pull over to allow another vehicle to pass in the opposite direction. I open the window and breathe in the dusty, grassy scent of the hedgerows as I drive. A warm breeze dips the cow parsley in my direction, and I sneeze at the sudden downdraught of pollen. I know country life isn't all bucolic vistas and pastoral idylls, I've seen abattoir footage, but it seems so beautiful and meandering out here – a world away from the rush and dirt of London.

Nick's farmhouse is the only one for several miles, bounded on three sides by fields and meadows, and on the fourth by a small copse of young saplings. It looks old and picturesque, if – as I drive nearer – rather in need of some TLC and modern wiring. No wonder he could hardly bear to leave it.

The gate is open. I park in the wide gravel space at the front of the house. My heart thumps wildly in my chest as I get out of the car. *Oh, shit. Suddenly I don't know if I've got the balls to go through with this.*

I can't bring myself to ring the doorbell. Instead, threading my way around several outhouses, I peer through the grimy kitchen window at the back. Inside, it's smaller and messier than I expected: I'd had visions of some *Sunday Times* Nigella Lawson supplement kitchen – all gleaming surfaces and shining saucepan racks. She is a bloody celebrity chef, after all. But the only things suspended above this ancient-looking Aga are some rather grey bras and several pairs of Bridget Jones knickers. The stone floor is covered with newspapers and what look like rabbit droppings, and dirty crockery is piled high in the sink A few chipped pots of dead herbs line the windowsill.

Sitting at the scrubbed pine kitchen table, head buried on her arms, is a small figure in a filthy, ratty old dressing-gown. Her wild tangle of dark hair is unbrushed. Every now and again, her thin shoulders heave.

Oh, God, I shouldn't have come. This was a huge mistake—

She looks up, and I feel a stab of shock. I barely recognize her. Her eyes are swollen and red from crying. Misery is etched on her face. Dark circles under her eyes speak of sleepless nights and long hours waiting for dawn to break. She looks bereft and heartsick, shrunken by grief. There's no trace of the flirty, lively woman who drops off the children every weekend before skipping merrily down to the car and her hot new lover.

I swallow. *I've done this to her.*

She unbolts the door, and turns back into the kitchen without speaking, wrapping her skinny arms around her-self. I step gingerly over a heap of muddy wellingtons.

And then I blurt out the question I came all this way to ask.

15

Malinche

Anger can take you a frighteningly long way, I discover: far from those who love and hurt you, far from everything that's familiar, and – it's this last I find so terrifying – far from everything you thought you knew about yourself.

After I have vomited on Sara's sofa, I wipe my mouth carefully on the back of my wrist. Without even glancing at my husband, now frantically throwing on shirt and shoes and jacket, or his mistress, still standing frozen in shock by the door, her cheap red kimono gaping, I walk out; and keep on walking.

I walk down New Fetter Lane towards Fleet Street, my feet starting to blister in the ridiculous gardening clogs I grabbed in haste from the scullery as I ran from the house, desperate to get to Nicholas before it was too late. Barely noticing the traffic or the fumes or the lewd remarks from hooded teenagers loitering in doorways, I concentrate on putting one foot in front of the other, terrified to stop even for a moment in case I cannot start again. My feet are raw and bloodied by the time I reach the Strand, and the left turn that will take me across Waterloo Bridge, back to the railway station and home; such as it is, now.

But I turn right. I hadn't known where I was headed, until now; but I keep walking, up Bow Street, with renewed purpose, and then, ducking through a maze of small narrow streets, I emerge abruptly in Covent Garden.

His beautiful gourmet shop is easy to find; but it is in darkness, of course, closed, and I realize with a shock that it's after nine-thirty, late; that if he is anywhere, he will be at home now: or else out of my reach entirely. Jostled by tourists and theatre-goers, I take a side turning out of the piazza, and within moments find myself in an elegant old street, lined with tall, narrow white houses; graceful, sophisticated houses that seem to close their eyes with pained expressions at the litter and the down-and-outs and the youths urinating into the street.

I mount the steps of his townhouse, knowing that if he's not in, or turns me away – we've barely spoken, after all, since Rome – I shall simply curl up in a corner and wait to be blown away, like the rest of the unwanted rubbish bowling along the street like urban tumbleweed.

But he *is* in. And when he opens the door, and I stumble across the threshold in my bare, bleeding feet, clutching the silly clogs in my hand, my hair whipped wild by the wind, my face streaked with tears I hadn't known I was weeping, he simply picks me up without a word and carries me upstairs.

I awake to the sounds and smells of a summer a long time ago. Nancy Sinatra's 'Sugartown' plays distantly in another room. Coffee and freshly squeezed orange juice scent the air – I sit up, realizing he has placed a breakfast tray at the foot of the bed, complete with croissants and muffins and a single white rose – and sunshine streams across the high, white brass bed from the bank of French windows, casting rhombuses of light on the hand-finished planked floor. One pair of doors is flung wide open; white muslin curtains billow in the light breeze, catching on the iron railing. Overhead, a woven plantation fan slowly turns. I feel like I have stepped into a Flake advert; all I need now is a lizard on the Bakelite telephone.

I sink back against the marshmallowy pillows, pulling the fluffy cloud of duvet up to my chin. Even my British winter pallor looks fetchingly honeyed against this much eye-watering white.

My thighs ache; there is a raw, sticky, unfamiliar throb between my legs.

Last night, after Trace ran me a bath in his clawfooted movie-bathroom tub, and soaped my back, and rinsed my hair free of vomit and street grime and tears, he took me to bed; and made love to me with such controlled passion, such gentleness, that the ice storm in my heart finally ceased blowing its frozen winds through my body.

At the thought of that erotic, blush-making sex – 'Lights *on*,' Trace said firmly, 'I want to see you, all of you, I want to see your face when you come' – I suddenly realize I'm ravenous.

I sit up in bed and pull the tray towards me. I am on my third croissant and raspberry jam when Trace comes in, towelling hair still damp from the shower. His white linen shirt and cornflower-blue linen pants would look outrageously *Men's Vogue* on anyone else. His feet are bare. Despite the satiating gymnastics of last night, a pulse beats somewhere in the region of where the knickers of a thirty-something married mother-of-three *should* be – which is *not* twisted inside out and hanging on the bedpost of her lover.

'Sleep well?' he asks, throwing aside the towel to sit on the edge of the bed.

I rescue my glass of orange juice as it tilts on the tray. 'Oh, *yes*,' I purr, stretching lazily, 'I can't remember when I last—'

I bolt upright, nearly sending everything flying. 'What time is it?' I grab his wrist to see his watch. 'Eleven-thirty! Trace, you should never have let me sleep in that long! – the children! – I need to get home. And Edward, *poor* Edward, I must speak to Daisy, I—'

'All taken care of,' he says, 'I rang Kit. He's arranged for Liz to keep the girls until tomorrow evening, they're all going to some gymkhana or another, having the time of their lives. And Kit checked with the hospital: no news yet, he'll call me back as soon as he hears anything. But in the meantime you,' he says briskly, taking the locusted tray from my lap and flipping back the duvet, 'need to get up. I have plans for you today.'

His gaze lingers appreciatively. Blushing furiously, I grab back the bedclothes.

He laughs and stands up.

'I took the liberty of getting Alice – my right-hand, Alice, couldn't manage without her – to nip along to Whistles and get you something fresh to wear. Five minutes, downstairs. And don't bother to shower,' he adds, with a wink, 'you're not going to need it where you're going.'

I wait until he leaves the room before getting out of bed (thirteen years and three children is a little too much water under the bridge in the cold light of day) and open the bag he's left propped against a beautiful cherrywood armoire. Alice, whoever she is, has taste; and common sense. In addition to the simple turquoise tunic and loose-fitting cropped cream trousers, she's included some flat, non-blister-rubbing (oh, bliss!) sandals, a pretty pair of pink-and-white knickers and a matching bra. All in the correct sizes. If I didn't know better, I'd think she'd done this kind of errand for Trace before.

I catch myself. *Of course she has.* He's hardly been living the life of a monk for the past ten years whilst I've been marrying and giving birth to three infants. I catch up my hair with a clip, feeling a little disoriented by the speed things are moving.

'Come on. You have no idea how many strings I had to pull to get you in at this short notice,' Trace urges, as soon as I come downstairs. He tenderly wipes a splodge of jam from the corner of my mouth with his thumb. 'Luckily the girl who takes the bookings is a friend of mine.'

That ugly twinge of jealousy again. I give myself a shake. *It was this kind of absurd paranoia that ruined everything last time.*

Five minutes later, I'm being propelled across the cobbles towards the glass door of the Sanctuary, a girls-only oasis of spoiling I have visited only in my dreams. Liz and I always said we'd treat ourselves and book a day there for our fortieth birthdays, get Giles and Nicholas to mind the children—

A fist of pain winds me. I take a deep breath, and open my eyes again.

Dear Lord, what am I *doing* here? Wandering around Covent Garden in strange clothes with aches in strange places from a night of sex with a man who is not my husband whilst my children are somewhere in the wilds of Wiltshire and Nicholas is – *Nicholas is*—

'Go on,' Trace prompts, 'I can't go in with you. You've got an entire day, booked and paid for – massage, aromatherapy, toe painting, belly-button cleaning, the works—'

'Belly-button cleaning?'

He grins, and my heart lurches as if I've just driven over a hump-backed bridge.

'Well, I don't know what they do in there, do I? I'll see you at five, a new woman.' His eyes gleam wickedly. 'Not that there's anything wrong with the old one, if last night is anything to go by—'

He kisses my flushed cheek, and I follow his long-limbed stride as it eats up the cobbled street.

There are so many confused thoughts whirling around my head, tangling into a Gordian knot of fear and panic, that the only way I can prevent myself from splintering into a thousand pieces is by refusing to acknowledge any of them. And so I meekly go inside and submit to the pampering that has been arranged for me, deliberately emptying my mind until it's as blank and cloudless as the sky on a sunny day.

At five, pummelled and polished and smoothed and painted, I am collected as promised, and taken straight to Michaeljohn, where my hair is smoothed and tamed and coiled on my head. And then to Gucci, where he has picked out a dress – black, thank heavens – which fits me beautifully, and is perfect for the film première (*a première!*) in Leicester Square, where I try not to hang on his arm too adoringly, too obviously. And then to Boujis, to dance until four a.m., when he finally takes me, drooping, home, and to bed; and, eventually, to sleep.

On Sunday, we drive out to Oxford for an afternoon picnic – roast pheasant, grilled asparagus, truffles stuffed with Bermuda onion *confit* and the smallest, sweetest early strawberries, washed down with a bottle of cold Krug Tête de Cuvée – lolling on a riverbank across from a beautiful, mellow stone college; not the one Nicholas went to, that was further in town—

Don't think don't think don't think.

Trace finally drives me home to Wiltshire a little before eight; and then calls me on his mobile before his car has even pulled out of the gravel driveway.

'I miss you,' he says.

'You've only been gone two minutes!'

'I *miss* you,' he says firmly.

'You too,' I say, sifting through the clutch of envelopes on the floor, hoping Liz will bring the children back soon, to fill this empty house – strangely cold despite the Aga – with laughter and noise. 'Now go, you mustn't talk to me whilst you're driving, I don't want you to crash.'

'I'll call you in the morning,' he says.

And he does. He rings me in the morning, and at lunch, and in the afternoon; he peppers my day with calls to see how I am, to check that the hours aren't dragging, and then at seven he scoops me up on his white charger (well, racing-green Aston Martin) and whisks me out to dinner. When he drops me off later, *much* later, that night,

I am so tired that I fall asleep the moment my head hits the pillow, my tears drying unnoticed on my cheeks.

Every day that week he calls me; every night, he takes me out whilst Kit babysits: to the theatre, the movies (a romantic comedy with a handsome new actor I haven't seen before, someone called Matthew McConaughey; it's *years* since I saw a film at the cinema), to an art gallery, to dinner. And afterwards, he takes me back to his cottage in the village, where we spend some energetic, pleasurable hours in bed – not quite as smooth, as practised, as with Nicholas, perhaps, not quite as *easy*; but then it *has* been a long time, we are having to learn each other all over again.

I never stay the night. The children need me home, at the breakfast table as I always am, constant and steady. Now that their father has gone.

Trace keeps me so busy, that what with the girls, and my work (for some reason the recipes come thick and fast, now; feverishly I race to write them down) I don't have a moment to dwell. To think or wonder what I'm doing, or where this is all going. I'm a dancer whose partner has spun away, out of her reach, only for another to take her hand, whirling her back into the reel with steps so fast she barely has time to register the change.

I feel as if I'm on a merry-go-round, colours and shapes spinning past me so quickly everything has become a blur.

Even if I wanted to, I wouldn't know how to get off.

It is Kit, of all people, who sounds the first warning note.

'It's happening too fast, darling,' he says, kneading my

shoulders as I sew in name-tapes, 'too *soon*; heaven knows I don't want to rain on your parade, but you can't just bounce from the marital bed to the arms of your admittedly toothsome lover. It's just not you.'

I bite off a thread.

'How do you know,' I demand, 'how do you *know* that about me?'

'Angel. It's barely three weeks since you marched into his girlfriend's flat and told your husband not to come home, before vomiting heroically all over her sofa. You then walked straight round to your childhood sweetheart—'

'Hardly childhood—'

'—and hopped into bed with *him*—'

'It's not as if Nicholas—'

'Since then,' Kit interrupts firmly, 'he's had you gallivanting all over town, rushing off to one glam junket after another. He's turned your head and blown your mind with premières and parties; he hasn't given you a moment to yourself.'

'I haven't wanted—'

Kit brooks no argument. I can't remember ever seeing him this serious.

'For the past month, your beautifully shod feet – *love* the Ginas, by the way, darling – have barely touched the ground. And let's not even get into the extraordinary pink paint job you've given your bedroom; what on earth possessed you, Malinche, did you give Barbie *carte blanche*?'

He releases my shoulders and drops into the chair opposite me. 'Look, darling, I'm not saying you shouldn't enjoy yourself a little,' he sighs, 'but for the best of motives Trace deliberately isn't giving you a moment's peace to think. And think, my darling, is what you really need to do before you let this go any further.'

'I can't,' I say, terrified. 'I can't, Kit. If I start to think, I'll break apart, I'll collapse, I'll be no good to anyone—'

'Malinche, apart from anything else, this isn't fair to Trace. If you two are going to make a go of it, it has to be honest. And sooner or later, you're going to have to face Nicholas—'

'Tomorrow, actually, Kit,' I say faintly. 'It's Edward's funeral.'

Kit is silent for a long moment. He lights a cigarette: now that Nicholas isn't here, I've given in and allowed him to smoke in the kitchen. Exhaling slowly, he blows a stream of smoke across the table.

He pounces with the speed and accuracy of a rattlesnake.

'Trace or Nicholas?'

'Nicholas,' I say instantly: and then gasp and cover my mouth.

'It doesn't count,' I whisper, 'it's just force of habit—'

'This,' says Kit, 'is why you need to think.'

My chair scrapes hideously across the stone floor.

'There's nothing to think about, is there?' I cry anguishedly. 'Because I don't actually have a choice! Nicholas has gone and he isn't coming back! He hasn't even called once to see how I'm doing, much less thrown himself at my feet and begged for forgiveness—'

'Do you still love him?'

'What does it matter, if *he* doesn't love *me*? And Trace *does*. Trace makes me feel special and wanted and cherished! I've loved him for as long as I can remember, I can't imagine ever not.'

'But you love *me*,' Kit says. 'Not quite the same thing, though, is it?'

I start to shake. Kit stubs out his cigarette and pulls me into a hug, resting his chin on the top of my head.

'Why are you doing this?' I sob into his shirt. 'You don't even *like* Nicholas. You've pushed and pushed me to be with Trace. Why are you doing this?'

'Because somebody has to make you face the truth,' Kit says simply. 'Whatever it is. You can't keep burying your head – and your heart – in the sand forever. You have to allow yourself time to grieve for your marriage. You can't just move on to Trace as if the two men are interchangeable. This isn't real.'

But it's not that simple, I think the next day, watching as Edward Lyon's casket is lowered into a gaping dark wound sliced into the bright green grass, tears streaming unchecked down my face. I used to believe that every one of us had a soul mate – 'A *bashert*,' I explained to Nicholas, not long after we first met, 'that's Yiddish for destined other' – but perhaps that's fanciful, too suggestive of order and purpose in a life that is really nothing but chaos and confusion. Thirteen years ago, I was convinced Trace was my soul mate; then I met Nicholas, and was suddenly certain that *he* was the man I was destined to be with. And now? Now I don't know what I believe. I'm not sure I believe in anything any more.

All I know is that Trace wants me. And Nicholas doesn't.

After the service, I stop by Nicholas as he helps his mother into the waiting car. For several moments, I struggle for words. What do you say to a man who has shared your bed for more than ten years, and now looks straight through you, as if you're not even there?

'This isn't what I wanted,' I manage, finally. 'I wanted to wait you out. I did *try*.'

'How long have you known?' he says shortly.

'Since the Law Society dinner.'

'How did you—'

How can he be so cold, so *clinical*? I choke back a sob on his name.

He shifts uncomfortably. 'Malinche, is there any chance I could come—'

I cut him off, not yet ready to have him at the house, emptying his wardrobe, clearing his book shelves; not yet ready to put away the framed wedding photographs – currently flat on their glass faces, but still *there*. Misery makes my tone harsher than I intend. 'No, Nicholas. I'm sorry.'

'I know how this must sound: but it didn't mean anything. Please—'

'Of course it *meant* something, to me, if not to you! You aren't the only one affected by this. It's not up to you to decide if it meant something or not.'

'I realize you're angry now, but—'

'Angry,' I breathe fiercely, 'doesn't begin to cover it.'

'You can't mean to go through with this. Separation. A divorce. Surely?'

Divorce. The word hits me like a hammer blow. Of course, I think bleakly. He'll want to marry *her* now. I shrug dully. 'What else did you expect, Nicholas?'

'Can't we at least *talk*? What about the children, did you think about what this will—'

'Did *you*?'

Two grave-diggers pass us, cigarettes and shovels in hand. The grief on my husband's face as his eyes follow them is so naked, so raw, that despite myself, my anger dissolves. 'Nicholas,' I say quietly, 'now isn't the time. I've told the children you're looking after Grandma at the moment. When the time is right, we can tell them that you – that we—'

'Can I see them?' he says, his voice cracking slightly.

'Of course you can see them! I would have brought them to see you before, but you were always either working or at the hospital. It didn't seem right to involve them in all of that.'

From the corner of my eye, I see Trace get out of the car – which I asked him to wait in; I don't want Nicholas to see him, not now, not here, at his father's funeral – and walk towards me. He stops twenty feet away, hovering on the edge of a knot of mourners. Waiting.

I turn back to Nicholas. A strange expression crosses his face; almost a look of yearning. Suddenly, dizzily, the years fall away, and I'm standing before him, at the altar, my hand in his, the gold of my wedding band shiny and new and foreign on my finger. And as we stand outside another church, ten years later, for a funeral, not a wedding, I understand, with startling clarity, that I still love him, that my love for him is stamped through me like a stick of rock, that even if I'm shattered into a thousand pieces by grief it will always be there, running through the centre of my being, an absolute certainty; and that all he has to do is tell me he loves me now and nothing else will matter: *nothing at all—*

But, 'I'd like to see them this weekend,' he says coolly, 'if that's all right.'

We arrange his painful, timeshare access to the children; at his mother's house – I can't quite bear to think of *her* with them yet. A part of me wants to fight him, to make it as difficult as I know how, to hurt him in the only way left to me. But that would hurt our daughters, too, and I can't do that. They are suffering enough as it is. And however angry I am with Nicholas, however much I hate him in the small hours of the morning, when Trace has gone and I am left to sob into my pillow, I can't do it to him either.

I say goodbye and walk away from him, towards Trace, who loves me, honestly and unreservedly, who will be the one I'm *with*, now, if not quite the one I *love*; and realize for the first time that I've lost my husband forever.

'But you said I could have it!'

'No, I never! I said you could have it later.'

'It *is* later! You've been ages. Give it to me, Mummy said we had to share—'

'I haven't finished with it yet! It's not *fair*.'

'But I want it now!'

'Give it back! Give it back, you'll break it! You can't do it anyway – *now* look what you've done! I'm telling on you! *Muu-uuu-mmmmy!*'

Louise marches into the sitting room. I hear her scary, Mary Poppins tones through a foot of thick cob wall. 'Stop it, the pair of you!' she says sharply. 'You'll wake the baby. One more word out of either of you and neither of you will see that PlayStation again.'

'I don't know *what* Nicholas was thinking,' she adds, coming back into the kitchen, 'buying them expensive electronic toys at their age. Buying their approval, if you ask me.'

'Well, it seems to be working,' I say despondently.

'Children aren't *stupid*, Malinche. They'll see through it—'

'Chessington was a roaring success last weekend,' I despair. 'The girls came back full of how *Sara* took them on all the big rides, *Sara* took them to have their faces painted, *Sara* didn't mind at all when she got absolutely soaking wet on the flumes.' I pick fretfully at my nails. 'She's practically half my age, she doesn't nag them to brush their teeth or do their homework, of course she's going to seem fun compared to their ancient dull mother, no wonder Nicholas upped and—'

Louise slams her palm on the kitchen table. I jump six feet; in the scullery, I hear the frantic scrabble of claws against wood as poor Don Juan nearly dies of fright.

'You can stop that nonsense right now,' she says fiercely. 'Self-pity will get you nowhere. Your eldest daughter has a great deal more sense than you give her credit for. She's pushing your buttons, that's all. Testing you, to see how you feel about all of this.'

I bite the inside of my cheek.

Louise folds her arms. 'Little Miss Drop-Her-Drawers is full of peace and love right now,' she says thoughtfully, 'whisking your adorable little girls off to theme parks and playing dress-up and braiding their hair. Easy to play the fairy godmother when you can throw money at the problem for a couple of hours and then send them home. It's all a little different when you have to live with them twenty-four/seven.'

I've never quite got used to my mother's easy appropriation of teenage slang.

'Tell me about it,' I say crossly, going into the scullery to soothe Don Juan. 'Metheny slept in my bed for two nights after they got back, and Sophie was an absolute swine for days. Wouldn't do her homework, refused to clean out the rabbit's cage, was beastly to her sisters—'

'Real life, in other words. Something Nicholas must be missing.'

I toss a carrot into the rabbit's cage. 'What are you getting at?'

Her mouth twitches. 'I think perhaps it's a little unfair to refuse to allow them to stay over at Madam's flat after all. Nicholas said his mother found it all a bit much, so soon after losing Edward. Maybe you should *let* them spend the weekends with the lovebirds at their bijou little nest after all. Their charming, one-bedroom, no-garden, white, minimalist London flat.'

I gasp delightedly. 'Louise, I can't, they'll run amok—'

'Well, come on, Malinche,' she says robustly. 'It's one thing to put the children first, but no one said you had to be a saint. The little trollop pinched your husband from right under your nose. It's about time you rubbed hers in a little reality. And it won't do any harm at all if you drag that ridiculously handsome new man of yours with you either. Nicholas could do with a taste of his own medicine. And before you start in about turning the other cheek and the rest of that nonsense,' she adds tartly, '*I'm* not the one who threw up all over her sofa.'

*

Trace and I sit in darkness, the three girls asleep, finally, on the back seat behind us. He cuts the engine, but neither of us can summon the energy to get out of the car.

'Well. That was a big hit, wasn't it?'

I start to laugh, end up on a half-sob. 'I'm so sorry. I don't know what else to say.'

'I think unmitigated disaster just about covers it. Hey,' he says, as I dissolve into tears, 'hey, relax. It's OK. No one expects children to be angels all the time. The more it matters to you that they behave, the less likely it is to happen, you know that. Come on, Mal. I hate it when you cry.'

'But they were awful!' I wail. 'The worst they've ever been! I don't know *what* got into them, I bet they're not like that for their father—'

He wraps his arms around me and I rest my head against his shoulder. I can feel his heart beating, strong and steady, beneath my cheek. 'Look,' he murmurs into my hair, 'it's been a tough time for them. Perhaps it was too soon for us to all go away together to France. I know they'll have to get used to it eventually, but maybe it was just too much, what with having to deal with Nicholas and Sara too. Give them a little time, and it'll sort itself out.'

I dash the back of my hand across my nose. Trace is right. The past few weekends have been dreadful; certainly for me. Watching my children – *my* children, *mine*! – walk into that woman's arms. Well, not literally, Nicholas did at least have the decency to keep her out of sight: but it might just as well have been. I don't know how I'd have borne it if it hadn't been for Trace.

And I deserve an Oscar for my performances on the

doorstep. Smiling, laughing like I haven't a care in the world, refusing to let Nicholas see the pain splintering my heart. I do have my pride.

I dress more carefully to drop off my children than for anything since my wedding day. *I am not a victim. I am not.*

'You've cut your hair,' Nicholas said, shocked, one Saturday.

'Kit persuaded me to go to his stylist in London.' Without thinking, I added, 'Do you like it?'

I could have kicked myself for sounding so needy. But, to my surprise, 'I love it,' Nicholas said. 'It's very short, very gamine, but it really suits you. I don't think I've ever seen you with your hair short like this before.'

It's funny how the pain catches you unawares, just when you think you are ready for it, have steeled yourself for the worst. In bed, Nicholas would often twine my hair around his fingers, telling me how much he loved it long, making me promise never to cut it. He said he loved the way it fell across my face when I was on top of him, claimed it made me seem wild and abandoned.

'I used to have it this way, before we met,' I said steadily. 'But you never let me cut it. You always insisted I keep it long.'

'Did I?'

He didn't even remember. *Oh, dear God, when will the pain stop?*

I smiled sadly. 'You used to insist on a lot of things, Nicholas.'

I got back into the car and sobbed for the entire hour it took us to drive to the beautiful country manor house in Kent that Trace had booked for the weekend. To his great credit, he never once indicated that he was anything other than thrilled to be rubbing my back as I snivelled and hiccoughed like a child. I don't know if I'd have been so phlegmatic if the boot had been on the other foot and it had been Trace bawling his eyes out over an ex-girlfriend.

When Nicholas rang last week to ask if I could keep the children this weekend, I was thrilled. Mondays to Fridays are such a slog, getting the girls ready for school, cleaning, laundering, helping with homework; it's the weekends with them that are the real treats. Well, usually. I've really missed them the past few weeks when they've been with their father. Nicholas and I are clearly going to have to come to some sort of arrangement to divide our time with them more fairly; perhaps a midweek visit and alternate weekends. Oh, Lord, the horrid, soul-destroying business of divorce.

Trace and I extended our original romantic reservation at the farmhouse in Normandy to include the children, and I had thought it might be the perfect time to introduce them properly to Trace. Not just as Mummy's friend, but as – well, Mummy's *friend*.

It started to go wrong the moment we got into the car. First the non-stop battery of questions – 'Why aren't we going to Daddy's this weekend? Doesn't he want to see us? Are we going *next* weekend? *Why* don't you know? Can we ring and ask him? *Why* can't we ring? Can we ring later? *When?*' – and then the sulks, punctuated by demands to stop the car every five minutes for the lavatory, a drink, to be sick. When Trace finally insisted that everyone do up their seatbelts and hold their bladders and their bile until we got to the Eurotunnel train, Sophie muttered, audibly, 'You're not our father. You can't tell us what to do.'

Once in France, it just got worse. The girls hated the farmhouse: the sheets were scratchy, the room too cold, the food too *foreign*; they were bored, they couldn't watch television, they had nothing to *do*. Did they want to go to the beach? Duh, raining! Well, how about a nice long walk along the river? I've got your anoraks, in some places it's shallow enough to paddle in – oh. All right. Maybe a pony ride, then; wouldn't that be nice? It'll be dry in the forest, under the trees. They're very friendly, you can feed them if you – well, what *do* you want to do? No, I've told you. Your father is busy this weekend. I don't *know* what he's doing. No, I can't ring and ask him. *No!*

When, on Sunday, the owner of the *pension* apologetically explained that her mother had been taken ill, she was *extrêmement désolé*, she couldn't cook us our lunch after all, *c'est bien dommage*, she'd quite understand if we wanted to leave early: we all *leapt* at the chance.

The drive home has been the only peaceful part of the entire trip, I think ruefully, glancing at the sleeping children in the back.

Trace carries the bags into the house, whilst I rouse Sophie and Evie, who stumble, drowsy and grumbling, up the garden path, and carry Metheny, still sleeping, upstairs to her bedroom. She doesn't wake even when I undress her and lay her gently in her cot.

For a long moment, I stand looking down at her, my hand resting possessively on the side of the rail, moonlight gilding the plump curve of her cheek, warm as a ripe peach.

Our last-chance baby: named for the jazz guitarist Nicholas loves so much. She still isn't yet two. *What* happened to us? How did it all go so wrong, so fast?

I sink onto the window seat, watching Trace unloading her pushchair from the car below. He looks so competent and assured, it's as if he's been doing this for years. *But he hasn't*, I remind myself. *He* isn't the father of your children. However much you have, at times, wished he were.

Kit was right when he said I hadn't got over Trace when I met Nicholas. That I loved Nicholas, I had no doubt. But I didn't give myself time to heal. I simply papered over the cracks, and threw myself headlong into Nicholas; *used* him, perhaps, to get over Trace and so started everything out on the wrong foot from the beginning. When Sophie was placed into my arms, even as Nicholas and I gazed at each other in awe at what we had made and I drank in her pink-and-white perfection, greedily, a tiny part of me wondered what my lost baby would have looked like: how it would have felt to give birth to Trace's child. Once a year, I slipped away to the tiny Catholic church in Salisbury to light a candle for him – it was a boy, I'm sure it was a boy – and thought of Trace. Every time Nicholas and I ever had a row, and we were married ten years, *of course* we rowed, a secret, black part of my heart turned, disloyally, towards Trace. Wondered if he would have cancelled a skiing trip because of work, or failed to buy a single Christmas present *again*, or undermined me with the children: whatever silly, domestic niggle had triggered the fight. My internal calendar observed his birthday, the day we met, the date we parted. I followed his exploits in the gossip columns, telling myself the ugly swirl of jealousy was maternal frustration at his refusal to grow up. I never acknowledged it, even to myself; but he was as much a part of my marriage as I was, an undercurrent always tugging, tugging me away from Nicholas.

If I hadn't been so focused on Trace, on his sudden physical presence in my life after a decade of imagining, I would have seen what was happening with Nicholas. Perhaps, even, in time to stop it.

I reach up to close the curtains. Trace glances up as he locks the car, smiles, lifts his hand. He really is startlingly handsome.

All these years, I've secretly believed Trace was my soul mate, wrenched from me by Fate. I've thought of Nicholas as the sensible choice, the husband of expediency, the safe, steady, reliable option; loving and loved, of course, but not passionately, not in the wild, untamed way I had loved and was loved by Trace.

But Trace and I weren't destroyed by jealous gods. The rather prosaic truth is that we were never right for each other. I was always convinced I didn't deserve him: which is why I was so ready to believe the worst. And he just wanted to *fix* me.

Nothing has changed. He is still racing around, bending life to suit him by sheer force of will. And if I no longer feel inadequate, I can see how wildly unmatched we are. Have always been. I don't want a saviour; I want a partner. A friend, an equal. *I want Nicholas.*

My hand shakes. All this time I've spent missing something I never had, letting what *really* mattered slip through my fingers.

Nicholas is the love of my life, not Trace. It is Nicholas I love with a real passion, born of years of loyalty and laughter and shared love; of tears and hardship, too. Frustration and joy, contentment and boredom: that's what makes up a marriage, that's what *real* love is all about.

I close Metheny's door softly. It's not that I don't love Trace: I do. But not enough to make this work, however easy and safe it would be for me.

He glances up as I walk into the kitchen and pushes a mug of tea towards me. 'Here, thought you could do with this—'

My eyes fill. *This is going to be so hard.*

'No,' I say softly.

He knows immediately that I am not talking about the tea. A shadow crosses his face, replaced in an instant by his usual, easy smile. 'It was just a bad day, Mal,' he soothes. 'A bad couple of days. It doesn't mean anything. Next time, it'll be easier—'

'*No.*'

Outwardly relaxed, smiling still, he leans back against the sink. Only by the whiteness of his knuckles can I see that this is just an act.

'Why don't I go home and give you a call in the morning?' he says, his voice carefully neutral. 'It's late, we're all tired, and it's been a long journey. Perhaps next week we should—'

'Trace,' I say gently. 'This isn't going to work. *Us.* You know that as much as I do.'

His eyes darken. A muscle moves in his jaw, but he doesn't speak.

'You know I'm right,' I press. 'We're just too different, Trace. We want different things. It's been fun for you playing at being a husband and father these last few months, and you've been wonderful with the girls, but it isn't you,' I say. 'Not yet, anyway. We don't really fit into your life. I'm not the person you should have on your arm. You should be escorting some glamorous, leggy model up the red carpet, not an old married woman like me.' I touch his arm; he doesn't respond. 'That life isn't *me*, Trace. Never was. It was exciting for a while, but it's not my world. And *this* world – ' I spread my arm, taking in the paintings Blu-tacked to the kitchen wall, the anoraks slung over the backs of chairs, the Lego in the fruit bowl ' – this isn't *yours*. We've both been stuck in the past, seeing each other the way we were thirteen years ago. But life has moved on since then. *We've* moved on.'

'I'd learn all of this,' he says, painfully. 'The nappies and the Pony Club and the rest of it, if that's what you wanted.'

'It isn't that—'

'Nicholas,' he says heavily.

'Nicholas,' I agree.

We both know there is really nothing more to be said.

Trace heaves himself away from the sink.

'I should go,' he says awkwardly. 'There is – there's someone I should call. Someone – nothing would have happened if – anyway. I said I might ring. And I should go.'

We both know there isn't anyone. But there will be.

'Friends?' he asks, his voice catching slightly.

'The best,' I whisper.

For a long time after he's left, I sit at the kitchen table, wondering if I have made the worst mistake of my life, pushed away the man I love for a second time. And then

I finger the wedding band on my finger, and I know that however terrifying it is to let him go, I'm right. I care too much for Trace to condemn him to life as second best. And for as long as I'm in love with my husband, that's all it would be.

Four days later Nicholas files for divorce.

I can't believe he's done this. Actually gone to a solicitor, sat in an office and regurgitated the story of our marriage to a virtual stranger, sifted through the dirty laundry of our lives together for something to fling at me, to make this outrageous charge of *unreasonable behaviour* stick.

How *could* he? How could he do this to me?

I bury my head on my arms, the ugly legal papers scattered over the table in front of me. I can't bring myself even to read them through; the first paragraph was enough. I can't bring myself to move. I know I should eat, get dressed, clear up the kitchen, but I'm unable even to summon the energy to lift my head from my arms. Thank God for Liz, answering my howl after I opened the morning post and called her, dashing over to take the girls to school.

It's real. It's really over. He isn't going to come back, throw himself at my knees and beg me to forgive him. He's left me, and he's going to marry this girl.

A bloom of hatred wells in my heart, and as suddenly dies, unable to find purchase. My despair and grief are so all-consuming, I have no room for anything else.

Suddenly I can't stop the tears. I keen like a wounded animal, crying for hours until I have no tears left, and still

I weep, dry, racking heaves. Darkness oozes through my soul. I cannot even imagine how it might feel to smile.

Hours later, dimly, I register the sound of a car on the gravel outside. A minute or two passes, and I become aware of a presence behind me. I look round and see Sara standing outside my kitchen door.

It doesn't matter any more. Nothing matters any more.

I open the door, then retreat to the safety of the Aga, wrapping my dressing-gown tighter about my body.

She takes a huge breath. I realize she's nervous. How strange. I can't imagine feeling nervous, or anything else, ever again.

'Do you want him back?' she asks.

She makes it sound as if she's returning my ball. *This landed in my garden, and I was just wondering—*

I stare at her for a few moments, at this girl – no, that lets her off the hook too easily, as if she is too young to know any better, as if she isn't responsible for what she's done – this *woman*, I think, this woman who has so casually picked up my life, shaken free what she wanted from it, and cast the rest aside. An angry red spot, like an insect bite, disfigures her chin.

I put the kettle on the hot plate of the Aga. 'Tea?'

She hesitates, then nods.

'It'll take a while. It's not like an electric kettle.'

'That's fine.'

'I'm sorry I'm not dressed. I wasn't expecting—'

'I know. I should have called, but I thought you wouldn't see me—'

'I wouldn't,' I say, 'if I had a choice.'

'No.'

The silence spreads.

I gesture to the table. 'Why don't you sit down. I'm sorry about the rabbit, one of the children let it out this morning and I haven't been able to persuade him to go back in his cage.' I rub at a patch of eczema on the inside of my left wrist. 'I can't say I blame him, I wouldn't want to be cooped up in there all day myself, I'd let him wander around in the garden but something might get him. Last time he was let outside he was nearly eaten by next door's dog—'

'Evie?' Sara hazards.

'She wanted him to go organic,' I say, sighing.

She smiles. Ambushed, I smile back.

We're like tourists, trapped in a foreign land, trying to find common ground – 'From which part of Wiltshire? Oh, how *extraordinary*, my son's godfather lives not far from you' – so that we feel less alone. Safety in numbers. The kettle boils; I busy myself making us tea, choosing two mugs that aren't chipped, setting out milk and sugar on the table. Hurriedly, I heap the divorce papers into a pile, and hide them beneath one of Metheny's paintings.

The link between us, such as it was, dissolves.

'What did you mean,' I ask abruptly, 'when you asked if I wanted him back?'

The grandfather clock ticks loudly in the hall. Somewhere beneath my feet, Don Juan scrabbles, his claws clicking on the stone floor. I don't like her perfume: strong and synthetic. It makes me feel slightly sick.

'I need to know,' she says finally, staring into her mug. 'I can't make a go of things until I do. I don't want to come home every night wondering if he's gone back home to you.' The strap of her bag slides off her shoulder and she pushes it back. 'That's all. I just want to know it's over between you.'

She isn't here to put things right. She hasn't come to apologize: *if you want him back, here you are, he's yours.* She isn't going to tell me it's all been a terrible mistake. She's here for reassurance: that I won't steal him back from her.

A bubble of hysterical laughter rises to my lips. I cover my mouth with my hand.

'You expect me to *help* you?' I demand incredulously.

Her cheeks stain. 'I know it seems ridiculous, me coming to you. I know you must hate me. I've given you every reason. But you have Trace now,' she pleads. 'You don't need Nicholas any more. Can't you let him go? Can't you let him be happy with me?'

I lean both arms heavily on the sink, my back towards her. 'I'm not stopping him.'

'But he needs to know you've moved on. He can't shut the door otherwise. You have to tell him—'

'I don't,' I say coldly, '*have* to do anything.'

She swallows hard. I pull the edges of my dressing-gown a little closer.

'I'm sorry,' she mumbles. 'I didn't mean it like that. Of course you don't have to say anything. It's just – I don't understand. Your marriage was dead, you have a new life now, I know you must be upset that things worked out as they did, but it wasn't my fault—'

I spin round.

'What makes you think my marriage was dead?'

'But—' she flounders. 'But there's Trace—'

'No,' I say tightly, 'there isn't. For a few weeks,

perhaps, after Nicholas left, he filled the gap. Or rather, tried to. Nothing, actually, can mend the rip in my heart that losing my husband to you has made. Nothing.'

She bites her lip. I'm suddenly reminded how young she is; how little she knows.

Old enough.

'Do you have any idea what you've *done*?' I demand fiercely. '*Do you?* The damage you've caused? Do you know what it's like to listen to your child sob herself to sleep in the next room because her father's left and she thinks that somehow it must be her fault?' My body trembles with anger. 'Do you know what it's like to face her in the morning and see the accusation in her eyes, because you couldn't protect her from this pain? You've taken away from my children the *one* thing I wanted to give them more than anything else: a happy, stable home.' I close my eyes, misery rising in my throat like bile. 'You're not a mother: you can't know. They'll carry the scars with them for the rest of their lives. They'll take this baggage with them into every relationship they ever have. A mother wouldn't do this. A mother wouldn't smash three little girls' childhoods just for the sake of a quick roll in the hay.'

She seems to shrink back in her chair with each word, as if I'm pelting her with rocks. *Good*, I think bitterly. Let it hurt. *Good*.

'You think my marriage is dead because he slept with you?' I challenge. 'Well, let me tell you something, Sara. Marriage is hard work. *Very* hard work. If you don't both put everything you have into making it a success, it fails. Sometimes it's wonderful and romantic and everything you ever dreamed it would be when you stood at the altar and made your vows to love and cherish until death parted you. And sometimes,' I say, my voice hard, 'it's dull and frustrating and difficult and you can scarcely bear the sight of each other. Sometimes you bore each other to tears. It only takes one trip, one stumble, and it can all come crashing down.'

I push my hair behind my ears, my hands shaking with anger. What can *she* know of seeing ten years of your life wiped out in a few short hours? Of watching the man you've loved, whose children you've borne, walk away from you to another woman?

'My marriage was very much alive until he met you,' I hiss. 'But you didn't care. You saw someone you wanted, and you took him. *You took him.*'

'I didn't make him,' she protests. 'He had a choice. He *wanted* me.'

'What man wouldn't?' I laugh shortly. 'You're beautiful. You're young. You're not his wife. Of *course* he wanted you. But did he make the first move, or did *you*?'

She looks away.

'You won't always be twenty-six,' I say bitterly, 'with your smooth unlined face and firm body. You think you'll be young forever at your age. Forty seems as far away as a hundred. But it sneaks up on you when you're not looking. Nothing happens for years and years – and then suddenly, *wham!*, you wake up one day and your hips have got bigger and your lips have got smaller and your breasts are halfway down to your stretch-marks and what the hell happened? But *he*,' I add, '*he* just gets distinguished wings of grey at his temples and *character* in his face and secretaries' eyes following him as he walks past their desks.'

I wrap my arms around myself, barely seeing her any more. 'You marry a man and give him children and tell yourself it doesn't matter that you're not so young now, that your body isn't as taut, your face as clear, because he loves you anyway. You let your guard down: you let him see you snivelling with a cold or with your hair in rat's tails because you haven't had time to wash it, and you think it doesn't matter.' I pace the length of the kitchen, frightening the rabbit under the table. 'At work you get out of the fast lane to make way for the bright young things without families, reminding yourself that giving him somewhere he wants to come home to is far more important than a corner office or a promotion, that *he'll* still find you interesting. You know that there are younger women than you, prettier women, more exciting women; but *you're* the one he chose to marry, *you're* the one he promised to love forever.' I shiver. 'You put him at the centre of your life, at the centre of your heart, where he should be; and then overnight, it's all gone. Gone.'

'I'm – I'm sorry. I didn't mean for this to happen,' she whispers.

I jump; I'd forgotten she was there.

'You could have had anyone you wanted,' I say help-lessly. 'Someone free to love you, without a wife and family. Why did you have to take my husband?'

'Because I fell in love with him,' she says simply.

For the first time, I notice the shadows beneath her eyes, the fatigue and weariness in her face. I recognize in her expression the fear and uncertainty that walk hand in hand with love. I can't bring myself to forgive what she's done. But with a sudden rush, I begin – just *begin* – to understand it.

'It's not just about love,' I sigh. 'Marriage.'

'No.' She folds her hands in her lap. 'No. I see that now.'

My nose starts to run. Using the sleeve of my dressing-gown, like a child, I wipe my face.

'I didn't mean to hurt you,' she pleads. 'I know that's no consolation. But I didn't mean this. I'm not a bad person. I didn't mean for any of this to happen. I kept thinking I could stop it, that no one would ever need to know—'

'Enough. Please.' Exhausted, I collapse into a chair. 'Why are you here, Sara? Does Nicholas know?'

'No.' She shoves herself back from the table and stands up. 'I told myself you were happy without him. Convinced myself he wouldn't have come to me if his marriage had been a good one. But that's not true, is it?'

I shake my head.

And then, 'He loves you, not me,' she says clearly.

I can't breathe.

'He's never loved me. Not enough, anyway.' She rubs the heels of her hands against her eyes, and I'm reminded of Evie. Somewhere, deep inside, I feel a dim tug of pity. 'He wasn't free to love me. I thought it didn't matter, that I could love enough for the both of us, but it doesn't work like that, does it? And it turns out,' she attempts a smile, 'that I have a conscience after all.'

She hitches her bag on her shoulder. Her hand shakes, and I realize how much this confrontation has taken out of her too.

'What are you doing here?' I ask again.

She shrugs, then gives me a sad half-smile. 'I've been trying to work that one out myself.'

A fragile tendril of intimacy unfurls between us. We are linked, after all, by love: for the same man.

'May I use the loo,' she says, 'before I go?'

I point her in the direction of the downstairs lavatory. She's come all the way here to offer me a choice: take him, or give him back to me. Free and clear.

But it's not up to me. I can't go to him. *He* has to come to *me*. He's the one who made the choice to leave: he is the one who has to make the choice to come back. Otherwise I'll never know; it will undermine everything we try to build. I have to hear that he loves me not from *her*, but from Nicholas himself.

She opens the lavatory door, and dips her head around it. Her expression is a strange mixture of pain, embarrassment – and an extraordinary, fierce relief.

'Do you have any Tampax you could give me?' she says. 'I wasn't expecting it, but my period just started.'

16

Nicholas

Divorce is a difficult business. Never more so, may I suggest, than when your lawyer looks at you with an expression that suggests in no uncertain terms that all men are bastards, and you're left shifting uncomfortably in your seat whilst your penis tries to make itself scarce.

Janis Schultz does not have a single photograph or personal memento anywhere in her spartan office. A thick slab of polished glass separates us, atop of which rests her computer and one slim manila folder: mine. Its contents currently number a single appointment slip and two sheets of foolscap upon which she has written her notes during this meeting in a uniform, precise hand. I know that once this process gets fully under way, that solitary folder will spawn letters, faxes, forms to be completed, affidavits to be sworn, until the paperwork fills a box eighteen inches deep. We will each, Malinche and I, be required to provide copies of bank and credit card statements, insurance policies and share certificates, details of our income and our outgoings – not just those you would expect, the standard, ubiquitous expenses like school fees and mortgages, but the intimate, private details of our lives, the window cleaner and the osteopath, gym membership and private proctology examinations: all of it laid bare for consideration and dry judgement.

The carpet is clearly new: the room smells pungently of rubber. It tastes acrid in my mouth. I pinch the bridge of my nose, my head aching.

Ms Schultz is known for her cool, detached professionalism and tempered approach. I haven't met her before – one reason I chose her – but by reputation she chases neither headlines nor precedent, and whilst naturally seeking congenial rulings for her clients, makes it plain from the outset that confrontational terms such as 'victory' do not belong in her chambers.

She is perceived as a wife's lawyer. Her legal obligation will be to me; but her hand may be stayed from the usual gladiatorial excesses by a modicum of sympathy for my wife. It will, perhaps, go some way towards ameliorating my natural advantage in being so familiar with this eviscerating process. I want, above all else, for this to be fair.

'And your wife can't be persuaded to file a petition herself?' Janis Schultz asks.

'I haven't asked her,' I say.

She taps her pen against the pad. 'You do not wish to wait for two years.'

It is no longer a matter of what I *wish*, but what is *right*. Sara is pregnant with my child; I cannot leave her to twist in the wind. My marriage to Mal is over, that much is clear. The only honourable thing now is to extract myself from it and attempt to do the right thing by Sara; whose only fault has been to love me.

'Very well. The grounds for our petition, Mr Lyon?'

I hesitate. Even though Malinche has found solace in the arms of another man, I cannot bring myself to sue her for divorce on the grounds of her adultery: it would be monstrously hypocritical. My options, however, as I am only too well aware, are limited.

'I find in instances such as this,' Ms Schultz says carefully, 'a charge of unreasonable behaviour is often cross-petitioned, where there is cause.'

I sigh heavily.

'There is cause,' I say.

We will provoke Malinche by charging her with unreasonable behaviour – 'On the fourth of this month, the Respondent rinsed out the milk bottles with tepid water instead of hot, as had previously been agreed with the Petitioner from the outset of the marriage' – and her lawyers will no doubt advise her to throw the book at me, to insist that she cross-petitions on the grounds of my adultery. At which point I will concede the issue of blame; and secure the divorce.

Ms Schultz recrosses her legs. Beneath the glass slab, her crisp grey wool skirt rides up a little, exposing an inch or two of thigh. She is close to sixty; my interest is academic.

I glance up, to find her steely gaze upon me.

'Mr Lyon. I think that's all,' she says knowingly.

Her handshake is firm, masculine. She ushers me briskly from her office.

I pause at the door. Atop a low bookcase is a small

cream cardboard box, of the kind in which handmade chocolates are presented. A gold label affixing a ribbon in place suggests these originated in Belgium.

A memory ambushes me: Malinche, waiting for me in my office, perhaps a month or two after we first met. It was late; everyone else had already gone home. She had persuaded the cleaner to let her in, and then sat in the darkness until I returned from Court, whither Fisher had despatched me with a vexatious case with which he did not wish to be troubled.

I walked into my office and smelled it instantly.

'Don't put on the light,' she said, as I reached for the switch.

I jumped as she stood up and took the briefcase from my hand. Streetlights gilded her skin as she unbuttoned her coat. Beneath it, she was naked, save for a coffee-coloured suspender belt and a pair of dark seamed stockings.

'Close your eyes,' she said, her voice curving. 'Now: open your mouth.'

It took a moment to discern the mix of orange and bitter chocolate. As it melted to a creamy puddle on my tongue, Mal sank to her knees and unzipped my trousers. She took my cock in her mouth, reaching up and feeding me another chocolate. Dark chocolate, this time with a cognac centre.

When I pulled away from her, fearing I would come too soon, and pushed her back onto my desk, kissing her hard on the mouth, I tasted white chocolate and mint on her lips. My cock throbbed as I moved lower. She had painted chocolate on her nipples; cocoa powder dusted her pubic hair. It seemed to me, when I bent my head between her thighs and plunged my tongue inside her, that she had become chocolate herself, her centre a rich, creamy liquid that made me long for more with every taste.

I can never smell chocolate without remembering that night.

I leave Ms Schultz's office and hail a taxi. Without giving myself a chance to think, I tell the driver to take me immediately to Waterloo.

Salisbury station is deserted when I arrive; I have to wait more than forty minutes for a cab to collect me and drive me to Stapleford. Forty impatient minutes in which the certainty which impelled me here evaporates, replaced by a knell of doubt and fear thudding in my stomach. This is madness. *Madness.* Mal would be quite within her rights not to permit me through the front door. May well do precisely that, in fact.

'Stop here,' I tell the driver suddenly, as we reach the village.

He pulls sharply onto the side of the road and I get out. 'Thirteen quid, mate.'

I hand him a twenty-pound note through the window. As he fumbles for change, I glance up the hill. The house appears to be in darkness; for all I know, she isn't even here.

I realize dispiritedly how ridiculous this enterprise is. Mal isn't going to want to see me. She's made it quite clear that she doesn't need me in her life any more – for which I have only myself to blame. I can't expect her to suddenly trade back, as if we are children in the playground negotiating an exchange of Yu-Gi-Oh! cards. And there's Sara to consider. She's sitting in London even now, wondering where the hell I've got to, pregnant with our child. What does my presence here say about my future with her?

I lean into the cab to tell the driver to take me back to the station, just as he puts his foot on the accelerator and roars away into the darkness.

A horse snickers softly in a nearby field. Shifting my briefcase to the other hand, I step onto the grass verge to avoid another car, headlights bucking and swaying as it picks its way down the country lane. A wash of ditch-water puddles over my socks and shoes.

In two days' time, my wife will be served with papers informing her that due to her *unreasonable behaviour*, I require a divorce. I know from experience that once that happens, there is no turning back. Our legal mercenaries will enter the ring on our behalf to do battle, and our positions will become entrenched. Such tentative cordiality as we have now will disappear under a storm of disclosures and Form Es and *our client believes* and *Without Prejudice*. However much I give her, it will be less than she needs or deserves. Whatever access I am permitted with my children, it cannot be enough.

If there is a window, one chance to turn back the clock, it is now.

Grasping my case more firmly, I strike out up the hill. *I love Mal.* I have to convince her of that. Throw myself at her feet and beg her forgiveness, whatever it takes. I'll sleep in the scullery with the bloody rabbit if she'll just agree to give me another chance. Counselling, therapy, church, castration, whatever she wants. I made one mistake: a huge mistake, of course, the worst; but I've learned from it. Surely she can understand that? *Errare humanum est,* after all. Of course it's going to take time to rebuild trust, I can't expect her to forgive me overnight, but if we both work at it, if we both really *want* it to work—

The front of the house is still in darkness when I reach it, but light spills from the back, by the kitchen.

I make my way around the outhouses, my shoes crunching on the gravel. God, my feet are cold. I brush past a bank of lavender; the silky leaves stroke the back of my hand, tickling. I have trodden this familiar path every night for nearly ten years, but I have never truly appreciated it until now. A balloon of nervous excitement rises. *She must understand, she must, she must.* I turn the corner and the back door opens; Mal steps into the rectangle of light cast from the warm glow of the kitchen. My steps quicken with hope. Perhaps she heard me outside; perhaps she is coming to meet me halfway—

And then Trace follows her out, pulls her into his arms for a lingering embrace, and I hear my wife laugh as she playfully ducks another man's kisses.

A cold wind blows through my heart. *It didn't take her long to find a replacement.* What was I thinking, coming here ready to prostrate myself like a repentant sinner? Heaping myself with sackcloth and ashes? *When all the time*—

I back away, trembling with bitter fury. I have known she is with him, but to see him, in my own home, with my wife. This man has been waiting in the wings since the day I married Malinche, ready to pounce, no doubt, the moment he had the chance. Or perhaps he hasn't waited in the wings at all; perhaps he's been centre stage with my wife all along. I always thought the candle she held for him – and I've always known about Trace Pitt, known *exactly* how much he meant to her – was just the nostalgic regret of a happily married woman for her first, lost, love. Perhaps I was wrong. Perhaps he wasn't *lost* at all.

Fine.

Fine.

As of now, he's welcome to her.

The anger abates before I even reach London, leaving me empty and bereft. On the morning the papers from Ms Schultz are due to thump onto the rabbit-chewed doormat in Stapleford, I feel an overpowering sense of loss, as if someone has died. In a sense, someone has. Everything I thought I was, everything I had planned to be, with Malinche at my side, is gone.

Sara is out of the office all day; no one seems interested in where she has gone when I ask, but that isn't unusual. Since word of our affair leaked out, she has been cold-shouldered like a Nazi collaborator in Vichy France.

I shut myself in my office and work, secretly glad of the respite.

When I get back to the flat a little after seven, I find Sara sitting in darkness, a glass in her hand and a bottle of wine, three-quarters empty, on the table in front of her.

I loosen my tie and throw my jacket over the back of a chair. 'Should you really be drinking?'

'It doesn't matter.'

'I suppose so. God knows how many babies are conceived when their mothers have had one too many, after all.' I reach for a glass. 'Go easy, though. The first twelve weeks are—'

'I saw Malinche today.'

The glass shatters on the marble counter.

'Christ! Where's the dustpan?'

'Your wife, Malinche.'

'Yes, I gathered that much!' I brush shards of glass into a newspaper. 'Where, for God's sake? Was she here? Did she come round?'

'No. I went to see her.'

Sara hasn't moved. Her head is bowed, so I cannot see the expression on her face.

I dispose of the broken glass in the plastic bag hanging from one of the cupboards and sink heavily onto the sofa next to her. 'What's going on, Sara?'

She runs a finger around the wet rim of the glass. It sings sharply.

'I told her you loved her, not me. I told her she should take you back – well, not in so many words. But she knew what I meant.'

I gape.

'You told her *what*?'

'Come on, Nick,' she says impatiently. 'I'm only saying what we both already know. It's not like this is news.'

I open my mouth to deny it, to plug the gap between us with another lie, another carefully crafted piece of wishful thinking: and discover I can't. Sara has found the courage that has so far eluded me and dared to acknowledge the pink elephant in the room. Useless now for me to keep on stepping around it.

I get up, find another tumbler, and pour myself a hefty measure of Scotch. The liquid burns a hot path to my stomach, its warmth spiralling out through my body. On the far side of the street, a teenager is panhandling, a filthy blanket wrapped, squaw-like, around her bony shoulders. Her shoes don't match: she's wearing one thick-soled trainer and one navy snaffle shoe, trodden down at the back. The imbalance gives her a curious gait as she shuffles down the street.

I close the blind.

'You went all that way to tell her that?'

'No. Yes. I don't know.' She slugs back some wine. 'I don't know what I planned to tell her, Nick. I didn't really think it through, if you want the freakin' truth. I just needed to know, one way or the other.'

'Know *what*, for Chrissake?'

Sara stares at me as if I'm being deliberately obtuse. 'Whether *she* still loved *you*.'

The room is suddenly very still. My heart pounds in my ears. I only realize how tightly I am holding the glass when my wedding ring bites into my palm.

'What did she say?'

She reaches for the bottle again. 'I'm not pregnant, Nick.'

I can't breathe. A kaleidoscope of possibility explodes behind my eyes.

'I don't know if I ever was. I never actually did the test – yes, I know,' she says tightly, 'I missed two periods, Nick, I was sick every bloody day, I'm sorry, I just assumed—'

'You assumed?' I slam my drink onto the table. '*You assumed?* Jesus Christ, Sara, this isn't a bloody game, people's *lives* are at stake here—'

'I realize that!'

'I asked you to *marry* me!'

'Well, now you don't have to, so that's all right then, isn't it!'

I push my face into hers, dropping my voice to a cold hiss: the words fall like hot stones into an icy lake.

'What was it, some kind of trick to keep me hooked? Like the bloody lipstick?'

She jerks, as if I've slapped her.

'I gave you the benefit of the doubt that time. But *this*. The oldest trick in the book,' I snarl, 'and I bloody fell for it! When were you going to tell me, Sara: as I walked you up the aisle with a fucking cushion under your dress? Jesus Christ!'

'I didn't make it up! I swear, Nick, I wouldn't do that, I'm not like that! I just made a mistake—'

'Why should I believe you?'

She leaps up to face me, eyes glittering with anger and tears. 'Go back to her, Nick! Go back to her!' She shoves me in the chest with the heel of her hand. 'I don't know why you've waited this long! You've had your fun, you've got your legover and reminded your dick what it was all about, so now you can go back and play house with your wife and your psychotic children and forget all about me. It's what you've wanted to do ever since you moved in, isn't it?' Her chest heaves. 'Well? Isn't it?'

Suddenly, she seems no older than Evie. Guilt thuds into me. My behaviour has been unforgivable: to my wife, to my children, and to Sara. None of them deserves this. And now I have lost them all. Mal has Trace, and Sara and I have nothing to offer each other but recrimination and regret. My daughters will despise me before they are very much older; if they don't hate me, the best I can expect from them is pity. And I am left to gnaw at wounds of my own making. *Christ, what a mess.*

I reach out to Sara, but she brushes me angrily away.

'Go on! What are you waiting for?'

'I didn't mean for any of this to happen, Sara. I didn't want you to get hurt. Someday you'll—'

'For fuck's sake, spare me the pep talk!'

'Yes. Sorry.'

Her chin comes up. 'Aren't you going to ask me what she said?'

I pick up my jacket. I don't need to hear Sara tell me what I already know. If Mal had one shred of feeling left for me, she'd have picked up the phone after she heard my answerphone message last weekend. She wouldn't have been nestling in Trace's arms two nights ago.

'I'll be at the Dorchester,' I say wearily, 'for tonight, at least.'

She doesn't move.

'I'll see you at work on Monday. We can talk then—'

'I quit,' Sara says defiantly. 'Fisher accepted my resignation over the phone about an hour ago—'

'Fisher!'

Her eyes sparkle with malice. 'He said he'll pick up the slack for a while, until you find someone to replace me. He did mention something about coming out of retirement, actually. To keep an eye on things. Given the – how did he put it? – "ruddy pig's ear" you've made of things since he's been gone.'

I digest this for a moment. 'And you?'

'I don't think that's any of your business, do you?' she challenges. 'Don't worry. I'll be fine. I have an interview with the BBC next week – a second interview, actually –

they're looking for another entertainment lawyer. It's a growing field, apparently. Very well paid; and rather more riveting than who gets which saucepan, don't you think? And if that doesn't work out,' she shrugs, 'I never did take a gap year. I've always wanted to go white-water rafting down the Grand Canyon.'

I hesitate at the door.

'Sara. If I hadn't been married – if we'd met before—'

'No,' Sara says fiercely. '*No.*'

Outside, the homeless teenager holds out a dirty hand, palm upwards, for money. I reach into my pocket, and hand her the small turquoise box I had been planning to give Sara this evening.

I have already crossed the road and hailed a taxi by the time the runaway opens it and discovers the two-carat diamond ring nestling inside it.

Tug-of-love cases are always the worst; the ones every divorce lawyer dreads. Hard not to feed off a mother's desperation as she sits across from you, twisting a hand-kerchief in her hands and begging you to find a way to bring back her children. Children who are, even as you unscrew your fountain pen and note the details – 'two boys, four and seven, born in Chepstow, eldest child allergic to peanuts, husband's family of significant means' – being spirited to a dusty, cramped apartment in Tehran or Rabat, told their mother is dead, given new names and new lives. Children you know she will, in all probability, never see again unless her husband takes pity and returns them to her himself.

I open the file in front of me. There is something about

Leila Sabra that moved me. Perhaps it was the loss of my own daughters sitting heavy on my heart – my plight incomparable to hers, of course, but grief is not quantifiable; one does not feel misery any the less because one has company.

My sympathy for Mrs Sabra, however, is not the reason I am closeted in my office at three o'clock on a Sunday afternoon, wiring large sums of American dollars around the globe – Beirut, this time – to grease the palm of a facilitator we have used, with a modest measure of success, in such cases before. I am here because, quite simply, I don't know where else to go.

My mother is wrapped up in her own grief; I cannot add to it. My wife is in love with her childhood beau, with whom she is currently enjoying a bucolic existence – in *my* home, at *my* expense, with *my* children – and clearly has no further need of me. My mistress, who has thrown me out, is in love with me: for all the good it does either of us, since I am, inconveniently for all concerned, still in love with my wife.

I rub my temples. The sorry mess I have made of my life is beyond parody.

I slot my iPod – for the discovery of this revolutionary piece of technology, at least, I may thank Sara – into my computer docking system and start to compose a brief for Counsel as the soothing strains of Pat Metheny fill the room. One of the advantages of working on a Sunday: no telephones, no interruptions, and the freedom to deafen oneself with 'Sueño con Mexico' – from *New Chautauqua*, arguably his best album – if one so chooses.

My gaze snags briefly on a picture of my youngest daughter. In the words of my wife: our last-chance baby, indulgently named for the jazz guitarist I love so much. She still isn't yet two. What happened to us? How did it all go so wrong, so fast?

It would be comforting to think there were undetected fractures in our relationship, fissures that took only a little pressure to widen suddenly into unbridgeable gulfs. But I am done with lying, even to myself. The unpalatable, unvarnished truth is that I made one mistake; and wrecked everything.

I force my attention back to the computer screen. The knot of misery in my stomach eases a little as I lose myself in the labyrinthine complexities of the Sabra finances. It's always so much easier, of course, to bring order to the domestic chaos of other people's lives than to my own. No doubt Freud would have a great deal to say about my choice of career, given the tragedy that scarred my early childhood. And right now, I would not gainsay him.

I wonder idly if there is a Minotaur waiting for me as I follow the thread from one bank account to the next in Beirut, Switzerland, the Cayman Islands and Cyprus. My attention is caught by a shady cash deposit in Guernsey. A little close to home, Guernsey, not quite the launderer's haven it once was, there's a chance we may be able to—

'I have always preferred,' Mal says from the doorway, 'the *Still Life (Talking)* album myself.'

I startle, spilling my cold coffee. My wife looks pale, but otherwise composed. She's wearing a clingy dress I haven't seen before: the colour of burnt coffee beans, it's sharper, sexier than anything I've seen her wear for years. There's something that reminds me uncannily of Sara; for a moment I think it must be the short, boyish haircut, and then I realize it's more in the defiant tilt of her head. It is impossible to tell, from her shuttered expression, what she is thinking.

Heels, too, I notice. And lipstick.

'Did you know he used his baby daughter's voice on that album?' I say hoarsely. 'He washed it through his computer, and then hooked it up to his guitar. Every time he played a note, it was his daughter's voice.'

'Such a Latin American sound, for a boy from Missouri,' Mal says.

Once more I understand how much I love her; how much I have lost.

'How did you know I was here?' I ask, after a moment of silence.

'You weren't with Sara, or Daisy. You hadn't asked to see the girls. And,' she adds, 'it's always been easier for you to sort out other people's problems than your own, hasn't it?'

She moves into my office and picks up the photograph of Metheny, touching our daughter's face with her fingertip.

'When I discovered you were having an affair,' she says slowly, 'I thought I would never get over it. I thought I would drown in the pain.'

'Malinche, I'm sorry, I'm so, *so* sorry. I can't begin to tell you—'

She puts down the photograph and whirls towards me.

'*No*,' she says fiercely, 'this isn't about *you*. Shut up, Nicholas. Shut up and *listen*.'

I close my mouth, awed by the force of her anger.

She turns her back on me, as if I no longer matter. I wait for her to speak again, but instead she moves to my

cluttered book shelves, examining the childish artefacts
I have collected over the years, the proud proof of my
fatherhood: macaroni Father's Day cards, cotton-wool
snowmen, a folded tea-towel covered with painted hand
prints, bits of pottery. Propped in front of the heavy,
unread leather law books are photographs spanning our
decade together: on Brighton Pier, the summer after we
first met; our wedding day; cradling each of our daughters
moments after they were born. Family holidays in Crete
and France, my fortieth birthday, my father's eightieth.
Framed certificates attesting to my qualifications as a
steward of family affairs – or at least of their sundering;
a small wooden box we bought on our honeymoon,
smelling still of the sweet, heavy church incense once
stored in it.

The high heels define her calves, give a sexy lift to her
buttocks. As my cock stiffens, it hits me: *she no longer looks
like my wife.*

But then she *isn't* my wife now, is she? In any sense
that matters.

'You broke my heart,' she says, without turning round.
'But I discovered something, Nicholas. Hearts are remarkably resilient. They heal.'

Not mine.

'Trace,' I say tightly.

'Trace is part of my past, Nicholas. He always was. I
just didn't realize it.' Finally she turns and looks me in
the eye. 'I'm not going to make this easy for you. I'm not
going to let you say that I didn't pay attention to you,
wasn't giving you something you needed, and that's why
you looked elsewhere. That might all be true, though

forgive me if my attention wandered whilst I brought up your three daughters and made a home for you; but even so it's no excuse. No excuse at all for what you did to me.'

She's shaking: from grief or anger – or perhaps both, I have no idea.

'We all get *bored*, Nicholas! We all feel neglected, that we aren't getting enough attention! Did you think ironing your shirts and knocking up a quick lasagne in between checking in with your mother and organizing the school run was fulfilling for me? Do you really think it was *enough* for me?'

'Of course not—'

'I had dreams too, Nicholas! I'm not just somebody's wife or somebody's mother! But you know what? *Being* a wife, a mother, mattered more to me than anything else. And so I *made* it enough.'

She grips the edge of the bookcase for support. The pulse at the hollow of her throat beats fast; she takes a deep, steadying breath.

'I wanted to kill myself when you left. And then I wanted to kill you. I was so angry with you, Nicholas. So *hurt*. It wasn't just my life you'd smashed to pieces, but Sophie's, Evie's and Metheny's too. Did you never stop to think about them?'

Her gaze lacerates. I have no answer; she knows it.

'You wrecked everything, and for what? A roll in the hay that didn't last five minutes once real life got in the way. Oh God, Nicholas, how could you be so *stupid*?' With a visible effort, she collects herself, swallows hard. 'But after a while, I realized I didn't want to spend my life angry and hating. And I'd spent years loving Trace. It was such an easy habit to fall back into.'

'Is he here?' I ask jealously. 'Downstairs, waiting for you?'

'She came to see me last week,' Mal says, ignoring my question. 'Sara.'

My throat closes.

'Yes. She said.'

'She asked me if I still loved you.'

I wonder if it is like this, the moment before you die. If every sense is sharpened, the world you are about to quit suddenly a thousand times more vivid. I smell her shampoo: oranges, mangoes, pineapples and lemons, mingling with the warm, fresh-sheet scent of her skin. My scratchy wool trousers chafe where they have ridden up around my groin. A faint hiss from the computer speakers – the album is old, even the wonders of iPod technology cannot work miracles – is overlaid by the thud of my heart in my chest. The smudge of mascara beneath her cinnamon eyes tells me she has cried before coming here.

'What did you tell her?'

'I told her to go home,' Mal says sharply. 'She has no place in our marriage. No right to know what I think or feel. I wasn't even going to talk to you again, Nicholas. I certainly had no intention of making the first move. But then,' her voice changes, 'Kit gave me this.'

She holds out her hand. A small cassette sits in her small palm. The kind of cassette you find in a telephone answering machine.

'He came to feed Don Juan and the bloody hamsters when I was in France. He saw I had a message and played it back in case it was something urgent—'

'Jesus Christ, he *took* it!' I exclaim. 'The *bastard*!'

'He was just trying to protect me, Nicholas. You left it

at three in the morning, for heaven's sake, you could have been drunk and changed your mind the next day, who knows. But when I told him it was over with Trace and explained what Sara had said—'

An explosion of fireworks occurs somewhere in the vicinity of my heart.

'It's over with Trace?'

'Nicholas, you never *listen*,' she says crossly.

The chocolate jersey of her dress clings to her slender frame, delineating her girlish silhouette. She isn't wearing a bra; her nipples jut against the delicate fabric. My cock throbs, and I force myself not to leap up and take her in my arms, to stay instead in my chair.

'You should know: I slept with Trace,' she says, eyes on mine. 'Not just once.'

The surge of rage is so strong that if he were here, I would reach down the man's throat and pull his balls out through his mouth.

'Yes,' I say, white-lipped.

'Can you deal with it?'

I swallow hard. 'I'm not in a position to—'

'It's different for a man. Pride is involved. Territory. There's a reason that men are *cuckolded*, that there's a special word for it. There isn't one for women who are betrayed, of course. This is why I'm asking you, Nicholas. I need to know if you can get past it.'

Suddenly I hear what she is saying.

'Be sure, Nicholas,' she warns. 'Before you answer, be sure.'

I remember watching her fold naturally into his arms the other night, her body slotting neatly into his. I picture her in bed with Trace, her small breasts pressed against his chest, his hands moving possessively over her skin, his cock buried inside her. Inside *my wife*. I feel sick at the thought.

And then I consider a life without Mal in it, and suddenly it's so simple I don't have to think at all.

'Trace is the past,' I say.

'Yes.'

I take a deep breath, force myself to let it go.

'The past is the past. It doesn't really matter if that is a week ago, or ten years, then, does it?'

She takes a step towards me. I stand up, but make no move towards her. Her face turns up to mine, a flower to the light, and I marvel again at the luminous beauty of the woman I fell in love with more than a decade ago. Extraordinary, that such ethereal fragility should conceal such tensile strength.

'So *did* you mean what you said,' she opens her hand on the cassette, 'on this?'

'I wasn't drunk,' I say. 'I haven't changed my mind.'

She looks at the tape, then at me.

'You *have* been a bloody fool. What you did *was* unforgivable. You don't deserve a second chance. Why shouldn't I shut you out, no matter how much you swear you love me?'

My own words, I realize, turned against me.

'*I* wish you could turn back the clock, too, Nicholas. I wish you'd told me before how happy I've made you, how much you loved coming home to me every night, and waking up next to me every morning. You're right: what you did was wrong, and there *are* no excuses.'

Her expression is cool, unflinching. Ice washes through my veins. *She hasn't come here to give me a second chance at all.* She's here to skewer me with my trespasses, to ensure I am fully cognizant of what I have lost. And she is doing it not out of spite or bitterness, but because she'd rather face me and have it out, fair and square, here, alone, than in a courtroom. Not for her the coward's way out. She won't use the children as weapons, or bleed me dry financially out of revenge. I can only imagine what it has cost her to come here; but I know that after today, she will draw a line beneath the score and walk away.

And I would give everything I own for her to stay.

'I know it's too late for us,' I say, 'I *know* that. And I will spend the rest of my life half-alive because of it. You're right. I had everything, and I let it slip through my fingers. I *chose* to do what I did, it didn't just happen, I have no one to blame but myself.' I realize I am crying; and that I don't care. 'I would never intentionally have hurt you or the girls, but my negligence amounted to the same thing. Oh, Mal. I deserve this, but you don't – you don't—'

'No,' she says, 'I don't. And nor,' she adds, in a quite different voice, 'do *you.*'

'But it's all my—'

'*Enough*, Nicholas. Enough of fault and blame and *I wish* and *you should*. I believe that you love me. I wouldn't be here if I didn't. And I certainly love you. If you still want that second chance, it's yours.'

I gape at her, slack-jawed. 'What?'

'Come home,' says my wife.

'Are you – are you sure? After everything I've done?'

'Nicholas, it wasn't *just* you. Mostly,' she smiles wryly, 'but not all. You weren't the only one who didn't appreciate what they had until they lost it. I realized last week that no matter what you've done, I'm happier being unhappy with you, than when I'm happy with anyone else. If you see what I mean.'

I do see, despite the tortured semantics.

'I don't want you unhappy at all.'

'No,' she says briskly. 'Well, neither do I. But that's rather up to you, isn't it?'

'She's left the firm. I won't be seeing her again. You know that, don't you? Not her, not anyone, you do understand that, I swear, Malinche, I will *never*—'

'Trace has gone back to London,' she offers. 'He came round one night last week and said he wanted me to buy him out of the restaurant in Salisbury. I'll have to borrow some money from the bank, of course, but – did you know? – your father very generously left me something, quite a lot, actually, and I think he would be rather pleased—'

'Yes, I did know. He told me he was going to.' I smile sadly. 'He would be very pleased.'

Malinche says, firmly, 'I want to work. Not full time, of course, I'll hire a manager and a chef: you and the girls will always come first; but I need to do this for *me*. How can I expect to interest you if I don't interest myself?'

'You *do* interest me,' I say feverishly, 'very much.'

'This is a second chance, Nicholas. It's not *carte blanche*. I can't promise I'll always be able to look at you and not see *her*. I can't promise I won't take it out on you sometimes. Throw it back in your face. I'm not a saint, you know. And I want us to *talk* about this, I don't want to brush it under the carpet in that public schoolboy way of yours; I know that's not your way, but this is no time for a stiff upper lip. We both have to find a way to live with the past. It's going to take time. We can't just go back to the way we were overnight.'

'I know. I don't expect that. I know I have to earn back your trust. And obviously I'll sleep in the spare room until—'

'Why,' she asks, 'would you do that?'

'Well, but you – I mean—'

I'm acutely aware of the closeness of her body, the flimsy jersey encasing her bare breasts, the glimpse of soft thigh at the part of her skirt. Her warm scent is at once achingly familiar and erotically exotic. *She has changed*. Or perhaps: simply rediscovered what was there all along.

There is challenge in her honey-swirled eyes. Challenge; and something else, something that seems almost like desire—

'Sex is where everything starts and ends, Nicholas,' she says clearly. 'If you want to sleep in the spare room, I might as well call your Ms Schultz now and—'

'Christ, no! No, that's not what I want! I want *you*, I've always wanted you, you're in my blood and my brain and my body, you're the reason my heart beats, you're why I get up in the morning. Jesus, don't you understand that still?'

She smiles. A slow, warm smile that reaches out to me.

'*That*,' she says, 'is what I wanted to hear.'

I move towards her, but she backs away. Holding my gaze, she unfastens the belt of her dress, and allows it to fall to the floor. She is naked beneath it, but for those heels. Her high breasts are as firm and pert as the day I met her. She has the legs of a dancer, the poise of a queen. Her belly is less taut, perhaps, than it used to be, but its softness speaks of sensual, erotic pleasure, of fecundity and libidinous, carnal satisfaction. Far rather this than the hard-bodied stomach of a gym maven.

She moves with a confidence I haven't seen for years. She is in control: not just of this moment, I see suddenly, but of herself, her life. She has made a choice.

'Close your eyes, Nicholas,' she says.

And shut out all of this?

She laughs at my expression. 'Come on. Close your eyes.'

I do as I'm bid. Her hands are at my trousers, unbuckling, unzipping.

'Now—' she says:

—just as I smell it; just as I realize that however hard the road ahead, however long it may take us to rebuild our marriage, we will succeed, and it will be stronger and better than it ever was, that we have endured, that I am the luckiest man alive—

'—open your mouth.'

Chocolate.

The Infidelity Chain

For my husband,

Erik.

Sometimes you are right,
and I am wrong.

Acknowledgements

I have been helped in so many ways by so many people; but in particular, I owe a deep debt of gratitude to Carole Blake, the most wonderful agent in the world, and Imogen Taylor, my brilliant editor. I am exceptionally lucky to be the beneficiary of their talent and friendship. Thank you for all you are and do.

Both are backed up by superb teams at Blake Friedmann and Pan Macmillan – Oli Munson, Trisha Jackson, Emma Giacon, Ellen Wood, Anna Bond and all the Pan team, you are all amazing. Without you, none of this would happen; this book is truly a team effort.

Dr Jerold Lucey, Professor of Paediatrics at the University of Vermont College of Medicine and Editor-in-Chief of *Pediatrics* magazine, and Professor David Edwards of the Department of Paediatrics at Hammersmith Hospital, provided invaluable information regarding the care of premature infants, and I am extremely grateful to them for their time, advice and kindness. Jerry, you are a wonderful and generous friend. Any errors in the book are entirely mine.

One of the main characters in this book endures frightening and debilitating panic attacks. I would thoroughly recommend the online book *Panic Away!* by Joe Barry (www.panicaway.com), whose simple, effective technique has transformed the lives of so many sufferers.

To Danusia, Michèle, Georgie and Charlie, Sarah, Peter and Jayne, Julie and Tony, Christina, Andrew and Susan, Robert, Grub – thank you so much for always being such marvellous friends, especially when I visit you with such chaos and disruption on my brief trips home. I love you all.

Kisses, too, to my father Michael and WSM Barbi, to my out-laws Sharon and Harry, to my sister Philippa, brother Charles (the original English gentleman), my nephews Christopher, Alexander, William and George: every novelist should have a family like mine.

My children Henry, Matthew and Lily – what can I say? I love you to pieces, though you drive me to drink. If only I could bottle your laughter.

My beloved mother, Jane – I miss you still. You're always in our hearts and prayers.

Above all, to my husband, Erik, for loving me more.

TESS STIMSON
Florida, September 2007
www.tessstimson.com

1

Ella

I've often wondered if adultery runs in the genes, like blue eyes or buck teeth. Am I unfaithful because it's written in my DNA?

The idea appeals to the scientist in me: we're all the sum of our genetic barcodes, no more, no less. See, yes, there it is, nestling between my red hair and tendency towards the pear-shaped (hips, life, take your pick) – there, *infidelity*, clear as day. Biological proof that I can no more stay faithful than shrink a shoe size, however hard I try.

William stirs next to me. He reaches for my breast, and my nipple peaks instantly beneath his touch. His cock jabs my hip, already hard again. I smile. After eight years, we don't have sex that often, but when we do, we get our money's worth.

He rolls on to his back and pulls me on to him; I wince slightly as he enters me. He isn't to know I had sex with Jackson – twice – last night.

As he thrusts upwards, I cling to the brass bedstead for

support, my breasts shivering tantalizingly above his mouth. His lips fasten on my nipple and there's a zig-zagging pulse between my legs. I tighten my grip. William is the more selfish lover; I've learned to take my pleasure from him without asking. Jackson is far more thoughtful: always seeking out new ways to please me, holding himself in check until I've come, sometimes three or four times.

I shunt Jackson out of my head. Contrary to popular myth, women *can* be good at adultery. All they have to do is learn to think like a man.

My clit rubs against William's pelvis, and the familiar heat builds. His teeth graze my breast; swift, greedy bites. I reach between his legs, skittering my fingernails along the inside of his thighs and across his balls. He bucks inside me, hitting my G-spot, and I stiffen, savouring the moment at the crest of the rollercoaster. Then my orgasm breaks over me in sweeping, almost painful, waves.

With one hand, I find the tiny sensitive spot between his balls and asshole, pressing just enough to send him wild. With the other, I reach for my beeping phone.

Only two people would text me this late at night. Jackson, or—

'Shit!' I tumble off William, groping for my clothes.

He slams his head against the pillow. 'Christ. I thought you weren't on call tonight?'

'Emergency.' I hook up my bra, and scrabble under the bed for my knickers. 'I'll be back as soon as I can.'

'Couldn't it have waited until *after* I came?'

I give up on the knickers, and pull on my grey pencil skirt before sliding my feet into a pair of skyscraper scarlet heels. I can only find a single topaz earring; I *hate* losing one of a pair.

Buttoning up my white silk shirt, I lean forward and drop a kiss on his sandpaper cheek. He smells of my sex. 'Happy Valentine's Day.'

William scowls. 'You owe me.'

'Get in line.'

Fifteen minutes later, I ease my toes from the to-die-in stilettos as the lift grinds its way up to the obstetrics floor. There must be another butter-wouldn't-melt little genome tucked away on that adulterous double helix to explain my uncontrollable fetish for pretty shoes. How else to explain the purchase of lust-have red Ginas in a size six (the only pair left – and no, they haven't 'stretched with wear' as the commission-only salesgirl promised) when I've been a size seven all my adult life?

My mother was always perfectly shod. Even when the French bailiffs evicted us from our little *appartement* on the Rue du Temple because my father had stopped paying the rent, her footwear (if not her reputation) was beyond reproach. We might starve as a result, but she could no more resist a new pair of polka-dot peep-toe slingbacks than she could him.

She brought her only daughter up in her likeness.

The lift doors open and I hobble towards the delivery suites, uncomfortably aware of the draught beneath my skirt. Lucy is my best friend, and I love her to death, but I really hope she isn't on duty tonight. I'm used to moral sermons from my mother; she speaks from fingers-burned experience, after all. But Lucy and I have been *les soeurs sous la peau* since we crossed scalpels over a half-dissected corpse as medical students at Oxford. She's the one I go to for a Xanax scrip before I fly. It's not like she hasn't known about my affair for years.

On the other hand, when your husband leaves you for a teenage choreographer (forget semantics: if you're thirty-six, as we are, twenty-three *is* teenage) I suppose it entitles you to take a more jaundiced than jaunty view of other people's adultery.

My mobile rings as I reach the labour ward. Peering through the glass porthole, I realize my patient must still be in the back of an ambulance trapped in stubborn traffic somewhere on the Fulham Road, and take the call.

'Jackson,' I say, 'I'm with a patient.'

'You're at work?'

'You knew I was on call.'

One of the perks of being a doctor (aside from delightful offers from strangers at parties to allow me to examine their thyroids or anal fissures in the guest bathroom, heedless of both the social niceties and the fact that I am a neonatologist) is the ability to stay out all night unquestioned. As paediatric consultant at the Princess Eugenie Neonatal Intensive Care Unit, I owe the hospital six nights on call each month. My husband has always believed it to be seven.

'You've got five minutes,' I tell Jackson.

'That's not what you said last night,' he teases, his Deep South drawl undiminished by nearly a decade in England.

I'm not having an affair because my sex life with my husband is either infrequent or unsatisfying. On the contrary: he's a conscientious lover. Though I have plenty of plausible reasons for my infidelity, I'm not sure that I can find an excuse that actually excuses me.

I shrug on my white coat. 'What is it?'

'I need to talk to you.'

'*Now*? Can't it wait?'

He hesitates. 'I just found this neat motorcycle on eBay, an Indian. The bids end at midnight, and I wanted to talk to y'all about it first—'

I can't help thinking he was going to say something else.

'A motorbike?'

'C'mon, Ell, you know I've always wanted one. It'd make it real quick to get to work. It's all right for you,' he adds, an edge creeping into his voice, 'living so close to the hospital. You're not the one gotta sit in traffic for an hour two times a day.'

'I'm sure DuCane Pharmaceuticals would still—'

'For Chrissakes, Ella! How many times?'

'No one's asking you to raise money for their pills,' I say tightly. 'We all know they're immoral drug-pushing pimps who'll go straight to hell, yada yada. But the research programme is different—'

'Suddenly stem-cell research is OK?'

'Jackson, I'm a doctor. What do you want me to say?'

'You don't have to leave your conscience at the door when you put on your white coat, Ella,' he says bitterly. 'Just your fancy shoes.'

I wish.

'I don't see what my conscience has to do with—'

'I thought you were supposed to be saving babies, not murdering them.'

'Not that it's anything to do with neonatology, Jackson,' I say, stung, 'but since when did messing about with zygotes become equivalent to baling infants with a pitchfork?'

'Stupid of me to think you'd care.'

'Stupid of me to think you'd be able to reason like a grown-up.'

Subtext whirls through the ether. We both know what this is *really* about.

I switch my mobile to the other ear, holding on to my temper with difficulty. Now is not the time to call him out for wanting to break our deal; we agreed from day one: no children. It's not as if the subject is going to go away, I think resentfully.

'Look. I only meant—'

'I know what you meant, Ella.'

It's one of the things I always admired about Jackson (particularly since I lack it myself): his steadfast, unfashionable integrity. A gifted fundraiser, charming, sincere and articulate, he has the kind of likeable persuasiveness that, were he politically minded, could have seen him in the White House (although his incurable honesty might have counted against him, of course). In the past couple of years, head hunters for several prestigious NGOs have offered him six figures and an open-ended expense account to run their capital campaigns or head up their development offices. All have come away disappointed – though only after Jackson has charmed them into donating hefty sums to One World, the lentils-and-hairy-armpit environmental charity for which he works.

It's one of the things that always irritates me about my husband: his rigid, my-way-or-the-highway Southern sense of honour.

I jam my mobile between chin and shoulder to button the white coat over my smart crêpe skirt. There's nothing I can do about the fuck-me red shoes. 'Fine. If you've made up your mind.'

'Think of it as a belated birthday present.'

I close my eyes, suddenly awash with remorse. 'Oh, Jackson. I'm sorry.'

'Forget it.'

'I've been so busy at the hospital – we're understaffed—'

'I said forget it.'

The silence lingers. How could I miss his birthday? It's Valentine's Day, for God's sake. You'd think I could manage to remember *that*.

Jackson coughs again. 'How's the cold?' I ask quickly; guiltily.

'Actually, I feel kinda lousy, to be honest. I think I'm spiking a fever.'

I suppress a smile. It's extraordinary, the way the same bug affects the male and female immune systems. I should write a paper on it: 'A virus that will just produce sniffles in the female of the species miraculously becomes an upper respiratory infection the moment it encounters macho Y chromosomes . . .'

'Look, Jackson, we'll go out at the weekend, I promise. I'll make up some excuse—'

'Sure.'

'You choose. Anywhere you like.'

'Yep. Whatever.'

'You'll enjoy it more when you're feeling better anyway.' Then, partly to appease my conscience, and partly because, despite William, despite everything, it *is* still true, I add, 'I love you.'

'Love you more.'

It's our catchphrase, one of those couply exchanges you develop in the early months together and then later cling to, like a lifebelt, out of mingled superstition and hope and fear when the going gets rough.

It is also, in six words, a synopsis of our marriage.

We met in America eleven years ago, at the perfect-storm moment; the one night when I was tired enough, and vulnerable enough, and (let's be honest) drunk enough for a window in my carefully nurtured cynicism to crack and give Jackson time to slip through.

I'd lost my virginity at seventeen (to my thirty-four-year-old tennis coach; the cliché embarrassed me more than being caught *in flagrante* by my grandmother, who'd merely nodded with the quiet triumph of one being proved right). Since then, all the men I'd dated had had just one thing in common: not one was remotely available, and that's just how I liked it.

A part of me knew my behaviour wasn't exactly well adjusted; but the rest of me figured it'd sort itself out when I met the right man.

It wasn't a *coup de foudre* when Jackson Garrett sauntered into the piano bar on Bourbon Street, in the French Quarter of New Orleans, and headed straight over to Lucy and me as if we'd been waiting there all night just for him. Love certainly didn't come into it.

Jackson was – *is* – the most handsome man I'd ever seen. He's got this all-American, dazzling-white movie-star smile, and the kind of skin that looks golden even in the middle of an English winter. Eyes a Tiffany turquoise, with obscenely long lashes and the kind of sparkle that makes your skin tingle and your clothes somehow unbutton themselves. And a mouth so mobile and sensual you have no choice but to throw your anal British reserve to the wind and demand that it kiss you. *Come on, it's my birthday, what are you, shy?* (Looking back, I believe that's where three Hurricanes came in.)

After we came up for air, I grabbed my cigarette lighter and fumbled for my poise, waiting for him to zero in on Lucy. Men always do. Hardly surprising, given her fifties curves, perfect skin and waist-length, old-gold hair; for the first year I knew her, I seriously considered a Sapphic conversion. The universal Law of Attraction, which dictates that people end up with partners of the same degree of attractiveness as themselves, plus or minus one point (unless money or power distort the equation), put Jackson firmly in her league, rather than mine.

But, bending his dark-blond head to mine, he murmured in my ear, his warm breath rum-sweet, 'I always knew you colonialists didn't play fair. I should warn y'all, I surrender easy.'

'I'm no Virginia myself.'

'I'd Nevada thought it.'

'I know there's something rude I could do with Kansas and Mississippi,' I mused, 'but these Hurricanes are stronger than they look.'

His skin smelled of leather and soap and pine trees just after it's rained. There was a quiver in the region of my knickers.

He took the unlit cigarette out of my fingers and guided me towards the door. 'I think we need to discuss the state of this union somewhere else.'

It was obviously never going to be more than a brief holiday fling, since Lucy and I were only down from North Carolina for the weekend. We planned to experience the

'Come as you are, leave different' philosophy of the Big Easy before we graduated from Duke and – her words – went home to London and stuck our heads back up our uptight British arses.

So while Lucy generously waved me on, I went back to his apartment and slept with him (oh, the brazen shame of me!) *the first night*, with none of that tedious game-playing, no-touching-below-the-waist-till-the-fifth-date routine.

Over breakfast the next morning – Creole beignets, fresh fruit fritters and cinnamon sopaipillas; dear Lord, the man could *cook*! – we exchanged some of the personal details we'd neglected in favour of energetic sex the night before, such as our names. Jackson was a fundraiser at New Orleans' Tulane University. When I told him I was studying medicine at Duke, he nearly spat out his (strong, black) coffee.

'I'll be damned. I just got a job at Duke, I'm movin' there in a couple weeks.'

Still aching pleasurably from the night's exertions, I decided Jackson was the perfect rebound lover (there'd been a brief and unhappy dalliance with a married history professor, recently ended and best not dwelt upon): the casual, restorative relationship that helps mend a broken heart after a romantic near-miss, or at least someone to play hooky with while you wait to meet The One. He was not, as he warned me at the time, supposed to be the man I *married*.

All relationships are intrinsically unequal; I'd learned that lesson as a small child. Whoever loves the least has the most power.

Growing up, I'd often wondered why my mother always seemed to be waiting for something that never came. I'd vowed into my pillow, as I listened night after night to my mother sobbing on the other side of the wall into hers, that I would not end up like she had. I would not wait *seventeen years* for a charismatic, faithless man who had no intention of ever leaving his wife for me, who would get me pregnant and not give our child so much as his name, who would die and leave me, at forty-six, not-quite-a-widow in a still-strange land with a nine-year-old daughter to support and no earthly means to do it.

Thrown unceremoniously on to the streets after the untimely death of *mon père*, my mother and I had slept in the back of her ancient green Peugeot for three weeks, living on day's-end baguettes and over-ripe cheese, before she'd admitted defeat and summoned the courage to go back home, beret in hand, to Northamptonshire. Her own father had died without ever forgiving her. Her mother referred to me as 'the French bastard'. It had seemed reasonable to me at the time.

For the next nine years, I'd watched my mother scrabble for scraps of approval from the old witch, struggling hopelessly to atone for her one doomed act of defiance (how she'd ever found the courage to escape to Paris in the first place, I'd never yet worked out). I'd stared into the speckle-backed mirror at my homely reflection, with its unattractive mass of red curls and eyes the colour of weak tea, so different from hers and therefore so clearly *his*, and wondered what she had seen in my father that could possibly make him worth this misery.

As soon as I turned eighteen I fled to Oxford, determined that, whatever happened, I would never depend on a man for anything: love or money.

Jackson had all the hallmarks of a toxic bachelor;

charming, sexy and footloose, he should have broken my heart. But right from the start, and against all reason (even with a streaming cold he was a definite 9½; on my wedding day, with a flotilla of *Vogue* make-up artists, I'd be lucky to scrape a 7), somehow I always knew I was the one in control.

It was no single thing, but a thousand tiny kindnesses. He filled our bedroom with Confederate jasmine because I mentioned that I liked its scent. He stayed up all night testing me before my exams, never taking offence when I yelled at him out of nerves or sheer bloody-mindedness. When I wanted to ski in Colorado, he was happy to take me, even though he hated the cold with all the fervour of a Southern boy who's never experienced a morning frost. Not just keep-the-peace happy. Child-on-Christmas-morning happy. Being with me was enough for him. No matter what I proposed, he smiled his easy smile which scrunched the corners of his blue blue eyes, and said that if it worked for me, it worked for him too.

Our light romance bridged the gap between Mardi Gras and real life with surprising success. We were very different people, and yet we understood each other. We both knew what it was like to suddenly lose a parent at a young age – in Jackson's case, both: his parents had died in a hotel fire when he was eleven, leaving him to be brought up by his brother Cooper, six years his elder. We'd both had to grow up hard and fast, and if our reactions to this hot-housed awareness of the fragility of life were very different – he chose to live for today, I to control tomorrow – we had a shared knowledge of the chaos that lay beneath. We both loved jazz and blues, Gregory Peck and baroque architecture. Jackson adored peaceably walking in the mountains almost as much as I loved the challenge of climbing them; we both relished the thrills of white-water rafting, kayaking and canoeing. Admittedly I missed the bright lights of London, but in those early days we were truly both happiest when we were far from the madding crowd, holed up in a cabin somewhere with just the odd harmless black bear for company.

Of course I loved him; it was impossible not to. He gave freely and asked nothing of me (the talk of babies came much later). He was always there for me, my confidant and companion, my dearest friend.

And I needed him; for many reasons, but most of all to counterbalance the fatal pull I felt towards men I couldn't handle, men who *didn't* make me feel safe. Men like my father, men who would catch me in their riptide and drag me under.

We all marry partly out of fear: of being alone, of dying unloved. Three months after we met I asked Jackson to marry me, knowing that whatever his reservations, he would be unable to say no, because I was afraid of what I might do if I didn't.

Lucy looks up from the nurses' station, where she's skimming a bulky manila folder. 'Nice shoes.'

I hesitate. She smiles ruefully and, relieved at the unexpected *détente*, I smile back.

She hands me the folder. 'Sorry I had to call you in. It's Anna Shore.'

Damn. Anna is one of Lucy's heartsink obstetric patients: thirty-nine, six miscarriages in five years, two of them distressingly late, at nineteen and twenty weeks. This pregnancy is her last chance to have her own child; she and her husband, Dean, have already decided that they cannot bear to go through the shattering cycle of hope and despair again if this attempt fails.

'Remind me. How far along?'

'Twenty-two weeks and six days.'

'Shit.'

I scan the notes, trying to get a read on how developed we think this baby is. It's hospital policy not to save babies of less than twenty-three weeks' gestation; born at the very cusp of viability, their chances of survival, even with our intervention, are minimal. I'm relieved Lucy called me in; William will get over it. This sort of case isn't something I'd want a senior house officer handling in my absence.

'Look, Ella,' Lucy says carefully, 'I'm sorry about going off at you the other day. It was just a shock, running into the two of you like that. Tell William I'm really sorry about the carrot juice. I'll pay for the dry-cleaning—'

'Forget it. At least it wasn't hot coffee.'

'It's just that you know how much I like Jackson, and what with – with Lawrence—'

'Did he agree to counselling?'

She seems to shrink inside her skin, so that suddenly it hangs loose and grey on her bones. 'He's asked for a divorce.'

'Oh, Lucy. Oh, darling, I'm *so* sorry.'

'*Shit*, Ella. Don't be nice to me or I'll lose it completely.' She pulls herself together with a visible effort. 'I know you don't want to hear this, but I'm worried about you. Jackson is such a good man. You two could be really great together. I don't want this thing with William to blow up in your face.'

'It's a bit of a mess, I know, but—'

'Eight years, Ella!'

'Look, all right. It kind of drifted. But it's not like we see each other that often.' I snap shut the file. 'Lucy, you know the score. This is about you and Lawrence, not—'

'Do you love him?'

'Jackson? Or William?'

'Either,' she exclaims, exasperated.

'It's not that simple. Life isn't black and white, you know that—'

'Actually, Ella, some things *are*.' She looks at me sharply. 'It was one thing playing with fire when we were at college, but it's different now. This is real life. I thought when you met Jackson you'd finally got whatever was eating you out of your system. Obviously I was wrong.'

I shift uncomfortably. How to explain in a way that makes any kind of sense? At twenty-five, when I married Jackson, I truly intended to be faithful to him for ever. I thought *wanting* to be in love with him was enough. But within a year, I discovered that getting what you wish for isn't all it's cracked up to be. Beautiful and careless, Jackson never, ever said no to me. But I soon realized he let me have my way less out of love than a desire to slough off responsibility for anything at all. I hadn't married an equal, but an emotional child; and why would I want to have a baby – already an enterprise I felt deeply ambivalent about, given my own parents' staggering incompetence – when I was already parenting my husband?

I'd hoped that moving back to London for my residency would help, that the buzz of the city would somehow jump-start things between us. But then, just a week shy of our third wedding anniversary, I met William.

He wasn't anywhere near as good-looking or charming as Jackson. Twelve years older, tough, cynical, sexist and controlling, he was everything my gentlemanly, easygoing husband was not. And unlike my husband, he just had *it*; in spades.

It was like being hit by a train. The sexual chemistry was tangible, but it was more than that. Meeting him made me realize how much I'd short-changed not just Jackson but myself when I took the safe way out and married him. I morphed into a different person when I was with William, the person I'd always wanted to be: confident, desirable, exciting. He challenged me; being with him was like walking a tightrope – terrifying and exhilarating at the same time. One slip and I could lose him; or, even worse, fall in love.

I never considered leaving Jackson. I married him to protect myself from men like William Ashfield. And I was very fond of my husband. None of this was his fault. But I couldn't face the thought of spending the rest of my life never experiencing anything stronger than *fond*.

William wanted the same as I did: an escape. A chance to play what-might-have-been, without jeopardizing what was.

To my astonishment, tears threaten. I blink furiously, surprised and shocked. I *never* bring my personal life into work.

'Ella, I'm sorry. I didn't mean to upset you—'

'You didn't. It's my problem, not yours.'

'I'm sure you know what you're doing,' Lucy says uncertainly.

'You'd think, after eight years.'

She folds her arms. 'Ella, you're the most self-controlled

person I've ever met, but even *you* can't expect to lead two separate lives and not have them collide now and again, if only in your head. Feelings have a way of coming to the surface, whether you like it or not.'

Lucy is my dearest friend, but she doesn't know what she's talking about. Things are absolutely fine. My life is perfectly organized. It's all beautifully balanced. William and I have the perfect arrangement. Jackson isn't going to find out; nothing's going to go wrong. I'm totally in control.

I jump at the asthmatic sound of the Victorian lift. Instantly, thankfully, my focus is on my patient. *You escape into work and call it altruism,* Jackson said once, in a rare moment of anger. *I call it the coward's way out.*

A flurry of medical personnel wheels a hospital bed from the lift. Anna Shore's frantic husband struggles to keep hold of her hand as the cavalcade steps up its pace. Behind them, Richard Angel, the hospital's chief number cruncher – known, without a trace of irony, as the Angel of Death – strides down the corridor. His fine blond hair is so badly cut it borders on rude. He snaps his fingers constantly at his sides, an irritating nervous tic.

'Shit,' Lucy mutters, 'I meant to warn you.'

'If I might have a word . . .' Angel starts.

Lucy disappears to a private room to examine Anna, while Angel and I glare at each other across the nurses' station. I'm acutely conscious of the fact that I'm not wearing any knickers.

The prognosis is written on her face when she returns. 'The drugs aren't working, Ella. She's in full-blown labour. I said you'd talk to her, and explain what happens next.'

Of course. I'm always the one who has to break bad

news. Lucy's far too beautiful for anyone to believe in her as the bearer of grim tidings. Clearly, awash with freckles and gifted with hideous ginger ringlets and my father's Depardieu nose, I have the right looks for tragedy.

I'm sluiced by a wave of sadness as I go into Anna's room and sit down on the edge of the bed. It's not the fear in her eyes that disarms me; it's the unremitting hope.

'Anna,' I say gently. 'We've tried to stop the labour, but it's not working. Your baby is going to be born in the next hour or so. We've given her steroids, to try to mature her lungs, but we haven't really had much time. She's very tiny, Anna. Not much more than a pound. Do you know how small that is?'

'Half a bag of sugar,' Anna whispers.

'She's so little, darling. Not quite twenty-three weeks. I need to talk to you about what that means, and you're going to have to be very brave. Can you do that for me?'

She glances up at her husband, then nods, her grip tightening on my fingers.

'At this age, we lose two-thirds of these tiny babies during delivery. They just can't cope, sweetheart, their little lungs aren't strong enough. If they do make it, we have to help them with their breathing. We give them something called surfactant, which keeps their lungs from sticking together and makes their breathing easier—'

'What about brain damage?' Dean, her husband, asks fearfully.

'When a baby is born this early, there is a risk she'll have an intracranial haemorrhage – bleeding of the brain.'

'How high a risk?'

'If the baby is really small, about one in three.'

Anna closes her eyes and turns her head away.

God, this never gets any easier. 'That doesn't necessarily mean that the baby will be brain-damaged, Anna. There's only a bad outcome in a small percentage of cases—'

'Wait. Wait. What do you call a bad outcome?' Dean interrupts. 'What are we talking about here?'

'Some type of limited motion, or intellectual trouble at school, that kind of thing.'

'So how long before you know if she's going to be – *normal*?'

'We can't tell with babies this small. I'm sorry, I know it's hard.' I pause, my heart aching as I search for the right words to help them. 'Sometimes when the baby is this little, it can be better to just let her go. Intervention can be very traumatic, for you and your baby, and when the outlook is as uncertain as this—'

'I don't care if she's not perfect!' Anna cries. 'I don't care if we have to spend the rest of our lives looking after her!'

Dean swallows. 'And if she makes it? What then, Dr Stuart?'

'Call me Ella, please.' I sigh. 'Look, Dean, I'm not going to lie to you. There are lots of hurdles a baby this premature has to face, but there's no point giving you nightmares by outlining every possibility. We really need to concentrate on the here and now, not on what might develop later down the line. I want you to clearly understand what's going to happen once we start to deliver your baby, because I may not be able to explain everything at the time. I might need you to make some very difficult decisions very quickly.'

He nods, jaw working as he fights to hold back tears. *Jesus, why would anyone want to be a parent and risk* going through this? Having a child must be like spending the rest of your life with your heart walking around outside your body.

'If you want us to stop at any point during resuscitation, you just have to say so,' I add gently. 'No one is going to think badly of you.'

Tears seep beneath Anna's closed eyelids. 'I don't care what you have to do. Just don't give up on her. Please.'

I spend the next forty minutes prepping with the neo-natal team, acutely aware that somewhere in this hospital another team of medical staff are preparing to abort a baby a week older than the infant we are trying to save. I know the chances are high that Anna's infant will die. I have dealt with a thousand cases just as tragic as hers. Why has this one got under my skin?

Richard Angel is lying in wait for me when Lucy pages me back to the obstetric suite. He glances at my scarlet heels, opens his mouth, then wisely thinks better of it.

'What are you still doing here?' I demand. 'No funny Valentine waiting at home?'

He scurries to keep pace with me, fingers clicking like a skeletal metronome. 'New policy. I expect to be notified whenever there's a borderline neonate.'

'Borderline?'

'You know hospital policy, Dr Stuart. It's a perfectly reasonable—'

'I'm sorry. Did I miss your graduation from medical school?' I hiss. 'Since when have *you* been qualified to determine viability, Richard? Is it just small babies you want to flush down the sluice, or do you plan to tour the geriatric ward pulling plugs, too?'

He looks like he wants to hit me. I watch him struggle

to keep his temper, knowing and not caring that I have just made a permanent and dangerous enemy.

'Someone has to be responsible for the operating costs of this hospital, Dr Stuart. If your department overspends, we have to make cuts elsewhere. One day in NICU costs the same as—'

'Do you expect me to stand by and watch this baby die?'

'This *foetus*,' he stresses, 'is too young to be viable.'

'Check your facts. It's ten past midnight,' I snap. 'Which means that, as of ten minutes ago, this *baby* is twenty-three weeks old and wins tonight's big prize: a shot at life. Now, if you'll excuse me, I have a patient waiting.'

I should be elated. Angel had both probability and statistics on his side. But against all the odds, Anna and Dean's baby – appropriately named Hope – snatched the chance we offered her. She'll spend the next four months in the NICU, a dozen lines snaking into her tiny body; it'll be weeks before she even breathes on her own, but she's alive. A brain scan hasn't shown up any obvious abnormalities, though we have a long way to go before we can relax. The risk of infection with a baby this young is acute. But so far, so good.

Yet the usual high eludes me. I let myself quietly into William's flat a little after four in the morning, my mood oppressed. A sense of unease drags at my heels. For the first time in years, I crave a cigarette.

Pouring myself a glass of tap water, I add four ice-cubes – thank you, America – and tiptoe through the darkened hallway towards the bedroom, wincing like a teenager as the ice clinks noisily in the sweating glass. For a long moment, I stand in the open doorway, leaning against the jamb. Asleep, William looks younger than his forty-eight years, the cynicism stripped from his expression. He is not conventionally handsome; his features are too uneven for that. A faded scar, three inches long, bisects his right jaw, the result of a climbing accident when he was eleven. He still nicks it when he shaves, one of the reasons he sports designer stubble – salt and pepper now, I notice, like his overlong hair. His head is heavy, leonine; when he smiles, his tawny eyes glow like copper. Angry, they darken to the colour of coffee beans. It is impossible to know the extent of his charisma, the force of his sexual energy, until he turns it on you.

I'm not in love with him. I knew from the beginning I couldn't allow myself that – especially after Cyprus. Divorce from Beth was not an option, given her problems, nor would I ever want it. That was never part of our arrangement.

Suddenly weary, I finish my glass of water and strip off my clothes, padding into the bathroom to brush my teeth. I notice my period has started a couple of days early; annoyed at being caught out, I grab an emergency tampon from my wash-bag and make a mental note to pick up a new box from the corner shop tomorrow; or rather, today.

It's four-thirty when I finally slip into bed beside William: too late to pick up where we left off. His alarm will go off in half an hour; despite owning a successful PR agency with a staff of over forty people, William is always the first to arrive at the office, and the last to leave. If I were married to Beth, no doubt I'd do the same. I'm very lucky to go home to a man I can at least respect.

Lucy's words have burrowed deeper than I care to

admit. For the first time in a very long time, I allow myself to think what it might be like to have to live without Jackson. I'm faintly surprised at how much I don't want that to happen. I know full well I deserve to lose him. I've always been very careful to control my feelings for William, to keep our relationship separate in my heart and head; I would never leave Jackson. But I know that would prove scant consolation to him if he ever found out about my affair. It would break his heart; and that would break mine.

I realize the unfamiliar feeling in the pit of my stomach is shame. This is not the kind of wife I ever wanted or intended to be. I've short-changed my husband; not only have I cheated on him, but I've denied him the only thing he has ever asked of me. Would a baby *really* be so bad?

My mobile rings, making me jump. I reach for it as William stirs, recognizing the hospital number on the caller ID. My heart sinks. Baby Hope seemed stable enough when I left the NICU—

But it's A&E on the other end of the line, not the NICU. And when I end the call a few minutes later, I am no longer any kind of wife, adulterous or otherwise.

I am a widow.

March 8, 1997

Chapel Hill Road
Durham
North Carolina 27707

Dear Cooper,

> *Well, I'm not dead yet, despite what you must be thinking! I'm sorry it's been so long since I touched base, but it's been a crazy couple months. It'd be easier if you got connected – once you're online you can get these whizzy little electronic letters, they call them emails, maybe you've heard of them?!*

Anyways, I'm back in the Land of Tar; you always said I couldn't stay away from the mountains for long! I'd have called you before I left New Orleans, but everything happened so fast, I didn't have time. My new condo hasn't got a phone yet and the landlord's dragging his heels, so I guess this letter is it for a while.

The thing is, I've met a girl. Her name's Ella Stuart, and she's the most beautiful woman I've ever seen. She's British (she has this cute accent!) and she's a doctor – well, studying to be one over at Duke.

I'm guessing you're putting the pieces together right now and shaking your head and wondering what trouble your kid brother's gotten himself into this time, but it's not like that. This girl is the real deal, Coop. There's just something about her; soon as you meet her, you'll know what I mean.

Anyways, couple weeks ago, first night of Mardi Gras, I went down the Famous Door (you remember, I took you there last time you were in the Easy, you got picked up by that

*transvestite) and soon as I walked in the bar, I saw her.
She's hard to miss, Coop, with this long wild red hair, like
the setting sun, and these big gold eyes that put me in
mind of Lolly's iced tea. She was laughing with her friend,
and right then she turned and caught my eye, and something
just clicked inside of me, like tumblers sliding into place.
I couldn't take my eyes off her. There was a look about her,
underneath all the sass: wary and sad at the same time. She
hides it well, but it's there. You think first off she's tough as
nails, but deep down she's sweet as pie.*

*So there I am, still trying to think of something smart to
say, when Ella just comes up and kisses me! I swear, I could
feel the tingling in my toes for ten minutes afterwards.
What's it called? A* coup de foudre, *something like that.
When you know the rest of your life is never going to be the
same again.*

*I bet you're laughing your ass off right now out on the
back porch, wondering how your brother has ended up all
misty-eyed over some girl like a lovestruck loon. Well, take
another pull on your Jack, brother, because that isn't the half
of it.*

*Next day, she tells me she's studying at Duke, and I just
come right out and say I've got a job there – don't ask me
what made me do it, Coop, I couldn't tell you, I just knew I
couldn't let her slip through my fingers. So I've spent the last
three weeks calling in every favor I ever chalked up and then
some, and two days ago I got a letter offering me a job in the
Department of Earth and Ocean Sciences, starting Monday!
It's less money than Tulane, but I like the idea of working for
the environment, I've had my fill of capital projects. So I gave
notice, quit my apartment, and drove up here yesterday.*

Now here I am sitting in a rental condo without a stick of furniture but a bed and a chair, wondering if I've gone and made the biggest fool of myself since Old Man Allen caught me buck-naked with Blair in the sawmill!

Thing is, Coop, I'm blown away by Ella, but I'm not so sure she's sold on me, and I don't know what all to do. Not to toot my own horn, but my problem's usually the other way round! I know she likes me, but I'm pretty sure she thought our hook-up was just a weekend fling. How do I close the deal, big brother? She blows hot and cold; one minute she's all over me, and the next I feel like I've got her foot in my ass and I'm being led out the door. I'm guessing she's been screwed over in the past by guys who never did the honorable thing, but the one thing you got to give me is that I say what I mean and I do what I say. If I can get her to trust me, I'll never give her cause to regret it.

Guess this is all part of your famous Karma Credit Plan, right? Payback for some of those hearts I broke along the way. I can't wait for you and Lolly to meet her. She's the one, Coop. I can see us sitting on the swing at Dad's old place by the lake, watching the sun set behind the mountains and knowing I've come home. I want to grow old with this woman, watch our kids grow up together, rock grandkids on my knee like Grandpa did with us. I can't blow it, bro.

I'd better close now, and go unpack some boxes before she comes round. I thought I might find some jasmine – she says she loves the scent, just like Mom used to. Lord, but I still miss her.

Write me soon, kiss Lolly for me, and see about that computer!

    Jackson

2

William

Christ Almighty, the poor bastard was only forty-one. Seven years younger than me. And a damn sight fitter, according to Ella: tennis, cycling, jogging down the Thames towpath at weekends. You're always reading about these health nuts keeling over in their running shorts, perfect specimens of physical fitness (apart from the unfortunate fact that they're dead); but it wasn't the running that gave him a heart attack. A fucking *virus*. Jesus.

It makes you think. Shit, it could happen to anyone; I could be next. Ella says it's not catching, it was just one of those freaky bugs that come out of nowhere, but let's face it, she's a paediatrician, not an immunologist—

'Mr Ashfield, is everything OK?'

I start. 'Sorry, Carolyn, miles away.'

My PA consults her notepad, nipples perking from the air-conditioning. 'Joe needs an answer on the Brunswick proposal. I told him you're still waiting to hear back from

Natasha, said you'd be in touch after the weekend. He's not happy, but he'll live with it.'

'Good. Did Sky get back to us yet about the Malinche Lyon interview?'

'Still waiting to hear. You've got about a dozen messages from Andammon, they're really keen—'

'Not interested. We'll have all our blue-chip clients beating a path out the door if we start representing footballers' wives. Tell them we're not taking anyone else on right now, and give them Clifford's number.'

Idly, I watch her pert derrière wiggle out of the room, then swivel my chair back towards the window, barely noticing the stunning floor-to-ceiling view of Canary Wharf. Funny how you can work towards something for years, and six months later it barely registers.

I can't get Ella's husband out of my head. Which is ironic, given I've been screwing his wife on a regular basis for the last eight years and until he checked into the morgue a week ago I'd barely spared him a thought.

I'm not bloody proud of it; messing about with another man's wife isn't something I take lightly. No question, if Jackson had twigged what was going on, he'd have been quite within his rights to nail my balls to a tree. But in my defence, it wasn't as if I was going to break up the marriage. Perhaps, if it hadn't been for Beth – if she wasn't the way she is . . .

It's always been clearly understood, right from the outset, that divorce wasn't an option for either of us; all the more so after Cyprus. Ella wouldn't have it any other way.

Still. She was in *my* bed when she found out her husband had turned up his toes. Hardly my fault, but it makes me feel a bit of a prick none the less.

Of course, now she's convinced it would've made a difference if she'd been with him. Says she might have seen the signs; though as I understand it, the whole problem is that there weren't any.

I've never known Ella feel guilty before. She doesn't experience the self-doubt that plagues us ordinary mortals; that kind of confidence is very sexy. Handy, too, for a doctor; if you second-guessed yourself over every life-or-death decision, you'd wind up off your head. But I suppose that kind of hubris catches up with everyone in the end. Even brazen, beautiful Ella.

I rub my hand over my face, trying to dispel a lingering weariness. Haven't been sleeping all that well lately. Beth isn't doing too brilliantly at the moment. I keep hoping she's just missing the boys, that we're not back on the slippery slope, but in the meantime there's a lot of slack for me to pick up at home, and of course Cate is at that stage – mothers and daughters, never easy even in a normal household.

And now Ella. Hard to know how things are going to go there. Suddenly single. Available, after all these years.

I hope she's not going to go getting any ideas about *us*. She seems to be taking it in her stride, as usual, but you never know. Even caught myself playing the old 'What if?' game once or twice. Jackson dying has rather put the cat amongst the pigeons, all in all—

My mobile buzzes. 'Cate,' I exclaim, pleased. An unsolicited phone call from my seventeen-year-old daughter is a rare honour. 'I was just thinking about you—'

'Dad,' she interrupts, 'I think you'd better come home. Quickly.'

*

The house is cold and silent when I open the front door. Instantly, I smell burning. I throw my briefcase on to the hall table and sprint into the kitchen. Inside the Aga are the charred remains of the steak-and-kidney stew I put in it at six o'clock this morning. I slam my fist against the wall. *Damn it, Beth!* I may not be Jamie Oliver in the kitchen, but I was up at sparrow's fart to peel bloody carrots in the dark! All I asked you to do was take the fucking casserole out mid-morning. Is that really too much to ask?

I throw the blackened dish in the sink and run the hot tap, holding on to my temper with difficulty. It's not her fault. *It's not her fault.* But Jesus Christ almighty, it isn't mine either.

Upstairs, Cate's bedroom door is closed. The faint back-beat of music echoes down the hall. I raise my hand to knock, and then think better of it. Cate's pretty savvy, but at the end of the day she's still a child. She should be obsessing over pop stars and clothes and worrying about her exams, not helping me hold it together while her mother falls apart on us. Again.

In our room, Beth is sitting on the edge of the unmade bed in her shapeless pink flannel nightdress, bare feet dangling over her towelling slippers. As far as I can tell, she hasn't moved since I left her here this morning.

Foreboding fills me. I haven't seen her like this for years, not since Sam was small. I call her name, but she doesn't respond. Even when I crouch down in front of her and say it again, she doesn't show by so much as a flicker that she's heard me.

'Beth, baby, come on, you can't do this to me. You have to *try.*'

Gently, I take her chin between my thumb and forefinger and turn her head to look at me. She blinks, as if I've shone a light into her eyes.

'I know you're in there, darling. I'm not letting you just give up.'

Her watery blue eyes are expressionless, but still lucid, I note with relief.

'Come on, sweetheart. I know you miss the boys, but they'll be back soon as term's over. Sam has an exeat weekend soon, and Ben will be down from Oxford in just a few more weeks—'

'I want to die,' my wife says.

Marvellous. Well, at least she's talking.

'You know you don't mean that.'

'I don't want to feel like this any more. I want this to be over. I want to just not *be*.'

I stand up and switch on the bedside lamp, flooding the room with light. Briskly, I draw the curtains that I flung open this morning. 'That's not an option, Beth. This isn't exactly a party for me, either. But we'll get through it, we always do. Perhaps we need to go back to Dr Stone and get another prescription. Up the dosage.'

'I don't want any more drugs.'

Well, I bloody do. The kind Ben is secretly growing under the cloche by the apple tree in between the tomato plants, so the spiky leaves don't give him away.

'Beth, darling, you must see you can't go on like this,' I say through gritted teeth. 'Look at you: you haven't moved in over twelve hours. You haven't even managed to get dressed or take dinner out of the oven, let alone look after Cate. Sweetheart, you can't even look after yourself!'

Her still-pretty face is a blank mask. I have no idea what – if anything – is going on inside her head. I hate it when she shuts down like this.

I resist the sudden urge to shake a response from her. She can't help it. I have to keep telling myself that.

'Look. If we need to change your medicine, darling, that's what we'll do. I'll take some time off work, God knows how, but we'll go away for a bit, do whatever we have to—'

'Don't you get it?' Beth cries unexpectedly. 'This isn't about the boys leaving. It's not *about* anything. It's *me*. It's who I am. It's not going to change. You can't cheer me up or jolly me out of it with a trip to the seaside. Don't you think I'd give anything not to be like this?' She thumps her thigh with her fist. 'I'd rather be dead than wake up one more morning feeling this way, and the only reason I'm still here is that I'm too much of a coward to do anything about it!'

She buries her face in her hands, and I'm about to comfort her, to put my arms around her as I always do; but for once all I can think of is Ella, who has been my lifeline for eight years; strong, fearless Ella, knocked sideways in an instant by death. I am scared shitless of what it may mean for us, of all that I suddenly now stand to lose.

Fear explodes into anger.

'Death may be better for you, but what about those you leave behind?' I demand. 'What about Ben, and Cate, and Sam? What about *me*?'

'You'd be better off without me.'

To my shame, I don't contradict her. I've soothed and calmed my troubled wife for twenty-one years, biting my tongue and getting on with things. I may not have kept all my vows, God forgive me, but I've stuck with the one that really mattered: she's my wife, in sickness and in health. Even at her worst, even when she doesn't know her own name. I've loved her as hard as I can, in the best way I know how. Of course I've had the odd fling – Christ, I'm only human – but nothing serious, not until Ella. And she made it clear from the start that she wasn't going to leave her husband, so that took divorce off the table once and for all.

But suddenly the well of sympathy has run dry. I'm exhausted from carrying Beth day after day after bloody day. I'm tired of her depression and inertia and sheer relentless fucking *misery*.

'Pull yourself together, Beth,' I say sharply, and walk out of the room.

It started when Cate was born. Beth had always been a bit highly strung, but until then I'd put it down to a mixture of PMT and artistic temperament – we'd met at her student exhibition at St Martin's, where a cousin of mine was also showing. I forget how we got talking. Beth didn't graduate, of course. Ben put paid to that, halfway through her final year.

At twenty, she was seven years my junior, and pretty, in a virginal, girl-next-door way. She had an old-fashioned air about her; it was partly the way she wore her fair hair in a shoulder-length bob held off her face with an Alice band, partly the way she dressed, in cashmere twinsets and pearls – more débutante than starving artist – but more than anything it was the vulnerability in her pale blue eyes. She seemed fragile, damaged, in need of fixing. I was looking for a science project, and Beth Llewellyn was it.

She also fucked like a rabbit. I'd never met a woman who wanted sex as often as Beth; it was all the more erotic for being so unexpected. I'd spent the previous ten years courting bankruptcy with flash dinners and flowers to get girls into bed; now here was this shy English rose practically ripping my clothes off every time I walked through the door.

Stupidly, I'd assumed she was taking precautions. It was only after she'd skipped two periods that she told me, in her artless way, that she'd stopped taking the pill because it made her feel sick. Of course I offered to marry her. I'd been searching for a way to stick it to my bitch of a mother – and she'd never liked Beth.

At our wedding, everyone agreed we made the perfect couple. Admittedly, I wasn't exactly head-over-heels, but we got on well, we were comfortable together – and the sex was frequent, if a little vanilla. I'd never made any secret of wanting to settle down with a nice ordinary girl who'd be happy to look after hearth and home while I went out and earned a crust. No tricky career women for me; I'd had enough of ball-breaking alpha females for one lifetime. I had no intention of ending up like my poor bloody father.

We'd barely brushed the confetti out of our hair when I began to realize that what I'd taken for agreeability was actually apathy; that Beth's acquiescence on every issue – other than sex – came less from a desire to please me than because she simply didn't care. About anything. Ever.

I chose the first house we bought, the furniture we put in it, even the cushions on the bloody sofa. I told myself it was just her hormones – everyone knew pregnant women were serene and unruffled. It was a good thing, surely? Better than throwing saucepans and demanding to know if I was having an affair.

That came when Ben arrived, four months after our wedding. Poor little sod, he must have wondered if he'd been born in Beirut. For his first few months, all we did was scream at each other. She burst into tears when I bought full-fat milk instead of skimmed. I nearly got my nose broken for forgetting to tape *Casualty* when she was at the shops. We smashed more plates than a Greek restaurant.

But between the rows, we screwed our brains out. And when Beth (unsurprisingly) found herself pregnant again when Ben was just nine weeks old, things calmed down once more. Apparently back to her placid self, Beth sat out in the garden rocking Ben in his pram for hours, stroking her swelling belly and seemingly content to immerse herself in motherhood and domesticity.

When Cate was born, I braced myself, ready for the airborne crockery, but it never came. Instead, Beth abruptly slid into a state of listless misery. I'd come home to find her standing at the sink with her arms in the washing up, tears pouring down her cheeks, unable to tell me what was wrong.

It soon became evident, even to an unreconstructed young male like me, that this wasn't your normal baby blues. She wasn't eating, she wasn't sleeping; her moods swung between biting my head off and near-catatonia.

'She's sinking, William,' Clara, Beth's capable mother, warned when Cate was about four weeks old. 'I'm sure you've done your best, but she needs professional help. It's no good sitting back and giving her time and waiting for her to get better. Beth's never been much good at managing her life. You have to take charge.'

Easier said than done. I tried to cut back at work, but I was still getting my fledgling company up and running, and I couldn't afford to sit at home minding the kids while my wife slumped comatose in front of *Neighbours*. I did manage to get Ben and Cate into a nursery two mornings a week at the local parish centre, and hired a cleaner we could ill afford to come in once a week and 'do'. Beth had got better last time; if we could just muddle through for a bit longer, I was sure things would sort themselves out again.

Six weeks later, I arrived home to find the police waiting on my doorstep. There had been some sort of accident – the children strapped into their car seats while Beth ran into the butcher's, a handbrake left off, the car parked on top of a hill . . .

'It's a miracle no one was seriously hurt, sir,' the young cop told me on our way to the hospital. 'Your wife's car crossed four lanes of traffic on the A22, knocked down a garden wall and ended up in an old lady's sitting-room.'

I thanked God the only casualty was the old dear's budgie, which apparently flew out of its cage in the confusion and was eaten by next door's cat, and hugged my children a little tighter than usual when I put them to bed.

'I didn't really want to *hurt* them, William,' Beth said piteously, later that night, 'it's just Cate wouldn't stop crying – then Ben started screaming too, I couldn't stand it any more, I thought if I could just – I only wanted them to *stop* . . .'

Appalled by her admission and secretly ashamed of my

neglect, the next day I took Beth to see a psychiatrist, who diagnosed severe post-natal depression and put her on a course of anti-depressants. When my wife started to refer to herself as the Virgin Mary and took to cleaning out the attic at three in the morning in preparation for the second coming, he switched her to anti-psychotic drugs. She responded by building a pyre in the back garden.

I took her back to the doctor. 'We may need to think about electroconvulsive therapy,' he advised grimly.

Repulsed at the thought of wiring my wife up to the mains, I told him where to stick his Frankenstein therapy. For the next week, I took turns with Clara to watch Beth in case she tried anything else with the children, and ground her pills into her food when I realized she'd been palming them.

Then one morning Clara rang me at work to say she'd caught Beth force-feeding four-month-old Cate table salt, to 'purify her'. Reluctantly, I agreed to the ECT.

For two months, I drove Beth to a private mental health clinic an hour from home three times a week, while Clara and Beth's best friend Eithne minded the children. I sat outside the clinic in my car with my clunking great mobile and attempted to keep my flat-lining business afloat, whilst my wife was anaesthetized, had electrodes glued to her scalp and was electrocuted into convulsions. She'd emerge so confused she didn't even know who she was. I'd drive her back home and put her to bed, thankful that at least the children would be far too young to remember the deranged, gibbering woman who wandered the house at all hours of the day and night in her dressing-gown.

It was the stuff of horror movies, but the ECT worked. Within weeks, Beth started to get better; by the time Cate was six months old, she was almost back to her normal self, albeit a dramatically subdued version.

But the treatment had wiped out huge chunks of her memory, some of which never came back – she didn't remember meeting me, for example, or giving birth to Ben and Cate. It had its plus sides: she forgot she'd loved *EastEnders*, thank Christ. But she became forgetful and uncertain; her confidence, never strong, ebbed to the point where she could be reduced to tears at the thought of entering a roomful of strangers.

Her mood swings were levelled out by a pick 'n' mix selection of anti-depressants and tranquillizers. Occasionally she complained she'd lost her sense of feeling – 'It's like my emotions are numb, William. I don't feel happy or sad, I don't seem to feel *anything*' – but whenever she tried to go cold turkey, the depression would creep back.

Unfortunately, the drugs also wiped out Beth's libido. Not only did she no longer want to have sex; she quite simply refused to.

The impact on our marriage was devastating. I couldn't communicate with my wife inside the bedroom or out of it; if it hadn't been for the children, I honestly don't know if I'd have stayed.

When Cate and Ben were three and four, I came back from a business trip to Dublin (with a rather pretty brunette who couldn't type to save her life; be fair, by that stage Beth and I hadn't had sex for two and a half *years*) to find my wife running through a neighbouring orchard stark naked, giving away five-pound notes to passers-by.

'Well, at least we know what the problem is now,' the doctor observed, diagnosing her with manic depression and writing her a prescription for lithium. 'This should help her get back to her old self. I'm surprised we didn't pick it up before, but it may have been the post-natal depression that triggered it. The drugs she's been on since then would have masked it. I don't suppose you ever noticed any manic tendencies before she got pregnant the first time?'

'Like what?'

'Oh, reckless behaviour, excessive energy, out-of-control spending, that sort of thing.'

'You've just described ninety per cent of my ex-girlfriends, but not Beth. Though she did paint a lot at night sometimes, now I think about it. She'd fill whole canvases at a single sitting, but that's just the way artists work, isn't it? Other than that, I don't—'

'Abnormally high libido?' the doctor asked, scribbling on his pad.

'Ah,' I said.

The lithium enabled Beth to control her moods without turning her into a zombie. Gradually she began to pick up the threads of her old life. Things improved in the bedroom, too, although sex was only ever at my instigation; her wild enthusiasm, it seemed, had gone for ever. Occasionally she still cried over nothing or threw herself into new projects with rather too much energy (the house was littered with half-finished tapestries and misshapen clay pots), but on the whole, if you hadn't been there during the darkest days, you'd never have known anything was wrong. I was confident Ben and Cate would have no memories of their mother as anything other than the way she was now.

And then when Cate was nine, Beth fell pregnant again.

When she went into premature labour at twenty-nine weeks, my first concern was for my wife, not the baby. The pregnancy had been closely monitored; Beth's lithium had been cut back, but not eliminated because of the risk of relapse. All I'd been able to think about since discovering the bloody unreliability of Greek condoms (purchased whilst on holiday in Rhodes) was whether the birth would trigger another psychotic episode.

But when we were led into a delivery suite, and a stunning blonde obstetrician with distracting breasts explained the possible complications, I was seized by a new and terrible fear: that after all the risks we'd taken to ensure his survival, I would lose my new son before he was even born.

'I've taken the precaution of calling a neonatologist down, just in case,' the doctor explained; 'she's one of the best. Your son will be in safe hands with her, I promise.'

Which was how I met Ella.

'I'm married,' she'd said.

'So am I.'

'I'm *happily* married,' Ella emphasized. 'I have no intention of leaving my husband.'

'I'm – married,' I grimaced, 'and I promise you, I've no intention of leaving my wife.'

'In that case,' said Ella, 'what are we doing here?'

'If I really have to explain, then I've just made the second big mistake of my life.'

Her strange gold eyes danced with amusement, crazy red hair spiralling out in all directions. She effervesced with barely contained energy, from the tips of her long, delicate fingers, now tapping a brisk tattoo with a packet of sugar on the Formica tabletop, to the razor-sharp toes of her bizarre purple high-heeled knee-boots (not the footwear one normally expected to see beneath a doctor's white coat). She certainly wasn't beautiful – the large nose and the freckles saw to that – but she was the most arresting woman I'd ever seen. Tall, maybe five-ten or so, she went in and out in all the right places. Her mouth was wide and full-lipped, her smile white and even – if it hadn't been for the idiosyncratic gap between her two front teeth, I'd have said she'd had work done. But it was the knowingness in her eyes that almost had me coming in my pants. This was a woman who knew what – and who – she wanted, and wasn't afraid to take it.

The chemistry between us had been obvious from day one. We'd both known, as we made eyes at each other across Sam's incubator, that as soon as he was discharged and any possible doctor–patient conflict removed (Ella was fiercely protective of her career), we'd end up in bed. The only question was whose.

Six weeks later, I'd picked Sam up from the hospital, taken him home to Clara, kissed Beth chastely on the cheek and turned the car straight back round to the hospital where Ella was waiting for me.

She stood up and hitched a huge leather bag on to her shoulder. 'What I meant,' she said as she threw four pound coins into her saucer, 'was what are we doing *here*?'

I followed her out of the hospital cafeteria, climbed into the black cab she hailed – by stepping out into the middle of the road and raising one autocratic arm, like Boudicca, heedless of the screeching brakes and hail of curses that ensued – and settled myself in the corner so that I could look at her for as long as it took us to get wherever she'd decided we were going.

Ella pulled her bag on to her cinnamon-suede lap and

rummaged around in it. 'Your wife never came to the NICU. What's the story there?'

'Beth has problems. Post-natal depression, bipolar disorder—'

'Yes, I saw that from her notes. But she's getting treatment?'

'Christ, yes. She nearly killed the kids last time round, so this time they dosed her up to the eyeballs as soon as she had the baby. Turns her into a bloody space cadet, which is why she never came in to see Sam, but it's better than—'

'Ah, here they are.' She tossed a small foil packet into my lap. 'Don't think they're time-expired, but you might want to check.'

'Condoms? Shy, aren't you?'

'Sorry. Love babies, but I couldn't eat a whole one.'

'I can't rule out a dose of the clap, but I'm not going to be sowing any seed, if that's what you're worried about. I got the snip the week we found out Beth was pregnant again.'

'All the same.'

'We've had one coffee,' I said, 'and you didn't let me finish that.'

Ella looked me in the eye, picked up my hand and slid it under her skirt. Her hard thighs, bare beneath the suede skirt, parted, and my fingertips brushed the crisp curls of her pussy. *No knickers. Jesus Christ.* 'You're not hiring me to be your children's nanny, William. What are you waiting for, references?'

The cab pulled up at Hyde Park. Ella thrust a couple of notes into the driver's hand as I tumbled out after her into the weak September sunshine, my dick tenting my trousers.

Without speaking, she pulled me into the eerie green shade of a chestnut tree, its leaves just beginning to turn. A few feet away, a mother fed the ducks with her two small children. A jogger ran past, barely breaking stride as a couple of teenagers on rollerblades tore up the pavement.

Backing up against the tree, Ella unzipped my trousers and lifted her skirt. My knuckles scraped against the rough bark of the tree as I gripped her arse with one hand. With the other, I rolled on the condom and plunged my dick into her slick, sticky wetness. Behind me, hooves thudded as a rider trotted past.

I buried my face in her neck, inhaling the scent of seawater, patchouli and fir, and ripped open her violet blouse without troubling with the buttons. She wasn't wearing a bra. Her nipples were as hard as the conkers at my feet.

'Ella, I'm going to—'

'Too late,' she gasped, her body shuddering, 'I'm there already.'

Later, as we walked past pensioners and tourists, I asked her, 'Do we do this again, or was it a one-off?'

'Which would you prefer?'

I stopped, watching the boaters on the Serpentine. Until now, I'd only ever had brief flings with girls I felt nothing for, none of which had lasted more than a few weeks. Once or twice things had got a little messy; one girl, a blonde PA who looked, accurately, like she'd been ridden hard and put away wet, had even turned up at the small bachelor pad I'd bought in Bayswater, a year or two after Cate was born, so that I didn't have to traipse home after a late night out with clients. Much as I'd appreciated the no-strings sex, I was growing increasingly wary of shitting on my own doorstep, and I was terrified that one of the gym bunnies would, sooner or later, turn out to be a bunny boiler.

Clearly I'd been going about things the wrong way. Single women naturally always wanted me to leave my wife, which I had no intention of doing. But a *married* woman, a happily married woman with as much to lose as me . . . A married woman, who got her kicks having sex in the park, who wasn't afraid to take the initiative, who had made it plain she didn't want to rock her marital boat either.

A woman who lifted my hand to her mouth as we stood in the sunshine amid a crowd of people, and tasted her juices on my fingers.

We sat down at a wrought-iron café table near an ice-cream kiosk and, over another cup of coffee, thrashed out the terms of our arrangement. No question of divorce on either side, *ever*; that was a given. Nothing that risked discovery: no phone calls at home, and to the mobile only in the event of an emergency (in eight years, there never had been); circumspect, and limited, emails, to our work accounts only; no personal gifts or photographs of us together. We agreed to meet no more than once a month, both to minimize the risk of arousing suspicion on the part of our spouses, and to prevent either of us become too entwined, or too involved, in the other's life. If either of us ever wanted to walk away, there would be no questions asked, and no comeback.

In another era, Ella would have made the perfect courtesan. Intelligent, witty, accomplished and accommodating, she was good company both in bed and out of it. Always civilized, always controlled: no demands or rows or histrionics. Apart from one little hiccup, that week in Cyprus – swiftly ironed out and never repeated – the arrangement worked perfectly.

I didn't ask Ella about her marriage; she didn't ask about mine. I knew her birthday only because I'd booked the flights to Cyprus. I could tell you her bra size and that she was allergic to strawberries, but I had no idea what really made her tick, and I was happy to keep it that way. It was bad enough having to pretend I cared about one woman's relationship with her mother. I was damned if I was going to do it for two.

We had the perfect set-up. And now Jackson has to die and fuck it all up.

When I get back downstairs, Cate is standing in front of the Aga, warming her bottom as she waits for the dented steel kettle to boil on the hotplate. Her boyfriend, Dan, has his arm wrapped around her waist, his fingers buried deep in the back pocket of her jeans. I want to punch his fucking lights out.

Cate was fourteen when she got her first boyfriend. Ever since she was born, blonde and blue-eyed and utterly perfect, I'd joked – only it wasn't funny – that I was putting her name down for a Romanian convent, and that any boy who wanted to date her would have to go through me first. Shovel or shotgun, I'd tell them. You mess with my baby, you dig your own grave.

I'd show her the drawing on the back of the cheap white wine her mother sometimes drank. 'Look,' I'd say, 'that's what you're going to be when you grow up.'

'A nun,' Cate would nod seriously.

Yet somehow I'd never actually considered how I might feel when she finally brought a boy home, how sick and angry the sight of a man's proprietary arm around her waist might make me. It had never occurred to me that she'd ever look at another man with that gold light in her eyes, turning to him like a flower to the sun, barely sparing a glance for me.

'How's your wife doing, William?' Dan asks concernedly.

Dan is twenty-three. Too old, apparently, to call me Mr Ashfield. Too old to have his hand tucked into my seventeen-year-old daughter's jeans.

How I let Cate talk me into using him for the firm's new logo . . .

'She's just tired,' I say tersely. 'A good night's sleep, and she'll be fine.'

'Dad, she needs to see Dr Stone,' Cate says. She detaches herself from Dan's grasp and busies herself with the tea. 'She's been getting worse since Christmas. He needs to change the pills again.'

Dan drops a kiss on the top of Cate's head. I know he wants to fuck my daughter. If he hasn't already.

Cate drops to her knees as Cannelle pads into the kitchen, and buries her face in the dog's silky golden coat. 'D'you fancy some very burnt stew?' she asks the animal. 'Daddy got up in the middle of the night and made it specially for you, didn't he, Cannelle?'

'I have to go,' Dan says. 'I promised I'd help set up the exhibition. Some of those sculptures are pretty heavy.'

'See you Friday?'

'Cate, I can't. Got to take the first-year life class, remember? It counts towards my teaching credits. Maybe Saturday. I'll call you.'

Cate shrugs moodily.

Dan catches my eye over her head as he leaves, and smiles as if to say, *Women*. But Cate isn't women, *she's my daughter*. I don't want some fucking randy art teacher in ripped jeans and a tight T-shirt – THIS IS BEAVER COUNTRY, for Christ's sake – rolling his eyes at me like we're best buddies: these birds, always trying to tie you down, good for a legover but a bloke's got to sow his wild oats, right? Who the *fuck* does he think he is? If he so much as *touches* her, I'll—

'Dad, for God's sake,' Cate snaps, standing up. 'Get with the programme, would you? I said I need you to take Mum's tea up to her.'

'Sorry, Kit-Cat.' I ruffle her hair. 'Been a long day.'

She scowls and pushes my hand away. 'Leave it, Dad. I'm calling out for pizza, OK? There's, like, *nothing* in the fridge. You said you were going shopping.'

'Pizza's fine. I'll go shopping at the weekend.'

'You'd better. Ben phoned to say he's coming down on Saturday, and he'll pick Sam up from school on the way. You know how much he always eats when he's home, he says the food at Corpus is worse than it was at school.'

'Fine.'

'If you don't get in some burgers and chips, he'll—'

'Cate, I said I'd do it,' I say irritably. 'Look, go and order the pizza, and I'll see if I can get your mother to come down. I don't suppose she's eaten anything all day.'

'She'd have a hard time *find*ing something,' Cate mutters, and flounces out.

I pick up Beth's mug of tea, straightening a crooked picture in the stairwell as I pass. This is all I need right now. Ella's taken it into her head to go off and scatter Jackson's bloody ashes in California or Carolina or wherever it is he comes from, which means it's going to be weeks before I see her again. *If* I see her again. There's no knowing how she's going to feel about us when the shock wears off and this really hits home.

Cate's right: Beth needs to go back to see Stone. We all know the routine by now. If this doesn't get nipped in the bud, she'll sink back into depression, and then – almost worse – the pendulum will swing the other way. She'll be seized by an unnatural manic energy, rushing around the house frantically tidying and painting and cleaning, until she crashes like a jet slamming into the ground. The last time she had a manic episode, she hired a helicopter on my company Amex to the tune of £49,000. Luckily they were very understanding.

'Beth?' I say, glancing round the empty bedroom.

I put the tea on the bedside table. The bathroom door is closed, and I can hear the sound of running water. Maybe she's feeling better, having a shower.

And then I see the empty Valium bottle on the floor.

'Beth?' I rattle the door handle. *'Beth!'*

Christ, she hasn't—'Pull yourself together' – oh dear God, not again, not on my watch, oh Jesus, *no*—

The door gives on the third shove, wood splintering beneath my weight.

At first I think the bathroom is empty. The claw-footed tub is overflowing, the hot tap still running; I paddle through an inch of water to turn it off, swearing as I nearly go arse over tip on the black and white tiles.

The Infidelity Chain

For a second, I see her, but I still don't understand.

My wife is lying at the bottom of the bath beneath a foot of water, her blue eyes wide and sightless, and I know instantly she's dead.

3

Beth

I'm not a victim. Dr Stone keeps telling me that. I'm not a victim, I'm a *patient*.

If anyone's the victim in this, it's William. I know I love him; actually, I'm quite sure I love him rather more than he loves me. The problem is that an awful lot of the time, I can't feel it. Which means I can't show it either.

It's the drugs. I don't feel much of anything any more.

'I'm off now, Beth. You'll be all right, won't you, darling?'

Nothing. It doesn't even hurt, these days.

'Sweetheart? Cate's spending the day studying at Dan's, but your mother said she'd pop round later this morning to see how you're doing. And I put a steak-and-kidney stew in the Aga for dinner. You just need to get it out mid-morning.'

If I could choose between another forty-one years of this bleak, soul-destroying emptiness, desolate and stripped of all feeling, or just *not being* at all . . .

'Right. I'd better get going. I'll see you later, then. Don't forget the stew.'

I curl into a tight ball on the bed, and watch the brittle winter sky lighten from black to grey. I've forgotten lots of things, what with the pills and the electric shocks, but I still remember every single detail of the moment we met, laid out before me like a *My Guy* photo-story. The nubby tweed of my skirt, hot and itchy at the waistband; the ladder in my brand-new tights; the gouache abstraction on papyrus I was hanging when he walked into the exhibition hall. I could tell you every word of our conversation, after William stopped to help steady the painting, and steady me. Word for word.

I knew right away he was the one I'd kept myself tidy for. Sometimes I wish I had someone to compare him with, and then I think, Why? What good would it do? If he was worse in bed (although I don't really know what 'worse' is – do you measure in orgasms? Minutes spent in foreplay? Whether he makes you a nice cup of tea afterwards?) then wouldn't I always feel a bit let down, disappointed, like turning up on the second day of the M&S sale and finding all the pretty colours had gone, and you're just left with the sludgy browns and greys? And if he was better, how would it help to know that? I'd simply regret I'd wasted myself on others who weren't quite up to the job.

He was *so* gorgeous. The sheets sizzled when we were in bed together, whatever anyone thinks now. The firm, muscled, hard-bodied strength of him; I'd never seen a man naked before. When he was inside me, it was the only time I stopped feeling alone.

'Mum! Didn't you hear me calling you? Your toast'll be well cold by now.'

Cate puts her head round the door, and then hangs there, swinging on the knob as if she doesn't want to come into the room for fear of catching something.

People are like that about depression. I read a poem, once: 'You are the modern leper, though you do not carry a bell.' I'm treated like an outcast, as if I've brought this on myself through some fault in my character. But nothing I could have done deserves this punishment. I wouldn't wish it on my worst enemy – I live in terror that I've passed it on to my children, as my father did to me. If I'd known beforehand, I'd never have had children at all. No one realized Dad was ill, of course. He was just a flamboyant, hail-fellow-well-met restaurateur who drank most of his profits until my mother left him and he found God (and Lillian); 'It's just Hector,' people used to say, 'such a *character*.'

I've watched Cate closely as she's grown up, far more than the boys; somehow I've always known they'd escaped it. Boys are so much easier to love, anyway, aren't they? Less rivalry. I haven't seen any signs of it in my daughter yet, but then no one did with me, they just thought I was artistic and creative; and then of course Cate was born and—

'Mum, stop staring at me like that, you're like freaking me out.'

Cate's closer to her father; she worships the ground he walks on. That's fine: I hate my mother too.

'Great, Mum, don't talk to me. Like I care. I'm off to Dan's, I'll be back this afternoon. Don't forget Dad's stew or he'll throw his toys out of his pram, you know what he's like.'

A few flakes of snow whirl against the windowpane. Grey outside, grey inside. This time of year, it never really seems to get properly light. How can February be the shortest month? It seems to last a year.

Later, when I wake to a knock at the front door, it's already turned to rain. My mother's sharp voice pricks and pokes through the letterbox. I roll myself in the duvet, its protective softness wound around me like a suit of armour.

Clara ruined my wedding day, just as she ruins everything. Even the name she chose for me was an act of spite. Louisa and Georgia for my sisters; just the one dull syllable for me, the middle sister. Beth. Not Bethany, or Elizabeth, which could have been shortened to so many other things; sassy Liz, glamorous Eliza. Beth, after one of the sisters in *Little Women*. The quiet, boring, mousy one who dies.

I wanted to marry William so much I nearly burst with excitement in the weeks before my wedding day. Nothing could dampen it, not even my mother or the hideous nylon empire-line dress she picked out to hide my 'condition'. (As Clara pointed out: why else would he be marrying me? Although even she didn't guess that a silly goose like me might be capable of doing something so clever on purpose. She doesn't really know me at all.) Her own mother-of-the-bride outfit was stunning, of course. A beautiful Jean Muir in matte gold silk, with sheer sleeves and small silk buttons on the side where it wrapped elegantly around her size-six hips.

The week after she showed it to me, pink with triumph, my father's new wife came round with the same dress (only four sizes larger). She'd already had it altered to fit her short frame, so she couldn't take it back.

Sick with fear and trepidation, I told my mother. 'Never mind,' she said graciously, 'I'll just get another dress. After all, it's your special day.'

A few days later, she returned with an even more beautiful suit from Chanel. 'Did you return the other dress?' I asked, as she twirled in front of the cheval looking-glass.

'Take it back? Of course not.'

'But it's so weddingy! Where on earth will you wear it?'

'Oh, I'll think of something,' Clara said, smiling secretively.

She turned up to our rehearsal dinner in it, the night before our wedding. Poor Lillian spent the evening in tears, knowing she couldn't possibly wear her dress the next day. My mother sat smugly at the head of the table at our reception, full of gracious charm and looking like she'd just swallowed the canary.

It gets dark so early in the winter. Four o'clock in the afternoon, and I'm still curled up in the duvet as the squares of glass behind me slowly darken from grey to black. I can smell burning. I should have gone downstairs and taken William's stew out of the Aga ages ago, but I didn't want to.

The bedroom door thunks as it hits the wall.

'Mum! You can't *still* be in bed! Gran rang my mobile and said you hadn't answered the door— Oh, for God's sake. I'm calling Dad.'

If only I could go to sleep one day and never wake up. I'm not really brave enough for suicide – it seems too calculated to contemplate, too wilful, its effect on the children would be too devastating – but if someone were to do it for me, to just come and flip the off switch . . .

Everyone thinks I'm wallowing in misery and self-pity

out of *choice*. If I had a pound for every time I've been told to pull myself together.

I'm woken again by William on the stairs; I'd recognize his tread anywhere. I force myself to sit up at last. I knew he wouldn't be pleased Cate called him home. I should have stopped her.

'Beth!'

You'd think I could let my husband make love to me, even if I'm not in the mood. But you don't know what it's like. You can't imagine how I feel. Or rather: don't. In the end, I couldn't bear it. All that stroking and touching and kissing and fondling, and I couldn't feel anything. Oh, not literally; my nerve endings hadn't died. But it gave me no pleasure. And that killed William's. I hated that more than anything. The concern in his eyes, the determination to do better, to make it better. Later, the irritation, quickly hidden (but not quickly enough). The *pity*.

'Beth, baby, come on, you can't do this to me. You have to *try*.' He kneels in front of me and turns my chin towards him, so that the light from the hallway gets in my eyes. 'I know you're in there, darling. I'm not letting you just give up.'

Easy for him to say.

'Come on, sweetheart. I know you miss the boys, but they'll be back soon as term's over. Sam has an exeat weekend soon, and Ben will be down from Oxford in just a few more weeks.'

Of course I miss the boys, especially Sam; he's only eight. I didn't want him to board, but William said it'd be good for him, so there wasn't much point in arguing.

Doesn't he understand how much it costs me to do what everyone else takes for granted? Of course I don't want to eat; it just prolongs the agony. If I get dressed, and come downstairs, and go through the motions of living, I'll only have to go back upstairs, and get undressed, and go back to bed so that I can not sleep, and then get up again and do it all the next day. Knowing that it will be exactly the same, that I'll feel exactly the same.

If only the world could be hit by an asteroid while I sleep. No pain, no mess, no family left to pick up the pieces. I want this to be over, I want to die—

'You know you don't mean that.'

I hadn't realized I'd spoken aloud. 'I don't want to feel like this any more,' I mutter, punishing him. 'I want this to be over. I want to just not *be*.'

'That's not an option, Beth. This isn't exactly a party for me, either. But we'll get through it, we always do. Perhaps we need to go back to Dr Stone and get another prescription. Up the dosage.'

The wretched *pills*! Pills to stop me going too high or too low, pills to help me sleep and prevent the paranoia, pills to stop my hair falling out as a result of all the mood stabilizers I have to take. Shake me – I know William wants to – and I'd rattle.

'I don't want any more drugs.'

'Beth, darling, you must see you can't go on like this. Look at you: you haven't moved in over twelve hours. You haven't even managed to get dressed or take dinner out of the oven, let alone look after Cate. Sweetheart, you can't even look after yourself!'

I deliberately say nothing, knowing it drives him mad.

He sighs heavily. 'Look. If we need to change your medicine, darling, that's what we'll do. I'll take some time off work, God knows how, but we'll go away for a bit, do whatever we have to—'

'Don't you get it?' I cry, provoked out of my silence. 'This isn't about the boys leaving. It's not *about* anything. It's *me*. It's who I am. It's not going to change. You can't cheer me up or jolly me out of it with a trip to the seaside.' Why doesn't he get it? *Why*? 'Don't you think I'd give anything not to be like this? I'd rather be dead than wake up one more morning feeling this way, and the only reason I'm still here is that I'm too much of a coward to do anything about it!'

'Death may be better for you, but what about those you leave behind? What about Ben, and Cate, and Sam? What about *me*?'

'You'd be better off without me.'

'Pull yourself together, Beth,' he snaps, and storms out of the room.

I'm stunned. William *never* gets cross with me. He soothes and tolerates and understands me. His pity is almost as hard to bear as his indifference. It's such an unexpected pleasure to be treated normally, to be shouted at, that the tears stop as suddenly as they started.

A crumb-strewn plate and an old Valium bottle fall from the tangle of bedclothes on to the floor as I get up and go into the bathroom. Maybe I'd feel better if I had a bath. Clean, at least.

I strip off my nightgown and stare dispassionately at my reflection as the bathwater runs. The weight's fallen off me in recent weeks, but not in a flattering way; I look like a shapeless, baggy sack of flesh. My fine blonde hair is cut in exactly the same bland style my mother chose when I was six. I'd never hear the end of it if I changed it. It makes me look like a woman from another age – from Clara's age, an age of girdles and aprons and cotton sanitary napkins on belt loops. My breasts sag, my cheeks sag, my stomach sags. *I* sag. I look like what I am: dried-up, used, no good to anyone. I wouldn't blame William if he had an affair. It's been years since we slept together. You'd have to be a saint not to want sex from *some*one.

The bathwater is still only tepid when I get in, so I leave the hot tap running for a bit. I love the feeling of being submerged beneath the water, the outside world muffled and far away. I used to be a good swimmer when I was a child. My PE teacher wanted me to compete in the school diving team, but Clara said I'd never cope with the pressure. My sisters used to count how long I could hold my breath under water, I could do it for twice as long as either of—

Suddenly William is looming over me, his face distorted by the bathwater. I gulp a lungful in shock as he grabs my shoulders, yelling my name. My ribs and hips and elbows and knees bang against the old iron bathtub as he clumsily yanks me out and on to the floor.

'Jesus Christ, Beth, what are you doing? Come on, Beth, stay with me, don't die, please don't die—'

I'm gasping for breath on the fluffy peach bathmat like a landed fish. I slap his hands off me as he tries to check my pulse.

'William,' I pant, when I'm finally able to speak, 'what on *earth* is going on?'

*

Honestly. You have to laugh, don't you? I couldn't help it, every time I tried to explain, I just dissolved again. I don't think the hysterical laughter helped my cause, actually, but by the time I'd got over my giggles, I couldn't be bothered to go through it. I don't suppose he'd believe me, anyway. After all, I do have what Ben would call 'previous'.

'You have to rescue me,' I tell my best friend Eithne three days later. 'They've all but got me on suicide watch. Mother's downstairs now, guarding the razor blades.'

Eithne snorts down the phone. 'An hour in her company, and anyone would want to top themselves.'

'It's ridiculous. Cate gave me plastic cutlery last night and told me everything else was in the dishwasher. Honestly, I'm depressed, not dim-witted. Although,' I add, 'I think the worst is over, for now. All that drama has rather perked me up. I haven't felt this upbeat in months.'

'Beth, darling, I don't want to rain on your parade, but you're not feeling *too* upbeat, are you? Only you know how you sometimes get—'

'I'm not manic,' I say crossly. 'Just full of the joys of spring, that's all. Oh, please, Eithne, they'll let you through the cordon, they're scared of you. I want to go to my studio, see if it's still standing. I thought I might even do a bit of work later.'

'Wonders never cease. OK, you've twisted my arm. I'll be over soon as I've finished soldering my roundhead. But if Clara tries to strip-search me, I can't answer for the consequences.'

I pace the bedroom impatiently, trying not to trip over the heaps of clothes I've been frantically sorting into piles: things to keep, things to throw away, things to donate to

Cate's school spring fête. The room smells of fresh paint, although I'm not sure about the slate green now it's on the walls. It looks rather too much like the bottom of the fish-pond. But then I didn't like the primrose either – in places you can see where I didn't give it long enough to dry and it's mingled with the green to look suspiciously like diarrhoea. I don't think William's going to be very pleased when he gets home. He liked the Colefax & Fowler wallpaper we had. Maybe I should have stuck to the taupe I started with in the first place—

As soon as I hear the crunch of Eithne's ancient orange 2CV on the gravel outside, I fly downstairs. Clara, resplendent in a grey wool trouser suit and pearls, stands guard in the kitchen.

'Blue and green, dear,' she reproves.

I glance down. 'Midnight isn't really blue, is it? And these trousers are so comfy.'

She gives me a look she's perfected over the years, one of mingled disappointment and resignation: this is her lot, the daughter she's been saddled with, but she'll stoically pick up her cross and make the best of it. I slink back upstairs and change into a pair of canvas dungarees I know she hates. Eithne will have parked her car by the time I come back down; Clara won't dare say anything if she's there.

It seems my daughter is less encumbered by good manners than my mother.

'God, Mum, you look like the window cleaner,' Cate exclaims when I appear.

They both turn pitying blue eyes upon me. It strikes me again how similar they are. We all share the same polar-pale colouring and blonde hair – a little ashier in Clara's case, these days, and rather too much henna in Cate's, I note, frowning – but I'm not really *like* them. I lack the confidence, the supreme self-belief that runs through my mother and daughter like a stick of rock. Good things fall into their laps because they believe they should. I expect nothing, and am never disappointed.

Eithne marches into the kitchen.

'Come back here, Beth, there's absolutely no need to go and change.'

'But maybe I—'

'Bollocks.'

My mother affects affront at Eithne's robust language. A papery hand flutters to her throat to fiddle with the pearls (third-generation; a coming-out gift to her grandmother from Queen Victoria, if Clara is to be believed).

'Keep low till we're past the fence,' Eithne whispers as she propels me through the back door, 'when you see the barbed wire, run for it.'

Eithne is a kindred spirit. She remembers Spangles and *Jackanory* and *Jackie* magazine. She knows what it's like to go upstairs to fetch something and forget what it was by the time you reach the landing. She understands perfectly that when you bend down to pick up something from the floor, it's only prudent to wonder what else you can do while you're down there. Eithne appreciates what it is to be forty-one and fallible.

She also knows what it's like to have the world think you've gone mad.

We met in my first year studying art at St Martin's – have you noticed how you stop making real friends sometime in your twenties? Friends of your *own*, I mean. After that, it's all about the mothers of your children's friends, or the wives of your husband's colleagues; colleagues of your own, too, I suppose, if you're lucky enough to have a job. But the friends you'd call upon in a crisis, the women you'd ring if your husband left you, or ask to look after your children if you were both killed in a plane crash; you stop making those kinds of friends much earlier than you'd think.

We didn't share many classes; my Fine Arts pathway was 2D, drawing and painting, whereas Eithne was 3D, sculpture and installation; now I think about it, that rather sums us up: compared to Eithne I do seem rather *flat*. But we were next-door neighbours at our hall of residence, and though neither of us really fitted in, somehow we fitted together. I couldn't help dressing like I was going for tea with the Queen, and while Eithne looked the art-student part, with her spiky cropped hair (dark naturally, but pink that first term) and kaftans and piercings and tall, rangy body, well, she wasn't quite as brave and fearless as she made out. Just how damaged, I didn't discover until our second year, when she had a passionate, showy affair with an aspiring actor called Kit Westbrook, which all ended rather horribly when she went round to his flat early one day and found him in bed with her brother.

I was the one who called the ambulance and held her hand when they pumped her stomach, and I was the one who listened to her when she screamed and shouted and wished she'd been left to die.

They called it a nervous breakdown, but I think she'd just turned inside-out with grief. And when she came back from the clinic, she was tougher and brighter and sharper than she'd ever been, and even though she dated like fury, she never – then or since – let anyone get close to her again. All that passion and energy she poured into her art, and long before she'd even graduated, people who mattered were starting to know who Eithne Brompton was.

She fidgets impatiently while I struggle to unlock the door to my studio, a converted folly at the end of the garden that's icy in winter and suffocating in summer. I haven't been here in months.

As soon as the door opens, Eithne pushes past me. She stops abruptly in front of a huge canvas that fills most of one wall, a monotype in blacks, purples and greys.

'Fuck. This is amazing. I feel like Alice falling down the rabbit hole.'

She pulls a charcoal-and-oil-pastel canvas from a rack, dislodging a cloud of dust, and steps back, her head (plum, these days) tilted to one side. 'This is stunning, too. And this. Shit, you've done so many since I was last here.'

'Some of those aren't quite finished . . .'

She whirls round, silver bracelets clanking. 'Look, Beth, why don't you let me arrange for you to exhibit? I'm owed a few favours, it would be so easy to organize a show—'

'I couldn't.'

'Why not? You've got enough art for one. You need to get out a bit. Break free from William. He makes you so damn *help*less.'

'Of course he doesn't. I couldn't manage without him, Eithne. You don't understand. I need him.'

'Yes. And he needs *that*.'

I put the canvases sullenly back in the rack. 'You don't understand.'

'What I don't understand, Beth, is why you keep your

talent hidden away in a mouldy old shed when you could be blazing across the London art scene. And with Sam at school now, you've got time—'

'Cate still needs me.'

'I've never met a seventeen-year-old who needed her mother less. Talk of the devil,' she adds, as Cate appears in the doorway.

Cate's in awe of Eithne, partly because she's scary (even to me, at times) and partly because of her winning the Turner Prize a few years ago and all that that implies.

'I don't mean to interrupt?' she says to Eithne, voice rising in the irritating way teenagers have these days. 'I was just wondering if I could, like, ask you something?'

'*Like* ask me? And how would that differ from *actually* asking?'

Cate turns pink. I know it's mean of me, but I can't help enjoying her discomfort a little. She's always so superior.

My daughter wraps her arms around her narrow torso, ducking her head so that her long hair falls across her face. 'Cate,' I exclaim, as her thin hooded sweatshirt lifts with the movement, 'is that what I think it is in your belly button?'

'She's had it pierced for a year,' Eithne says, 'where have you been?'

'Your father's going to go spare.'

'Only if you tell him,' Cate mutters.

She thinks she's making a point by rebelling. It's not that I'm jealous. I'm just trying to protect her from a world that doesn't treat rebels kindly. You have to keep your head down, and try to fit in. She'll learn.

I wish I had her courage.

Eithne picks up a daguerreotype I was experimenting with last summer. 'What was it you wanted, Cate?'

'Well, it's, like, our – I mean, it *is*,' she amends hastily, 'our spring fête in a couple of weeks, and my class has to organize the charity auction. I was wondering if maybe you'd let us have something, you know, a piece of art, to auction. It's in a really good cause, we're like raising funds for this environmental charity called One World who—'

'I know who they are,' Eithne says coolly, 'I designed their Green Scene awards a few years ago. Who're they sending down?'

'No one. Well, this guy *was* coming, but he died, bummer for him.'

'Caitlin!'

Eithne frowns. 'Jackson Garrett? I read about it in their newsletter. I met him a few times – nice guy. American, married to a doctor. He was only the same age as us, Beth.'

'Oh, dear, how sad. His poor wife must be—'

'So can we?' Cate interrupts. 'Have something, I mean.'

Eithne shrugs. 'Why not? I'll look something out for you and bring it down.'

'I might pop along,' I say brightly. 'To the fête.'

Cate pulls a face. 'Great, Mum. Trash my cred, why don't you.'

'Cate—'

The door slams in my face.

When Eithne leaves, I'm seized by a sudden burst of energy, flinging open shutters and poring over half-finished canvases until it's too dark to see. My mind races all night with images and inspiration; I'm up at dawn and back in the studio before William even wakes up.

For the next ten days I do nothing but paint, filling canvas after canvas with abstract images worked in water-colours, oils, charcoal and gouache, consumed by a burning need to get the maelstrom in my head down on paper before the creative door slams shut again. I don't sleep, I barely eat. Obviously I don't need my pills any more; I'm clearly over the depression at last, thank goodness, so I stop taking them. I'm not manic, just having a few good days, that's all. William tries to get me to rest, but I can't, my brain is on fire, so he leaves me to it, to 'let it burn out in its own time', he says. 'I'll be here for you afterwards, Beth, don't worry.'

I order more paint, more canvases, recklessly putting a professional Nikon camera costing thousands of pounds on my credit card when I decide to photograph black-and-white images on to glass and then paint them. Working with a luscious mocha pigment, I suddenly fancy some Belgian chocolates. Without thinking twice about it, I simply arrange for a box to be couriered from Brussels. William won't mind. Eithne is right, I *am* good, what I'm doing now is some of the best work I've ever done, I *should* let her exhibit my paintings. Why on earth have I been so shy? To think that the fear of being judged stopped me going back to college, when I was one of the best students they'd ever had. Perhaps I should finish my degree, just to prove – I don't know, prove *some*thing.

The studio is soon crowded with canvases, and then I realize that of course it's too small. What I need is some-thing more like Eithne has in London, a huge bright airy space four times the size of my horrid little studio, with plenty of room to spread out. This garden is big enough for an extension – no, we might as well knock down this folly altogether and start again. If we're going to do this, we should do it right. Yes, a big, open studio; if we get rid of William's greenhouse there'll be plenty of room, he never uses it anyway – of course we'll have to move the garage, it's in the way and I need *light*, lots and lots of natural light—

The architect is very accommodating when I contact him and explain what I need to do, and that time is of the essence and money is absolutely no object.

Within days, I'm poring over plans and discussing options. Of course Murray's right when he says that I shouldn't just be thinking about my current needs, I must plan for the future. In that context, cathedral ceilings and a separate photographic loft are actually an economy. There's no point bothering William with it all now, especially given the mood he's in. I've never known him so tetchy. He got *so* cross about the bulldozer earlier (poor Murray, he was very upset about it, after all our hard work), and then rushing off when he got that phone call from work, didn't even stop to say goodbye, it's not like him at all.

No. We might as well wait until everything's finalized, and in the circumstances, a 50 per cent deposit is entirely reasonable – Sam won't be needing his college funds for years yet, and by then I'll have paid him back ten times over: sales from my work will make all this minor expense seem like a drop in the ocean.

I bounce back up to the house in exuberant mood, throwing my arms around my daughter as she messes about at the Aga with the kettle, trying not to notice the way she flinches within my hug.

'Darling, I've had a marvellous idea! I need to go down to Brighton tomorrow, I have to see the sea – I need that colour in my mind's eye, nothing else works, I have to *be* there. Why don't you come too, Cate? We'll have a wonderful time and—'

'Mum, I can't. I've got exams soon, I can't just bunk off.'

She's looking peaky, poor thing. She works far too hard. I know exams matter, but sometimes you just have to take a little time out and enjoy life!

'Of course you do, darling,' I soothe. 'I hadn't forgotten, I just thought you could do with a break. We don't spend enough time together, I miss you, sweetheart, and silly old school will still be there next week—'

'You're not getting it, Mum,' she snaps, washing her hands under the tap. 'I don't want to go to bloody Brighton and see the sea. I'm not five years old, I'm seventeen and I've got to study!'

'All right, darling. No need to get quite so huffy. I just thought it would be fun, I was only trying to help take your mind off—'

'Look, if you really want to help, call Eithne and ask her about the artwork she promised us! The auction's on Saturday and her name's in all the brochures and if she doesn't turn up I'm just going to die!'

'I'm sure she'll—'

'Oh, never mind! I'm going over to Clem's!'

I don't know what's got into her lately. She's been in a funny mood for days; it must be the pressure of her exams.

I call Eithne about the artwork; 'Oh, Christ!' she says, 'I did promise, didn't I? Only I'm in the middle of something, I really can't get away. I don't suppose if I send the bloody statue down in a cab you could take it instead?' And I say of course, because actually, for once, I feel like I *can*.

Obviously I didn't expect to be called on to the stage to present the wretched thing. But on Saturday I'm in such a good mood I don't feel shy at all, so I clamber up the steps at the end of the playing fields with the artwork Eithne's donated, an exquisite (and rather heavy) abstract bronze statue two feet high.

Despite a smattering of polite applause, no one is really paying much attention. Even Cate's whispering furiously with Dan as the bidding gets under way.

The headmistress does her best: 'An Eithne Brompton,' she says gamely, 'surely we have some takers? At the back there? Come on, ladies and gentlemen, it's for a good cause! Now, who'll start me at a thousand pounds?'

The crowd shifts on its feet. It's not that they don't have the money (after all, fees at Cate's school are currently running close to £20,000 a year); but these aren't the sort of people who appreciate art. They just want a nice painting of something they can recognize, trees on a hill, cows in a field. Something that goes with the new curtains.

'Five hundred, then.'

What they need is something to wake them up, get them in the mood, make them sit up and take notice— Of course! Why didn't I think of it before? It's always worked in the past.

I put down the statue and lean into the microphone. 'Come on, everyone. This is an Eithne Brompton. Do you know how much her artwork is worth on the open market? There's a waiting list two years long for commission pieces.'

I catch Cate's eye, and wink.

Then I unbutton my neat navy shirt-waister, whip off my bra and knickers, and, before anyone has even realized what's happening, I'm streaking naked across the playing field.

For a moment, there's stunned silence. Then a roar of enthusiastic applause breaks out, and the bidding for Eithne's statue has reached £4,000 before I'm halfway to the sports pavilion. I'm sure Cate will be thrilled when she realizes how much we've raised for her favourite charity.

I'm just starting to appreciate that it's still only March and actually jolly cold when someone throws a coat over me and whisks me out of sight around the side of the pavilion.

'Dan! Thank you so much, I was beginning to get a little chilly – but wasn't it worth it? Did you hear the bidding – terrific, isn't it? Not that I'm anything terribly exciting to look at, of course, not any more, rather frightening, I should imagine, actually, but I really think I put everyone in the mood, jazzed things up a little – I remember we used to do this sort of thing when I was at St Martin's, Eithne and me, you should have seen us one year at the Edinburgh Fringe—'

And then Dan silences me.

It's not his kiss that horrifies me, warm and smoky and delicious though it is, because after all, the most effective way to shut a woman up is to give her mouth something else to do. But the fact that, with a passion I haven't felt in twenty years, I kiss my daughter's boyfriend back.

4

Cate

'C'mon, Cate. Relax,' Dan murmurs. 'I'm not going to make you do anything you don't want to.'

'I know, but . . .'

He strokes the side of my cheek with the back of his hand, tilts my head and kisses me softly on the lips. It's like being in a movie; I could do this all day.

Then his hand slides up my calf, and I quickly cross my knees so he doesn't get the wrong idea.

'Hey. It's OK, you know. My students won't be here for ages. We're cool.' He drops gentle, nuzzling kisses down my neck; it tickles, and I giggle. 'Just go with the flow, baby. Soon as you want me to stop, say so, and I will.'

His knuckles brush my breast, back and forth, back and forth, and even though I'm wearing a bra and a school blouse and a gross woolly jumper, my nipple goes all hard, and a warm wet feeling spreads between my legs.

'You're so beautiful, Cate,' Dan says thickly. 'Please, can

I just look at you properly? I won't do anything, I swear. I just want to see you. Let me undo your blouse, please. That's all, I promise.'

'I don't—'

'You're not scared, are you?'

'No!'

'At least take off your sweater. That's not going to do any harm, is it?'

Why did I tell him I was a virgin? Talk about red rag to a bull. He's even more determined to get into my knickers now. It's Mum and Dad's fault. First they make me go to a girls' school, and then they send Ben off to board. What's the point of having an older brother if all his hot friends live, like, three hundred miles away? Honestly. Dad wasn't joking when he said he'd send me to a Romanian convent. He might as well have done. How am I supposed to get any real experience when I never meet any boys?

In a private act of defiance, I pull up the hem of my jumper with both hands, feeling unexpectedly sexy and grown-up as Dan's eyes darken and he touches his tongue to dry lips. I struggle to get the sweater over my shoulders, and he helps me, his hands pulling and touching and smoothing a bit more than I need, actually, somehow he's untucked my blouse at the same time, and I know I didn't leave that many buttons undone—

'God, Cate. Feel what you do to me.'

He grabs my hand and puts it on his *thing*. I'm kind of grossed out, but it's cool at the same time. I can't believe how hard it is under his jeans. I mean, *totally* hard, like a bone or something. I squeeze it a bit, just to feel, and he rocks back on his heels and closes his eyes and moans.

'You have no idea how sexy you are, Cate. You're driving me crazy.'

I undo another button on my blouse, just to see the effect it has. He gulps, rubbing his hand against his chin. I can't believe I have this *power* over him, it's a total trip.

I try out this sexy look my best friend Fleur taught me, and daringly unfasten another button, so my shirt falls open to my waist. I'm so glad I wore my new lacy pink bra from Miss Selfridge. I hadn't planned to let Dan see it, exactly, but then, I hadn't planned not to either. God, imagine if I was wearing my period pants – not that it matters, I'm not letting him go below the waist yet, but still. No one feels hot and sexy in their period pants.

I suck in my stomach as Dan's eyes travel up and down my body, and sit up a bit straighter. I wish I wasn't wearing my school uniform. He must think I'm such a baby. I mean, he's twenty-three. His students are older than I am.

He pushes me gently back against the sofa pillows and slides his body over mine, his hands crushing and squeezing my breasts. I like it, but I stop him when he tries to pull them out of my bra. I sort of ache between my legs, and when his knee pushes my thighs apart, I rock my hips a bit against him, as if I'm scratching an itch. It feels really good, like having a hot drink on a cold day.

It's getting a bit warm in here, so I don't mind too much when Dan slips my blouse off my shoulders. My pleated grey skirt has somehow got rucked up around my waist, and I hook one bare leg around his hips as he pulls me close, his hands roaming all over my back. God, this is really good. I must stop in a minute, though. I don't want things to go too far. In a minute, I'll stop him.

He leans up on one elbow, staring at me with such intensity I barely recognize him. Then he dips his head to my breast, and I realize with a gasp of shock and pleasure that my bra has somehow come off, and his lips are on my nipple, *my naked nipple*, I'm naked from the waist up, and his hand is between my thighs, oh God, that's good, I've got to stop now, but that's so good—

'Dan . . .'

His fingers slip beneath the edge of my cotton panties, and they're stroking me *there*, he's touching me *there*! It feels so much better than when I do it, it's hot and wet and heavy and—

'Dan, no . . .'

Every time he sucks my nipples, I can feel a zing down below, oh, God, this is so good, but I have to stop him, I have to stop—

Suddenly he leans back and unbuckles his jeans. I have a brief glimpse of his thing, red and swollen and totally huge, and suddenly all the warm lovely feelings vanish as if someone's thrown a bucket of cold water over me. I struggle up from the sofa, pulling down my skirt and grabbing my jumper from the floor.

'I can't, Dan. I'm sorry, I just—'

'Cate, come on, I'll be careful, it won't hurt.'

I pick up my bra from the floor and clutch it to my chest. 'I'm sorry, Dan,' I mumble, cheeks flaming. 'I have to go home. My mum will be wondering where I am.'

He leaps to his feet, his thing sticking out of his jeans. It looks purple and angry. I can't take my eyes off it.

'Are you kidding me? You can't come on to me like that and then stop! I'm not a fucking robot, Cate!' His expression hardens, and he turns and tucks himself away. 'I can't just switch it on and off like a tap, even if you can!'

'I didn't mean—'

'Christ! This is what I get for dating a kid!'

'Dan, that isn't fair—'

'Nor is behaving like a prick-tease. Do you have any idea how much my fucking balls ache right now?'

All of a sudden, I start to cry. Dan hesitates, then exhales and slowly runs his hand through his hair. 'Look, I'm sorry,' Dan says, as I sniff miserably. 'I shouldn't have pushed you, I obviously got it wrong. I didn't mean to make you do something you weren't ready for.'

He hands me my blouse, waits until I've turned around and put it on, then pulls me into his arms and rubs my back gently. 'You've got to be more careful, Cate. I'm a decent guy, and I stop when I'm asked. But there are some men out there who think that when you set something in motion, you've got to follow through.'

'I'm sorry. I didn't mean to—'

'Yeah, I know. It's OK.'

I hiccup. 'You're not going to dump me?'

'You think I'd do that because you won't sleep with me?' He holds me away from him, his expression serious. 'What kind of man do you think I am? I care about you, Cate. You're beautiful and funny and totally nuts. I love being with you. And besides,' he grins, 'I'm depending on you. Who else is going to keep me on the straight and narrow?'

My breath frosts in the cold March air as I walk home. I'm so embarrassed, I wish the ground would just open up and swallow me. It's not as if I'm saving myself for Prince William or something. Basically I want to get on with it and then I can forget about it – well, not forget about it, exactly, but tick it off the list. Lose virginity, check.

So why does it feel like such a big deal? I mean, Dan's really nice and totally hot, and he's twenty-three, at least one of us'll know what we're doing. Fleur's right, he'd be a great person to do it with the first time.

I wish she hadn't gone back to France last summer. I really miss her. She's so cool, and she knew all these really neat places to hang out after school. Plus, she didn't think I was sad for wanting to study hard so I can get into NYU and be a journalist. The only thing the other girls at school care about is when they'll get into a size zero.

Last year, I gave up chocolate for Lent, like everyone does, but my best friend, Clem, gave up everything containing sugar. *Everything*. Pretty much all food has *some* sugar in it, right? Basically, she had to live on celery and lettuce, so then everyone else in the class copied her. It was like this weird virus. For weeks, no one could think about anything but diets. People were, like, fainting all over the place. The swimming team had a total crisis, because everyone stopped swimming in case it gave them muscles. Girls would sit round me at breaktime and watch me eating an apple – an *apple*, for God's sake – with their eyes totally focused on my mouth, until I couldn't even chew. All they read were stupid glossy magazines with pictures of skinny stars in them, and they'd talk and talk and *talk* about celebrities and what they ate and how thin they were.

Most of them gave up after a few weeks, but a few kept going. Clem even wrote this whole pro-ana blog on her

Facebook page, until Mrs Buchanan, our headmistress, found out and made her take it down.

Dan calls them the girls from St Thinian's. He says men don't like skinny girls, or women who obsess about their weight. He says older women can be really sexy because they're not always worrying about how they look. Yeah, right. Like you wake up one morning and think, *Oh, I'm thirty, I'm just going to let it all hang out from now on.* Total BS.

I should stop thinking about it and just sleep with him. Get it over with.

Dad hates him. Every time he comes over, he gives Dan this laser-beam glare. He's like, *Are your intentions honourable, young man, because if not I'm going to chop up your body and feed it to the fishes.*

It took me for ever to talk Dad into letting him design the new logo for the company. But Dan was really cool, he knew all this stuff about Ashfield PR, so in the end Dad gave in. I wish he'd stop acting like this Victorian paterfamilias, it's so embarrassing.

I think Mum quite likes him, though it's hard to tell with her. When she's acting like a zombie she doesn't even talk to you; you can be like, 'The house is on fire and I just stuck an axe in my foot' and she'll just sit on the bed and like *look* at you and not even move. Or else she can be this nutso freak, painting all night and jabbering on at you at a million miles an hour and doing crazy stuff, like when she decided to knock down the conservatory last summer and build an open-air theatre for this stupid triptych she was doing. Luckily I came home early the day the demolition crew arrived or we'd have ended up with half the house gone. I wish I could just talk to Mum sometimes. I really envy Clem that. Her mother is so normal. You can talk to her about school and boys and stuff and she really *listens*.

But it's thanks to Mum I met Dan in the first place. Like, a few months ago, she'd promised to go to the opening of Eithne's new show in London, but when it came to it she couldn't face the thought of going alone. Dad was too busy, as per, so she dragged me along, which actually wasn't too lame after all because all these cool people turned up, it was in all the papers the next day and everyone at school was seriously impressed. Clem even asked for my autograph; I worry about that girl sometimes.

So anyway, we're in this huge hall, and I kind of left Mum alone for a bit to sneak a quick glass of wine, and when I go back, she's yakking with this guy about art or something, and I'm like, *Wow! he's hot,* and I give him my best smile, but he just keeps droning on about expressionism or individualism or whatever, and I'd had enough by then and dragged Mum away.

Then a week later, I'm at home on study leave and Mum's gone Christmas shopping, and Hot Guy turns up on the doorstep! He'd obviously gone to a lot of trouble to track me down, so I couldn't leave him sitting there. He was actually a lot more interesting once you got him off the subject of art. Anyway, I asked him if he wanted to come to our New Year's Eve party, and he said yes straight away. So that was it, really.

I wish Eithne would send us that statue she promised. I'm going to be *so* dead if she doesn't come through.

I bump open the garden gate and trudge up the drive. I've got a ton of work to do. I shouldn't have gone over to

Dan's. Now I'm going to have to stay up all night if I want to finish that stupid essay on the American Revolution.

Cannelle leaps up to welcome me as I let myself into the kitchen. I give him a big hug, then throw my bag on the kitchen table and put the kettle on the Aga hotplate. I wish we had a proper electric one, like everyone else does. I loathe this crappy thing.

My nerves are totally jangling. I've got a headache, and I'm all achey. It's like PMT, or something. God, I hate being a woman.

Mum bursts through the back door and I jump, spilling hot water on my hand.

'Darling, I've had a marvellous idea! I need to go down to Brighton tomorrow, I have to see the sea – I need that colour in my mind's eye, nothing else works, I have to *be* there.' She swoops me around the kitchen, and I nearly trip over the dog. 'Why don't you come too, Cate? We'll have a wonderful time and—'

I prise her off me. 'Mum, I can't. I've got exams soon, I can't just bunk off.'

'Of course you do, darling. I hadn't forgotten, I just thought you could do with a break. We don't spend enough time together, I miss you, sweetheart, and silly old school will still be there next week—'

It's as if she still thinks I'm in kindergarten. *I nearly had sex with my boyfriend on his sofa this afternoon, Mum! Why don't you know to ask me about that?*

'You're not getting it, Mum,' I snap, going to the sink and running cold water over my scald. 'I don't want to go to bloody Brighton and see the sea. I'm not five years old, I'm seventeen and I've got to study!'

'All right, darling. No need to get quite so huffy. I just

thought it would be fun, I was only trying to help take your mind off—'

Suddenly I'm so angry I want to scream. Why can't she just be normal for once? Why does she always have to be like this?

'Look, if you really want to help, call Eithne and ask her about the artwork she promised us!' I yell. 'The auction's on Saturday and her name's in all the brochures and if she doesn't turn up I'm just going to die!'

She looks bewildered. 'I'm sure she'll—'

'Oh, never mind! I'm going over to Clem's!'

I grab my bag and storm back outside. Tears blur my vision. It's like I don't belong *anywhere* – not at school; not at home; not with Dan. I wish I could just do my own thing and not have to be responsible for anyone.

I take the short-cut to Clem's, ducking down an alley-way that runs past the railway station. My breath forms smoky plumes as I jog quickly along the path in the dark, imagining rapists and murderers lurking in every shadow. I wish I'd brought Cannelle. My heart's racing by the time I get to the car park and turn towards Clem's street, though it slows a bit when I spot a couple snogging in one of those disgusting 4x4s parked near the platform gate (Dad bought one last year; like doesn't he even *care* about the planet?). At least someone's around if I get jumped by the mad axeman. God, look at them, they're really going for it—

They suddenly separate, and the woman flings open her door, so the light comes on inside. I think I know her. She's got the kind of mad hair you don't forget, like rusty bedsprings – shit! She was the doctor who looked after Sam when he was little! I got dragged along to his annual check-ups every year until he was about five.

I recognized Dad instantly, of course.

'Christ,' Dan mutters. 'Are you *sure*?'

'Of course I'm sure. I've only lived with him, I don't know, *my whole life*.'

'You couldn't have made a mistake? Maybe he was just giving her a lift—'

'A lift? From where I was standing, she looked ecstatic.'

'There's probably an innocent—'

'Look, I didn't like get it wrong or imagine it or anything, all right?' I snap. 'Basically, my dad had his tongue down another woman's throat, and he wasn't giving her mouth-to-mouth, OK?'

'Are you going to tell your mum?'

I watch my mother stagger on stage with Eithne's stupid bronze statue. She usually hates this sort of thing, but she'd do anything for Eithne. It's bizarre, it's as if that hippy lezzie has some strange hold over her— Yeah. That'll be the day. My mum do anything blackmail-worth.

'Course I'm not telling her,' I retort. 'You want her to flip out again and try to slash her wrists with the loofah?'

'So what are you going to do?'

As if I know. It's so confusing. I mean, I should be mad at Dad, and I *am*; but at the same time, I can't really blame him. Basically, Mum's a complete basket case most of the time. And she's so *boring*. She never wants to do anything, she just sits around all the time crying or feeling sorry for herself. OK, sometimes she gets all manic and paints and stuff, like she has this last week or two, but then she never does anything with it. It never goes anywhere. Eithne says she could be this huge artist if she wanted to, but she just gets all depressed again and goes back to being helpless and pathetic. I know she's ill, but couldn't she make a bit of an *effort*?

She'll never cope on her own if he leaves. Which means I'll be the one stuck looking after her.

Up on stage, Mrs Buchanan points to the statue. 'An Eithne Brompton,' she says with this fake enthusiasm, 'surely we have some takers? At the back there? Come on, ladies and gentlemen, it's for a good cause! Now, who'll start me at a thousand pounds?'

'She'll be lucky to get a fiver,' Dan whispers.

'Whatever.' I scuff my boot on the grass. 'Stupid auction. I only came to get her off my back.'

Mrs Buchanan looks beaten. 'Five hundred, then.'

'Come on, Dan. This is so gay, I don't know why you wanted to come. Let's get out of here,' I plead.

'We can't. I promised your dad I'd give your mum a ride home.'

'Yeah, well, he'd know all about *rides*.'

'Come on, everyone,' Mum urges into the microphone. 'This is an Eithne Brompton. Do you know how much her artwork is worth on the open market? There's a waiting list two years long for commission pieces.'

Behind me, two girls from my class snigger.

'Great, Mum,' I mutter, closing my eyes. 'Just great. *Now* you decide to come out of your shell.'

'Cate—' Dan begins.

Which is when my mother strips off all her clothes and, in front of my entire class, my teachers and my boyfriend, runs naked across the playing fields waving her arms in the air.

Dan whips off his coat and chases after her. I don't bother to follow him. My eyes are dry and hard as I shoulder my way through the excited, buzzing crowd towards the exit.

I'm never going to forgive her for this. Never, never, *never*.

I'm so humiliated I want to die, except I'm not going to give her the satisfaction. How could she do this to me? I'll never be able to show my face at school again. Thank God it's the Easter holidays, and I can just shut myself in my room with Cannelle. I don't want to see anyone, even Dan. I hate her. She's ruined my entire life. The only good thing is that I've dropped six pounds, but since I'm going to spend the rest of my life hidden from the world, even that doesn't cheer me up.

For as long as I can remember, I've had to make allowances for Mum. *She's sick. She can't help it. She doesn't know what she's doing.* When she sits all day staring out of the window, or doesn't even bother to get dressed, 'It's the pills,' Dad says. 'It's not her fault.'

But he gets to escape to the office. He's not the one who has to come home and mop up the kitchen floor because she's left the tap running for eight hours. He didn't have to repaint my bedroom after Mum decided on the spur of the moment to paint it orange. He didn't save his pocket money for three months to buy a journalist's Billington bag, only to watch her give it all away to the Salvation Army when she was having one of her highs.

He wasn't the one to come home and find her That Day.

I wonder what she's like. His girlfriend. She always seemed OK, but that was before I knew she was shagging my dad. How can she be having an affair with him when she knows he's got kids? Doesn't she care?

What if he leaves us for her? He'll have a baby with her, a whole new family, and forget about us. Mum'll go to pieces. Or worse. If his girlfriend knew how much we need him, she'd have to leave him alone and find someone else. She's a *baby* doctor. She can't be that much of a bitch, surely?

Only one way to find out.

She's not hard to find. Still at the same hospital, though she's moved offices. Less than an hour from home, door to door. Handy for Dad.

She's got *cojones*, that's for sure. She doesn't even look surprised to see me when I turn up outside her office.

'It's Caitlin, isn't it?' she says.

'Cate.'

'Cate.' She nods. 'Well, you'd better come in.'

I follow Doctor Ella Slapper Stuart into a bright, cramped room that reminds me of Dad's new office, but without the amazing view. Her fancy glass desk is covered with heaps of forms and papers, weighted down with coffee mugs and books; two thin computer screens dovetail neatly in the centre of the desk, like a book that's been left propped open. The walls are filled with shelves of thick, boring-looking leather-bound books.

There are no photographs anywhere.

She waves me to a squishy grey chair on my side of the desk, but doesn't sit down herself, perching on the edge of her desk instead. 'What was it you wanted to talk to me about?'

'Dad,' I say.

She unclips her long red hair, scrapes it back more firmly from her face, then clips it up again. 'What exactly did you—'

'Don't pretend you don't know what I'm talking about. I saw the two of you last week in the station car park. You were *kissing*,' I accuse.

For a long moment, we just look at each other.

'You were about thirteen the last time I saw you,' she says finally. 'You were angry – I think you'd had to miss a concert or something to come up with your little brother—'

'Fourteen. Were you sleeping with my dad then?'

'Still angry,' she observes.

'Well? Were you?'

She fiddles with a row of books, straightening their spines. She looks thinner than I remembered, and kind of pale, as if she's been sick or something. I shake myself. God, I'll be feeling sorry for the cow in a minute.

'How did you get here?' she asks.

'Train. Tube. Then I walked. Finding the hospital wasn't exactly rocket science. I'm not a kid any more. You still haven't answered my question.'

'What exactly do you want me to say?'

I open my mouth: *I want you to say sorry, that you'll stop, I want you to promise you're not going to steal my dad away from me.* Instead, 'Do you love him?' I ask.

'I don't think that's any of your business,' she says softly.

'He's my dad. He's married to my mum. I think that makes it my business.'

'No. That just makes them your parents.'

'Aren't you at all sorry?' I demand hotly.

'For what?'

'You're having an affair with my dad! How can you just sit there and act as if it doesn't matter? You're basically a – a home wrecker!'

She leans back against her desk and folds her arms. She's wearing the coolest knee boots, kind of chocolate and orange and cinnamon paisley suede, with little kitten heels. 'I haven't wrecked your home. I would never do that.'

'How do you *know*? What if my mum finds out?'

'Are you going to tell her?'

Why does everyone keep asking me that? 'I won't need to, if you keep snogging Dad all over the place. You were practically doing it in our back garden! Anyone could've seen you!'

'I'm sorry about that,' she acknowledges. 'I shouldn't have gone down there. I'd had a bad— Never mind. It won't happen again.'

She twists a ring nervously on her left hand. It takes a moment for the gesture to register.

'You're married!' I exclaim. 'Does your husband know?'

She hesitates. 'He died.'

'Oh. I'm sorry. I didn't know.'

'Why should you?' She digs her fists deep in the pockets of her white coat. 'He died a month ago today. And no, he didn't know.'

'Was he really old?'

'No. Though he might seem it to you, I don't know. He was forty-one. Two,' she corrects herself. 'I keep forgetting it was his birthday.'

'Did he have an accident?'

'A virus attacked his heart. It was just one of those things. Chance in a million. No one could have known—'

'Do you have kids?'

She ducks her head. For a moment, she doesn't seem any older than me or Clem. 'No. He wanted them, but I didn't.'

'Bet you're glad now.'

'Not really.'

I don't know what else to say. This isn't going the way I thought it would. I had some hazy idea that she'd be so shocked and embarrassed when she saw me, she'd break down and promise never to go near Dad again. I suppose I thought she might put up a bit of a fight and argue, maybe even cry a little, but in the end she'd realize the game was up and go quietly.

Her husband's just died. Shit. And she's so normal, giving me proper answers and not treating me like a stupid kid. She seems almost – well, *nice*.

I ask her quickly, before I totally lose my bottle.

'So are you and Dad going to go off together?'

'Is that what you're worried about?' Her cheeks are flushed. 'I'm not going to run off with Will – with your dad. I'm not a home wrecker. I know how it seems, but I loved my husband. I never meant for anyone to get hurt—'

'Doesn't it worry you that he's cheating on my mum?' I ask curiously. 'I mean, he could be cheating on you, too. He might have loads of girlfriends.'

'You could say the same about me,' she says, with a strained smile.

God, she looks awful. Her hands are shaking. 'Are you . . . Dr Stuart, are you OK?'

She sucks in a breath. 'Could you pass me – some water . . .'

There's an unopened bottle of mineral water on the desk.

I unscrew the top and hand it to her. She's panting like she's been running: she's starting to freak me out.

'Dr Stuart? Ella? Would you like me to get someone?'

'Oh, Cate. I'm so sorry,' Ella manages.

She collapses like a rubber doll. I try to catch her, but it all happens too fast. There's a sickening thud as her head hits the corner of her glass desk.

'Ella! Ella! Are you OK?'

She doesn't move. I crouch down and gently turn her head towards me. Oh, God, there's so much blood! I can't see if she's actually poked out her eye – my stomach turns – or simply hit her head. I call her name again, but she doesn't respond. She's so pale. I can't even tell if she's breathing.

I open the door to the corridor and scream my head off.

5

Ella

I'm not scared of flying. Terrified of crashing, yes. 'In the event of an emergency, ladies must remove high-heeled shoes' – only a man would come up with that rule. What if I happened to be wearing my favourite pair of Manolos? Maybe they'd let me carry them; other women take their babies down the emergency chute, so why not—

An unexpected jolt of terror-laced adrenalin almost bounces me out of my seat.

I inhale deeply, and focus on the steward as he fastens his demonstration life-jacket. Of course I'm upset. My husband's just died. Pollyanna would be hard put to get in the holiday mood, given the circumstances.

The aircraft pulls away from the stand: the point of no return. A warm wash of sweat sweeps over me. I reach up and fiddle with the air vent, but it doesn't seem to make any difference.

'Miss?' The steward taps me on the shoulder. 'Excuse me, but we need to put that in the overhead locker for take-off.'

'It's OK, I'll hold it.'

'I'm sorry, miss. I'm afraid we have to—'

'It's Mrs.'

'Sorry?'

'It's not Miss, it's Mrs.'

'Yes, ma'am. If I could take that from you now . . .'

My chest tightens. A knot twists my stomach: nausea and fear. The passenger on my left shifts irritably in his seat. He's about five stone overweight; the armrest won't go down over his massive thigh. His flab spills into my seat, invading my space. I'm hemmed in, trapped. It's not fair – I bet *he* hasn't been charged £240 for excess baggage. It wasn't my fault, I couldn't decide what to pack; I spent a full twenty minutes this morning sobbing on the floor by my wardrobe, unable to choose between charcoal wool trousers or black. In the end, it was easier to pack everything.

Another wave of adrenalin surfs through me. My arms tingle with pins and needles. I start to feel really scared. Dear God, am I having a heart attack? Is this how Jackson felt?

The steward reaches across me. 'I really need to take that—'

'No! I'll hold it.'

'I'm afraid I can't let you do that, miss.'

'It's Mrs!' I shout. 'Mrs Garrett! *Mrs!*'

The steward backs nervously down the aisle. I can't breathe. I scrabble with my belt buckle as the aircraft gathers speed. I can't breathe, I have to get out of here, *I have to get off the plane—*

A cool, steady hand reaches across the aisle for mine.

'You're going to be fine,' a woman's voice says reassuringly. 'You're hyperventilating. You need to breathe slowly. In through the nose, out through the mouth. *Slowly*. In through the nose. Out through the mouth. In through the nose. Out through the mouth . . .'

Hyperventilating. Yes. I know what that is. A page from my med notes swims in front of my eyes: 'hyperventilation (or hyperpnoea) is the state of breathing faster or deeper (hyper) than necessary, and thereby reducing the carbon dioxide concentration of the blood below normal . . .'

Gradually the feeling of suffocation eases. For several moments, I can't speak.

'You had a panic attack, dear,' the woman says gently. 'I used to have them, after my mother died. It's very frightening, but they won't actually do you any harm.'

I yank my hand free. 'I don't have panic attacks.'

'Sometimes they come on out of the blue, if you're stressed or over-anxious. Anyone can get them. It's nothing to be ashamed of.'

'It's probably just the altitude. I feel fine now.'

She doesn't need to point out that we're barely off the ground.

The steward comes back down the aisle. '*Mrs* Garrett,' he emphasizes nastily, 'we really can't permit you to endanger yourself and other passengers like that again. You need to stow your belongings during—'

'It's my husband,' I say.

'I'm sorry?'

I shelter the wooden box in the curve of my arm. A sunlit memory flickers across my mind's eye: Jackson crouching by the side of a red dirt road in Paraguay, laughing as he barters with a young boy of no more than eight, knowing that whatever price he pays in the end, it'll be ten times what the cumbersome carved box is worth. 'But how on earth will we get it home?' I'd asked him, already planning, organizing. 'We'll find a way,' Jackson said carelessly. 'It'll be part of the fun.'

'It's my husband's ashes,' I tell the steward, taking bleak pleasure in the way his jaw drops. 'I'm taking him home.'

I've never met Jackson's brother, but I recognize him instantly. He has the same features: the Caribbean-blue eyes, the wide, full mouth, the square jaw. But whereas Jackson's beauty is so much more than the sum of his parts, Cooper's manages to be just that little bit less.

His expression is flinty and unwelcoming; the deep grooves between his brows and bracketing his mouth suggest it's habitual, rather than personal. He nods unsmilingly when I introduce myself, and leaves me to push my trolley after him as he turns on his heel and heads towards the airport exit. Clearly Jackson scooped the family charm lottery too, I think crossly.

I follow Cooper out to the car park. My heart sinks when he stops by a battered two-door Ford pick-up. It looks as if its last passengers were a pair of mud-wrestling hippos.

He climbs into the driver's seat without bothering to help me load my suitcase into the filthy truck bed, but reluctantly gets out again when he sees me struggling.

'Thank you,' I pant, as he tosses the case over the tailgate.

He ignores me and gets back into the pick-up. So much for the fabled Southern manners. I can't believe how different Jackson is from his brother—

Was. *Was.*

Cooper swings the truck on to the busy interstate, leaving his window open so that conversation is impossible over the rush of air. My hair whips around my face, getting into my mouth and eyes. Four lanes of huge American cars belch out clouds of grey fumes as they overtake us on both sides – the one thing Jackson really loved about England, apart from Maltesers and double-decker buses, was our small, neat little cars. I shiver as the air whistles round my shoulders. When I turn the car heater on, Cooper immediately reaches past me and turns it back off. No wonder Jackson's brother never married, if this is the way he goes about winning friends and influencing people.

Slumping against the hard bench seat, I pull my jacket close and shut my eyes. His driving is as aggressive as his attitude, but I'm just too damn tired and miserable to care. In the two weeks since Jackson died, I've deliberately pulled back-to-back double shifts at the hospital: work is the only thing that helps right now. Even on the days I haven't been on duty, I've found myself gravitating towards the warmth of the NICU anyway, spending hours hunched over baby Hope's incubator, willing her to keep on battling. For some reason, the tiny baby has touched the part of me I'd call my soul, if I still believed in God. It's as if, in saving her life, I have somehow made her a part of mine.

My stomach lurches. Sitting here next to Jackson's brother, I'm literally sick with guilt. William says I've got to stop blaming myself for Jackson's death, but how can I? I'm a doctor; if I'd been home, instead of with William, I might have realized how serious it was. If only—

If only *what*, Ella? He'd got to the hospital in time?

You'd got the chance to say goodbye? You hadn't spent the last eight years cheating on him?

'That him?' Cooper says suddenly, jerking his thumb at the box on my lap.

I start at the sound of his voice. His expression is sour. Can he tell just from looking at me what kind of woman his brother married?

I nod. Cooper's jaw sets, but he says nothing further.

After an hour of driving we turn off the interstate and on to a series of increasingly narrow and neglected roads, the last of which isn't even paved. The pick-up jolts over deep ruts and potholes, spraying me with a fine mist of dirt through the open window. Live oaks looped with grey skeins of Spanish moss arch across the track, plunging us into a deep, green gloom. The air is still, oppressive. The damp smell of mould and decay seeps into my bones. I'd often wondered why Jackson never found time to take me home. I'm beginning to understand.

Cooper swings the truck into an overgrown dirt drive running alongside a peeling post-and-rail fence. A horse snickers in the distance as he pulls up in front of a surprisingly large and well-kept antebellum mansion straight out of *Gone with the Wind*. I'd expected some grim, Gothic horror, but this is beautiful.

I lean out of the pick-up window, trying to picture Jackson growing up here – a six-year-old boy perched on the balustrade, a teenager kissing his first girl on the porch. An eleven-year-old wriggling uncomfortably in his stiff new mourning clothes, his hair wet and slicked against his head, trying to be brave like his big brother as he buries his parents.

Cooper grabs my suitcase from the truck bed and heads

into the house. I clamber out of the cab, clumsily cradling the awkward box.

A small black woman in her mid-seventies is waiting for me in the airy hall at the bottom of a sweeping curved staircase, hands folded against her crisp white apron. There's no sign of either Cooper or my suitcase.

'You must be Miss Ella,' she says warmly, her Southern accent painfully familiar. 'I'm Lolly. Y'all must be wore out now after your journey. Let me show you up to your room, so you can freshen up before dinner.'

'It's so good to meet you at last, Lolly. Jackson's told me so much about you—'

Her gaze rests on the box in my arms. 'Oh, Miss Ella. I can't believe he's gone.'

'Me neither,' I whisper.

'He was such a strong boy. Could run outside all day and still have plenty of fizz left in him when he got home. Always playing pranks – frogs and bugs and I don't know what-all in my bed. Once, he got this hognose snake in a burlap sack—' Her brown eyes fill with tears, and she dashes them away with the back of her hand. 'Listen to me, chattering on like a silly old woman, with you all but dead on your feet. You follow me, now. Cooper's put you in the Blue Room at the end of the hall. There's fresh towels laid out in the bathroom, but y'all must tell me if there's anything else you need.'

She shows me upstairs and into a bright, high-ceilinged room. On the far side, a pair of French windows leads on to a small balcony. In the centre of the room, an old brass bed is cloaked in a drift of white duvet and mosquito netting. The polished oak floor gleams gold with the patina of age.

I place Jackson's ashes carefully on the wooden dresser,

next to a pair of silver-backed hairbrushes and a hand-mirror monogrammed with initials too worn to read. Beside the bed is a simple rag rug in the same shade of pale blue as the papered walls. My suitcase stands on it at a dislocated angle, as if it had been thrown from the doorway. Knowing Cooper, it probably has.

Lolly watches as I kneel on the floor and yank the case flat to unzip it.

'You mustn't mind Cooper,' she says hesitantly. 'He can be a little ornery, but it's just his way. This has hit him hard. He loved Jackson like he was his own son.' Her eyes wander to the box on the dresser. 'After their parents died, he gave up everything to raise him. You know Cooper had won himself a place at Juilliard just a month before the fire? He came home so excited that day, I swear he was a foot off the ground. He was such a talented musician. Even now, when he sits down at the piano, it's like the world stands still.'

I sit back on my heels. 'Jackson never mentioned that.'

'Oh, he never knew. Cooper didn't want the boy feeling guilty. Never mentioned Juilliard again. Lord knows how much that cost him.'

'And he never married?'

'There was a girl, once.' She sighs. 'Jackson was still just a boy, and she didn't want to be stuck raising him. After that, I guess Cooper gave up on the idea of a family of his own. Jackson was all the family he needed.'

She tells me that dinner is at six-thirty, and leaves me to unpack. It doesn't take long; I leave most of my clothes in the suitcase, since I'm only going to be here a couple of days. Just long enough to scatter Jackson's ashes and say goodbye.

When I've finished, I glance longingly at the bed. I'd like nothing more than to slide under the crisp covers, but I know if I do that now, I'll be wide awake at three in the morning with jet-lag.

Instead, I splash water on my face and run my fingers through my hair, already kinking even tighter than usual after the plane journey. Maybe I'd feel better if I went for a walk. My muscles ache from being crammed into the cattle truck that passes for economy these days.

Downstairs, the sound of a piano drifts through the hall. I pause on the bottom step, arrested by the music, the world pouring through me like light. Cooper's grief and sorrow is given voice by the plaintive notes spilling from his fingers. My heart swells with pity. I loved Jackson as well as I knew how, but the ties of blood are different. I've seen enough bereaved parents to know that the loss of a child is visceral, akin to having your heart cut out. Cooper mourns his brother the same way. Listening to him play, I'm strangely embarrassed, as if I have stumbled on a private grief I have no right to witness.

Quietly, I open the front door and let myself into the garden.

'We're here?' I ask, as Cooper parks the truck.

He nods brusquely. After three hours together driving up into the Smoky Mountains, during which we've exchanged no more than five words, I didn't really expect actual conversation.

I open the pick-up door, and reach back for Jackson's ashes. Cooper makes no move to follow me. 'You're not coming?' I ask in surprise.

He stares ahead impassively.

Suddenly, unexpectedly, he reminds me of his brother. Something about the stubborn set of his mouth, the angry, defensive tilt of his chin. I realize that if Jackson hadn't had the path of his life smoothed by his protective elder brother, this is the kind of man he might have become: worn, cynical, closed off. I wonder what Cooper would look like if he smiled.

I leave him smouldering in the truck, and shield my eyes as I glance up the path I have to climb. Oh, Jackson. It had to be a four-hundred-foot vertical rock, didn't it?

'If I check out while I'm living on this godforsaken island,' he'd said cheerfully over breakfast one wet Sunday morning, shortly after we'd moved to London, 'don't y'all dare bury me in one of your gloomy English boneyards. I want you to take me back home and scatter my ashes from Chimney Rock.'

'Chimney what?'

He dipped his cereal spoon into my Ben & Jerry's, grinning when I slapped his hand away. 'Chimney Rock. It's a rock, and it's shaped like a chimney—'

'Carry on like this and I'll just flush your ashes down the loo.'

'I love the way you say that. "The loo." It's so British, like "bugger" and "*shed*ule". And red buses and Marmite and—'

'You sound like a bloody tourist.'

'I *am* a bloody tourist. Chimney Rock, you ignorant Brit, is on the edge of the Blue Ridge Smoky Mountains in North Carolina, the most beautiful spot on God's green earth. Y'all can see a couple hundred miles from the top on a good day. I'm surprised you never checked it out when you were at Duke.'

'Scared of heights,' I confessed. 'I've never liked going anywhere near mountains – all those narrow hairpin bends and sheer drops.'

I stare up at the wall of rock in front of me now, and feel sick. Fortunately, I don't have to don a climbing harness or equip myself with ropes; a winding staircase has been cut into the rock. But it's still nearly four hundred feet high, and I've barely reached the first landing when the vertigo hits.

Oh, Jesus. I'm not sure I can do this.

Focus. One foot in front of the other. Don't look up, and it'll be fine. If these stairs can stand the weight of the average American, they can stand you.

Clinging to the stair rail, I climb steadily for twenty minutes, and emerge panting at the top. It's quite sheltered here, and I begin to feel better. That wasn't so bad. And there's a nice stone wall at the edge, not some rickety parapet—

Shit. Shit shit *shit*. This isn't the top. I've got to go up more stairs and – Jesus. Across some kind of Indiana Jones plank bridge. You have *got* to be kidding me.

I sink on to a bench. Oh, Jackson. Aren't *you* having the last laugh.

William thought I was mad coming all this way to scatter his ashes. Heaven knows, I did little enough for my husband when he was alive; maybe it is pointless to go to all this trouble now. But (and at the risk of sounding like a talk-show victim) I need closure. If I do this one last thing, perhaps I can start to move on.

Wearily, I get up and climb the last set of stairs, stopping when I reach the bridge. It must be a thousand feet down to the valley.

There's only one thing to do. When the going gets tough, the tough shut their eyes.

As soon as I'm over the bridge, I collapse on to the rock. And stay there. Nothing is going to get me to stand at the flimsy guard rail by the edge. I'm on a narrow rock the size of my kitchen, four hundred feet up. It's not even flat. I could just topple over the side.

My throat closes. I grip the box tighter, my heart racing. A clammy sweat swamps me. I can't do this. I can't move. *I can't do this*.

An arm cradles my elbow, and propels me on to my feet.

Gently but firmly, Cooper leads me towards the guard rail. The Smoky Mountains are spread out before me, the blue haze that gives them their name softening and blurring the landscape. A silvery river twists its way towards the horizon. The air smells cleaner, more fresh, than anything I've ever experienced. Jackson was right; it is the most beautiful place on God's green earth.

Together, his brother and I open the box. A light wind lifts the ashes, scattering them like rainfall.

Cooper turns to me, his blue eyes navy with grief. I only realize I'm crying myself when the tears splash on to my shirt.

He holds out his hand, and leads me back over the bridge.

*

The evening is unseasonably warm for the first week of March. I open my French windows and step on to the balcony as a cool breeze rustles the live oaks, stirring the Spanish moss. The black night presses down on me, starless. Clouds scud across a nail-paring new moon. Out here there are no streetlights, no neon. Nothing but darkness and the beat of wings.

I lean on the balustrade and sip my bourbon nightcap, enjoying the balmy caress of the night air on my bare skin. In the morning, I'll leave and go back home to London, grey in every sense of the word, shutting this door for ever. For the first time in my life, I'll be truly alone.

It sounds ridiculous – he was my husband, after all – but I hadn't realized quite how much space Jackson took up in my life until he left it. His quiet, reassuring presence was the solid rock on which I built my house of cards. Without him, it's just a matter of time before it comes tumbling down.

I could fool myself that my heart is broken, but that would just pile lie upon betrayal. There are people whose deaths make you ache with misery. And there are people whose deaths are the end of everything, a biblical darkness descending on the land, deaths that send a scream through your head like the keening of lost souls. Hard as it is to admit, losing Jackson hasn't come close to this second kind of grief.

My eyes have adjusted to the dark. On the far side of the lawn is a small lake; as I watch, an owl swoops low over it.

I mourn my husband more than I would have thought possible, but it's fear that's uppermost now, not Cooper's raw kind of anguish. I've already lost Jackson; will I lose William too?

Our relationship worked because it was perfectly balanced. We each had as much to lose; we shared the power. But now, instead of being an equal partner, I've suddenly turned into a needy cliché: the Other Woman.

Whether William knows it or not, part of my attractiveness to him has always been my unavailability. I never needed to play hard to get, because with Jackson in the picture, I actually *was*. But that's changed now. William's probably shit-scared and ready to run for the hills. And to be perfectly honest, I can't blame him. If he ever left Beth, I'd be the same.

Lucy thinks I'm shameless (the unfortunate thing about best friends is that they tend to know you rather well), but that's not entirely true. An affair with William was one thing – if not with me, it would've been someone else, maybe a woman who'd want Beth's wedding ring on her finger and would stop at nothing to get it. That's never been me. I've always sworn I'd never steal another woman's husband.

Easy to do when you're not tempted. I can dress it up as altruism, but the simple truth is I was too much of a snivelling coward to leave Jackson.

Now that he's gone, the moral high ground looks decidedly less bucolic.

For a moment, I allow myself to imagine what it might be like to share a real life with William. Waking up together every morning, spending weekends lazing around with the papers, getting the Eurostar to Paris for the bank-holiday weekend on a whim. Now I'm a widow (I still can't get used to that word; it conjures Greek crones in black picking olives) I'm going to have to get used to doing so many things alone. Unless—

What is it you want, Ella? What do you *want*?

For the first time, I can't give myself an honest answer.

I'm startled by a noise in the room behind me. I spin round, dropping the empty bourbon glass and instinctively covering my nakedness with my hands.

Cooper is framed in the bedroom doorway, his expression unreadable. I recognize that I'm not surprised. The air between us has been charged since we left Chimney Rock two days ago.

When I walk into a room, he leaves. We don't speak, except the briefest banalities at dinner. But every time I look at him, I see Jackson. Every time he looks at me, it's like he can plumb my soul.

Something primitive and visceral in me takes over. I want this man in a way that has nothing to do with who he is, nothing to do with who I am; everything to do with lust and escape and anger and bourbon and the need to remind myself that I am living, breathing, beating flesh, not a box of grey ashes tipped over a mountainside.

I drop my hands and meet his gaze, allowing his eyes to travel over me. My nipples stiffen in the cool breeze from the window.

I don't know what it is I see in his eyes as he crosses the room, and I don't care. Stepping over the broken bourbon glass, I rip at his denim shirt; buttons rattle on the floor. He pushes me roughly back on to the bed, unbuckling his jeans, shucking them off.

In moments he's inside me; I'm already wet. I claw at his back, pulling him harder, deeper within me. He bites my shoulder, his callused hands rough on my breasts. Our bodies are slick with sweat. The brass bed bangs rhythmically against the wall as Cooper pounds angrily into me, his blond hair drenched with perspiration. We come together in an explosion of grief and heat.

His body is heavy on mine. I ease myself free, spent and strangely soothed.

Cooper stands up and pulls on his jeans; we haven't spoken a word from start to finish. He walks towards the door, then abruptly stops and turns, his eyes dark. For an insane moment, I wonder if he's going to tell me he loves me.

'I always wondered what kind of woman my brother married,' he says coldly. 'Now I know.'

I've never been so humiliated and furious in my life. What kind of fucked-up bastard sleeps with his brother's widow just to prove he can? Jesus. I thought *I* was screwed up.

It's not the first time I've regretted having sex for the wrong reasons, but I've never felt as dirty and ugly afterwards as I do now. Ashamed, as if I've been publicly caught naked.

I'm so disturbed I forget to take any Xanax before boarding the plane home. Eight hours later, tired, anxious and depressed, the panic hits. I suddenly find myself standing in the middle of the concourse at Gatwick, clinging to my suitcase and unable to move, terror blossoming inside me like a mushroom cloud. A hot band tightens around my chest. The airport is suddenly airless, suffocating. People press all around me. I'm buffeted from every direction. I drop my case and gasp for air, clawing at my chest, trying to undo my buttons, desperate for breath.

Somehow, I contain the fear. Scrabbling through my bag, heedless of the coins and papers and keys I scatter on the floor, I grab my phone, and for the first time in eight years I call William at home.

His expression is stony when he meets me at his local railway station, where he's told me to come. Wordlessly, he picks up my suitcase and walks me out to his car. My relief at seeing him fades as a newer fear grips me.

I don't want to be alone.

'I'm sorry,' I say, as soon as we're in the car.

'You can't call me at home,' William says tightly. 'Please don't do it again.'

The seatbelt cuts into my shoulder as I twist towards him. 'Jesus, William. Thanks for the tea and sympathy.'

'Come on, Ella. You know the score.'

'One call in eight y—'

'My wife was next to me in the kitchen, Ella!' he exclaims.

I'm appalled by his lack of understanding. 'William, I've just flown halfway across the world and back to scatter my husband's ashes from a mountaintop, and in a moment of weakness, I just thought that seeing you would make me feel better! Clearly I was wrong!'

I gaze out of the window at the ill-lit station car park, so that he won't see the sudden tears filling my eyes. Damn it, what's *wrong* with me? Dragging him from his home in the middle of the evening for no reason. No wonder he's angry. I've got to get a grip. I don't want to drive him away with this nonsense. I'll end up in adjoining beds with his wife at the nuthouse.

'Ella—'

'I'm sorry. I shouldn't have called.'

'Ella, it's not that I don't care. You know I do. But things are so difficult at home right now.' He rubs the side of his face. 'Beth's in one of her manic phases, it's impossible to reason with her—'

A train pulls into the station behind us, briefly drowning out his voice.

'. . . some damn contractor was just about to bulldoze the garage as I pulled into the drive,' William is saying. 'God knows how much she's blown this time. I should have paid more attention to what she was up to, but things have been so insane at work with the takeover bid I lost track.'

'James Noble?' I say, grateful for the distraction.

'Bastard. I didn't build up my company from scratch so some eviscerating card sharp could march in and take it over when he felt like it.'

He's been fending off friendly and not-so-friendly feelers from Noble's company for more than a year. Six months ago, William was in a position to tell him where to get off, but Ashfield's has lost several key accounts in the past few months. The company is vulnerable to attack, and much as William tries to put a brave face on it, I know it's eating him up.

I unbuckle my seatbelt and slide towards him, brushing a clump of dried mud from his shirt without pausing to wonder how it got there, and inhaling his familiar woody, lemon scent. God, I've missed him. I need to remind him why he's missed me.

My hand slips between his legs. Briefly, I wish I'd had a chance to shower after the plane as he pulls my head to him and kisses me, mouth hard and insistent. Heat spreads through my body. Cooper was about meeting a physical need, but this is so much more—

I freeze. How *much* more, Ella? Jackson isn't here to safeguard you now. Are you sure you know what you're doing?

Without warning, the panic returns. The weight of the night presses in on me. Suddenly the car is stifling. I push William away from me, fumbling at the door handle. His hand catches my wrist, and I wrench it painfully away.

'Ella, what is it? Ella!'

The light comes on as I open the door. The chilly air revives me, and instantly I feel better. I sit half in and half out of the car, hands on my knees, breathing deeply the way the woman on the plane showed me. *In through the nose, out through the mouth.*

In the distance, a cat yowls. Someone runs quickly across the car park in the dark. A couple of teenagers kick a can across the station platform. Slowly, my heart rate returns to normal.

William looks distinctly fed up. Hardly surprising, given the way I'm blowing hot and cold. He gets enough tears and histrionics at home – the last thing he needs is more of the same from me. I need to get things back on track with him, and then perhaps I can figure out what my next move needs to be.

I don't want to be alone.

I slam the car door shut and pour every ounce of the old Ella into my smile. 'Let's go back to my place,' I say.

'Ella?'

I'm lying on my back, floating on the warm ocean. A gentle wave sends me drifting towards the white spun-sugar beach, then tugs me back out to sea again. I'm a frond of seaweed, a piece of driftwood, at the mercy of wind and tide. The salt water laps against my face, splashing in my eyes. The sun warms my skin. I can't remember the last time I felt this relaxed, and at peace.

'Ella? Can you hear me?'

The water splashes my face again, cold this time. Something tugs at me, pulling me down. I begin to choke. The sun is so hot, it's *burning*. God, it hurts, it *hurts*—

'Don't try to move,' a voice says in my ear.

It feels as if a giant is pushing his thumbs against my eyes. It takes a huge effort to force them open. 'Lucy? Have I been in an accident?'

'You fell, and hit your head against the corner of your desk. You've been out cold for about five minutes. Can you remember what happened?'

'What's going on?'

She peers into my eyes with her penlight. 'Nausea? Double vision?'

I flinch from the bright light. 'It feels like there's a road-drill in my head, but that's all. What happened?'

'What's the last thing you remember?'

'I remember the flight from North Carolina, and meeting William at the station – were we in a car crash?' I sit bolt upright, and the room spins wildly. 'Is William OK? Oh, God, please tell me he wasn't hurt—'

Lucy frowns. 'Ella, that was a week ago. There wasn't any crash, the accident happened here, at the hospital—'

'A *week*?'

'You don't remember anything about today? We did our rounds this morning, Ella – remember, Hope's doing so well, she's made amazing progress – and then you had a row with Richard Angel over closing the NICU beds.'

I shake my head, and instantly regret it as the room tilts again.

'Afterwards, you came down to your office to do some paperwork. Gina said there was someone waiting for you, a blonde girl. She was with you when it happened. Apparently the two of you were talking, and then you fainted mid-sentence. You hit your head on your desk as you went down. The girl screamed the bloody place down, it sounded like someone was being murdered.'

'Cate,' I breathe.

'You remember?'

A tape fast-forwards in my head: William's daughter, the panic attack, her question: *Do you have kids*? And my instinctive response – despite the fact that I've never wanted children – my first visceral, gut response: *If I'd given Jackson the baby he wanted, I wouldn't be alone now.*

I haven't told Lucy about the panic attacks, or the constant knot of anxiety lodged below my ribcage. For weeks, I haven't been able to eat: I'm too sick with nerves. I wake three, four, five times a night with adrenalin flooding my body, my heart pounding, feeling as if a suffocating weight is pressing on my chest. I'm so exhausted I can't see straight. I look in the mirror and I don't recognize myself.

I've always been in such control of my life. I've never been remotely nervous or anxious about anything. I sailed through my finals. How can this be happening to *me*?

'I remember now,' I say painfully. 'Not all of it, but at least the edited highlights.'

'The rest will come back. That cut's going to need a couple of stitches.' Lucy snaps on some gloves and opens a suture kit. 'You were lucky you didn't lose an eye. You need to start eating properly,' she adds crossly. 'Look at you: you must have lost fifteen pounds in the last couple of weeks. No wonder you fainted.'

I wince as she sterilizes my forehead. 'The girl was Cate,' I say, 'William's daughter – ow! Watch what you're doing, Lucy!'

'Sorry. What on earth was she doing here?'

'She found out about us. Came to warn me off, I think. Although . . .' I hesitate. Her hostility didn't seem quite real; almost as if I wasn't its focus. It must have taken a lot of courage to come and confront me. I wish she hadn't, but I can't help liking her for it. 'I'm not really sure what she wanted. I'm not sure she knew, either.'

'So what now?'

For the briefest moment, I think of Cooper, and the straightforward, if brutal, need that brought us together.

Since when did my free-and-easy relationship with William become so *complicated*?

'I have no idea,' I sigh.

'Are you going to tell him?'

He needs to know that his daughter has discovered us; but I promised her I wouldn't say anything, and, stupid as it may sound, I don't want to let her down. Oh, God, I'm so *tired* of all the lies.

Knowing he had a family was one thing; being confronted by his teenage daughter, seeing the pain and confusion in her eyes, is another. She may affect a tough front and take her daddy's side, but she loves her mother too, whether she acknowledges it or not. How can I let things go on, now that Cate knows?

How can I bear to lose William too?

'Look, Lucy. Thanks for putting me back together, but

I need to get going. I've got to finish this paperwork for Angel, or he'll shut down half the hospital.'

'Ella, forget work! You just knocked yourself unconscious! Don't even think about going back to your office. And you're getting a taxi home. I'm not having you wandering around the District & Circle Line in a daze asking people what your name is. Besides,' she adds, peeling off her gloves, 'Richard will understand. He's not as bad as people think.'

'"Richard"?'

'If you give him a chance, he's actually OK,' she mutters.

'I thought *I* was the one with concussion,' I say, narrowing my eyes.

She doesn't meet them. 'I'll call you a taxi.'

Today is taking on a surreal quality. First Cate turns up, and now Lucy's defending the Angel of Death. Maybe when I hit my head, I woke up in a strange parallel universe where all this actually makes sense.

I allow myself to be bundled into a cab, and give the driver William's address. Thirty minutes later, I let myself into his flat; he gave me a key years ago, though obviously I never turn up uninvited. The apartment's in darkness; he's clearly still at work. Thanks to my little medical drama, I'm an hour early.

I sink into the sofa without turning on the lights. My forehead throbs. This is not what I wanted from this evening. I meant to be fun and sexy for William, back to the old Ella, to wipe out the neurotic impression I've been giving over the past few weeks. The last thing I wanted was to sit here with my head swathed in gauze, looking like romantic roadkill—

Something is digging into my back. I reach beneath the sofa cushions and pull out the TV remote, but there's still something—

A boned slither of lace and silk falls into my lap. A very sexy, very expensive black basque, at least two sizes too small for me.

He could be cheating on you, too. He might have loads of girlfriends.

It doesn't belong to his wife.

October 24, 2000

Felden Street
Fulham
London SW6

Dear Cooper,

   You've no idea how good it was to get your letter, bro. I thought you were going to stay mad at me for ever. I wish we'd made up before I left the States; I hated not being able to say a real goodbye. But wild horses couldn't stop me coming home for Thanksgiving, so you'd better get Lolly started in on her baking! What I wouldn't give right now for a mouthful of her sweet potato pie!

 Look, I shouldn't have said the things I did, and I'm sorry. You know it was just the Jack talking. You've been the best brother a man could have, and I owe you a lot. But Ella is my wife, and I love her. It's killing me that the two people I love most in the world can't love each other.

 She keeps asking to meet you, and I'm fast running out of excuses. I wish you'd just give her half a chance. I don't know why you've taken against her so when you haven't even met her. She isn't what you think, Coop. She's a good wife. I know you've always held a woman ought to stay home and take care of her man like Mom did, but if you could just see the way she talks about her babies at that hospital, you'd think different. What she does is real important. I'll admit, sometimes I wish I got a bigger slice of her time, but those tiny ones need her as much as I do.

 It's not fair to blame her for us moving to London – that was my idea. Thing is, I reckon if she's in her home town, she'll feel differently about us starting a family of our own.

She always says she doesn't want children, but I know she can't mean it. She just needs to feel settled and secure, is all. After what happened to her mom, you can't blame her. She needs a lot of gentling, like a skittish mare. Remember how I got Star to trust me, how long that took? Man, but I took some hard falls from her before I was done! For a time there, seemed like Lolly was always rubbing liniment on one bruise or another!

Jackson Junior – how about that for a wild idea! Bet you never thought you'd see the day when your crazy-ass brother would be looking forward to changing a diaper!

I'm not saying it's been plain sailing. We got our troubles, same as everyone. She works too hard, for a start, and she's always pushing me to climb the greasy pole. But you know me, my job's never been the be-all, end-all. I don't deny, she gets me all fired up at times. She's not the easiest woman in the world to live with, but I can't do without her, Coop.

Why don't you come over and stay with us awhile, get to know her properly? This is an amazing city, for all it's so crowded a man can scarce breathe for tripping over his neighbor. And the cars! Man, I love their cute cars. Our townhouse is so small I can touch both sides of the kitchen without shifting, but it's in a real neat neighborhood and I've already met so many interesting folk. Ella says I gotta stop bringing home my 'strays', but how you ever going to make friends if you don't talk to people? No one has any time for each other any more. That's one thing I miss about home. You could spend all day just passing the time of day with your neighbors and no one's going to think badly of you for it.

I guess I'd better haul ass if I want this to reach you

before Christmas. You gotta go find yourself a 'letterbox'
over here – they don't collect mail from home like they do in
the good old US of A. There's a lot of stuff here takes some
getting used to. Did you ever hear of something called
Marmite? Tastes like shit rolled in salt and looks like tar,
but these Brits are addicted to the stuff! Makes me feel queasy
just thinking about it. I'll take Lolly's biscuits and cranberry
sauce any day!

    Give her a smacker for me, and tell her I'll be home soon.

    Jackson

6

William

Carolyn was definitely giving me the eye this morning. Christ, that skirt. Any shorter and I'd have seen her breakfast.

I ease the Land-Rover out of the station car park, drumming my fingers on the steering wheel as I hit rush-hour traffic. Carolyn's a nice girl, bright, but I don't shit on my own doorstep; not any more. She can't be much older than Cate, for heaven's sake. Twenty-four, max. Amazing body (you could lose yourself for a week in those tits), but the *ingénue* thing doesn't do it for me. I like a woman who knows what she's doing in bed, and tells you what she wants. Isn't afraid to get down and dirty. Carolyn's not the type to take it up the arse or let you come all over her face, far too proper.

God, I miss Ella. Apart from the obvious, I could use her company. No one makes me laugh like Ella. What with Beth painting like Tigger on speed, Ben demanding another two grand to clear his college bar bill (what's he drinking?

Bloody Moët?), Cate making bedroom eyes at that fucking luppy boyfriend of hers and James Noble breathing down my neck in the boardroom, I need some down-time. If Beth knew how close we are to the whole bloody house of cards collapsing—

I slam on the brakes as a cement mixer reverses out into the road. Where the hell is Ella when I need her? She's the only one who understands. Why she had to scatter the poor sod's ashes in person I don't know. Couldn't she have FedExed them or something?

OK, that was a bit harsh. I take it back. Anyway, she's home today, that's the main thing. With any luck, I'll see her next weekend.

I turn into our road. Got to be very careful I don't let things get out of hand. Be a bit too easy to start seeing Ella more often, now she doesn't have to answer to the husband, and tempting though it is, I don't want to rock the boat at home. Once a month is one thing. But Beth might ask questions if I had to 'take clients out' every week—

What the fuck?

I abandon the car, engine running, and race up the driveway, silk tie flapping over my shoulder. The bulldozer raises its claw, ready to smash down into the garage. I shout to attract the driver's attention, waving my arms and getting as close to the caterpillar treads as I dare.

My life flashes before me. I'm reminded, amongst other things, of the reason I don't return my mother's calls. A bloody great clod of mud falls from the bulldozer bucket on to my shoulder, and I close my eyes, bracing myself for the groan of metal, glass, brick and, quite possibly, flesh.

'You want to get out of the way, mate,' the driver calls. 'You could get hurt.'

'Beth!' I yell, as I slam into the kitchen five minutes later.

There's no sign of my wife. There is every sign, however, of her latest manic episode: tubes of paint and dirty paintbrushes fill the sink, milky jars of white spirit are ranged along the windowsill, and half a dozen squares of paint-smeared glass are spread over the Aga to dry. Of dinner, laundry, shopping or, in fact, I notice as I go to put it on, the coffee percolator, there is no sign.

'*Beth!*'

She bumps open the back door with her hip, her arms full of photographic equipment. 'All right, William. There's no need to shout.'

'Christ almighty. I'm putting in an eighty-hour week to put a roof over our heads. Is it really too much to expect for it to still be there when I get home?'

She beams. 'Oh, did you meet Murray?'

'If you mean the sadistic bastard intent on knocking down my house and demanding my first-born in payment, yes, I have,' I say darkly.

'Now you're being silly.' She puts down the equipment and pushes her hair back off her face in a gesture that reminds me of Cate. 'I need to expand my studio, and since you wouldn't let me move the conservatory last year – well, it's not as if we need the garage—'

'Need it?' I yelp. 'Where am I supposed to put the car?'

'For heaven's sake, I don't know. You can't expect me to take care of everything. Did you see Cate on your way up from the station? She should be back from school by now – she must've gone over to Dan's. I wanted to ask her about Brighton.'

She's making even less sense than usual. It's like stepping into a Dali painting.

My mobile rings. I pull it out, and nearly drop it into the nearest jar of turps when I see Ella's number come up. In eight years, she's never called me on it at home.

'Who is it?' Beth says brightly.

'Work.'

'Aren't you going to answer it?'

'It's a client. Confidential.'

She pulls a face. 'Oooh, all right. I can take a hint. I'll be in my studio if you need me.'

I wait till Beth's safely out of earshot.

'Ella? Are you there? What's wrong?'

'William, you have to come and get me. You have to come. William, William, can you come? Can you come and get me, now, please. Please, William—'

'It's OK,' I say, alarmed. 'Ella, it's OK. Just tell me where you are.'

When I find her sitting on her suitcase like Little Orphan Annie at the edge of the station platform, I almost don't recognize her. She's lost a huge amount of weight; her face is drawn, her eyes bruised by tiredness. But what really throws me is her air of uncertainty. She looks as if she's woken up in a country she doesn't recognize, and no matter how hard she keeps trying, she can't find her bearings. I've never seen Ella anything but brazenly confident before.

'I'm so sorry,' she says, as soon as we're in the car.

I start the engine, but don't put it in gear. I'm thoroughly unnerved, and anxiety makes my tone sharper than I intend. 'You can't call me at home. Please don't do it again.'

'Jesus, William. Thanks for the tea and sympathy.'

'Come on, Ella. You know the score.'

'One call in eight y—'

I expect this kind of neediness from Beth, but not Ella. Her unexpected vulnerability has thrown me more than I care to admit.

'My wife was next to me in the kitchen, Ella!'

'William, I've just flown halfway across the world and back to scatter my husband's ashes from a mountaintop, and in a moment of weakness, I just thought that seeing you would make me feel better! Clearly I was wrong!'

She turns her back on me. Shit. As if I don't have enough emotional, neurotic women at home.

I remind myself she's just lost her husband. How would I feel, if it were Beth?

'Ella—'

'I'm sorry,' she says tightly. 'I shouldn't have called.'

'Ella, it's not that I don't care. You know I do. But things are so difficult at home right now. Beth's in one of her manic phases, it's impossible to reason with her. She's up all hours of the day and night painting, and ordering thousands of pounds' worth of canvases and who knows what else on my credit cards, which are already maxed out from paying off Ben's student loans. We're up to our ears in debt – it's only the overdraft keeping Sam at school. Then today I find out she's spent a fortune on architect's fees to build a bloody new studio. Some damn contractor was just about to bulldoze the garage as I pulled into the drive.' Wearily, I rub my hand over my face. 'God knows how much she's blown this time. I should have paid more attention to what she was up to, but things have been so insane at work with the takeover bid I lost track.'

She looks up, alert. I wish Beth showed half as much interest. 'James Noble?'

'Bastard. I didn't build up my company from scratch so some eviscerating card sharp could march in and take it over when he felt like it.'

Ella unbuckles her seatbelt and moves into my lap, her hand reaching between my legs. I kiss her, hard. She smells sweaty and slightly stale from the plane; bizarrely, it turns me on. My palm slides up her calf. I want to fuck her, right here in the middle of the car park. Anyone could see. Eight years and it's still as exciting as the first—

Suddenly she goes rigid in my arms and pulls away, grabbing the door handle. I try to catch her, but she yanks her hand free.

'Ella, what is it?' *God damn it, what now*? 'Ella!'

A blast of cold air puts a brake on my ardour, and my dick shrivels to Squirrel Nutkin proportions. Ella sits on the edge of her seat and sticks her head between her knees, breathing in short little pants as if she's about to give birth. Her face looks green in the dim interior light. Fuck, I hope she isn't going to puke everywhere.

I wonder if I should get her out into the fresh air, or drive her somewhere for coffee. Maybe it's something she ate on the plane. Sometimes I wonder if having two women in my life doesn't just mean twice the bloody hormones.

Clearly a fuck is now out of the question!

'Let's go back to my place,' Ella breathes.

I don't need asking twice.

The workings of a woman's mind are mystery understood only by God. The working of her body, on the other hand . . .

'Shit, that was good,' I pant, two hot and sweaty hours later.

'You have *no* idea,' Ella agrees.

She swings her long legs out of bed. Beautiful arse. Great tits, too. No breastfeeding, of course.

'Sorry about earlier,' she says ruefully, twisting her wild Pre-Raphaelite hair into a knot and starting the shower. 'I guess this whole grief thing is a bit more complicated than I thought. Staying at his childhood home freaked me out.' She shivers. 'Too many ghosts.'

I'd noticed there are no photos of Jackson anywhere in the flat; no sign a man has ever even lived here, apart from the state-of-the-art sound system and forty-two-inch flat-panel plasma TV. No bike in the hall, no jacket on the banister. No tacky fishing trophies on the wall, or car magazines on the coffee table. It's as if he never existed. I wonder what she's done with it all.

In the morning, Ella's up before I am, brewing coffee in the kitchen. She hands me a mug with a smile; her old self again, I'm relieved to note. 'Got to run, William, sorry. Mother at twenty-six weeks with pre-eclampsia has just been admitted, and it looks like we're going to have to deliver the baby.' She grabs her keys from the fruit bowl. 'Just let the door slam behind you when you leave.'

'You free this weekend?'

'Sorry. Double shifts for the next week, payback for the time I took off. But I'm around next Friday, if that works for you.'

Bugger. I've already told Beth I have to be in London on Saturday. If I cancel now, she'll drag me along to that bloody school fête of Cate's.

'I don't suppose,' Carolyn says shyly to me later that morning, 'you're going to be in town this weekend? Only a friend of mine is in this band – they're doing rather well, actually – and he's thinking of going solo, but I thought he should talk to you first. He's coming down from Manchester on Saturday. I was wondering if you'd have time for a quick drink with us. If you're in London, of course. I wouldn't want you to come up specially.'

I don't look up. The latest quarterly accounts make worrying reading. Malinche Lyon, my star signing, and Equinox Hotels are the only accounts making any real money. That bastard Noble. He's poached two of my best rainmakers this past few months; no wonder the company's suffering.

'Which band?' I ask absently.

'WdLuv2Meet. I don't know if—'

Suddenly she's got my full attention. 'Who's your friend?'

'Davy Kirkland. We were at school together . . .'

You've got to be kidding me. Cate's bedroom wall is plastered with posters of the kid. Cross Robbie Williams with Brad Pitt, throw in a dash of the young Paul McCartney, and you've got Davy Kirkland. The group isn't bad, as boy bands go, but the other three lads are nothing special; they're holding Kirkland back. He's headed for the stratosphere once he breaks free.

Thank you, God.

I could kiss Carolyn. The little star has all but got Kirkland in the bag. I'll have to take her out somewhere really hot this time to celebrate.

Let's face it, I needed a bit of good news after the shitstorm that went down at the weekend. What *possessed* Beth to strip off and streak across the fucking playing fields, for God's sake?

Cate's been a bloody hermit ever since, holing up in her room; can't say I blame her. Obviously she's not speaking to her mother, who's treating the whole thing like some kind of joke. Thank God it's the Easter holidays. With any luck, the fuss will have died down by the time she goes back to school. Sometimes, I could bloody murder Beth.

I let myself into the apartment block, taking the stairs two at a time. I'm surprised to find my flat in darkness when I unlock the front door. Strange. Ella said she'd be here by seven-thirty, and it's gone eight—

'Christ Almighty, Ella! What are you doing sitting in the dark! Are you trying to give me a bloody heart attack?'

She winces. Shit. Not the best thing to say, in the circumstances.

'Sorry I'm late. Meeting ran over.' I throw my jacket over the back of a chair, and pour myself a Scotch. 'Let me jump in the shower, and I'll be right out—

I pause. Ella's sitting unnaturally upright on the sofa, hands in her lap, spiky lovat-green boots pressed neatly together as if she's having tea with the Queen. She hasn't taken off her jacket. I switch on the lamp, and suddenly see the gauze taped to her right temple. 'Ella! What in hell happened?'

She ducks away from me. For the first time, I register the chill in her expression.

'Ella, sweetheart, is everything OK?'

'I was rather hoping you'd tell me.'

'Sorry. I don't get it.'

'Prescient of you,' Ella says drily. She holds up a lacy black corset, and waits. I realize I'm supposed to say something, but I haven't a clue what.

Ella sighs with exaggerated patience 'This isn't mine, William. I found it down the back of the sofa.'

'Whose is it?'

'Ah. Straight to the heart of the matter.'

'It's probably Beth's—'

'Come on, William. We both know it's not your wife's.'

'Well, it's not mine,' I say tersely. 'Who knows how long it's been there? Ben stayed here last month; one of his girlfriends probably left it behind. I still don't—'

'The thing is, William,' Ella says pleasantly, 'it's the lying I've always hated most. Having to lie to Jackson about where I was and who I was with. You lying to Beth every time you see me. Lying to my friends by omission – there's a whole side of my life most people know nothing about, and that makes me a fraud. But I've come to terms with all of that, because I always thought that at least we never had to lie to each other.'

The penny finally drops.

'Wait. Are you asking – Ella, do you think there's *someone else*?'

She smiles. 'I know. Ironic, isn't it?'

'No, it's bloody ridiculous!' I explode. 'Of course there isn't!'

'Why "of course"? We never said this was an exclusive arrangement.'

'Because I never thought it needed to be said! Do you think I've got some sort of revolving-door policy at this flat? A different girl every night of the week? What sort of man do you think I am?'

'The sort who cheats on his wife,' she says coolly.

I'm taken aback. Doesn't she know what this – what *she* – means to me? How can she think there'd be anyone else?

'Oh, don't look so shocked. I'm no better, am I?' she laughs. 'Come on, William. We're not Romeo and Juliet. We've always known what this is about, haven't we? If you've met someone else—'

'I bloody haven't, Ella!'

'Look, you're free to see who you please. I'd just—'

An unpleasant thought surfaces. 'Ella, are you trying to tell me something?'

She smiles sweetly. 'Such as what, William?'

'Are you – have you – is there . . .'

'Would you mind?'

Mind? Of course I'd bloody mind! I never much liked the thought of her in bed with Jackson, but I could hardly tell her not to grant her own husband his conjugals. The thought of her fucking someone else makes me want to reach down the bastard's throat and choke him on his own balls.

'As you said, we're free agents,' I say stiffly.

'Absolutely.'

'So *you* wouldn't be jealous if there were someone else, then?'

She meets my gaze head-on. 'Not at all.'

'Fine, then.'

'Yes, fine.'

I knock back my Scotch. 'So, just out of curiosity. Have you slept with someone else?'

'No one important.'

I nearly choke on my drink. I didn't bloody expect her to say yes!

I want to slam my fist into the wall. I force a casual smile. 'And are you still—'

'It was a one-off.'

I get up and pour myself another drink. My hand shakes with suppressed fury. I have no idea what to do with this information. Jealousy eats at me like acid. Now Jackson's gone, they'll be swarming like bees to a honeypot. Christ. Christ! And I just have to sit and take it. It's not like I can offer her anything permanent. I can't leave Beth. I wouldn't want to. Obviously.

The irony is that Ella's the only woman I've slept with in more than eight years. Unlike most adulterers, I really *don't* have sex with my wife.

She curls her feet under her on the sofa. 'So,' she says conversationally, 'whose underwear is this, then, William? I'm sure she'll want it back. It's so annoying when you lose half a matching set.'

'I've told you, I've no—'

Oh, shit.

'William?'

I pick up the ridiculous Spongebob backpack from behind the sofa. I'd recognize it anywhere. Somehow she's got a key to the flat and come up here behind my back and – with that fucking hippy bastard – prancing around in black underwear – I'll kill him, *I'll rip his fucking throat out*—

'Cate,' says Ella.

I hammer on my daughter's bedroom door. 'Cate! Phone!'

She doesn't respond. Hesitating briefly, I try the door-knob. Locked.

'Cate!' I thump the door again. 'It's Paris! Are you coming out to take it or shall I—'

The door opens.

'There's no need to shout,' Cate says primly.

She snatches the phone and waits. I get the hint. 'Send Fleur's parents my best.'

The door slams in my face. Charming. I pay twenty grand a year for these manners.

I stomp back downstairs, nearly tripping over the dog, and wonder what the hell my daughter's up to now. That friend of hers has always been trouble. She and Cate palled up when Fleur's father was posted to the French Embassy in London and she went to Cate's school for a couple of years. Cate was devastated when the family moved back to Paris last summer, though I'll admit I was rather relieved. A bad influence, Fleur. Too clever by half. And she has a disconcerting way of looking at you: altogether too knowing for a seventeen-year-old.

Reminds me of Ella, in a way. Must be the French influence.

I pull a couple of T-bones out of the fridge, setting them out of Cannelle's reach, and put a bottle of white in to chill. Beth's got her art class tonight, Ben's staying with his posh Oxford totty and Sam's on a school trip, so it's just Cate and me. Thank God she grew out of the vegan phase. There are only so many things you can think of to do with tofu that are strictly legal.

Maybe tonight would be a good time to have our father–daughter chat. I can't put it off any longer. It's already been a week, and I still haven't tackled her about the bloody corset – Beth said she'd deal with it, but Cate's my daughter too. I don't want things going on in her life I know nothing about. I want her to feel she can tell me anything.

Even if it's the last thing I want to hear.

The back door slams open and Beth whirls into the

kitchen on a gust of cold air. She looks pink and flushed, as if she's been running.

'Oh! William! You're home already. I'm not stopping, just needed to get a few bits, then I'm going back for the life class – I did tell you I'd be out tonight, didn't I?'

I nod briefly.

'You don't mind, do you, darling? I don't have to go, of course, but they don't like us to miss classes and I did promise—'

'Of course I don't mind,' I say irritably. 'I told you, I think it's good for you to get out a bit.' I stop tenderizing the steaks, throwing her a suspicious glance. She looks rather excited. 'You are taking your pills, aren't you, Beth? We don't want another repeat of—'

'Yes, yes, all right.'

I reach for the pepper. Beth hovers by the Aga, fiddling nervously with her charm bracelet. Changed her mind about going, no doubt. I can probably stretch the steaks to three.

'William,' she blurts suddenly, 'I invited your mother down for lunch on Sunday.'

My hand stills.

'It's Easter Sunday, William, and she's eighty on Tuesday. You can't let this silly row go on for ever. I mean, twenty *years*. I thought now was as good a time as any to let bygones be bygones, and since Ben and Sam will be home tomorrow too—'

'You – did – *what*?'

' – and I knew you'd just say no if I asked,' she gabbles. 'Come on, darling. I know you don't get on with her, but my mother isn't all sweetness and light either, and I manage to—'

'It's hardly the same thing!'

'Yes, but I understand how you—'

'Your mother didn't kill your father!'

Beth flinches, but stands her ground. 'Nor did yours, William.'

'You weren't there,' I grind out.

'She's your mother, William,' Beth says staunchly.

There are times when I actually hate my wife. 'Cancel.'

'I can't, it'd be too—'

'I said, *cancel*.'

'Please, William. If something happens to her and you still haven't—'

'Aren't you going to be late for your class?' I ask coldly.

She opens her mouth to say something, then thinks better of it. I turn my back, my hands gripping the Aga rail so hard my knuckles turn white, and moments later hear the soft click of the back door.

Twenty years, and I can still smell the metallic stench of fresh blood.

It happened just a few months before I met Beth. (No doubt the trick-cyclists would make something of that, but cod psychology didn't get her pregnant, I did.) Dad had been out of work for three years by then, one of the victims of Thatcher's victory over the miners' unions. He was a small-town Nottinghamshire solicitor who'd made a modest living from writing wills and settling minor local disputes; when the miners had nothing left to leave or fight over, the firm he'd built up over nearly forty years collapsed almost overnight.

It destroyed him. He aged about twenty years in the space of a week. As far as he was concerned, his life was over; without purpose or hope.

For three years, he sat in his favourite armchair and just

stared into the distance. I got used to having one-sided conversations; very useful, as it's turned out.

My mother (whose estate agency went from strength to strength as the buy-to-let market took off) taunted him daily with his failure, demeaning him at every opportunity. Useless. Hopeless. Worthless. Wish I'd never married you. Always knew you wouldn't amount to anything. He said she wouldn't let up. *She wouldn't bloody let up.*

I knew as soon as he called the morning of his sixty-fifth birthday that this was goodbye. I knew; and I couldn't do a bloody thing about it.

When he told me he loved me and put down the phone, I got in the car and drove like the hounds of hell were behind me. I only lived ten minutes away back then. I was nearly in time. I nearly made it.

I heard the gunshot as I pulled into the drive.

You have no idea how much blood and brains a human head contains until you see your father's splashed over the floor, and walls, and ceiling, and doors, and windows, of your family home.

'Dad? Are you going to cook those steaks or shall I give them to Cannelle?'

I jump and stare uneasily at the pulped and bloody flesh in my hands. 'Changed my mind. D'you fancy Chinese?'

Cate shrugs.

'Find me the takeaway menu, and I'll call them. You can give these to the dog, but don't tell your mother. What did Fleur want?'

'Nothing special.'

She lurks in the doorway, twisting the rope bracelet on her wrist, her mother's *doppelgänger*. 'Dad, can I talk to you about something without you flipping out?'

Dear God, she's pregnant.

'I'm not pregnant, Dad, if that's what you're thinking,' Cate snaps. 'This is serious.'

'Fine. I'm listening.'

'The thing is, Dad, I need to get my applications in for uni soon, and we still haven't had a chance to—'

'Have you decided what you fancy? I thought I'd go with the hot-and-sour soup, and then maybe a beef chow mein—'

She snatches the menu out of my hand. 'Dad, why do you always do this?' she cries. 'Every time I try to talk to you about it, you pretend it's not going to happen! I'm not twelve any more!'

'I know that,' I sigh.

'Look, Dad,' she pleads. 'I don't want to keep fighting you, but you're not giving me any choice. Sometimes it feels like I can't breathe around here. You've got to give me some space.'

I pull out a kitchen chair and sink heavily into it. 'OK, Cate. Let's talk.'

'I want to study journalism,' she says firmly.

'But you're so good at science! What happened to being a doctor?'

'I wanted to be a doctor when I was, like, seven, Dad.'

'OK. But a science degree would be so much more useful—'

'Dad, I want to be a journalist.'

I note the set of her jaw, the resolute squaring of her shoulders, and realize who she reminds me of. I had the same battle with my mother a few years before Dad died, when I refused to join her property business and insisted on a 'useless' history degree.

'Journalism it is,' I say brightly. 'I don't know which colleges are best for that, but we can easily find out—'

'Not Oxford, Dad. And not Cambridge, either,' she adds quickly.

'I see. Well, at least if you're in London we'll still see plenty of you—'

'I want to go to NYU.'

'NYU? But that's in New York.'

'No shit, Sherlock,' Cate mutters. 'Dad, it's the best in the world for journalism. I probably won't get in, but I really want to try. I've got quite a good portfolio from editing the school paper, and those local stories I wrote, and if I can get some serious work experience this summer, like at the *Mail* or something, I might—'

'New York! No, Cate. Out of the question, I'm afraid.'

'But you'd have let Ben!'

'That would've been different.'

'Why?'

'Ben can look after himself. It's girls who get attacked and raped, or murdered. It might not be fair, but that's the way it is. The answer's no, Cate.'

'I'll be eighteen soon, Dad! You can't stop me—'

'True. But since I'm the one paying for your education, I do still have some say in the matter. And I say no to New York. There are plenty of good universities in this country. You don't need to go halfway across the world—'

'Has it ever occurred to you I might *want* to go halfway across the world?' Cate cries. 'I hate it here! I'm fed up with looking after Mum! Every day I come home and wonder if she's going to be running naked round the garden cos she hasn't taken her pills! I'm too embarrassed to bring my friends home, I never go anywhere, and you're never here!

Everyone depends on me! I'm always the one left to handle everything, and I'm sick of it!'

'It's not your mother's fault—'

'It's not mine either!'

I sigh. 'I know, sweetheart. And I'm sorry. If I could do anything about it—'

'You could come home a bit more often! Why do you think she acts this way? It's not just the illness. She's lonely! You're never here for her!' She takes a breath. 'You think because you haven't actually left her, that's enough. Don't you get it, Dad? She *loves* you. She knows you don't love her back. No wonder she goes a little mad sometimes.'

'Cate, that's not true—'

'Does she know you're screwing Sam's doctor?'

I stare at her, ashen-faced.

'I saw you,' she accuses tearfully. 'A couple of weeks ago. In the car park by the station. You were kissing her—'

'Oh, Jesus.' I get up and go to her, but she shrugs me off. 'Cate, I am *so* sorry, I never meant for you—'

'Oh, forget it, Dad.' She knuckles her eyes, looking nearer seven than seventeen. 'I don't really blame you, I guess. I mean, Mum's not exactly easy to live with, is she? But you're the one who married her, not me. It's not fair if I've got to pick up the pieces when you leave.'

'I'm not going to leave, Cate. I promise.'

'You're not that good at keeping promises, Dad,' she sniffs.

I wince.

'Daddy, *please*. I really want to go to NYU. It's not just about getting away from all this. I'd come back every holidays, you know I would—'

'Is that your price, Caitlin?' I say sharply. 'I let you go to New York, or you'll tell your mother about Ella?'

She gasps, as if I've punched her in the stomach.

'Cate, look, I didn't mean—'

'I'm going to New York, Dad. I don't care if you support me or not. You can't stop me.' Her expression is suddenly hard. 'Just because you screwed up your life, doesn't mean I have to waste mine. You only married Mum so you could fix her and make up for what happened to Grandpa. Well, fine. Just don't expect me to hang around any more and share suicide watch with you!'

Her feet thunder up the stairs. Moments later, her bedroom door slams.

She knows about Ella. How in hell did that happen? After all this time. We've always been so careful.

She's still only a child. How can I possibly let her go off to New York? Who'd be there to look out for her if I wasn't?

Atoning for Dad? Is that what I've been doing all these years?

I'm still standing shell-shocked in the kitchen when Ben saunters in ten minutes later, munching a wedge of pizza. 'Just saw Cate storming off down the road,' my son mumbles through a mouthful of melted cheese. 'You two have a row?' He slings his backpack on the table. 'Leave her to it, Dad. She'll get over it.'

'She wants to go to New York next year,' I manage. 'To study journalism.'

'Oh, she finally told you?' Ben says. 'Good for her.'

'You knew?'

'Course. Don't sweat it, Dad. She'll be fine. She's tougher than you think.'

'Doesn't seem much I can do about it, either way. Looks like she's made up her mind.' I put the kettle on the hob. 'What are you doing home tonight, anyway? We weren't expecting you back till tomorrow.'

'Candida bailed. Her parents are taking her to Aspen. Figured I might as well come home. Not a problem, is it?'

'Frankly, Ben, I couldn't be happier to see you. I could do with a bit of testosterone round here. If you want, we could – shit, sorry. I really need to take that call.'

Ben raises a hand and ambles cheerfully towards the stairs as I flip open my mobile. If only Cate was as even-tempered as my oldest son. Mind you, that probably has more to do with the spiky plants at the end of the garden than any natural Pollyanna temperament.

'Hi, Andrew. What's up?'

My lawyer gets straight to the point. 'You lost Kirkland. Noble just signed him up; it's all over the wires.'

'Shit! I thought we had that one in the bag!' I close my eyes in despair. 'How the hell did Noble find out? Davy said he wasn't talking to anyone else; this was to be kept strictly under wraps till he told the rest of his band he was leaving.'

'Well, someone leaked. Noble's representing him for half his usual percentage. And it gets worse.'

'How much worse?'

'Looks like he's been putting out feelers to Equinox. I don't have to tell you how hard that'll hit your bottom line. God knows how he discovered their contract is up for renewal, but if I were you I'd get myself on a plane to New York ASAP and turn this around before it's too late.'

My gut spasms. If I lose the international hotel group, I might as well give up and go home.

'Listen, William,' Andrew says cautiously. 'I'm not making any wild accusations, but if I were you, I'd review your internal security. This is the fourth time in the last two months that sensitive information has reached Noble before it's become public knowledge. It's really beginning to hurt you.'

'Plain English, Andrew.'

'Someone very close to you is screwing you over.'

After he rings off, I go into my study and pour myself a neat Scotch. It's not Carolyn; apart from the fact that she was the one who brought Davy Kirkland to me in the first place, she didn't know anything about the Equinox contract. The only person other than me to work on that account is Harry Armitage, and he's been hiking in New Zealand for the last three weeks. He's out of the loop on Kirkland, which rules him out too.

I knock back my drink. There are only two people who knew about both those deals.

Beth. And Ella.

7

Beth

No more pills. No more pills!

Except I promised William.

I hate them. Oh God, how I *hate* taking them. I can't paint, I can't think, I can't feel. It's like a fog envelops my brain. I fumble for the right word, forget friends' faces, pick up a corkscrew and can't remember how to use it. Someone will tell me their mother's just died, and I'll stare at them in puzzlement, like an autistic child, not even knowing what my response should be. It's like I'm trapped in a glass bubble: nothing can get in, and I can't get out.

I unclench my fist. The pretty, brightly coloured drugs in my palm iron out the highs and lows and save me from the worst depression – but, oh, the price! No sadness, but no happiness either. No misery, and no joy. Who wants to experience a life without love, grief, fear, ecstasy? That's not living, it's existing.

I tip them into the sink and turn on the waste disposal.

In the end, I'll have to take them again, or I'll get so

manic they'll lock me up. But while I have this window where I am truly *me*, this brief interval between stupor and madness, I'm going to make the most of it.

Dress like *you*, Eithne said when I asked her what to wear today. They're coming to the gallery to look at your art, not your shoes.

How can I dress like me when I don't know who I am? I've never had a chance to find out. Clara's daughter, William's wife, the children's mother – all my life I've been defined in terms of my relationships to other people. What would Beth Ashfield, brilliant new about-to-be-discovered artist, wear to the most critical meeting of her life?

Not this shapeless turquoise suit, chosen by her mother for her sister's wedding, nor the shoes her husband picked out because he liked the high heels (never mind that they pinched her toes unmercifully). Certainly not the foul feathered hat. It looks like a pheasant died on my head. I snatch it off, and send it spinning across the unmade bed.

But the necklace? Yes. She'd wear the sea-glass and platinum necklace. She'd appreciate the irony: broken pieces of glass no one wanted, reclaimed from the sea, placed in an expensive setting and passed off as a work of art.

Well, never mind what Beth-the-Artist would choose, I think crossly as I shoulder my ugly old handbag and double lock the front door. It's this suit or my usual uniform of baggy T-shirt and supermarket jeans.

By the time I emerge from Green Park tube station ninety minutes later, I remember why I pensioned off the outfit after one wearing. The cheap skirt rides up over my flabby tummy, while the sloppy jacket constantly slides off one shoulder or the other. And it *itches*.

A splatter of rain hits my face. I glance up and another

fat raindrop slugs me in the eye. Oh, dear, that's all I need. I'm going to look like a bedraggled tropical parakeet by the time I get to—

Suddenly, I'm careening into the newspaper stand. Dozens of glossy magazines slide on to the wet pavement as I tumble across the plywood counter. Flushing scarlet, I apologize profusely to the startled vendor, wondering what on earth I tripped over.

Then I try to take a step, and realize: my heel has snapped.

No need to panic. I don't have to be at Cork Street for an hour – thank heavens I allowed myself plenty of time. Shoes. Shoes. Where to buy a new pair of—

William's flat! Bayswater is less than five minutes away by cab; I've left several pairs there from trips to the theatre and whatnot. Silly to buy new if I don't have to. The black courts will be perfect, and a lot more comfy too, which is what really matters. I've never understood the way some women get obsessed with what they put on their feet. Long as they get me from A to B with a minimum of blisters.

First, though, I call ahead on my mobile. I've learned the hard way: surprises aren't good for any marriage.

But the answer-machine picks up, which means William's at work; I leave a message, just in case, and jump into a taxi. The black flatties are exactly where I thought they'd be, and my feet thank me for them as I plonk on the sofa and slip them on.

I check my reflection in the mirror. A bit crumpled, but that just adds to the artist thing, doesn't it? Five-past three. My meeting with Eithne and the gallery owners isn't till three-thirty. It's only round the corner. Lots of time.

Goodness, I'm nervous. Eithne said they liked the canvases she took up to London, but liking isn't loving. Liking isn't agreeing to finance and organize a show. I know an artist has to be commercial these days. Marketable. I'm not a glamorous rebel like Eithne, all piercings and pink hair and headlining attitude. I'm just a fat, middle-aged housewife, more suburban than urban rebel. If you ran me over in the street, you probably wouldn't notice.

Sighing, I pick up my keys, open the front door and let out a blood-curdling scream when I see Dan standing there.

'It's all right,' I tell the young lady who's very kindly (and rather bravely) run out from the flat next door to see who's being murdered, 'I know him. I didn't mean to cause a panic; he made me jump, that's all.'

'Someone was leaving the building as I arrived,' Dan apologizes. 'They let me in, so I didn't buzz up first.'

He saunters past me into the flat before I have a chance to gather my addled wits. I can understand what my daughter sees in him. He really *is* dishy: his eyes have that lovely blue David Essex twinkle, I remember I had *such* a crush on him when I was Cate's age – David Essex, obviously, not Dan—

'Cate's not here,' I blurt.

'I know that,' Dan says. 'I came to see you.'

My heart beats faster. It's just the fright.

'How did you know where I was?'

'I – followed you,' he admits.

'You *followed* me?'

'I thought I was going to lose you when you hopped in that cab,' he adds unrepentantly. 'And I do mean hopped. What happened to your shoe?'

'Never mind my shoe! Why are you following me?'

'I've told you. I wanted to see you.'

'You can't.'

'And yet here I am.'

He folds his arms and watches me put on the kettle and hunt about for teabags and sugar (tea: first refuge of the discombobulated). He smells of smoke and trouble. I try not to think about how good his kiss tasted last Saturday: cool and sweet like home-made lemonade. I'm not manic at the moment; I'm very definitely in my right mind. There'll be no stripping off and streaking down Marble Arch this afternoon. Absolutely no kissing of daughters' boyfriends, no matter how close they stand or how delicious they smell, even if they run their fingers down my spine in a way that makes my insides turn to liquid and my heart beat faster than a – a – than a—

'Dan, stop,' I gasp.

It's so long since anyone just *touched* me. The children all think they're too old, even Sam, you know how they get once they go to school; and when William and I stopped having sex, the cuddles and hugs stopped too. I can't remember the last time he even held my hand.

Dan's lips feather the nape of my neck. 'Don't you like it?'

'No – yes – that's not the point!'

His erection presses the small of my back. An answering pulse beats unexpectedly between my legs. The long-forgotten sensation makes me giddy, and without really knowing what I'm doing, I'm spinning willingly in his arms, pulling him closer, fitting my body to his. His mouth meets mine, his kiss ripping along my nerve endings, jolting my body awake.

It takes every ounce of willpower to break away.

I clutch the sink. This is insane. It can't happen. We can't possibly do this. He's half my age. I'm married. He's my daughter's boyfriend—

'Oh, my God! Cate!'

'This has nothing to do with her. I'm very fond of her, of course, but it's always been about you, Beth, from the first moment at Eithne Brompton's show, I should never have—'

'No! Outside! It's Cate!'

'*What*?'

'Look! I'd know that silly backpack anywhere. She must be coming here! Oh, God, she mustn't find us together! Go, go!'

'I can't. She'll see me.'

'You'll have to hide! Quick, the bedroom!'

'Beth, this is ridiculous—'

'You followed me here, Dan! How do you plan to explain that? Or do you want to tell her we'd arranged a secret rendezvous?'

I fling open the bedroom wardrobe. It's crammed not just with clothes, but with boxes of files and papers, the work William brings home. I panic. Cate hasn't spoken to me all week (and now that the mania has passed, how can I blame her? If my mother had done that to me, I'd never forgive her either).

If she finds me here with her boyfriend, she'll never speak to me again, no matter how innocent the explanation. Although frankly I'm hard pushed even to think of one that doesn't sound very damning indeed.

'Under the bed!' I cry, shoving Dan's head down.

Still protesting, he nevertheless slides beneath the bed.

I thank God we have an old-fashioned brass bed in the Bayswater flat, rather than an expensive modern divan like we have at home. You couldn't hide a piece of paper under that, never mind a young man in a, well, rather *obvious* state of arousal.

Keys rattle in the front door. Dan sticks his head back out. 'Beth, I really don't—'

I throw myself flat on my stomach, wriggle under the bed and clamp my hand over his mouth.

Cate's voice echoes down the hall. 'Hi, it's only me.'

I feel sick. It's too late. She's seen us. Oh, how am I ever going to—

Dan shakes his head, and prises my fingers loose. 'Phone,' he mouths.

He's right. I squirm further under the bed, out of sight.

'Well, I did it, Fleur, I went to see her – no, for real, I swear—'

Dan smooths his hand along my hip, snaking beneath my blouse. At a time like this!

' – you'll never *believe* what happened,' Cate says. 'It was total drama! I'm in the middle of telling her – oh, really nice, actually, and she was wearing these really cute boots, all swirly orangey purply colours – anyway, so we're talking, and suddenly she goes all weird and—'

I hear her moving about the flat. What on earth is she doing here, anyway? I didn't even know she had a key to the apartment.

Dan nudges me. I twist round, and he dangles a lacy black basque an inch or two above my face with a grin.

'It's not mine!' I hiss indignantly.

He puts a finger to his lips, as Cate's chatter stills.

'Hang on,' she says, 'thought I heard something.'

I daren't breathe. Through the gap between the edge of the coverlet and the floor, I see her silver trainers return to the bedroom. Oh, God, if she finds us now – I shouldn't have panicked, after all, there is a perfectly innocent – well, not innocent exactly, but nothing *happened*—

'No, must have been next door. Look, I'd better get going. I only came here to nick some cash from Dad's desk, he'll never miss it. I'm supposed to meet Dan at the Tate in an hour—'

Dust is getting up my nose, and I suddenly feel the urge to sneeze. I cover my face with my hands, as Dan shakes with suppressed laughter. How can he find this funny? Doesn't he care about Cate at all?

In a sudden moment of clarity, I realize that whatever *Graduate*-style nonsense is going on between us, I'm no Mrs Robinson. No matter how much I'm attracted to Dan, even if I could bring myself to betray William, I could never hurt my daughter.

' – I haven't asked her yet. She'll only say no, like she always does. I hate her, Fleur. She's such a hypocrite. She bangs on about what's good for me, she's only thinking of me, blah blah blah, then she goes out and, like, ruins my entire life. I can't wait to get away from her—'

The front door slams. Dan prods me, but I don't move.

You don't expect gratitude from teenagers. They're supposed to hate you; if they don't, you're not doing your job.

How much easier it would be to be a bad parent and say yes. Yes, you can pierce your navel, have a cigarette, stay out till two a.m. on a school night, sleep with your boyfriend at fifteen. But you say no, and deal with the tantrums and 'I hate you!' because you love them and want to protect them. You want to save them from the mistakes you made.

Of course I haven't always got it right. Children don't come with instructions. You muddle your way through in a mixture of trial and error. All right, lots of error, in my case. But I always thought, until now, I was doing all right. I made their packed lunches and ironed their school uniforms and read them stories and stayed up all night when they had earache. I took them to ballet and football, cooked nourishing meals and picked up wet towels. I've never been a jam-tarts-and-finger-painting kind of mother, but I've always been there when they got home from school, and I never missed a sports day or school play, even when I wanted to curl up in a ball under the duvet and never come out.

The irony is, before I actually had babies, I wanted to be a mother *so* much. No one ever tells you how dull and repetitive it is (although to be fair to Clara, she did try. I just thought she meant mothering *me*). But I did everything I was supposed to. I did the best I could.

To learn from my own daughter that I've comprehensively failed in the most important job of my life is almost too painful to bear.

'Come on, Beth. She's gone.'

I crawl out from under the bed, brushing dust from my clothes. Dan looks shame-facedly pleased with himself, a little boy nearly caught scrumping. I'm horribly ashamed of the whole farcical episode.

'So,' he smiles, twirling the corset around one finger, 'want to tell me about this?'

'I told you, it's not mine—'

We both suddenly realize what that means. I snatch it away from him and shove it out of sight down the side of the sofa.

Set against the conversation I've just overheard, the fact that I have cast-iron proof of my husband's affair seems almost irrelevant.

'I'm sorry, Eithne,' I say, 'please don't shout at me any more. I didn't mean to let you down. I wanted to be there. I did *try*. I know you went to a lot of trouble to arrange it for me, and it was terribly sweet of you, but I think we both know I'm not really cut out to be an artist. I never have been. I've got a little bit of a knack with a paintbrush sometimes, but that's all it is. Clara's right, I was getting above myself, thinking I could have a show and actually sell my paintings. I'm just a housewife, at the end of the day. This isn't one of those lovely Cinderella films where the dull little mouse suddenly turns out to be an amazingly talented genius and gets discovered. This is real life, and the truth is, I'm not a star, and never will be. It was silly to think I could be anything else. I *am* sorry, Eithne. Now can we please forget all about shows and paintings and just be friends?'

There's nothing very unusual about William not coming home all night. He often stays in London when he has to entertain clients in the evening, and I know he's very keen to get that young lad from the boy band signed to Ashfield PR.

But this time, it's different. This time, I know he's not

with his lawyer, or some teen pop star, but the owner of that very glamorous black corset.

I stare at the ceiling. It's one thing to suppose, in theory, that your husband may have had the odd fling here and there. After all, eight years is a long time to expect a normal red-blooded man to go without sex. There must have been – perhaps on trips abroad – and of course there was that upsetting business in Cyprus, though I never had any actual *proof*—

There was that pretty English teacher, who seemed strangely keen to discuss Ben's progress at school in her own time. And I've always wondered about that striking Titian-haired doctor who helped look after Sam when he was little. William talked about her endlessly, and then very suddenly never mentioned her again. There were others before that: secretaries, PAs, assistants who came and went over the years. All rather lovely girls, who looked at William adoringly and blushed whenever he walked past and then, after a while, abruptly left without working their notice. Little Carolyn worships the ground he walks on. It'd be impossible not to suspect that there must have been, at times, something with one or two of them.

But knowing is very different from suspecting. Knowing keeps you up all night, and leaves you no place to hide.

'You've only yourself to blame,' Clara says sharply, when she turns up (uninvited) for breakfast the next morning and prises it out of me. 'You've driven him to it with your selfishness and moods. Why the poor man stays with you I have no idea. The fellow's a saint.'

I put the kettle on the hotplate.

'Of course, he'd never have married you in the first place if you hadn't got yourself caught. You're lucky he's not a bolter. Not like your father. When I think of what I put up with from that man, and look how he repaid me.'

'Toast?'

'You're just like him, you know. Weak. I could tell as soon as you were born. You were a difficult, fretful baby. The doctors said it was just colic, but I knew.'

'There's some home-made marmalade from the tea shop in town,' I say brightly, 'so much better than the supermarket stuff. Lovely big pieces of peel.'

'I hope you're taking your pills, Beth. Poor Cate. She'll never forgive you, you know.'

Carefully, I put down the breadknife.

Then I go outside, walk quietly to the orchard at the end of the garden, and smash flowerpots against the low stone wall until I no longer want to murder my mother.

When I've finished, I sweep up the broken shards and spilled potting soil, wrap them in old newspaper and put them neatly in the dustbin. I don't need my mother to remind me how lucky I am to have William. Infidelity is no reason to end a marriage. Sex isn't love.

As long as he doesn't actually *leave*. I couldn't let that happen.

I'm not quite the pushover everyone thinks. I can fight for what I want, in my own way. I got William, didn't I? Any niggling doubt I might have felt about that was wiped out the instant Ben was placed in his arms and I saw the love light up his face. I knew then I'd been right: we were meant to be a family.

I'm not so proud of what I did when he was in Cyprus. But I had no choice. I thought he was going to run out on me – silly, really. Still. It all worked out in the end.

The thing is, I know William better than anyone. I know he needs me just as much as I need him.

When he finally comes home a little before six in the evening, I can tell immediately from the careful way he shuts the front door that he's in a towering rage. No one knows his moods like I do.

He storms into the kitchen and flings something on the table.

'You know what this is?' he demands.

Fortunately, he doesn't wait for me to answer. 'D'you want to know where I found it?'

I suck air.

'Down the side of the sofa in London!'

He waits, clearly expecting something more than gawping astonishment from me. But until ten seconds ago, I thought the undergarment in question belonged to his mistress. If *he's* asking *me*—

'Whose is it?' I gasp.

He looks at me as if I'm an imbecile. 'Cate's, obviously!'

Cate's? Cate's! Oh, why didn't I think of that?

'You know what this means?' he rants. 'Our daughter is running off up to London and having sex with that bloody gypsy in my bed!'

Cate's!

Cate and Dan.

I'm not jealous. Just concerned, as any mother would be.

'*Our* bed, surely, William?' I ask mildly. 'And they all have rather long hair these days, dear, it doesn't necessarily make him a gypsy—'

'Our daughter's been sneaking off behind our backs, dressing up like a hooker to indulge that hippy's perverted fantasies, and all you can talk about is his *hair*?'

I wonder curiously if he'll actually froth at the mouth.

'She's seventeen, Beth. Seventeen!'

'Yes, darling, I know, I was there the night she was born—'

'Who knows what else he's dragging her into – drink, drugs – she'll end up with a criminal record! That'll put paid to Oxford – she'd have made a wonderful doctor – before we know it, she'll be pregnant, stuck on her own in some appalling council flat with kids leaving syringes on the stairs and dealing drugs – that boy's not going to stay around, you can see it in his eyes, shifty, I've thought that from the moment I first—'

'William,' I say firmly, 'please stop pacing. I'll speak to her. Well,' I amend, 'once she starts talking to me again, obviously.'

William growls and retreats to his den. I lift the saucepan off the hotplate, add a knob of butter and mash potatoes for the shepherd's pie.

As a mother, I expected to feel many things when I discovered my daughter had started having sex; but relief wasn't one of them.

'Of course it's not mine,' Cate snaps, when I finally dredge up courage and corner her a few days later.

'Are you quite sure, darling?'

'Get real. Like I'd wear anything that sad.'

'So you haven't been to the Bayswater flat recently?'

Her eyes slide away. 'I told you, not for months.'

Now I know she's lying.

'Cate,' I venture, 'you and Dan, you will be careful, won't you? I'd hate to see you—'

'What? Trapped like you were?'

She doesn't mean it. She's a teenager. She doesn't realize how much it hurts.

'Miss out on chances you could have had,' I say calmly.

Her pretty face twists. 'I'm so sorry to have been such an inconvenience, *Mother*. If I'd known I was depriving the world of the next Picasso, I'd have taken care not to have been born.'

'Cate—'

'Give it up, Mum. We all know how much you wish you'd never had us. Well, don't worry, there's only me left at home now, you've managed to get rid of Sam and Ben. I'll be out of your way soon. Then you'll have Dad all to yourself, just like you've always wanted.'

'That's not—'

'You know, if that corset isn't mine and it's not yours, whose can it be, I wonder?'

I realize with shock that she *wants* me to think it belongs to another woman. She's enjoying this. Does she really hate me that much?

'Caitlin, I've never wished I hadn't had you for a second,' I say with sudden passion. I grip her fiercely by the shoulders. 'I *love* you and your brothers. You've brought more happiness into my life than you can possibly know. Motherhood is much harder than you expect, but I wouldn't undo a second of it. I just wish I'd had a bit more time to find out who *I* was before I took on responsibility for someone else, that's all.'

Cate trembles. With anger, misery or impatience, I don't know.

I let her go, and she immediately puts the width of the

kitchen between us. Much as I want to, I resist the urge to chase after her and hug her like I used to when she was small.

'Cate, you've got your whole life ahead of you,' I say. 'The world's your oyster. Don't be in such a rush. Do all the things I never had time to do,' I add, trying not to sound bitter. 'Follow your dreams. Be a journalist if you want to. Win that Pulitzer – oh, Cate, I'm not blind. I know how much it means to you to go to NYU. If that's what you really want, I'll support you. It's your father you have to convince, not me. But don't think I won't worry about you and miss you every second you're away, because I will.'

Confusion and yearning chase across her pale features. For a second, I almost think I've reached her.

Then the phone rings, and the moment is broken.

'Cate, darling, wait, please wait—'

The door slams. I want to go after her, but realize I'll only chase her further away. She has to come to me.

Miserably, I pick up the phone.

'Beth, it's Anne.'

Oh, Lord. The last person I want to talk to now is William's mother. I never know what to say to her. Her son's refused to speak to her for twenty years; against his wishes, I've maintained sporadic contact, mainly for the sake of the children, but also for Anne, as one mother to another. I just have to think how I'd feel if Ben or Sam were to cut me out of their lives.

Or Cate, of course.

I try to sound welcoming. 'Anne, how are you?'

'Not that good, actually, Beth,' she says briskly. 'I've just come from the doctor.'

'Oh dear, poor you. Is everything OK?'

'Actually,' she says, 'that's what I wanted to talk to you about.'

Fortunately, given the appalling way I let her down last week, Eithne doesn't stay angry with me for long – 'It's lucky I love you,' she sighs, 'or I wouldn't tell you about the three red SOLD stickers currently adorning your paintings; oh, calm down, Beth, I *told* you they were good' – and it's she who gets me to see the funny side of the fiasco with Dan.

'Why *wouldn't* he fancy you?' she demands, tilting her head (green this week, in honour of St Patrick's Day) to one side in that way she has. 'You're the experienced, exciting older woman Cate will grow into one day. No wonder he's smitten. And before you ask, he's the spitting image of William twenty years ago, which explains *your* damp knickers.'

She makes it sound so safe; so *normal.* I cheer up immensely. Every foolish, ever-so-slightly-lovestruck middle-aged woman should have a friend like Eithne.

So when Dan rings my mobile and begs me to model for our life class this evening – 'Please, Beth, it's for my teaching credits, my usual girl ran away with a trapeze artist, no, don't laugh, please, it's *true*' – well, how can I refuse? Frankly, after that depressing conversation with William's mother, I could do with letting my hair down. And if there's a little guilty *frisson*, well, where's the harm? It's not like I'd ever *do* anything.

I go home to change. Well, not quite change – after all,

it's not like I'm going to be wearing clothes – but *tidy up*. Exactly.

I burst into the kitchen feeling rather giddy and light-headed.

'Oh! William! You're home already.' I blush to the roots of my hair. 'I'm not stopping, just needed to get a few bits, then I'm going back for the life class – I did tell you I'd be out tonight, didn't I?'

He gives his steak a grumpy bash with the hammer.

'You don't mind, do you, darling?' I venture. 'I don't have to go, of course, but they don't like us to miss classes and I did promise—'

'Of course I don't mind. I told you, I think it's good for you to get out a bit.' He shoots me a suspicious look. 'You are taking your pills, aren't you, Beth? We don't want another repeat of—'

'Yes, yes, all right,' I say crossly.

I fidget, screwing up my courage to tell him about Anne. Got to tell him, got to, got to. Can't leave it any longer. Maybe, I think in burst of wild optimism, he'll even be pleased, once he's got over the surprise.

The words come out in a rush. 'William, I invited your mother down for lunch on Sunday.'

The blood drains from his face.

Oh, God. Oh, God, this is going to be even worse than I thought.

I gabble nervously. 'It's Easter Sunday, William, and she's eighty on Tuesday. You can't let this silly row go on for ever. I mean, twenty *years*. I thought now was as good a time as any to let bygones be bygones, and since Ben and Sam will be home tomorrow too—'

'You – did – *what*?'

' – and I knew you'd just say no if I asked. Come on, darling. I know you don't get on with her, but my mother isn't all sweetness and light either, and I manage to—'

He looks like he wants to brain me with the tenderizer. 'It's hardly the same thing!'

'Yes, but I understand how you—'

'Your mother didn't kill your father!'

Why is he so pig-headed? I appreciate that he needs to blame someone, but the only person responsible for his father's suicide is his father. No one drives another person to suicide. They choose it despite – to spite – you. I know that better than anyone.

'Nor did yours, William.'

'You weren't there.'

He wasn't there either: a child never knows the reality of its parents' marriage. But of course I can't say that to him. I wouldn't dare.

'She's your mother, William,' I say faintly.

'Cancel.'

There are times I almost hate my husband. 'I can't, it'd be too—'

'I said, *cancel*.'

'Please, William. If something happens to her and you still haven't—'

'Aren't you going to be late for your class?' he snaps.

She has leukaemia! I want to cry. She won't reach her eighty-first birthday and if you don't make it up with her, you'll feel even worse about her than you do about your father!

But I know this isn't a battle I'm going to win. I hoist

my bag on to my shoulder, and quietly let myself back into the night.

'Is it warm enough in here?' Dan asks.

I nod nervously, still strung out by my row with William.

The six students sitting in a semicircle around me are suddenly very busy with their paper and pencils.

Dan hands me a long red silk robe. 'You might want to put this on for now. Easier to slip it off when you're ready.'

I shut myself in the tiny bathroom to change. Oh, Lord. *Why* did I agree to this?

Get a grip, Beth. This is ridiculous. You stripped off happily in front of a thousand people the other weekend. Bit late to come over all shy.

Quickly, before I lose all confidence, I whip off my clothes and fold them into a small, neat pile on the loo, tucking my greying granny knickers out of sight beneath my jeans. Maybe if I pose carefully I can hide the floppiest bits of my tummy. Sort of lose them beneath the chenille throw on the chaise longue. I could squinch my bosoms together with my arms so they don't splay sideways like two fried eggs. And if I tilt my head back, that'll get rid of the double chin—

Oh, for heaven's sake. I'm forty-one, and the mother of three children. Short of turning out all the lights and blindfolding the students, I can't hide it.

I put on the silk robe and mentally gird my (rather cellulity) loins. I don't care what Dan thinks. It's not like he hasn't seen it all before.

I settle myself on the chaise longue in the centre of the

room. At least we're in Dan's private studio, not the huge one at the school. Though I do wish it wasn't *quite* so bright and revealing in here—

'Are you ready, Beth? Can I get you anything?'

I gulp and shake my head.

'OK. Whenever you're ready.'

I untie the belt of my robe, and let it fall from my shoulders. There are no indrawn gasps of horror. No one runs screaming from the room. Six pencils scratch at six easels, and I slowly start to relax. This isn't going to be so bad. It's only one class. I can do this.

'Feel free to chat, everyone,' Dan says, moving between the students. He puts on some music; I recognize it as Davy Kirkland from Cate's endless playing. 'Let's keep this nice and relaxed. Beth, how's your painting coming along? Finished that triptych yet?'

'Last panel's almost done,' I say, pathetically grateful for the distraction.

'Can't wait to see it. Did you try out that ochre pigment I told you about?'

We discuss light, and fresco techniques, and then the conversation moves on to more general topics: books we've read, films we've seen, the new logo he's designed for William's firm. Before I know it, the hour's flown past and Dan's telling the students to put their pencils down. 'You can get dressed, Beth,' he says absently, leaning over a student's shoulder to study his work. 'Make yourself a cup of tea next door if you want. I won't be long.'

I get up and knot my robe, wincing at the pins and needles in my legs. I could do with something hot to drink, actually. I'm rather chilled from sitting still so long without moving.

As I let myself into his flat, my silk belt catches on the door. Twisting round, I try to free it, but succeed only in tangling it further.

'You'll have to step out of it,' Dan calls, 'the fabric's hooked on the hinge.'

Flushing, I shrug out of the robe. Dan frees the snagged belt, then holds it up for me to slip on. His hands linger a fraction too long on my shoulders. My nipples harden automatically. It would be so easy to turn and fold myself in his arms, to give myself up to this – so easy—

But wrong.

I pull away, wrapping the dressing-gown tightly around my body. 'Dan, what are you doing?'

'Yes, Dan,' says my daughter from the doorway, 'what *are* you doing?'

8

Cate

'Mum? I'm going to sleep with Dan tonight – well, lose my virginity actually – and I was wondering if we could talk about it? Like, if you've got any advice or anything? Only I'm a bit nervous, so . . .'

Yeah, right. Not the kind of thing you can say to your mother, is it?

Not that mine's the type you can say anything to; at least, not if you want a clued-up response. We hardly have this great mother–daughter thing going on.

Clem's always complaining that her parents interfere in her life, but at least they *care*. At least they're involved. I'm not sure mine notice I'm there half the time. And when they do, they act like I'm still six years old. Well, Dad does. He thinks he's so on top of things, with his stupid 'Bed at ten on a week night, young lady,' but he's got no idea what's really going on in my life.

At least Mum sort of gets it. Yesterday was cool, actually. I think it's the first time she's ever taken my side against Dad. Maybe, if she talks to him about going to New York, he might come round.

Mind you, that whole thing with the corset. Like, what was *that* about?

Weird. Fleur reckons Mum's having this secret lesbian fling with Eithne, and asking me about the corset was a major double-bluff to throw Dad off the scent. That girl has *way* too much time on her hands.

Fleur did It the first time when she was fifteen. She's been telling me to get on with it for ages, and she's right, there's not really much point waiting any longer. I mean, Dan and I have been together ages; God, it's nearly four months now. OK, I don't love him, we're not talking marriage and babies, but he's fun and everything. At least I'll finally understand what everyone's talking about—

Suddenly there's a hammering at the door. 'Cate! Phone!'

I ignore him. It's probably Clem, she's been freaking out about the Chaucer essay—

'Cate! It's Paris! Are you coming out to take it or shall I—'

I quickly flip the duvet over the shiny Debenhams bag on my bed, and open the door. 'There's no need to shout.'

I wait for Dad to go away. I'm not discussing my sex life in front of him, if that's what he's thinking.

He sighs. 'Send Fleur's parents my best.'

Whatever. I kick the door shut and curl up on my bed with the phone. Must remember to paint my toenails, can't have sex for the first time with them all chipped, Dan'd think I'm a total slut. Clem's got this really cool purple from Hard Candy. I'm sure she'll let me borrow it.

Oh, God. This time tomorrow, I will no longer be *virgo intacta*.

'*Enfin!*' Fleur exclaims in my ear. 'I got your email! What are you going to wear? Where will you do it? Did you buy condoms?'

'Fleur!'

'What? You 'ave to think of these things. He's a man. It's not his problem.'

I jam the phone between shoulder and ear and take off my old toenail polish. 'Well, to be fair, I haven't actually told him yet. I thought I'd, like, go round after his stupid art class and surprise him—'

'*C'est parfait!* You 'ave to wear a trenchcoat, like Ingrid Bergman in *Casablanca*. But nothing underneath. Just sexy underwear.'

'Fleur, I can't go wandering around town in my knickers. I'll get arrested.'

'No one will see. It will be perfect! Very *film noir!* You arrive at his 'ouse. He will be surprised to see you. You will say nothing. You smile, and look mysterious. Then you undo the belt, you slide the coat from your shoulders – *merde*, it will be so sexy, just like a movie!'

I giggle. 'I don't have a trenchcoat.'

'Your mother must 'ave one. Did you get stockings?'

'Yes,' I say, putting down the nail-polish remover and pulling the bag out from beneath my duvet. A tremor of nervous excitement ripples through me. 'I went shopping this afternoon after school. And I got this really gorgeous body lotion too, it smells like chocolate oranges.' I hesitate, stroking the silky French knickers on my knee. It took me ages to decide what colour to buy; black seemed too obvious, red too tacky. In the end I went for a delicate coffee-coloured silk edged with antique cream lace. 'Fleur,' I say uncertainly. 'You know all those stories you hear, about the first time. The – the blood and everything. Does it really hurt a lot?'

'A little,' Fleur admits. 'But not for long. Don't worry, *chérie*. You just have to relax, and it will be fine.'

Relax. Yes. I can do that.

As if.

I push open the gate to Dan's semi, then hesitate. No going back after this.

I check my watch. I'm way earlier than I'd planned, thanks to that screaming match with Dad. Dan will still be teaching. But I couldn't stay at home another minute. Dad'll have me in a chastity belt next. Honestly, he treats me like a stupid kid sometimes. I'm nearly eighteen. When's he going to *get* it?

An old guy walking his dog throws me a dirty look as he goes past. Nervously, I retie Mum's black trenchcoat a bit tighter. (I can't believe all the cool stuff she has at the back of her wardrobe. It's, like, totally vintage. Sometimes I forget she went to art college.) It's OK for Fleur, going on about Ingrid Thingy and *Casablanca*. Now I'm actually here, I feel a bit gay. These stockings are really uncomfortable, for a start. I can totally see why they invented tights. Why do men find all this stuff sexy? I don't get it—

Shit, I hope he *does* find it sexy. Supposing he laughs?

No, Fleur knows what she's talking about. She's French. Everyone knows they're the chicest, coolest women in the world.

After a quick check to make sure no one's watching,

I slip down the side alley. I'll just let myself in through the back – he never locks the kitchen door – and wait in the sitting-room for him to finish teaching. I can sit on the sofa with my legs crossed, and kind of dangle my heel like they do in the movies. I wish I smoked. It's disgusting and makes me feel really sick, but it looks *so* cool.

It takes me a moment or two to understand what I'm seeing.

My boyfriend has his arms wrapped round my mother, and he's helping her take off this slutty red dressing-gown, and underneath she's naked, and his hands are all over her, and she's enjoying it, I can see it in her face, she's pink and sort of sighing and he's panting and I hate her, I hate her, how *could* they—

'Dan,' my mother moans, 'what are you doing?'

I bite down on my lip until I taste blood, and my legs stop shaking.

'Yes, Dan,' I say coolly, 'what *are* you doing?'

The look on their faces: it'd be funny if it wasn't so sad.

'Cate!' my mother cries, clutching at her robe. 'This isn't – I was modelling – Dan's life class—'

'I bet this looks really weird,' Dan says, giving me his best cute smile. 'I can imagine what you must be thinking—'

' – the class just finished – I was getting dressed—'

'Your mum did a great job, Cate. Everyone really enjoyed working with her. You should come through and see what they—'

'Get off me!' I scream. 'Don't you dare touch me!'

He backs away, hands raised. 'C'mon, Cate. You can't seriously—'

'How could you! With her! She's so – so *old*! It's disgusting!' I whirl round to my mother 'And what about Dad? How could you do that to him? How could you do it to *me*?'

'I didn't – Cate, nothing happened! I promise!'

'He's my boyfriend! He's young enough to be your son! How *could* you?'

She starts to cry. Watching her, my own throat aches with misery.

'Why do you have to ruin everything for me? Why can't you just let me be happy?' I yell. 'I trusted you! All that stuff yesterday about not wasting my chances and helping me to go to New York! You don't really want me to have a life! You want me to end up as sad and lonely and pathetic as you are!'

'Of course I don't! I love you, Cate, you know that—'

I shake her off. She collapses on to the sofa, rubbing the back of her hand across her runny nose like a child. Her face is red and blotchy. She looks ugly. Old.

'You don't,' I say bitterly. 'You never have. You spoil *every*thing.'

'Cate,' Dan says, 'why don't we all just calm down and—'

'You're just a mean, wicked, jealous old woman. I wish you *had* died when Dad was in Cyprus. I wish I'd never come back and found you.'

She blanches. 'You don't mean that.'

'You *are* dead, as far as I'm concerned. I never want to speak to you again!'

Then I turn to Dan, and slap him as hard and furiously as I can.

Outside, I run, stumbling and tripping in the dumb heels. I take my shoes off, tearing through the empty streets in my stockinged feet, not caring how much it hurts. My chest heaves painfully, but I don't stop running. Everything feels strange and unreal, as if I'm moving under water. My whole life is disintegrating. It's all a lie. Nothing is real. Everyone is busy lying and cheating and no one cares what happens to me. No one would even notice if I was gone.

I want things to go back to the way they were. I want not to know all this grown-up stuff. I'm sick of protecting them. I want them to protect *me*.

Slamming into the kitchen, I catch sight of the corset, still lying on the kitchen table where Mum left it after our fight last night. My head explodes with rage. I pick it up and hurl it across the room, where it slaps against the dresser so hard the cups rattle.

I jump as my brother wanders in from the den, munching from a handful of tortilla chips cupped in his palm.

'Cool,' Ben says, picking up the corset, 'Candida was wondering where she'd left that. I thought it was at Dad's flat.'

I gape disbelievingly at him, and laugh. Suddenly, I can't stop.

'By the way,' Ben adds, spraying a fine mist of chips across his T-shirt, 'like the get-up, sis. You look like Ingrid Bergman in *Casablanca*. Way to go.'

I stay in the shower, tears mingling with the water, till it runs cold and I can't cry any more. Cleansing off the remains of my ruined make-up, I pull on a pair of cosy pink-flannel PJs, and scrape my wet hair back into a ponytail. The stockings and underwear, even the trenchcoat, I shove into the bin.

Downstairs, I knock on Dad's study. 'You busy?'

'Nothing that won't wait,' he sighs. 'Come on in, Cate. I could do with the distraction.'

Cannelle follows me into the room. I kneel and bury my face in his gold coat, as he closes his eyes and rumbles with pleasure. I'll miss him more than anyone. 'He's more like a cat than a dog,' I say. 'Listen to him. He's almost purring.'

Dad snaps his laptop shut. 'Is everything all right, Cate? I thought you were going over to Dan's this evening?'

'Didn't feel like it.'

'You're not still upset about the New York business, are you? I'm sorry, Cate, but—'

'Forget it, Dad.'

'Worried about your exams?'

'Bit.'

I pick up the bronze Buddha on the bookshelf, absently rubbing his fat tummy for luck. Dad brought him back from Tibet when I was four; over the years, I've worn a little shiny spot on his stomach. 'What were you and Mum arguing about last night?'

He doesn't answer for a moment, busying himself with the files and papers on his desk. He looks really tired: there are huge black bags under his eyes, and he's lost tons of weight. It's as if Superman suddenly turned mortal. It's kind of scary to see him like this. Who's going to take care of things, if he can't?

He summons a smile. 'Nothing that need worry you, Kit-Cat.'

'Dad—'

'It wasn't what you think. We were discussing Granny Anne.'

I chew my thumb. 'You and Mum – are you . . .'

'We're fine. Everything's fine. Now, Cate, if there's nothing else, I really need to get on.'

'I was wondering,' I blurt, 'if I could go to Fleur's? Just for a week or so. I wouldn't need to miss school. We're on study leave soon, and—'

He stops sorting papers. 'Out of the question.'

'But Dad—'

'Cate, be reasonable. You can't just skip school in the middle of term. Your exams are coming up soon, and you said it yourself, you need to get started on sorting out your university applications.'

'What's the point?' I mutter. 'You won't let me apply where I want to go.'

'There are plenty of excellent places here, we've been through this. First New York, now Paris: I really don't understand this sudden obsession with fleeing the country.' He checks his BlackBerry. 'Unless there's something wrong, Cate?'

I want to tell him. I really do. But I don't know where to start.

'You can trust me, darling,' he says, scrolling through his emails. 'I'm always here for you.'

'I thought you were going to New York on Friday?'

'Well, yes. But I'm here now. Come on, darling.' He finally puts his BlackBerry down and holds out his arms. 'What's on your mind?'

After a brief hesitation, I snuggle on to his lap. I'm safe here; suddenly none of that other stuff matters. It's like I'm four again, and Daddy can make everything better. I want it to stay this way. Why can't it stay this way?

'Hey, Kit-Cat. Are these real tears?' He tucks my head

under his chin, and rubs my back. 'Sweetheart, come on. Tell me. What is it?'

I can't stay here any more. Not with *her*.

'Take me with you to New York, Daddy,' I sniffle. 'Please?'

'You know I can't do that,' he says irritably. 'Cate, what's this about?'

If I tell him, he'll leave Mum. He'll leave, but I'll have to stay. I've got to tell him, or I'm going to burst. All these secrets are doing my head in.

I can't. I want to, but I *can't*.

'Come on, darling. Tell your old daddy.'

Maybe I should just spit it out. It would be such a relief. He'll know what to do. He'll sort it all out.

'Cate? You're starting to worry me. I'm sure it's nothing we can't – oh, shit. Oh, darling, I've got to take this call. I'm sorry, but it's really important.'

'It's OK.' I climb off his knee. 'Never mind. It didn't matter anyway.'

Fleur throws open her arms and envelops me in a gorgeous waft of jasmine and apples. '*Chérie!* It's so good to see you! But you've lost weight? A little from the chest, *merde*, but from the face, it's good. Very chic. Come, we take a taxi. Where's your luggage?'

'I only brought this.'

'One bag? We must go shopping. *Immédiatement!*' She tucks my arm through hers. 'Well, perhaps not immediately. But as soon as you are rested. Cigarette?'

I shake my head. Fleur lights up, heedless of the

DEFENSE DE FUMER signs posted around the Gare du Nord. She looks so wonderfully French.

I struggle to keep up as she skitters across the busy station concourse, marvelling at the speed she can move at in three-inch heels. Suddenly I feel a bit scruffy in my combats and silver Pumas. She looks so glam. Like, how does she get her long black hair that shiny? If I wore that shirt and pencil skirt, I'd totally look ridiculous, but she looks amazing, miles older than seventeen. And what is it about the French and scarves? She's twisted two through her belt loops, giving her classic outfit this brilliant funky edge. I'd look like a homeless squatter if I tried it.

'I love your combats,' she sighs, as we join the taxi queue. 'You look so cool.'

'Swap you,' I grimace.

She giggles. 'Why not? You give me London style, and I will teach you French chic. Fair, no?'

It's ages since I've been to Paris. Last time was about five years ago, when Dad took us all to EuroDisney for a special treat. I stick my head out of the open car window, not caring if I look like a hick from the sticks. I'd forgotten how different abroad is. All the signs are in French, for a start. PHARMACIE. BOULANGERIE. TABAC. It's so cool. The buildings are tall and elegant with their shutters and everything. It even smells different from London. And everyone looks so amazing, like they've stepped out of a magazine; even the men, with their leather satchels and purple shirts, not boring old white ones. You can tell straight away who the tourists are: the fat ones in T-shirts and trainers.

The taxi drops us off in a smart-looking part of town. Fleur drags me up some white stone steps and an actual maid opens the shiny black door when she rings, in a smart black-and-white uniform and everything.

'Papa!' Fleur yells, throwing her bag and keys on to the hall table. They slide straight on to the marble floor, but Fleur doesn't even notice. '*Cate est arrivée!*'

The maid picks up Fleur's things and holds her hand out for my giant rucksack. I feel a bit guilty, till I clock her expression. She's got the same arsey look on her face as one of those assistants in a posh shop. Skinny cow.

I trail Fleur into a huge high-ceilinged sitting room filled with museumy furniture, all spindly gold legs and teeny chair-backs. I'm scared to sit on anything in case I break it and it used to be Marie Antoinette's and is worth, like, a million pounds or something. The walls are this deep womb-red, though it's hard to see them properly because of all the gilt mirrors and paintings. It's like being on a movie set.

Her dad comes in and my stomach boomerangs all over the place. Fleur's dad is totally gorgeous: killer good looks mixed with this amazing French rumpled sexiness, all three-day-old stubble and dishevelled dark hair. He must be at least forty, but I've had the hugest crush on him for *years*.

'Cate, welcome,' he says, kissing me on both cheeks. 'Did you have a good journey?'

I nod, blushing furiously. Damn! That is *so* not cool.

'How are your parents? Would you like to telephone and let them know you arrived safely?'

'Dad flew to New York on Friday, Monsieur Lavoie,' I say quickly, hoping he doesn't ask about Mum. 'He knows where I am, though.'

Well, that's more or less true. I haven't *really* run away.

Dad'll figure out where I've gone straight away once Mum discovers I'm missing and tells him. He'll be really mad, but he's not going to interrupt his precious trip to New York just to come and get me. And Mum will be glad to see the back of me. She and Dan can have the place to themselves.

Like she's *really* gone to stay with Eithne.

Fleur's dad smiles deep into my eyes, and my palms are suddenly sweaty. 'Call me Hugo, please,' he murmurs. '"Monsieur Lavoie" makes me feel so old.'

'Hugo,' I mutter, crimson to the tips of my ears.

Fleur watches me with interest. 'You like 'im!' she giggles, once we tumble through the doorway to her bedroom.

'I do not!'

She shrugs. 'He has a mistress at the moment, so you are quite safe.' She picks up a scarlet lipstick from her vanity and holds it consideringly against my face. '*Mais non*. Too orange. She is very beautiful, his girlfriend. Very clever. My mother 'ates her, but she has a boyfriend 'erself, so she lives with it. *C'est la vie.*'

I throw myself stomach-down on the bed. 'Fleur, don't you *mind*?'

'It's better than divorce. Ah, I think this colour is better for you. I don't want to spend my time going from one 'ouse to the other. This way, they are both happy.' She laughs. 'Just not with each other.'

They certainly *seem* happy, I think, as they chat pleasantly to each other – in English, as a courtesy to me – from opposite ends of a shiny mahogany table bigger than our whole dining-room at home. I'm seated on Hugo's left, which basically means I can't eat anything, opposite me is Michel, Fleur's younger brother. He looks just like his father; in a few years he'll be totally hot, but right now he's only sixteen, still a kid.

'You don't like quails' eggs?' Hugo asks me. 'They're a little difficult to shell; let me help you.'

He reaches across and picks up one of the tiny eggs, his hand brushing mine. I jump as if I've been burned.

Fleur digs me in the ribs. 'I think she's lost her appetite,' she teases.

'You must be so tired after your journey,' says Mme Lavoie. She pins me with a glacial stare. 'Le Chunnel is an experience *terrible*.'

She's really beautiful, but her eyes are so cold. Even though she's smiling at me, I can tell she doesn't want me here. She's like the ice queen, with her white hair (very Cruella) and pale, pale skin – 'Forget St Tropez, no true Frenchwoman really likes the sun,' Fleur told me once, 'so bad for the skin, so *ageing*.'

I nod and duck my head so Mme Lavoie can't see my expression. I bet the old witch can read minds.

The maid clears our plates, then returns with the main course, a huge fish on an enormous silver plate that's almost as big as she is. It's still got the head on. It's staring at me. Oh, God, it's got *teeth*—

Don't look at it. It's just a big fish finger. With teeth and eyes.

I'm fiddling with the knives and forks on either side of my plate, wondering how to flee the table without seeming rude, when the maid comes back and whispers in Hugo's ear.

'Cate, your father is on the telephone,' he says pleasantly. 'Amélie will show you to the study, so you may take it in private.'

Shit. I didn't think he'd be this hot on my tail.

'What the hell do you think you're playing at?' my father yells as soon as I pick up the receiver.

'Dad, if you'll just let me explain—'

'For God's sake, Cate! Sneaking off to Paris without a word to anyone, not even a bloody note, your poor mother was worried sick' – frankly, I doubt that – 'on the verge of calling the police! I can't believe you'd do something this irresponsible! You can just get yourself on the next train back home, young lady, or you're going to find yourself in a world of trouble!'

'Please, Daddy, I only want to stay a few days. I promise I'll practise my French—'

'Screw your French! I want you home now!'

'Dad, I need a break!' I cry. 'I'm fed up with you and Mum arguing all the time! I can't cope with her any more!'

'You think *you've* got problems? I've got your mother on the phone in hysterics saying you've been kidnapped or murdered, while I'm in New York trying to save my company from going belly-up and throwing us all out on the streets! And you go and pull a stupid stunt like this!'

'You knew where I was,' I say sulkily.

'Luckily for you, the Lavoies are good people, but you can't just turn up unannounced on their doorstep, Caitlin! Grow up! This isn't just about you!'

'It never is, is it?'

'Don't be so damn childish! And I'd like to know where you got the money in the first – oh, Jesus.'

'What?'

'Keep still. Don't move.' His voice sounds distant, as if he's dropped the phone and is talking to someone else. 'Stay there, I'll get someone. Hold on.'

There's a scrabble as he picks up the phone again. 'Cate, I've got to go. Get yourself home. We'll talk when I get back at the end of the week.'

I'm left listening to the dial tone. I stare at the receiver in astonishment. Fuck knows what's going on his end, but whatever it is, I think it's just bought me some time.

'Cate? You didn't go out with Fleur?'

'Didn't really feel like dancing. Thought I'd get an early night.'

Hugo shuts the door of the tiny study – the only room in the house, other than the loo, that's less than a thousand miles across – and perches on the arm of the polished-conker leather sofa in front of the fire. He's wearing this thin black silk polo-neck and black jeans, and he looks *totally* fit.

'A beautiful young girl who doesn't want to go dancing? Either she is ill, or she is very sad. Which is it, *chérie*?'

He called me beautiful! 'I'm fine, honestly—'

'Cate. For three days, you don't leave the house. This is Paris! No woman comes to Paris to hide away and read books!'

'I can't really afford to go shopping—'

'Since when has that stopped a woman?' His voice softens. '*Chérie*, I don't know why you are here – *bien sûr*, perhaps you are just visiting your very dear friend Fleur, as you say?' He shrugs elegantly. 'Or perhaps there is trouble at home, something that is making you unhappy?'

I pull a cushion into my lap and pick fretfully at the fringe.

'I don't wish to poke, Cate. Your business is your business. You are welcome to stay with us as long as you like. Three days, or three months, you must stay until you feel ready to go home.'

Tears prick the back of my eyes.

Hugo sighs. *'Ma petite*, your mother telephones every day, and you don't want to speak to her. Your father doesn't call, and I think you do want to speak to him.' He leans forward and squeezes my hand. 'Sometimes, it's better to talk to someone, a friend, instead of keeping everything inside. Whatever it is, your secret will be safe with me.'

The logs in the grate snap, and I startle. Hugo unfolds gracefully and jabs them with the poker, adding more wood. It's April, but this big old house is cold, and I'm grateful for the warmth as it flares.

He opens a small drinks cabinet and pours two drinks, then hands one to me. *'Tiens.* To warm you inside, too.'

It smells disgusting, but I knock it back in one go.

'Doucement, Cate! Easy! That's Armagnac, not water!'

I cough and splutter for a good five minutes after it's burned its way down my throat. Hugo laughs, and once I finally catch my breath, I laugh too; for the first time in what seems like years.

'Here,' he says, pouring me another drink. 'Slowly, this time. Armagnac should be savoured, never rushed. Like good food. Or,' he smiles, 'a good woman.'

The two of us sit peaceably, staring into the fire. There's something very soothing about watching the flames leap and dance. The knot in my stomach slowly loosens.

I sip the drink carefully.

'Dad's having an affair,' I blurt suddenly.

Hugo nods, but says nothing.

'And I found Mum with my boyfriend – she wasn't wearing anything – they said nothing happened but I could *see* – I want to go to New York but no one will listen to me—'

'I am,' Hugo says.

For the next forty minutes, he doesn't say a word. When I start bawling, he hands me his gorgeous green silk handkerchief and lets me snivel into it. He tops up my drink, throws another log on the fire, and really seems to care how I feel. I wish Dad could be more like this. I used to think he was too busy with work, but he wasn't too busy to find time for Ella, was he?

When I finally run out of words, Hugo gives me a warm hug. I bury my head in his chest. God, he smells yummy, kind of like toffee apples—

All of a sudden, I stop feeling cosy and comforted, and begin to feel something very different. A tingle spreads to my fingers and toes. He really *is* sexy. His hand brushes the nape of my neck as he strokes my hair, and my body goes into meltdown. My heart's pounding, my hands are clammy, and there's a little fish of excitement leaping hotly in my knickers.

I tilt back my head, and kiss him.

For a moment, he kisses me back. Then he breaks away, holding me at arm's length. 'Cate, no.'

'Why not?'

'*Chérie*, this isn't the answer. You're looking for something else, not this. It would be wrong of me to take such advantage – much as I might want to,' he adds ruefully.

'Don't you like me?'

'But of course. You're a beautiful girl. Charming.' He stands and rubs his jaw, eyeing me regretfully. 'If you were a little older, a little more experienced—'

'I'm experienced enough.' I fling my arms round his neck, stumbling slightly. 'Fleur said you liked girls like me.'

He fends me off. 'Fleur has a vivid imagination. Cate, you're very tired. And perhaps the Armagnac wasn't such a good idea. I think it's time for bed—'

'That's a very good idea,' I slur.

'*Alone*, Cate.'

My eyes fill with tears. Hugo doesn't want me. Dan didn't want me. He preferred my own mother. There must be something wrong with me.

I hate myself. I hate my life. I wish I was dead.

I run out of the room, my chest heaving. I'm crying so hard, I can't see where I'm going, and run full-tilt into Fleur's brother as he comes out of the sitting-room, spilling his cup of coffee over both of us.

He puts out a hand to steady me.

And doesn't let go.

9

Ella

Hope's mother carefully lifts her tiny daughter from the incubator on to her lap, delicately mindful of the tubes and wires snaking into the fragile body. In an automatic, instinctive gesture, she drops her face into her daughter's dark hair, breathing in the scent of her child.

The baby yawns and shoots out a tiny pink fist. Anna strokes it, and the miniature fingers unfurl like sea fronds, and then curl back around Anna's finger. She glances up at me, and smiles radiantly.

I want that.

The thought – visceral and unexpected – knocks me off balance. I busy myself with the disinfectant dispenser. Hormones, that's all. I don't want children. I never have.

'Ella,' Anna says, concern shadowing her voice. 'Can you come here a minute?'

I examine the baby with my eyes. Anna's instinct is right. Something is wrong, I can sense it. Nothing obvious, but—

'Gina,' I call to the nurse on duty. 'How's she been feeding?'

'Actually, not so well today.'

'Stools?'

'Only one, early this morning.'

Gently, I palpate the baby's tummy. Abdominal distension and redness. Slightly elevated temperature. Alarm bells ring. She shouldn't have it; NEC typically occurs within the first two weeks of life, usually after we withdraw the feeding tube and milk feedings have begun, but—

'I want a CBC, full panel, CHEM-7 and X-ray of her abdomen,' I say briskly. 'Monitor for hematochezia.'

The nurse nods and takes Hope from her mother, placing her carefully back into the incubator.

'What's wrong?' Anna asks nervously.

'It may be nothing—'

'Ella, please, what is it?'

'You remember we talked about some of the challenges that face babies as little as Hope?' I say carefully. 'One of those challenges is a gastrointestinal disease called necrotizing enterocolitis, or NEC—'

Her eyes widen. 'The flesh-eating bug? Oh, God, she's going to die, isn't she? That's what you're telling me—'

'Anna, calm down. That's *not* what I'm telling you. You're thinking of something called necrotizing fasciitis, which is quite different. Forget what you read in the newspapers. NEC involves infection and inflammation of the bowel, and although it's serious, it's also quite common with babies this small.'

'Will she be all right?'

'We don't even know if she has it yet, but if she does,

it's extremely treatable. The majority of infants recover fully and have no further problems—'

'But if she doesn't . . .'

I rub Anna's cold hands between mine. 'She's only five weeks and one day old, darling,' I say softly. 'If you were still carrying her, you'd only be twenty-eight weeks pregnant by now. You know there are no guarantees. But we'll do our very best for her, and there's absolutely no reason to panic. I'm sure she's going to be just fine.'

I study the X-rays a couple of hours later. I had hoped I'd be proved wrong, but the diagnosis of NEC is confirmed by the presence of an abnormal gas pattern in the walls of the intestine and air in the abdominal cavity. It's a serious setback, but there's no reason to think Hope will make anything other than a full recovery. We'll start her on intravenous fluids, antibiotics and nasogastric drainage. Her condition should start to improve dramatically.

But it doesn't. The antibiotics slow the rate of her deterioration, but there's no doubt she's still getting worse. I don't go home for forty-eight hours, cat-napping on the sofa in my office when I can. By the third day, Hope's abdomen is so swollen that it interferes with her breathing, and we have no choice but to put her on a ventilator, something I've done my best to avoid up to now.

'Can't you do something to help her?' Anna begs tearfully.

'We're doing everything we can—'

Dean grabs my arm. 'You're not feeding her! She'll starve to death if this goes on much longer!'

'She won't starve, Dean,' I say, gently freeing myself. 'She's getting all the nutrients she needs through the IV.

Her tummy needs to rest so it can heal. I know it's frightening not to see her being fed, especially when she's so small to begin with. But it's for her own good, I promise.'

'What if she doesn't heal?' he demands. 'What if she doesn't start to get better?'

'If she doesn't improve soon, we may have no choice but to operate,' I say quietly.

I'm caught between a rock and a hard place. I don't want Hope on the IV longer than absolutely necessary because of the risk of nosocomial infections or other complications. Neither do I want to operate on an infant this vulnerable unless I've got no option. There's a very real chance she won't survive the trauma of anaesthetic and surgery.

But if we do nothing and her bowel *does* perforate, allowing faecal matter to leak into her abdomen, the infection will spread very quickly to all her major organs and she will certainly die.

'How long do we wait?' Dean asks.

'Please, Dean. Let me worry about that,' I say, with more confidence than I feel.

I go back to my vigil, filled with foreboding. Somehow, even in the most high-pressure, life-or-death situations, I've always known instinctively what to do. When to intervene, and when to pull back. When to medicate, and when to let nature take its course. When to resuscitate; and, hardest of all, when to let go. I haven't always been right, of course, but I've been able to weigh up the pros and cons in a moment and somehow know exactly which course has the best possible chance of a good outcome.

But suddenly, I'm floundering. I know I'm over-thinking

this case I'm too close to my patient. I just have to pray that, should it come to it, instinct will take over and something will tell me what to do.

I spend another sleepless night at the hospital, monitoring Hope every half-hour. By six the next morning, her condition has finally stabilized, but she still shows no positive sign of improvement.

I watch her chest rise and fall with the ventilator. At least she's no longer getting any worse. Perhaps the tide is slowly turning. She was extremely premature, after all. No point putting her through the trauma of surgery if the antibiotics are able to do their stuff.

But if her bowel has been weakened by days of infection – if it perforates now—

A cold wash of panic engulfs me.

Dear God, not now.

I struggle to hold the monster at bay. I know its signs: the surge of adrenalin, the painful prickling along my arms and legs, the tightening around my chest, the shortness of breath. I'm woken by it every night, sometimes two or three times, my heart pounding, drenched in sweat. It's got so that I dread going to bed; I stay in the armchair in the sitting-room, watching mindless television, until exhaustion finally takes over and I fall into a restless sleep.

Sometimes I can control it, push it back into its box by sheer force of will; but other times it overwhelms me, and I give in to the panic, gasping and choking and witless with terror, until, eventually, it passes, leaving me limp with exhaustion.

I've started to avoid anything that might trigger an attack. I can't cope any more with the tube, or an underground car park. I'm afraid of bridges, crowds, the dark, going to a movie. I'm beginning to understand how people become trapped in their own homes for years.

But I've always been safe working. Until now.

Fear wreaths my chest like smoke as I watch Hope struggle to breathe. *I don't know what to do for the best.* For the first time in my life, my legendary certainty has deserted me.

The night-duty nurse checks the baby's vital signs. 'What do you think?' she asks.

I don't know.

'She's certainly a fighter, this one. Reckon she's turned the corner?'

I don't know.

'Let's just wait and see,' I prevaricate.

Maybe Hope will get better and I won't need to do anything. Maybe (God forbid) she'll get worse, and I'll have no choice but to send her for surgery.

Maybe I'll wake up tomorrow and know what to do.

For the rest of the day, we watch and wait. And then at quarter to midnight, three and a half days after my unofficial vigil started, Hope's temperature begins to climb. And climb.

I don't need the surgeon to insert a needle into her abdominal cavity to withdraw fluid so that we can determine whether there's a hole in her intestines. I know immediately her bowel has perforated. We need to remove the diseased section as soon as possible, before it infects her entire abdomen and causes sepsis. Depending on the location and extent of the bowel removed, she may need a colostomy, or repeated surgical procedures; she may have problems with blockages or malabsorption in the future. But if her entire intestine is involved, we won't be able to do anything. Which will mean—

I'm hopelessly involved with my patient. It's unprofessional and counter-productive. It's utterly unlike me.

But as Hope is wheeled to the operating room, I feel as if my heart has gone with her.

William's phone call the next morning comes as I'm writing up Hope's case notes.

'New York?' I repeat. 'Tomorrow?'

'Please, Ella. It's make-or-break time for the company. I really need you there.'

I put down my pen. It's seven years since we went away together. To risk reopening that very dangerous can of worms, William must be truly desperate.

We'd been seeing each other for just over a year when he took on a new client, a prestigious multinational Arab bank based in Cyprus. William's business trip coincided with Thanksgiving in the US; Jackson was flying home, as he did every year, to spend the holiday week with his brother. Since Cooper hadn't seen fit to include me in the invitation, as usual, I'd been left kicking my kitten heels alone in London until William suggested I join him in Cyprus.

Aware that we were taking our casual affair to a new – and hazardous – level, whilst pretending I knew no such thing, I told Jackson I was going to Oxford for a girls' week with Lucy, and switched my mobile to international roam.

During the day, I lounged by a glittering pool while

William went hunter-gathering in the corporate jungle. In the evenings, we ate by candlelight on a terrace beneath the stars, or got a taxi out to the beach and walked hand-in-hand along the moonlit sand. It was like a slushy montage from a Hollywood rom-com – we even rented a sit-up-and-beg bicycle, and I sat on the handlebars as William cycled along the shore – but we revelled in the cliché of it all. It never occurred to us, as we ironically pastiched falling in love, that it might actually *happen*.

On the last day, William decided we should go wind-surfing. As we skinned up in wetsuits, my zip jammed. I tried to free myself, and instead caught my breast in the plastic teeth. Blood welled, and I gasped in pain.

William reached over and caught the drop of blood on his fingertip. I glanced up, and saw it in his eyes. I knew, from the confusion chasing across his features, that in the same moment, he'd seen it in mine.

Outwardly, it was a very prosaic moment. No drumroll, no explosion of fireworks. A fraction of time: in which everything changed.

If he'd asked me, then, to leave Jackson, I would have gone.

He didn't. And when we got back to the hotel, the message from Beth's friend Eithne was waiting.

After that, there was no question of love coming into it. If there had ever been a tiny part of me that had once hoped for that Hollywood ending, a sliver of me unregulated by my sensible, realistic, self-preserving instincts, Cyprus had extinguished it. The original, pragmatic terms of our agreement still stood. But there would be no going beyond its boundaries. What we had now was all we would ever have.

I realized I was trapped in a paradox of my own making. If I wanted to keep William in my life, I had to excise every shred of love I felt for him.

I succeeded. But that sort of radical emotional surgery is indiscriminate. It wasn't just my feelings for William that ran up against a brick wall whenever they tried to get a purchase. Slowly, what I felt for Jackson dimmed too. Somewhere along the line, I lost touch with the best part of myself.

'Ella?' William's voice prompts now.

My instinct is to say no. Getting over what happened in Cyprus took reserves of strength I don't have any more. And just thinking about getting on a plane is enough to set my heart pounding with fear. Plus I've had so much time off recently. Richard Angel's baying for my blood; if I take any more unscheduled leave, I could hand him the ammunition he needs to get me fired.

My case notes swim in front of me. After everything that's happened in the last six weeks, losing my job doesn't seem to matter much any more in the grand scheme of things. And William *needs* me.

I close the file on my desk. 'Of course I'll come.'

I can't stop thinking about Hope. Or, despite everything, wishing she'd been mine.

William wakes me from my pharmacological coma when we land at JFK. We take a yellow New York taxi to a small boutique hotel serendipitously close to Fifth Avenue and my personal shopping nirvana, while I try to shake off my Xanax hangover.

A skinny Hispanic girl with disfiguring acne shows us

to a large wood-panelled room with red-oak floors and a vast white-linen four-poster bed. Fresh flowers scent the room; in the bathroom is an old-fashioned claw-foot tub, surrounded by unlit scented candles, and a heap of marsh-mallow towels. In the heart of Manhattan: I can only imagine how much this must cost.

'I like your style,' I comment, biting into a ripe peach from a bowl on the antique credenza. 'Going down in a blaze of glory.'

'All guns firing,' William agrees. 'And talking of going down . . .'

Laughing, I evade his amorous advance. Peach juice dribbles down my chin. 'Let me shower first, then we'll see.'

'Story of my life.' He pulls off his tie, and checks his BlackBerry. 'OK, I've got to make a couple of calls, so I'll see you downstairs. Italian work for you this evening?'

'Depends. Can he breathe through his ears?'

William snorts. I blow him a kiss, go into the bathroom and lock the door. For a moment, I simply lean back against it, too drained to move. Now that I'm alone, I don't need to keep up the pretence.

I lever myself forward and start the bath running; I haven't got the energy to shower. As the room fills with steam, I slide to the tiled floor and rest my forehead against the edge of the bath. William needs me to be bright and cool and distracting; the careless, carefree Ella he's always known. His whole life is on the line: the next few days will decide if his company, his baby, survives, or is swallowed whole by Noble. I have to send him out refreshed, ener-gized and ready to do battle. I may want to curl into a ball and cry my eyes out, but this isn't about me.

I allow myself the blessed relief of a therapeutic five-minute pity bawl in the bath, then get out and pull my emotional corset back on. Carefully, I apply make-up to hide any trace of tiredness or tears, and slither into an iridescent pink, turquoise and black Pucci swirl of a dress.

Perching on the edge of the bed, I open my new Gina shoebox with the reverence that is its due, and slip on the sparkling silver sandals.

'Blaze of glory,' I tell my reflection.

William whistles as I walk into the hotel reception. If we'd run off together in Cyprus, he wouldn't be whistling like that, would he? We'd have grown complacent by now, taking each other for granted, in and out of the bedroom. Far better this way.

Later, after dinner, we go back to our room, and William eases the delicate spaghetti straps over my bare shoulders; my dress ripples down my body and pools at my feet. He kisses my neck, my collarbone, my navel, his stubble grazing my skin as he unhooks my strapless bra and eases my panties down my thighs and over my feet. I step clear, naked but for my silver shoes and the aquamarine pendant we bought together in London. I've never dared wear it before, in case Jackson asked where it came from.

William unpins my hair, running his fingers through it as it spirals on to my shoulders.

'You are so goddamn beautiful,' he sighs.

I help him undress, enjoying his tensile strength as he pushes me back on to the linen sheets and hovers over me like a panther. His body is hard and brown, the body of a man who keeps himself fit not out of vanity, but practicality.

He kisses me: I taste zabaglione on his lips.

My body stirs, anticipating his touch. His hands skim my skin – I feel the calluses from years of tennis on his palms – and a wetness spreads between my legs. I arch towards him, but he smiles and holds my wrists over my head with one hand, dipping his head to my breasts. My nipples tighten beneath his tongue. He smells of sweat and city dirt and lemons. I lose any sense of time and place as pleasure ripples through my body. Hooking one leg around his waist, I draw him towards me, aching to have him inside me, but he pulls away and slithers down the bed.

Gripping my buttocks, he tugs me to the edge of the bed and drops to his knees, drinking from my pussy as if it were a flute of champagne.

I twist my fingers in his thick hair, keeping him there. He kneads my breasts with a firmer touch now, and I groan at the sensory overload. In a rush, my orgasm sweeps over me, and I jerk against his mouth, driven higher and further by the rasp of his stubble against my clitoris.

William flips me expertly on to my stomach and slides his fingers into me, his cock thrusting against my pussy. The motion skates my nipples back and forth against the cool linen, and I come once more, wetly, against his hand.

I turn in his arms, kissing him and tasting myself on his lips. His cock brushes against my stomach as he licks the sweat in the hollow of my throat. I pull him towards me, the delicious ache rising in me again. Parting my thighs, I guide him into me with my hips. He thrusts inside me and I rock with him, our eyes locked as firmly as our hands above our heads.

In that moment, something cracks and breaks inside me. Without warning, I'm open to him, heart and soul, and even though I know it's the worst thing that could happen, *the absolute worst thing I could do*, a part of me wants this surrender more than I ever thought possible.

Afterwards, he curls against my back, spooning: the classic position of lovers down the centuries. I clasp my hands over his, dizzy with self-knowledge. While I could tell myself that it was just an affair, I was safe. He had his life to go back to, and I had mine. But I can't fool myself any longer. I love him. Without Jackson to hide behind, sooner or later, I'm going to want more. I'm going to want all of him, and that can't happen. I can't destroy his marriage, and his family, and attempt to build my happiness on another woman's misery. That's what having William for myself would cost.

I love him.

I have no choice but to let him go.

I love him.

'Crazy badger,' William whispers in my ear.

I want to ask him what he means, but he's already asleep.

When all else fails, a girl still has shopping.

With every swipe of my credit card, I'm a little more in control. Purchasing power is better than no power at all. First the élite department stores: Henri Bendel, Bergdorf's, Neiman Marcus; and then the funky vintage shops: Alice Underground, Screaming Mimi's. I buy a stunning coral necklace from Anthropologie, a striking bottle-green ankle-length velvet coat from Anna Sui. I can't afford it, any of it, but I don't stop until I am so laden I literally can't carry anything else. There's nothing quite as effective as a glossy, rope-handled bag to help mend a broken heart, and mine is in a million tiny pieces.

I bump into William in the hotel lobby – literally, as a cascade of bags slither off my shoulders at his feet. There is one upside to being single: I don't have to apologize for my extravagance. *No, darling, I haven't had it ages, and I didn't get it half-price in the sale.*

'How did the meeting go?' I ask.

He peers into a bag from La Petite Coquette. 'It went. Is that for me?'

'Only if you're very bad. What did they say?'

'They're going to think about it over the weekend,' he says tightly. 'We'll meet again on Monday. One of the three directors is a lost cause, but I think the other two are genuinely undecided. I pointed out to them that if Noble uses these kinds of practices to win their business, they can't expect him to play by the Queensberry Rules once they've signed with him.'

'How did that go down?'

'Christ knows. I think it struck a chord, but he's offering them a hell of a deal. I can't compete financially. I just have to hope my track record speaks for me.'

'D'you want me to go and give them all Chinese burns?'

'It may yet come to that. So,' he says, shrugging off his dejection with a visible effort, and pulling me close, 'looks like we're stuck in New York with nothing to do tomorrow. How *will* we fill the time?'

The contents of the La Petite Coquette bag help. Late on Sunday morning, we finally stumble out of bed and emerge into a brilliant spring day, the kind that lifts the spirits and soothes the soul. A cool breeze sweeps gently through the Manhattan streets, freshening the workaday city. We take our papers to an outdoor café, and William tucks into a fluffy mushroom omelette – morels, shiitakes and oysters; simple but delicious – while I enjoy a fresh berry fruit salad and hot, crispy *pain au chocolat*. There's a dull, pleasurable ache between my legs. Every so often, William looks up from his newspaper and smiles, and the thought of saying goodbye to him for ever is almost more than I can bear.

At a nearby table, a young couple struggle to contain their shrieking children, twin girls aged about four and a boy of about eighteen months. All three have streaming colds and freely wipe their snotty noses on anything that comes to hand – their sleeves, each other, their mother's skirt. Then the toddler picks up his mother's coffee and pours it over his nearest sister's head. She retaliates by upending the table, spilling pastries, milk and more coffee.

As the wailing reaches a crescendo, the parents wearily get to their feet and gather children, pushchairs, hats, jackets, bags, toys.

William snaps his *New York Times*. 'Thank God mine are past that stage.'

I watch them leave. I'd be a dreadful mother. A newbie shrink could point out the keloids on my psyche. Abandonment by a philandering father, a passive mother who abdicated responsibility to her nine-year-old daughter: who knows what damage I'd inflict in my turn on an innocent infant? It'd be like opening a fridge and throwing random ingredients into a bowl blindfold, stirring them for twenty years, and waiting to see what resulted.

A good-looking man in his mid-thirties takes the young

family's table, and gives me an openly appraising glance as he sits down. He clearly likes what he sees; he smiles and tilts his coffee in salutation.

Beside me, William stiffens.

It was a calculated risk, telling him about Cooper. Whether William realized it or not, Jackson's death must have changed the way he saw me; my availability was bound to make me seem needy, demanding, even pitiable. At a stroke, the knowledge that I'd slept with someone else dispelled that notion; he hasn't been this attentive since our first year together.

But jealousy is a dangerous game. I hit where it hurt most: his pride. I've made my point; no need to overplay my hand.

I turn carefully towards William, not even glancing in the stranger's direction.

Later, he takes my hand and we stroll through Central Park, walking off our brunch, just another ordinary couple on just another ordinary Sunday.

The mild weather has brought the blossom out early; the air smells sweet and clean. I lean on the parapet of Bow Bridge, enjoying the feel of smooth warm stone beneath my palms. William wraps his arms around me, his chin resting gently on the top of my head.

'Damn it!' I say suddenly. 'I left my book in the café.'

'Forget it. It'll be long gone by now. Buy it again at the hotel bookshop.'

'You don't understand. It was one of a special set, Lucy gave it to me for my thirtieth birthday. I have to go back, I have to find it.'

'Ella, sweetheart—'

'I can't lose it,' I panic, 'we have to go back. You know

194

how much I hate losing one of a pair, I need to find it, we—'

'Ella,' William says, tucking me against him and stroking my back as if I were a child. 'Forget the book. It's time to tell me about Hope.'

Even after the surgeons discovered her bowel had perforated, as we'd feared, I didn't lose hope; I was so sure they'd save her.

So sure; but in the end the sepsis was too widespread, there was nothing they could do. She didn't even make it out of the OR. Her brave little heart gave out there, on the operating table, and she died surrounded by monitors and machines and medics who didn't even know her name. Alone, without anyone to hold her and tell her they loved her, that even having known her for just five weeks and six days, they'd miss her.

I broke the news to her parents myself. Dean toppled like Saddam's statue, collapsing forward into a chair, smashed by grief. Anna slapped my face.

When I tell William, dry-eyed, that it was my indecision that killed Hope, he doesn't say it's not my fault, it couldn't be helped. He doesn't serve up the usual platitudes, or tell me I shouldn't feel responsible. He knows there's nothing he can say that will take the grief and guilt away. He simply holds me tight against him, and somehow, for the moment, it's enough.

William slams into the hotel room the next afternoon, his expression grim. I pause in my packing, my heart sinking.

The meeting went against him, then. He's lost the Equinox contract. Lost his company.

'I could bloody strangle her!' he cries. 'What the hell does she think she's playing at? As if I haven't got enough on my plate!'

I rock back on my heels, a shoebox in each hand.

'Cate!' he explodes, finally noticing my mystified expression.

'I don't understand. What does she have to do with Equinox?'

'What? Oh, the meeting with Equinox went fine. They'll let me know tomorrow, but I think I swung it. It's Cate who's giving me the bloody headache! Running off to Paris! What on earth does she think she's playing at!'

He slumps on to the end of the bed and loosens his tie. 'Beth rang an hour ago in hysterics. Cate's run away, no note, but she's taken her bloody silver trainers and that damn backpack, so she's clearly gone of her own free will. Beth was on the verge of calling the police before I talked her out of it.' I hand him a bourbon from the mini-bar and he knocks it back in one gulp. 'I know where she is. She was on at me before I left to let her go and stay with her best friend in Paris. Bloody Fleur. I knew the two of them were up to something.'

'What are you going to do?'

'Cancel her credit card, for a start! I should never have given in to Beth and let her have one. I'm paying for this bloody nonsense!'

I picture the determined white face of his daughter in my office, as she tried to make sense of the mess a bunch of adults who should know better have made of her life.

'Don't do that. You don't want her stranded in a foreign country with no money. Have you tried calling her mobile?'

'Switched off. I tried ringing Fleur's parents, but the bloody French maid answered the phone, either doesn't understand English or doesn't want to—'

'Give me the number.'

I speak briefly to the maid in French, and then hand the phone to William. 'She's there. Amélie has just gone to get her.'

I tune him out as he yells at his daughter. I've got a headache already, and to be honest, I'm not feeling too brilliant. Hot and dizzy. My shoulder is aching as if I've been playing tennis for a month. And I've felt nauseous since I got up this morning. Probably the thought of having to get on the plane again, although the panic attacks have abated these last few days. Perhaps I just needed something real to worry about—

I'm knocked sideways by the worst pain I've ever known.

It's like my insides are being twisted by a giant fist. For a moment, it's so intense, I can't breathe. I cling to the back of a chair, my knuckles whitening. Too vicious for food poisoning. It must be appendicitis – only I had mine out when I was twelve—

William is still shouting at his daughter. If I can just get to the bathroom—

A film of sweat sheens my face. I'm going to be violently sick.

I try to make it to the lavatory, but my legs refuse to work, and I crumple to the floor. William turns and drops the phone.

I vomit uncontrollably where I lie, in too much agony even to feel embarrassed.

'Oh, Jesus.' William yanks the coverlet from the bed, and tucks it around me, then wipes my face with his shirt. 'Keep still. Don't move.'

I shiver convulsively, and the room begins to spin. I didn't think it was possible to be in this much pain and stay conscious.

'Stay there, I'll get someone. Hold on.'

Dimly, I hear him sign off with Cate and tell someone to call an ambulance. Then he's scooping my head into his lap, and stroking my damp hair back from my face.

'They'll be here soon. Whatever it is, we'll get you sorted out. The best care money can buy. Don't worry, darling. I'm here. It's probably something you ate. Nothing to worry about.'

You're wrong! I scream silently. *It is something to worry about!*

William wouldn't be nearly so solicitous, wouldn't be tenderly wiping the vomit from my lips with his linen shirt, if he realized what was really wrong with me.

November 25, 2001

Felden Street
London SW6
England

Dear Cooper,

  This is the hardest letter I ever sat down to write. But you got to know the truth, and tough as this is, saying the words out loud would be a hundred times harder, else I'd pick up the phone. Just read it through, Coop. Once I'm done, I don't ever want to talk about this again.

  She's made a fool out of me. How could you see what kind of woman she was, Coop, when you never even laid eyes on her? How could I live with her, eat with her — Jesus, <u>sleep</u> with her — for four years and never realize?

  I wouldn't believe it still, if I hadn't seen her with my own two eyes. Lolly would say it's all part of the Lord's plan, that I was meant to fly back two days early to bring her home to you for Thanksgiving, and find her right there, in the airport, kissing the face off some bastard in a fancy suit. All I can say is, the Lord has a fine sense of humor. I just spent the last week telling you how wonderful my lovely wife is, and begging you to give her a chance. Turns out you were right about her all along.

  God's will or not, if I'd had my twelve-gauge with me I'd have put a slug straight between the asshole's eyes.

  But instead I hid so she wouldn't see me; she never even knew I was there. Daddy would have turned the gun on himself before he let a carpetbagger treat him that way. I'm shamed, Coop, and the worst of it is, I don't give a damn. If I could turn back the clock and go back to not knowing, I would.

How could she do this to me? I've given her everything she ever wanted. Hell, I'm not perfect, I know that, but I thought I made her happy. How could I not <u>know</u>?

It's killing me. Every time I look at her, I see her in bed, spreading her legs for another man. It's been three days, and I still can't face her. I can't bear to say her name, I can't stand to touch her. I'm sick to my stomach every time she smiles at me. It's got so I can't stand to be in the same room. She's so lost in her own world, I don't think she's even noticed. What kind of marriage do we have, that we can have such secrets from each other?

My head's buzzing with so many questions, I can't think straight. Did she take him home, did they do it in our bed? How long has it been going on? Is he better in bed than me? Smarter, richer, funnier? Is he married, too? Does he love her?

Does she love him?

I'm so scared, big brother. Right now I'm numb, like after Mom and Dad died. But I know what comes next. It's like having your arm cut off and looking at the bloody stump and knowing it's going to hurt more than you can imagine, but you can't feel it yet. I'm not sure what I'll do when the pain hits. I don't know if I can go through it again.

You know the worst thing, the very worst of it? Even more than picturing the two of them in bed, even more than the shame and humiliation and anger?

God help me, I still love her.

How is it possible to love someone who gives you so much pain? She's not the kind of wife I ever planned on; she lies and cheats, she blows hot and cold, she won't even have my babies. I should kick her to the curb. If I stay, she'll cause me nothing but more grief. Maybe I'll wind up hating her. It'd almost be a relief. This kind of love, it's more than I can bear.

I don't want your pity, Coop. I know what you'll say: same as any right-minded person would. But a part of me wants her so bad I'd settle for just a piece of her, if it means I don't lose her. And another part of me knows it'll kill me in the end. She'll break my heart.

You're the only one who's never let me down. I know I don't tell you this as often as I should, but I love you, bro.

Jackson

10

William

I'm screwed. My company is about to go to hell in a hand-basket, and there's bugger-all I can do to stop it.

'Wonderful news!' I exclaim, leaping up from behind my desk.

Malinche blushes. 'Isn't it? Although the girls think it's terribly embarrassing, proof positive their parents are having sex – well, Sophie does, she goes absolutely *scarlet* whenever anyone mentions the baby. Evie is another kettle of fish entirely, as you can imagine: she keeps answering the phone and saying Mummy and Daddy are too busy making a baby to speak to anyone, Nicholas' poor mother was rather shocked when she called the other day—'

'He must be thrilled,' I say, when I can get word in.

'Oh, he *is*, especially when the scan said it was a boy, at *last* – although of course they said that last time, and then along came darling Metheny.'

She settles herself into the inhospitable black leather chair opposite me and beams radiantly. Despite the financial bombshell she's just lobbed my way, I beam back. Malinche Lyon is one of the few clients on my books I actually like.

Her career as a celebrity chef is undergoing a surprising renaissance at the moment. Fifteen years ago, Mal was a hot property, with a shelf-full of best-selling cookbooks and a cable-TV deal, but then she married a rather dull divorce lawyer, moved to the country and more or less vanished off the radar overnight. She and Nicholas hit a bit of a rocky patch a year ago, but it blew over, and next thing I know, she's opening a shit-hot gourmet restaurant down in Salisbury. Off the back of it, she's got a new cookbook at number one, another in the pipeline, and a hit BBC show that's put her right back at the top.

Naturally, her success has been good for my agency (a lifesaver, actually); but, hand on heart, I can think of few people I'd rather see good things happen to.

'I know it messes things up for the new series,' she says apologetically, 'but I really don't think I can juggle the three girls and a tiny baby and work, even with the new nanny – Nicholas was so sweet about that, he absolutely wouldn't take no for an answer, positively insisted we hire her—'

I grasp at straws. 'Could they shoot round you?'

'They could, they've been terribly sweet about the whole thing, but actually, William,' she says, dimpling, 'I do rather want to take a bit of time off – after all, I am thirty-nine, this is a bit of last-chance baby – and I want to enjoy every minute without worrying about film schedules and recipes and things. I realize it leaves everyone in rather a muddle – ' understatement *du jour*, ' – but I promise it'll only be for a year. Of course, if you really need me to—'

'Mal, please don't worry. I'm delighted for you both,

couldn't be happier. I'll issue a press release tomorrow to take the heat off you, and I'm sure the BBC will be more than happy to take you back whenever you're ready. You just concentrate on looking after yourself, and leave the rest to me.'

She levers herself awkwardly out of the chair. 'You are a poppet, William.'

I'm not sure the taxman will see it quite like that when I can't pay my next bill.

'By the way,' she adds, shouldering a huge black bag and absently spilling half its contents on the floor, 'who was that rather beautiful blond young man chatting up your secretary just now? He looks *terri*bly familiar, but I can't quite place him.'

I help her pick up keys, mints, tampons (clearly it's been a while since she used this bag) and assorted fluffy toys. 'That would be my daughter's boyfriend.' I scowl. 'She sweet-talked me into letting him design the new company logo. I hate to admit it, but the bastard's actually bloody good.'

'Oh, dear. Fathers and daughters. I've got all this to come with the girls. Nicholas is already muttering about shotguns and convents—'

'There's a good one in Romania. I can give him the number if he likes.'

Malinche peals with laughter as she kisses me goodbye.

I tell Carolyn to hold my calls and stare broodingly out over the glittering Canary Wharf skyline. Losing Mal, even temporarily, is a body blow. We still have a decent bedrock of bread-and-butter clients, but I have forty-two staff to pay, and crippling overheads. These new offices are a good investment, but it's going to take time to reap the rewards.

For the past six months, we've been haemorrhaging cash, thanks to Noble's poaching, we're barely keeping our heads above water. Tomorrow's trip to New York is more vital than ever. Thank God Ella agreed to come. I need the kind of moral support only she can give me.

Without Malinche, the grim reality is that if I can't persuade Equinox to stay loyal, we're not even going to make it to next Christmas.

While Ella sleeps on the plane, I review the notes I've pulled together on the three key players at Equinox. I'm fairly sure John Torres, the chairman and CEO, is in our corner: we've worked well together over the years, and he's already intimated over the phone that he wants to stay with Ashfield PR. But he's barely a year from retirement; his vote counts for less than it used to. And his finance director, Drew Merman, is pushing hard for fresh blood. Charming and slippery, he's cast from the same mould as Noble himself. I wouldn't be surprised if they've already done some sort of back-room deal.

The new V-P, Mina Gerhardt, is the real unknown quantity. She's only been with Equinox eight months, so we haven't had the chance to build up much of a working relationship, and she has a reputation for ruthless unsentimentality. Who knows which way she's going to jump?

Damn it, who the hell is selling me out to Noble? *Who?* I can't believe it's Ella. What possible reason would she have? Unless he's her mystery one-night stand—

Ridiculous. Beth, then? If she's found out about Ella, she might want revenge. But if she sinks us, she'll be cutting off her nose to spite her face. The house is mortgaged to the hilt; if the firm goes down, we'll be left with nothing. No juicy divorce settlement. She wouldn't want that, surely?

I rub my hand across my face. I'm nearly forty-nine. Too old to start again. If the firm goes under, where will that leave me?

Ashfield PR has been my life for twenty years. The kids have their own lives; they'll be gone soon, even Sam. Christ knows what'll happen when it's just Beth and me rattling round that huge house on our own. If we didn't have Cate to referee, we'd be at each other's throats already.

I won't have Ella for ever, either. Not now Jackson's gone. She'll find someone else, someone free; she's young and beautiful, she won't be a widow for long.

I reach over and tuck the thin airline blanket more securely around her shoulders. Funny that she's scared of flying; she's usually so sensible. Rather endearing, in a way. I've always found her confidence exciting, but it can be a little disconcerting at times. I know she hates showing any sign of weakness, but actually, far from putting me off, it just makes me love her more—

In the ordinary way you love those close to you, of course. Ella wouldn't stand for any of that soulmate, can't-live-without-you stuff. She's not the sort to get swept away by feelings. If I was so pathetic as to declare myself madly in love with her, she'd run a bloody mile.

I unscrew my miniature Scotch and top up my glass. There was a moment, years ago, when I *did* wonder, though. The trip to Cyprus: something happened that week. I don't know if it was the sun or the booze or all that romantic walking along the beach (enough to give anyone daft ideas; I even hired a bicycle and did the whole *Butch*

Cassidy and the Sundance Kid thing, cycling through fields with Ella perched on the handlebars. Thinking about it still brings a smile to my face). It was the first time we'd spent more than a night together, and it must have gone to my head, because I found myself wondering what it'd be like if this was real, if I could fall asleep every night with Ella beside me, knowing that I had a lifetime of waking up to her the next morning.

I took her wind-surfing the last day we were there, and she managed to catch the bloody zip of her wetsuit on her skin. Daft thing to do, and not in the least romantic; but when I saw her wince, saw the blood, it twisted my guts in the kind of primitive, knee-jerk way it does when one of the kids gets hurt. And even though I was married, with three young children – Sam was barely a year old at the time – in that moment, none of it mattered. If she'd crooked her finger, given me the merest hint, I'd have left Beth in an instant.

On the way back to the hotel afterwards, the question rattled around my brain; I couldn't think of anything else. *Would she leave Jackson if I asked?*

Then, as we walked up the hotel steps, the concierge came running out to meet us. Cate had been the one to find her mother, Eithne told us over the phone. She'd forgotten something she needed for school, and had come back to get it. She'd found Beth in the kitchen, barely conscious in a pool of blood. My wife had slit her wrists.

Cate was just ten years old, but she'd bandaged her mother's arms with a couple of tea-towels and called 999, and sat there staunching the flow with her small hands until the paramedics arrived. What must it have done to her, to find her mother like that? I'd been in my twenties when my father killed himself, and I still regularly wake screaming from the nightmares.

'I didn't mean for her to find me,' Beth had said sullenly from her hospital bed. 'Eithne was coming over, I thought Cate would be safely at school—'

'But *why*, Beth?' I demanded. 'You've been doing so well since Sam was born. Why now?'

She turned her head into the thin pillow. 'I thought you were going to leave me. I couldn't bear that. I didn't want to live without you.'

'Of course I'm not going to leave you—'

'I wouldn't blame you. You must hate me.'

I sighed. 'I don't hate you, Beth.'

I sank on to the edge of her narrow bed and took one of her bandaged wrists in mine. Clearly this wasn't just a cry for help: if she'd simply wanted attention, it would have been much easier, and safer, to have taken an overdose; she certainly had access to enough pills. No one slits their wrists, and takes the trouble to do it lengthwise, along the vein, unless they're serious.

The room suddenly seemed smaller and darker. 'I'm not going to leave you,' I said.

Beside me, Ella stirs restlessly in her plane seat. On our way back from Cyprus, she asked me if I wanted to end things, without a trace of self-pity. Calm and collected, she was sanity itself. She made everything so easy. Of course I couldn't let her go. Not then; not now. She's the only one keeping me sane.

After we land at JFK and check in at the hotel, I leave Ella to take a shower and go down to the lobby to make my duty call to Beth. Cate answers the phone; to my surprise, she tells me Beth's staying in London with Eithne for a couple of days. Beth never mentioned that. I'm not sure I like the idea of Cate being left alone in the house right now. She sounds tense and unhappy. It could just be the pressure of exams, of course, but I get the feeling it's something more. When I mention Dan, she quickly changes the subject. I want the bastard out of the picture more than anyone, but if he's used and dropped her like a snotty tissue, I'll string the fucker up by his balls.

Damn it. I knew something was up when she came to my study the other night. I should've made time to listen to her, but this thing with Equinox – I *had* to take that call from John Torres – it'll be different once this contract is sorted . . .

I tell Cate to call if she needs me, and spend the next twenty minutes setting up the Equinox meeting. Christ. Power breakfasts on a Saturday morning. Welcome to America, Land of the Workaholic.

I nearly drop the phone altogether when Ella walks into the lobby. She's pulled out all the stops this evening: a clinging silky multi-coloured dress that skims her thighs and barely covers her nipples, and sky-high silver fuck-me shoes. I'm tempted to forget dinner and take her straight back upstairs.

We eat at a laid-back restaurant in Little Italy which serves the best zabaglione I've ever tasted. Ella is at her sparkling, witty best; if you didn't know her, you'd miss the giveaway signs of tension hidden beneath cleverly applied make-up. Sometimes she's so self-controlled it's fucking scary.

By the time we get back to our hotel room, you could run the Stars and Stripes up my erection. I unclip Ella's hair, fanning it out across her shoulders. She looks like an erotic Renaissance painting. 'You are so goddamn beautiful,' I mutter thickly.

I push her back on the vast bed, holding her down lightly as she arches impatiently towards me. Not yet, Ella. Not yet.

Taking my sweet time, I mouth my way down her body, her sweat salt on my tongue. I stroke her heavy tits as they splay either side of her ribcage, pink nipples darkening to mulberry beneath my touch. Dipping my tongue into her navel, I trace delicate whorls down her pale belly, then spread her legs and pull her to the edge of the bed, burying my face enthusiastically in her wet pussy. She tastes sweet and clean, and as she comes in shivering waves, I lap noisily, relishing the uninhibited way she gushes into my face.

Before she's even spent, I flip her on to her stomach, lifting her arse so that I can drive my thumb deep inside her, the way I know she likes. I love her big arse. Can't stand skinny bitches. A man needs something to get hold of.

Ella claws at the bed, her body going rigid as she comes again. I can't wait any longer. She spins slickly in my arms and I thrust my cock inside her, pinning her hands above her head with mine as we move together. Technically, she's not the best I've ever had – Christ, there was a Spanish girl my third year at Oxford, she had a cunt that could crack walnuts – but no one has ever made me feel like Ella. She's under my skin and inside my head; there are moments when I have no idea where she ends and I begin.

Afterwards, I pull her into my arms, stroking her glorious hair. Something was different tonight. I'm inexplicably sad, as if Ella's grief has leached into me.

'Crazy 'bout you,' I whisper before falling into a dreamless sleep.

When Beth's number is displayed on my mobile for the fourth time in ten minutes, I realize I've got no choice but to interrupt the most crucial meeting of my life and call her back.

I push my chair back from the table. 'Sorry, got to take this.'

John Torres stands with me. 'Go right ahead. I think we could all do with a ten-minute break. Mina, how about you call down for some fresh coffee? Tell them to go out to Café Dora, none of that machine piss.'

'Thanks, John,' I mutter, as he shows me to an empty conference room. 'Sorry about this—'

'Forget it. Take your time, you shouldn't be interrupted here. And quit worrying about the contract, William. It's a done deal. Let me tell you, Mina was very impressed by your presentation Saturday. She's with us. Drew may kick up some, but in the end, he'll come round.'

Relief engulfs me. 'You won't regret it, John.'

'I know that.' He claps me on the shoulder. 'Go make your call, buddy.'

For a minute or two after the door closes, I stare dazedly out of the window at the rainy New York streets forty-one floors below. I hadn't realized until the axe was lifted just how fucking terrified I was. We came *this* close to disaster . . .

I hit the speed-dial. 'Beth? What's up?'

'Oh, William, thank God! I've been going out of my mind, I've been calling and calling you – I know we have to ring the police but I wanted to talk to you first. You have to come home—'

Don't tell me she's pranged the bloody car again.

'Beth, calm down! What the hell is going on?'

'Cate's gone – I just got back from Eithne's and she's not home, oh, God, William, what are we going to do—'

'What makes you think she's not at Dan's, or out with friends?'

'She's not at Dan's, they broke up – oh, William! Supposing she's been abducted, she could be lying in a ditch somewhere—'

'Beth, get a grip, for God's sake. She's probably just gone shopping with Clem, and forgotten to leave you a note.'

'But she hasn't been home for two days!'

'How do you know?'

'She left Cannelle with the Franks across the road on Saturday—'

'Well, she can't have been kidnapped then, can she!' I exclaim, exasperated. 'For heaven's sake, Beth! If she left the dog with the neighbours, she's obviously gone off somewhere. Has she taken anything with her?'

'Like what?'

'I don't know! Her silver trainers, for a start, they're practically welded to her feet. And that bloody yellow backpack.'

I tap my fingers in an impatient tattoo on the conference table while I wait for Beth to come back on the line. Bugger Cate, for putting her mother through all this unnecessary upset. And bugger Beth, for overreacting as usual.

'She's taken them,' Beth pants a moment later. 'And her make-up bag and the Diesel jeans I bought her for her birthday—'

'I don't need a bloody inventory,' I snap. 'All right, we know she's run off. And I can guess where she's gone. She was nagging me before I left to go and see Fleur.'

'But Fleur's in Paris!'

'I'm aware of that. Give me the number, and I'll ring and put a bloody rocket up her arse. She'll be on the next train home, believe me.'

I punch in the number as soon as I hang up with Beth. I could swing for Cate. As if I haven't got enough on my plate with the Equinox deal, and poor Ella, breaking her heart over that baby—

'*Allo?*'

'*Bonjour.* May I speak to Cate Ashfield, *s'il vous plaît?*'

'*Je ne comprends pas.*'

The bitch! She just hung up on me!

I redial. 'Cate Ashfield, please—'

'*Parlez français.*'

'*Je veux parler à Cate Ashfield,*' I say again, through gritted teeth.

'*Je ne comprends pas.*'

'No, don't hang—'

I have steam coming out of my ears by the time I get back to the hotel. Bloody maid! Bloody Cate! Bloody women!

'I could bloody strangle her!' I yell, as I burst into our room. 'What the hell does she think she's playing at? As if I haven't got enough on my plate!'

Ella looks up from her packing in bewilderment.

'Cate!' I shout.

'I don't understand. What does she have to do with Equinox?'

'What? Oh, the meeting with Equinox went fine. They'll let me know tomorrow, but I think I swung it. It's Cate who's giving me the bloody headache! Running off to Paris! What on earth does she think she's playing at!'

'Beth rang an hour ago in hysterics,' I say, a little more calmly. 'Cate's run away, no note, but she's taken her bloody silver trainers and that damn backpack, so she's clearly gone of her own free will. Beth was on the verge of calling the police before I talked her out of it.' Ella hands me a bourbon from the mini-bar, and I knock it back. 'I know where she is. She was on at me before I left to let her go and stay with her best friend in Paris. Bloody Fleur. I knew the two of them were up to something.'

'What are you going to do?'

'Cancel her credit card, for a start! I should never have given in to Beth and let her have one. I'm paying for this bloody nonsense!'

'Don't do that,' Ella says quickly. 'You don't want her stranded in a foreign country with no money. Have you tried calling her mobile?'

'Switched off. I tried ringing Fleur's parents, but the bloody French maid answered the phone, either doesn't understand English or doesn't want to—'

'Give me the number.'

I'd forgotten Ella speaks fluent French. She rattles off a few rapid-fire sentences, then hands the phone to me. 'She's there. Amélie has just gone to get her.'

She's safe. Thank God.

She's safe, while we've all been running around like headless chickens—

As soon as Cate comes to the phone, I give her both barrels. I don't care if she saw Ella and me writhing naked by the light of the silvery moon! It doesn't excuse her putting her mother and me through such grief. Nor am I mollified when she starts on about improving her French. Improving her French my arse!

'You knew where I was,' Cate mutters sulkily.

I want to reach down the phone and throttle her. 'Luckily for you, the Lavoies are good people, but you can't just turn up unannounced on their doorstep, Caitlin! Grow up! This isn't just about you!'

'It never is, is it?'

'Don't be so damn childish!' I shout. 'And I'd like to know where you got the money in the first—'

There's a sound behind me. I turn just in time to see Ella crumple to the floor.

I gape in shock.

'Oh, Jesus,' I whisper, as she vomits uncontrollably on the carpet. Suddenly I'm galvanized into action. Yanking a blanket from the bed, I tuck it round her and wipe the puke from her face with the tail of my shirt. 'Keep still. Don't move. Stay there, I'll get someone. Hold on.'

I hang up with Cate, dial zero and yell at the hotel receptionist to call an ambulance. Ella's doubled up with pain, her lips white and bloodless. Fear sluices through me as I cradle her head in my lap. I can't stop thinking about Jackson. Supposing the virus *was* contagious? Supposing Ella has it too? I can't lose her. She means the world to me.

Who am I trying to kid? She *is* my world.

This woman. This one woman: of course, of course. I love her. Not in a controlled, organized, tidy fashion. Not once a month, when she can be fitted into the spaces of my tidy, comfortable life. I love her because I can't help myself, because it comes as naturally to me as breathing, because she's the only woman I've ever met who knows more about jazz than I do.

I can't believe I've fooled myself for so long. Of course I love her; there's never been a moment when I didn't.

'They'll be here soon,' I tell her, stroking her damp hair back from her face. She's barely conscious. 'Whatever it is, we'll get you sorted out. The best care money can buy. Don't worry, darling. I'm here. It's probably something you ate. Nothing to worry about.'

My voice sounds hollow even to me. I've never seen anyone collapse like this, as if the life's been sucked out of them. I cling to Ella's hand as paramedics arrive and load her into an ambulance. We rocket around the streets of New York, and I feel strangely detached, as if I'm watching an episode of *ER* on television. This can't be happening. None of it seems real.

When we reach the emergency room, Ella is whisked out of sight by the paramedics. I try to follow her, but a security guard bars my way. I'm shunted, protesting, towards a glassed-in counter near the door.

'Insurance card,' the receptionist barks.

'What? I don't – I'm not sure—'

'Credit card?'

Dazedly, I hand it to her. She shoves a clipboard with a dozen multi-coloured forms towards me, and waves me to one side. 'Next.'

'Where have they taken—'

'Someone will be with you shortly. Next!'

A passing nurse takes pity and hands me a ball-point

pen. There's nowhere free to sit down, so I lean against the peeling wall and fill in the forms, ad-libbing when I don't know the answer. It's not like we've ever discussed whether she's had her tonsils out. I don't even know her full address.

When it comes to next of kin, I hesitate a moment, then put down my name.

Four hours later, I still have no idea what's happening. I've drunk a dozen cups of ersatz coffee from the machine, accosted anyone and everyone in a white coat, including the vending-machine filler, and been escorted firmly back to the waiting area twice by the menacing security guard, who's clearly of the thump-first-ask-questions-later school. No one seems able to tell me anything. I only know Ella's alive because I haven't yet been taken to the sinister windowless room off the long hallway.

The stroppy receptionist won't even speak to me. Actually, she threatened to call the cops if I went near her again. Even the wild-eyed methadone junkies are giving me a wide berth.

My phone rings, and I quickly take it outside. 'Christ, Beth, I'm so sorry. Cate's with Fleur, I meant to call you back—'

'For God's sake, William! I've been beside myself! I had to call the Lavoies myself in the end and get them out of bed! What on earth have you—'

'Look, I said I'm sorry,' I snap irritably. 'Something came up.'

'Something more important than your *daughter*?'

'Look, she's OK, that's the main thing. She'll be home in a day or two—'

'A day or two? When? What's she doing? Are you sure she's all right?'

'Mr Ashfield?'

I swing round. A doctor roughly the same age as my eldest son motions me to follow him inside.

'Look, Beth. I have to go. I'll talk to you tomorrow.'

I snap shut my phone and hasten into the hospital.

'Your wife is doing much better,' the doctor smiles, flashing orthodontic braces. 'She's in recovery. It was dicey for a bit, but she's gonna be fine. You can see her now.'

I don't bother to correct his assumption: *my wife*. If only.

Ella is several shades whiter than her hospital sheets, but produces a wan smile when I burst into the recovery room. 'I wouldn't recommend the fish,' she says thinly.

'I'll bear that in mind.' I perch gingerly on the edge of the bed, painfully aware of the last time I visited a woman in hospital. 'You gave me quite a scare back there.'

'I gave myself one,' she grimaces. 'I'm so sorry, William. You've got enough on your plate without—'

'Don't be bloody ridiculous! Christ, Ella. I thought I'd lost you!'

'Sorry. You'll have to try a bit harder next time.'

'Not funny, Ella. I had no idea if you were even dead or alive. No one would tell me anything. What in hell happened? '

She shifts, wincing, against the pillows. 'Let's just say, if your appendix ever puts in a formal complaint, listen to it.'

'Talk about "Physician, heal thyself." '

I hesitate. Ordinarily, Ella would slap me down if I so much as hinted the L-word, but she's changed since Jackson died. There's a softness to her, a vulnerability, that wasn't there before. It gives me the balls to tell her the truth. 'Ella, you've no idea what it did to me, seeing you like that,' I say carefully. 'I realized this afternoon how much you mean to me, how much I—'

'William, I'm sorry, but could you ask the nurse for some more codeine?'

I summon a candy-striper, who bustles in with some pills. Ella sips slowly from a paper cup, her features etched with pain. I notice for the first time how much weight she's lost recently. She's got cheekbones like Katharine Hepburn.

'Ella—'

She covers my mouth. 'Don't say it.'

'I've spent the last eight years not saying it! It's time we—'

'All this drama,' Ella says lightly. 'It's enough to make anyone get carried away and say things they might regret later.'

'But I—'

'William,' she cries fiercely. 'You're *married*. It doesn't matter what either of us feel, or think we feel. We agreed at the beginning that this wasn't going to go anywhere. Beth needs you. Your children need you. Talking like this just makes everything worse.'

'I can't keep on pretending I don't care, Ella! It'll make things a total farce!'

Her eyes are bright. Fear swirls around me like fog.

'William. I think we both know it's over—'

'Of course it's not over! Look, I'll leave Beth. If that's what you want. I'll leave her, she'll be fine, she'll still have the children—'

'No! That's not what I meant!' She struggles to sit

upright. 'We should never have let it get this far. We should have ended it after Cyprus; *I* should have ended it. Think what Beth might do if—'

'I'm to spend the rest of my life held to ransom?'

'She's your *wife*. Please, William. Don't make this more difficult than it has to be.'

I stand up. 'Look, you've just had surgery. God knows what drugs are still in your system. You're probably still in shock. Hormones all over the place. We'll talk about this sensibly when you've calmed down.'

'I am calm!' Ella yells.

'Of course you are. I'll be back tomorrow morning. Sleep well, darling.'

A pillow thumps against the door behind me.

She doesn't mean it. It's just post-traumatic stress, or whatever the bloody hell they call it these days. Emergency surgery, on top of the last few weeks she's just had. It's guilt and grief talking. She probably doesn't know whether she's coming or going. She doesn't mean it. She can't.

The teenage doctor stops me as I'm about to leave. 'I wanted to say how sorry I am, Mr Ashfield. It's a real shame.'

'Well, yes. But she's on the mend now, that's the main thing.'

'Sure. Good. You got a great attitude, sir. You keep saying that sort of thing to her. She needs to know she's just as much of a woman to you now as she always was. It can be a terrible blow if—'

'Excuse me,' I say, 'but what the hell are you talking about?'

He looks horrified. 'She didn't tell you?'

'What didn't she tell me?'

'I think maybe you should speak to '

'Look, doctor. I've had enough of this. I don't mean to be rude, but if you don't tell me what the fuck is going on, I won't be responsible for my actions. Do you follow me?'

He swallows.

I open the door to the sinister death room. 'After you.'

'I really shouldn't—'

I take a step forward.

'Mr Ashfield, as you know, your wife had an ectopic pregnancy,' he says quickly, shutting the door behind us. 'That's when the embryo implants in the fallopian tubes, rather than the womb. Unfortunately, we only found out about it when the tube burst. Ordinarily, that wouldn't be the end of the world, as she'd still have had the other tube. It'd make pregnancy more difficult, certainly, but not impossible.'

Pregnant? *Ella*?

'The problem,' he adds nervously, 'is that in your wife's case, there was already considerable scarring on her other tube. She must have gotten an infection at some point, probably years ago. She might not even have known about it. It means she'll never conceive naturally. I'm so sorry.'

I sink into a chair. Clearly it can't be mine; we took care of that the week after Beth discovered she was pregnant with Sam. Jackson died, what, six weeks ago? Christ. A posthumous baby.

Why didn't she *tell* me? Why pretend she had appendicitis? Did she think it'd make any difference to the way I feel about her?

'There's always IVF,' the young doctor says encouragingly. 'She still has plenty of eggs for a woman her age, which is good news. You could—'

'We've never wanted children,' I say faintly.

'Well. Look. I need to get back to my patients . . .'

'You go. I'll be fine. I just need to take a minute.'

The door shuts softly behind him. I bury my head in my hands, trying to get my mind around what he's just told me.

Jackson's baby. Dear God. And now she's lost even that.

I wait for Ella to tell me. For three days, we discuss the weather, the news, the origins of man and the latest series of *American Idol*, but we studiously avoid any mention of the future, and Ella doesn't tell me she's lost Jackson's child and will never have any man's baby again.

When I arrive at the hospital to collect her and sign her discharge papers, I wonder if this is finally it. I should never have tried to tell her I love her. She hates that kind of clinginess. I've driven her away.

I just thought – I had a feeling – she seemed more *open*, somehow.

If we can just go back to the way things were, I'll take it. Whatever her terms.

My mobile rings as I pay off the taxi. It's an international number; I head towards the parking lot to take the call.

'Beth! Where are you?'

'Paris. Cate didn't come home, so I came to get her.'

'I hope you gave her hell,' I exclaim. 'She needs to grow up and think of other people for a change. I can't believe she's been so irresponsible—'

'Shut up, William! Would you just shut up!'

I'm taken aback. It's not like Beth to get angry. Sad is

what Beth does. Sad, defeated, depressed. 'There's no need—'

'Cate's not here!' Beth cries.

'Of course she's there. I spoke to her on Monday.'

'She left this morning. No one knows where she's gone!'

I jam the phone against my other ear. 'She's probably on her way back to you. I bet you crossed each other in the Chunnel.'

'She hasn't gone home, William! She could be anywhere. She's only seventeen.' Beth's voice cracks. 'Anything could happen to her. We have to find her!'

'I'm sure she'll—'

'William! Would you just *listen* instead of talking! Your daughter is missing, and no one has any idea where she is! I don't care what you're doing or how important you think it is. For once in your life, you need to put Cate first. I expect you to get a plane to Paris the moment you arrive in London, and I'll pick you up at the airport, do you understand?'

She hangs up with a sharp click. I'm speechless. I can't remember Beth ever talking to me like that in her life. Who knew she had *that* in her?

Ella is waiting for me at the hospital reception. 'Don't wait till tomorrow,' she urges, when I tell her about Cate. 'There's bound to be a flight to Paris this afternoon. You could be there by tomorrow morning.'

For the first time, the reality of the situation sinks in. I picture my daughter, alone in a foreign country, too scared to come home. Seventeen is so young. She thinks she knows it all, but she's not one of those street-wise teenagers you see hanging around shopping malls or falling out of nightclubs. I suppose I'm to blame for that, protecting her too much. Wrapping her up in cotton wool.

I'm torn. 'But you've just come out of hospital—'

'William, don't fuss. I'll be fine. I *am* a doctor,' she says. 'You need to put your family first. Call me when you find Cate.'

The next flight to Paris via Philadelphia leaves in four hours. I book myself on it, and drop Ella at the hotel. She kisses me goodbye. I ask when I'll see her again, but she doesn't answer: a reply in itself.

Maybe she's right, I think bleakly. Maybe it *is* over. We've driven Cate to this, Ella and I. If anything happens to my daughter, I'll never forgive myself.

I'm exhausted by the time I arrive in Paris the next morning. Beth is waiting for me at Charles de Gaulle, as arranged. She waves when she sees me, and I push my trolley towards her, then freeze with shock.

I haven't seen her in twenty years, but she looks exactly the same.

Standing behind Beth is my mother.

11

Beth

Cate wasn't supposed to be the one to find me. It should have been Eithne, I knew she was coming round that morning for coffee (laced, as always, with vodka, even at 10 a.m.); it wouldn't have been pleasant for her, of course, but she owed it to me. One-all, as it were.

Eithne would've known I didn't mean it. She'd have understood I had to do *some*thing to get William's attention.

It was all Clara's fault, of course. She knew how much I hated leaving the house on my own, but William was in Cyprus and the baby needed milk and nappies and Clara simply refused to go shopping, so I had no choice but to drive to the supermarket myself. Naturally the car park was terribly crowded, I couldn't find a space, and of course I got into one of my panics. I only hit a wall, nothing serious. But I needed to find the insurance papers, and when I got home I realized I had no idea where they were.

I'd never have dreamed of going through William's desk, so I had to phone him at his hotel, even though I knew how much he hated being disturbed by domestic trivia when he was away on business.

The receptionist couldn't find his reservation at first. 'No Mr Ashton,' she said in thick English—

'It's Ash*field*,' I corrected in relief. 'William Ashfield.'

'*Εδώ είναι!* Here is, Mr and Mrs Ashfield, room two-oh-one. But they gone out, I call them the taxi myself. You want take message me?'

I put down the telephone and sat quietly thinking for a very long time. The girl could have made a mistake – her English was quite atrocious – but somehow I knew she hadn't. Mr and Mrs Ashfield. This wasn't just a fling with some floozie William had picked up in a Cypriot bar; a one-night stand. This was planned. She was staying with him, he'd booked her into the hotel with him, which meant this was something altogether more serious.

I knew what I had to do. I was fighting for my marriage the only way I knew how. I didn't have much else to offer William. As Clara often reminded me.

Guilt can be more powerful than love, sometimes.

An overdose would have been the easiest way, but that's so unpredictable, and too easy to dismiss as a cry for help. William had to believe I *meant* it. I had to choose a way that left no room for doubt – whilst making sure, of course, that there was plenty of room for doubt after all.

I was very careful. I knew where to cut, and how deep. (It didn't hurt. I expected it to, but it didn't. There was something rather soothing about watching the blood flow out of my wrists, though when I saw the sticky red mess, so *much* blood, I felt a moment of absolute terror. If Eithne didn't come—)

What I didn't know was that Cate would forget her

school project that morning, the one she'd spent weeks and
weeks working on with William, that she'd catch the bus
back home and burst into the kitchen to find me on the
floor (where Eithne would be sure to see me, through
the kitchen window, when I didn't answer the door). I
didn't know she'd be the one to rip up tea-towels to bind
my wrists, and call 999, and explain to the doctors and
policemen – and later, no doubt, to a therapist – that her
mother had tried to kill herself when she was ten years old,
and she'd been the one to find her.

'You were *ill*,' Eithne groans now, for the umpteenth
time. 'You couldn't help it.'

'She was only ten,' I fret, pacing the length of her studio.
'How could I do that to her? I'm her mother! I'm supposed
to *protect* her!'

Eithne stretches out on the filthy, paint-smeared sofa,
hands behind her head. Sunshine streams through the
grimy windowpanes, blocking the studio floor with faded
gold diamonds. The room shakes as a train rattles along
the Northern Line beneath us. It may not be quiet here, but
I envy her all this space. I should never have had children.

'Why do you keep worrying at it?' she demands. 'You're
like a dog with a bone. Yes, you fucked up, but haven't we
all? It was seven *years* ago, Beth. Let it go.'

I chew at my nails. 'Cate can't. I see it in her eyes, every
time she looks at me. She doesn't trust me. She never has.
Even before—' I hesitate.

'Your little *flagrante*?'

'It wasn't—'

She flaps her hand laconically. 'Yes, yes, I know. Look,
she'll come round. Give it a few days—'

'She won't, Eithne. You know she won't. She hasn't

spoken to me since it happened. I thought, if I stayed with you for a few days and gave her time – but she's not even picking up the phone when I call. How can I explain what happened if she won't speak to me?'

'You have to let her work it out in her own time, Beth. You and William have over-compensated with that child. It won't do her any harm to grow up a little.'

I open my mouth to object.

'Look.' Eithne swings herself upright. 'Shit happens, Beth. You did something stupid, but you were ill, and Cate knows that. She's seventeen now, not ten. Old enough to see beyond the myth that Daddy's a conquering hero and you're a nutty old bat who should be locked up in an attic.' She gets up and pours herself an inch of neat vodka. 'William, Cate, Clara – none of them takes you seriously. They all treat you somewhere between an old lady in her dotage and the village idiot. And you just *let* them.'

'Eithne, stop. This isn't helping.'

'I give up. You're so damn *passive*, Beth! You're taking a back-row seat in your own life. When are you going to step up to the plate and take some responsibility?'

I take a pace backwards. 'I've tried—'

'Don't you dare hide behind your illness!'

'You were the one who just said I couldn't help it!'

'You can't help being ill, but you can help what you do about it,' Eithne says sharply. 'Plenty of people have manic depression and achieve all sorts of things. Winston Churchill had it, and saved the bloody country!' She gesticulates wildly, spilling her drink. 'Some of the greatest artists and writers and scientists have been bipolar – Mozart, William Blake, Isaac Newton, Mark Twain – it didn't keep them from using their talents and living their lives to the full, did it?'

'They were all men,' I mutter. 'It's different for women. I have three children, don't forget—'

'Beth, sometimes I want to slap you! You could do so much! You could *be* so much! And you won't even *try*!'

'It's the drugs!' I shout suddenly. 'It's easy for you to say! You don't understand! They take everything! Mozart and Churchill didn't have to spend their lives feeling dead and numb, just so they could function! They didn't have to drug themselves into oblivion just to give the semblance of being a normal wife and mother—'

Eithne puts down her glass, cups my face with her hands, and kisses me with such force my teeth graze my lips. All the passion and anger and frustration I see in her art, she pours into that kiss.

I'm too shocked to kiss her back, but it doesn't seem to matter. My arms stiffen. Something unexpected stirs inside me: neither revulsion, nor the kind of desire that drenches me when I think of Dan; it takes me a moment to identify it as curiosity. I've never kissed a woman before. I close my eyes, but it's still – different. *Other*. Eithne is taller than I am, as tall as any man, and broad-shouldered from years of heaving stone and iron sculptures; flat-chested and crop-haired and rangy, she could pass for a man from a distance. And yet she is more womanly than any woman I've ever met, and her kiss so clearly feminine in a way I can't begin to explain.

She steps back, her expression defiant, and waits.

'Oh,' I squeak.

'Is that all you have to say?'

'I'm a little surprised, I suppose—'

She snorts.

'Well. It's just – the thing is, Eithne. First Dan, and now you. It's not as if I – I'm hardly – it's never happened quite so – I mean, *why*?'

Eithne takes me by the shoulders and propels me towards the florid rococo mirror taking up two-thirds of a wall on the far side of her studio. 'What do you see, Beth?' she demands.

'Oh, you know,' I mumble, ducking my head. 'Just me.'

'You really have no idea, do you?' She leans over my shoulder, lifting my chin and meeting my eyes in the mirror. 'You're too used to seeing yourself through the eyes of your bloody mother, or that bratty daughter of yours, or the man who's been sharing your bed and taking you for granted for twenty years.' She gives me a gentle shake. 'Look at you! You're beautiful. And you don't even know it! That's what's so amazing about you! You don't even realize how lovely you are!'

For a moment, I almost see it. Sometimes, years ago, I'd see a photo of myself, taken in an unguarded moment, and think, *Goodness, I nearly look pretty* . . .

But that was a long time ago.

'You love me,' I say wonderingly.

'Well, of course I do,' she retorts crossly.

I turn from the mirror, looking into her angular, intelligent face. Eithne Brompton has been my dearest friend for two decades; we've weathered loss and grief, enjoyed happiness, survived children and marriage, disaster and success, our lives as opposite as it's possible for two women's to be, and yet she's closer to me than anyone; William included. There's nothing we haven't shared. How could I not have known this about her?

I knew it.

'I love you, too,' I say, 'but not like that—'

'It's all right,' she says. 'I didn't expect you to.'

'I know,' I say.

And then I kiss her back.

I don't love her *like that*, but I love her enough. And she loves me. Love, even from the wrong person in the wrong circumstances, has a rightness all its own. Not to receive it with gratitude seems like arrogance of the worst kind.

I've never been a very bohemian sort of artist. More the Tupperware kind, if truth be known. Just once, I'd like to see myself the way Eithne sees me. To be the person she seems to think I am.

And – and it wouldn't really *count*, would it? With a woman. Not like it would, oh, God, with Dan.

So I lead her towards the low Japanese bed in the corner of the vast, dusty studio, her fingers running up and down my spine like a nun counting rosary beads. I untie the belt of my neat shirt-waister, and help her with her own buttons when her hands shake too much to undo them herself. My hands flutter over her bare bony shoulders as she unfastens my bra and cups my heavy breasts. It's impossible to be touched by someone with such love and not feel anything. Impossible to remain *un*touched.

But when she pushes me back on the bed and slides down between my legs and touches and tongues and strokes me to the first orgasm I've had since before Cate was born, my gratitude is no longer theoretical.

I kiss her and taste myself on her lips, and wonder if I can love her like that after all.

'I'm sorry,' I say, leaning up on one elbow. 'I wish I was a lesbian. I'd really *like* to be.'

Eithne nearly chokes with laughter. 'Oh, Beth. This isn't netball. It's not like picking whether you want to be reds or yellows.'

'It was very nice, and everything—'

'Next you'll be thanking me for having you.'

'It's just – well. I don't think it's exactly *me*.'

She sits up, bare-breasted, and stubs out her cigarette. Despite everything we did last night – my cheeks flame – I primly avert my gaze from her nakedness.

'Look, Beth. I'm not under any illusions here. I know you're not what William would no doubt term a rug-muncher. I wish it were otherwise,' she smiles ruefully, 'but you don't have to apologize for being the way you are. I've loved you since the moment you picked me back up off the floor after Kit, but I've always known I hadn't got a cat in hell's chance. Don't start blaming yourself. You've never given me false hope. Last night was unexpected, the most wonderful gift, a dream come true, but I realize that's all it was.'

She gathers the sheet around herself, and perches on the edge of the platform bed next to me. 'Nothing's changed, Beth,' she says softly, linking her fingers with mine. 'We're still OK, aren't we?'

I look at our entwined hands, and nod.

'Separate beds in Italy next month, though,' she adds wryly. 'I'm not that much of a saint. This was just a one-off, Mrs Suburban wife-and-two-point-four. Nothing to get your sensible knickers in a twist about, OK? No going home and immersing yourself in yet more guilt and self-doubt.'

'I'm not sure William would see it quite that way—'

'William would just sulk because we didn't let him watch.'

I can't help but laugh.

'You're a much happier person when he isn't around,' she sighs. 'I'd never ask you to leave him for me, Beth, but I wish you'd consider leaving him for *you*. He's made you so helpless. He's just taken over control of your life from where Clara left off. I'm sure he thinks he's doing you a favour, but—'

'No,' I say firmly.

There are places even Eithne isn't allowed to go.

She stands up, still wrapped awkwardly in the damp sheet, and hugs me. 'It'll be fine, Beth. Go home. And talk to Cate. Even if she doesn't talk to you.'

Eithne is right, I think, as I let myself into the house later that afternoon. I can't expect Cate to make the first move. I have to go to her, even if she spits on my olive branch. Surely, if I give her enough time, prove that I'm here for her . . .

The hallway is cold and dark. I feel a moment of concern, before remembering that it's Monday, and Cate will still be on her way home from school.

I'm expecting the usual pile of dirty plates in the kitchen sink and butter-smeared knives left on the counter – why are teenagers physically incapable of reaching that extra ten inches to the dishwasher? – but the kitchen is as neat and tidy as when I left it on Saturday morning. I smile in surprise. Perhaps this is Cate's way of saying she's sorry, too.

Someone knocks at the back door as I go to put the kettle on the hob. A moment later, Cannelle bounds into the kitchen, buffeting me with enthusiasm and rank doggy breath. 'Hey! Where have you been?' I say, ruffling his glossy coat. 'Did you miss me, boy? Did Cate take good care of you?'

'Sorry to pounce the moment you get back,' my neighbour, Jean, apologizes, 'only I've got to take my mother to the dentist at five, and I saw your car pull up—'

'You've been looking after Cannelle? That's very kind, Jean, but Cate didn't need to ask you. He's all right on his own for a couple of hours. She knew I'd be back this afternoon—'

Jean looks confused. 'But she left him with me on Saturday. She said she had to go away for a few days. I thought you knew. She said you'd be back to pick him up sometime today.'

I feel the first stirrings of alarm. 'Did she say where she was going?'

'No. I assumed she was going to stay with you— Oh, dear. Beth, is there a problem?'

'No, no,' I say, mustering a smile. 'Thanks so much, Jean. I'm sure it's just a few crossed wires, that's all.'

I run upstairs, and check Cate's room. The bed hasn't been slept in: the pile of clean laundry I left on her duvet on Saturday morning is still there.

The panic escalates. She's been gone nearly three days; anything could have happened. She could have been kidnapped, murdered – even now, she could be lying in a ditch somewhere. We might never know what happened to her. That poor estate agent girl, it's been twenty years and she's never been found, what her mother must have gone through—

'For heaven's sake, Beth!' William exclaims five minutes later. 'If she left the dog with the neighbours, she's obviously gone off somewhere. Has she taken anything with her?'

'Like what?'

'I don't know! Her silver trainers, for a start, they're practically welded to her feet. And that bloody yellow back-pack.'

I run upstairs with the phone, and fling open her wardrobe. Relief engulfs me. William's right: half Cate's favourite clothes are missing.

'She's taken them,' I confirm, almost giddy at the reprieve. 'And her make-up bag and the Diesel jeans I bought her for her birthday—'

'I don't need a bloody inventory. All right, we know she's run off. And I can guess where she's gone. She was nagging me before I left to go and see Fleur.'

'But Fleur's in Paris!'

'I'm aware of that. Give me the number, and I'll ring and put a bloody rocket up her arse. She'll be on the next train home, believe me.'

I sink on to the edge of Cate's bed, cradling the phone between my knees. Thank God William's so sensible, thank God, thank God. He's right. Of course he's right. A kidnapper wouldn't have let her take the dog over to the Franks! She's just bunking off. Gone to see Fleur in Paris. William will bawl her out, and she'll be on the next train home.

He'll call me back in a minute and tell me she's safe with Fleur.

Twenty minutes later, when he still hasn't rung, I start to worry again. I get up and put away Cate's clean laundry, willing myself not to get carried away again. It could be as simple as the Lavoies' phone being engaged.

I twitch her duvet into place, then go downstairs, feed Cannelle and water the plants. It's nearly an hour since I spoke to William. If she definitely wasn't with Fleur, he'd have called me back by now. He must still be trying to get hold of the Lavoies. No news is good news. Perhaps they've taken Cate out to dinner or something. No need to read anything sinister into it.

Another hour passes. I leave an anxious message on William's mobile, and wander distractedly around the dark house, straightening pictures and book spines. This is all my fault. If I'd stayed home this weekend, got her to see reason over Dan—

I leap on the phone, but it's only Eithne. I promise to call her back in the morning, and then hang up, in case William's trying to get through.

By eleven, I'm frantic. Why hasn't he phoned? What can he be doing all this time?

It's only midnight in Paris, I tell myself as I dial the Lavoies' number. *I have to know she's safe.* Everyone knows they go to bed later in Europe.

Five minutes later, fear has been replaced by fury.

'Christ, Beth, I'm so sorry,' William says, when he finally answers his mobile. 'Cate's with Fleur. I meant to call you back—'

'For God's sake, William! I've been beside myself! I had to call the Lavoies myself in the end and get them out of bed! What on earth have you—'

'Look, I said I'm sorry. Something came up.'

My outrage is so consuming, it takes me a moment to recover my voice. 'Something more important than your *daughter*?'

'Look, she's OK, that's the main thing. She'll be home in a day or two—'

'A day or two?' I cry. 'When? What's she doing? Are you sure she's all right?'

'Look, Beth. I have to go. I'll talk to you tomorrow.'

He hangs up. I stare at the phone in disbelief. Our daughter's run away to France! What kind of father is he? Doesn't he *care*?

But then he isn't the one riven with guilt.

I jump at the sound of the back door opening. Cannelle immediately leaps up, barking madly. Standing in the kitchen is the last person I expected to see.

'Beth, please, let me speak before you throw me out,' Dan says urgently. 'There's something very important I have to tell you.'

I clench my fist around the pills. A handful of poison. God knows I don't want to take them. I know what that will mean.

But I also know what it will mean if I don't.

Cate needs me in my right mind. It's been three days since William spoke to her, and she still isn't home. I have to go to Paris and find her. For once, I have to be the mother Cate needs and deserves.

I'm not just swinging from one extreme to the next now; I'm living all kinds of extreme at the same time. Despair and mania and a spinning, tilting reality. Water-sprites in the bathroom; Jesus's face in a hunk of Stilton. I can't control it any more.

I take a large gulp of water and knock them back.

My throat closes. I can't swallow. I hold the pills and water in my mouth, my cheeks bulging. I can't bear it. To surrender to the fog, to lose touch with everything that makes life worth living. Especially now, after Dan—

Maybe I'm a fool for believing him. It could just be another lie. At the very least, I should tell William. Warn him.

Swallow!

Coughing and choking, I lean over the kitchen sink and spit out the pills. Failure heaves itself into my mouth, more bitter than the medication.

I push my hair back from my face with my wrist, and run the tap, watching the last of my pills spiral down the drain. That's it, then. No going back.

When I look up, William's mother is standing in the doorway.

'Of course I'll come with you,' Anne says.

'Are you sure you're well enough?'

'For the moment,' she says, taking the kettle from my hand, 'and frankly, my dear, as things stand, I don't have a lot to lose.'

I drift towards a chair while Anne bustles about the unfamiliar kitchen as if it's her home, not mine. I watch helplessly. 'I don't know how long we'll be gone—'

'Don't worry, dear.' She nods towards the small blue

BOAC bag by the door. 'I've got everything I need in there, and I'm not above rinsing my smalls in the basin if needs be.'

She sets two clean mugs on the table and briskly warms the pot, trim and neat in her pressed cream blouse and calf-length tweed skirt. I know she's already been through two gruelling rounds of chemotherapy, but her silver hair is still perfectly coiffed, her discreet make-up flawless. Her only concession to illness is an antique silver-topped ebony cane. I'm certain that when we reach Paris, everything will emerge pristine from her holdall, her slacks creaseless and newly dry-cleaned, crisp shirts sporting the full comple-ment of buttons, polished shoes stuffed with newspaper and carefully packed in their own cloth shoe bags so there's no chance of the immaculate heels marking any of her clothes. Even before I had children I never went anywhere without at least two bulging and battered suitcases, and no matter how carefully I pack, everything always emerges looking like crumpled Oxfam rags.

I'm perfectly capable of getting myself to Paris (my teenage daughter managed it, for heaven's sake) but Anne smoothly takes over, booking our train tickets, organizing my packing – 'Now, dear, it may be springtime in Paris, but I think *two* sweaters, don't you?' – and arranging for Cannelle to spend his second holiday in a week with the neighbours.

Despite her well-meaning kindness, I feel helpless and diminished. There's a rebuke to her efficiency, an *If you want a job doing well* . . . This is exactly what William does, I realize suddenly. He takes control, suffocating me with his capability.

I want to tell Anne to leave me alone, let me run my own life, but of course I don't.

I never do.

Sabine Lavoie shrugs her elegant shoulders. 'If you had telephoned first, it would have saved you a wasted journey.'

'I didn't want to frighten Cate away,' I say.

'Instead, she has already left.'

Next to me, Anne's eyes are as Arctic as the Frenchwoman's. 'Perhaps we could come in, rather than discuss this in the street.'

Mme Lavoie hesitates, then nods curtly and turns. We follow her into an overdone, rococo drawing-room crammed with gilt chairs and ornate furniture. It might seem impressive, were the pieces of the same period, or even from the same country. A Louis XVI tri-fold mirror is hugger-mugger with a Spanish baroque tabernacle and two Italian Renaissance armchairs. A pair of mid-nineteenth-century majolica bottleneck vases sit atop a sixteenth-century Florentine credenza. The effect is a cross between an Arab souk and a country-house car-boot sale.

'Coffee would be perfect,' says Anne, as though Mme Lavoie had spoken. 'Thank you so much.'

Mme Lavoie signals to the maid, who scuttles out of the room, eyes wide with delight. I suspect her mistress isn't discomforted in her own home too often. If I weren't so concerned for my daughter, I might enjoy this clash of the titans too.

'Where is she?' I burst out. 'She was here last night, wasn't she?'

Another Gallic shrug. 'I had an engagement. She was here when I left at five.'

'Your daughter must know,' Anne says firmly. 'We need to talk to her.'

'My daughter was also out last night, I believe.'

'Your husband, then.'

'*Désolée*. He is working. Perhaps, if you come back after six—'

'Madame Lavoie,' Anne says, rapping her cane sharply against the marble floor. 'I don't think you understand. My granddaughter is missing. She is only seventeen years old. The last time anyone saw her was here, at your house. We appreciate your hospitality, but things are more serious now. Naturally, we're reluctant to involve the police in a private matter, but we must find her as soon as possible. I'm sorry if that causes you embarrassment, but—'

Sabine Lavoie stands. 'I'll see if I can reach my husband.'

'I'm going to talk to that maid,' Anne says, *sotto voce*. 'Servants always know what's really going on.'

'I need to call William,' I say. 'My mobile doesn't work here—'

'There's a phone in the hall. Don't let him off the hook,' Anne warns. 'That boy needs to be brought to heel. Stand up to him, Beth. It's the only way to earn his respect. Men don't love where they don't esteem, remember that.'

I can quite see why, after growing up with a mother like Anne, William felt the need to marry a woman like me. And why he's been regretting it ever since.

'Beth!' William exclaims. 'Where are you?'

'Paris. Cate didn't come home, so I came to get her.'

'I hope you gave her hell. She needs to grow up and

think of other people for a change. I can't believe she's been so irresponsible—'

Irresponsible? I want to scream. Who's the one living it up in New York doing who-knows-what with who-knows-whom, while his daughter is missing? Who couldn't even be bothered to call me back to say he'd found her because *something came up*? Where did she learn *irresponsible* from, if not from you?

Suddenly, my simmering anger reaches boiling point.

'Shut up, William! Would you just shut up!'

He sounds as startled as I am at my tone. 'There's no need—'

'Cate's not here!' I yell.

'Of course she's there. I spoke to her on Monday.'

'She left this morning. No one knows where she's gone!'

'She's probably on her way back to you. I bet you crossed each other in the Chunnel.'

'She hasn't gone home, William!' I say impatiently. 'She could be anywhere. She's only seventeen. Anything could happen to her. We have to find her!'

'I'm sure she'll—'

'William!' I shout. 'Would you just *listen* instead of talking! Your daughter is missing, and no one has any idea where she is! I don't care what you're doing or how important you think it is. For once in your life, you need to put Cate first. I expect you to get a plane to Paris the moment you arrive in London, and I'll pick you up at the airport, do you understand?'

I slam the phone into its cradle. 'About time,' Anne says behind me.

'Did you speak to the maid?'

'We had a very interesting conversation. Apparently, Medusa in there *did* see Cate after last night: they had a screaming row this morning, which ended with Cate slamming out of the house just after eight.'

'The bitch,' I breathe.

I start towards the *salon*, then turn.

'Anne,' I say, 'I don't want to be rude, but I need to talk to Fleur's mother by myself, if you don't mind.'

She forces a smile. 'Of course.'

Mme Lavoie is on her mobile when I find her. I shut the *salon* door behind me, and she looks up, then mutters something unintelligible in French and snaps her phone shut.

I fold my arms and channel Clara into my expression.

'Now,' I say grimly. 'How about you tell me what *really* happened this morning between you and my daughter?'

'What the fuck is *she* doing here?' William snarls.

Anne stiffens, but her smile doesn't slip. 'Hello, dear,' she says calmly.

He starts to push his suitcase trolley past us, but I block his way. 'She came to help me find our daughter,' I say sharply. 'Since *you* weren't available. And right now, I don't give a damn whether Anne beat the soles of your feet with bamboo canes or force-fed you slugs in castor oil when you were a baby. Cate is our priority, and until she's found, she's the only one I care about.'

Astonishment, fury and confusion chase each other across William's features.

'Same goes for you, Anne,' I add, more gently. 'Whatever you need to say to William, it waits until Cate's back.'

'May I ask where we're going?' my husband enquires icily as I lead the way to the taxi rank. 'Or would you like a group hug and a quick round of "Kumbaya" first?'

'Sabine Lavoie thinks Cate may have gone to Marseille,' I reply. 'Fleur was showing her pictures of their holiday home the other night, apparently. I suggest we go back to the hotel Anne and I stayed at last night, and work out what we're going to do from there.'

No need to mention that Mme Lavoie threw Cate out of her house, or why. William has had enough shocks for one day.

'Sounds like a wild goose chase, if you ask me—'

'No one did, William. Unless you have a better idea?'

'Fine,' he snaps.

He climbs into the taxi, his anger evident in the rigid set of his shoulders. I don't care. For the first time in as long as I can remember, pleasing William isn't top of my concerns.

'Go and check in,' I tell him, when the taxi drops us off at the hotel, a short walk from the Lavoies'. 'I'm going for a walk, to clear my head. I won't be long.'

He stalks up the steps. My heart shivers, watching him. Whatever our differences, there's nothing I wouldn't do for this man.

I've always known he doesn't feel the same about me. Over the years, I've grown to accept his tepid, damning-with-faint-praise affection; to see it as my due.

Maybe it's because I haven't taken my pills for a few weeks; perhaps Cate's disappearance has stripped everything down to the bone. But suddenly affection isn't enough. I don't want to settle for the same careless fondness he bestows on the dog. I'm his *wife*! I want him to long for me the way I ache for him; to race home at the end of the day eager to see me. If I can't have that, I don't want second-best.

I cross the Seine, heading towards the Jardin des Tuileries. The air smells of traffic fumes and cut grass and springtime. William and I should be strolling along the Left Bank hand-in-hand, enjoying a second honeymoon. Instead, thanks to my reckless stupidity, we're here to search for our missing teenage daughter. Dear Lord, how did it come to this?

I should have stood up to William long ago. Eithne was right. I've let him treat me like an incapable, pitiable fool. And in the end, that's what I've become.

I sink on to a bench beneath a block of linden trees. What if Cate's not in Marseille? *What if we never find her?*

A teenage girl is huddled on a bench near me, knees drawn up under her chin, cheek resting on them. She looks dishevelled and unkempt, as if she's slept in her clothes. It could be Cate, I think despairingly. She's about the same age. Still not much more than a child—

The girl wearily unfolds herself, and picks up the bag at her feet.

Silver feet.

She hoists her filthy yellow back-pack on to her shoulder, glancing listlessly in my direction. I get up as if in a dream. For a moment her gaze drifts past me; and then suddenly her eyes widen with recognition and shock.

'Cate, please,' I cry.

She hesitates. I reach out my hand, too terrified to move. And watch her run.

12

Cate

No one ever tells you how, like, *clumsy* sex is. The first time
I kissed a boy – Patrick Corcoran, when I was thirteen and
a half, at the bus stop by the cemetery – I didn't even know
which way to tilt my head so we didn't bump noses. How
do people find out this stuff? Is there some rule, like driving
on the right? Or is it in your genes, like being left-handed?

Mum and I had the birds-and-the-bees conversation, of
course, and we all sniggered over the drawings of long-
haired hippies getting it on in Biology (you'd think they
could update the pictures once in a while). But I don't
remember anyone saying Prince Charming would stick his
finger in your eye trying to get your bra off, or you'd knee
him in the balls when he got on top of you, or that when
he'd finally stopped swearing, your sweaty bodies wouldn't
just fit together neatly like two pieces of a jigsaw puzzle,
but that you'd have to shuffle up-a-bit, down-a-bit, going
Excuse me and *Oops sorry* till you got it right. Or that his
thing would bang blindly around down there like a dis-

orientated mole trying to find the right burrow. I'm sorry, but God is definitely a man. No woman would come up with such a dumb idea. I mean, how much thought's really gone into it? Fleur always says if their stuff tasted of chocolate milkshake instead of yukky and salty, men would get a lot more blow-jobs.

I don't care what it tastes of. No way am I *ever* putting a man's willy in my mouth. I mean, they don't even wash their *hands*.

In the end, I reach down and sort of help Michel before he ends up in the wrong hole. He doesn't seem to know what he's doing any more than I do, but I've got to give him props for enthusiasm. I guess there's a lot to be said for instinct, after all.

I flinch as he pushes into me and meets resistance. He smells a bit of BO. 'It's OK?' he asks anxiously.

I nod, bracing myself.

He thrusts again, and there's a kind of sharp, searing pain, like putting a tampon in when you're dry, only a hundred times worse; and then suddenly he's moving inside me. I wait for some kind of lightning-bolt moment, but it just *hurts*. A lot. It's like having someone stick their finger up your nose. We rock together, banging hipbones and chins, totally out of time. It's as if I'm dancing with someone who's got zero sense of rhythm and two left feet. In the end I keep still, and let him bang away by himself. My head thumps the padded headboard with each thrust; every time I try to wriggle down the bed, he jolts me back up. It's not really painful any more, but I can't say I'm exactly hooked, either. It isn't even as nice as kissing, to be honest. There's none of the fizzy, tingly anticipation. In fact, now it's stopped hurting, it's a bit, well. Boring, actually.

Is this *it*? Is this what all the flirting and butterflies and snogging come down to? This damp, kind of lame in-and-out, in-and-out?

He starts to move faster, and I squirm uncomfortably. His elbow is on my hair. I hope he hurries up and finishes soon. I thought teenage boys were supposed to come as soon as they unzipped their trousers.

Suddenly he goes rigid and yelps, sounding just like Cannelle when you accidentally step on his tail. *Finally.*

He flops heavily on to the bed beside me. '*Merde.*'

Stuff trickles stickily between my legs. I'm cold and sore; I swear I've got third-degree friction burns. I can't believe how *crap* that was. Fleur says it gets better after the first time, but frankly I'm not sure how it could get worse. If this is sex, I'm sorry, I really can't see what all the fuss is about.

Michel lights two cigarettes, and hands one to me. I'm about to tell him I don't smoke, but I don't run away from home or get pissed on Armagnac or lose my virginity as a rule either.

'Good, *oui*?'

I exhale, coughing. 'I guess.'

'Next time, it will be better,' he says confidently.

The cigarette makes me feel sick. The room starts to whirl, and suddenly I know I'm going to throw up. I leap out of bed and run to the *en suite* bathroom, semen running down the inside of my thighs.

The Armagnac burns even more coming up than it did going down. I retch until I'm just dry-heaving, then flush the toilet and flip the lid down, resting my head against it. Oh God, what have I just done?

It seemed like a good idea an hour ago, when I ran into

him and spilled coffee all over us. I could tell from the hot way he was looking at me that he fancied me; I knew exactly what he really meant when he asked if I wanted to come to his room to fix my shirt. I just wanted someone to *want* me for a while.

My thighs are smeared with blood. I turn on the shower. The water's freezing, but it sobers me up in an instant. I never thought my first time would be like this. I imagined ... I don't know what I imagined. Soft music and candles and kisses that made me melt. Romance and fireworks and a feeling like you've just won the lottery.

I wash carefully, my skin goosefleshing with cold. No point getting all girly and hysterical about it. This isn't a Mills & Boon novel.

When I return, Michel flips back the covers and pats the damp bed. 'Come.'

'I should go back to my room—'

'Later,' he says, with a surprising grin that tells me he's going to be just as irresistible as his father before long. '*Maintenant*, is your turn.'

The first thing I notice when I wake is the ache between my legs. I smile. He really *was* a fast learner. The next go round was much better, and the third—

The third. *Wow.*

The second thing I notice is the time.

I double-check the bedside clock. Seven-fifteen! *Shit!* I must've fallen asleep after that last sesh. Hardly surprising, but—

Michel is lying on my coffee-stained shirt and jeans. I kneel up, trying to yank them out from under him without waking him up. There's no doubt it was fun in the end last night, but I don't think I'm ever going to be a morning-sex kind of person. Oh, come on, *come on*.

There's a light tap at the door. I freeze.

'*Michel? Es-tu prêt?*'

Oh, fuck. Fuck, fuck and double fuck.

'*C'est sept heures et quart, Michel. Tu seras en retard pour l'école.*'

'Michel!' I hiss. 'Michel, wake up!'

He grunts and rolls on to his side, snoring loudly. Quickly, I grab my clothes as he moves off them. I'll have to hide in the bathroom until she's gone and sneak back to my room later—

His mother knocks again. 'Michel?'

I'm halfway to the loo when I spot my pink bra lying brazenly in the middle of the floor for the world to see. I run back in a Neanderthal crouch and scoop it up.

The doorknob turns.

I am *so* dead.

I don't know exactly what '*putain*' means, but I don't think it's very nice.

I stand on the doorstep, wondering what the hell to do now. I've only got about twenty euros in cash – that won't even get me a taxi to the station. I've still got Dad's credit card, of course, but I've no idea where the nearest ATM is. I don't know where *any*thing is; this is the first time I've been outside the house since I got here. If only Fleur hadn't already left for school, I bet her mother wouldn't have dared throw me out.

God, what a bitch. It's not like I was the only one

involved. Michel was there too. She didn't say a bloody word to him. I can't believe she's just chucked me on the streets like this.

Shit. I can't go home, and I can't stay here. Maybe if I go south to Provence, I can get a job or something while I figure out what to do. Picking grapes, maybe. Are grapes ripe in April?

The front door opens again and I dart down the steps before Cruella flays me alive.

'Cate, *attend*!' Michel pads after me barefoot, wearing nothing but a pair of jeans.

I wait. God, he *is* hot. Next to him, Dan's got all the sex appeal of Mr Bean.

'*Ma mère*,' he shrugs. 'She is a beetch. I'm sorry she do this.'

'Yeah, sure. Whatever.'

'Please, Cate. I worry for you. We 'ave a villa in Marseille. I write for you *l'adresse*.' He shoves an envelope into my hand. 'I 'ave telephone Lauren, the 'ousekeeper, and tell 'er is OK.'

In the envelope is a thick wad of euros. 'I can't take this—'

'You give me back after, OK? I tell Fleur what 'appen when she come 'ome. She come see you at *le weekend*. I'm sorry, Cate. I like you *beaucoup*.'

'I like you *beaucoup*, too, Michel,' I smile.

He runs back up the steps and, with a brief wave, disappears inside.

I shove the money and address into my backpack, pick up my holdall and trudge towards the nearest main road. OK. I can do this. I'll hail a taxi, go to the station, and get a sleeper to Marseille. If I use cash to pay for my ticket, Dad won't be able to track me through his credit card. I'm not staying away for ever; I just need to get my head together before I'm ready to go home and face the music.

As I turn a corner, three teenage boys are lounging against a wall. When they see me, they step forward, not quite blocking my path, but crowding me all the same.

I keep my head down, trying to shrink into myself. I hate it when guys do this. They think it's just a bit of fun, but actually, it's really scary. They cat-call in French, laughing and jeering, but not actually touching me. Then, just as I get past them and think the worst is over, a fourth boy steps out from the shadows of a doorway, right in front of me.

Without stopping to look, I run across the road. Cars swerve round me, blaring their horns. I keep running, until I'm sure they haven't followed me.

Finally I stop to catch my breath, hands on my knees. A second later, I scream when someone taps me on the shoulder.

'Hey, are you OK?'

A girl not much older than me, with sun-bleached cropped hair and a huge, travel-stained rucksack on her back, peers into my face. 'You been crying?'

'I'm fine.'

'Sorry, didn't mean to scare ya.' She grins and sticks out a tanned hand. 'Jodi Crane. Originally from Oz, as you can prob'ly tell. I was doing Europe with some mates, but we kinda fell out a while back. I'm making my way down to Damascus to hook up with my sister. What's your name?'

'Cate Ashfield. I was staying with some friends, but we – we fell out too.'

'Fancy a coffee? You look like you could use a bit of cheering up.'

I hesitate. I don't even know this girl—

I sound just like my mother.

'I'd love one,' I say firmly.

Jodi leads the way to a small pavement café near the river. Over coffee and croissants, we exchange notes – 'Your mother sounds like a right nutter, but at least she didn't drag you to church eight times a week like mine' – and swap tips: 'Never trust a bloke who says "Trust me,"' Jodi says, '*especially* if it has anything to do with contraception.' She's forthright, funny, and outrageous. It's impossible not to warm to her. By the time we order a second round of espressos, it's as if I've known her for years.

'Look,' she says suddenly, 'if you ain't got any plans, why doncha come to Damascus with me? It's much safer travelling with a mate, and we'll have a great time. Whaddya say?'

I'm taken aback. Syria is a *really* long way away. Don't you need visas, or something? I won't be able to just jump on a train and go home when I've had enough. What about my exams? They start in a couple of weeks. I never meant to be gone that long.

But what's the point of doing exams if Dad won't let me go to NYU? I want to be a journalist. Who says I have to have a piece of paper to do that? I could get some real-life experience and work my way up instead. I might even be able to sell a few travel pieces to the *Mail* on the way. I'm never going to get anywhere if I don't learn to take a few risks. Woodward and Bernstein didn't get Pulitzers sitting at home playing Scrabble. I don't want to end up like Mum, scared to travel to the end of the road.

It's about time I took charge of my own life.

'OK. Why not?'

Jodi breaks into a huge smile. 'Neat! This is going to be so cool! We should get going straight away, head south. We can get you a visa at the British Embassy in Rome. Ever done any bar work?'

'Not yet.'

'It's real easy, and looking the way you do,' she winks, 'your tips are gonna be great.'

Her enthusiasm's contagious. This could be the best thing that's ever happened to me! Mum and Dad have babied me for too long. An adventure like this will prove to them I *can* cope on my own.

I push back my chair. 'Just need to use the bathroom—'

'In the back, towards the kitchen. Only don't use the john on the left, I was in there earlier and it sucked big-time, if you know what I mean.'

I leave Jodi minding my bags, and thread my way between the crowded tables to the back of the restaurant. Damascus! It sounds so biblical and exotic. It's not like I'm taking that much of a risk. Jodi's been around, she clearly knows what she's doing. It'll be fun travelling with her. And it's not like Mum and Dad are going to miss me.

The loo isn't exactly clean, but I tell myself I'd better get used to roughing it for a bit. I don't know much about Syria, but I've a feeling sanitation isn't high on their list of priorities.

I emerge into the sunshine, and realize I've come out the wrong side of the café. Jodi must be on the other side.

It takes ten minutes before I acknowledge the truth.

She's disappeared. So too have my backpack and holdall, along with all my money, my credit card, my passport and my mobile phone.

She didn't even pay for the coffee.

I collapse on to a chair. I can't believe I was so stupid. How could I trust a girl I'd known for half an hour with all my stuff? And I was going to run off to Syria with her! Maybe Dad's right. If I can't last five minutes on my own in Paris, how could I survive alone in New York?

The waitress tucks the bill beneath my saucer. I drop the last of my euros into it, and drift aimlessly through the park, fighting a rising tide of panic. What am I going to do? I don't even have a jacket: it was in my holdall, along with the rest of my clothes. I'll have to wait until it gets late, then go back to Fleur's. I'm sure she'll lend me enough money to get down to Marseille. After that – well, I don't know what I'll do after that. But I'll think of something.

Except that when I go back to the Lavoies', after spending all day wandering around the Tuileries, the house is in darkness. When the maid finally answers the door, she takes great pleasure in telling me the family has gone to Geneva for the weekend, before slamming it in my face.

I traipse back to the park, not knowing what else to do. It's starting to get dark. Fear ices my veins at the thought of staying out all night.

I climb over a low wall and hide in some thick bushes. I'd rather risk being disturbed by foxes in here than get attacked by a rapist or worse out in the open.

I trip over something soft, and nearly scream. Then I see a glimpse of yellow fur.

Near by, I find my holdall too. A sound, half laugh, half sob, escapes me. Jodi must have thrown my bags here when she'd taken what she wanted. The money and my phone and credit card have gone, but she's left my passport and clothes. At least I'm not going to freeze tonight.

I pull on my Gap sweatshirt, and try to sleep, but it's impossible. Every sound sets my heart racing. I shuffle over to a tree and sit with my back against it, so that no one can sneak up behind me. Oh, God, I'm so scared. Part of me wants to call it quits and go home, but Mum and Dad will be so mad, I just can't face them. Maybe I can get hold of Ben in the morning. He might be able to find a way to get some money to me without grassing me up. And then—

There is no 'and then'.

The night is full of terrifying sounds and snuffles. Every distant footstep is a mad axeman coming to get me. Each cracked twig is a killer on the prowl. My eyes ache with the strain of peering into the darkness. I can't stop shivering, from fear as much as the cold. Eventually, I fall into a fitful, exhausted sleep just before dawn.

I'm woken by bright sunshine slanting through the trees. I scramble to my feet, and brush the leaves and mulch from my clothes. Jodi's left my washbag; I squirt some toothpaste on my finger and rub it around my teeth, then feel stupid for bothering.

I'm bone-achingly tired, cold, stiff, and sick from lack of food. The only meal I've had in the last thirty-six hours was that croissant with Jodi. I've got to eat. Maybe if I look on the pavement near the café, I can find enough dropped coins to get a sandwich and ring Ben.

It takes me three hours to collect enough loose change for a small cheese baguette. I wolf it down, then curl up miserably on a park bench. It's hopeless. I can't do this. I'm not even sure why I ran away now.

Mum was telling the truth about Dan. Of course she was. She wouldn't do that to me. She loves me. I know that. She can't help that she's got an illness that makes her do strange things sometimes.

What the hell am I doing here?

She must be worried sick about me. I remember how she used to freak out if the school bus dropped me off late, thinking there'd been an accident. She'd sit outside ballet class and Brownies rather than leave me on my own, even for an hour. She was always lecturing me about accepting sweets from strangers, and going on about not taking the alleyway to the station after dark. OK, she screwed up big-time too. But she was *sick*. She couldn't help it. I've told myself this a thousand times before, but for the first time I actually believe it.

How could I ever have thought she didn't care?

If I can find a phone – call her – I bet she'll – I bet she'll—

I grab my bag and stand up, tears running down my face. *I want my mum.*

And suddenly she's there.

It's like a mirage. She's really here.

She reaches out her hand. 'Cate, please—'

For a moment, I can't even move. And then I'm running into her arms, sobbing into her shoulder, saying her name over and over again.

'I'm so sorry, Mum,' I mumble, when I finally stop howling.

'Don't cry any more, darling. Please. I can't bear to see you so unhappy.'

'But after everything I did! Aren't you mad?'

'Of course not!' She hugs me tighter. 'How could I be angry now? I've been half out of my mind with worry.'

'But why? I've been such a bitch—'

'Because you're safe,' she says simply.

I duck my head, thoroughly ashamed. What have I put my mother through? Her eyes are puffy and red from crying, and she looks, like, ten pounds thinner. She can't have slept for days.

Mum picks up my rucksack. 'You must be famished. Why don't we go and get something to eat, before we go back and face the music?'

'Have you – have you spoken to Dad?' I ask.

'Of course. He got the first plane from New York when I told him you weren't with Fleur. I just picked him up from the airport.'

'Dad *came*?'

Mum dumps my bag on the café table and waves a waitress over. 'Oh, we're mob-handed on this one,' she says drily. 'I've got Granny Anne in tow as well. I'm sure she and Daddy are having a lovely heart-to-heart right now.'

'Mum! You didn't!'

'Things are going to be a bit different from now on, darling.'

The waitress takes our order, and returns a few minutes later with two coffees and a *croque monsieur*. I grab the toasted sandwich, scalding my mouth on the hot cheese and ham.

'Cate,' Mum says, 'I owe you an apology.'

'Mum, of course you don't! I was the one who—'

'Please, darling. Just hear me out.'

She picks up a packet of sugar, tapping it nervously against the side of her cup.

'I don't blame you for thinking the worst about me and Dan,' she says. 'I've never given you any reason to trust me, have I? Nothing happened with him, but why should you believe that?'

'I do, Mum,' I say quickly. 'I was just being a stupid cow—'

'I would never intentionally do anything to hurt you, Cate. But I know I haven't been fair to you, and I can't just blame the illness,' she adds, swallowing hard. 'You've suffered more than either of the boys, and I can't forgive myself for that. I treated you the way my mother treated me, the way I always swore I'd never treat a child of mine: like some kind of second-class citizen. I didn't mean to, Cate, I promise. I've always loved you just as much as Ben and Sam. It's just—'

She puts down the sugar and twists her fingers together. I hold my breath; I can't remember my mother ever having a real conversation like this with me.

'I was jealous of you,' she whispers. 'Such an appalling thing to admit, being jealous of your own daughter. Oh, not because you're young and pretty, though you are, of course. But I was young and pretty too, once, hard as that is to believe now. I was jealous because you have energy and optimism and such a huge capacity for happiness. You're so determined to enjoy your life. You showed me what I *could* have been, if only I hadn't been born with this – this—'

'Mum, you're a brilliant artist,' I say helplessly. 'I haven't got half your talent.'

'But I've never done anything with it, have I?' she cries in frustration.

For the first time, I look and really *see* her. She's only

forty-one; just five years older than Ella. And still lovely, beneath the layers of worry and disappointment, her tropical blue eyes warm, her skin clear and unlined. Suddenly she's not just my mother, the boring, middle-aged housewife who's scrubbed and cooked and kept for me all my life, but a beautiful, still-young woman with her own dreams and fears. This can't have been the way she expected her life to turn out when she was seventeen. We both know Dad doesn't take much notice of her – she might as well be part of the furniture for all the attention he pays her. And part of that's my fault, I realize suddenly. I wanted to be the most important girl in his life. I elbowed Mum out of the way.

I remember when she planned for the two of us to go camping at the end of the garden as a birthday surprise; I can't have been more than six or seven. She'd bought a little tent for us, and sleeping bags and even a tiny camping stove. She must have been so excited about it; she'd been arranging it for weeks.

When I opened my presents and saw the tent, I was thrilled. 'But I want to go camping with Daddy,' I said, running over and climbing on to his lap.

I watched her face fall, and knew how much I'd hurt her. She never said a word, though. She packed our sandwiches and rolled up our sleeping bags and waved us off cheerily on our Big Adventure.

What a brat.

'Mum, it's not too late,' I urge. 'You could still do something with your painting. Eithne said you could do a show, didn't she? You could—'

'Cate, darling, we both know it's not going to happen.' She squeezes my hand. 'I need to start taking my pills again. Sooner or later I'm going to go off the rails if I don't. Sooner, probably. Once I go back on them, I won't be able to paint. I'll let everybody down.'

'Have you,' I ask, 'ever *really* tried?'

She picks up her coffee, then puts it back down untouched. An elderly couple at the next table crumble some bread and throw it on the ground. Birds peck at their feet, just inches away.

Mum's eyes fill with tears. 'Cate, I'm sorry. Sorry for so many things. I put far too much responsibility on your shoulders – what I did to you when your father was in Cyprus—'

I feel sick. I always try not to think about That Day. All the blood. I was so scared – oh, God, *so* scared. I had to shut down and pretend it wasn't real, I was watching a video, I could just press STOP any time and it'd all go away. It was the only way I could save her. I ripped up some tea-towels – *Granny Clara gave Mummy these for Christmas, she's going to be so mad* – and wrapped them round her wrists like they do on TV, and it all seemed so weird, like it was happening to someone else. When the ambulance men arrived, I almost expected Mum to get up and laugh, say it had all been a silly joke, it wasn't real, she hadn't actually tried to kill herself rather than be my mum any more.

Afterwards, I was so *angry*. And frightened. Even when the doctors said they'd given her medicine so she'd get better, and Dad brought her home, the knot of fear in my stomach didn't go away. She could do it again. Any time, she could do it again, and I might not be there to save her.

I had to keep watch. I didn't dare let down my guard, even for a moment. I hid all the sharp knives in the cupboard under the stairs. I emptied the bottles of aspirin and paracetamol. I threw out the weedkiller and bleach, though of course she just kept buying more. When Dad was home, at weekends or in the evening, it was OK, I knew she wouldn't try anything then, but when she was on her own – when it was just the two of us—

I never knew what I might find when I came home from school. I'd drag my feet as I walked up the path, dreading opening the back door.

'I was so scared, Mum!' I cry, unable to keep it in any longer. 'I didn't dare love you, I couldn't take the risk! It wasn't that I didn't want to – it wasn't that I didn't care—'

Mum stares at me, white-faced.

'I *had* to hate you. Don't you see? I had to make myself believe it wouldn't matter if you – if you weren't there. I didn't mean it,' I plead, tears streaming down my cheeks. 'I thought it was my fault you did it. I didn't know how to stop you doing it again. I was so terrified I'd lose you, I had to stop loving you – I had to protect myself—'

She throws herself out of her chair and pulls me into her arms. 'Cate, oh, Cate. It wasn't because of you, it had *nothing* to do with you,' she whispers fiercely into my hair. She disentangles herself, and cradles my damp face between her palms. 'Cate, listen to me. I didn't mean it. I never meant to kill myself. I would never have left you, do you understand that? I love you and the boys more than anything. I was sick. I didn't really know what I was doing.'

'But supposing – supposing you get sick again?'

'No matter how sick I am, I would never do that again. I didn't understand then what I was doing to you. I thought it was all about Daddy and me, and I was wrong.'

'I love you, Mum,' I sob. 'I'm sorry I ran away.'

'I love you too, Cate,' she says. 'I told you, it's going to be different from now on. No more being scared, darling. Not for either of us. I promise.'

I don't know what Mum says to Dad when we get back to the hotel, but when he comes to see me, he doesn't scream or yell or do any of the things I'd expected, but hugs me tightly like I've been gone for years.

I go to bed and sleep for eighteen hours straight, and when I wake up, I experience a flood of relief, like you do when you open your eyes after a terrible nightmare and discover none of it was real. It's like a huge weight has been lifted from my shoulders. I'm no longer filled with dread. It's going to be OK, I realize. I throw back the covers, giddy with happiness. *It's going to be OK.*

When I shower, I spot a series of tiny bruises, like fingermarks, on the inside of my thighs. I put what happened with Michel firmly to the back of my mind. What's done is done.

Over breakfast, I notice something different about Mum and Dad. I don't know what it is, but they're both being really weird. She insists we all go home together on the Chunnel train, and won't let Dad stay on in Paris for some business meeting, but what's really amazing is, he never says a word. He went out and bought her this beautiful pale blue Hermès scarf when we were shopping with Granny Anne; it's exactly the same colour as her eyes. He *never* buys her presents like that.

At first I think it's just because of the *Days of Our Lives* drama of the last few weeks and the whole running-away-to-Paris thing, but even after we get home and go back to normal (or what passes for it in our house), it doesn't wear off. He's coming home every evening before seven, and he doesn't stay up in London once. Mum's more chilled, too; she's taking her happy pills again, of course, but it's not just that. She's not exactly full of the joys, skipping around and crocheting friendship bangles; she's more like someone who's been in a terrible car crash and thought they were maimed for life, and then checked and realized they weren't that badly hurt after all. But it's a start.

It's all kind of freaky, but in a good way. I can go to school and have panic attacks over my exams like normal people. I don't know how long the peace-in-our-time routine will last, but I finally feel like I can breathe.

Three weeks after we come back from Paris, I take my last exam, go to bed and sleep for, like, a week.

When I finally get up around lunchtime, I mooch downstairs in a pair of Ben's boxers and an old T-shirt. Mum's been painting in her studio for days, so I'm not surprised when I don't find anyone in the kitchen. I've made myself some toast and Marmite, and I'm sitting at the kitchen table, flicking through the *Mail* and waiting for the kettle to boil, when Mum and Dad come in together and sit down opposite me like some kind of interview board.

I look from one to the other. 'What's going on?'

'I thought you didn't like Marmite,' Mum says nervously.

'I don't usually, I just fancied some today. Mum, why's Dad home from work? Is something wrong?'

'Nothing's wrong,' Dad sighs. He looks grey and tired. 'We've got something important to tell you, we've just been waiting for you to finish your exams—'

'I knew it. You're getting divorced, aren't you? That's what all this is—'

'This is about you, Cate. We want to talk about university.'

I look away. 'What's the point?'

'Hear your father out,' Mum says sharply.

Sometimes, I'm not totally sure this New Mum is a good thing.

'Your mother and I have discussed it at length. We realized – I realized – that this is your decision. We don't have the right to stop you doing what you want to do. But,' he adds quickly, 'we want you to be safe. Cate, you're still so young. Moving to New York is such a huge step. It's not like nipping over to Paris. You'll be so far from home if anything goes wrong.'

'So you've said,' I say, trying not to sound bitter. 'Why the big song and dance now?'

'Ben finishes at Oxford in two years,' Mum puts in. 'He wants to do a postgraduate course at Columbia, and his tutors think he'll have no trouble getting in.'

I shrug. 'So? What's that got to do with me?'

'Columbia's in New York—'

'She knows that, Beth. Look, Cate,' Dad says, 'what we're trying to say is that if you really want to go to NYU, we'll give you our full support if you'll wait a year and go with Ben. You don't have to live there together – I know you'll be doing your own thing, and so will he – but your mother and I would feel so much better just knowing he was near by.'

'You mean, take a gap year after my A levels?'

'Lots of students do it. And I could use a keen pair of

hands and eyes at the agency. How do you fancy coming to work for me?'

'Are you *serious*?'

'I might even be able to get you some work with one or two of the papers, too, if I pull a few strings—'

I throw myself at him. 'Daddy, that's fantastic! I don't mind waiting – it'll give me time to build up my portfolio – I can't believe it! Oh, thank you! I promise I'll take care.' I hug my mother. 'I know you talked him into it, Mum. I'll be really careful. Oh, God, this is so amazing—'

'Look, I'd better get going,' Dad says, standing up. 'I've got a meeting.'

He kisses Mum on the cheek as he leaves; something else he wouldn't have done a month ago. He smiles at me, but it doesn't quite reach his eyes. He looks defeated, somehow. For the first time, I wonder what this family harmony has cost him.

I'm not a baby. I don't want my parents to stay together for my sake. I just want them both to be *happy*, so I can get on with my own life without worrying about them.

Mum gets up to make some tea. 'Sometimes it's easy to forget how hard your dad works,' she says, watching him through the kitchen window. 'He's been under so much strain recently. James Noble has had it in for him since Dad turned down his takeover bid last summer. He's not finished yet, either. Several of Dad's key accounts have—'

'James Noble?' I interrupt.

'Sorry, darling. He's the man causing all the trouble.' She takes the lid off the kettle and peers inside. 'Wretched thing's boiled dry. I wish your father would just let me get a plug-in.'

Nausea pushes its way into my throat 'Mum,' I say urgently.

'Cate? Darling, are you all right? You look like you've seen a ghost—'

I shove back my chair. It slams against the dresser, toppling plates, but I don't even notice.

'James Noble,' I gasp. 'I know him. He's Dan's stepdad.'

13

Ella

'They're *suing* me?'

'I'm so sorry, darling,' Lucy says helplessly. 'I know how hard you tried to save her. They're just looking for someone to blame, and you're the easiest target. I'm sure it's not personal—'

'They think I killed their baby! How can that not be personal?'

I push my chair back and pace towards the window, struggling to take it in. A lawsuit! How can Anna and Dean think it's my fault Hope died? I did everything I could to save her! I didn't leave the hospital for a single second after their daughter became ill. If she'd been my own child, I couldn't have tried harder.

Except I couldn't save my own child either, could I?

'*Is* it my fault?' I cry, scrabbling through the folders on my desk for Hope's file. 'You were there. Was there something I missed, something I should have done—'

'Stop second-guessing yourself, Ella. You shouldn't even

be back at work yet, never mind poring over paperwork Go home and get some rest.' She takes Hope's folder out of my hands. 'The Shores may not even go through with it. They're in shock at the moment. And so are you,' she adds gently. 'It's only been two weeks since you lost your own baby, Ella. Look at you, working all hours of the day and night, running yourself ragged. You need to give yourself time to grieve.'

She thinks the baby was Jackson's, of course. There was a brief moment, as I lay on the floor of the hotel room in New York and realized what was happening to me, when I'd thought that too; and then I'd had a sudden, clear memory of standing in William's bathroom the morning I got the news that Jackson had died, hunting through my bag for an emergency tampon, annoyed that my period had started early, unaware that in a few minutes my mobile would ring and everything in my life would change.

Even as pain had snatched the air from my lungs, my mind raced. *William's, then*?

Vasectomies weren't 100 per cent reliable. It wasn't impossible. I shouldn't be pregnant at all; I wasn't some foolish teenager, taking chances. I hadn't missed a single pill, and yet here I was. Who was to say that William—

And then I'd remembered.

That night when Cooper had come to my bedroom, and we'd fucked each other in every sense of the word.

It hadn't been Jackson's baby I'd lost, but his brother's.

Lucy jumps as my office door opens. 'I think you should see this, Dr Stuart,' the duty nurse says, picking up the remote on my desk and pointing it at the flat-screen TV on the wall. 'Sky has been running it for the last half-hour.'

I clutch the edge of my desk. 'Oh God,' I breathe.

Anna Shore looks directly into the camera, as if she can see me watching. 'We placed our trust in what we were told would be the best hands at the Princess Eugenie,' she says, her voice breaking. 'We trusted them with our daughter. We were promised she'd get the very best care. But she was left to die by doctors who didn't think she was worth saving. She was just a number to them, an expense they could do without.'

My fingernails dig into my palms. She doesn't think – she *can't* think—

On screen, Dean steps forward and hugs his wife as she turns and sobs into his shoulder. He reads awkwardly from a piece of paper in his hand.

'We hope the General Medical Council will apportion the appropriate discipline in answer to the levels of negligence of the staff involved, and that hospital procedures are enforced to ensure such devastating failures never happen again,' he says stiffly. 'The mark of a civilized society is the way it cares for its most vulnerable members, the very young, the very old, and the disabled. No other parents should have to go through what we've been through in the past few weeks.'

A reporter picks up the story as Richard Angel walks out of the hospital towards a cluster of microphones. 'The Princess Eugenie Trust offered an apology to the Shore family, and promised an investigation was under way into the affair.'

'I wish immediately to apologize for any distress to Mr and Mrs Shore,' Angel says smoothly. 'We have not yet received a formal complaint, but an internal investigation was launched as soon as their case was brought to my attention, and we will of course keep you updated.'

'That's *it*?' I exclaim, as Angel swivels on his heel, fingers snapping. 'That's all he has to say? No vote of confidence in his own staff?'

'It's just a formal statement,' Lucy says uncomfortably. 'I'm sure he'll make certain you have every legal—'

'You're right,' I interrupt coldly. 'I should go home and get some rest.'

'Ella—'

My throat closes as I slam the door furiously behind me. For the first time, it dawns on me that this lawsuit will put not just my job and career on the line, but my dearest friendship as well. Not once has Lucy said she believes in me. Does she think I'm to blame, too? That I brought my personal life into work, and made a mistake that cost my tiny patient her life?

I need her to believe in me, because I can't.

The following Saturday, I get up early, throw on an old pair of jeans and a T-shirt and pull down the trap-door to the attic. I hesitate for a moment, my hand on the tread of the ladder, gazing up into the stuffy darkness. I wish I'd swallowed my pride and asked Lucy to come round and help me.

Don't bottle out now.

Carefully, I climb the ladder, my healing stitches pulling painfully with the unaccustomed exertion, and play my torch across the rafters.

The cramped, airless space is filled with cardboard boxes and black bin bags, thrown haphazardly on top of one another. Jumbled inside them are Jackson's clothes and books, his collection of antique hunting knives and a treasured ivory chess set, framed photographs of our wedding day, CDs, fishing rods, clay-pigeon trophies, tennis racquets, ski boots, defunct computer parts, DVDs, tapes, dog-eared outdoor-equipment magazines, the American flag folded neatly in a triangular display case, stars uppermost, a four-foot carved wooden fish – all the detritus of his forty-one – no, forty-two – years on this planet.

I haul down each bag and box, one by one, and lug them, panting, into the bedroom. After Jackson died, I couldn't bear to see anything that reminded me of him. But I have to deal with it if I'm to move on. I can't put it off any longer.

I start to sort slowly through it all. My cheeks are soon wet with memories. Even sadder are the keepsakes that mean nothing to me: a spray of pressed flowers that still carry a faint trace of jasmine, a pair of worn cream evening gloves I've never seen before, a small Tiffany box containing a silver baby's rattle. What did these things mean to Jackson? What are their stories?

I throw open the battered leather steamer trunk at the end of the bed – inherited from his parents, it's one of the few things Jackson shipped over when we moved here – and toss aside the spare blankets stored inside. Carefully, I fill it with the things I can't bear to give or throw away: the wedding pictures, his notebooks and knives. I add a worn pale blue cotton shirt that I used to love him in, and the college sweatshirt he wore every day when he went running. The rest of his clothes I'll give to the One World charity shop on the King's Road, along with most of his books and CDs.

On impulse, I place the pressed flowers, the gloves and the Tiffany rattle in the trunk. Perhaps I'll send them to

Cooper. If they meant enough to Jackson for him to bring to London, they're too important to throw away.

By the end of the day, I'm physically exhausted and emotionally drained. Summoning my last reserves of energy, I load Jackson's eco-friendly Toyota hybrid with cardboard boxes, and slide into the driving seat, adjusting it so that I can reach the pedals. We used to joke that Jackson's legs were so long, he could have reached the pedals from the back seat. When I turn on the engine – to my astonishment, after two months sitting in the garage, it starts first time – his favourite CD, Rascal Flatts' *Feels Like Today*, automatically begins to play. I eject it, slip it into its cover and add it to the nearest box on the front seat.

I double-park on the pavement outside the charity shop. A middle-aged woman in a hideous pansy-print dress and blue rinse comes out to help me unload.

'Thank you, dear,' she says, in ringing Home Counties tones, as I dump the last of the boxes near the shop counter. 'D'you mind holding the fort a moment while I take some of these things out to the back?'

She disappears before I have a chance to say no. I hover near the window so I can keep an eye on the car and make sure I don't get clamped. You can tell this is Chelsea, I think drily, glancing round the shop: all the donated bags are Louis Vuitton and the suits last season's Chanel.

A beautiful white linen layette is displayed in the window. I lean forward, marvelling at the tiny clothes and exquisite stitching. It's so beautiful. Utterly impractical, but beautiful. I hardly ever see babies in anything but miniature hospital gowns or the ubiquitous babygro.

A little pair of pale pink leather shoes embossed with

minute gold suns sits on a shelf near my shoulder. I pick them up and balance them in the palm of my hand.

The grief bursts over me like a tsunami, whipping in out of nowhere. I stand there in the shop window, huge, wrenching sobs convulsing my body as I howl like a child, in ugly, gasping wails, hiccupping and struggling for breath. I cry for Jackson, and my poor barely-there lost baby, and all the children I'll never be able to have. Snot and tears mingle on my cheeks. I cling on to the nearest shop rail and give myself up to it because I simply can't do anything else, the enormity of my loss is so utterly over-whelming.

I'm barely aware of the saleswoman taking me in her arms and leading me towards the rear of the shop, where she pulls me to her capacious floral bosom and pats my back as if I'm an infant.

'Get it all out, dear,' she soothes. 'It helps. That's it. Go on, you have a good cry.'

I bawl against her shoulder until I have no tears left. Two months ago, I'd have been appalled and embarrassed at breaking down like this in public. I've always prided myself on my self-control. But grief has transported me to a new world, where self-discipline and professional success count for nothing. I've always been the one dispensing hope and saving lives. Now I'm dependent on the kindness of strangers just to get from one day to the next.

Moments ago, I pitied this woman in her sitcom blue rinse and suburban smock. Now I'm clinging to her as if she's all that stands between me and the end of the world.

I've always seen vulnerability as some kind of weakness. How could I have been so *arrogant*?

'I lost my son three years ago,' the woman says unexpectedly, as the storm of grief finally blows itself out and I sink, exhausted, on to a wooden stool near the storeroom. 'He was blown up in a roadside bomb in Iraq. I coped well the first few months, it was like he was still away on duty. It was when I went to get the Christmas decorations down it hit me. He was the only one tall enough to reach the top shelf of the cupboard.'

I blow my nose loudly on a tissue. 'My husband died two months ago,' I say. 'He caught a virus and died, there was no warning. I never even got a chance to say goodbye.' I take a deep breath, and look her straight in the eye. 'I wasn't in love with him. He was my best friend but I didn't love him the way I should, the way a wife should love her husband.'

'Oh, my dear,' she says softly. 'I'm so sorry.'

She doesn't mean she's sorry he died. She's sorry for me, because I didn't know how to love him first.

I wrap my arms tighter around my knees in the darkness, drawing my feet up under me on the sofa. It's two in the morning, but I can't sleep. Of all the things to set me off. Baby clothes. I'm a walking cliché.

In my work at the hospital, I've met dozens of women who've spent years desperately chasing the dream of a child of their own: IVF babies are more likely than those conceived naturally to be premature, especially since so many are multiple births. For mothers like Anna Shore, the wizened infant in the Perspex butter dish represents the culmination of years of tests, injections, failures and disappointments; often, this treasured, fragile baby is their last hope. They've told me stories of falling apart in the babycare aisle of the supermarket; of crossing the road to avoid walking past BabyGap; of flinching at the cry of a child on an aircraft, and fantasizing about seizing the baby left unattended in his pushchair for a few brief moments. I've listened sympathetically, and then wondered how empty their lives must be that they need a child to complete them.

Baby hunger. I never understood the term until now. This visceral gnawing at your insides, an agonizing emptiness that nothing can fill.

I smile bitterly into the dark. I've spent most of my adult life working with babies, and never felt a single maternal pang. I wrecked my marriage by refusing, amongst other things, to give my husband a child. Now I'm a barren widow, my hormones have finally woken up and leaped into action. If there is a God up there, She has a sick sense of humour.

I get up and pour myself a large glass of white wine from the fridge. I thought I had my life all worked out. A high-flying career, child-free independence, a charming husband I was very fond of, and – the icing on the cake – a passionate, worldly older lover when I needed a quick thrill. I thought I could have it all; I thought I could keep all the plates spinning at once without dropping any of them. The word 'hubris' could have been invented for me.

Jackson had a theory: the Karma Credit Plan. He believed you built up karmic points, good and bad, depending on how you lived your life. Sooner or later, you'd be called to account.

It's all slipping away from me. Husband, lover, career, children – all gone.

I knock back the wine and pour another glass. I was so

terrified of ending up like my mother, or like Lucy, or any of the other thousands of women who get kicked in the teeth by men on the lookout for someone younger, prettier, perkier. I thought I'd ring-fenced myself from hurt by marrying a man I didn't really love. All I did was shut out everything that makes life worthwhile.

I must have fallen asleep, because I'm startled into wakefulness by the sound of the phone. I sit up, my heart racing. It's not even light yet. I glance at the set-top box on the television – 05:35. My chest tightens with panic, and I struggle for control. *It's just the phone.*

The answer-machine kicks in, and I listen to myself tell callers to leave a message.

'Ella? Are you there?'

Despite myself, I experience a miserable thrill of pleasure at the sound of his voice. It's two weeks since we last spoke, when he told me Beth had found Cate sleeping rough in Paris. I know I'm taking the coward's way out by dodging his calls, but I haven't trusted myself not to give in if I speak to him.

'Look, I know it's the middle of the night, and I'm sorry if I've woken you. I can't sleep. I don't know if you're busy, or if you just don't want to talk to me, but you can't leave it like this, Ella. If you're there, please pick up the phone.'

His voice echoes round the flat. I back quietly away from the answer-machine, as if he can hear me.

'Ella, we have to talk. There's something important I have to tell you. If it's really over, I can accept that, but I need to know what happened first. You owe me that, at least.'

Oh, God. This is so hard. *Why* did I have to fall in love with the one man I can't have?

'Ella, I know about Jackson's baby,' William says quietly.

The room tilts.

'I know how hard this must be for you. Actually, I don't, but I can imagine.' He sighs. 'It doesn't affect how I feel about you, Ella. Nothing could. You may not want to hear it, but I love you. You don't have to do anything with that information; I'm not even sure if I want you to. I just had to say it, that's all.'

There's such a long silence I think William's hung up.

I jump when he speaks again. 'We always said we'd stay friends. I never thought of you as a deal breaker, Ella.'

It took me eight years to admit I was in love with this man. Now I have to give him up, because I've finally understood that doing the right thing – at last – is the only way I can put my life back together.

He's right. I owe him an explanation, if nothing else.

I pick up the phone. 'I'm not,' I say.

'God, you look like hell,' William says.

'Thank you. I feel so much better now.'

He grins and pulls out a chair. I'm glad he chose somewhere public and upbeat like the Chelsea Brasserie for lunch. It makes this easier.

No it doesn't. Nothing could make this anything other than sheer desperate agony.

I edge my chair into the shade. The English weather is up to its usual tricks, seducing us with blistering August sunshine in late April, which no doubt will become freezing November fog by May. It's taken me thirty-six summers, but I've finally learned the hard way that, as a redhead, I *never* tan.

'Flip-flops?' William snorts, eyeing my footwear.

'Gold leather flip-flops. Metallics are very in this summer,' I say defensively.

'You hate sandals. I hadn't realized things were so serious. If I'd known you were reduced to sackcloth and flip-flops, I'd have acted sooner.'

William has already ordered wine, an expensive Montrachet. He pours me a cool glass and I sip it, fiddling uncomfortably with the stem. Neither of us seems willing, or able, to start a real conversation.

We order lunch – spatchcocked partridge for William, and the salade quercynoise with a confit of duck gizzards for me – and watch the foot traffic around Sloane Square. A crocodile of children from nearby Hill House School file past in their trademark cinnamon knickerbockers and beige shirts, giggling and jostling. A little girl of about five with thick red plaits and a splatter of freckles catches my eye. She looks just like I did at her age.

If I'd had a daughter, I wonder if she'd have looked like that.

I snap a breadstick, and line the pieces up neatly on the table. 'How's Cate doing?'

'Good,' he says, his tone surprised. 'I've no idea what went on in Paris – I'm not sure I want to know. But she's been much happier since we got back. Of course, Beth is levelling out again, so that helps.'

'She didn't miss any exams?'

'Got back just in time. Her last one's tomorrow. You know how focused she is, you never get much out of her at the best of times. But she's given the bloody boyfriend the elbow, which is the best news I've had in a long time.' He hesitates. 'She knows about us, Ella. She saw us that night in the station car park.'

I busy myself with my napkin, playing for time.

'You knew,' William accuses suddenly.

'She came to see me,' I admit. 'A few weeks ago. She asked me not to say anything.'

He pours us both another glass of wine, then stares into the bottom of his as if the answers to everything are written there.

'Is that what's behind all this?' he says finally. 'What's happening with you and me?'

'Partly.' I sigh. 'It's *everything*, William. When we started, no one was supposed to get hurt. It was supposed to be fun.' I push my salad away untouched, suddenly sickened by the thought of food. 'I thought this was just about the two of us, but it isn't, is it? There's a whole chain of people affected by our affair. Beth, of course, and Jackson – he didn't even know about you, but it still poisoned everything between us. And now Cate. We're the reason she ran away. She could have been raped or murdered because of us. We can't pretend it doesn't matter.'

'Of course it matters, Ella. But Cate understands. She knows her mother and I—'

'She's seventeen, William. She's still a child.'

'She's lived with Beth all her life,' he says soberly. 'She understands.'

'It's not just Cate. There's Ben, and Sam—'

'Ben's away at university, he has his own life. He'll be going to Columbia as soon as he finishes Oxford. He doesn't need his parents any more. And Sam is at boarding school. He'll always have a home to come back to, whatever happens, but his day-to-day life is bound up in his school, not us.' He frowns. 'Ella, my children aren't the issue. You've known about them for eight years. What's really going on inside your head?'

'You're married, William. Suddenly, that matters. I can't explain it.'

'I told you. I'll leave her.'

'William, you know that's not—'

'I've already discussed it with her.'

I knock over my glass, spilling wine across the table.

'Well, in a manner of speaking,' he amends. Suddenly he won't quite meet my eye. 'Cate running away brought everything to a head, in a funny kind of way. Beth doesn't actually know about you, but I think she's guessed there's someone. She asked me not to leave until Cate finishes her exams next summer.' He reaches for my hand, but I pull away. 'Ella, please. Wait for me. It won't be much longer. We've waited eight years, surely you can—'

'William, I never asked for this!' I exclaim, aghast. 'You can't leave because of me!'

'What do you think all this has been about?'

'I never wanted to break up your marriage—'

'For Christ's sake, Ella! Take some damn responsibility!' he cries with sudden fury, slamming his fist on the table. 'You can't sleep with me for eight years and let me fall in love with you and then back away with your hands up and say it's got nothing to do with you! The moment you kissed me in the park, it became something to do with you! Why else would I leave, if not for you?'

I stare at him, appalled. *I did this.* I set all this in motion. I started a chain reaction that's wrecking the lives of everyone connected to me.

William pulls himself together with a visible effort, and produces a wary smile. 'Ella, can we put this behind us, please? Let's think about the future, not the past.'

I have to put things right.

'Ella? In a couple of weeks, Beth's going off on a painting holiday in Italy with Eithne, it's been arranged for months. We could—'

'I don't love you, William,' I say clearly.

He recoils, as if I've punched him.

'I'm sorry,' I say, my gaze unflinching. 'I'm very fond of you, of course. We've had a great time. But I don't love you. I don't want you to leave your wife for me. There's no point.'

'I don't believe you,' he says hoarsely.

My hands are shaking. I hide them beneath the table.

'We always said that if either of us wanted to end this, we'd walk away, no questions asked. It's just not working any more, William. I need someone with less baggage—'

'You don't think I'll leave her, do you? That's it, isn't it? I can't blame you, it sounds like the oldest line in the book.' He leans forward eagerly. 'I mean it, Ella. Just give me a chance, and I'll come through. I know you love me—'

'It wasn't Jackson's baby.'

He stares at me, stunned.

'You haven't been the only one, William, you know that. After all, we're not married to each other, are we?'

I watch the light in his eyes die. The pain and disillusion

that replace it are almost more than I can bear. Instinctively, I reach out to him, and he looks at my hand on his arm as if my touch is poison.

'You bitch,' he breathes.

He stands up so abruptly his chair topples backwards, and plucks half a dozen notes from his wallet, flinging them on the table. 'This should just about cover your fee.'

'William—'

He looks at me with disgust. 'Jackson was the lucky one,' he says stonily, and walks away without a backward glance.

'You idiot,' Lucy sighs, when I turn up on her doorstep and fling myself, sobbing incoherently, into her arms, 'you can't just hand him back to his wife like he's a toy you've got tired of, it doesn't work that way. I know you're trying to do the right thing, Ella, but it's gone too far for that. Sometimes staying and living a lie is more dishonest than having the guts to leave. I should know. I thought when Lawrence walked out, it was the worst thing that had happened to me, but once the shock wore off I realized he was right to go. We'd been faking our marriage for years. By leaving, he gave me the chance to have an honest relationship with someone else. You and William love each other, Ella. I don't want to come over all Mills & Boon, but love is so precious. You don't have the *right* to throw it away.'

'Oh, God,' I cry despairingly. 'What have I done?'

*

He doesn't return my calls. After ten days, I stop making them. I wanted to make the break irreversible. How marvellous that I've succeeded.

I go to work because I don't know what else to do, but it's no longer an escape. I'm terrified of making another mistake. It's like I've suddenly forgotten how to walk; what once came to me instinctively, I now ridiculously over-analyse, hobbling myself with my own fear. I'm painstakingly thorough, checking and double-checking the most basic procedures. Hope isn't the first baby I've lost by making the wrong call; every doctor lives with the stark reality that their errors and misjudgements *will* kill a patient at some point. Her death didn't cause my loss of confidence; my self-doubt is what led to her death. How can I trust my judgement at work when it's so clearly lacking in every other area of my life?

I volunteer to work the May Day bank holiday because I can't bear to be at home. I'm sitting in my office, staring at Hope's autopsy report without reading it – I don't need to: I know every word by heart – when Richard Angel walks in without knocking.

'Dr Stuart. May I have a word?'

I shrug.

He jerks the leather chair on the other side of my desk further away from me, as if my proximity is toxic, and sits down. Given my recent run of luck, perhaps he's wise.

'I'm here at Dr Nicholson's request,' Angel opens sharply. Naturally: he doesn't want me to mistake his presence for anything approaching professional solidarity. 'Lucy has prevailed upon me – against my better judgement, I might add – to ask the Trust to convene a meeting to discuss the Shore case in advance of our official inquiry.'

He grimaces as if he's sucked a lemon. 'This will be your opportunity – your *only* opportunity – to put your case before we decide what level of support the hospital will be able to offer you. I don't need to tell you that your future depends on its outcome.'

'You're not settling with the Shores?' I ask in surprise.

'They have already gone public with their complaint, which, I am sure you are aware, is extremely serious,' he says unpleasantly. 'This is most unfortunate. Clearly a swift and discreet resolution of the matter is now impossible.' What he means is that the hospital trust can't just pay up to minimize the negative press coverage, thereby throwing me to the wolves by effectively admitting liability.

I'm not fooled by his promises of an impartial inquiry. If he has his way, I'll be left to sink or swim on my own, at the mercy of the red-top newspapers, which love nothing better than a tragic dead-baby story to boost circulation.

'You don't like me, do you?' I say conversationally.

He stiffens. 'My personal preferences don't come into it.'

'Oh, come on, Richard,' I jeer. 'You've made your "personal preferences" very clear. You've been waiting for an opportunity like this ever since you took over.'

'If you're referring to my dislike of your intuitive approach to your work, then yes, I have indeed feared just such a development as we now have,' he snaps. 'You are emotional, instinctive in your approach to client diagnoses, and wilfully empathetic—'

'Wilfully empathetic?'

'This is not a charity, Dr Stuart. This is a business. Our clients expect the very best—'

'Our *patients* expect to be treated as human beings, not

battery-farmed chickens on some sort of medical conveyor belt!' I exclaim. 'Three-quarters of the time an accurate patient history will give you a correct diagnosis before you even put on your stethoscope. To do that you have to know who your patients are and what's brought them to you. Of course you have to be empathetic—'

He stands up. 'This is pointless. I can see we have a fundamental divergence in our approach to client care. Regardless of the outcome of the inquiry, you may wish to consider, Dr Stuart, if your philosophy is entirely compatible with that of this hospital.' He pauses at the door. 'The board will convene on the twenty-third of this month. I cannot emphasize enough how crucial it is for your sake that you are there.'

My paperweight hits the door as it shuts behind him, shattering. Bastard. *Bastard*! What the hell is Lucy doing with him?

I know the answer to that question, of course. Richard Angel is everything Lawrence Nicholson was not: predictable, organized, morally upright – in his own way; he would never break a promise, or a rule – and disconcertingly honest. He truly believes that his way of running the hospital is in the best interests of his 'clients'. If he were a forensic pathologist, I'd find his dedication and attention to detail admirable. It's just unfortunate, given his dismal bedside manner, that our patients still have a pulse.

By the time I get home, my anger has given way to despair. If the hospital doesn't support me, my chances of winning a lawsuit are slim. And if I lose that . . .

All doctors are covered in theory by NHS indemnity for mishaps whilst working, but in practice it's not worth the paper it's written on. Like most medics working in a high-risk specialty, I've got extra insurance, which I pay for myself. Or at least I had. What with everything that's happened over the past three months, I've rather lost track of the paperwork.

I fumble for my door keys. I could lose my licence to practise medicine, my job, everything.

Just twelve weeks ago, I'd have been in a frenzy of terror. Now, it doesn't matter. My career seems almost unimportant next to everything I've already lost.

A figure steps out of the shadows. His face catches the light, and I scream.

Jackson.

'I didn't mean to scare you,' he says.

'What do you expect when you hide in the shadows and leap out at me! What the hell are you doing here?'

'I've been waiting on you to get home.'

'You'd better come in before someone calls the police.'

I'm shivering with shock. I drop my bag in the hallway, and am about to go into the kitchen to put on some coffee, but turn towards the drink cabinet in the sitting-room instead. I need alcohol.

I pour us both a generous double measure of Scotch, and hand him a glass without bothering to ask if he wants one. 'You scared me half to death. Why didn't you tell me you were coming?'

'You'd have set the dogs on me.'

He has a point.

I drain my drink, and pour another. 'Look, Cooper. It's late, and I'm really tired. I've had a miserable day at work, and I need to sleep. I don't know what it is you want from me, but I can't deal with it tonight. If you need a place to stay, there's a spare room—'

'I came to give you these.'

He thrusts a bundle of papers awkwardly towards me. I put down my glass, but make no move to reach for them.

'Take them,' Cooper says, almost angrily.

I stare at him, this fierce, bitter, beautiful man who is so much like my dead husband to look at, so like William in his absolute, arrogant certainty, and yet utterly different from both of them. I barely know him; I certainly don't like him. And yet I'm drawn to him in a way I can't explain. He has a brooding intensity that sucks you in, a dark, dangerous charisma that's almost hypnotic. An unexpected pulse beats between my legs.

I take the bundle of envelopes, my hand trembling: from fear, or desire, I can no longer tell. There are about thirty; judging by the postmarks, they date back more than ten years. All are addressed to Cooper in Jackson's familiar, flamboyant script.

'I don't understand. Why are you giving me these?'

He ignores my question. 'Keep them. I don't want them back.'

'Why are you really here, Cooper?' I ask tiredly. 'You could have sent these. You didn't need to bring them yourself. Is there something you want? I've given most of Jackson's things to his charity, but I kept a few bits and pieces in case you wanted them.'

He doesn't reply.

I touch his arm. 'Cooper?'

'If I'd posted them,' he says, his cobalt eyes blazing, 'I couldn't have done this.'

His kiss is hard, hot, passionate, searing. My breasts

crush painfully against his chest, and there's a slippery rush of wetness between my legs.

'I've hated you since the moment I saw you,' Cooper murmurs into my hair. 'Oh God, how I hate you.'

Gently, I kiss his angry mouth. 'I hate you too,' I whisper back.

February 14, 2008

Felden Street
London SW6

Dear Cooper,

      *Happy Valentine's Day, bro! And thanks for
the b-day card. Ella forgot again; like this is news. Guess I'm
buying my own present this year. Time this letter reaches
you, I should be the proud owner of a 1972 250cc Indian
Cub! Gonna cost, but not as much as it should, thanks to
eBay. I reckon I can talk Ella round if I play the guilt card!*

    *She doesn't know it yet, but I'm giving her a fair trade.
Something she's wanted for years, too. I'm coming home,
Coop. For good.*

    *Hope you and Lolly could use the company because I'm
going to need somewhere to lay my head for a bit. Sorry to
spring it on you like this, but I didn't want to say anything
till I'd gotten things sorted my end. Turns out One World
have a new office opening a short ways out of Charlotte, so
I'm transferring there soon as I hire a replacement for my old
job. They even threw in a raise, but it's still going to take a
while to put away enough cash for a place of my own. I don't
want anything from Ella. This house in London has never
felt like my home anyways. I'll bring the Indian and my
books and Grandpa's chest, but I'm leaving the rest. I don't
need any reminders.*

    *Seven years is a long time for a man to wait for a woman
to love him. I don't just mean me; I'm talking about William
Ashfield too. There was a time I wanted to string him up,
but I can't find it in me to be angry any more. A part of me
almost feels sorry for him, poor bastard. Must be going soft*

in my old age. I went to his house once, did I tell you that? Years ago. Stood outside in the rain and watched him flipping pancakes with his little girl in the kitchen.

Ella's not mine. She never was. You knew it, didn't you, bro? Tried to warn me, but I wouldn't listen. All this time I've been fooling myself I had enough love for the both of us. I never should have married her. I knew I wasn't the one for her, same ways as I knew she was the only one for me. Love works like that sometimes, doesn't it? We all like to think we got a soulmate out there, just waiting to be found. No one says they gotta love you back, though.

Remember when I was a kid, I found that stray, the one with the broken leg? Man, I loved that mongrel. Stayed up night after night nursing him. I couldn't have been more than seven. Spent all my allowance buying him treats and whatnot, even skipped school till Mom caught me out in the old barn, playing ball with him. But soon as he was healed, he wanted to be off. He'd pull at his leash, whining fit to bust. He didn't belong with me, I just didn't want to see it.

Mom said then that if you loved something, you should let it free; if it came back to you, it was yours. And if it didn't, then it never was.

Well, I'm setting Ella free. I should have done it years ago.

Guess I've only clung on so long because I wasn't ready to say goodbye. I knew she'd never leave me, she's got too much stubbornness in her. She's like you, Coop. Reckon you'd have been better for her than me, come to think of it. I rolled over too easy, gave her what she wanted. A woman doesn't respect you if she always has the upper hand. Hindsight's 20/20, right?

I should have stood my ground when I first found out

*about William, and told her to choose. Maybe back then she'd
even have chosen me, but I guess I'll never know now. I've
been weak, bro. All I can say is, love makes fools of us all.
You never know what you'll do for it until the time comes.*

*Figure you're wondering, why now? I'm not sure I know
the answer to that one. Daddy would say I'm finally growing
some balls, and maybe he's right, but it's not just that. Sure,
I got dreams. I want to know what it's like for a woman to
love you, really love you, like you're her reason for
breathing. I want to see that in my woman's eyes. I want
babies, I want to take all that love and see what we make of it
between us. Ella's never going to give me any of that. All the
time I'm loving her, there's no room for me to love anyone
else. What I feel, it's like a creeper, strangling everything else
before it has a chance to take root. I don't know if I can
change that, yet it seems I've gotta try, before it's too late.*

*But the simple truth is, I love Ella too much to stay. She's
not happy with me, not the way a woman should be happy.
I've tried my damnedest but I can't give her what she needs.
I've got to step aside, and give her a chance to be with
someone who can.*

*If I can see her happy, I reckon that'll be the first step to
being happy myself. You know what I'm talking about, Coop.
It's no more than you did for me.*

*You've been the best brother a man could have. If I
screwed up, it's not because of anything you did. I hope
I haven't disappointed you too much.*

*I'll be telling Ella at the weekend. Soon as I work out
when I'm coming home, I'll let you know. Reckon it won't be
more than a few weeks. I can't tell you how much I'm looking
forward to leaving the British weather behind me! You
wouldn't think the world had this many shades of gray.*

The Infidelity Chain

Seems I most always have a cold these days. Couple weeks of Lolly fattening me up with her home cooking, and I'll be a new man!

Fire up the grill, bro. I'll soon be home.

Jackson

14

William

Christ! This is all I fucking need!

I storm into the hotel room. My daughter's missing, my girlfriend's just lost her dead husband's baby, I'm fighting to save my company from going tits-up, and my wife has picked this moment, of all moments, to come off her drugs and start rapid-cycling her moods. Now, to top it off, my bitch of a mother has just crawled out from whatever rock she's been hiding under for the past twenty years.

Any more liquid ordure coming my way?

My mother tips the porter and shuts the door carefully behind him.

'So,' I say tightly, 'to what do I owe this honour?'

'I'm dying, William.'

As opening gambits go, it's a showstopper.

I crack open the mini-bar. 'Here's to you, Mother,' I say, downing a miniature of Bell's in a single gulp and unscrewing another.

She takes it away and pours it down the bar sink. 'Get a

grip, William. I didn't come all this way to watch you fall apart. If I can deal with it, so can you. No wonder your daughter ran off, if *this* is the kind of thing that's been going on at home.'

'Don't worry, Mother. You haven't driven me to drink. This is the first good news I've had in a week.'

'Sit down, William.'

I'd forgotten how much taller I am. In memory, she still towers over me—

'I said, sit *down*!'

I fling myself into an armchair. 'Fine. Keep your bloody wig on.'

'How observant of you. I could have gone for something a little younger, of course, but one doesn't want to draw attention. Chemotherapy, William,' she adds acidly, as I gawp. 'Pay attention, I don't wish to go through this twice. I have acute myeloid leukaemia. It's terminal.' She smooths her skirt over her lap, picking off an imaginary piece of lint. 'I was diagnosed eleven months ago; I've already had two courses of chemotherapy and radiation, but the cancer has come back. If I were younger, I'd be a candidate for a bone-marrow transplant – oh, don't worry, William, I'm far too old. You won't be called upon to make a display of filial devotion and donate.' Her thin lips twist. 'That would have been an interesting moral dilemma for you, though, wouldn't it?'

I hate the bitch, but she's got balls. We could be discussing the weather.

'The prognosis is bleak – well, from my point of view.' Another tart smile. 'The doctors are talking now in terms of weeks. Curious, isn't it, how we measure the start and end of our lives in weeks, not years, every day precious.'

I find my voice. 'So what's this about, Mother? Looking for a deathbed reconciliation?'

'Oh, I didn't come for me, dear. Well, not as far as you're concerned. I wanted to see my grandchildren again, I must admit; I have a particular fondness for Caitlin. Girl's got more balls than all the men in our family put together.'

I grimace at the ironic echo of my own thoughts.

'No, I came, William, because there are things that need to be said.'

'Sorry to disappoint, but I don't give a damn what you need to get off your miserable chest before you check out,' I say coldly, getting to my feet. 'My daughter is *missing*. Right now, salving your conscience is the last thing on my mind. Whatever self-serving crap you came to dish up, save it. As far as I'm concerned, the next time I see you, you'll be in a wooden box.'

She doesn't flinch. 'I'm not here to salve my conscience, dear. You're the one in trouble.'

I fold my arms contemptuously, waiting.

'I'm quite aware what you think of me, William. You've made that very clear. I've watched you turn your father into a saint, while you pushed me firmly in the other direction. I've sat by and said nothing while you made a complete mess of your life, because you wouldn't have listened anyway.' She waves her hand dismissively. 'Oh, I'm not talking about Ashfield PR – you've made exactly the same mistake I did, and poured all your energies into your company: of course it's a success. I'm talking about your marriage. You're more like me than you realize.'

My hackles rise. 'I've spent the last seven years trying to *stop* my wife committing suicide. You *drove* Dad *to* it!'

'You'd like to believe that, William. And perhaps there's

even a grain of truth in it. But your real problem is that deep down, it's not me you blame, but yourself.'

I feel the air rush from my lungs. Punctured, I deflate on to the edge of the bed.

'It's much easier to tell yourself I harangued your father into his grave, isn't it? You've certainly done your best to convince yourself that's how it happened. Trouble is, it won't wash. You still believe it's *your* fault. It's why you married Beth.'

'Oh, please. Don't give me the fucking cod psychology,' I snap, but my voice lacks conviction. 'You haven't got a clue—'

'You weren't to blame for what your father did, William.'

'I bloody know that! *You* pushed him over the edge, not me! Telling him he was a failure, going on about how useless and pathetic he was—'

'When?'

'When *what*?'

'When did you hear me tell him that?'

'Christ, what does it matter now?' I slump forward, my head in my hands. 'Whatever he needed to hear, I didn't give it to him, he blew his brains all over the shagpile, end of story. And spare me the California psychobabble, Ma. I got a woman pregnant and married her. Forget the redemptive bullshit. She was up the duff, I did the honourable thing. I had no idea I was a bloody suicide magnet till it was too late.'

'I've never heard anything so ridiculous. Suicide magnet indeed. It's part of the illness, you know that—'

'What illness? What are you talking about?'

'Your father was manic depressive, William.'

My head jerks up. 'No. I'd have – he can't – I *know* about manic depression!'

'Then you should understand. I thought you realized. It ran in his family, though I didn't know that till after he died, of course. I found an old family photograph in the attic when I was sorting out his things, a boy in the back row who didn't look quite right; and there was an aunt who was locked up and died young.' She gives a self-mocking smile. 'I thought I could save him. We're not so different, you see.'

I'd have known. Surely.

I can't have got it so wrong.

I attempt to rally. 'You expect me to believe this shit?'

'I'm many things, William, but a liar isn't one of them.'

I revisit my childhood, observing it through the lens of my life with Beth. Dad's extraordinary bursts of energy; the endless unfinished DIY projects. The dark, inexplicable moods: 'Your dad's having a bad day. Let him sleep.' Twice, when I was still very young, he disappeared altogether for several months; probably to a clinic, I realize now.

Dear Christ. If my mother endured half of what I've had to put up with from Beth . . .

The silence between us stretches.

'Your father wasn't a fool. He knew I didn't mean some of the things I said; he understood I was angry at the illness, not him. But I still shouldn't have said them. In that sense, perhaps his death *was* partly my fault. But it certainly wasn't yours. He stopped taking his medicine when he lost his job. You've lived with Beth long enough to know what that means. Nothing you could have said or done would have made any difference.'

Medicine?

It wasn't my fault?

It wasn't my fault.

'William, I spent more than thirty years trying to fix something that couldn't be mended,' my mother says urgently, grasping my sleeve. 'It turned me into someone I didn't recognize, eaten up with anger and bitterness. In the end, I lashed out at him not because I hated him, but because I hated what his illness had made *me*. I don't want you to make the same mistake, son. I don't want you to become bitter and resentful. I know you have the children to consider, but don't do what I did. Don't become someone they despise.'

I shake her off, but without venom. Dear God, a bloody shrink would have a field day with this. I thought it was women who married men like their fathers.

She's right, of course; but what she doesn't realize is that she's too late. I hate myself already. I'm a one-woman man; I believe in faithfulness and loyalty and love. And I've been cheating on my wife for most of our marriage.

My mother struggles to her feet, leaning heavily on a silver-topped cane. I'm struck suddenly by how frail she's become.

'Beth's a good woman,' she says firmly, 'but she's not good for you.'

I laugh disbelievingly. 'You really are a viper, aren't you? She's played fair with you all these years, let you see the kids, brought you to Paris, and now you're telling me to leave her!'

'I'm just warning you what will happen if you don't.'

I lock eyes with the woman who gave birth to me, who gave me her chin and colouring and ruthless ambition, and feel nothing. Which is progress, of a sort, given my feelings towards her for the past twenty years.

So much left unsaid.

'This doesn't change anything,' I manage. 'You can't just waltz in and say your piece and expect everything to be OK between us overnight.'

'Certainly not,' she says crisply. 'You're my son. A tough negotiator. I wouldn't expect anything less.'

'She's my daughter too, Beth! I want to see her!'

'She's not ready to see you,' my wife says, with infuriating calmness. 'She needs to sort herself out first. Not to mention shower; the state of her, quite extraordinary, she'll need sandpaper, not soap. Anyway,' she adds, 'we need to talk before you go rushing off like a bull in a china shop and scare her away again.'

I've had just about enough of women and their cosy little chats for one day.

'I didn't fly halfway round the world to twiddle my thumbs in another bloody hotel room!' I snap, pushing past her towards the door. 'There's nothing we need to discuss that can't wait.'

'What about your affair, William?'

Ah. Except that.

'Well. Affairs, plural, I should say,' my wife amends, 'I'm sure there's been more than one. After all, we haven't had sex for eight years. You'd have to be made of stone not to want it from someone, and trawling King's Cross isn't really your style.' She pulls back the curtain and looks down at the Paris streets, her back ramrod straight. 'Cate ran away because we let her down. A lot of that's my fault,

I know. I've damaged her, and that's something I have to live with. But a lot of it has to do with *us*. You and me. She's still a child, William. She still needs us.'

'Beth,' I say carefully, 'I never meant to hurt you—'

'I'm not blaming you, William. That's not what this is about.'

I pinch the bridge of my nose. 'It's been a hell of a day. Do we have to talk about this now?'

'Cate's afraid everything's going to fall apart,' she continues, as if I haven't spoken. 'She's running away so she doesn't have to see it happen. You're too wrapped up in your – work. I'm too wrapped up in my own problems. We've both failed her.'

Screw these miniatures. What I wouldn't do for a bloody stiff drink.

'What is it you want from me, Beth?' I say wearily to my wife's back.

'We've got two choices. We can paper over the cracks, pretend everything's OK, and watch our daughter lurch from one crisis to another and wreck her life. Or we try to do something about it.'

'Fine. I'll cut back at work—'

'I'm not talking about work.' Finally, she turns from the window to face me. '*We're* the problem, William. I told you. This pathetic apology of a marriage isn't doing anyone any good, least of all Cate. We've got to start being honest. Either we try to fix it, or we give up and call it a day.'

The words hang in the air. She's pale, but in control. No tears. No histrionics.

I can't quite believe it's *Beth* who's finally daring to acknowledge the elephant in the room.

'Are you talking *divorce*?'

'If that's what you want, yes. I won't stop you,' she adds. 'I won't fight it or – do anything silly. Ben's left home, Sam's at boarding school; it'll be tough on them, but they'll survive.'

'This – this is what you want?'

'No! Of course it's not what I want! William, I love you more now than the day you offered to help straighten my picture at the exhibition,' she cries fiercely. 'But even I can see this isn't working the way it is. Sooner or later you'll meet someone who won't put up with sharing you. If you don't want to be with me, I'd rather end things now, while we can still be friends.' She takes a deep breath. 'I just want one thing.'

Here it comes. The house? Half the company?

'A year.'

She rushes on. 'Do it for Cate, if not for me. She'll be going to university next year and getting on with her own life. If we can just see her through her A levels. Give our marriage one last, final chance. If we both give it our best shot and you still feel the same in a year, if you still want to leave, I won't stand in your way.'

She's offering me freedom. A way out without guilt or recrimination. The promise of a new start with Ella, without having to worry if my wife's going to slit her wrists again or jump off a cliff.

I can't leave her—

It's not my fault my father killed himself.

She's giving me a choice. Marriage as penance short-changes us both.

Ella will wait twelve months for me, surely.

'A year?'

'No more lying,' Beth says quickly. 'If we're going to do this, we have to mean it. You have to honestly try, William. You have to *notice* me.'

'And you'll take your pills?'

She hesitates.

'It won't work if you don't, Beth. You know that. You know what you get like.'

'Yes. I'll take my pills.'

'A year,' I say.

It doesn't even occur to me I might want to stay longer.

'There's one other thing,' Beth says, moving towards me.

Slowly, nervously, she unbuttons her neat blouse. She unfastens her plaid skirt, and lets it fall to the floor. She's wearing underwear I haven't seen before: lacy, pink and cream. Her whole body is trembling.

Her blonde hair swings forward, hiding her face, as she reaches behind and unhooks her bra. I'm suddenly reminded of the first time she undressed for me, more than twenty years ago. Her hands shook so hard she dropped her watch, then knocked over a full wineglass when she bent to retrieve it.

My cock springs to life. *She's beautiful.* I'm ashamed how much that surprises me.

Her breasts sway lushly as she bends to peel off her knickers. Gravity and three children have taken their toll, but they've given her curves she didn't have before, a voluptuousness I don't remember. It suits her. There's something else different about her, too. It takes me a moment, and then with a shock I realize: she's shivering not from nerves, but desire. She *wants* this.

She sinks to her knees and reaches for my flies. She reeks of sex, I think suddenly. Where the hell has *that* come from?

Her lips close around my cock.

I can't – she's rapid-cycling – it would be taking advantage – she's manic, it's not her – I can't – oh, God, that feels—

'Beth – are you sure . . . ?'

She looks up. 'No more papering over the cracks, William. If we're going to do this,' she adds, returning to the task in hand, 'we're going to do it *properly*.'

For once, I don't mind letting let my wife have the last word.

'For God's sake, Ella, pick up,' I mutter, drumming my fingers on my desk.

I glance apprehensively at the closed study door. It's five-thirty in the morning; if Beth wakes up, she's bound to wonder why I'm not in bed beside her.

Come on, pick up! It's been two weeks since I got back from Paris, and I still haven't had a chance to tell her the news. My initial excitement has been gradually leached away by worry. She can't mean what she said in New York, surely? If I can just tell her what's happened. I realize she's avoiding me, but I'm starting to get desperate. I've already called the hospital; she's not working today. She has to be home. Where else would she be at this time of night?

I swear under my breath as her answer-machine kicks in. 'Look, I know it's the middle of the night, and I'm sorry if I've woken you. I can't sleep. I don't know if you're busy, or If you just don't want to talk to me, but you can't leave it like this, Ella. If you're there, please pick up the phone.'

Nothing but the crackle of static.

'Ella, we have to talk,' I say urgently. 'There's something important I have to tell you. If it's really over, I can accept that, but I need to know what happened first. You owe me that, at least.'

The floorboards above my head creak. *Shit*.

'Ella, I know about Jackson's baby. I know how hard this must be for you.' I correct myself. 'Actually, I don't, but I can imagine. It doesn't affect how I feel about you, Ella. Nothing could. You may not want to hear it, but I love you. You don't have to do anything with that information; I'm not even sure if I want you to. I just had to say it, that's all.'

I picture her hunched up in bed, refusing to pick up the phone.

I can't leave it like this. I have to know she's at least OK.

Playing my final card, I take aim at her pride. 'We always said we'd stay friends. I never thought of you as a deal breaker, Ella.'

'I'm not.'

'Ella! Thank God! I've been going frantic—'

'Sorry. I've been – busy . . .'

Her voice sounds thick, disused.

'Is everything all right? Are you OK?'

'Not really. What is it you need to tell me?'

'Not over the phone.'

A sigh. Then, 'Where?'

'How about the Chelsea Brasserie? Thursday, say seven-thirty—'

'Thursday's OK. But not dinner. Lunch.'

'But—'

'Lunch, William.'

She's not going to make this easy. But I can win her round. As soon as she hears the news, she'll change her mind.

I'm counting on it.

Ella looks at me in horror. 'William, I never asked for this! You can't leave because of me!'

A waiter tops up our wineglasses. I wait impatiently for him to go.

'What do you think all this has been about?' I hiss through gritted teeth.

'I never wanted to break up your marriage—'

Bitter disappointment swamps me. *This isn't how she was supposed to react.*

'For Christ's sake, Ella! Take some damn responsibility!' I slam my fist on the table; an elderly couple walking past the pavement café leap as if they've been shot. 'You can't sleep with me for eight years and let me fall in love with you and then back away with your hands up and say it's got nothing to do with you! The moment you kissed me in the park, it became something to do with you! Why else would I leave, if not for you?'

She recoils as if I've slapped her. In the harsh April sunshine, the fine lines sketched around her eyes and mouth are clearly visible. Her eyes are bruised, her expression hunted. I tell myself it's only been a couple of months since her husband died; less than four weeks since she lost his baby. No wonder she looks like death.

Ironically, Beth's blooming. She's never looked better, in fact.

With a supreme effort, I settle back in my chair and summon a smile. 'Ella, can we put this behind us, please? Let's think about the future, not the past.'

Her gaze drifts. I suppress a resurgent beat of anger. Doesn't she understand? *I'm going to leave my wife for her.* 'Ella? In a couple of weeks, Beth's going off on a painting holiday in Italy with Eithne, it's been arranged for months. We could—'

'I don't love you, William.'

My stomach goes into freefall.

'I'm sorry. I'm very fond of you, of course. We've had a great time. But I don't love you. I don't want you to leave your wife for me. There's no point.'

Is this some sort of *joke*?

I laugh uncertainly. 'I don't believe you.'

She folds her hands in her lap and regards me coolly. 'We always said that if either of us wanted to end this, we'd walk away, no questions asked. It's just not working any more, William. I need someone with less baggage—'

'You don't think I'll leave her, do you? That's it, isn't it?' Silly girl; why didn't she just *say*? 'I can't blame you, it sounds like the oldest line in the book. I mean it, Ella. Just give me a chance, and I'll come through. I know you love me—'

'It wasn't Jackson's baby.'

I search her eyes for some sign she's kidding.

'You haven't been the only one, William, you know that.' She shrugs carelessly. 'After all, we're not married to each other, are we?'

She's fucking serious.

I want to be violently sick. Bad enough that she screwed someone else, but that she got pregnant by him – *pregnant*—

Jesus Christ almighty. I held her hand in the ambulance, I was the one pacing up and down all night at the fucking hospital!

Anger courses through me like a molten river. I want to kill someone. The conniving, cheating, deceitful whore! I should have bloody seen this coming. She opened her legs eagerly enough for me. I was an idiot to think I was the only one.

'You bitch,' I spit, shaking her hand off my arm and standing up so sharply my chair falls backwards. I throw a fistful of twenties on the table. 'This should just about cover your fee.'

'William—'

'Jackson was the lucky one,' I snarl.

I walk blindly without a fucking clue where I'm going. I can't believe I've been so comprehensively *had*. I got it all wrong. No wonder my company is going under. My judgement's shot to shit.

She's played me for a fool. It was all fine and dandy while she could invoke the sainted Jackson, but now she's on her own she hasn't got anywhere to hide. She never really wanted me. She just wanted to get her kicks, taste a bit of forbidden fruit. Of course she didn't want me to leave Beth. I was just her bit on the side. She's probably got another married sucker on the line already.

How could I have been so fucking *blind*?

*

I sleepwalk through the next few weeks. It's my turn to ignore Ella's calls; I delete her number from my phone and put a block on my email. If only I could block out the pain as easily.

I cling on to my anger as long as I can, but in the end grief forces its way to the surface. It's like having my heart fed through a shredder. The fact that she's made a patsy of me into the bargain rubs salt in a mortal wound.

The irony is that if this had happened any time in the past eight years, it wouldn't have killed me. Until three months ago, our relationship was a two-dimensional, compartmentalized fling. Outside of our nights together once a month, it didn't really exist. I made sure I knew nothing about her life, or what went on in her head, and she never asked about mine.

Jackson's death changed everything. For the first time I met the real Ella, the vulnerable, fallible woman behind the perfectly controlled façade. I fell in love with her in a way I never could have done with the confident old Ella. I fell in love with her fear of flying, her ridiculous shoes, her hatred of losing half a pair of anything – gloves, books, earrings – the way her nose ran when she cried, her mercurial and unpredictable moods.

Except I hadn't met the real Ella at all, had I? It was all an act.

I pick up the red leather box on my desk and put it in my pocket. A gold love bangle from Cartier; my fashionista daughter will appreciate its cachet, even if Beth doesn't. I've had it inscribed with my wife's name.

She's really trying. The sex isn't ground-breaking, but it's regular, and she even makes the first move sometimes.

She's gone shopping for new clothes with Cate, and changed her hairstyle for the first time in twenty years; the *gamine* crop suits her. It's not just the way she looks, either. In her own quiet way, she's made it clear she's not taking any shit from anyone. She overruled me on the new Hummer and insisted on a bloody hybrid, for God's sake (I see Cate's hand in that). It's all taking a bit of getting used to, but I have to admit I rather like the bolshy new attitude. I hadn't realized how tired I've been, carrying this marriage on my own. It's the first time in all these years I've felt as if we're in things together.

Beth was the one who came up with the compromise on New York. I'd still rather Cate didn't go at all, but at least if she's with Ben, it'll go some way towards putting my mind at rest.

When Beth asked me to wait a year, all I saw was a way out. Maybe, just maybe, it's actually a way forward.

I'm half out the office when the phone goes. I look for Carolyn, but she's already left.

'William? It's Malinche Lyon. William, it's been bothering me for days, but it finally came to me – in the supermarket, of all places, they've got the most extraordinary range of spices these days, I remember when I had to get Kit to bring me sumac from Dubai, it was the only way to get it fresh – anyway, I was dithering over the cumin, whether to go for whole or ground, and then I remembered where I'd seen that lovely boy in your office: Cate's boyfriend, I mean. I *thought* he looked familiar. I know it probably doesn't matter, but Nicholas said he'd heard something on the grapevine, you'd been having some problems with a hostile takeover bid, and the name rang a bell—'

'Mal,' I say patiently, 'what *are* you talking about?'

She giggles. 'Oh, dear, baby brain again, Nicholas says I'd forget my name if it wasn't sewn into my knickers. Dan, of course. He came to my restaurant just before Easter with his real father, I've known Simon for years. Dan is James Noble's stepson, William. I just thought you ought to know.'

'Dan's not the mole,' Beth says.

'What are you talking about? Of course he bloody well is!' I storm across the kitchen, nearly tripping over the dog. 'And I bloody *employed* him, for fuck's sake! I gave him a job at my office!'

Beth puts another dirty plate in the dishwasher. 'It's not Dan,' she repeats stubbornly.

'Haven't you been listening? It must've been a set-up from the beginning. Look at the way he turned up here out of the blue! Obviously Cate had no idea he was using her to get to me, but—'

'William, would you shut up for *one minute!*'

There are times when I'm not entirely sure about this new assertiveness.

She slams the dishwasher shut and turns to face me. 'It isn't Dan! You can't go charging off to his house in the middle of the night accusing him of industrial espionage! What do you plan to do, drag him out of bed and lynch him from the nearest apple tree?'

'Don't be so bloody melodramatic.' I stop pacing, my eyes narrowing. 'Why are you so sure it's not him?'

'It's not me either, if that's what you're thinking,' Beth snaps.

I'm aware of Cate watching TV in the next room. I lower my voice.

'Look, Beth. It all makes sense. For the last six months, James Noble has been one step ahead of the game, poaching my best members of staff and stealing clients out from under me. He has to have someone on the inside, someone privy to more than the usual office information. Some of the stuff he's got hold of was just too damn sensitive. And Dan mysteriously appeared on the scene just before Christmas. You do the maths. No one else fits the bill.'

Beth busies herself with wiping down the kitchen counter. For a long moment, neither of us speaks.

'There is one person,' Beth says.

I sit in my car in the darkness, staring at her house. The lights are on downstairs; through the wooden shutters, I see her shadow move around the sitting room. I have no idea how long I wait, or why I'm even here. A gentle wind stirs the branches of a tree overhead; May blossom falls like confetti on the bonnet of my car.

God defend me from my friends; from my enemies, I can defend myself.

In the distance, a church bell chimes eleven. A cat yowls; moments later, a dustbin lid clatters to the ground.

Unexpectedly, Ella's front door opens. I duck down in the car, but she can't see me. She's wearing a pale silk dressing-gown; the breeze sculpts the flimsy fabric to her form, silhouetting her against the light spilling from the doorway. She looks like a goddess: beautiful, and treacherous.

A second figure appears behind her, tall and broad-shouldered. As he steps into the pool of light, I curse beneath my breath. He looks so like Jackson, there's only one person he can be.

Ella turns. Her face lifts to his, and he kisses her. I feel the passion, the intensity, in that kiss, even from here.

I start the car, angrily forcing it into gear. It's time to stop fooling myself. Ella and I were never real. A hothouse romance, unable to survive in the real world. She gave me passion and excitement and challenged me in ways I can't begin to explain, but those aren't the proper foundations of a marriage. She was the perfect mistress. And that's all she was.

Beth loves me. It's not perfect, but she's my wife. We've got three children and twenty years between us. She's right: it's worth fighting for.

It's past midnight by the time I let myself quietly into the house. I toss the car keys on to the hall table. Cannelle whimpers softly, and I fondle his golden head as he slumbers in his basket in the warm kitchen.

Pouring myself two fingers of single malt, I shut myself in my study. Time to grow up, Will, old son. Be grateful you didn't make a bloody arse of yourself and dump the wife for a cheap bit of totty.

She cheated on Jackson with me, and now cuckolds me with his brother. It's fitting: almost biblical.

It also hurts like fuck, but I'll get over it. I'm not a callow youth in the flush of first love. I've been around the block enough times to know that, much as you might want it to at times, a broken heart doesn't kill you. I still have Beth. She adores me. We're still good together. There's a lot to be said for the companionship and security that come with two decades of shared experiences. She still laughs at my jokes, no matter how many times she's heard them.

I knock back my drink, and turn out the light. It's about time I tried a bit harder with Beth. She's been pulling out all the stops for the last month, but if I'm honest, my contribution has been a bit half-hearted. Apart from the sex, of course. I don't think she could fault me there.

To my surprise, Beth's sitting up in bed, reading. When she sees me, she lays the book aside and puts her glasses on the bedside table.

'You didn't have to wait up, darling. I told you I'd be late.' I yank off my tie, and perch on the edge of the bed to unlace my shoes. 'Something wrong?'

'Yes, William, I'm sorry.'

I look up. 'Sorry for what?'

'My mind's made up, I'm afraid,' Beth says clearly. 'I'm leaving you.'

15

Beth

Seeing Jesus in the cornflakes is a warning sign by anybody's standards.

I've been given a second chance with my daughter. I won't get a third.

I always knew I'd have to start taking the pills again, sooner or later. I wouldn't have brought them to Paris with me, tucked into the lining of my handbag where I could pretend I'd forgotten all about them, if I hadn't known time was running out. This morning I spent €900 on exquisite Meerschaum pipes for William in the hotel shop. He doesn't even smoke.

I can't afford another manic episode. I took the drugs. Now I just have to make sure it's worth the price.

My husband tries to push past me to the door. I screw up the courage to take the biggest gamble of my life, knowing I could lose everything.

'What about your affair, William?'

The blood drains from his face. Guilty as charged. I realize how much I'd still hoped it wasn't true.

I turn to the window, so he can't see my face. 'Well. Affairs, plural, I should say,' I add lightly. 'I'm sure there's been more than one. After all, we haven't had sex for eight years. You'd have to be made of stone not to want it from someone, and trawling King's Cross isn't really your style.' I'm surprised how normal my voice sounds. 'Cate ran away because we let her down. A lot of that's my fault, I know. I've damaged her, and that's something I have to live with. But a lot of it has to do with *us*. You and me. She's still a child, William. She still needs us.'

I sense William wondering how to handle this, how to handle me. He hates scenes.

'Beth, I never meant to hurt you—'

'I'm not blaming you, William. That's not what this is about.'

When I tell him what I want, I'm ready for him to affect surprise; to protest at the idea of leaving me, even. Perhaps, at some level, he might actually mean it: William is a man, after all. Used to his creature comforts, the familiar routine of home. He won't want to leave unless he has somewhere – some*one* – to go to. Most men don't.

I'm not ready for the raw, desperate hunger in his eyes.

I watch him weigh my future in his mind. I know he isn't seriously considering my offer – at least, not in the sense I want him to. If he agrees, it won't be because he wants to give our marriage a chance to work, but because he's looking for a guilt-free, no-strings way out.

But a lot can happen in a year.

'A year,' William repeats slowly.

Now or never, I tell myself. Dan wanted me. Eithne

wanted me. If I'm to hold on to my husband, I must make him want me too. Somewhere out there is a faceless woman who knows how to sigh and flatter and please my husband, who has stolen him away from me with her long legs and come-to-bed eyes and pliant body. I have to win him back. I have to make him want me again.

Whether *I* want *him* is irrelevant.

'There's one other thing,' I say.

I don't take my eyes off him as I undress. My mouth is dry; I can't seem to stop my hands trembling. He hasn't seen me, really *seen* me, for a long time. I'm forty-one. (How old is *she*?) My breasts sag; my stomach is pleated and covered in stretch marks. (Does *she* have children?) Will he be repulsed at the thought of making love to me? Will he *laugh*?

I can't meet his eye. I drop my gaze as I unhook my bra, but find myself staring straight at his crotch. There's no mistaking the bulge.

You're beautiful. That's what's so amazing about you! You don't even realize how lovely you are! If I'm beautiful to Eithne, I can be beautiful to William, too.

I strip off my knickers and close in on William, reaching for his flies. His penis springs into my hand, bucking beneath my touch. What do all those sexpots in shiny beach novels usually do next? Something the old Beth would never try. I fall to my knees and take him in my mouth. It doesn't taste *too* bad. He shudders violently, gripping my shoulders so hard it almost hurts. I've never been very good at this, but I do my best, licking his penis like it's an ice-lolly melting in the sun. He groans, so I'm obviously doing something right.

'Beth – are you sure . . . ?'

'No more papering over the cracks, William,' I say firmly. 'If we're going to do this, we're going to do it *properly.*'

I open my jaw wide, praying I don't gag. Experimentally, I stroke his testicles. His response is to pull me to my feet, scoop me up and almost throw me on the bed.

For the first time, I actually start to feel aroused myself. William parts my thighs, and puts his head between them. I sit up, about to protest – *I haven't washed! I'm not ready!* – and then remember the sexpots. Perhaps, when men talk about wanting dirty sex, they mean it literally.

I've never been very adventurous in bed. Having one's bottom whacked with a wooden spoon sounds so unhygienic. And I've never really seen the point of handcuffs.

But in the last few months, I've been propositioned by a boy young enough to be my son, and fallen into bed with my oldest girlfriend. I think a little cunnilingus is allowed.

'A bit faster, please,' I say firmly.

He's not as silver-tongued as Eithne, I think absently; and then, quite suddenly, I find I'm pleasantly unable to think at all.

'He's not really *trying*, of course,' I say, 'apart from in the bedroom, naturally.'

Eithne slugs back another shot of vodka from her silver hip-flask. 'I wouldn't call *that* trying at all,' she says waspishly.

'You're very sweet, darling, but we both know I'm not Cirque du Soleil material in the boudoir, and never will be. No, William's been very conscientious in that department, but it's quite clear his mind's not on the job.'

'I wish I could say the same,' Eithne sighs.

I turn back to the carrots. 'He was fine for the first week or two after we came back from Paris – rather *too* fine, actually,' I say painfully, 'like a child waiting for Christmas. And then last week he came home in a foul mood, and he's been in a complete funk ever since. I've no idea what's the matter with him, he won't tell me. He just sits brooding in his study for hours. To be honest, Eithne, I'm beginning to think the business is about to collapse and he's scared to come clean. And to make things even worse, he keeps buying ridiculously expensive presents to make up for being so miserable, then forgetting what he's bought, and giving me the same thing again.' I stop peeling to move tonight's roast further out of Cannelle's reach. 'I've had to take back two Cartier bangles already, much to Cate's disapproval. She was all for selling them on eBay and buying herself a car.'

'Smart girl. She's rather gone up in my estimation, I must say.'

'Not necessarily a good thing,' I observe.

'She's not pining over the boyfriend, then?'

'Dan?' I'm suddenly very busy with my root vegetables.

'Yes, *Dan*,' Eithne mocks. 'You really are a terrible liar, Beth.'

'I didn't say anything—'

'You didn't need to.'

I finish the carrots, and reach for a string bag of sprouts. 'He keeps calling me,' I confess. 'He's left dozens of messages on my mobile since we got back from France. Obviously I haven't returned any of them—'

'Why "obviously"?'

'Why?' I splutter. 'Eithne, it's – well, it's obvious!'

'Oh, absolutely. I can quite see why you'd prefer to abase yourself for your worthless husband rather than entertain the idea of a gorgeous young man who's completely infatuated with you and would no doubt happily go down on you for *hours*. It makes perfect sense. Honestly, Beth. Haven't I taught you anything? You should be biting his bloody hand off in gratitude – and I say this as one who has a vested interest,' she adds grumpily.

'He's not infatuated—'

'Adultery *really* isn't your forte,' Eithne says, 'you're the colour of a tomato.'

'Pass me that saucepan,' I say crossly.

She hands it to me, and lights a cigarette. 'Is it because of Cate?'

'No! Well, yes, of course. She may be over him, but she'd hardly be terribly pleased if her mother – if he— Anyway, that's not the point!'

'I'm sorry. What *is*?'

'Eithne,' I say, exasperated, 'I'm *married*. That still means something to me, even if it doesn't to anyone else these days. And even if I wasn't, Dan is half my age! What do we have in common? I was studying light and colour at St Martin's when he was still trying to stack plastic bricks!' I drop the carrots in the water and put the saucepan on the Aga. 'He was barely out of nappies himself when I had my first baby! You know it'd never work. And it's bound to be me who'll end up heart-broken,' I add realistically, 'you know I never do anything by halves.'

'You're making too much of this. It's just *sex*,' she says. 'Isn't it?'

I hesitate. Eithne is never without a metaphoric bucket

of very chill water to hand. I know Dan is just flattering me, to get what he wants, but he seemed genuine—

Suddenly, I feel very foolish. I *need* a moral drenching. I've let that young man lead me up the garden path. In the cold light of day, it all seems very different. I should've told William as soon as Dan confessed. If he loses his company now, it'll be my fault.

'There's something very important I have to tell you,' Dan had said, when he turned up at the house the afternoon Cate went missing. 'Actually, two things. Please, will you just hear me out?'

I'd assumed he was talking about Cate, of course.

I'd watched Dan pick up a pot of thyme on the windowsill, put it down, then take a paring knife from the rack and test it against his thumb before laying it back on the butcher's block. He was so clearly cat-on-hot-bricks, I'd actually smiled. Cannelle lifted his head from his paws, panting. Dan knelt down and gave him a couple of the doggy treats he always kept in the pocket of his cargos.

The dog trusts him, I remember thinking, *he can't be all bad*.

'Dan, please, I don't have much time—'

He'd stood up and fixed me with those amazing green eyes.

'I think I'm in love with you,' he said simply. 'I've tried very hard *not* to be. No offence, but this isn't exactly a result for me. A married woman twice my age, with grown-up kids and everything—'

'Yes. I can see that,' I said faintly.

'Cate wasn't a game,' he added quickly. 'I never meant to hurt her. It's just, she's so *like* you. I thought I could find in her what I felt about you, but—'

I couldn't really take it in. All I'd cared about was finding my daughter. At the time.

'What's – what's the other thing, Dan?'

'You have to believe me,' he'd pleaded, 'I didn't know what James was doing. It was nothing to do with me, I had no part in it, I swear—'

'And *do* you believe him?' Eithne asks now, when I've finished telling her everything.

'I should never have trusted him,' I say bitterly. 'I let him persuade me he had nothing to do with James Noble because I wanted to think he'd meant the rest of what he said. I've just been fooling myself. Of course he doesn't love me! It sounds ridiculous, even to me—'

'Is it really so ridiculous that someone might fall in love with you?'

'He's just trying to buy time, so I don't go running to William. He's using me, like he used Cate.'

Eithne looks at me strangely. 'And if he *wasn't* James Noble's stepson?'

I start to protest, but Eithne's right: I'm a terrible liar. I've been drawn to Dan from the first moment we met at the art gallery. I just haven't acknowledged it before.

I'm not going to rip my family apart for a fling with a young boy who'll swiftly tire of his Mrs Robinson moment and move on. I'm not *that* much of a fool. But his attention has meant more to me than I care to admit. He made me believe in myself, if only for a moment. It hurts to know it was just another lie.

I shrug, my eyes glittering with tears.

'Dan does love you,' Eithne says flatly.

'No. It's time I stopped—'

'It's not Dan who's been spying for James Noble,' Eithne says, 'it's me.'

'I always told you that girl was trouble,' Clara snipes. 'All those piercings and tattoos.'

'She doesn't have tattoos, Mother. And actually, you never said—'

'I don't take any pleasure in being proved right, Beth. You know me. Live and let live, that's my motto.'

I yank a weed out of the flowerbed with more force than is strictly necessary.

'I'm not surprised William's hardly talking to you – that's not a weed, dear, you'll have no flowers left if you carry on like this – the poor man's been working all the hours God sends, and all the time you've been undermining him, harbouring a viper in your bosom.'

Haven't I just, I think grimly, shooting her a glare. I count to ten and pray for patience.

'You can't blame him for being upset. It shows such lack of judgement on your part, Beth. You take after your father, of course. He's always been a *dreadful* judge of character—'

I rock back on my heels and brush dirt from my forehead with the heel of my gloved hand. 'Aren't the roses doing well this year, Mother? Dad sent you roses every week for a year when you were courting, didn't he? He was absolutely mad about you in those days. Quite head over heels,' I add meaningfully.

My mother sucks lemons. *One to me.*

'I do wish you hadn't cut your hair,' she says pettishly. 'I'll never get used to it.'

'I was thinking of getting a tattoo next. A dolphin, on my right shoulder—'

'Really, Beth. I'm surprised you're in a mood to joke.' She tucks a stray tendril of pink clematis neatly beneath the kitchen windowsill. I immediately free it again. 'I assume the girl was being paid? Eithne, I mean. Thirty pieces of silver, or whatever the going rate for betraying your friends is these days.'

'Actually, I think in a funny way she was just trying to help,' I sigh.

'I don't know how you can possibly defend her,' Clara snaps. 'She's practically put you out on the streets.'

'It's complicated. Look, Mother, I really do need to get on—'

'At least you won't still be going ahead with this ridiculous Italian nonsense,' she sniffs, 'not now that woman's shown herself in her true colours. Absurd idea in the first place. Jetting off to the Continent to mess about "discovering art" at your age. Lord knows what would have happened to your poor family when you were gadding about Europe.'

I contain my simmering temper.

'They'd have been fine. Cate's perfectly capable—'

'Perfectly capable! She's a delinquent! You should've taken a much firmer hand with her when she was young. I'm sorry to be the one to say I told you so, but—'

I pick up my trug, and get to my feet. 'Cate is *not* a delinquent. She's beautiful, and funny, and bright, and I'm so proud of her it hurts to breathe!' Suddenly, I can't contain my anger. 'My daughter has determination and talent and ambition, and she's already twice the woman you or I could ever hope to be! I will not have you coming to my house and pouring your poison on my family! You've made my life a misery since the day I was born. I won't have you turning your venom on my daughter!'

I'm trembling. I've never spoken to my mother like that in my life. I half expect her to stand me in a corner, or wash my mouth out with soap.

'Well! It's no wonder she's run off the rails if this is the example she gets at home!' Clara snatches the edges of her quilted jacket together. 'I won't be treated this way by my own flesh and blood! *When* you're ready to apologize, you know where I am!'

I sink on to the stone steps by the rose garden as she storms away, a half-laugh-half-sob dying in my throat. It's taken me forty-one years to find the courage to stand up to Clara, and I know already I've wasted my breath. I'll just have to apologize to her now, and she'll make me crawl over hot stones before she'll accept it.

Oh, Eithne. What *possessed* you?

She's never approved of William, I know that, but I had no idea she'd go this far to sabotage us. Did she really think that wrecking his company would force me to stand on my own two feet – 'If he wasn't there to prop you up all the time, Beth, you could do so much more, *be* so much more; please, you must believe me, I would never do anything to hurt you, I was only trying to *help*' – or was it simply revenge?

The awful irony is: in some ways Eithne was actually *right*. As William's struggled to keep his company afloat, his confidence has gradually leached away. For the first time in all these years of marriage, I don't feel overwhelmed by him.

I look up at the sound of footsteps.

'Mum? Are you OK?'

I give my daughter a lopsided smile. 'I'm not quite sure.'

Cate plonks herself on the step next to me. She looks a bit pale; I think she stayed up too late last night when she slept at Clem's. 'Is it true?' she asks. 'Is Eithne really the mole?'

I nod.

'But why? I thought she was your friend?'

'She's never really forgiven me for marrying Daddy,' I sigh. 'She thinks it's his fault I stopped painting.'

'Well, it is, a bit,' Cate says.

I stare at her in astonishment.

'Come on, Mum. You've got to admit he's a bit of a control freak. You always let him have his own way, same as you do with Granny Clara.'

'He's always been very encouraging about my painting—'

'Yeah, as a *hobby*. Can you imagine what he'd have said if you'd wanted to, like, do it as a career or something? He'd have gone ape.' She picks a fragile white climbing rose and smells it. 'Gorgeous. They're amazing this year—'

'Cate, it's not your father's fault,' I interrupt. Suddenly it's important she understands. 'I *let* him take over. I blamed him, and I blamed the illness, but the truth is it's *my* fault I stopped painting.'

It's the first time I've admitted it even to myself.

'I was afraid to fail,' I confess. 'It was easier not to try.'

Cate picks up the secateurs, and cuts a dozen white blooms, filling the trug. Their scent, sweet and strong, drifts towards me.

'Are you still going to Italy on Saturday?'

'No. I was in two minds about leaving you anyway. I suppose Eithne and I will get over this eventually, but it's going to take time. She had no business interfering the way she did, whatever her motives. I trusted her, Cate. She's the one always telling me not to be such a doormat and let people walk all over me.' I smile sadly. 'She's got a lot of grovelling to do before we can be friends again. I sort of understand why she did what she did, but I don't think we'll ever be quite the same.'

'You don't need her, Mum.'

I ruffle her hair. 'Not when I've got you.'

Cate shrugs me off. 'Mum! I meant, to go to Italy. You should go on your own.'

'Darling, I couldn't.'

'Why not? It's only for three weeks. Mrs Ghedini can come in and clean and stuff. Dad and me can manage.'

I open my mouth to tell her not to be so silly, and then pause. I'd been looking forward to Rome *so* much. The 'Pietà' – the Sistine Chapel – the catacombs of St Callistus – hours and hours to walk and look and think and maybe even paint. Eithne would've been great company, of course, but she can be very – well, *demanding*. I've never had a holiday by myself; not even a weekend away. And the children *would* be fine—

'What about your father? I couldn't leave him, it wouldn't be fair.'

'Mum, it's time to think about *you* for a change,' Cate says.

I look into her silvery-blue eyes, the colour of the sea just after a storm has passed, and suddenly realize she's not just talking about three weeks in Italy.

'You don't have to stay for me,' she says softly. 'I'll be

gone soon. If you don't leave now, you may never bring yourself to do it. I want you to be happy, Mum. I don't want to worry about you any more. When we did the *Titanic* at school,' she adds, looking down and fiddling with the secateurs, 'Mrs Buchanan said some of the people who drowned might have survived if they'd stopped clinging to each other. Sometimes you – you just have to let go.'

I'm washed by a wave of love for this brilliant, difficult, unique child of mine.

'Since when did you get to be so wise?' I gasp.

'Mum, it's OK,' Cate says. 'Go. I'll be fine. Dad'll be fine. We'll all be OK.'

'I do love your father, Cate. Very much.'

She nods, her eyes suspiciously bright. 'Not always enough, though, is it, Mum?'

'No.' I pull her into my arms, grieved that she's had to learn this lesson so young. 'No, it isn't.'

What was the turning point? I wonder. That brief, unguarded moment in Paris when his eyes told me, clearer than lipstick on his collar ever could have done, that he was having an affair? Seeing his longing for *her* written on his face when I offered him a chance of escape? Was it when he stood over me while I took my pills, a jailer, not a lover?

Virginia Woolf lies unread on my lap. Perhaps it was Cate bringing home our failure as parents when she ran away to France. Or when I begged William not to send Sam to boarding school, and he sent him anyway.

Maybe it was when he took the children skiing, but left me home because he said I played up to their fears.

Or perhaps it came the day he laughed at the idea of me opening a little art shop. Or when he ordered for me at a Vietnamese restaurant because he assumed I couldn't cope with the menu.

Did I finally start to get angry when I went to bed with Eithne, and saw myself, just for a moment, through her eyes instead of his? Or when Dan told me he loved me, and I realized how much William has denied me?

No. It goes back beyond that. Back to Cyprus, when William booked another woman into a hotel with my name.

Back further: to that dreadful place where they held me down, strapped me to a table with leather buckles and glued electrodes to my head.

Back to the beginning: when I built a marriage on a lie, the biggest lie of all.

It's not William I'm really angry with.

The pages of *Mrs Dalloway* blur. For years I've accepted a second-rate, second-hand love because I was too scared to demand better. I've cheated both of us. I used a lie to trap William, and I've used pity and guilt to bind him to me. All I've done is make us both miserable. Cate's right. I need to set us free now, before it's too late.

William's tyres crunch on the gravel drive. I glance at the digital clock on the bedside table. Nearly midnight. Where on earth has he been?

I check myself. What does it matter now?

It's another twenty minutes before he comes upstairs, smelling of bitterness and whisky. I take off my reading glasses and put my book aside.

'You didn't have to wait up, darling,' he says wearily. 'I told you I'd be late.'

Yanking off his tie, he tosses it on to the floor for me to pick up and put away tomorrow, and slumps on the end of the bed to unlace his shoes. 'Something wrong?'

'Yes, William, I'm sorry.'

'Sorry for what?'

Suddenly, it doesn't seem hard at all.

'My mind's made up, I'm afraid. I'm leaving you.'

For a moment, he doesn't react. Then he laughs.

He laughs.

I'm engulfed by a fury so incendiary I'm surprised the bedclothes don't burst into flames. I spring out of bed, planting myself right in front of him where he can't ignore me, or pat me on the head and send me away.

'Do you think my life is so wonderful with you I couldn't dream of leaving? Do you think I *enjoy* it when you look at me like shit on the sole of your shoe?'

He looks taken aback. 'That's not what—'

I'm shaking with indignation. 'You've treated me like a charity case for twenty years, as if I should be grateful to have you, and, fool that I am, I've let you! You, Clara, even the children – you all act as if I'm the village idiot, incapable of independent thought or feelings of my own! For forty years, I didn't even dare to change the way I did my hair! Did it ever occur to you how difficult *you* are to live with?'

He pushes past me into the bathroom and throws cold water on his face. 'What's this really about, Beth? Is it your pills? Because it's been one hell of a day, and I really don't need to come home to a fucking harpy who wants to use my balls for target practice.'

'This is not about the *pills*, or your affairs, or the hours you spend nursing your bloody company instead of being where you should be, with your family. It's about *me*.'

'Did it ever occur to you that *you're* the reason I don't want to be with my family?'

'Did it ever occur to you that that's bullshit?'

We glare at each other. A pulse beats in his forehead; my chest heaves. We haven't felt this passionately about each other for twenty years.

Suddenly my anger evaporates. 'William, we've both used my illness as an excuse for far too long,' I say tiredly, sinking on to the edge of the bath. 'Let's be honest with each other for once. If I hadn't been pregnant with Ben, you'd never have married me. You never loved me, and I knew it. *That's* the truth at the heart of this marriage. My illness gave you the excuse you needed to opt out of it, and it gave me a reason to stop trying. It's time to stop kidding ourselves. This marriage was over before it even began.'

'And whose fault's that?'

'Mine.' I swallow, hard. 'Ben wasn't an accident, William.'

He stares at me for a long moment, then swivels on his heel and leaves.

I follow him downstairs into his study, and shut the door quietly behind me. No need for Cate to hear any of this.

Neither of us speaks.

'Aren't you – aren't you angry?' I venture.

'Would it help if I were?'

'I did a terrible thing to us, William,' I whisper.

He pours slugs of whisky into two crystal tumblers, and hands me one without looking at me. The alcohol burns my throat without melting the block of ice in the pit of my stomach.

William slumps forward in his chair, cradling the glass

between his palms, defeat written in every line of his body. He looks utterly exhausted, as if he can't even find the energy to argue. Only the certainty that I'm doing the right thing prevents me from throwing my arms around him and begging for forgiveness.

'Are you sure about this?' he asks, without looking up. 'We could try again – *make* it work—'

'I think we both know we've passed that point, don't you?'

'What happened to waiting a year, for Cate?'

'Cate needs me to be happy more than she needs me to be here,' I say quietly.

William nods, once. When he speaks again, his tone is resigned. 'What do you want me to do?'

'Answer me honestly. Do you love me, William?'

He closes his eyes, and tilts his head back against the chair. Outside, an owl hoots. The grandfather clock in the hall ticks in time with my own heart. 'No. Not the way you deserve.'

'Thank you for that,' I say softly.

'So. What do we do now?'

I sink on to the window seat, leaning my head against the cool glass. The moon is full, bathing the garden in an eerie white light. A fox runs on to the lawn, scents the air, and disappears into the darkness.

'I'll go to Italy on Saturday,' I say. 'It'll give us both the time and space we need to sort out where we go from here. When I get back, we can discuss all the details, the practicalities. I don't want much, William—'

'You should keep the house. The flat in London is enough for me. What do you want to tell the children?'

'Sam doesn't need to know anything just yet. We can wait until I come back from Italy, and break it to him together in the summer holidays. Ben and Cate are old enough to know the truth now.'

He turns tired eyes towards me. 'And what is that?'

'That their parents love them, and always will. That they are the best of us, that they make us proud, that we'll always be there for them.'

'I didn't just marry you because of Ben,' William says. 'I'd have done it anyway.'

'I hope she makes you happy, William. Whoever she is.'

'There's no one,' he says bleakly. 'No one at all.'

A week later, I'm floating in a sea of pink, almost drunk on the scent of azaleas covering every inch of the Spanish Steps behind me. I had no idea the Romans did this every May. The carpet of flowers stretches all the way up the stone steps to the French church at the top, the Trinità dei Monti, where, in the eighteenth century, the most beautiful women and men of Italy gathered, waiting to be chosen as an artist's model. I remember my own foray into modelling, and think briefly of Dan.

Pushing my new sunglasses on top of my head, I thread my way between the couples sitting below me on the steps, and join the throng of tourists in the Piazza di Spagna taking pictures and throwing coins for luck into the boat-shaped fountain at the heart of the square.

A couple in their late forties catch my eye. The crisp creases of new clothes fresh from the cellophane tell me this is probably their first time away together in years, perhaps decades. I imagine children newly flown from the nest, a second honeymoon. When they stroll away, they're holding hands.

I miss William dreadfully; there hasn't been a moment in the last four days when I haven't ached for him. Every morning I wake wondering if I've done the right thing.

It's just as well I put some distance between us. I don't know how strong my resolve would have proved if I'd stayed.

I push William from my mind. Dodging the mopeds whizzing like mosquitoes along the narrow streets, I head down the Via Bocca di Leone towards the tiny cheap flat I've rented on the fifth floor of a crumbling old apartment building. I'm sharing a cramped, spider-filled bathroom with five other apartments, there is no lift, and the building smells of other people's cooking; but the light in my tiny bedroom is extraordinary. I've already filled three canvases; I have to climb over them to reach my bed.

I know I'll never have a career as a painter. The day before I left England, Eithne returned my paintings; only four had sold, probably to Eithne herself, though she'd die before she'd admit it. This isn't a Hollywood movie; I'll never be 'discovered'.

But it doesn't matter. My mania has ebbed; the depression is rolling in again, like a fog from the sea. Its first wisps already wreath and twist around my ankles. Soon I won't be able to see my hand in front of my face. When I paint, I'm able to believe it will lift again, if I can just be patient.

I reach my building and push open the small post door cut into the vast great double doors, towering twenty feet tall. The steps up to my apartment have been worn into hollows by countless pairs of feet over the centuries. Behind closed apartment doors, children screech, couples argue. I had thought I might feel lonely, travelling by myself, but it turns out I love my own company. I'm at peace, for the first time in my life.

My apartment is unlocked; there's nothing to steal. Panting slightly from the climb, I push open the door, and cross straight to the open window. I can still see the mass of pink flowers on the steps, if I lean out over the balcony.

I reach back into the room for my camera, and jump, startled.

Life's full of surprises.

16

Cate

Jelly shots *suck*.

I crawl into the bathroom and clasp the toilet bowl. This is all Clem's fault. She said she hadn't made them too strong. I don't think I've ever been so drunk in my life as I was last night. I even smoked half a pack of cigarettes – my mouth tastes like an ashtray, and I've burned my oesophagus practically down to my stomach.

Oh, God. Surely I can't be sick *again*?

I puke into the loo, and wipe my mouth with a wet flannel. There's nothing left to barf up. I am never, *ever* going near vodka or strawberry jelly again.

Actually, I feel a bit better now. Maybe I've finally got it all out of my system.

I throw on some old clothes, and scrape my hair into a ponytail. Where's a bit of parental discipline when you need it? Dad should never have let me go round to Clem's when her parents are away. Has the man no sense of responsibility?

I hear the sound of raised voices outside, and peer out of my bedroom window.

Poor old Mum is bent over her weeding, while Granny Clara waves her arms and chases her along the flowerbeds like Lady Macbeth. Bitching about the whole Eithne drama, I bet. She couldn't wait to come and say 'I told you so.' Bloody ambulance chaser.

Dad, like, totally freaked last night when he found out what Eithne had been up to. He and Mum had a huge row. They've barely spoken since. I guess whatever deal they cooked up in Paris is off now. It was never going to work, anyway. OK, he's bought her all this fabulous stuff and came home early for a few weeks, but he looks like someone's cut out his heart. We did *Doctor Faustus* at school last term. You'd think Mephistopheles had just paid Dad a call.

I open the window for some fresh air. Granny Clara's voice drifts towards me like sulphur.

'. . . Absurd idea in the first place. Jetting off to the Continent to mess about "discovering art" at your age. Lord knows what would have happened to your poor family when you were gadding about Europe.'

'They'd have been fine,' Mum says. She sounds really tired. 'Cate's perfectly capable—'

'Perfectly capable! She's a delinquent! You should've taken a much firmer hand with her when she was young. I'm sorry to be the one to say I told you so, but—'

'Cate is *not* a delinquent,' Mum yells unexpectedly. 'She's beautiful, and funny, and bright, and I'm so proud of her it hurts to breathe! My daughter has determination and talent and ambition, and she's already twice the woman you or I could ever hope to be! I will not have you coming to my house and pouring your poison on my family! You've made my life a misery since the day I was born. I won't have you turning your venom on my daughter!'

My cheeks redden, even though no one can see me. I don't think I've *ever* heard Mum talk back to Granny Clara, never mind stick up for me like that.

It's strange. I know Mum really loves Dad, but it's like she's Superman and he's some kind of romantic kryptonite. Usually, he takes charge of things and she just fades into the background. But with him all weird and zoned out like he's been this last few weeks, she's been getting stronger and stronger. Without him telling her what to do all the time, she's even started to boss *him* about a bit. She stopped him getting that disgusting Hummer (does he want his grandchildren to be living on a charred rock?) and she put her foot down over going on holiday to Italy, though I s'pose that's off now because of Eithne.

Her new hair's really cool. And she let me take her shopping somewhere other than M&S – she bought this gorgeous red wrap dress online from Boden, and some bootcut jeans; like, *finally*. It's really nice to see her standing up for herself for a change.

Everything blurs. I want Mum to be happy. Dad, too. I bet Ella's got something to do with his miserable mood. They've probably split up or something. I don't want Mum and Dad to stay together just because of me. I'll be gone soon, anyway. I don't want that kind of responsibility.

I get up and go downstairs. Granny storms furiously into the kitchen. 'Your mother has taken leave of her senses!' she cries. 'Like mother, like daughter!' she adds, as I ignore her and go outside.

Mum is sitting on the garden steps, looking like she doesn't know whether to laugh or cry.

'Mum? Are you OK?'

She throws me a watery smile. 'I'm not quite sure.'

'Is it true? Is Eithne really the mole?'

She nods miserably, and I perch on the steps next to her.

'But why? I thought she was your friend?'

Mum bites her lip. 'She's never really forgiven me for marrying Daddy. She thinks it's his fault I stopped painting.'

'Well, it is, a bit.' I smile. 'Come on, Mum. You've got to admit he's a bit of a control freak. You always let him have his own way, same as you do with Granny Clara.'

'He's always been very encouraging about my painting—'

'Yeah, as a *hobby*. Can you imagine what he'd have said if you'd wanted to, like, do it as a career or something? He'd have gone ape.' I reach past her and pick one of her roses. 'Gorgeous. They're amazing this year—'

She puts a detaining hand on my arm. 'Cate, it's not your father's fault. I *let* him take over. I blamed him, and I blamed the illness, but the truth is it's *my* fault I stopped painting.' She hesitates. 'I was afraid to fail,' she admits quietly. 'It was easier not to try.'

'Are you still going to Italy on Saturday?'

'No.'

She starts making excuses for the old lezzie, but I'm not really listening. I cut a few more roses and drop them in her basket, trying to work up my courage to tell her how I feel. Of course I don't want my parents to split up, but I need her to know she doesn't have to worry about me any more. If it has to happen, I can deal with it. I'd rather have them both happy and doing their own thing than have to live this fake happy-families routine any more. I'm fed up with the lies and pretending. I just want things to be *real*.

'... but I don't think we'll ever be quite the same.'

'You don't need her, Mum.'

'Not when I've got you.'

I duck as she ruffles my hair. 'Mum! I meant, to go to Italy. You should go on your own.'

'Darling, I couldn't.'

'Why not? It's only for three weeks. Mrs Ghedini can come in and clean and stuff. Dad and me can manage.'

I know she's tempted. She's never been away on her own before; I bet she'd have a brilliant time. I've half a mind to go with her.

'What about your father? I couldn't leave him, it wouldn't be fair.'

'Mum,' I say carefully, 'it's time to think about *you* for a change.'

She looks at me sharply. 'You don't have to stay for me,' I say, feeling my way. 'I'll be gone soon. If you don't leave now, you may never bring yourself to do it. I want you to be happy, Mum. I don't want to worry about you any more.' I drop my gaze, not wanting her to see me cry. 'When we did the *Titanic* at school, Mrs Buchanan said some of the people who drowned might have survived if they'd stopped clinging to each other. Sometimes you – you just have to let go.'

For a long moment, she doesn't say anything. Oh, fuck. I shouldn't have interfered, should I, it's none of my business—

Except the pair of them have *made* it my business, haven't they?

She makes a little 'oh' sound, and covers her mouth with her hand. 'Since when did you get to be so wise?'

'Mum, it's OK. Go. I'll be fine. Dad'll be fine. We'll all be OK.'

'I do love your father, Cate. Very much.'

I swallow. 'Not always enough, though, is it, Mum?'

'No.' She hugs me so tight I can hardly breathe. 'No, it isn't.'

She releases me with a kiss, and I run upstairs to my bedroom. An unexpected idea has occurred to me, but I need to get myself together first. I can't go anywhere looking like this.

It takes a hot shower, half a can of hair gel and a ton of MAC, but an hour later I look recognizably human again. You'd never guess this was a girl with seven vodka jelly shots in her extremely recent past.

I turn side-on to the mirror. I'm not sure about this empire-line top, though. I bought it when I went shopping with Mum on Saturday, and it's totally cool with all this embroidery and beads and stuff, but it makes me look pregnant—

I grab my bag. Who cares what I look like? This isn't about *me*.

As soon as I see him, I wish I'd changed into the pink Fat Face T-shirt after all. I don't want him to think I've totally let myself go.

'Cate!'

I push past him before I lose my bottle. 'Can I come in?'

'Would it make a difference if I said no?'

I smile sheepishly. Dan smiles warily back.

For a moment we both stand in the centre of the living-room, not quite sure what to do next. I try not to think about the last time I was here.

'D'you want a coffee or something?'

I hate coffee. 'Sure.'

I follow him into the tiny kitchen. It's full of dirty plates and pizza boxes, and there's a line of jars filled with murky turps and paintbrushes on the windowsill like Mum's.

Dan messes with the coffee machine. Grounds scatter all over the grimy Formica; when he opens the cupboard beneath the sink to throw away the old filter, I notice the bin is overflowing with beer cans and mouldy teabags.

'So,' he says, his back towards me, 'how did the exams go?'

'Fine, thanks. French was a bit tough, but I think I did OK.'

'Well, you should. You've had a bit of practice.'

'You heard about that?'

He turns and grins. 'Village jungle drums, you know how it is.'

'I – I met someone,' I say, my cheeks flaming, 'in Paris. He's going to be spending the summer in Bath on a student exchange. We might meet up.'

'Great. That's great.'

I fiddle nervously with the fringe on my top. 'Look, I'm sorry about—'

'I'm sorry you had to—'

We both laugh nervously. I nod to indicate he should go first. 'Cate, what happened that day, I should've come to find you and explained. Nothing happened, I swear—'

'I believe you.'

'You do?'

The coffee machine hisses and burbles on the counter. A steady stream of water leaks from a crack in its side and drips on to the stained floor.

'Mum's going to Italy on Saturday for three weeks. On her own,' I add.

Dan nods, but says nothing.

'She and Dad – well. I think they're splitting up. He'll probably go up to London when she gets back, and stay in the flat he's got there. Mum's been doing a lot of painting recently. She seems to be really into it. I think she'll be OK about Dad leaving. In the end, anyway.'

'What about you?'

'I'll be fine. I'm not a kid any more,' I say, realizing it's true. 'Look, Dan. I just came to say sorry and to – to give you something.'

I hand him a scrap of paper.

'It's Mum's address in Rome. She's renting an apartment from a friend of Eithne's. It can get a bit lonely on your own. Sometimes it's wonderful when friends drop by unexpectedly.' I smile. 'I just thought you might like to know.'

It's not the jelly shots. Or nerves about Mum leaving.

I wrap my arms around my waist, rocking to and fro as I perch on the edge of the bath. I'm so scared I'm shivering.

It was just one time! I can't be pregnant! *I can't be!*

I've been sick every morning for a week, but that could be tension, or something I've eaten. My jeans won't do up, but I've been pigging out on doughnuts and chocolate. I'm really tired all the time, but my parents have just split up, my Mum's in Italy, and I'm not sleeping well. My breasts are sore, but that could just be hormones, couldn't it, it happens a lot when I get my period—

I can't even remember when I last had my period.

We only did it once – well, three times, but it was just one night! People try for *years* to get pregnant. What are the chances I managed it first time?

Fleur says every time you have sex, you have a fifty–fifty chance. Either you get pregnant, or you don't.

I wish I could call her, but I don't want Michel to know. I don't want anyone to know.

It must be five minutes by now.

I glance at my watch. Only two.

Why didn't I think about contraception? I know I was a bit drunk – OK, a lot drunk – but I've carried condoms in my bag, just in case, since I was fourteen! How could I have been so *stupid*?

I can't keep it. I don't want a baby. I want to finish my exams, go to NYU, become a journalist, there's no room in my life for a baby.

I pick up the little stick.

Oh, God. *Oh God oh God oh God*.

Everyone's very nice at the clinic. They don't treat me like a stupid little schoolgirl who's made a total screw-up of her life. The counsellor fills in all the paperwork and writes down the date of my last period (the 19th of March! And it's already the end of May! How could I not have *noticed*?) and doesn't even bat an eyelid when I tell her I had a one-night stand on holiday in France, and fib and say I don't know the name of the father.

I give her the urine sample they told me to bring to the consultation, and she tests it. I didn't quite believe I was really pregnant until she confirms it. Secretly, I'd still hoped all those stick things had been wrong.

She explains nicely that I'm eight weeks pregnant (it's only the size of a walnut, but I know from Biology it's already got arms and legs and tiny hands and feet) and asks me if I'm sure I want to end my pregnancy. She makes it sound so straightforward, like I'm terminating a lease. Which, in a way, I am.

It's way too late for a morning-after pill, of course (it's got eyes, too, and tiny nails, maybe it's even sucking its thumb), so she outlines the different options.

Vacuum. Aspiration. Dilatation and evacuation.

My head starts to swim. It all sounds so gruesome and medieval. I picture Sam when he was a baby inside Mum, being sucked into a vacuum cleaner, his arms and legs ripped off, his tiny body broken.

'Are you sure this is really what you want, Cate?' the counsellor asks.

'I can't have a baby,' I gasp.

'A termination isn't your only option. Have you considered adoption? And if you did decide to keep the baby, there are lots of support groups and—'

'No,' I choke out. 'I can't.'

'Cate,' the counsellor says, 'I know it sounds terrifying, but these procedures are much less painful than you think—'

'For me? Or the baby?'

'The foetus,' she corrects gently, 'won't feel anything. Cate, I really think you should go home and talk this through with Mum. Lots of parents are upset at first, but once they've got used to the idea, they nearly always come round. Many actually look forward to being grandparents.'

I can't tell Mum. She'd be so disappointed. She'd come rushing back from Italy, it'd ruin everything for her. She'd think it was all her fault. I got myself into this. It's up to me to sort it out.

'Can't – can't I just take a pill, or something?' I ask desperately.

She sighs. 'An abortion isn't like getting rid of a headache. First we need to be sure you really understand what you're doing, and can live with the consequences. This is a big decision, Cate. You'll have to live with it for the rest of your life.'

I nod, trying not to cry. She'll never give it to me if I cry.

'If you do decide to go ahead, you can have EMA – an early medical abortion – up to nine weeks' gestation. You'd take medication to cause an early miscarriage. It doesn't involve any surgery, and you won't need an anaesthetic.'

'I'll do that,' I say, dizzy with relief. 'Can I take it now?'

She smiles. 'It's not quite that simple, I'm afraid. If you're really sure this is what you want to do, I'll arrange for you to see a doctor now. She'll complete the legal paperwork with you, and she'll probably want to confirm gestation with an ultrasound since you're near the nine-week limit. After that, she'll need to take a blood test, and discuss any possible risks and complications—'

'Risks? What sort of risks?'

'She'll explain those to you. An EMA is a very safe procedure, Cate. Most girls experience no more than some nausea, vomiting, that kind of thing.'

'How long do I have to wait?'

'You can see her right now.' She hesitates. 'I take it you haven't seen your own GP yet? If you want to have the procedure on the NHS, you'll need him to refer you to us. Otherwise, we'll have to treat you as a private patient.'

'I have to pay?'

'It'd be quicker that way. We could make your appointment for early next week, which would keep you within the time limit for an EMA. Otherwise, if we wait for your NHS referral—'

'I'll pay,' I say quickly.

'You can bring a friend or relative with you if you'd like.'

'No. I don't want anyone to know.' I shake my head violently. 'No one can know.'

The night before my appointment, I can't sleep. I toss and turn in bed, haunted by images of chopped-up babies and big blue eyes gazing up at me pitifully from black plastic bags. *It's just a bunch of cells*, I tell myself. *It's not a real baby*.

Two years ago, a couple from one of those anti-abortion groups came to our school and showed us photographs of babies in the womb, sucking their thumbs and running on the spot like tiny hamsters on wheels, and even hiccuping. They were a bit odd-looking, with their huge heads and everything, but they already seemed like real little babies, even the tiny ones: you could tell which ones would have big noses or need braces on their teeth.

They played a video of the unborn babies listening to Vivaldi; you could see them waving their tiny arms just like they were keeping time. Heavy metal got them bouncing around and kicking all over the place.

Then they showed us babies after they'd been vacuumed

out of their safe, warm hiding places. Some of them had had poison injected into their hearts. Others were born alive, and left in cold metal bowls to die.

I get out of bed and curl on the window seat, my hand instinctively fluttering to my stomach. It's still so flat; how can there be a baby in there?

After I saw the counsellor, the doctor put this probe thing inside me and I saw my baby on the screen. I heard its heartbeat.

Taking a pill's different, isn't it? It's not like chopping the baby up or anything. I read the leaflet. It says the drugs work by blocking the essential hormones that make the lining of the uterus hold on to the pregnancy. It just lets go. That's the same as having a period, right?

My cheeks are wet with tears. I can't have a baby. I'm only seventeen. I've got no money, no job. How can I look after a baby when I can't even look after myself?

In the morning, I dress in black, to suit my mood, and carefully pull back my hair into a neat French plait. I put on just enough make-up to hide the dark circles beneath my eyes. Dad's been going all-out to take proper care of me since Mum left for Italy; even though his head's all over the place these days, I don't want to take any chances. He stayed home from work last week when I said I had a headache; the last thing I need is him deciding we need to spend some quality father–daughter time together today.

I can't eat any breakfast. As soon as Dad turns his back, I give my bacon and eggs to Cannelle. He's going to have trouble fitting in his basket soon.

'No school today?' Dad asks.

At least I don't have to make up a lie about that. I shake my head. 'Half-term.'

'You could come up to London with me, if you like,' Dad offers. 'Do a bit of shopping, and then meet me for lunch—'

'I promised Clem I'd go round to hers,' I say, 'sorry.'

Dad looks genuinely disappointed. He must be lonely, I realize, with Mum gone and everything.

'Another time?'

I nod. Dad drops a kiss on the top of my head, and leaves for work.

I flit around the house, unable to settle to anything, trying to kill time until it's late enough to leave. I never thought I'd ever have to make this decision; I've always been sort of anti-abortion. But it's different when it happens to you. I can't give a child the kind of life I'd want to give it. I'm not ready to put my life on hold because I made a mistake; *one* mistake. With other mistakes you get the chance to go back and fix them. Why not this?

I'm doing the right thing.

The counsellor I saw the first time isn't there when I arrive. The admissions staff are perfectly nice, but brisk. I sit in the waiting room, surrounded by other girls not much older than me, none of us able to look each other in the eye.

Someone calls my name. I let them take my blood pressure and check my details, and it's like it's happening to someone else. They hand me a small tablet and a glass of water, and I sit there on the edge of the examination table with the pill in the palm of my hand.

'You'll need to come back in three days for the second dose,' the doctor tells me. 'You may experience some bleeding and cramping before then, but that's perfectly normal.'

This baby's already part of me. It has my genes; my blood is keeping it alive. I can't feel it yet, but it's had a profound effect on my body already. Does it know its mother is about to kill it?

I'm not ready to be a mother.

I swallow the pill.

I'll never even know if it was a girl or a boy.

I'm on the platform at Waterloo waiting for my train when the cramps begin. Within minutes, I'm doubled up with pain. I stagger towards the toilets and throw up before I can even make it to the loo. No one asks how I am or offers to help me.

Somehow I manage to make it outside and fall into a taxi. I tell the driver to take me back to the clinic, and collapse back against the seat.

I deserve this. *I've killed my baby, and now it's killing me.*

An allergic reaction, the doctor says. My body has rejected the pill, and because I vomited so much it hasn't been absorbed properly. After all that, I'm still pregnant.

I can't take another pill, so now I have no choice but to suck my baby out in bits.

You'd think after what had happened I'd keep it, wouldn't you? You'd think I'd decide it was clinging to life with all its might and deserved a chance to live, but if anything this has just made me more determined. I'm not fit to be a mother. I can't even do this right.

So three days later I go back to the clinic, where two nurses help me change into one of those hideous gowns that shows your bottom at the back, and they take me to an examination room, where I lie down on a table with my fect in some kind of rubber bands that are up in the air. They help me scoot to the edge of the table, and gently hold my legs apart. Their hands are so cold. The doctor comes in and chats to the nurses about the weather as she puts her fingers inside my vagina to check the position of my uterus, and then she shows me a speculum and tells me she's going to put it in and it might hurt a little. I feel the cold metal sliding inside me and opening me out, and it feels so horrid, so *invasive*, I wonder for a moment if my baby is just going to fall out on its own. Then she takes a long, scary-looking needle and inserts it into my open vagina and up into my cervix; it stings a little, but it's not too bad. She shows me something she calls the dilators and explains she's going to put them into my cervix to help it open wider and she reaches between my legs—

'Stop!' I yell.

'Is it hurting? We can give you some more meds—'

'I've changed my mind,' I gasp, struggling to sit up.

'Cate, we've just paralysed your cervix,' the doctor says, frowning. 'If we stop now, you'll miscarry anyway, because your cervix will open on its own.'

'I don't care,' I sob. 'I can't do this. I'm sorry, I'll pay you and everything, but I can't do this.'

The doctor nods to one of the nurses, and snaps off her gloves. They help me out of the stirrups, and one of them sits beside me on the examination table and rubs my back as I weep uncontrollably.

'Is there anyone you'd like us to call?' she asks gently.

I start to shake my head, then catch her arm. 'Wait. There is someone.'

*

'You're all dressed up,' I say. 'Are you sure I'm not interrupting something important?'

'Cate, it's fine.' She turns to the nurse. 'She's OK to leave?'

'You'll be staying with her, Dr Stuart?'

Ella nods. 'I'll keep her with me overnight. Has she had any meds?'

'Just codeine for the cramps. I'm afraid she waited rather too long before changing her mind,' she adds quietly; 'her cervix will probably dilate on its own now. After she miscarries, she'll need to return for a D&C to ensure there's no material left inside the uterus. The biggest danger now is an infection—'

'I understand,' Ella says coolly.

She turns and hugs me hard. 'I'm so sorry,' I sob into her shoulder. 'I've been so stupid, I've ruined everything. I didn't know who to call, I can't tell Dad, he'll be so disappointed, he'll blame Mum and she'll have to come back from her holiday—'

'Sssh. Cate, it's OK. I'm here now. It's going to be fine, we'll get through this.' She releases me and picks up my bag. 'Do you think you can walk a little way to the car?'

I nod. 'Ella, you won't tell Dad, will you?'

'I'm a doctor, remember? We're like priests, we can't tell anyone anything.'

'I'm going to lose the baby now, aren't I?'

'Yes, darling,' Ella says gently. She helps me down the front steps, and slips her arm through mine for support as we walk slowly towards the underground car park. My legs are rubbery, and now that the internal anaesthetic is starting to wear off, it feels like someone's shoved a red-hot poker up inside me.

'Will I still be able to have another one?'

A shadow crosses her face. She shivers, as if someone's walked over her grave.

Then she seems to collect herself, turning to me with a reassuring smile. 'There's no reason why you shouldn't, especially if we make sure you don't get an infection. But we need to think about contraception after this, Cate. Your parents don't have to know, but you can't take these sorts of risks with your health.'

A police siren screams a few streets away. Ella glances briefly at her watch, and hitches my bag on her shoulder.

'Can I ask you a personal question?' I ask after a moment.

'I think we know each other well enough now, don't you?'

'Why didn't you ever have children?'

'Oh, Cate. You don't pull your punches.'

'I'm sorry.' I bite my lip. 'You don't have to tell me if you don't want to.'

She sighs. 'No, I don't mind. This seems to be a day for exchanging secrets. OK, we have to cross here.' She presses the button, and we wait for the lights to change. 'I never wanted children with my husband. I could probably spend a solid year in therapy and never get to the bottom of why, but I think it's partly to do with my own parents, how they never seemed quite ready for me, and partly to do with me, my career, my need to prove something to myself; and partly to do with me and Jackson. I always knew I didn't love him the way I should. It seemed wrong to bring a baby into the world like that, almost under false pretences.'

The light flashes green for us to cross. Neither of us moves.

'What about Dad? Do you love him that way?'

She swallows. 'It's too late for us, Cate. I got in the way of your mum and dad, and I shouldn't have done. They've got a chance to—'

'Mum's left him,' I say baldly.

Ella jerks as if I've slapped her. 'She found out about me?'

'No.' I shake my head. 'In the end, it had nothing to do with anyone else.'

We've missed the lights. Ella presses the button again.

'Will you and Dad get back together now?'

'I can't have children. I got some kind of infection when I was younger,' Ella muses, as if she hasn't even heard me. 'It's why we have to take such care with you. I don't want you ever to have to stand in my shoes.' She smiles sadly. 'Ironic, isn't it? I mean, there's never been a time in my life when I've been less prepared for a child, and I've never wanted one more.'

'I'd have given you mine,' I say impulsively. 'If I hadn't . . .'

'Oh, Cate—'

The traffic signal beeps, telling us to cross. It's almost drowned by the police sirens a street or two away. I'm about to step on to the crossing when a souped-up car on elevated wheels jumps the red light and races past, music blaring from its open windows. Someone lobs a beer can from the car, and it bounces across the road, coming to a stop by my foot.

'That was close,' I laugh, as Ella's eyes widen. 'Do you think we could—'

I never get the chance to finish my sentence.

17

Ella

It's rained in the last half-hour. The night air smells of wet grass and acrid city streets: the scent of London. In the distance, a clock chimes eleven. A light breeze shivers the May tree outside the front gate, spattering me with wet blossom, and I wrap my kimono more tightly around me. Somewhere down the street, a car guns its engine and roars off into the darkness.

Cooper pulls me into his arms and kisses me goodbye. It occurs to me I've never met a man able to say so much with so few words.

'Sure you don't want me to call you a cab?' I ask softly.

He shakes his head, shouldering his battered rucksack. The wind slaps the hem of my kimono against my legs.

'Will you – will you at least let me know you're OK?'

'I'm OK,' he says simply.

I watch him until he turns the corner. He doesn't look back. *What did you expect, Ella? Flowers and a declaration of undying love?*

Later, after I've showered and thrown on a pair of old pyjamas, I pour myself a glass of Scotch and curl up on the sofa. Jackson's letters are heaped in my lap. It's three days since Cooper arrived and gave them to me, but I still haven't read them. Partly because of Cooper, of course; but mainly because I'm cravenly afraid of what I might discover, and what I might feel.

I turn the packet over in my hands. Cooper didn't give them to me to hurt me, I know that now. This is something I need to do if I'm ever to get my life back.

Pulling off the elastic bands holding the letters together, I riffle through the envelopes. There must be at least thirty of them. I had no idea Jackson wrote proper letters; emails and texts were more his style. But of course Cooper doesn't have a computer. I smile wryly. He was born a hundred years too late for the age that would've suited him best.

The first letter is postmarked March 1997 – the month we met. The last is dated the 14th of February this year.

I shiver. He wrote it the day he died.

I take a fortifying sip of Scotch, and pull the first letter from its envelope.

My first reaction is a shame so profound, I can hardly bear to wear my own skin. Jackson knew all along. *Seven years.* Every time I looked him in the eye and told him another lie, every night I said I was working late, he knew, and never said a word.

My deceit was a thousand times worse than I ever realized.

I put the letters down and stand up, my limbs aching as the blood rushes to them. It's not quite light; across the road, the newsagent's shutters rattle as he opens up to take delivery of today's papers. I thought I had Jackson all figured out. I knew he loved me, but I thought it was a child's love: needy, careless and demanding. I thought I deserved more.

The truth is, he loved me far more than I merited. How could he have kept silent all those years? How could he not have hated me?

I make myself a coffee, and prop myself at the kitchen table. My head swims with conflicting emotions. Dying confers a strange inviolability on its disciples: 'Don't speak ill of the dead.' For the past three months, I've heaped coals of fire on myself, unwilling to allow a whisper of criticism about Jackson even to cross my mind. I was the adulteress who betrayed a good and loving husband. I was to blame. I didn't deserve happiness with William, or anyone else. I didn't deserve a child. I put my career before my marriage; it was only just and fitting that I should end up with neither.

But Jackson's right. He *should* have called me on William.

For the first time since he died, I feel a flicker of anger at my husband. He knew I was only staying with him out of stubbornness and guilt, and he used that knowledge to keep me prisoner. Why couldn't he have had the balls to confront me? He trapped us both in a dead marriage. So much grief and pain on both sides, and for what?

Of course I shouldn't have had an affair, nothing excuses that; but by keeping quiet for so long, Jackson let himself become part of it.

I was right not to have a child with him.

A baby doesn't glue a relationship together. It would have been the worst thing, the most selfish thing, we could have done; Jackson knew that as well as I did. And yet he used my refusal to give him a child as a weapon against me for years.

Coffee splashes on to my hand; I find I'm shaking with anger. *Damn it, Jackson! Look what you did to us!*

We never should have married. Jackson knew that even better than I did. We both fooled ourselves I could learn to love him. We both knew, deep down, it would end in disaster.

Why didn't he say something?

I glance at the brightening sky. I should get ready for work; the last thing I need is to give Richard Angel any more ammunition in advance of the board meeting.

I dress on automatic pilot. *We both screwed up.* Jackson knew that. And he forgave me for my part in it.

He wanted me to be happy.

The realization is so startling, I drop the bottle of foundation I'm holding; the glass shatters on the tiled floor.

Jackson proved he loved me, not by staying with me all those years, but by finally having the courage to let go.

I clean up the spilled make-up. Cooper gave me the letters so that Jackson could finish what he'd set out to do: to set me free. No more guilt. No more regret. It's time to get on with my life.

I owe it to my husband.

Lucy chooses my clothes for the board hearing. She spends half an hour sorting through my wardrobe before deeming it all wildly inappropriate – 'For heaven's sake, Ella, don't you have anything that's not purple, slashed to the waist, fringed, beaded, or all four? If you didn't wear a white coat at work, you'd have been fired years ago' – and dragging me out to the one circle of hell Dante forgot to mention: the upmarket department store.

'It's not *supposed* to look sexy, that's the whole point,' she sighs, when I reject the latest in a line of identical neat, knee-length black suits in synthetic, sweaty fabrics.

'I'm sorry. But suppose I get knocked down by a bus? People might think I *meant* to dress like that.'

In the end, we compromise on a charcoal-silk trouser suit from Emporio Armani. The nipped-in waist is still too figure-hugging for Lucy, but at least it's black (well, nearly) and depressingly conservative. I'll team it with my vintage grey alligator boots. That should take the sensible edge off it.

She hauls me to an upmarket hair salon – 'Just do your best,' she sighs – and two hours later I emerge feeling like I've been mugged: my wallet is empty, and I'm strangely light-headed. But I have to admit it suits me. Cut short, my curls hang in becoming ringlets round my face instead of spiralling crazily in all directions like rusty bedsprings.

'Do you think any of this is really going to help?' I ask Lucy when we get home.

'You're a good doctor,' Lucy says. 'Everyone knows that. You did your best.'

'You didn't answer my question.'

She hands me my new lipstick, a thrilling shade of nude. 'Despite what you believe, Ella, Richard thinks you're a good doctor too. One of the best, in fact. Just turn up on time, play the game his way, and it'll be fine.'

My eyes suddenly fill with tears. I don't bother to hide them.

'I still miss him, Lucy,' I whisper.

She squeezes my hand. 'Of course you do,' she says, knowing better than to ask who I mean.

The night before the hearing, I can't sleep. I pace my bedroom, replaying the events in my mind. I shouldn't have to justify myself to a roomful of hostile pen-pushers. I *am* a good doctor. I did my best for baby Hope. We're doctors, after all, not miracle workers. Some things are just meant to be.

I glance thoughtfully at the huge vase of lilies on the coffee table. The whole room breathes with their scent. Cooper sent them to me this morning, to wish me luck for the hearing tomorrow. I don't know if Jackson told him they're my favourite flowers, or if it was just blind luck.

I'm ready long before I need to leave. Zipping up my boots, I check my reflection in the mirror. Even with the benefit of make-up, I still look like I haven't slept in a week. Maybe that'll play in my favour: Angel will know I've been up all night worrying. Showing due respect to his kangaroo court.

The phone rings as I'm double-locking the front door. I check my watch. I have time.

The answer-machine has already kicked in before I can pick up; a tinny voice echoes round the living room. 'This is Linda Biss at the Pregnancy & Planned Parenthood Advisory Centre. I'm calling on behalf of Ms Caitlin Ashfield—'

I switch off the machine. 'Hello?'

'Dr Stuart?'

'Sorry, I was halfway out the door. Who did you say you were?'

'I'm calling from the PPPA Centre in central London, Dr Stuart. We have a patient—'

I straighten my collar. 'I'm sorry, I think you've got the wrong number. I'm a paediatric consultant—'

Wait. Did she say *Cate*? Cate *pregnant*?

'Put her through,' I say sharply.

'Ella, I'm so sorry, I thought I could do it but I can't, and you're the only person I could think of to call—'

In my bag, my mobile beeps twice. It's Lucy, checking up on me. In less than one hour I have to be at the most important meeting of my life; my entire career hangs in the balance. Richard Angel isn't one to give second chances. There's no way I can make it into central London, collect Cate and then get to the hospital in time for the hearing.

She isn't my daughter; she's not even my stepdaughter, but the child of my ex-lover. She has two perfectly good parents of her own. I'm not her friend; in fact, she has every reason to hate me.

She's killing a baby I'd kill to have.

As Cate herself would say: it's a no-brainer.

'Give me your address,' I say.

'Ella, you won't tell Dad, will you?'

She looks so *young*. I smile, and give her a quick hug. 'I'm a doctor, remember? We're like priests, we can't tell anyone anything.'

'I'm going to lose the baby now, aren't I?'

'Yes, darling,' I say gently.

I pick up her silly yellow backpack and help her down the front steps. Cate always struck me as so *sensible*. How did she let this happen?

I check myself. At her age, I was leading a much wilder life. Who knows where I picked up the infection that wrecked my own chance of motherhood?

'Will I still be able to have another one?' Cate asks, eerily echoing my thoughts.

With an effort, I push the grief away. This isn't about me.

'There's no reason why you shouldn't, especially if we make sure you don't get an infection,' I reassure her. 'But we need to think about contraception after this, Cate. Your parents don't have to know, but you can't take these sorts of risks with your health.'

'Can I ask you a personal question?' Cate says.

'I think we know each other well enough now, don't you?'

'Why didn't you ever have children?'

'Oh, Cate. You don't pull your punches.'

'I'm sorry. You don't have to tell me if you don't want to.'

'No, I don't mind,' I sigh, as we reach the pedestrian crossing. 'This seems to be a day for exchanging secrets. OK, we have to cross here.'

She pushes her hair out of her eyes. I've always thought she looked so like Beth, but in this moment, it's William I see in her expression.

I try to find the right words to explain. 'I never wanted children with my husband. I could probably spend a solid year in therapy and never get to the bottom of why, but I think it's partly to do with my own parents, how they never seemed quite ready for me, and partly to do with me, my career, my need to prove something to myself; and partly to do with me and Jackson.'

Talking about it doesn't hurt as much as I thought it would. I realize I've finally started to reach some sort of acceptance; and that Jackson's letters have played a part in that. I offer him a silent prayer of thanks.

'I always knew I didn't love him the way I should,' I admit. 'It seemed wrong to bring a baby into the world like that, almost under false pretences.'

The pedestrian light flashes green, telling us to cross. I can't move.

'What about Dad? Do you love him that way?'

'It's too late for us, Cate,' I say painfully. 'I got in the way of your mum and dad, and I shouldn't have done. They've got a chance to—'

'Mum's left him.'

'She found out about me?' I whisper, appalled.

'No. In the end, it had nothing to do with anyone else.'

My mind whirls. William's free? Beth left *him*?

Except – it's too late. I've put a gulf between us nothing can bridge.

No point feeling sorry for myself. I can't change the past. I set this chain of events in motion the first time I kissed William. The game has played itself out; the cards I'm left holding are the ones I deserve. I hit the pedestrian button again.

'I can't have children. I got some kind of infection when I was younger,' I say. 'It's why we have to take such care with you. I don't want you ever to have to stand in my shoes. Ironic, isn't it? I mean, there's never been a time in my life when I've been less prepared for a child, and I've never wanted one more.'

'I'd have given you mine. If I hadn't . . .'

My heart twists. 'Oh, Cate—'

A boy racer jumps the lights, speeding past us in his souped-up Ford. Cate says something, but it's drowned out by the police sirens screaming towards us. She's laughing as she steps on to the pedestrian crossing.

She doesn't see the police car racing along the street in hot pursuit of the speeding Ford. She doesn't realize the young man at the wheel lost control as he hit a sharp turn in the road, trying to keep up with the car ahead of him. She is still laughing as he mounts the pavement, desperately trying to wrest back control of his vehicle, panic in his eyes——

She never even sees it coming.

Lilies.

For a moment, I think I'm still at home, half asleep on the sofa.

I try to open my eyes, but my lids refuse to work. Panicked, I try again. This time I succeed, and am rewarded with dazzling white brightness. I flinch; the movement sends a searing pain shooting through my neck and down my spine. I wait for it to pass, battling to stay calm. I can't seem to think properly. Disjointed words and pictures drift across my mind. *Focus*. I'm flat on my back; the pain and the grim ceiling tiles tell me I'm in a hospital bed. A bank of flowers surround me: clearly not A&E, then. I must have been here at least a day.

An IV pole on my left side tethers me to the bed. My right arm is heavily bandaged; my right foot is cradled in a sling a foot above the covers. I've broken my ankle. I move my left leg a little; the bedclothes wrinkle. I'm not paralysed, and I don't seem to have lost any limbs.

The fog starts to descend again. I try to fight it. There's something else – something I'm forgetting ... something important ...

I sleep.

'How are you feeling?'

I open my eyes. This time, it's easy.

Lucy strokes my hair back from my forehead. Her hand is cool.

'Would you like some water?'

She feeds me water from a sippy cup, like a baby. I want to speak, but my throat is too raw. I've been intubated, I realize.

'You were in an accident,' Lucy says gently. 'A car hit you. Do you remember?'

A jumble of shredded images blur in my head. The little green man telling us to cross. A beer can skittering down the street. Music, loud and distorted. *If it be love indeed, tell me how much.* Police sirens – the bite of a heavy bag on my shoulder – *There's beggary in the love that can be reckoned* – Cate laughing—

'Cate,' I whisper.

She doesn't hear me.

'Get some sleep,' she says, straightening my covers. 'I'll be back later.'

'*Cate*,' I scream; but the sound echoes only in my head.

Once more, I sleep.

*

The next time I wake, my mind is clear. I hurt all over, but the drug-induced fugginess has gone. I take a mental inventory of my injuries. The heavy bandage on my arm is now a straightforward dressing. My throat still rasps when I swallow, but my head no longer aches. The flowers next to me are wilting; I must have been here for days. A week, perhaps.

I hit the call button by my fingertips.

A nurse bustles in. 'Oh, we're awake. Feeling better?'

'Where's—' I cough, and try again. 'Where's Cate?'

'Don't try to talk, now. You've been very sick, you know, we nearly lost you—'

I struggle unsuccessfully to sit up. *'Where's Cate?'*

Her lips purse.

'Get me Dr Nicholson!'

The nurse stalks out.

I fall back against the pillows, trying to remember. I dredge up an image of the police car careering towards us, out of control; the young boy at the wheel, terror in his eyes; and then nothing until I wake up here. I thump the bed in frustration. What happened to Cate? *Why* can't I remember?

'Same old Ella,' a voice says from the doorway. 'Still giving everybody grief.'

William looks twenty years older than the last time I saw him.

'Doctors make the worst patients,' I say hoarsely.

He pulls out a chair and sits down without meeting my eye. 'Looks like I owe you for two of my children now, Doctor Stuart.'

It takes a moment for the words to register. 'Cate's OK?'

'They didn't tell you? Christ, Ella. Yes, she's fine—'

'Thank God,' I breathe, my eyes closing in relief. 'Oh, thank God.'

'Yes. And thank *you*.'

My confusion must show.

'You pushed her clear of the car, Ella,' William says quietly. 'Don't you remember? It didn't touch her. You saved her life. She sprained her wrist when she fell against the pavement, but that's it. You're the one who took the full force of the impact.' He swallows. 'You saved her life,' he says again.

'I don't remember—'

'I'm not surprised. You've been out of it for nine days. Cate says you were thrown twenty feet down the road. One of the nurses from the PPPA Centre came out and gave you CPR, or you wouldn't even have made it to the ambulance. It's OK,' he adds, seeing my expression, 'Cate told me why you were there. She told me everything.'

'I'm so sorry, William—'

'What on earth for?'

'I didn't mean to interfere—'

Tears clog my throat. William squeezes my hand, and I realize he can't speak either.

We gaze at each other across a landscape of pain and betrayal. For the first time in eight years, we're both free; and yet we're further apart from one another than we've ever been.

There's so much I want to say, I don't know where to begin.

'I know,' William whispers, as if I've spoken aloud.

We both jump when Lucy appears in the doorway. 'What's so urgent I had to— Oh. William.'

'It's OK. I was just going. I came to thank Ella.' He

stands and drops a quick kiss on my forehead. 'Keep in touch. Let me know how you're doing.'

No! Don't go, I urge silently.

'Nice flowers. Cooper?'

I stiffen.

He smiles sadly. 'Take care, Ella,' William says; and then he's gone.

My heart blisters. I turn away, so Lucy won't see my tears.

She twitches my covers into place. 'He's been here every day,' she says casually, 'waiting for you to wake up. He's sat here for hours at a time, reading and talking to you. Shakespeare, mostly. The first couple of nights, he slept in a chair next to you, wouldn't leave. We had to promise to call him the moment you came round, just to get him to go home and shower.'

> *Doubt thou the stars are fire,*
> *Doubt that the sun doth move,*
> *Doubt truth to be a liar,*
> *But never doubt I love.*

'I remember,' I say quietly.

'Ella—'

'Don't, Lucy,' I beg. 'Don't say it. Please.'

She busies herself with my chart. I don't point out that she's not my doctor, and that she shouldn't even be here. I know she's probably spent almost as many hours in the past week sitting next to my bed as William has.

'There's a TV news crew who want to interview you,' she says, after a few minutes. 'They've been calling every day. Someone got pictures of the accident on their phone and put it up on YouTube—'

'I don't want to talk to anyone.'

'Richard was very impressed,' she adds drily. 'Especially when it got him and the hospital all over the evening news. He's managed to persuade the Shores to come to terms with their loss in private, rather than have it all raked over again in open court. I believe he pointed out that it doesn't look good accusing an injured heroine of being a baby murderer.'

I'm not fooled. I know she must have pulled out all the stops to persuade Richard to do that for me.

She clips my chart to the end of my bed. 'I'm sorry, Ella,' she says suddenly. 'I know you don't want to talk about it, but William has sat here for nine days begging you not to die. All he wants is some sign from you. Why is that so hard?'

'That was for Cate—'

'He knows what you did for her,' Lucy says. 'Not just saving her life. He knows you were prepared to put his daughter before your career. Don't you think that says a lot to him? You've been given another chance. Don't throw it away. He's still here,' she adds, gesturing towards the window. 'Speak to him. If you let him leave now—'

'He'll leave anyway!' I cry suddenly. 'Sooner or later! He'll leave! He'll make me love him and then he'll leave! He'll break my heart and I'll be left with nothing! Don't you understand? I can't! *I can't!*'

Lucy stares at me for a long moment. I can't bear the pity in her eyes. I turn away, but she sits carefully on the edge of my bed, so that I have no choice but to look at her.

'Ella, love doesn't come with guarantees. There's no safe way to do it. It takes you hostage, it gets inside you and opens up your heart and means you're no longer in control.' She sighs. 'You think you're safe, you build a wall around yourself and you think no one can get in, and then one day, somebody does, and your life isn't your own any more. Love is a risk, Ella,' she says urgently. 'Loving someone means risking failure, but not loving someone is the greatest risk of all. Don't you see?'

'He'll never forgive me,' I whisper.

Her gaze doesn't flinch. 'Maybe not,' she says. 'But can you spend the rest of your life not knowing?'

I shiver with fear. And then, without warning, I'm in the middle of the worst panic attack I've ever known. Adrenalin zips through my body, instantly shutting everything down but the instinct to fight or flee. My heart pounds in my ears. I have pins and needles; I'm so dizzy I feel sick. My vision blurs. My mouth is dry, and my mind races. I can't breathe; my body is smothering itself. I hyperventilate, trying to pull in enough air. Oh, God, this is it. The big one. I'm going to lose control, it's going to win, I can't fight it any more—

What's so bad about losing control?

The thought slices like a laser through the static in my head.

Where, exactly, has being in control got me?

Alone. Widowed, rejected by my lover, pitied by my dearest friend. Cut off from everything that makes life worthwhile. The more I've tried to control my life, the more the chaos has taken over.

Fine. Have it your way.

I let go. And in that instant the panic stops.

The tightness around my chest loosens. I can breathe. My heartbeat slowly returns to normal. The dizziness has gone.

I probe gingerly, like a tongue prods an aching tooth. There is pain, yes, and loss, certainly; but the panic has dissolved like salt in water.

It can't be that simple. Can it?

Come on, Jackson says in my head. *Take a chance, Ella. What've you gotta lose?*

'Is he still here?' I ask Lucy.

She glances out of the window, and nods.

'Help me up,' I say.

'You can't get out of bed—'

'Why? Too much of a risk?'

'Can't you just phone him and—'

'He'll never answer. *This is the moment!*' I grab her hands. 'Please, Lucy!'

She lowers the sling cradling my ankle, and helps me stand. My head swims. I take a deep breath, and the room stops tilting.

It's only four paces from my bed to the window, but it feels like a thousand miles. By the time I reach it, I'm sweating and dizzy. I cling to the windowsill. Four floors below me, William is walking towards his car.

I bang on the glass, but of course he can't hear me.

'Help me open it!'

'This is mad,' she says, but pushes against her side of the Victorian sash window. I do the same on mine. It shifts a little, but still doesn't open. William is searching through his pocket for his keys.

We shove again. He unlocks the car.

The window opens. I lean out, and yell his name as loudly as I can.

My voice is carried away on the breeze. William opens the car door. Lucy yells with me, but we're drowned out by the scream of an aeroplane overhead.

I grab the nearest thing to hand and throw it at him.

Then I collapse into a chair, and wait.

It doesn't take long.

'What the hell do you think you're doing?' William shouts, storming into the room. Lucy discreetly leaves, but he doesn't even notice her. 'You could've killed me!'

'I needed to get your attention,' I say.

'Well, you've bloody got it!'

'Why didn't you return any of my calls?'

'Why d'you think, Ella?'

'William,' I say desperately, 'that day at the Chelsea Brasserie, I made a mistake. I said terrible things to you, things I shouldn't have said and didn't mean. I wanted to apologize, to explain—'

'Not necessary. You made yourself perfectly clear.'

'But you don't understand—'

'Ella, you saved my daughter's life. I'll always be in your debt for that.' He turns away, so I can't see his face. 'But we've hurt each other too many times. How can you trust me, knowing I'm capable of cheating on my wife for eight years? How can I trust you, after you got pregnant by another man?'

There'll always be a question at the back of his mind. Unless, somehow, I can persuade him otherwise.

I only have one chance to get this right. I search for the words that will persuade him to stay. Jackson had just died,

I was so scared of being alone, Cooper happened to be there, I'd had too much bourbon. It'll never happen again; it's in the past. All true. All good reasons.

I step out on to the tightrope, and say the only words that matter.

'I love you.'

His back shivers.

'Why should I believe you?' he whispers finally.

'Why would I lie?'

'What about – ' he waves blindly to the flowers – 'about Cooper?'

'Cooper came to collect some of Jackson's things, and give me some letters. He kissed me,' I admit, knowing that honesty is my only option now. 'I kissed him back. But then I stopped. I told him I loved *you*.'

Finally, he turns around. His face is white and twisted with pain.

'I saw you kissing him!'

'You saw me kissing him goodbye!'

'You were pregnant with his baby!'

'*One* mistake, William! Haven't you ever made one mistake?'

'How can I trust you again?' he cries furiously. 'How do I know?'

'The same way I trust you! The same way any of us trust the ones we love! By choosing to! By taking a leap of faith, William! What else is there?'

'I can't do this any more, Ella,' William says, his voice raw. 'I don't want this kind of part-time love. I want to fall asleep with the woman I love, to breathe the same air as she does, for hers to be the face I see when I wake in the morning. I want to be the most important thing in her life.

I want to know her inside and out, for there to be nowhere I can't go, nothing I can't ask. That's not you, Ella. It never will be. You're too independent, too self-contained—'

'Do I look independent and self-contained to you?' I cry. I force myself to my feet, ignoring the bolt of white pain that shoots up from my ankle. 'I'm so far out on a limb here, I can't even see the ground! I'm fucking terrified, William! I love you so much, I'm too scared to breathe!' My cheeks are wet. 'Don't you *get* it? I've loved you from the moment I saw you, and this is the first time I've stopped running away from the truth long enough to admit it!'

'For Christ's sake, Ella, sit down before you fall down,' William says sharply.

'William, please—'

'It's OK, Ella. I get it,' he says tiredly.

In that moment, I know I've lost.

I collapse on to the edge of the bed. I'm out of words, out of ideas. My ankle throbs. My head aches. I'm sore all over. Even my fingertips feel raw.

'Cate didn't lose the baby,' William says. 'They're both going to be fine.'

For a moment, I'm too stunned to speak. 'I can't believe it,' I manage finally. 'William, that's amazing. It's – it's a miracle.'

'So Lucy said.'

Our eyes meet. In the midst of all the loss and anguish we've inflicted on each other, this tiny new life represents hope, no matter the circumstances of its existence.

'What will Cate do?' I ask. 'Is she going to keep it?'

He sits next to me, close enough that all I have to do is reach out and touch. 'She knows she's not ready to become a mother. She's got so many plans and dreams – university,

New York, journalism. So much she wants to do. She's decided to give the baby up for adoption.'

'Oh, William. How hard. For you, too—'

'Cate wants to give her baby to us, Ella.' He turns to me. 'I told her there wasn't an us.'

His eyes blaze with intensity. My heart heaves itself into my mouth.

'Ella? Was I wrong?'

It takes a moment to understand what he's saying.

He pulls me into his arms, burying his face in my hair. 'Dear God, Ella, we've been so bloody reckless,' he says fiercely. 'We could have lost each other for good. I love you so much. I never want to take that chance again.'

I feel the pulse of his blood beneath warm skin, hear the oxygen flowing in and out of his lungs, taste the scent and feel and essence of him, and know that I will never be safe again.

I search his face. 'Why . . . why did you come back?'

Without letting go of me for a moment, he places a single grey alligator boot on the bed. 'Firstly, you threw this at me. I know how you hate to lose one of a pair.'

'And secondly?'

'Secondly,' he murmurs, drawing me towards him, his lips hovering a fraction above mine, we're surviving on each other's breath, *there is no life but this*, 'secondly, I hate it too.'